Preface

With the dozens of short story anthologies available for use in literature courses, it might legitimately be asked why there is need for another, especially when its orientation seems to be psychological rather than "literary" and when roughly half its stories are translations from non-English-speaking cultures—cultures that often differ radically from one another and that span such a very long period of time. Of course we might reply that our collection, precisely because its approach and organization are untraditional and because it does not serve up familiar material in a familiar way, has at least the advantage of freshness and novelty; but this is not really an adequate answer to the question. We would not have undertaken a project of this scope had we not been convinced that the archetypal approach, in addition to providing a fresh perspective from which to study the short story, is also capable of offering other rewards as well, rewards whose nature is genuinely and specifically literary.

Oliver Evans
Harry Finestone

NORTHRIDGE, CALIFORNIA
AUGUST 1970

The World of the Short Story:

Archetypes in Action

Edited with introductions by

Oliver Evans

and

Harry Finestone

both of

San Fernando Valley State College

Alfred · A · Knopf: Publisher *New York*

THIS IS A BORZOI BOOK
Published by Alfred A. Knopf, Inc.

 Published in the United States by Alfred A. Knopf, Inc., New York, and simultaneously in Canada by Random House of Canada Limited, Toronto. Distributed by Random House, Inc., New York.

Library of Congress Catalog Card Number: 79–144004

ISBN: 0–394–31038–1

Manufactured in the United States.

First Edition
4 5 6 7 8 9

Acknowledgments

The editors are indebted to their colleagues and friends in the Department of English, San Fernando Valley State College, who suggested stories for this volume. They owe a debt to Nell Almquist, Margaret Bratcher, Jeffrey Hershenson, Carol Imlay, Delia Rüdiger, and Edith Smith for help, research, and clerical tasks too numerous to record. To Ardis Blackburn they are particularly grateful for reading their manuscript with a careful and judicious eye. They also wish to thank James B. Smith and Stephanie Gloger Wald for believing in the value of the archetypal approach and for preparing a long and complex manuscript for the printer. They are grateful to Eve Finestone for her patience and support.

Contents

The World
of the Short Story

Introduction

I

That certain literary motifs are universal has, of course, long been acknowledged; it is a common-sense observation based on the fact that identical characters, themes, and situations are found in the literature (particularly of myth, religion, and folklore) of cultures separated widely in time and space. In some cases—by no means all—it is possible to account for this phenomenon by various processes of cultural transmission, but where this is impossible, an alternative explanation is required. We cannot dismiss the problem merely by saying that human nature is essentially the same in all places and at all times, and therefore that the phenomenon is not so phenomenal; for, even if it were true that human nature exhibits this degree of constancy, the questions of why there are universal human qualities and why some elements in human nature are apparently less variable than others would still remain.

Although the use of the term *archetype* in literary criticism is relatively recent, the concept of the archetype as denoting a primordial idea, an idea preformed and universal, is very ancient, in Western civilization dating at least from Plato. The word itself occurs as early as the first century A.D. in the writings of Dionysius the Areopagite, who used it in a religious sense. This use of it is found also in various medieval theologians, particularly those of Neoplatonic persuasion, who took the existence of archetypes for granted. But the concept of the archetype was never a monopoly of religion. In philosophy it dominated the thinking not only of Plato but also of Kant, and in anthropology the term *représentations collectives* was used by Lévy-Bruhl to designate the symbolic figures in the primitive view of the world. More recently, in psychology, Carl Jung formulated an hypothesis of archetypes that has been enormously influential.

When we review the writings of the great literary critics, it is interesting to note that many of them, though they did not use the word, seemed often to assume the existence of archetypes. They were implicit in the classical concept of Nature and in the notion that art should somehow "imitate" it.

It is ironical that Aristotle, an arch-rationalist, subscribed emphatically to this notion; he was also the first to suggest, in *The Poetics,* the theory of organic or inevitable literary form, in which a "beginning, a middle and an end" were a condition for a masterpiece. Longinus, a Platonist, argued that just as Nature, "the first originating principle which underlies all things," was "no creature of random impulse delighting in mere absence of method," literature likewise was subject to certain immutable laws. And no one before or since Longinus, in his famous treatise *On the Sublime,* has stated so clearly the principle by which archetypal criticism chiefly justifies itself:

> You may take it that those are beautiful and genuine effects of sublimity which please always, and please all. For when men of different habits, lives, ambitions, ages, all take one and the same view about the same writings, the verdict and pronouncement of such dissimilar individuals give a powerful assurance, beyond all gainsaying, in favor of that which they admire.

In the Renaissance, Sir Philip Sidney, who was only partially a Platonist and who maintained that it was the special virtue of art to improve upon Nature, nevertheless observed in *An Apologie for Poetrie:*

> There is no art delivered to mankind that hath not the works of Nature for his principal object, without which they could not consist, and on which they so depend, as they become actors and players, as it were, of what Nature will have set forth.

Similarly Alexander Pope, that bastion of the Age of Reason, wrote in the *Essay on Criticism:*

> When first young Maro [1] in his boundless mind
> A work t'outlast immortal Rome designed,
> Perhaps he seem'd above the critic's law,
> And but from Nature's fountain scorn'd to draw;
> But when t'examine every part he came,
> Nature and Homer were, he found, the same.
> Convinced, amazed, he checks the bold design,
> And rules as strict, his labour'd work confine
> As if the Stagyrite [2] o'erlooked each line.
> Learn hence for ancient rules a just esteem;
> To copy Nature is to copy them.

And again:

> Those rules of old, discover'd, not devis'd,
> Are Nature still, but Nature methodiz'd;
> Nature, like Liberty, is but restrain'd
> By the same laws which first herself ordain'd.

---

[1] Virgil (Publius Virgilius Maro).
[2] Aristotle.

These passages clearly imply the existence of natural forms that are universal and eternal, that every artist "rediscovers," when he creates a masterpiece.

The tests of universality and survival as criteria for literary greatness, which were first articulated by Longinus, were restated by yet another rationalist, Samuel Johnson:

> Nothing can please many, and please long, but just representations of general nature . . . What mankind have long possessed they have often examined and compared; and if they persist to value the possession, it is because frequent comparisons have confirmed opinion in its favor.

Notwithstanding the most sophisticated attempts of professional criticism, these are still the most valid criteria of literary greatness, but even they are somewhat relative, as Johnson well knew: "Some seem to admire indiscriminately whatever has been long preserved, without considering that time has co-operated with chance." There is revival as well as survival, and each age and each culture has its own reasons for admiring a masterpiece from another age or another culture.

As might be expected, because of the influence of Transcendentalism, it is among the poets and critics of the nineteenth century that the concept of archetypes was most pronounced and most persistent. Coleridge defined the "primary" imagination in Platonic terms as "a repetition in the finite mind of the eternal act of creation in the infinite I AM" while the "secondary" imagination was an "echo" of it, and Keats implied the existence of inevitable forms in his correspondence with J. H. Reynolds. (See letter of February 19, 1918.) Shelley, an ardent Platonist, was quite explicit. In "The Defence of Poetry," he defined poetry as "the creation of actions according to the unchangeable forms of human nature, as existing in the mind of the Creator, which is itself the image of all other minds." The poet, he wrote, "participates in the eternal, the infinite, and the one; as far as relates to his conceptions, time and place and number are not," adding that "he would do ill to embody his own conceptions of right and wrong, which are usually those of his place and time, in his poetical creations which participate in neither." Using a familiar Neoplatonic image, Shelley thus described the humanizing effects of poetry:

> The sacred links of that chain have never been entirely disjoined, which descending through the minds of many men is attached to those great minds, whence as from a magnet the invisible effluence is sent forth, which at once connects, animates, and sustains the life of all.

Stripped of their mystical terminology, Shelley's ideas very much resemble those of modern Jungian psychology.

The romantic theory of inspiration, incidentally, which derives ultimately from Plato and in which mystics like Blake and Whitman were devout believers, seems often to invite archetypal explanation. Shelley wrote:

> Poetry is not like reasoning, a power to be exerted according to the determination of the will. A man cannot say, "I will compose poetry." The greatest poet even cannot say it; for the mind in creation is like a fading coal, which some invisible influence, like an inconstant wind, awakens to transitory brightness; this power arises from within, like a colour of a flower which fades and changes as it is developed, and the conscious portions of our natures are unprophetic either of its approach or departure. Could this influence be durable in its original purity and force, it is impossible to predict the greatness of the results; but when composition begins, inspiration is already on the decline, and the most glorious poetry that has ever been communicated to the world is probably a feeble shadow of the original conceptions of the poet.

These "original conceptions" are the archetypes, which according to Jung inhabit the collective unconscious and are altered in the process of being projected into actual behavior—or, in the case of literature, into particular motifs.

T. S. Eliot, perhaps the most important critic of the present century, is ordinarily identified with the moral rather than the psychological approach to literature; yet the "impersonal" theory of poetry which he expounded in "Tradition and the Individual Talent," and which for many readers is difficult to grasp, may perhaps be better understood if we assume that archetypes are involved. "This essay proposes to halt at the frontier of metaphysics or mysticism," Eliot declared, but actually he invaded the area of the metaphysical when he asserted that the literary masterpieces of the past formed an "ideal order among themselves" and that the creation of a new masterpiece altered this order. "We do not quite say," he continued, "that the new is more valuable because it fits in, but its fitting in is a test of its value." In this essay Eliot argued that it was wrong to insist, when evaluating a poet, on "those aspects of his work in which he least resembles anyone else," and maintained that "not only the best, but the most individual parts of his work may be those in which the dead poets, his ancestors, assert their immortality most vigorously."

According to Eliot, a genuine poet writes

> not merely with his own generation in his bones, but with a feeling that the whole of the literature from Homer and within it the whole of the literature of his own country has a simultaneous order.

The "mind of Europe," he stated, is much more important than the poet's own mind: "What happens is a continual surrender of himself as he is at the moment to something which is more valuable." Compare this with Jung:

> This re-immersion in the state of *participation mystique* is the secret of artistic creation and of the effect which great art has upon us, for at that level of experience it is no longer the weal

> or woe of the individual that counts, but the life of the collective. That is why every great work of art is objective and impersonal, and yet profoundly moving.
>
> The essence of a work of art is not to be found in the personal idiosyncrasies that creep into it—indeed, the more there are of them, the less it is a work of art—but in its rising above the personal and speaking from the mind and heart of the artist to the mind and heart of mankind. The personal aspect of art is a limitation and a vice.[3]

It is interesting that Eliot recognized the transcendent quality of great literature in time, but limited it in space: if in fact for "mind of Europe" we substitute "mind of man" there is not a single one of these ideas with which the archetypal critic would not agree.

Robert Frost, a poet who steadfastly refused identification with any school of a theoretical tendency, nevertheless observed that for him the act of writing a poem was a "voyage of discovery" in which the problem was to give a conscious form to that which was already preexistent in the unconscious. Frost's own poems are full of archetypal images. Perhaps the most persistent of these is the Tree, either singly, as in "Tree at My Window," or collectively, as in "Birches," "Stopping by Woods on a Snowy Evening," and "Come In," the last two of which are dominated by the archetype of the Enchanted Forest.

Among living critics who have postulated the existence of literary archetypes, one of the most active is Kenneth Burke, who, though his classification of them is unique and bears little resemblance to Jung's (he arranges them under various rubrics, one of which is literary form), nevertheless defines the concept of archetype in precisely the same terms. In "The Poetic Process," speaking of such rhetorical devices as contrast, balance, and crescendo, Burke observes:

> Art has always appealed, by the changing individuations of changing subject matter, to certain potentialities of appreciation which would seem to be inherent in the very germ-plasm of man, and which, since they are constant, we might call innate forms of the mind. These forms are the "potentiality for being interested by certain processes of arrangements." [4]

These "innate forms of the mind" are clearly archetypes in the sense that Jung used the term, in that they are both universal and inherited.

After observing the disgrace into which Platonic thought had fallen at the hands of the rationalists, and approving what he calls the essential justice of Plato's doctrines, Burke continues:

---

[3] C. G. Jung, *The Spirit in Man, Art and Literature* in *The Collected Works of C. G. Jung*, ed. by Sir Herbert Read, *et al.*, and trans. by R. F. C. Hull, Bollingen Series XX (Princeton: Princeton Univ. Press, 1966), Vol. 15, p. 105.

[4] Kenneth Burke, "The Poetic Process," *Counter-Statement*, 2nd. ed., (Los Altos, Cal.: Hermes, 1953), p. 45.

> We need but take his universals out of heaven and situate them in the human mind (a process begun by Kant), making them not metaphysical, but psychological. Instead of divine forms, we now have "conditions of appeal." There need not be a "divine content" in heaven for me to appreciate a contrast; but there *must be* in my mind the sense of contrast.[5]

Leaving the rubric of rhetoric for a broader principle of classification, he declares:

> The researches of anthropologists indicate that man has "progressed" in cultural cycles which repeat themselves in essence (in form) despite the limitless variety of specific details to embody such essences, or forms. Speech, material traits (for instance, tools), art, mythology, religion, social systems, property, government, and war—these are the nine "potentials" which man continually reindividuates into specific cultural channels, and which anthropologists call the "universal pattern." And when we speak of psychological universals, we mean simply that just as there is inborn in the germ-plasm of a dog the potentiality of barking, so there is inborn in the germ-plasm of man the potentiality of speech, art, mythology, and so on. And while these potentialities are constantly changing their external aspects, their "individuations," they do not change in essence. Given the potentiality for speech, the child of any culture will speak the language which it hears. There is no mental equipment for speaking Chinese which is different from the mental equipment for speaking English. But the potentiality externalizes itself in accordance with the traditions into which the individual happens to be born.[6]

Though Burke nowhere mentions Jung in this particular essay, the debt is very plain, as the reader who is unfamiliar with Jung's views will discover in the next section of this introduction, where these views are summarized.

Among other professional critics who have recently shown a tendency to speculate along archetypal lines we might mention Ernst Cassirer, for whom myth is a form of thought as autonomous as science, art, and language; Mario Praz, who based his monumental study of European romanticism (*The Romantic Agony*) on archetypal principles, though his approach was essentially Freudian; Maud Bodkin, who tested Jung's hypotheses on a number of literary masterpieces; Sit Herbert Read, whose focus has been primarily on the visual arts but who has provided occasional valuable insights into literary archetypes; Northrop Frye, who attempted a correlation between the primary modes of literature and the solar cycle of the day, the seasonal cycle of the year, and the organic cycle of human life; and W. H. Auden, who in 1950 contributed importantly to the literature of archetypes with a little-known book entitled *The Enchafèd Flood:*

---

[5] *Ibid.*, p. 48.
[6] *Ibid.*

A Romantic Iconography of the Sea. This list is by no means complete, and the critics differ considerably in their assumptions and in their conclusions; but they are similar in their general approach to the problem of literary value. There has thus been considerable professional activity in this area.

II

By far the most ambitious systematic investigation into the nature of archetypes was undertaken by the psychoanalyst Carl Jung. In his essay "Archetypes of the Collective Unconscious," first published in 1934, he attempted to classify those which he encountered most frequently in his patients: this classification was modified and expanded in succeeding studies, most of which have been included in Volume 9 (*The Archetypes and the Collective Unconscious*) of *The Collected Works of C. G. Jung.* Jung's interest was thus essentially clinical, and he was more concerned with the manifestation of archetypes in general behavior than in literature.

Early in his career Jung had been closely associated with Freud. He agreed with Freud's theory of a personal unconscious and with his explanation of how the unconscious is formed: conscious experience that caused conflict or that for some reason was unacceptable was repressed, thus becoming unconscious. Freud had also noted that there was a part of the unconscious that apparently had never been in consciousness; he labeled the contents of this portion "archaic remnants" and considered them to be of minor importance. Jung, however, became convinced that these remnants indicated the existence of another whole layer of the unconscious, one that was suprapersonal and hereditary. He never discarded the concept of a personal unconscious, but he complicated it considerably:

> A more or less superficial layer of the unconscious is undoubtedly personal. I call it the *personal unconscious.* But this personal unconscious rests upon a deeper layer, which does not derive from personal experience and is not a personal acquisition but is inborn. This deeper layer I call *collective unconscious.* I have chosen the term "collective" because this part of the unconscious is not individual but universal; in contrast to the personal psyche, it has contents and modes of behavior that are more or less the same everywhere and in all individuals. It is, in other words, identical in all men and thus constitutes a common substrate of a suprapersonal nature which is present in every one of us.[7]

Jung called the contents of the personal unconscious, complexes; the contents of the collective, archetypes. Not only were they impersonal, but they were inherited as well:

---

[7] Jung, *The Archetypes and the Collective Unconscious* in *The Collected Works, op. cit.,* 1959, Vol. 9, Part 1, p. 3.

> Like every animal, he [man] possesses a preformed psyche which breeds true to his species and which, on closer examination, reveals distinct features traceable to family antecedents. We have not the slightest reason to suppose that there are certain human activities or functions that could be exempted from this rule.[8]

In *Psychological Reflections*, he declared that the archetypes are "older than historical man, . . . have been ingrained in him from earliest times, and, eternally living, outlasting all generations, still make up the groundwork of the human psyche."[9] Jung was convinced that the psyche evolved simultaneously with the body, and just as the human body exhibits a basic conformity in spite of environmental differences, so does the human mind. He believed that discoveries in the development and structure of the mind would eventually result in a science that would correspond in the psychic area to comparative anatomy.

Archetypes, as such, cannot be expressed consciously; we know them only in the forms they assume as they project in human behavior. On the unconscious level we may experience them directly in dreams, and so dreams, as in Freudian psychology, are enormously revealing as clues to the content and functioning of the unconscious. "The archetype," Jung explained, "is essentially an unconscious content that is altered by becoming conscious and by being perceived, and it takes its color from his individual consciousness in which it happens to appear."[10] For practical purposes, therefore, Jung found it necessary to distinguish between archetype and "archetypal idea," the former a "hypothetical and irrepresentable model, something like the 'pattern of behavior' in biology,"[11] and the latter a manifestation of the archetype in conscious experience.

Because of its numinous nature, the concept of the pure archetype is somewhat difficult to grasp. It is not form so much as it is the *possibility* of form, or, as Jung phrased it, form without content: "An archetype in its quiescent, unprojected state has no exactly determinable form but is in itself an indefinite structure which can assume definite forms only in projection."[12] Jung had to cope repeatedly with the misconception that an archetype was determined in regard to its content. "A primordial image," he insisted, "is determined as to its contents only when it has become conscious and is therefore filled out with the material of conscious experience."[13] To describe exactly how an archetype functions, he used an analogy from chemistry that is strongly reminiscent of the one Eliot used in the above-mentioned essay to describe the process of poetic creation:

> Its form . . . might perhaps be compared to the axial nature of a crystal, which, as it were, preforms the crystalline structure in the mother liquid, although it has no material nature of its

---

[8] *Ibid.*, p. 78.
[9] Jung, *Psychological Reflections* (New York: Harper Torchbooks, 1961), p. 42.
[10] *Ibid.*, p. 5.
[11] *Ibid.*
[12] *Ibid.*, p. 70.
[13] *Ibid.*, p. 79.

> own. This first appears according to the specific way in which the ions and molecules aggregate. The archetype in itself is empty and purely formal, nothing but a *facultas praeformandi,* a possibility of representation which is given *a priori.* The representations themselves are not inherited, only the forms . . . Our comparison with the crystal is illuminating inasmuch as the axial system determines only the stereoscopic structure but not the concrete form of the individual crystal. This may be either large or small and it may vary endlessly by means of the different size of its planes or by the growing together of two crystals. The only thing that remains constant is the axial system, or rather, the invariable geometric proportions underlying it. The same is true of archetypes.[14]

In other analogies, Jung spoke of the archetype as "an instinctive *trend,* as marked as the impulse of birds to build nests, or ants to form organized colonies." And the collective unconscious, that matrix of psychic existence, he likened to an "ocean of images and figures which drift into consciousness [15] in our dreams or in abnormal states of mind." [16]

Besides dreams, other sources for the study of archetypes are paranoid delusions, trance states, the fantasies of small children, the behavior of primitive tribes living at a low level of consciousness, the visions of religious mystics and artists, and the myth and folklore of various cultures transmitted either orally or in literary form. These last are of particular interest to the literary critic, who normally lacks access to the sources available to the professional psychologist or anthropologist. Myths are archetypal representations on the racial scale:

> Just as the archetypes occur on the ethnological level as myths, so also they are found in every individual, and their effect is always strongest, that is, they anthropomorphize reality most, where consciousness is weakest and most restricted, and where fantasy can overrun the facts of the outer world.[17]

The prevalence of similar motifs in the myths of the world renders the existence of archetypes a plausible if not a necessary assumption:

> From the unconscious there emanate determining influences which, independently of tradition, guarantee in every single individual a similarity and even a sameness of experience, and also of the way it is represented imaginatively. One of the major proofs of this is the almost universal parallelism between mythological motifs, which, on account of their quality as primordial images, I have called archetypes.[18]

---

[14] *Ibid.,* pp. 79–80.

[15] Since dreaming is an unconscious process, Jung was apparently referring to the conscious process by which we recollect our dreams.

[16] C. G. Jung, "The Basic Postulates of Analytical Psychology," in *Modern Man in Search of a Soul* (New York: Harcourt Brace Jovanovich, 1950), p. 186.

[17] Jung, *Collected Works, op. cit.,* Vol. 9, p. 67.

[18] *Ibid.,* p. 58.

Classification of archetypes, based on the forms they assume in projection, is immensely difficult. For one thing, their number appears almost infinite, for, as Jung observed, there are as many archetypes as there are typical characters and situations in life. For another, it must be remembered that they undergo alteration in the projection process. Thirdly, it is possible for them to exist in combination—and it is our observation that, in literature at least, this may be the rule rather than the exception. The first archetype that Jung identified he called the *Shadow,* because it frequently appears in dreams as a dark personification, sometimes veiled or hooded. It represents those aspects of the personality that one is reluctant to admit to oneself and thus acts as a corrective to the *persona,* which is the mask one wears in public, the outer self that represents the conscious ego. When an individual tends to identify too completely with his persona, neglecting the claims of his deeper self, the Shadow rears itself. Like other important archetypes, it may operate either as a beneficent or malignant influence; when the latter, it takes the form of compulsive behavior of a destructive kind, as in the phenomenon known as daemonic possession. Robert Louis Stevenson's *The Strange Case of Dr. Jekyll and Mr. Hyde* (which was inspired by a dream) is a classical literary specimen of this archetype.

In Jung's system the problem of classification is further complicated by his conviction that the masculine psyche differs from the feminine in much the same way that the body does. Thus, while certain archetypes, like the Shadow, are the common property of both sexes, others are a monopoly of the male or female psyche. Jung had always been impressed with the fact that biologically each sex contains certain characteristics of its opposite, and he believed the same was true of the psyche. On this basis he distinguished two more archetypes: the *Anima* and the *Animus.*

The Anima is the female element in the male psyche—as Jung defined it, "the psychic representation of the minority of female genes in a man's body." [19] In dreams it is personified as a female figure or image. The materials composing this archetype come from two sources: the male's experience of his mother and the racial idea of woman that he inherits as a part of his collective unconscious, derived from man's experience of woman in the past. The resultant image, or archetype, he carries about with him as part of his psychic equipment and projects it upon persons of the opposite sex in whom he conceives an interest because they correspond to this image, little suspecting that its source is in himself. (The image is sometimes so powerful that it may force itself upon someone who actually bears little resemblance to it—the cause, Jung believed, of much friction both marital and extramarital.) The Anima is typically enigmatic or Sphinx-like: in art she may appear as a Mona Lisa, in myth as a Siren or a Lorelei, and in literature as a *femme fatale.* In everyday life this archetype seems to manifest itself most commonly in the form of erotic fantasy. In her beneficent aspect, the Anima, as the feminine element in man's unconscious, frequently rescues him from logical dilemmas because of her superior intuition, and sometimes leads him, as Beatrice led Dante, to a knowledge of the highest spiritual values.

---

[19] Jung, *The Archetypes and the Collective Unconscious, op. cit.,* p. 30.

The Animus is the counterpart of the Anima; it is the masculine element in the female psyche, formed from the woman's experience of her father and from the inherited image of man in her collective unconscious. In myths and fairy tales he often appears as a prince who has been transformed by sorcery into a beast or monster and who is enabled to recover his identity through a woman's love. In romantic novels he may assume the role of a Byronic hero. In his negative aspect he may be a robber or a murderer. Animus figures are frequently dangerous (Bluebeard in folklore) and sometimes multiple,[20] while the Anima is always solitary. Often he possesses a devilish sort of charm for the woman who has thus constituted him in her unconscious, like Heathcliff in *Wuthering Heights*, who may well have been an archetypal projection of Emily Brontë. The case of Heathcliff is interesting, for it shows that archetypes may exist in combination with other archetypes: Heathcliff could also legitimately be considered as a Shadow figure. On the personal level, the Animus, as the masculine element in woman's unconscious, may function positively as a corrective to impulsiveness, moodiness, and indecision; negatively, it may express itself in an unnatural rigidity of outlook or in the form of unalterable convictions that often have little relation to reality. Under Animus domination a woman becomes stiff and unyielding; she complains constantly of being "misunderstood" by men (the wife in Frost's "Home Burial" is an excellent case in point); and because of her domineering tendencies sometimes acquires the reputation of being a shrew or termagant, like Katherine in *The Taming of the Shrew*. Projection of the Animus onto eligible males (and some who are not so eligible) follows exactly the same pattern as for the opposite sex, sometimes with the same unfortunate consequences.

Other important archetypes in the Jungian system include the Mother, the Wise Old Man, the Trickster Figure, the Child, and the Hero. Some of these will be referred to in the introductions to the separate sections of this book.

III

In *The Masks of God*, Joseph Campbell notes that newly-hatched chickens, fresh from their shells, will dart for cover when a hawk flies over them, but that other birds will not produce this effect upon them; moreover, a wooden model of a hawk mounted on a wire suspended overhead for that purpose will cause them to run if it is drawn forward, but not if drawn backward. He inquires: "Whence this abrupt seizure by an image to which there is no counterpart in the chicken's world? Living gulls and ducks, herons and pigeons, leave it cold; but the work of art strikes some very deep chord." [21] Some critics, seeing an analogy with literature, have commented as follows on Professor Campbell's observation:

---

[20] This aspect of the Animus would appear to be derived from the woman's inherited image of man.

[21] Joseph Campbell, *The Masks of God: Primitive Mythology* (New York: Viking, 1959), p. 31.

> It is with the relationship of literary art to "some very deep chord" in human nature that mythological criticism deals. The myth critic is concerned to seek out those mysterious artifacts built into certain literary "forms" which elicit, with almost uncanny force, dramatic and universal reactions. He wishes to discover how it is that certain works of literature, usually those that have become, or promise to become, "classics," image a kind of reality to which readers give perennial response—while other works, seemingly as well constructed, and even some forms of reality, leave us cold. Speaking figuratively, the myth critic studies in depth the "wooden hawks" of great literature: the so-called "archetypes" or "archetypal patterns" which the writer has drawn forward along the tensed structural wires of his masterpiece and which vibrate in such a way that a sympathetic resonance is started deep within the reader.[22]

Perhaps this analogy will serve to return us to the problem of literary value. From what has been said, it is clear that the presence of archetypal contents in a literary work is one factor in determining its greatness if in the concept of greatness we include—as surely we must—relevance to the psychological needs of human beings. It is certainly not the only factor; it may not even be the principal one. We are aware of the very real and obvious danger in the archetypal approach that the aesthetic quality of a work may be overlooked in favor of its psychological interest—that an inferior work, by reason of its archetypal content, may be elevated above a superior work in which archetypal elements seem either to be lacking or difficult to identify. A number of psychologists have fallen into this error, Jung among them, who, though he recognized the value of *Moby Dick,* was almost equally ready to assert what he thought was the importance of Rider Haggard's *She*.

So as not to be guilty of this kind of naïveté, we have selected stories that we feel succeed first of all by literary standards. In all honesty we must admit that there are two or three exceptions we felt worth making to this rule; they involve pieces of very early literature. Except for these they are all, we feel, stories of genuine literary merit. Actually it is rather surprising that so many of them succeed so well in translation, which is perhaps testimony to the power of the archetypes to transcend the barrier of language as well as of time.

Granted the limitations of our approach, we think the archetype must be reckoned with in any serious discussion of literary value. William Empson once observed apropos of Cleanth Brooks's analysis of John Crowe Ransom's poem, "Janet Waking," that he admired it enormously as literary criticism but that the subject of the poem (which he took to be the grief of a little girl over the death of her pet chicken) was essentially trivial, so that Brooks's ingenuity, so to speak, had been wasted. It happened that Empson was wrong; the real subject of the poem is death and the inability of innocence to cope with its meaning. Empson was wrong,

---

22 Wilfred Guerin, Earle Labor, Lee Morgan, and John Willingham, *A Handbook of Critical Approaches to Literature* (New York: Harper & Row, 1966), pp. 115–116.

but he might have been right, and he *was* right to the extent that there are major and minor themes in literature. And the major themes, somehow, seem always to involve the presence of archetypes.

As to the system of classification that we follow, it was suggested in a general way by Jung, but it is much less highly schematized. In its specifics, Jungian psychology sometimes makes assumptions that seem hazardous and somewhat arbitrary. Jung was constantly revising his own system, and had he worked primarily with literary materials rather than with the dreams of individual patients, his classifications would probably have been somewhat different. We have been mindful, for our part, of the studies of other researchers, especially in the area of literature. These touch Jung's at some points but not at others, and we were interested in abstracting what they seemed to have in common. But most of all, the archetypes we finally selected are those which we ourselves found to appear repeatedly in the hundreds of stories which we read: in this sense, they might almost be said to have chosen themselves. It should go without saying that we have not attempted to be exhaustive in any sense and have been content to deal with only a few of the more persistent characters and themes.

The tendency of archetypes to overlap and combine has already been commented upon. Kafka's "A Hunger Artist," for instance, could almost as well have been placed in the category of Return to the Womb as in the Search, while the protagonist in Lawrence's "The Woman Who Rode Away" is perhaps as much a Search figure as a Scapegoat.

Severe limitations were naturally imposed by the fact that we are dealing exclusively with the short story. This prevented our using material that is formally of a mythological or religious character. Thus, while the literatures of Greece and Rome are normally a rich source for archetypal illustrations, the fact that we are not concerned with either epic or lyric poetry, nor with the drama, ruled out selections from these periods. Again, had the size of our project permitted us to draw upon the novel, innumerable excellent examples would have presented themselves.

Another limitation, dictated less by matters of form than by personal scruple, we imposed upon ourselves by deliberately avoiding stories that we felt had been over-anthologized. The seriousness of this restriction may be appreciated when it is understood that the archetypal qualities of such stories had, we felt, more or less proved their worth. We were tempted to include Shirley Jackson's "The Lottery" and Hawthorne's "My Kinsman, Major Molineux" in the Scapegoat category; Faulkner's "A Rose for Emily" and Hemingway's "The Snows of Kilimanjaro" in the Fatal Woman archetype; and Joyce's "Araby," Sherwood Anderson's "I Want to Know Why," and Hemingway's "My Old Man" as examples of Initiation. But we resisted the temptation, using instead other, less familiar stories—some of them by these same authors—that were perhaps as good on literary ground and that illustrated the archetype perhaps as effectively.

Another scruple involved the use of material that consciously exploited archetypal motifs. Archetypes tend to be more impressive when they emerge naturally from the author's mind than when he consciously recognizes them for what they are and deploys them explicitly as such. This was another reason for omitting "The Lottery," for example. But it is not always so easy to know when this has happened, and again we have probably been guilty of an occasional exception: Anaïs Nin's story, "Hejda," where symbols of transformation are employed with conscious artistry—and, let it be admitted, with considerable effect—is probably an example of this synthetic use of archetypal materials.

Considering the restrictions of the form, the range of selections is extremely wide. We felt that this diversity was required by our approach and that it supported emphatically the concept of the archetype. In this collection, writers of different color and different culture join in a common cause: to provide an aesthetic satisfaction that is based on their experience of what it is to be human. To a younger generation that has shown a very real and legitimate concern for the increasing loss of human values in contemporary society, this approach, we feel, has much to recommend it.

Part One

SOME ARCHETYPAL CHARACTERS

The Fatal Woman

THE *femme fatale* is one of the most important of all the archetypes; she occurs not only in *belles lettres,* but also in the literature of religion, mythology, and folklore, where she figures sometimes as a temptress, sometimes as a witch, sometimes as a vampire or succubus. She is traditionally destructive, though not always consciously so, and usually chooses for her victims men whom she delights in torturing in various ways. She does not always destroy them physically, preferring often to keep them alive while forcing them to submit to various humiliations; sometimes she destroys their souls instead of their bodies.

Perhaps the best discussion of the Fatal Woman in Western literature is by Mario Praz in *The Romantic Agony,* referred to in the Introduction. Praz notes the presence of this archetype in ancient Greece, in mythology and fables (Lilith, Scylla, the Sphinx, Harpies, and Furies) and in epic and dramatic poetry (Homer and Aeschylus), and traces it through the Renaissance into the modern period, where it achieved a kind of culmination in the literature of Romanticism. Flaubert's Salammbô and Queen of Sheba, Mérimée's Carmen, Gautier's Cleopatra, Dostoyevsky's Nastasia Filippovna, Swinburne's Mary Stuart and Atalanta, Rossetti's Sister Helen, Coleridge's Geraldine, and Keats's La Belle Dame Sans Merci—all these bear witness to the abundance of this type in nineteenth-century European literature.

We might supplement this list by adding to it, on this side of the Atlantic, Hawthorne's Lady Eleanore Rochcliffe and Beatrice Rappaccini and James's Princess Casamassima, Madame de Mauves, and Madame Merle. In the twentieth century the American type continued to flourish in Fitzgerald (Judy Jones in "Winter Dreams"); in Faulkner (Emily Grierson in "A Rose for Emily"); and in Hemingway (Margot Macomber in "The Short, Happy Life of Francis Macomber," and Helen, the "rich bitch" in "The Snows of Kilimanjaro"). Examples are almost as numerous in poetry and drama.

As was pointed out in the Introduction, the Fatal Woman is identified with the Anima in Jungian psychology. Evidently referring to the novel by Heinrich Mann, *Professor Inrat* (of which the famous film *The Blue*

Angel was an adaptation), Jung says of this archetype: "When a highly esteemed professor in his seventies abandons his family and runs off with a young red-headed actress, we know that the gods have claimed another victim."

Traditionally the power and authority of the Fatal Woman are conferred upon her by the victim himself, who nevertheless feels peculiarly powerless to act otherwise—as in four of the five stories that follow. Perhaps partly for this reason, supernatural powers are sometimes attributed to her, as in the stories by Verga and Hawthorne, and her beauty is often of an exotic kind (Lady Eleanore is a good example). Praz notes that the male victim is typically lacking in aggressiveness:

> The lover is usually a youth, and maintains a passive attitude; he is obscure, and inferior either in condition or in physical exuberance to the woman, who stands in the same relation to him as do the female spiders, the praying mantis, etc., to their respective males: sexual cannibalism is her monopoly.

Fatal Women are traditionally pale: Frau von Rinnlingen, in "Little Herr Friedemann," has a "dead-white skin," and Verga's protagonist is "pale, as if always plagued by malaria."

But Fatal Women do not always give themselves away so easily: the American lady in "A Canary for One" seems innocuous, but in reality she is quite worthy of the company she keeps in this collection. Actually this story is a hybrid: the Fatal Woman archetype often coexists with that of the Earth-Mother.

THE SHE-WOLF
by Giovanni Verga

She was tall, thin; she had the firm and vigorous breasts of the olive-skinned—and yet she was no longer young; she was pale, as if always plagued by malaria, and in that pallor, two enormous eyes, and fresh red lips which devoured you.

In the village they called her the She-wolf, because she never had enough—of anything. The women made the sign of the cross when they saw her pass, alone as a wild bitch, prowling about suspiciously like a famished wolf; with her red lips she sucked the blood of their sons and husbands in a flash, and pulled them behind her skirt with a single glance of those devilish eyes, even if they were before the altar of Saint Agrippina. Fortunately, the She-wolf never went to church, not at Easter, not at Christmas, not to hear Mass, not for confession.—Father Angiolino of Saint Mary of Jesus, a true servant of God, had lost his soul on account of her.

Maricchia, a good girl, poor thing, cried in secret because she was the She-wolf's daughter, and no one would marry her, though, like every other girl in the village, she had her fine linen in a chest and her good land under the sun.

One day the She-wolf fell in love with a handsome young man who had just returned from the service and was mowing hay with her in the fields of the notary; and she fell in love in the strongest sense of the word, feeling the flesh afire beneath her clothes; and staring him in the eyes, she suffered the thirst one has in the hot hours of June, deep in the plain. But he went on mowing undisturbed, his nose bent over the swaths.

"What's wrong, Pina?" he would ask.

In the immense fields, where you heard only the crackling flight of the grasshoppers, as the sun hammered down overhead, the She-wolf gathered bundle after bundle, and sheaf after sheaf, never tiring, never straightening up for an instant, never raising the flask to her lips, just to remain at the heels of Nanni, who mowed and mowed and asked from time to time:

"What is it you want, Pina?"

One evening she told him, while the men were dozing on the threshing floor, tired after the long day, and the dogs were howling in the vast, dark countryside.

"It's you I want. You who're beautiful as the sun and sweet as honey. I want you!"

From *The She-Wolf and Other Stories*, translated by Giovanni Cecchetti, pp. 3–9. Reprinted by permission of The Regents of the University of California.

"And I want your daughter, instead, who's a maid," answered Nanni laughing.

The She-wolf thrust her hands into her hair, scratching her temples, without saying a word, and walked away. And she did not appear at the threshing floor any more. But she saw Nanni again in October, when they were making olive oil, for he was working near her house, and the creaking of the press kept her awake all night.

"Get the sack of olives," she said to her daughter, "and come with me."

Nanni was pushing olives under the millstone with a shovel, shouting "Ohee" to the mule, to keep it from stopping.

"You want my daughter Maricchia?" Pina asked him.

"What'll you give your daughter Maricchia?" answered Nanni.

"She has all her father's things, and I'll give her my house too; as for me, all I need is a little corner in the kitchen, enough for a straw mattress."

"If that's the way it is, we can talk about it at Christmas," said Nanni.

Nanni was all greasy and filthy, spattered with oil and fermented olives, and Maricchia didn't want him at any price. But her mother grabbed her by the hair before the fireplace, muttering between her teeth:

"If you don't take him, I'll kill you!"

The She-wolf was almost sick, and the people were saying that when the devil gets old he becomes a hermit. She no longer roamed here and there, no longer lingered at the doorway, with those bewitched eyes. Whenever she fixed them on his face, those eyes of hers, her son-in-law began to laugh and pulled out the scapular of the Virgin to cross himself. Maricchia stayed at home nursing the babies, and her mother went into the fields to work with the men, and just like a man too, weeding, hoeing, feeding the animals, pruning the vines, despite the northeast and levantine winds of January or the August sirocco, when the mules' heads drooped and the men slept face down along the wall, on the north side. "In those hours between nones and vespers when no good woman goes roving around," * Pina was the only living soul to be seen wandering in the countryside, over the burning stones of the paths, through the scorched stubble of the immense fields that became lost in the suffocating heat, far, far away toward the foggy Etna, where the sky was heavy on the horizon.

"Wake up!" said the She-wolf to Nanni, who was sleeping in the ditch, along the dusty hedge, his head on his arms. "Wake up. I've brought you some wine to cool your throat."

Nanni opened his drowsy eyes wide, still half asleep, and finding her standing before him, pale, with her arrogant breasts and her coal-black eyes, he stretched out his hands gropingly.

"No! no good woman goes roving around in the hours between nones and vespers!" sobbed Nanni, throwing his head back into the dry grass of the ditch, deep, deep, his nails in his scalp. "Go away! go away! don't come to the threshing floor again!"

---

* An old Sicilian proverb, which refers to the hours of the early afternoon, when the Sicilian countryside lies motionless under a scorching sun and no person would dare walk on the roads. Those hours are traditionally believed to be under the spell of malignant spirits.

The She-wolf was going away, in fact, retying her superb tresses, her gaze bent fixedly before her as she moved through the hot stubble, her eyes as black as coal.

But she came to the threshing floor again, and more than once, and Nanni did not complain. On the contrary, when she was late, in the hours between nones and vespers, he would go and wait for her at the top of the white, deserted path, with his forehead bathed in sweat; and he would thrust his hands into his hair, and repeat every time:

"Go away! go away! don't come to the threshing floor again!"

Maricchia cried night and day, and glared at her mother, her eyes burning with tears and jealousy, like a young she-wolf herself, every time she saw her come, mute and pale, from the fields.

"Vile, vile mother!" she said to her. "Vile mother!"

"Shut up!"

"Thief! Thief!"

"Shut up!"

"I'll go to the Sergeant, I will!"

"Go ahead!"

And she really did go, with her babies in her arms, fearing nothing, and without shedding a tear, like a madwoman, because now she too loved that husband who had been forced on her, greasy and filthy, spattered with oil and fermented olives.

The Sergeant sent for Nanni; he threatened him even with jail and the gallows. Nanni began to sob and tear his hair; he didn't deny anything, he didn't try to clear himself.

"It's the temptation!" he said. "It's the temptation of hell!"

He threw himself at the Sergeant's feet begging to be sent to jail. "For God's sake, Sergeant, take me out of this hell! Have me killed, put me in jail; don't let me see her again, never! never!"

"No!" answered the She-wolf instead, to the Sergeant. "I kept a little corner in the kitchen to sleep in, when I gave him my house as dowry. It's my house. I don't intend to leave it."

Shortly afterward, Nanni was kicked in the chest by a mule and was at the point of death, but the priest refused to bring him the Sacrament if the She-wolf did not go out of the house. The She-wolf left, and then her son-in-law could also prepare to leave like a good Christian; he confessed and received communion with such signs of repentance and contrition that all the neighbors and the curious wept before the dying man's bed.—And it would have been better for him to die that day, before the devil came back to tempt him again and creep into his body and soul, when he got well.

"Leave me alone!" he told the She-wolf. "For God's sake, leave me in peace! I've seen death with my own eyes! Poor Maricchia is desperate. Now the whole town knows about it! If I don't see you it's better for both of us . . ."

And he would have liked to gouge his eyes out not to see those of the She-wolf, for whenever they peered into his, they made him lose his body and soul. He did not know what to do to free himself from the spell. He paid for Masses for the souls in purgatory and asked the priest and the Sergeant for help. At Easter he went to confession, and in penance he publicly licked more than four feet of pavement, crawling on the pebbles in front of the church—and then, as the She-wolf came to tempt him again:

"Listen!" he said to her. "Don't come to the threshing floor again; if you do, I swear to God, I'll kill you!"

"Kill me," answered the She-wolf, "I don't care; I can't stand it without you."

As he saw her from the distance, in the green wheat fields, Nanni stopped hoeing the vineyard, and went to pull the ax from the elm. The She-wolf saw him come, pale and wild-eyed, with the ax glistening in the sun, but she did not fall back a single step, did not lower her eyes; she continued toward him, her hands laden with red poppies, her black eyes devouring him.

"Ah! damn your soul!" stammered Nanni.

DOUBTFUL HAPPINESS

by Guy de Maupassant

I can tell you the name neither of the country nor of the man. It was far, far from here, upon a hot, fertile coast. We followed, since morning, the shore and the wheat fields and the sea covered with the sun. Flowers grew down very near the waves, the light waves, so sweet and sleepy. It was very warm, but a gentle heat, perfumed with the fat, humid, fruitful earth; one could believe that he was breathing germs.

I had been told that this evening I would find hospitality in the house of a Frenchman who lived at the end of the promontory in a grove of orange trees. Who was he? I do not know yet. He had arrived one morning, ten years before this, bought the land, planted his vines and sown his seed; he had worked, had this man, with passion and fury. Month after month and year after year he had added to his domains, making the fertile, virgin soil yield without ceasing and amassing a fortune by his indefatigable labor.

It was said that he worked constantly. Up with the dawn, going through his fields until night, superintending everything without rest, he seemed

---

From *The Complete Short Stories of Guy de Maupassant,* with an introduction by Professor Artine Artinian (New York: Collier, 1903), pp. 3–22.

harassed by a fixed idea, tortured by an insatiable desire for money which nothing could distract or appease.

Now he seemed to be very rich.

The sun was setting when I reached his dwelling. This dwelling was at the end of a point in the midst of orange trees. It was a large, square house, very simple, overlooking the sea.

As I approached, a large, bearded man appeared in the doorway. Having saluted him, I asked for shelter for the night. He extended his hand and said, smiling:

"Enter, sir, you are at home."

He led me to a room, gave some orders to a servant with the perfect ease and good grace of a man of the world, then he left me, saying:

"We will dine when you are ready to come down."

We dined, tête-à-tête, upon a terrace opposite the sea. At first I spoke of his country, so rich, so far away, so little known! He smiled, answering in an abstracted way:

"Yes, this is a pretty country. But no country pleases one much when it is far from those they love."

"You regret France?"

"I—I long for Paris."

"Why not return there?"

"Oh! I am going to return there."

And gradually we began to talk of the French world, of the boulevards and of the many features of Paris. He asked me about men he had known, cities, names, all of them familiar names upon the vaudeville stage.

"Who does one see at Tortoni's these days?"

"The same ones, except the dead."

I looked at him with marked interest, pursued by some vague remembrance. Certainly I had seen that head somewhere! But where? And when? He seemed fatigued, although vigorous, sad, though resolute. His great blond beard fell upon his breast, and sometimes he would take it near his chin and draw it through his closed hand, slipping it along to the very end. He was a little bald but had thick eyebrows and a heavy mustache which mingled with the hair of his beard.

Behind us the sun was disappearing in the sea, throwing upon the coast a cloud of fire. The orange trees, in flower, exhaled a powerful, delicious fragrance on the evening air. Seeing nothing but me and fixing his look upon me, he seemed to discover in my eyes, to see at the depth of my soul, the well-known, much loved image of the broad walk, so far away, that extends from the Madeleine to the Rue Drouot.

"Do you know Bourtelle?" he asked.

"Yes, certainly."

"Is he much changed?"

"Yes, he is all white."

"And the Ridamie?"

"Always the same."

"And the women? Tell me about the women. Let us see. Did you know Suzanne Verner?"

"Yes, very well, to the end."

"Ah! And Sophie Astier?"

"Dead!"

"Poor girl! Can it be—— Did you know——"

He was suddenly silent. Then in a changed voice, his face growing pale, he continued:

"No, it is better not to speak of her; it disturbs me so."

Then as if to change the trend of his thought, he rose and said:

"Do you wish to go in?"

"I am willing to go." And I followed him into the house.

The rooms downstairs were enormous, bare, sad, and seemed abandoned. Some glass dishes were set upon the table by the tawny-skinned servants who constantly roamed around this dwelling. Two guns hung upon two nails on the wall, and in the corners were to be seen some spades, some fishlines, dried palm leaves and objects of every kind, placed there at random by those entering, that they might find them at hand should they chance to have need of them on going out.

My host smiled.

"This is a lodge, or rather the lodging place of an exile," he said, "but my chamber is more as it should be. Let us go in there."

I thought, on entering, that I was in a curiosity shop, so filled was the room with all kinds of things, things disconnected, strange and varied, that one felt to be souvenirs of something. Upon the walls were two pretty engravings of well-known paintings, some stuffs, some arms, swords, pistols; then, in the middle of the principal panel, a square of white satin in a gold frame.

Surprised, I approached to look at it, when I perceived a pin which held a hair in the middle of the shining silk.

My host placed his hand on my shoulder and said, smiling:

"That is the only thing that I see here and the only thing I have seen for ten years. M. Prudhomme exclaims: 'This sword is the most beautiful day in my life.' But I say: 'This pin is all of my life.' "

I sought for a commonplace phrase and ended by saying:

"You have suffered through some woman?"

He replied brusquely: "You may say I have suffered miserably, but come out on my balcony. A name has suddenly come to my lips that I have not dared to pronounce, because if you had answered 'dead' as you did when I spoke of Sophie Astier, my brain would be on fire, even to-day."

We were upon a large balcony where we could see two gulfs, one on the right and the other on the left, shut in by high, gray mountains. It was the hour of twilight, when the sun, entirely out of sight, no longer lights the earth, except by reflection from the sky.

He continued: "Do you know if Jeanne de Limours still lives?"

His eye, fixed on mine, was full of trembling anxiety. I smiled and answered:

"Yes indeed, and prettier than ever."

"You know her?"

"Yes."

He hesitated. Then asked: "Completely?"

"No."

He took my hand. "Tell me about her," he said.

"I have nothing to tell; she is one of the most charming women, or rather girls, in Paris, and the most courted. She leads an agreeable, princesslike existence; that is all."

He murmured: "I love her," as if he had said: "I am going to die." Then, brusquely: "Ah! For three years that was a frightful but delicious existence of ours. I was very near killing her five or six times, and she tried to put out my eyes with that pin you were just looking at. Wait! Do you see the little white point under my left eye? That shows how we loved each other! How can I explain this passion? You could never comprehend it.

"There should be such a thing as a simple love, born of the force of two hearts and two souls, and assuredly there is such a thing as an atrocious love, cruelly torturing, born of the invincible rapture of two beings totally unlike, who detest while they adore each other.

"This girl ruined me in three years. I possessed four millions which she squandered in her calm way, tranquilly, and destroyed with a sweet smile which seemed to fall from her eyes upon her lips.

"You know her? Then you know that there is something irresistible about her! What is it? I do not know. Is it those gray eyes, whose look enters into you and remains there like the barb of an arrow? Or is it rather that sweet smile, indifferent and seductive, which stays on her face like a mask? Her slow manner penetrates little by little and takes hold of you like a perfume, as does her tall figure, which seems to balance itself as she passes, for she glides instead of walking, and her sweet voice, which drags a little and is so pretty that it seems to be the music of her smile; her gestures, too, her always moderate gestures, always right, which intoxicate the eye, so harmonious are they.

"For three years I saw only her upon the earth! How I suffered! Because she deceived me as well as everybody else. Why? For no reason, only for the sake of deceiving. And when I found it out and accused her of being a street girl, a bad woman, she said tranquilly: 'Well, we are not married, are we?'

"Since I have come here I have thought much about her and have succeeded in understanding her; that girl is Manon Lescaut over again. Manon could never love without deceiving, and for her love, pleasure and money were all."

He was silent. Then after some minutes he added:

"When I had squandered my last sou for her she simply said to me: 'You understand, my dear, that I cannot live on air and weather. I love you very much; I love you more than anyone, but I must live. Misery and I can never dwell in the same house.'

"And if I could only tell you what an atrocious life I led by her side! Whenever I looked at her I had as much desire to kill her as I had to embrace her. Whenever I looked at her there came to me a furious desire to open my arms, press her to me until I strangled her. There was something about her, behind her eyes, something perfidious and unseizable which made me furious against her, and perhaps it was for that very reason that I loved her so much. In her the Feminine, the odious, frightful

Feminine, was more prominent than in any other woman. She was charged and surcharged with it, as with a venomous fluid. She was Woman, more than anyone else has ever been.

"And whenever I went out with her she would cast her eyes over all men in such a fashion that she seemed to give herself to each one with only a look. This exasperated me but attached me more strongly to her, nevertheless. This creature belonged to everybody from merely passing through the street, in spite of me, in spite of herself, from her very nature, although the allurement was most modest and sweet. Do you understand?

"And what torment! At the theater, in a restaurant, it seemed to me that everyone possessed her before my eyes. And whenever I left her alone others did, in fact, possess her.

"It is ten years now since I saw her, and I love her now more than ever."

Night had spread over the earth. A powerful perfume of orange flowers was in the air.

I said to him: "Will you try to see her again?"

He answered: "Surely! I have here now, in money and land, seven or eight hundred thousand francs. When the million is completed I shall sell all and set out. With that I can have one year with her, one good, entire year. And then—adieu; my life will be finished."

I asked: "And after that?"

"After that," he answered, "I don't know. It will be finished. Perhaps I shall ask her to take me as a *valet de chambre*."

LITTLE HERR FRIEDEMANN

by Thomas Mann

It was the nurse's fault. When they first suspected, Frau Consul Friedemann had spoken to her very gravely about the need of controlling her weakness. But what good did that do? Or the glass of red wine which she got daily besides the beer which was needed for the milk? For they suddenly discovered that she even sank so low as to drink the methylated spirit which was kept for the spirit lamp. Before they could send her away and get someone to take her place, the mischief was done.

Reprinted from *Stories of Three Decades*, by Thomas Mann, translated by H. T. Lowe-Porter, pp. 3–22, by permission of Martin Secker & Warburg Ltd. and Alfred A. Knopf, Inc., publishers.

One day the mother and sisters came home to find that little Johannes, then about a month old, had fallen from the couch and lay on the floor, uttering an appallingly faint little cry, while the nurse stood beside him quite stupefied.

The doctor came and with firm, gentle hands tested the little creature's contracted and twitching limbs. He made a very serious face. The three girls stood sobbing in a corner and the Frau Consul in the anguish of her heart prayed aloud.

The poor mother, just before the child's birth, had already suffered a crushing blow: her husband, the Dutch Consul, had been snatched away from her by sudden and violent illness, and now she was too broken to cherish any hope that little Johannes would be spared to her. But by the second day the doctor had given her hand an encouraging squeeze and told her that all immediate danger was over. There was no longer any sign that the brain was affected. The facial expression was altered, it had lost the fixed and staring look. . . . Of course, they must see how things went on—and hope for the best, hope for the best.

The grey gabled house in which Johannes Friedemann grew up stood by the north gate of the little old commercial city. The front door led into a large flag-paved entry, out of which a stair with a white wooden balustrade led up into the second storey. The faded wall-paper in the living-room had a landscape pattern, and straight-backed chairs and sofas in dark-red plush stood round the heavy mahogany table.

Often in his childhood Johannes sat here at the window, which always had a fine showing of flowers, on a small footstool at his mother's feet, listening to some fairy-tale she told him, gazing at her smooth grey head, her mild and gentle face, and breathing in the faint scent she exhaled. She showed him the picture of his father, a kindly man with grey side-whiskers—he was now in heaven, she said, and awaiting them there. Behind the house was a small garden where in summer they spent much of their time, despite the smell of burnt sugar which came over from the refinery close by. There was a gnarled old walnut tree in whose shade little Johannes would sit, on a low wooden stool, cracking walnuts, while Frau Friedemann and her three daughters, now grown women, took refuge from the sun under a grey canvas tent. The mother's gaze often strayed from her embroidery to look with sad and loving eyes at her child.

He was not beautiful, little Johannes, as he crouched on his stool industriously cracking his nuts. In fact, he was a strange sight, with his pigeon breast, humped back, and disproportionately long arms. But his hands and feet were delicately formed, he had soft red-brown eyes like a doe's, a sensitive mouth, and fine, light-brown hair. His head, had it not sat so deep between his shoulders, might almost have been called pretty.

When he was seven he went to school, where time passed swiftly and uniformly. He walked every day, with the strut deformed people often have, past the quaint gabled houses and shops to the old schoolhouse with the vaulted arcades. When he had done his preparation he would read in his books with the lovely title-page illustrations in colour, or else work in the garden, while his sisters kept house for their invalid mother. They went out too, for they belonged to the best society of the town; but unfortunately they had not married, for they had not much money nor any looks to recommend them.

Johannes too was now and then invited out by his schoolmates, but it is not likely that he enjoyed it. He could not take part in their games, and they were always embarrassed in his company, so there was no feeling of good fellowship.

There came a time when he began to hear certain matters talked about, in the courtyard at school. He listened wide-eyed and large-eared, quite silent, to his companions' raving over this or that little girl. Such things, though they entirely engrossed the attention of these others, were not, he felt, for him; they belonged in the same category as the ball games and gymnastics. At times he felt a little sad. But at length he had become quite used to standing on one side and not taking part.

But after all it came about—when he was sixteen—that he felt suddenly drawn to a girl of his own age. She was the sister of a classmate of his, a blonde, hilarious hoyden, and he met her when calling at her brother's house. He felt strangely embarrassed in her neighbourhood; she too was embarrassed and treated him with such artificial cordiality that it made him sad.

One summer afternoon as he was walking by himself on the wall outside the town, he heard a whispering behind a jasmine bush and peeped cautiously through the branches. There she sat on a bench beside a long-legged, red-haired youth of his acquaintance. They had their arms about each other and he was imprinting on her lips a kiss, which she returned amid giggles. Johannes looked, turned round, and went softly away.

His head was sunk deeper than ever between his shoulders, his hands trembled, and a sharp pain shot upwards from his chest to his throat. But he choked it down, straightening himself as well as he could. "Good," said he to himself. "That is over. Never again will I let myself in for any of it. To the others it brings joy and happiness, for me it can only mean sadness and pain. I am done with it. For me that is all over. Never again."

The resolution did him good. He had renounced, renounced forever. He went home, took up a book, or else played on his violin, which despite his deformed chest he had learned to do.

At seventeen Johannes left school to go into business, like everybody else he knew. He was apprenticed to the big lumber firm of Herr Schlievogt down on the river-bank. They were kind and considerate, he on his side was responsive and friendly, time passed with peaceful regularity. But in his twenty-first year his mother died, after a lingering illness.

This was a sore blow for Johannes Friedemann, and the pain of it endured. He cherished this grief, he gave himself up to it as one gives oneself to a great joy, he fed it with a thousand childhood memories; it was the first important event in his life and he made the most of it.

Is not life in and for itself a good, regardless of whether we may call its content "happiness"? Johannes Friedemann felt that it was so, and he loved life. He, who had renounced the greatest joy it can bring us, taught himself with infinite, incredible care to take pleasure in what it had still to offer. A walk in the springtime in the parks surrounding the town; the fragrance of a flower; the song of a bird—might not one feel grateful for such things as these?

And that we need to be taught how to enjoy, yes, that our education is always and only equal to our capacity for enjoyment—he knew that too, and he trained himself. Music he loved, and attended all the concerts that were given in the town. He came to play the violin not so badly himself, no matter what a figure of fun he made when he did it; and took delight in every beautiful soft tone he succeeded in producing. Also, by much reading he came in time to possess a literary taste the like of which did not exist in the place. He kept up with the new books, even the foreign ones; he knew how to savour the seductive rhythm of a lyric or the ultimate flavour of a subtly told tale—yes, one might almost call him a connoisseur.

He learned to understand that to everything belongs its own enjoyment and that it is absurd to distinguish between an experience which is "happy" and one which is not. With a right good will he accepted each emotion as it came, each mood, whether sad or gay. Even he cherished the unfulfilled desires, the longings. He loved them for their own sakes and told himself that with fulfilment the best of them would be past. The vague, sweet, painful yearning and hope of quiet spring evenings—are they not richer in joy than all the fruition the summer can bring? Yes, he was a connoisseur, our little Herr Friedemann.

But of course they did not know that, the people whom he met on the street, who bowed to him with the kindly, compassionate air he knew so well. They could not know that this unhappy cripple, strutting comically along in his light overcoat and shiny top hat—strange to say, he was a little vain—they could not know how tenderly he loved the mild flow of his life, charged with no great emotions, it is true, but full of a quiet and tranquil happiness which was his own creation.

But Herr Friedemann's great preference, his real passion, was for the theatre. He possessed a dramatic sense which was unusually strong; at a telling theatrical effect or the catastrophe of a tragedy his whole small frame would shake with emotion. He had his regular seat in the first row of boxes at the opera-house; was an assiduous frequenter and often took his sisters with him. Since their mother's death they kept house for their brother in the old home which they all owned together.

It was a pity they were unmarried still; but with the decline of hope had come resignation—Friederike, the eldest, was seventeen years further on than Herr Friedemann. She and her sister Henriette were overtall and thin, whereas Pfiffi, the youngest, was too short and stout. She had a funny way, too, of shaking herself as she talked, and water came in the corners of her mouth.

Little Herr Friedemann did not trouble himself overmuch about his three sisters. But they stuck together loyally and were always of one mind. Whenever an engagement was announced in their circle they with one voice said how very gratifying that was.

Their brother continued to live with them even after he became independent, as he did by leaving Herr Schlievogt's firm and going into business for himself, in an agency of sorts, which was no great tax on his time. His offices were in a couple of rooms on the ground floor of the house so that at mealtimes he had but the pair of stairs to mount—for he suffered now and then from asthma.

His thirtieth birthday fell on a fine warm June day, and after dinner he sat out in the grey canvas tent, with a new head-rest embroidered by Henriette. He had a good cigar in his mouth and a good book in his hand. But sometimes he would put the latter down to listen to the sparrows chirping blithely in the old nut tree and look at the clean gravel path leading up to the house between lawns bright with summer flowers.

Little Herr Friedemann wore no beard, and his face had scarcely changed at all, save that the features were slightly sharper. He wore his fine light-brown hair parted on one side.

Once, as he let the book fall on his knee and looked up into the sunny blue sky, he said to himself: "Well, so that is thirty years. Perhaps there may be ten or even twenty more, God knows. They will mount up without a sound or a stir and pass by like those that are gone; and I look forward to them with peace in my heart."

Now, it happened in July of the same year that a new appointment to the office of District Commandant had set the whole town talking. The stout and jolly gentleman who had for many years occupied the post had been very popular in social circles and they saw him go with great regret. It was in compliance with goodness knows what regulations that Herr von Rinnlingen and no other was sent hither from the capital.

In any case the exchange was not such a bad one. The new Commandant was married but childless. He rented a spacious villa in the southern suburbs of the city and seemed to intend to set up an establishment. There was a report that he was very rich—which received confirmation in the fact that he brought with him four servants, five riding and carriage horses, a landau and a light hunting-cart.

Soon after their arrival the husband and wife left cards on all the best society, and their names were on every tongue. But it was no Herr von Rinnlingen, it was his wife who was the centre of interest. All the men were dazed, for the moment too dazed to pass judgment; but their wives were quite prompt and definite in the view that Gerda von Rinnlingen was not their sort.

"Of course, she comes from the metropolis, her ways would naturally be different," Frau Hagenström, the lawyer's wife, said, in conversation with Henriette Friedemann. "She smokes, and she rides. That is of course. But it is her manners—they are not only free, they are positively brusque, or even worse. You see, no one could call her ugly, one might even say she is pretty; but she has not a trace of feminine charm in her looks or gestures or her laugh—they completely lack everything that makes a man fall in love with a woman. She is not a flirt—and goodness knows I would be the last to disparage her for that. But it is strange to see so young a woman—she is only twenty-four—so entirely wanting in natural charm. I am not expressing myself very well, my dear, but I know what I mean. All the men are simply bewildered. In a few weeks, you will see, they will be disgusted."

"Well," Fräulein Friedemann said, "she certainly has everything she wants."

"Yes," cried Frau Hagenström, "look at her husband! And how does she treat him? You ought to see it—you will see it! I would be the first to approve of a married woman behaving with a certain reserve towards the other sex. But how does she behave to her own husband? She has a way of fixing him with an ice-cold stare and saying 'My dear friend!' with a pitying expression that drives me mad. For when you look at him—upright, correct, gallant, a brilliant officer and a splendidly preserved man of forty! They have been married four years, my dear."

Herr Friedemann was first vouchsafed a glimpse of Frau von Rinnlingen in the main street of the town, among all the rows of shops, at midday, when he was coming from the Bourse, where he had done a little bidding.

He was strolling along beside Herr Stephens, looking tiny and important, as usual. Herr Stephens was in the wholesale trade, a huge stocky man with round side-whiskers and bushy eyebrows. Both of them wore top hats; their overcoats were unbuttoned on account of the heat. They tapped their canes along the pavement and talked of the political situation; but half-way down the street Stephens suddenly said:

"Deuce take it if there isn't the Rinnlingen driving along."

"Good," answered Herr Friedemann in his high, rather sharp voice, looking expectantly ahead. "Because I have never yet set eyes on her. And here we have the yellow cart we hear so much about."

It was in fact the hunting-cart which Frau von Rinnlingen was herself driving today with a pair of thoroughbreds; a groom sat behind her, with folded arms. She wore a loose beige coat and skirt and a small round straw hat with a brown leather band, beneath which her well-waved red-blond hair, a good, thick crop, was drawn into a knot at the nape of her neck. Her face was oval, with a dead-white skin and faint bluish shadows lurking under the close-set eyes. Her nose was short but well-shaped, with a becoming little saddle of freckles; whether her mouth was as good or no could not be told, for she kept it in continual motion, sucking the lower and biting the upper lip.

Herr Stephens, as the cart came abreast of them, greeted her with a great show of deference; little Herr Friedemann lifted his hat too and looked at her with wide-eyed attention. She lowered her whip, nodded slightly, and drove slowly past, looking at the houses and shop-windows.

After a few paces Herr Stephens said:

"She has been taking a drive and was on her way home."

Little Herr Friedemann made no answer, but stared before him at the pavement. Presently he started, looked at his companion, and asked: "What did you say?"

And Herr Stephens repeated his acute remark.

Three days after that Johannes Friedemann came home at midday from his usual walk. Dinner was at half past twelve, and he would spend the interval in his office at the right of the entrance door. But the maid came across the entry and told him that there were visitors.

"In my office?" he asked.

"No, upstairs with the mistresses."

"Who are they?"

"Herr and Frau Colonel von Rinnlingen."

"Ah," said Johannes Friedemann. "Then I will—"

And he mounted the stairs. He crossed the lobby and laid his hand on the knob of the high white door leading into the "landscape room." And then he drew back, turned round, and slowly returned as he had come. And spoke to himself, for there was no one else there, and said: "No, better not."

He went into his office, sat down at his desk, and took up the paper. But after a little he dropped it again and sat looking to one side out of the window. Thus he sat until the maid came to say that luncheon was ready; then he went up into the dining-room where his sisters were already waiting, and sat down in his chair, in which there were three music-books.

As she ladled the soup Henriette said:

"Johannes, do you know who were here?"

"Well?" he asked.

"The new Commandant and his wife."

"Indeed? That was friendly of them."

"Yes," said Pfiffi, a little water coming in the corners of her mouth. "I found them both very agreeable."

"And we must lose no time in returning the call," said Friederike. "I suggest that we go next Sunday, the day after tomorrow."

"Sunday," Henriette and Pfiffi said.

"You will go with us, Johannes?" asked Friederike.

"Of course he will," said Pfiffi, and gave herself a little shake. Herr Friedemann had not heard her at all; he was eating his soup, with a hushed and troubled air. It was as though he were listening to some strange noise he heard.

Next evening *Lohengrin* was being given at the opera, and everybody in society was present. The small auditorium was crowded, humming with voices and smelling of gas and perfumery. And every eye-glass in the stalls was directed towards box thirteen, next to the stage; for this was the first appearance of Herr and Frau von Rinnlingen and one could give them a good looking-over.

When little Herr Friedemann, in flawless dress clothes and glistening white pigeon-breasted shirt-front, entered his box, which was number thirteen, he started back at the door, making a gesture with his hand towards his brow. His nostrils dilated feverishly. Then he took his seat, which was next to Frau von Rinnlingen's.

She contemplated him for a little while, with her under lip stuck out; then she turned to exchange a few words with her husband, a tall, broad-shouldered gentleman with a brown, good-natured face and turned-up moustaches.

When the overture began and Frau von Rinnlingen leaned over the balustrade Herr Friedemann gave her a quick, searching side glance. She wore a light-coloured evening frock, the only one in the theatre which was slightly low in the neck. Her sleeves were full and her white gloves came up to her elbows. Her figure was statelier than it had looked under the loose coat; her full bosom slowly rose and fell and the knot of red-blond hair hung low and heavy at the nape of her neck.

Herr Friedemann was pale, much paler than usual, and little beads of perspiration stood on his brow beneath the smoothly parted brown hair. He could see Frau von Rinnlingen's left arm, which lay upon the balustrade. She had taken off her glove and the rounded, dead-white arm and ringless hand, both of them shot with pale blue veins, were directly under his eye—he could not help seeing them.

The fiddles sang, the trombones crashed, Telramund was slain, general jubilation reigned in the orchestra, and little Herr Friedemann sat there motionless and pallid, his head drawn in between his shoulders, his forefinger to his lips and one hand thrust into the opening of his waistcoat.

As the curtain fell, Frau von Rinnlingen got up to leave the box with her husband. Johannes Friedemann saw her without looking, wiped his handkerchief across his brow, then rose suddenly and went as far as the door into the foyer, where he turned, came back to his chair, and sat down in the same posture as before.

When the bell rang and his neighbours re-entered the box he felt Frau von Rinnlingen's eyes upon him, so that finally against his will he raised his head. As their eyes met, hers did not swerve aside; she continued to gaze without embarrassment until he himself, deeply humiliated, was forced to look away. He turned a shade paler and felt a strange, sweet pang of anger and scorn. The music began again.

Towards the end of the act Frau von Rinnlingen chanced to drop her fan; it fell at Herr Friedemann's feet. They both stooped at the same time, but she reached it first and gave a little mocking smile as she said: "Thank you."

Their heads were quite close together and just for a second he got the warm scent of her breast. His face was drawn, his whole body twitched, and his heart thumped so horribly that he lost his breath. He sat without moving for half a minute, then he pushed back his chair, got up quietly, and went out.

He crossed the lobby, pursued by the music; got his top hat from the cloak-room, his light overcoat and his stick, went down the stairs and out of doors.

It was a warm, still evening. In the gas-lit street the gabled houses towered towards a sky where stars were softly beaming. The pavement echoed the steps of a few passers-by. Someone spoke to him, but he heard and saw nothing; his head was bowed and his deformed chest shook with the violence of his breathing. Now and then he murmured to himself:

"My God, my God!"

He was gazing horror-struck within himself, beholding the havoc which had been wrought with his tenderly cherished, scrupulously managed feelings. Suddenly he was quite overpowered by the strength of his tortured longing. Giddy and drunken he leaned against a lamp-post and his quivering lips uttered the one word: "Gerda!"

The stillness was complete. Far and wide not a soul was to be seen. Little Herr Friedemann pulled himself together and went on, up the street in which the opera-house stood and which ran steeply down to the river, then along the main street northwards to his home.

How she had looked at him! She had forced him, actually, to cast down his eyes! She had humiliated him with her glance. But was she not a woman and he a man? And those strange brown eyes of hers—had they not positively glittered with unholy joy?

Again he felt the same surge of sensual, impotent hatred mount up in him; then he relived the moment when her head had touched his, when he had breathed in the fragrance of her body—and for the second time he halted, bent his deformed torso backwards, drew in the air through clenched teeth, and murmured helplessly, desperately, uncontrollably:

"My God, my God!"

Then went on again, slowly, mechanically, through the heavy evening air, through the empty echoing streets until he stood before his own house. He paused a minute in the entry, breathing the cool, dank inside air; then he went into his office.

He sat down at his desk by the open window and stared straight ahead of him at a large yellow rose which somebody had set there in a glass of water. He took it up and smelt it with his eyes closed, then put it down with a gesture of weary sadness. No, no. That was all over. What was even that fragrance to him now? What any of all those things that up to now had been the well-springs of his joy?

He turned away and gazed into the quiet street. At intervals steps passed and the sound died away. The stars stood still and glittered. He felt so weak, so utterly tired to death. His head was quite vacant, and suddenly his despair began to melt into a gentle, pervading melancholy. A few lines of a poem flickered through his head, he heard the *Lohengrin* music in his ears, he saw Frau von Rinnlingen's face and her round white arm on the red velvet—then he fell into a heavy fever-burdened sleep.

Often he was near waking, but feared to do so and managed to sink back into forgetfulness again. But when it had grown quite light, he opened his eyes and looked round him with a wide and painful gaze. He remembered everything, it was as though the anguish had never been intermitted by sleep.

His head was heavy and his eyes burned. But when he had washed up and bathed his head with cologne he felt better and sat down in his place by the still open window. It was early, perhaps only five o'clock. Now and then a baker's boy passed; otherwise there was no one to be seen. In the opposite house the blinds were down. But birds were twittering and the sky was luminously blue. A wonderfully beautiful Sunday morning.

A feeling of comfort and confidence came over little Herr Friedemann. Why had he been distressing himself? Was not everything just as it had been? The attack of yesterday had been a bad one. Granted. But it should be the last. It was not too late, he could still escape destruction. He must avoid every occasion of a fresh seizure; he felt sure he could do this. He felt the strength to conquer and suppress his weakness.

It struck half past seven and Friederike came in with the coffee, setting it on the round table in front of the leather sofa against the rear wall.

"Good morning, Johannes," said she; "here is your breakfast."

"Thanks," said little Herr Friedemann. And then: "Dear Friederike, I am sorry, but you will have to pay your call without me, I do not feel well enough to go. I have slept badly and have a headache—in short, I must ask you—"

"What a pity!" answered Friederike. "You must go another time. But you do look ill. Shall I lend you my menthol pencil?"

"Thanks," said Herr Friedemann. "It will pass." And Friederike went out.

Standing at the table he slowly drank his coffee and ate a croissant. He felt satisfied with himself and proud of his firmness. When he had finished he sat down again by the open window, with a cigar. The food had done him good and he felt happy and hopeful. He took a book and sat reading and smoking and blinking into the sunlight.

Morning had fully come, wagons rattled past, there were many voices and the sound of the bells on passing trams. With and among it all was woven the twittering and chirping; there was a radiant blue sky, a soft mild air.

At ten o'clock he heard his sisters cross the entry; the front door creaked, and he idly noticed that they passed his window. An hour went by. He felt more and more happy.

A sort of hubris mounted in him. What a heavenly air—and how the birds were singing! He felt like taking a little walk. Then suddenly, without any transition, yet accompanied by a terror namelessly sweet came the thought: "Suppose I were to go to her!" And suppressing, as though by actual muscular effort, every warning voice within him, he added with blissful resolution: "I will go to her!"

He changed into his Sunday clothes, took his top hat and his stick, and hurried with quickened breath through the town and into the southern suburbs. Without looking at a soul he kept raising and dropping his head with each eager step, completely rapt in his exalted state until he arrived at the avenue of chestnut trees and the red brick villa with the name of Commandant von Rinnlingen on the gate-post.

But here he was seized by a tremor, his heart throbbed and pounded in his breast. He went across the vestibule and rang at the inside door. The die was cast, there was no retreating now. "Come what come may," thought he, and felt the stillness of death within him.

The door suddenly opened and the maid came towards him across the vestibule; she took his card and hurried away up the red-carpeted stair. Herr Friedemann gazed fixedly at the bright colour until she came back and said that her mistress would like him to come up.

He put down his stick beside the door leading into the salon and stole a look at himself in the glass. His face was pale, the eyes red, his hair was sticking to his brow, the hand that held his top hat kept on shaking.

The maid opened the door and he went in. He found himself in a rather large, half-darkened room, with drawn curtains. At his right was a piano, and about the round table in the centre stood several arm-chairs covered in brown silk. The sofa stood along the left-hand wall, with a landscape painting in a heavy gilt frame hanging above it. The wall-paper too was dark in tone. There was an alcove filled with potted palms.

A minute passed, then Frau von Rinnlingen opened the portières on the right and approached him noiselessly over the thick brown carpet. She wore a simply cut frock of red and black plaid. A ray of light, with motes dancing in it, streamed from the alcove and fell upon her heavy red hair so that it shone like gold. She kept her strange eyes fixed upon him with a searching gaze and as usual stuck out her under lip.

"Good morning, Frau Commandant," began little Herr Friedemann, and looked up at her, for he came only as high as her chest. "I wished to pay you my respects too. When my sisters did so I was unfortunately out . . . I regretted sincerely . . ."

He had no idea at all what else he should say; and there she stood and gazed ruthlessly at him as though she would force him to go on. The blood rushed to his head. "She sees through me," he thought, "she will torture and despise me. Her eyes keep flickering. . . ."

But at last she said, in a very high, clear voice:

"It is kind of you to have come. I have also been sorry not to see you before. Will you please sit down?"

She took her seat close beside him, leaned back, and put her arm along the arm of the chair. He sat bent over, holding his hat between his knees. She went on:

"Did you know that your sisters were here a quarter of an hour ago? They told me you were ill."

"Yes," he answered, "I did not feel well enough to go out, I thought I should not be able to. That is why I am late."

"You do not look very well even now," said she tranquilly, not shifting her gaze. "You are pale and your eyes are inflamed. You are not very strong, perhaps?"

"Oh," said Herr Friedemann, stammering, "I've not much to complain of, as a rule."

"I am ailing a good deal too," she went on, still not turning her eyes from him, "but nobody notices it. I am nervous, and sometimes I have the strangest feelings."

She paused, lowered her chin to her breast, and looked up expectantly at him. He made no reply, simply sat with his dreamy gaze directed upon her. How strangely she spoke, and how her clear and thrilling voice affected him! His heart beat more quietly and he felt as though he were in a dream. She began again:

"I am not wrong in thinking that you left the opera last night before it was over?"

"Yes, madam."

"I was sorry to see that. You listened like a music-lover—though the performance was only tolerable. You are fond of music, I am sure. Do you play the piano?"

"I play the violin, a little," said Herr Friedemann. "That is, really not very much—"

"You play the violin?" she asked, and looked past him consideringly.

"But we might play together," she suddenly said. "I can accompany a little. It would be a pleasure to find somebody here—would you come?"

"I am quite at your service—with pleasure," said he, stiffly. He was still as though in a dream. A pause ensued. Then suddenly her expression changed. He saw it alter for one of cruel, though hardly perceptible mockery, and again she fixed him with that same searching, uncannily flickering gaze. His face burned, he knew not where to turn; drawing his head down between his shoulders he stared confusedly at the carpet, while there shot through him once more that strangely sweet and torturing sense of impotent rage.

He made a desperate effort and raised his eyes. She was looking over his head at the door. With the utmost difficulty he fetched out a few words:

"And you are so far not too dissatisfied with your stay in our city?"

"Oh, no," said Frau Rinnlingen indifferently. "No, certainly not; why should I not be satisfied? To be sure, I feel a little hampered, as though everybody's eyes were upon me, but—oh, before I forget it," she went on quickly, "we are entertaining a few people next week, a small, informal company. A little music, perhaps, and conversation. . . . There is a charming garden at the back, it runs down to the river. You and your sisters will be receiving an invitation in due course, but perhaps I may ask you now to give us the pleasure of your company?"

Herr Friedemann was just expressing his gratitude for the invitation when the door-knob was seized energetically from without and the Commandant entered. They both rose and Frau von Rinnlingen introduced the two men to each other. Her husband bowed to them both with equal courtesy. His bronze face glistened with the heat.

He drew off his gloves, addressing Herr Friedemann in a powerful, rather sharp-edged voice. The latter looked up at him with large vacant eyes and had the feeling that he would presently be clapped benevolently on the shoulder. Heels together, inclining from the waist, the Commandant turned to his wife and asked, in a much gentler tone:

"Have you asked Herr Friedemann if he will give us the pleasure of his company at our little party, my love? If you are willing I should like to fix the date for next week and I hope that the weather will remain fine so that we can enjoy ourselves in the garden."

"Just as you say," answered Frau von Rinnlingen, and gazed past him.

Two minutes later Herr Friedemann got up to go. At the door he turned and bowed to her once more, meeting her expressionless gaze still fixed upon him.

He went away, but he did not go back to the town; unconsciously he struck into a path that led away from the avenue towards the old ruined fort by the river, among well-kept lawns and shady avenues with benches.

He walked quickly and absently, with bent head. He felt intolerably hot, as though aware of flames leaping and sinking within him, and his head throbbed with fatigue.

It was as though her gaze still rested on him—not vacantly as it had at the end, but with that flickering cruelty which went with the strange still way she spoke. Did it give her pleasure to put him beside himself, to see him helpless? Looking through and through him like that, could she not feel a little pity?

He had gone along the river-bank under the moss-grown wall; he sat down on a bench within a half-circle of blossoming jasmine. The sweet, heavy scent was all about him, the sun brooded upon the dimpling water.

He was weary, he was worn out; and yet within him all was tumult and anguish. Were it not better to take one last look and then to go down into that quiet water; after a brief struggle to be free and safe and at peace? Ah, peace, peace—that was what he wanted! Not peace in an empty and soundless void, but a gentle, sunlit peace, full of good, of tranquil thoughts.

All his tender love of life thrilled through him in that moment, all his profound yearning for his vanished "happiness." But then he looked about him into the silent, endlessly indifferent peace of nature, saw how the river went its own way in the sun, how the grasses quivered and the flowers stood up where they blossomed, only to fade and be blown away; saw how all that was bent submissively to the will of life; and there came over him all at once that sense of acquaintance and understanding with the inevitable which can make those who know it superior to the blows of fate.

He remembered the afternoon of his thirtieth birthday and the peaceful happiness with which he, untroubled by fears or hopes, had looked forward to what was left of his life. He had seen no light and no shadow there, only a mild twilight radiance gently declining into the dark. With what a calm and superior smile had he contemplated the years still to come—how long ago was that?

Then this woman had come, she had to come, it was his fate that she should, for she herself was his fate and she alone. He had known it from the first moment. She had come—and though he had tried his best to defend his peace, her coming had roused in him all those forces which from his youth up he had sought to suppress, feeling, as he did, that they spelled torture and destruction. They had seized upon him with frightful, irresistible power and flung him to the earth.

They were his destruction, well he knew it. But why struggle, then, and why torture himself? Let everything take its course. He would go his appointed way, closing his eyes before the yawning void, bowing to his fate, bowing to the overwhelming, anguishingly sweet, irresistible power.

The water glittered, the jasmine gave out its strong, pungent scent, the birds chattered in the tree-tops that gave glimpses among them of a heavy, velvety-blue sky. Little hump-backed Herr Friedemann sat long upon his bench; he sat bent over, holding his head in his hands.

Everybody agreed that the Rinnlingens entertained very well. Some thirty guests sat in the spacious dining-room, at the long, prettily decorated table, and the butler and two hired waiters were already handing round the ices. Dishes clattered, glasses rang, there was a warm aroma of food and perfumes. Here were comfortable merchants with their wives and daughters; most of the officers of the garrison; a few professional men, lawyers and the popular old family doctor—in short, all the best society.

A nephew of the Commandant, on a visit, a student of mathematics, sat deep in conversation with Fräulein Hagenström, whose place was directly opposite Herr Friedemann's, at the lower end of the table. Johannes Friedemann sat there on a rich velvet cushion, beside the unbeautiful wife of the Colonial Director and not far off Frau von Rinnlingen, who had been escorted to table by Consul Stephens. It was astonishing, the change which had taken place in little Herr Friedemann in these few days. Perhaps the incandescent lighting in the room was partly to blame; but his cheeks looked sunken, he made a more crippled impression even than usual, and his inflamed eyes, with their dark rings, glowed with an inexpressibly tragic light. He drank a great deal of wine and now and then addressed a remark to his neighbour.

Frau von Rinnlingen had not so far spoken to him at all; but now she leaned over and called out:

"I have been expecting you in vain these days, you and your fiddle."

He looked vacantly at her for a while before he replied. She wore a light-coloured frock with a low neck that left the white throat bare; a Maréchal Niel rose in full bloom was fastened in her shining hair. Her cheeks were a little flushed, but the same bluish shadows lurked in the corners of her eyes.

Herr Friedemann looked at his plate and forced himself to make some sort of reply; after which the school superintendent's wife asked him if he did not love Beethoven and he had to answer that too. But at this point the Commandant, sitting at the head of the table, caught his wife's eye, tapped on his glass and said:

"Ladies and gentlemen, I suggest that we drink our coffee in the next room. It must be fairly decent out in the garden too, and whoever wants a little fresh air, I am for him."

Lieutenant von Deidesheim made a tactful little joke to cover the ensuing pause, and the table rose in the midst of laughter. Herr Friedemann and his partner were among the last to quit the room; he escorted her through the "old German" smoking-room to the dim and pleasant living-room, where he took his leave.

He was dressed with great care: his evening clothes were irreproachable, his shirt was dazzlingly white, his slender, well-shaped feet were encased in patent-leather pumps, which now and then betrayed the fact that he wore red silk stockings.

He looked out into the corridor and saw a good many people descending the steps into the garden. But he took up a position at the door of the smoking-room, with his cigar and coffee, where he could see into the living-room.

Some of the men stood talking in this room, and at the right of the door a little knot had formed round a small table, the centre of which was the mathematics student, who was eagerly talking. He had made the assertion that one could draw through a given point more than one parallel to a straight line; Frau Hagenström had cried that this was impossible, and he had gone on to prove it so conclusively that his hearers were constrained to behave as though they understood.

At the rear of the room, on the sofa beside the red-shaded lamp, Gerda von Rinnlingen sat in conversation with young Fräulein Stephens. She leaned back among the yellow silk cushions with one knee slung over the other, slowly smoking a cigarette, breathing out the smoke through her nose and sticking out her lower lip. Fräulein Stephens sat stiff as a graven image beside her, answering her questions with an assiduous smile.

Nobody was looking at little Herr Friedemann, so nobody saw that his large eyes were constantly directed upon Frau von Rinnlingen. He sat rather droopingly and looked at her. There was no passion in his gaze nor scarcely any pain. But there was something dull and heavy there, a dead weight of impotent, involuntary adoration.

Some ten minutes went by. Then as though she had been secretly watching him the whole time, Frau von Rinnlingen approached and paused in front of him. He got up as he heard her say:

"Would you care to go into the garden with me, Herr Friedemann?"

He answered:

"With pleasure, madam."

"You have never seen our garden?" she asked him as they went down the steps. "It is fairly large. I hope that there are not too many people in it; I should like to get a breath of fresh air. I got a headache during supper; perhaps the red wine was too strong for me. Let us go this way." They passed through a glass door, the vestibule, and a cool little courtyard, whence they gained the open air by descending a couple more steps.

The scent of all the flower-beds rose into the wonderful, warm, starry night. The garden lay in full moonlight and the guests were strolling up and down the white gravel paths, smoking and talking as they went. A group had gathered round the old fountain, where the much-loved old doctor was making them laugh by sailing paper boats.

With a little nod Frau von Rinnlingen passed them by, and pointed ahead of her, where the fragrant and well-cared-for garden blended into the darker park.

"Shall we go down this middle path?" asked she. At the beginning of it stood two low, squat obelisks.

In the vista at the end of the chestnut alley they could see the river shining green and bright in the moonlight. All about them was darkness and coolness. Here and there side paths branched off, all of them probably curving down to the river. For a long time there was not a sound.

"Down by the water," she said, "there is a pretty spot where I often sit. We could stop and talk a little. See the stars glittering here and there through the trees."

He did not answer, gazing, as they approached it, at the river's shimmering green surface. You could see the other bank and the park along the city wall. They left the alley and came out on the grassy slope down to the river, and she said:

"Here is our place, a little to the right, and there is no one there."

The bench stood facing the water, some six paces away, with its back to the trees. It was warmer here in the open. Crickets chirped among the grass, which at the river's edge gave way to sparse reeds. The moonlit water gave off a soft light.

For a while they both looked in silence. Then he heard her voice; it thrilled him to recognize the same low, gentle, pensive tone of a week ago, which now as then moved him so strangely:

"How long have you had your infirmity, Herr Friedemann? Were you born so?"

He swallowed before he replied, for his throat felt as though he were choking. Then he said, politely and gently:

"No, *gnädige Frau.* It comes from their having let me fall, when I was an infant."

"And how old are you now?" she asked again.

"Thirty years old."

"Thirty years old," she repeated. "And these thirty years were not happy ones?"

Little Herr Friedemann shook his head, his lips quivered.

"No," he said, "that was all lies and my imagination."

"Then you have thought that you were happy?" she asked.

"I have tried to be," he replied, and she responded:

"That was brave of you."

A minute passed. The crickets chirped and behind them the boughs rustled lightly.

"I understand a good deal about unhappiness," she told him. "These summer nights by the water are the best thing for it."

He made no direct answer, but gestured feebly across the water, at the opposite bank, lying peaceful in the darkness.

"I was sitting over there not long ago," he said.

"When you came from me?" she asked. He only nodded.

Then suddenly he started up from his seat, trembling all over; he sobbed and gave vent to a sound, a wail which yet seemed like a release from strain, and sank slowly to the ground before her. He had touched her hand with his as it lay beside him on the bench, and clung to it now, seizing the other as he knelt before her, this little cripple, trembling and shuddering; he buried his face in her lap and stammered between his gasps in a voice which was scarcely human:

"You know, you understand . . . let me . . . I can no longer . . . my God, oh, my God!"

She did not repulse him, neither did she bend her face towards him. She sat erect, leaning a little away, and her close-set eyes, wherein the liquid shimmer of the water seemed to be mirrored, stared beyond him into space.

Then she gave him an abrupt push and uttered a short, scornful laugh. She tore her hands from his burning fingers, clutched his arm, and flung him sidewise upon the ground. Then she sprang up and vanished down the wooded avenue.

He lay there with his face in the grass, stunned, unmanned, shudders coursing swiftly through his frame. He pulled himself together, got up somehow, took two steps, and fell again, close to the water. What were his sensations at this moment? Perhaps he was feeling that same luxury of hate which he had felt before when she had humiliated him with her glance, degenerated now, when he lay before her on the ground and she had treated him like a dog, into an insane rage which must at all costs find expression even against himself—a disgust, perhaps of himself, which filled him with a thirst to destroy himself, to tear himself to pieces, to blot himself utterly out.

On his belly he dragged his body a little further, lifted its upper part, and let it fall into the water. He did not raise his head nor move his legs, which still lay on the bank.

The crickets stopped chirping a moment at the noise of the little splash. Then they went on as before, the boughs lightly rustled, and down the long alley came the faint sound of laughter.

LADY ELEANORE'S MANTLE

by Nathaniel Hawthorne

Not long after Colonel Shute had assumed the government of Massachusetts Bay, now nearly a hundred and twenty years ago, a young lady of rank and fortune arrived from England, to claim his protection as her guardian. He was her distant relative, but the nearest who had survived the gradual extinction of her family; so that no more eligible shelter could be found for the rich and high-born Lady Eleanore Rochcliffe than within the Province House of a transatlantic colony. The consort of Governor Shute, moreover, had been as a mother to her childhood, and was now anxious to receive her, in the hope that a beautiful young woman would be exposed to infinitely less peril from the primitive society of New England than amid the artifices and corruptions of a court. If either the Governor or his lady had especially consulted their own comfort, they would probably have sought to devolve the responsibility on other hands; since, with some noble and splendid traits of character, Lady Eleanore was remarkable for a harsh, unyielding pride, a haughty consciousness of her hereditary and personal advantages, which made her almost incapable of control. Judging from many traditionary anecdotes, this peculiar temper was hardly less than a monomania; or, if the acts which it inspired were those of a sane person, it seemed due from Providence that pride so sinful should be followed by as severe a retri-

From *The Complete Works of Nathaniel Hawthorne,* Vol. 1, Riverside Edition, with introductory notes by George Parsons Lathrop (Boston and New York: Houghton Mifflin and Co., 1886), pp. 309–26.

bution. That tinge of the marvellous, which is thrown over so many of these half-forgotten legends, has probably imparted an additional wildness to the strange story of Lady Eleanore Rochcliffe.

The ship in which she came passenger had arrived at Newport, whence Lady Eleanore was conveyed to Boston in the Governor's coach, attended by a small escort of gentlemen on horseback. The ponderous equipage, with its four black horses, attracted much notice as it rumbled through Cornhill, surrounded by the prancing steeds of half a dozen cavaliers, with swords dangling to their stirrups and pistols at their holsters. Through the large glass windows of the coach, as it rolled along, the people could discern the figure of Lady Eleanore, strangely combining an almost queenly stateliness with the grace and beauty of a maiden in her teens. A singular tale had gone abroad among the ladies of the province, that their fair rival was indebted for much of the irresistible charm of her appearance to a certain article of dress—an embroidered mantle—which had been wrought by the most skilful artist in London, and possessed even magical properties of adornment. On the present occasion, however, she owed nothing to the witchery of dress, being clad in a riding habit of velvet, which would have appeared stiff and ungraceful on any other form.

The coachman reined in his four black steeds, and the whole cavalcade came to a pause in front of the contorted iron balustrade that fenced the Province House from the public street. It was an awkward coincidence that the bell of the Old South was just then tolling for a funeral; so that, instead of a gladsome peal with which it was customary to announce the arrival of distinguished strangers, Lady Eleanore Rochcliffe was ushered by a doleful clang, as if calamity had come embodied in her beautiful person.

"A very great disrespect!" exclaimed Captain Langford, an English officer, who had recently brought dispatches to Governor Shute. "The funeral should have been deferred, lest Lady Eleanore's spirits be affected by such a dismal welcome."

"With your pardon, sir," replied Doctor Clarke, a physician, and a famous champion of the popular party, "whatever the heralds may pretend, a dead beggar must have precedence of a living queen. King Death confers high privileges."

These remarks were interchanged while the speakers waited a passage through the crowd, which had gathered on each side of the gateway, leaving an open avenue to the portal of the Province House. A black slave in livery now leaped from behind the coach, and threw open the door; while at the same moment Governor Shute descended the flight of steps from his mansion, to assist Lady Eleanore in alighting. But the Governor's stately approach was anticipated in a manner that excited general astonishment. A pale young man, with his black hair all in disorder, rushed from the throng, and prostrated himself beside the coach, thus offering his person as a footstool for Lady Eleanore Rochcliffe to tread upon. She held back an instant, yet with an expression as if doubting whether the young man were worthy to bear the weight of her footstep, rather than dissatisfied to receive such awful reverence from a fellow-mortal.

"Up, sir," said the Governor, sternly, at the same time lifting his cane over the intruder. "What means the Bedlamite by this freak?"

"Nay," answered Lady Eleanore playfully, but with more scorn than pity in her tone, "your Excellency shall not strike him. When men seek only to be trampled upon, it were a pity to deny them a favor so easily granted—and so well deserved!"

Then, though as lightly as a sunbeam on a cloud, she placed her foot upon the cowering form, and extended her hand to meet that of the Governor. There was a brief interval, during which Lady Eleanore retained this attitude; and never, surely, was there an apter emblem of aristocracy and hereditary pride trampling on human sympathies and the kindred of nature, than these two figures presented at that moment. Yet the spectators were so smitten with her beauty, and so essential did pride seem to the existence of such a creature, that they gave a simultaneous acclamation of applause.

"Who is this insolent young fellow?" inquired Captain Langford, who still remained beside Doctor Clarke. "If he be in his senses, his impertinence demands the bastinado. If mad, Lady Eleanore should be secured from further inconvenience, by his confinement."

"His name is Jervase Helwyse," answered the Doctor; "a youth of no birth or fortune, or other advantages, save the mind and soul that nature gave him; and being secretary to our colonial agent in London, it was his misfortune to meet this Lady Eleanore Rochcliffe. He loved her—and her scorn has driven him mad."

"He was mad so to aspire," observed the English officer.

"It may be so," said Doctor Clarke, frowning as he spoke. "But I tell you, sir, I could well-nigh doubt the justice of the Heaven above us if no signal humiliation overtake this lady, who now treads so haughtily into yonder mansion. She seeks to place herself above the sympathies of our common nature, which envelops all human souls. See, if that nature do not assert its claim over her in some mode that shall bring her level with the lowest!"

"Never!" cried Captain Langford indignantly—"neither in life, nor when they lay her with her ancestors."

Not many days afterwards the Governor gave a ball in honor of Lady Eleanore Rochcliffe. The principal gentry of the colony received invitations, which were distributed to their residences, far and near, by messengers on horseback, bearing missives sealed with all the formality of official dispatches. In obedience to the summons, there was a general gathering of rank, wealth, and beauty; and the wide door of the Province House had seldom given admittance to more numerous and honorable guests than on the evening of Lady Eleanore's ball. Without much extravagance of eulogy, the spectacle might even be termed splendid; for, according to the fashion of the times, the ladies shone in rich silks and satins, outspread over wideprojecting hoops; and the gentlemen glittered in gold embroidery, laid unsparingly upon the purple, or scarlet, or sky-blue velvet, which was the material of their coats and waistcoats. The latter article of dress was of great importance, since it enveloped the wearer's body nearly to the knees, and was perhaps bedizened with the amount of his whole year's income, in golden flowers and foliage. The altered taste of the present day—a taste symbolic of a deep change in the whole system of society—would look upon almost any of those gorgeous figures as ridiculous; although that evening the guests sought their reflections in the pier-glasses, and rejoiced to catch their own glitter amid the glittering crowd. What a pity that one of the stately mirrors has not preserved a picture of the scene, which, by the very traits that were so transitory, might have taught us much that would be worth knowing and remembering!

Would, at least, that either painter or mirror could convey to us some faint idea of a garment, already noticed in this legend,—the Lady Eleanore's embroidered mantle,—which the gossips whispered was invested with magic properties, so as to lend a new and untried grace to her figure each time that she put it on! Idle fancy as it is, this mysterious mantle has thrown an awe around my image of her, partly from its fabled virtues, and partly because it was the handiwork of a dying woman, and, perchance, owed the fantastic grace of its conception to the delirium of approaching death.

After the ceremonial greetings had been paid, Lady Eleanore Rochcliffe stood apart from the mob of guests, insulating herself within a small and distinguished circle, to whom she accorded a more cordial favor than to the general throng. The waxen torches threw their radiance vividly over the scene, bringing out its brilliant points in strong relief; but she gazed carelessly, and with now and then an expression of weariness or scorn, tempered with such feminine grace that her auditors scarcely perceived the moral deformity of which it was the utterance. She beheld the spectacle not with vulgar ridicule, as disdaining to be pleased with the provincial mockery of a court festival, but with the deeper scorn of one whose spirit held itself too high to participate in the enjoyment of other human souls. Whether or no the recollections of those who saw her that evening were influenced by the strange events with which she was subsequently connected, so it was that her figure ever after recurred to them as marked by something wild and unnatural,—although, at the time, the general whisper was of her exceeding beauty, and of the indescribable charm which her mantle threw around her. Some close observers, indeed, detected a feverish flush and alternate paleness of countenance, with a corresponding flow and revulsion of spirits, and once or twice a painful and helpless betrayal of lassitude, as if she were on the point of sinking to the ground. Then, with a nervous shudder, she seemed to arouse her energies and threw some bright and playful yet half-wicked sarcasm into the conversation. There was so strange a characteristic in her manners and sentiments that it astonished every right-minded listener; till looking in her face, a lurking and incomprehensible glance and smile perplexed them with doubts both as to her seriousness and sanity. Gradually, Lady Eleanore Rochcliffe's circle grew smaller, till only four gentlemen remained in it. These were Captain Langford, the English officer before mentioned; a Virginian planter, who had come to Massachusetts on some political errand; a young Episcopal clergyman, the grandson of a British earl; and, lastly, the private secretary of Governor Shute, whose obsequiousness had won a sort of tolerance from Lady Eleanore.

At different periods of the evening the liveried servants of the Province House passed among the guests, bearing huge trays of refreshments and French and Spanish wines. Lady Eleanore Rochcliffe, who refused to wet her beautiful lips even with a bubble of Champagne, had sunk back into a large damask chair, apparently overwearied either with the excitement of the scene or its tedium, and while, for an instant, she was unconscious of voices, laughter and music, a young man stole forward, and knelt down at her feet. He bore a salver in his hand, on which was a chased silver goblet, filled to the brim with wine, which he offered as reverentially as to a crowned queen, or rather with the awful devotion of a priest doing sacrifice to his idol. Conscious that some one touched her robe, Lady Eleanore started, and unclosed her eyes upon the pale, wild features and dishevelled hair of Jervase Helwyse.

"Why do you haunt me thus?" said she, in a languid tone, but with a kindlier feeling than she ordinarily permitted herself to express. "They tell me that I have done you harm."

"Heaven knows if that be so," replied the young man solemnly. "But, Lady Eleanore, in requital of that harm, if such there be, and for your own earthly and heavenly welfare, I pray you to take one sip of this holy wine, and then to pass the goblet round among the guests. And this shall be a symbol that you have not sought to withdraw yourself from the chain of human sympathies—which whoso would shake off must keep company with fallen angels."

"Where has this mad fellow stolen that sacramental vessel?" exclaimed the Episcopal clergyman.

This question drew the notice of the guests to the silver cup, which was recognized as appertaining to the communion plate of the Old South Church; and, for aught that could be known, it was brimming over with the consecrated wine.

"Perhaps it is poisoned," half whispered the Governor's secretary.

"Pour it down the villain's throat!" cried the Virginian fiercely.

"Turn him out of the house!" cried Captain Langford, seizing Jervase Helwyse so roughly by the shoulder that the sacramental cup was overturned, and its contents sprinkled upon Lady Eleanore's mantle. "Whether knave, fool, or Bedlamite, it is intolerable that the fellow should go at large."

"Pray, gentlemen, do my poor admirer no harm," said Lady Eleanore, with a faint and weary smile. "Take him out of my sight, if such be your pleasure; for I can find in my heart to do nothing but laugh at him; whereas, in all decency and conscience, it would become me to weep for the mischief I have wrought!"

But while the by-standers were attempting to lead away the unfortunate young man, he broke from them, and with a wild, impassioned earnestness, offered a new and equally strange petition to Lady Eleanore. It was no other than that she should throw off the mantle, which, while he pressed the silver cup of wine upon her, she had drawn more closely around her form, so as almost to shroud herself within it.

"Cast it from you!" exclaimed Jervase Helwyse, clasping his hands in an agony of entreaty. "It may not yet be too late! Give the accursed garment to the flames!"

But Lady Eleanore, with a laugh of scorn, drew the rich folds of the embroidered mantle over her head, in such a fashion as to give a completely new aspect to her beautiful face, which—half hidden, half revealed—seemed to belong to some being of mysterious character and purposes.

"Farewell, Jervase Helwyse!" said she. "Keep my image in your remembrance, as you behold it now."

"Alas, lady!" he replied, in a tone no longer wild, but sad as a funeral bell. "We must meet shortly, when your face may wear another aspect—and that shall be the image that must abide within me."

He made no more resistance to the violent efforts of the gentlemen and servants, who almost dragged him out of the apartment, and dismissed him roughly from the iron gate of the Province House. Captain Langford, who had been very active in this affair, was returning to the presence of Lady Eleanore Rochcliffe, when he encountered the physician, Doctor Clarke, with whom he had held some casual talk on the day of her arrival. The Doctor stood apart, separated from Lady Eleanore by the width of the room, but eying her with such keen sagacity that Captain Langford involuntarily gave him credit for the discovery of some deep secret.

"You appear to be smitten, after all, with the charms of this queenly maiden," said he, hoping thus to draw forth the physician's hidden knowledge.

"God forbid!" answered Doctor Clarke, with a grave smile; "and if you be wise you will put up the same prayer for yourself. Woe to those who shall be smitten by this beautiful Lady Eleanore! But yonder stands the Governor—and I have a word or two for his private ear. Good night!"

He accordingly advanced to Governor Shute, and addressed him in so low a tone that none of the by-standers could catch a word of what he said, although the sudden change of his Excellency's hitherto cheerful visage betokened that the communication could be of no agreeable import. A very few moments afterwards it was announced to the guests that an unforeseen circumstance rendered it necessary to put a premature close to the festival.

The ball at the Province House supplied a topic of conversation for the colonial metropolis for some days after its occurrence, and might still longer have been the general theme, only that a subject of all-engrossing interest thrust it, for a time, from the public recollection. This was the appearance of a dreadful epidemic, which, in that age and long before and afterwards, was wont to slay its hundreds and thousands on both sides of the Atlantic. On the occasion of which we speak, it was distinguished by a peculiar virulence, insomuch that it has left its traces—its pit-marks, to use an appropriate figure—on the history of the country, the affairs of which were thrown into confusion by its ravages. At first, unlike its ordinary course, the disease seemed to confine itself to the higher circles of society, selecting its victims from among the proud, the well-born, and the wealthy, entering unabashed into stately chambers, and lying down with the slumberers in silken beds. Some of the most distinguished guests of the Province House—even those whom the haughty Lady Eleanore Rochcliffe had deemed not unworthy of her favor—were stricken by this fatal scourge. It was noticed, with an ungenerous bitterness of feeling, that the four gentlemen—the Virginian, the British officer, the young clergyman, and the Governor's secretary—who had been her most devoted attendants on the evening of the ball, were the foremost on whom the plague stroke fell. But the disease, pursuing its onward progress, soon ceased to be exclusively a prerogative of aristocracy. Its red brand was no longer conferred like a noble's star, or an order of knighthood. It threaded its way through the narrow and crooked streets, and entered the low, mean, darksome dwellings, and laid its hand of death upon the artisans and laboring classes of the town. It compelled rich and poor to feel themselves brethren then; and stalking to and fro across the Three Hills, with a fierceness which made it almost a new pestilence, there was that mighty conqueror—that scourge and horror of our forefathers—the Small-Pox!

We cannot estimate the affright which this plague inspired of yore, by contemplating it as the fangless monster of the present day. We must remember, rather, with what awe we watched the gigantic footsteps of the Asiatic cholera, striding from shore to shore of the Atlantic, and marching like destiny upon cities far remote which flight had already half depopulated. There is no other fear so horrible and unhumanizing as that which makes man dread to breathe heaven's vital air lest it be poison, or to grasp the hand of a brother or friend lest the gripe of the pestilence should clutch him. Such was the dismay that now followed in the track of the disease, or ran before it throughout the town. Graves were hastily dug, and the pestilential relics as hastily covered, because the dead were enemies of the living, and strove to draw them headlong, as it were, into their own dismal pit. The public councils were suspended, as if mortal wisdom might relinquish its devices, now that an unearthly usurper had found his way into the ruler's mansion. Had an enemy's fleet been hovering on the coast, or his armies trampling on our soil, the people would probably have committed their defence to that same direful conqueror who had wrought their own calamity, and would permit no interference with his sway. This conqueror had a symbol of his triumphs. It was a blood-red flag, that fluttered in the tainted air, over the door of every dwelling into which the Small-Pox had entered.

Such a banner was long since waving over the portal of the Province House; for thence, as was proved by tracking its footsteps back, had all this dreadful mischief issued. It had been traced back to a lady's luxurious chamber—to the proudest of the proud—to her that was so delicate, and hardly owned herself of earthly mould—to the haughty one, who took her stand above human sympathies—to Lady Eleanore! There remained no room for doubt that the contagion had lurked in that gorgeous mantle, which threw so strange a grace around her at the festival. Its fantastic splendor had been conceived in the delirious brain of a woman on her death-bed, and was the last toil of her stiffening fingers, which had interwoven fate and misery with its golden threads. This dark tale, whispered at first, was now bruited far and wide. The people raved against the Lady Eleanore, and cried out that her pride and scorn had evoked a fiend, and that, between them both, this monstrous evil had been born. At times, their rage and despair took the semblance of grinning mirth; and whenever the red flag of the pestilence was hoisted over another and yet another door, they clapped their hands and shouted through the streets, in bitter mockery: "Behold a new triumph for the Lady Eleanore!"

One day, in the midst of these dismal times, a wild figure approached the portal of the Province House, and folding his arms, stood contemplating the scarlet banner which a passing breeze shook fitfully, as if to fling abroad the contagion that it typified. At length, climbing one of the pillars by means of the iron balustrade, he took down the flag and entered the mansion, waving it above his head. At the foot of the staircase he met the Governor, booted and spurred, with his cloak drawn around him, evidently on the point of setting forth upon a journey.

"Wretched lunatic, what do you seek here?" exclaimed Shute, extending his cane to guard himself from contact. "There is nothing here but Death. Back—or you will meet him!"

"Death will not touch me, the banner-bearer of the pestilence!" cried Jervase Helwyse, shaking the red flag aloft. "Death, and the Pestilence, who wears the aspect of the Lady Eleanore, will walk through the streets to-night, and I must march before them with this banner!"

"Why do I waste words on the fellow?" muttered the Governor, drawing his cloak across his mouth. "What matters his miserable life, when none of us are sure of twelve hours' breath? On, fool, to your own destruction!"

He made way for Jervase Helwyse, who immediately ascended the staircase, but, on the first landing-place, was arrested by the firm grasp of a hand upon his shoulder. Looking fiercely up, with a madman's impulse to struggle with and rend asunder his opponent, he found himself powerless beneath a calm, stern eye, which possessed the mysterious property of quelling frenzy at its height. The person whom he had now encountered was the physician, Doctor Clarke, the duties of whose sad profession had led him to the Province House, where he was an infrequent guest in more prosperous times.

"Young man, what is your purpose?" demanded he.

"I seek the Lady Eleanore," answered Jervase Helwyse, submissively.

"All have fled from her," said the physician. "Why do you seek her now? I tell you, youth, her nurse fell death-stricken on the threshold of that fatal chamber. Know ye not, that never came such a curse to our shores as this lovely Lady Eleanore?—that her breath has filled the air with poison?—that she has shaken pestilence and death upon the land, from the folds of her accursed mantle?"

"Let me look upon her!" rejoined the mad youth, more wildly. "Let me behold her, in her awful beauty, clad in the regal garments of the pestilence! She and Death sit on a throne together. Let me kneel down before them!"

"Poor youth!" said Doctor Clarke; and, moved by a deep sense of human weakness, a smile of caustic humor curled his lip even then. "Wilt thou still worship the destroyer and surround her image with fantasies the more magnificent, the more evil she has wrought? Thus man doth ever to his tyrants. Approach, then! Madness, as I have noted, has that good efficacy, that it will guard you from contagion—and perchance its own cure may be found in yonder chamber."

Ascending another flight of stairs, he threw open a door and signed to

Jervase Helwyse that he should enter. The poor lunatic, it seems probable, had cherished a delusion that his haughty mistress sat in state, unharmed herself by the pestilential influence, which, as by enchantment, she scattered round about her. He dreamed, no doubt, that her beauty was not dimmed, but brightened into superhuman splendor. With such anticipations, he stole reverentially to the door at which the physician stood, but paused upon the threshold, gazing fearfully into the gloom of the darkened chamber.

"Where is the Lady Eleanore?" whispered he.

"Call her," replied the physician.

"Lady Eleanore!—Princess!—Queen of Death!" cried Jervase Helwyse, advancing three steps into the chamber. "She is not here! There, on yonder table, I behold the sparkle of a diamond which once she wore upon her bosom. There"—and he shuddered—"there hangs her mantle, on which a dead woman embroidered a spell of dreadful potency. But where is the Lady Eleanore?"

Something stirred within the silken curtains of a canopied bed; and a low moan was uttered, which, listening intently, Jervase Helwyse began to distinguish as a woman's voice, complaining dolefully of thirst. He fancied, even, that he recognized its tones.

"My throat!—my throat is scorched," murmured the voice. "A drop of water!"

"What thing art thou?" said the brain-stricken youth, drawing near the bed and tearing asunder its curtains. "Whose voice hast thou stolen for thy murmurs and miserable petitions, as if Lady Eleanore could be conscious of mortal infirmity? Fie! Heap of diseased mortality, why lurkest thou in my lady's chamber?"

"O Jervase Helwyse," said the voice—and as it spoke the figure contorted itself, struggling to hide its blasted face—"look not now on the woman you once loved! The curse of Heaven hath stricken me, because I would not call man my brother, nor woman sister. I wrapped myself in PRIDE as in a MANTLE, and scorned the sympathies of nature; and therefore has nature made this wretched body the medium of a dreadful sympathy. You are avenged—they are all avenged—Nature is avenged—for I am Eleanore Rochcliffe!"

The malice of his mental disease, the bitterness lurking at the bottom of his heart, mad as he was, for a blighted and ruined life, and love that had been paid with cruel scorn, awoke within the breast of Jervase Helwyse. He shook his finger at the wretched girl, and the chamber echoed, the curtains of the bed were shaken, with his outburst of insane merriment.

"Another triumph for the Lady Eleanore!" he cried. "All have been her victims! Who so worthy to be the final victim as herself?"

Impelled by some new fantasy of his crazed intellect, he snatched the fatal mantle and rushed from the chamber and the house. That night a procession passed, by torchlight, through the streets, bearing in the midst the figure of a woman, enveloped with a richly embroidered mantle; while in advance stalked Jervase Helwyse, waving the red flag of the pestilence. Arriving opposite the Province House, the mob burned the effigy, and a strong wind came and swept away the ashes. It was said that, from that very hour, the pestilence abated, as if its sway had some mysterious connection, from the first plague stroke to the last, with Lady Eleanore's Mantle. A remarkable uncertainty broods over that unhappy lady's fate. There is a belief, however, that in a certain chamber of this mansion a female form may sometimes be duskily discerned, shrinking into the darkest corner and muffling her face within an embroidered mantle. Supposing the legend true, can this be other than the once proud Lady Eleanore?

A CANARY FOR ONE
by Ernest Hemingway

The train passed very quickly a long, red stone house with a garden and four thick palm-trees with tables under them in the shade. On the other side was the sea. Then there was a cutting through red stone and clay, and the sea was only occasionally and far below against rocks.

"I bought him in Palermo," the American lady said. "We only had an hour ashore and it was Sunday morning. The man wanted to be paid in dollars and I gave him a dollar and a half. He really sings very beautifully."

It was very hot in the train and it was very hot in the *lit salon* compartment. There was no breeze came through the open window. The American lady pulled the window-blind down and there was no more sea, even occasionally. On the other side there was glass, then the corridor, then an open window, and outside the window were dusty trees and an oiled road and flat fields of grapes, with gray-stone hills behind them.

There was smoke from many tall chimneys—coming into Marseilles, and the train slowed down and followed one track through many others into the station. The train stayed twenty-five minutes in the station at Marseilles and the American lady bought a copy of *The Daily Mail* and a half-bottle of Evian water. She walked a little way along the station platform, but she stayed near the steps of the car because at Cannes, where it stopped for twelve minutes, the train had left with no signal of depar-

---

ture and she had only gotten on just in time. The American lady was a little deaf and she was afraid that perhaps signals of departure were given and that she did not hear them.

The train left the station in Marseilles and there was not only the switch-yards and the factory smoke but, looking back, the town of Marseilles and the harbor with stone hills behind it and the last of the sun on the water. As it was getting dark the train passed a farmhouse burning in a field. Motor-cars were stopped along the road and bedding and things from inside the farmhouse were spread in the field. Many people were watching the house burn. After it was dark the train was in Avignon. People got on and off. At the news-stand Frenchmen, returning to Paris, bought that day's French papers. On the station platform were negro soldiers. They wore brown uniforms and were tall and their faces shone, close under the electric light. Their faces were very black and they were too tall to stare. The train left Avignon station with the negroes standing there. A short white sergeant was with them.

Inside the *lit salon* compartment the porter had pulled down the three beds from inside the wall and prepared them for sleeping. In the night the American lady lay without sleeping because the train was a *rapide* and went very fast and she was afraid of the speed in the night. The American lady's bed was the one next to the window. The canary from Palermo, a cloth spread over his cage, was out of the draft in the corridor that went into the compartment wash-room. There was a blue light outside the compartment, and all night the train went very fast and the American lady lay awake and waited for a wreck.

In the morning the train was near Paris, and after the American lady had come out from the wash-room, looking very wholesome and middle-aged and American in spite of not having slept, and had taken the cloth off the bird-cage and hung the cage in the sun, she went back to the restaurant-car for breakfast. When she came back to the *lit salon* compartment again, the beds had been pushed back into the wall and made into seats, the canary was shaking his feathers in the sunlight that came through the open window, and the train was much nearer Paris.

"He loves the sun," the American lady said. "He'll sing now in a little while."

The canary shook his feathers and pecked into them. "I've always loved birds," the American lady said. "I'm taking him home to my little girl. There—he's singing now."

The canary chirped and the feathers on his throat stood out, then he dropped his bill and pecked into his feathers again. The train crossed a river and passed through a very carefully tended forest. The train passed through many outside of Paris towns. There were tram-cars in the towns and big advertisements for the Belle Jardinière and Dubonnet and Pernod on the walls toward the train. All that the train passed through looked as though it were before breakfast. For several minutes I had not listened to the American lady, who was talking to my wife.

"Is your husband American too?" asked the lady.

"Yes," said my wife. "We're both Americans."

"I thought you were English."

"Oh, no."

"Perhaps that was because I wore braces," I said. I had started to say suspenders and changed it to braces in the mouth, to keep my English character. The American lady did not hear. She was really quite deaf; she read lips and I had not looked toward her. I had looked out of the window. She went on talking to my wife.

"I'm so glad you're Americans. American men make the best husbands," the American lady was saying. "That was why we left the Continent, you know. My daughter fell in love with a man in Vevey." She stopped. "They were simply madly in love." She stopped again. "I took her away, of course."

"Did she get over it?" asked my wife.

"I don't think so," said the American lady. "She wouldn't eat anything and she wouldn't sleep at all. I've tried so very hard, but she doesn't seem to take an interest in anything. She doesn't care about things. I couldn't have her marrying a foreigner." She paused. "Some one, a very good friend, told me once, 'No foreigner can make an American girl a good husband.' "

"No," said my wife, "I suppose not."

The American lady admired my wife's travelling-coat, and it turned out that the American lady had bought her own clothes for twenty years now from the same maison de couturier in the Rue Saint Honoré. They had her measurements, and a vendeuse who knew her and her tastes picked the dresses out for her and they were sent to America. They came to the post-office near where she lived up-town in New York, and the duty was never exorbitant because they opened the dresses there in the post-office to appraise them and they were always very simple-looking and with no gold lace nor ornaments that would make the dresses look expensive. Before the present vendeuse, named Thérèse, there had been another vendeuse, named Amélie. Altogether there had only been these two in the twenty years. It had always been the same couturier. Prices, however, had gone up. The exchange, though, equalized that. They had her daughter's measurements now too. She was grown up and there was not much chance of their changing now.

The train was now coming into Paris. The fortifications were levelled but grass had not grown. There were many cars standing on tracks —brown wooden restaurant-cars and brown wooden sleeping-cars that would go to Italy at five o'clock that night, if that train still left at five; the cars were marked Paris-Rome, and cars, with seats on the roofs, that went back and forth to the suburbs with, at certain hours, people in all the seats and on the roofs, if that were the way it were still done, and passing were the white walls and many windows of houses. Nothing had eaten any breakfast.

"Americans make the best husbands," the American lady said to my wife. I was getting down the bags. "American men are the only men in the world to marry."

"How long ago did you leave Vevey?" asked my wife.

"Two years ago this fall. It's her, you know, that I'm taking the canary to."

"Was the man your daughter was in love with a Swiss?"

"Yes," said the American lady. "He was from a very good family in

Vevey. He was going to be an engineer. They met there in Vevey. They used to go on long walks together."

"I know Vevey," said my wife. "We were there on our honeymoon."

"Were you really? That must have been lovely. I had no idea, of course, that she'd fall in love with him."

"It was a very lovely place," said my wife.

"Yes," said the American lady. "Isn't it lovely? Where did you stop there?"

"We stayed at the Trois Couronnes," said my wife.

"It's such a fine old hotel," said the American lady.

"Yes," said my wife. "We had a very fine room and in the fall the country was lovely."

"Were you there in the fall?"

"Yes," said my wife.

We were passing three cars that had been in a wreck. They were splintered open and the roofs sagged in.

"Look," I said. "There's been a wreck."

The American lady looked and saw the last car. "I was afraid of just that all night," she said. "I have terrific presentiments about things sometimes. I'll never travel on a *rapide* again at night. There must be other comfortable trains that don't go so fast."

Then the train was in the dark of the Gare de Lyons, and then stopped and porters came up to the windows. I handed bags through the windows, and we were out on the dim longness of the platform, and the American lady put herself in charge of one of three men from Cook's who said: "Just a moment, madame, and I'll look for your name."

The porter brought a truck and piled on the baggage, and my wife said good-by and I said good-by to the American lady, whose name had been found by the man from Cook's on a typewritten page in a sheaf of typewritten pages which he replaced in his pocket.

We followed the porter with the truck down the long cement platform beside the train. At the end was a gate and a man took the tickets.

We were returning to Paris to set up separate residences.

The Earth-Mother

THE omnipresence of an earth goddess in the mythologies of the world is proof of the universality of the Mother archetype. For example, in Greek mythology Gaea, or the Great Mother, is the first deity to emerge from Chaos. It is surprising, in comparative mythology, how frequently an Earth-Mother deity is joined to a Sky-Father deity to produce a divine progeny; thus, Gaea became the wife of Uranus, who—just as Gaea personified the spirit of the earth—personified the spirit of the starry heavens. Later the Greeks distinguished between the Great Mother (Gaea) and the Earth-Mother (Demeter); and the latter, as goddess of agriculture, came to supersede the former in importance. During the Roman Empire, the Italians identified Demeter with their own mother goddess, Ceres. Viewed psychologically, however, all of these deities have the same source, the Mother archetype, of which they are mythical projections. We use the term Earth-Mother as describing most accurately the form in which this archetype projects in literature.

Like other archetypes, the Earth-Mother is recognized by means of the specific symbols she assumes in projection. She may appear not only as a personification of nature or the creative source, but also as a superhuman being or goddess—although this frequently is a personification through anthropomorphosis (the Virgin Mary, for example). She may also appear as an abstraction, disguised in the form of an ultimate ambition or goal, especially when the goal takes the form of a longing for Heaven or a death-wish; in these cases, overlapping with two other archetypes may occur: the Search and the Return to the Womb. She may appear in the form of a political, religious, or social institution that offers the protection of a collective identity (a nation, religion, school, or fraternity). Frequently in dreams and myths she appears associated with or in the form of certain objects, mother-symbols, of which the commonest are caves, wells, and still water generally; gardens and ploughed fields; eggs and milk; grain (especially corn and wheat), gourds and baskets; fruit (especially pomegranates); vessel-shaped flowers (roses and lilies); and animals of a helpful kind, such as cows and bees. Baskets are found in three of the five stories that follow, and both Mrs. Grimes and Yanda carry sacks.

Archetypal characters usually have a dual aspect, and the Earth-Mother is no exception. Gaea plotted the mutilation of her husband, and in Oriental art there are many examples of mother images that have two faces—one benign, the other terrifying. In her negative aspect the archetype may appear as a witch, may combine with the archetype of the Fatal Woman, and may be represented symbolically by a devouring or entwining animal, such as a dragon, a large fish, or a serpent.

Jung analyzed the Earth-Mother archetype in some detail, and Sir James Frazer discussed its importance to cultural anthropology in *The Golden Bough.* No systematic study of its appearance in literature, however, is available in English. Perhaps the myths of Greece and Rome furnish us with the best examples, but there are others much closer to hand in contemporary literature: Lawrence's Ursula (*Women in Love*); Steinbeck's Ma Joad (*The Grapes of Wrath*); Tennessee Williams' Amanda Wingfield (*The Glass Menagerie*); and Faulkner's Dilsey (*The Sound and the Fury*), Lena Grove (*Light in August*), and Eula Varner (*The Hamlet*). The type is, for some reason, found more frequently in long fiction than in short and tends to be especially prominent in proletarian novels.

In literature, the Earth-Mother, in addition to being fecund, is typically self-sacrificing and forbearing; she accepts everything and usually forgives everyone. Since these are qualities that invite exploitation, she is often paired with a mate whose character is parasitical and whose function, within the framework of the narrative, is to demonstrate through contrast the degree of her selflessness. She is inclined to be attracted to failures. Like Yanda, in Isaac Bashevis Singer's fine story, she need not be respectable—she is usually too generous to be completely respectable—nor intelligent, though she often possesses, perhaps by way of compensation, a kind of intuitive wisdom. She is usually of a placid and serene disposition, sometimes exhibiting astonishing strength in adversity. Her general influence is to sustain and nourish, and her peculiar virtue is that she endures.

The negative aspects of this archetype have been much publicized lately. The phenomenon of Mom-ism, which Philip Wylie attacked in *Generation of Vipers,* is a manifestation of it, as is also the syndrome of the Jewish Mother, who is a subtype. In this aspect the mother proves domineering and possessive; the relationship is reversed and it is she who becomes the parasite: spiritually she devours her progeny and threatens to destroy anyone who attempts to come to their rescue.

DEATH IN THE WOODS

by Sherwood Anderson

She was an old woman and lived on a farm near the town in which I lived. All country and small-town people have seen such old women, but no one knows much about them. Such an old woman comes into town driving an old worn-out horse or she comes afoot carrying a basket. She may own a few hens and have eggs to sell. She brings them in a basket and takes them to a grocer. There she trades them in. She gets some salt pork and some beans. Then she gets a pound or two of sugar and some flour.

Afterwards she goes to the butcher's and asks for some dog meat. She may spend ten or fifteen cents, but when she does she asks for something. Formerly the butchers gave liver to anyone who wanted to carry it away. In our family we were always having it. Once one of my brothers got a whole cow's liver at the slaughterhouse near the fairgrounds in our town. We had it until we were sick of it. It never cost a cent. I have hated the thought of it ever since.

The old farm woman got some liver and a soupbone. She never visited with anyone, and as soon as she got what she wanted she lit out for home. It made quite a load for such an old body. No one gave her a lift. People drive right down a road and never notice an old woman like that.

There was such an old woman who used to come into town past our house one summer and fall when I was a young boy and was sick with what was called inflammatory rheumatism. She went home later carrying a heavy pack on her back. Two or three large gaunt-looking dogs followed at her heels.

The old woman was nothing special. She was one of the nameless ones that hardly anyone knows, but she got into my thoughts. I have just suddenly now, after all these years, remembered her and what happened. It is a story. Her name was Grimes, and she lived with her husband and son in a small unpainted house on the bank of a small creek four miles from town.

The husband and son were a tough lot. Although the son was but twenty-one, he had already served a term in jail. It was whispered about that the woman's husband stole horses and ran them off to some other county. Now and then, when a horse turned up missing, the man had also disappeared. No one ever caught him. Once, when I was loafing at Tom Whitehead's livery barn, the man came there and sat on the bench

---

in front. Two or three other men were there, but no one spoke to him. He sat for a few minutes and then got up and went away. When he was leaving he turned around and stared at the men. There was a look of defiance in his eyes. "Well, I have tried to be friendly. You don't want to talk to me. It has been so wherever I have gone in this town. If, some day, one of your fine horses turns up missing, well, then what?" He did not say anything actually. "I'd like to bust one of you on the jaw," was about what his eyes said. I remember how the look in his eyes made me shiver.

The old man belonged to a family that had had money once. His name was Jake Grimes. It all comes back clearly now. His father, John Grimes, had owned a sawmill when the country was new, and had made money. Then he got to drinking and running after women. When he died there wasn't much left.

Jake blew in the rest. Pretty soon there wasn't any more lumber to cut and his land was nearly all gone.

He got his wife off a German farmer, for whom he went to work one June day in the wheat harvest. She was a young thing then and scared to death. You see, the farmer was up to something with the girl—she was, I think, a bound girl and his wife had her suspicions. She took it out on the girl when the man wasn't around. Then, when the wife had to go off to town for supplies, the farmer got after her. She told young Jake that nothing really ever happened, but he didn't know whether to believe it or or not.

He got her pretty easy himself, the first time he was out with her. He wouldn't have married her if the German farmer hadn't tried to tell him where to get off. He got her to go riding with him in his buggy one night when he was threshing on the place, and then he came for her the next Sunday night.

She managed to get out of the house without her employer's seeing, but when she was getting into the buggy he showed up. It was almost dark, and he just popped up suddenly at the horse's head. He grabbed the horse by the bridle and Jake got out his buggy whip.

They had it out all right! The German was a tough one. Maybe he didn't care whether his wife knew or not. Jake hit him over the face and shoulders with the buggy whip, but the horse got to acting up and he had to get out.

Then the two men went for it. The girl didn't see it. The horse started to run away and went nearly a mile down the road before the girl got him stopped. Then she managed to tie him to a tree beside the road. (I wonder how I know all this. It must have stuck in my mind from small-town tales when I was a boy.) Jake found her there after he got through with the German. She was huddled up in the buggy seat, crying, scared to death. She told Jake a lot of stuff, how the German had tried to get her, how he chased her once into the barn, how another time, when they happened to be alone in the house together, he tore her dress open clear down the front. The German, she said, might have got her that time if he hadn't heard his old woman drive in at the gate. She had been off to town for supplies. Well, she would be putting the horse in the barn. The German managed to sneak off to the fields without his wife seeing. He told the girl he would kill her if she told. What could she do? She told a lie about ripping her dress in the barn when she was feeding the stock. I remember now that she was a bound girl and did not know where her father and mother were. Maybe she did not have any father. You know what I mean.

Such bound children were often enough cruelly treated. They were children who had no parents, slaves really. There were very few orphan homes then. They were legally bound into some home. It was a matter of pure luck how it came out.

II

She married Jake and had a son and a daughter, but the daughter died.

Then she settled down to feed stock. That was her job. At the German's place she had cooked the food for the German and his wife. The wife was a strong woman with big hips and worked most of the time in the fields with her husband. She fed them and fed the cows in the barn, fed the pigs, the horses and the chickens. Every moment of every day, as a young girl, was spent feeding something.

Then she married Jake Grimes and he had to be fed. She was a slight thing, and when she had been married for three or four years, and after the two children were born, her slender shoulders became stooped.

Jake always had a lot of big dogs around the house, that stood near the unused sawmill near the creek. He was always trading horses when he wasn't stealing something and had a lot of poor bony ones about. Also he kept three or four pigs and a cow. They were all pastured in the few acres left of the Grimes place and Jake did little enough work.

He went into debt for a threshing outfit and ran it for several years, but it did not pay. People did not trust him. They were afraid he would steal the grain at night. He had to go a long way off to get work and it cost too much to get there. In the winter he hunted and cut a little firewood, to be sold in some nearby town. When the son grew up he was just like the father. They got drunk together. If there wasn't anything to eat in the house when they came home the old man gave his old woman a cut over the head. She had a few chickens of her own and had to kill one of them in a hurry. When they were all killed she wouldn't have any eggs to sell when she went to town, and then what would she do?

She had to scheme all her life about getting things fed, getting the pigs fed so they would grow fat and could be butchered in the fall. When they were butchered her husband took most of the meat off to town and sold it. If he did not do it first, the boy did. They fought sometimes and when they fought the old woman stood aside trembling.

She had got the habit of silence anyway—that was fixed. Sometimes, when she began to look old—she wasn't forty yet—and when the husband and son were both off, trading horses or drinking or hunting or stealing, she went around the house and the barnyard muttering to herself.

How was she going to get everything fed?—that was her problem. The dogs had to be fed. There wasn't enough hay in the barn for the horses and the cow. If she didn't feed the chickens how could they lay eggs? Without eggs to sell how could she get things in town, things she had to have to keep the life of the farm going? Thank heaven, she did not have to feed her husband—in a certain way. That hadn't lasted long after their marriage and after the babies came. Where he went on his long trips she did not know. Sometimes he was gone from home for weeks, and after the boy grew up they went off together.

They left everything at home for her to manage and she had no money. She knew no one. No one ever talked to her in town. When it was winter she had to gather sticks of wood for her fire, had to try to keep the stock fed with very little grain.

The stock in the barn cried to her hungrily, the dogs followed her about. In the winter the hens laid few enough eggs. They huddled in the corners of the barn and she kept watching them. If a hen lays an egg in the barn in the winter and you do not find it, it freezes and breaks.

One day in winter the old woman went off to town with a few eggs and the dogs followed her. She did not get started until nearly three o'clock and the snow was heavy. She hadn't been feeling very well for several days and so she went muttering along, scantily clad, her shoulders stooped. She had an old grain bag in which she carried her eggs, tucked away down in the bottom. There weren't many of them, but in winter the price of eggs is up. She would get a little meat in exchange for the eggs, some salt pork, a little sugar, and some coffee perhaps. It might be the butcher would give her a piece of liver.

When she had got to town and was trading in her eggs the dogs lay by the door outside. She did pretty well, got the things she needed, more than she had hoped. Then she went to the butcher and he gave her some liver and some dog meat.

It was the first time anyone had spoken to her in a friendly way for a long time. The butcher was alone in his shop when she came in and was annoyed by the thought of such a sick-looking old woman out on such a day. It was bitter cold and the snow, that had let up during the afternoon, was falling again. The butcher said something about her husband and her son, swore at them, and the old woman stared at him, a look of mild surprise in her eyes as he talked. He said that if either the husband or the son were going to get any of the liver or the heavy bones with scraps of meat hanging to them that he had put into the grain bag, he'd see him starve first.

Starve, eh? Well, things had to be fed. Men had to be fed, and the horses that weren't any good but maybe could be traded off, and the poor thin cow that hadn't given any milk for three months.

Horses, cows, pigs, dogs, men.

III

The old woman had to get back before darkness came if she could. The dogs followed at her heels, sniffing at the heavy grain bag she had fastened on her back. When she got to the edge of town she stopped by a fence and tied the bag on her back with a piece of rope she had carried in her dress pocket for just that purpose. That was an easier way to carry it. Her arms ached. It was hard when she had to crawl over fences and once she fell over and landed in the snow. The dogs went frisking about. She had to struggle to get to her feet again, but she made it. The point of climbing over the fences was that there was a short cut over a hill and through a woods. She might have gone around by the road, but it was a mile farther that way. She was afraid she couldn't make it. And then, besides, the stock had to be fed. There was a little hay left and a little corn. Perhaps her husband and son would bring some home when they came. They had driven off in the only buggy the Grimes family had, a rickety thing, a rickety horse hitched to the buggy, two other rickety horses led by halters. They were going to trade horses, get a little money if they could. They might come home drunk. It would be well to have something in the house when they came back.

The son had an affair on with a woman at the county seat, fifteen miles away. She was a rough enough woman, a tough one. Once, in the summer, the son had brought her to the house. Both she and the son had been drinking. Jake Grimes was away and the son and his woman ordered the old woman about like a servant. She didn't mind much; she was used to it. Whatever happened she never said anything. That was her way of getting along. She had managed that way when she was a young girl at the German's and ever since she had married Jake. That time her son brought his woman to the house they stayed all night, sleeping together just as though they were married. It hadn't shocked the old woman, not much. She had got past being shocked early in life.

With the pack on her back she went painfully along across an open field, wading in the deep snow, and got into the woods.

There was a path, but it was hard to follow. Just beyond the top of the hill, where the woods was thickest, there was a small clearing. Had someone once thought of building a house there? The clearing was as large as a building lot in town, large enough for a house and a garden. The path ran along the side of the clearing, and when she got there the old woman sat down to rest at the foot of a tree.

It was a foolish thing to do. When she got herself placed, the pack against the tree's trunk, it was nice, but what about getting up again? She worried about that for a moment and then quietly closed her eyes.

She must have slept for a time. When you are about so cold you can't get any colder. The afternoon grew a little warmer and the snow came thicker than ever. Then after a time the weather cleared. The moon even came out.

There were four Grimes dogs that had followed Mrs. Grimes into town, all tall gaunt fellows. Such men as Jake Grimes and his son always keep just such dogs. They kick and abuse them, but they stay. The Grimes dogs, in order to keep from starving, had to do a lot of foraging for themselves, and they had been at it while the old woman slept with her back to the tree at the side of the clearing. They had been chasing rabbits in the woods and in adjoining fields and in their ranging had picked up three other farm dogs.

After a time all the dogs came back to the clearing. They were excited about something. Such nights, cold and clear and with a moon, do things to dogs. It may be that some old instinct, come down from the time when they were wolves and ranged the woods in packs on winter nights, comes back into them.

The dogs in the clearing, before the old woman, had caught two or three rabbits and their immediate hunger had been satisfied. They began to play, running in circles in the clearing. Round and round they ran, each dog's nose at the tail of the next dog. In the clearing, under the snow-laden trees and under the wintry moon they made a strange picture, running thus silently, in a circle their running had beaten in the soft snow. The dogs made no sound. They ran around and around in the circle.

It may have been that the old woman saw them doing that before she died. She may have awakened once or twice and looked at the strange sight with dim old eyes.

She wouldn't be very cold now, just drowsy. Life hangs on a long time. Perhaps the old woman was out of her head. She may have dreamed of her girlhood, at the German's, and before that, when she was a child and before her mother lit out and left her.

Her dreams couldn't have been very pleasant. Not many pleasant things have happened to her. Now and then one of the Grimes dogs left the running circle and came to stand before her. The dog thrust his face close to her face. His red tongue was hanging out.

The running of the dogs may have been a kind of death ceremony. It may have been that the primitive instinct of the wolf, having been aroused in the dogs by the night and the running, made them somehow afraid.

"Now we are no longer wolves. We are dogs, the servants of men. Keep alive, man! When man dies we become wolves again."

When one of the dogs came to where the old woman sat with her back against the tree and thrust his nose close to her face he seemed satisfied and went back to run with the pack. All the Grimes dogs did it at some time during the evening, before she died. I knew all about it afterward, when I grew to be a man, because once in a woods in Illinois, on another winter night, I saw a pack of dogs act just like that. The dogs were waiting for me to die as they had waited for the old woman that night when I was a child, but when it happened to me I was a young man and had no intention whatever of dying.

The old woman died softly and quietly. When she was dead and when one of the Grimes dogs had come to her and had found her dead all the dogs stopped running.

They gathered about her.

Well, she was dead now. She had fed the Grimes dogs when she was alive, what about now?

There was the pack on her back, the grain bag containing the piece of salt pork, the liver the butcher had given her, the dog meat, the soupbones. The butcher in town, having been suddenly overcome with a feeling of pity, had loaded her grain bag heavily. It had been a big haul for the old woman.

It was a big haul for the dogs now.

IV

One of the Grimes dogs sprang suddenly out from among the others and began worrying the pack on the old woman's back. Had the dogs really been wolves, that one would have been the leader of the pack. What he did, all the others did.

All of them sank their teeth into the grain bag the old woman had fastened with ropes to her back.

They dragged the old woman's body out into the open clearing. The worn-out dress was quickly torn from her shoulders. When she was found, a day or two later, the dress had been torn from her body clear to the hips, but the dogs had not touched her body. They had got the meat out of the grain bag, that was all. Her body was frozen stiff when it was found, and the shoulders were so narrow and the body so slight that in death it looked like the body of some charming young girl.

Such things happened in towns of the Middle West, on farms near town, when I was a boy. A hunter out after rabbits found the old woman's body and did not touch it. Something, the beaten round path in the little snow-covered clearing, the silence of the place, the place where the dogs had worried the body trying to pull the grain bag away or tear it open—something startled the man and he hurried off to town.

I was in Main Street with one of my brothers who was town newsboy and who was taking the afternoon papers to the stores. It was almost night.

The hunter came into a grocery and told his story. Then he went to a hardware shop and into a drugstore. Men began to gather on the sidewalks. Then they started out along the road to the place in the woods.

My brother should have gone on about his business of distributing papers but he didn't. Everyone was going to the woods. The undertaker went and the town marshal. Several men got on a dray and rode out to where the path left the road and went into the woods, but the horses weren't very sharply shod and slid about on the slippery roads. They made no better time than those of us who walked.

The town marshal was a large man whose leg had been injured in the Civil War. He carried a heavy cane and limped rapidly along the road. My brother and I followed at his heels, and as we went other men and boys joined the crowd.

It had grown dark by the time we got to where the old woman had left the road, but the moon had come out. The marshal was thinking there might have been a murder. He kept asking the hunter questions. The hunter went along with his gun across his shoulders, a dog following at his heels. It isn't often a rabbit hunter has a chance to be so conspicuous. He was taking full advantage of it, leading the procession with the town marshal. "I didn't see any wounds. She was a beautiful young girl. Her face was buried in the snow. No, I didn't know her." As a matter of fact, the hunter had not looked closely at the body. He had been frightened. She might have been murdered and someone might spring out from behind a tree and murder him. In a woods, in the late afternoon, when the trees are all bare and there is white snow on the ground, when all is silent, something creepy steals over the mind and body. If something strange or uncanny has happened in the neighborhood all you think about is getting away from there as fast as you can.

The crowd of men and boys had got to where the old woman had crossed the field and went, following the marshal and the hunter, up the slight incline and into the woods.

My brother and I were silent. He had his bundle of papers in a bag slung across his shoulder. When he got back to town he would have to go on distributing his papers before he went home to supper. If I went along, as he had no doubt already determined I should, we would both be late. Either Mother or our older sister would have to warm our supper.

Well, we would have something to tell. A boy did not get such a chance very often. It was lucky we just happened to go into the grocery when the hunter came in. The hunter was a country fellow. Neither of us had ever seen him before.

Now the crowd of men and boys had got to the clearing. Darkness comes quickly on such winter nights, but the full moon made everything clear. My brother and I stood near the tree beneath which the old woman had died.

She did not look old, lying there in that light, frozen and still. One of the men turned her over in the snow and I saw everything. My body trembled with some strange mystical feeling and so did my brother's. It might have been the cold.

Neither of us had ever seen a woman's body before. It may have been the snow, clinging to the frozen flesh, that made it look so white and lovely, so like marble. No woman had come with the party from town; but one of the men, he was the town blacksmith, took off his overcoat and spread it over her. Then he gathered her into his arms and started off to town, all the others following silently. At that time no one knew who she was.

V

I had seen everything, had seen the oval in the snow, like a miniature race track, where the dogs had run, had seen how the men were mystified, had seen the white bare young-looking shoulders, had heard the whispered comments of the men.

The men were simply mystified. They took the body to the undertaker's, and when the blacksmith, the hunter, the marshal and several others had got inside they closed the door. If Father had been there perhaps he could have got in, but we boys couldn't.

I went with my brother to distribute the rest of his papers and when we got home it was my brother who told the story.

I kept silent and went to bed early. It may have been I was not satisfied with the way he told it.

Later, in the town, I must have heard other fragments of the old woman's story. She was recognized the next day and there was an investigation.

The husband and son were found somewhere and brought to town and there was an attempt to connect them with the woman's death, but it did not work. They had perfect enough alibis.

However, the town was against them. They had to get out. Where they went I never heard.

I remember only the picture there in the forest, the men standing about, the naked girlish-looking figure, face down in the snow, the tracks made by the running dogs and the clear cold winter sky above. White fragments of clouds were drifting across the sky. They went racing across the little open space among the trees.

The scene in the forest had become for me, without my knowing it, the foundation for the real story I am now trying to tell. The fragments, you see, had to be picked up slowly, long afterward.

Things happened. When I was a young man I worked on the farm of a German. The hired girl was afraid of her employer. The farmer's wife hated her.

I saw things at that place. Once later, I had a half-uncanny, mystical adventure with dogs in an Illinois forest on a clear, moonlit winter night. When I was a schoolboy, and on a summer day, I went with a boy friend out along a creek some miles from town and came to the house where the old woman had lived. No one had lived in the house since her death. The doors were broken from the hinges; the window lights were all broken. As the boy and I stood in the road outside, two dogs, just roving farm dogs no doubt, came running around the corner of the house. The dogs were tall, gaunt fellows and came down to the fence and glared through at us, standing in the road.

The whole thing, the story of the old woman's death, was to me as I grew older like music heard from far off. The notes had to be picked up slowly one at a time. Something had to be understood.

The woman who died was one destined to feed animal life. Anyway, that is all she ever did. She was feeding animal life before she was born, as a child, as a young woman working on the farm of the German, after she married, when she grew old, and when she died. She fed animal life in cows, in chickens, in pigs, in horses, in dogs, in men. Her daughter had died in childhood and with her one son she had no articulate relations. On the night when she died she was hurrying homeward, bearing on her body food for animal life.

She died in the clearing in the woods and even after her death continued feeding animal life.

You see, it is likely that when my brother told the story that night when we got home and my mother and sister sat listening I did not think he got the point. He was too young and so was I. A thing so complete has its own beauty.

I shall not try to emphasize the point. I am only explaining why I was dissatisfied then and have been ever since. I speak of that only that you may understand why I have been impelled to try to tell the simple story over again.

AN IDYLL

by Guy de Maupassant

The train had just left Genoa, in the direction of Marseille, and was following the rocky and sinuous coast, gliding like an iron serpent between the sea and the mountains, creeping over the yellow sand edged with silver waves and entering into the black-mouthed tunnels like a beast into its lair.

In the last carriage, a stout woman and a young man sat opposite each other. They did not speak, but occasionally they would glance at each other. She was about twenty-five years old. Seated by the window, she silently gazed at the passing landscape. She was from Piedmont, a peasant, with large black eyes, a full bust and fat checks. She had deposited several parcels on the wooden seat and she held a basket on her knees.

The man might have been twenty years old. He was thin and sunburned, with the dark complexion that denotes work in the open. Tied up in a handkerchief was his whole fortune; a pair of heavy boots, a pair of trousers, a shirt and a coat. Hidden under the seat were a shovel and a pickax tied together with a rope.

He was going to France to seek work.

The sun, rising in the sky, spread a fiery light over the coast; it was toward the end of May and delightful odors entered into the railway carriage. The blooming orange and lemon trees exhaled a heavy, sweet perfume that mingled with the breath of the roses which grew in profusion along the railroad track, as well as in the gardens of the wealthy and the humble homes of the peasants.

Roses are so completely at home along this coast! They fill the whole region with their dainty and powerful fragrance and make the atmosphere taste like a delicacy, something better than wine, and as intoxicating.

The train was going at slow speed as if loath to leave behind this wonderful garden! It stopped every few minutes at small stations, at clusters of white houses, then went on again leisurely, emitting long whistles. Nobody got in. One would have thought that all the world had gone to sleep and made up its mind not to travel on that sultry spring morning. The plump peasant woman from time to time closed her eyes, but she would open them suddenly whenever her basket slid from her lap. She would catch it, replace it, look out of the window a little while

---

From *The Collected Novels and Short Stories of Guy de Maupassant*, Vol. 6, translated and edited by Ernest Boyd (New York: Alfred A. Knopf, 1923), pp. 73–9.

and then doze off again. Tiny beads of perspiration covered her brow and she breathed with difficulty, as if suffering from a painful oppression.

The young man had let his head fall on his breast and was sleeping the sound sleep of the laboring man.

All of a sudden, just as the train left a small station, the peasant woman woke up and opening her basket, drew forth a piece of bread, some hard-boiled eggs, and a flask of wine and some fine, red plums. She began to munch contentedly.

The man also wakened, and he watched the woman, watched every morsel that traveled from her knees to her lips. He sat with his arms folded, his eyes set, and his lips tightly compressed.

The woman ate like a glutton, with relish. Every little while she would take a swallow of wine to wash down the eggs and then she would stop for breath.

Everything vanished, the bread, the eggs, the plums and the wine. As soon as she had finished her meal, the man closed his eyes. Then, feeling ill at ease, she loosened her blouse, and the man suddenly looked at her again.

She did not seem to mind and continued to unbutton her dress.

The pressure of her flesh causing the opening to gape, she revealed a portion of white linen chemise and a portion of her skin.

As soon as she felt more comfortable, she turned to her fellow traveler and remarked in Italian: "It's fine weather for traveling."

"Are you from Piedmont?" he asked. "I'm from Asti."

"And I'm from Casale."

They were neighbors, and they began to talk.

They exchanged the commonplace remarks that working people repeat over and over and which are all-sufficient for their slow-working and narrow minds. They spoke of their homes and found out that they had a number of mutual acquaintances.

They quoted names and became more and more friendly as they discovered more and more people they knew. Short, rapid words, with sonorous endings and the Italian cadence, gushed from their lips.

After that, they talked about themselves. She was married and had three children whom she had left with her sister, for she had found a situation as nurse, a good situation with a French lady at Marseille.

He was going to look for work.

He had been told that he would be able to find it in France, for they were building a great deal, he had heard.

They found nothing to talk about after that.

The heat was becoming terrible; it beat down like fire on the roof of the railway carriage. A cloud of dust flew behind the train and entered through the window, and the fragrance of the roses and orange blossoms had become stronger, heavier, and more penetrating.

The two travelers went to sleep again.

They awakened almost at the same time. The sun was nearing the edge of the horizon and shed its glorious light on the blue sea. The atmosphere was lighter and cooler.

The nurse was gasping. Her dress was open and her cheeks looked flabby and moist, and in an oppressed voice, she breathed:

"I have not nursed since yesterday; I feel as if I were going to faint."

The man did not reply; he hardly knew what to say.

She continued: "When a woman has as much milk as I, she must nurse three times a day or she'll feel uncomfortable. It feels like a weight on my heart, a weight that prevents my breathing and just exhausts me. It's terrible to have so much milk."

He replied: "Yes, it must be very annoying."

She really seemed ill and almost ready to faint. She murmured: "I only have to press and the milk flows out like a fountain. It is really interesting to see. You wouldn't believe it. In Casale, all the neighbours came to see it."

He replied: "Ah! really."

"Yes, really. I would show you, only it wouldn't help me. You can't make enough come out that way."

And she paused.

The train stopped at a station. Leaning on a fence was a woman holding a crying infant in her arms. She was thin and in rags.

The nurse watched her. Then she said in a compassionate tone: "There's a woman I could help. And the baby could help me, too. I'm not rich; am I not leaving my home, my people and my baby to take a place, but still, I'd give five francs to have that child and be able to nurse it for ten minutes. It would quiet him, and me too, I can tell you. I think I would feel as if I were being born again."

She paused again. Then she passed her hot hand several times across her wet brow and moaned: "Oh! I can't stand it any longer. I believe I shall die." And with an unconscious motion, she completely opened her waist.

Her right breast appeared all swollen and stiff, with its brown teat, and the poor woman gasped: "Ah! my God! my God! What shall I do?"

The train had left the station and was continuing its route amid the flowers that gave forth their penetrating fragrance.

Once in a while a fishing shack glided over the blue sea with its motionless sail, which was reflected in the clear water as if another boat were turned upside down.

The young man, embarrassed, stammered: "But—madame—I—might perhaps be—be able to help you."

In an exhausted whisper, she replied: "Yes, if you will be so kind, you'll do me a great favor. I can't stand it any longer, really I can't."

He got on his knees before her; and she leaned over to him with a motherly gesture as if he were a child. In the movement she made to draw near to the man, a drop of milk appeared on her breast. He absorbed it quickly, and, taking this heavy breast in his mouth like a fruit, he began to drink regularly and greedily.

He had passed his arms around the woman's waist and pressed her close to him in order not to lose a drop of the nourishment. And he drank with slow gulps, like a baby.

All of a sudden she said: "That's enough, now the other side!" And he obeyed her with alacrity.

She had placed both hands on his back and now was breathing happily, freely, enjoying the perfume of the flowers carried on the breeze that entered the open windows.

"It smells mighty good," she said.

He made no reply and continued to drink at the living fountain of her breast, closing his eyes to better taste the milk fluid.

But she gently pushed him from her.

"That's enough. I feel much better now. It has put life into me again."

He rose and wiped his mouth with the back of his hand.

While she replaced her breasts inside her dress, she said:

"You did me a great favor. I thank you very much!"

And he replied in a grateful tone:

"It is I who thank you, for I hadn't eaten a thing for two days!"

AMY FOSTER

by Joseph Conrad

Kennedy is a country doctor, and lives in Colebrook, on the shores of Eastbay. The high ground rising abruptly behind the red roofs of the little town crowds the quaint High Street against the wall which defends it from the sea. Beyond the sea-wall there curves for miles in a vast and regular sweep the barren beach of shingle, with the village of Brenzett standing out darkly across the water, a spire in a clump of trees; and still further out the perpendicular column of a lighthouse, looking in the distance no bigger than a lead pencil, marks the vanishing-point of the land. The country at the back of Brenzett is low and flat; but the bay is fairly well sheltered from the seas, and occasionally a big ship, windbound or through stress of weather, makes use of the anchoring ground a mile and a half due north from you as you stand at the back door of the "Ship Inn" in Brenzett. A dilapidated windmill near by, lifting its shattered arms from a mound no loftier than a rubbish-heap, and a Martello tower squatting at the water's edge half a mile to the south of the Coastguard cottages, are familiar to the skippers of small craft. These are the official seamarks for the patch of trustworthy bottom represented on the Admi-

From *Typhoon and Other Stories*, Vol. 20, by Joseph Conrad (Garden City: Doubleday, Page & Co., 1924), pp. 105–42. Reprinted by permission of J. M. Dent & Sons Ltd., publishers, and the trustees of the estate of Joseph Conrad.

ralty charts by an irregular oval of dots enclosing several figures six, with a tiny anchor engraved among them, and the legend "mud and shells" over all.

The brow of the upland overtops the square tower of the Colebrook Church. The slope is green and looped by a white road. Ascending along this road, you open a valley broad and shallow, a wide green trough of pastures and hedges merging inland into a vista of purple tints and flowing lines closing the view.

In this valley down to Brenzett and Colebrook and up to Darnford, the market town fourteen miles away, lies the practice of my friend Kennedy. He had begun life as surgeon in the Navy, and afterwards had been the companion of a famous traveller, in the days when there were continents with unexplored interiors. His papers on the fauna and flora made him known to scientific societies. And now he had come to a country practice—from choice. The penetrating power of his mind, acting like a corrosive fluid, had destroyed his ambition, I fancy. His intelligence is of a scientific order, of an investigating habit, and of that unappeasable curiosity which believes that there is a particle of a general truth in every mystery.

A good many years ago now, on my return from abroad, he invited me to stay with him. I came readily enough, and as he could not neglect his patients to keep me company, he took me on his rounds—thirty miles or so of an afternoon, sometimes. I waited for him on the roads; the horse reached after the leafy twigs, and, sitting high in the dogcart, I could hear Kennedy's laugh through the half-open door of some cottage. He had a big, hearty laugh that would have fitted a man twice his size, a brisk manner, a bronzed face, and a pair of gray, profoundly attentive eyes. He had the talent of making people talk to him freely, and an inexhaustible patience in listening to their tales.

One day, as we trotted out of a large village into a shady bit of road I saw on our left hand a low, black cottage, with diamond panes in the windows, a creeper on the end wall, a roof of shingle, and some roses climbing on the rickety trellis-work of the tiny porch. Kennedy pulled up to a walk. A woman, in full sunlight, was throwing a dripping blanket over a line stretched between two old apple-trees. And as the bobtailed, long-necked chestnut, trying to get his head, jerked the left hand, covered by a thick dogskin glove, the doctor raised his voice over the hedge: "How's your child, Amy?"

I had the time to see her dull face, red, not with a mantling blush, but as if her flat cheeks had been vigorously slapped, and to take in the squat figure, the scanty, dusty brown hair drawn into a tight knot at the back of the head. She looked quite young. With a distinct catch in her breath, her voice sounded low and timid.

"He's well, thank you."

We trotted again. "A young patient of yours," I said; and the doctor, flicking the chestnut absently, muttered, "Her husband used to be."

"She seems a dull creature," I remarked, listlessly.

"Precisely," said Kennedy. "She is very passive. It's enough to look at the red hands hanging at the end of those short arms, at those slow, prominent brown eyes, to know the inertness of her mind—an inertness that one would think made it everlastingly safe from all the surprises of imagination. And yet which of us is safe? At any rate, such as you see her, she had enough imagination to fall in love. She's the daughter of one Isaac Foster, who from a small farmer has sunk into a shepherd; the beginning of his misfortunes dating from his runaway marriage with the cook of his widowed father—well-to-do, apoplectic grazier, who passionately struck his name off his will, and had been heard to utter threats against his life. But this old affair, scandalous enough to serve as a motive for a Greek tragedy, arose from the similarity of their characters. There are other tragedies, less scandalous and of a subtler poignancy, arising from irreconcilable differences and from that fear of the Incomprehensible that hangs over all our heads—over all our heads. . . ."

The tired chestnut dropped into a walk; and the rim of the sun, all red in a speckless sky, touched familiarly the smooth top of a ploughed rise near the road as I had seen it times innumerable touch the distant horizon of the sea. The uniform brownness of the harrowed field glowed with a rose tinge, as though the powdered clods had sweated out in minute pearls of blood the toil of uncounted ploughmen. From the edge of a copse a waggon with two horses was rolling gently along the ridge. Raised above our heads upon the sky-line, it loomed up against the red sun, triumphantly big, enormous, like a chariot of giants drawn by two slow-stepping steeds of legendary proportions. And the clumsy figure of the man plodding at the head of the leading horse projected itself on the background of the Infinite with a heroic uncouthness. The end of his carter's whip quivered high up in the blue. Kennedy discoursed.

"She's the eldest of a large family. At the age of fifteen they put her out to service at the New Barns Farm. I attended Mrs. Smith, the tenant's wife, and saw that girl there for the first time. Mrs. Smith, a genteel person with a sharp nose, made her put on a black dress every afternoon. I don't know what induced me to notice her at all. There are faces that call your attention by a curious want of definiteness in their whole aspect, as, walking in a mist, you peer attentively at a vague shape which, after all, may be nothing more curious or strange than a signpost. The only peculiarity I perceived in her was a slight hesitation in her utterance, a sort of preliminary stammer which passes away with the first word. When sharply spoken to, she was apt to lose her head at once; but her heart was of the kindest. She had never been heard to express a dislike for a single human being, and she was tender to every living creature. She was devoted to Mrs. Smith, to Mr. Smith, to their dogs, cats, canaries; and as to Mrs. Smith's gray parrot, its peculiarities exercised upon her a positive fascination. Nevertheless, when that outlandish bird, attacked by the cat, shrieked for help in human accents, she ran out into the yard stopping her ears, and did not prevent the crime. For Mrs. Smith this was another evidence of her stupidity; on the other hand, her want of charm, in view of Smith's well-known frivolousness, was a great recommendation. Her short-sighted eyes would swim with pity for a poor mouse in a trap, and she had been seen once by some boys on her knees in the wet grass helping a toad in difficulties. If it's true, as some German fellow has said, that without phosphorous there is no thought, it is still more true that there is no kindness of heart without a certain amount of imagination. She had some. She had even more than is necessary to understand suffering and to be moved by pity. She fell in love under circumstances that leave no room for doubt in the matter; for you need imagination to form a notion of beauty at all, and still more to discover your ideal in an unfamiliar shape.

"How this aptitude came to her, what it did feed upon, is an inscrutable mystery. She was born in the village, and had never been further away from it than Colebrook or perhaps Darnford. She lived for four years with the Smiths. New Barns is an isolated farmhouse a mile away from the road, and she was content to look day after day at the same fields, hollows, rises; at the trees and the hedgerows; at the faces of the four men about the farm, always the same—day after day, month after month, year after year. She never showed a desire for conversation, and, as it seemed to me, she did not know how to smile. Sometimes of a fine Sunday afternoon she would put on her best dress, a pair of stout boots, a large gray hat trimmed with a black feather (I've seen her in that finery), seize an absurdly slender parasol, climb over two stiles, tramp over three fields and along two hundred yards of road—never further. There stood Foster's cottage. She would help her mother to give their tea to the younger children, wash up the crockery, kiss the little ones, and go back to the farm. That was all. All the rest, all the change, all the relaxation. She never seemed to wish for anything more. And then she fell in love. She fell in love silently, obstinately—perhaps helplessly. It came slowly, but when it came it worked like a powerful spell; it was love as the Ancients understood it: an irresistible and fateful impulse—a possession! Yes, it was in her to become haunted and possessed by a face, by a presence, fatally, as though she had been a pagan worshipper of form under a joyous sky—and to be awakened at last from that mysterious forgetfulness of self, from that enchantment, from that transport, by a fear resembling the unaccountable terror of a brute. . . ."

With the sun hanging low on its western limit, the expanse of the grass-lands framed in the counter-scarps of the rising ground took on a gorgeous and sombre aspect. A sense of penetrating sadness, like that inspired by a grave strain of music, disengaged itself from the silence of the fields. The men we met walked past, slow, unsmiling, with downcast eyes, as if the melancholy of an over-burdened earth had weighted their feet, bowed their shoulders, borne down their glances.

"Yes," said the doctor to my remark, "one would think the earth is under a curse, since of all her children these that cling to her the closest are uncouth in body and as leaden of gait as if their very hearts were loaded with chains. But here on this same road you might have seen amongst these heavy men a being lithe, supple and long-limbed, straight like a pine, with something striving upwards in his appearance as though the heart within him had been buoyant. Perhaps it was only the force of the contrast, but when he was passing one of these villagers here, the soles of his feet did not seem to me to touch the dust of the road. He vaulted over the stiles, paced these slopes with a long elastic stride that made him noticeable at a great distance, and had lustrous black eyes. He was so different from the mankind around that, with his freedom of movement, his soft—a little startled, glance, his olive complexion and graceful bearing, his humanity suggested to me the nature of a woodland creature. He came from there."

The doctor pointed with his whip, and from the summit of the descent seen over the rolling tops of the trees in a park by the side of the road, appeared the level sea far below us, like the floor of an immense edifice inlaid with bands of dark ripple, with still trails of glitter, ending in a belt of glassy water at the foot of the sky. The light blurr of smoke, from an invisible steamer, faded on the great clearness of the horizon like the mist of a breath on a mirror; and, inshore, the white sails of a coaster, with the appearance of disentangling themselves slowly from under the branches, floated clear of the foliage of the trees.

"Shipwrecked in the bay?" I said.

"Yes; he was a castaway. A poor emigrant from Central Europe bound to America and washed ashore here in a storm. And for him, who knew nothing of the earth, England was an undiscovered country. It was some time before he learned its name; and for all I know he might have expected to find wild beasts or wild men here, when, crawling in the dark over the sea-wall, he rolled down the other side into a dyke, where it was another miracle he didn't get drowned. But he struggled instinctively like an animal under a net, and this blind struggle threw him out into a field. He must have been, indeed, of a tougher fibre than he looked to withstand without expiring such buffetings, the violence of his exertions, and so much fear. Later on, in his broken English that resembled curiously the speech of a young child, he told me himself that he put his trust in God, believing he was no longer in this world. And truly —he would add—how was he to know? He fought his way against the rain and the gale on all fours, and crawled at last among some sheep huddled close under the lee of a hedge. They ran off in all directions, bleating in the darkness, and he welcomed the first familiar sound he heard on these shores. It must have been two in the morning then. And this is all we know of the manner of his landing, though he did not arrive unattended by any means. Only his grisly company did not begin to come ashore till much later in the day. . . ."

The doctor gathered the reins, clicked his tongue; we trotted down the hill. Then turning, almost directly, a sharp corner into High Street, we rattled over the stones and were home.

Late in the evening Kennedy, breaking a spell of moodiness that had come over him, returned to the story. Smoking his pipe, he paced the long room from end to end. A reading-lamp concentrated all its light upon the papers on his desk; and, sitting by the open window, I saw, after the windless, scorching day, the frigid splendour of a hazy sea lying motionless under the moon. Not a whisper, not a splash, not a stir of the shingle, not a footstep, not a sigh came up from the earth below—never a sign of life but the scent of climbing jasmine: and Kennedy's voice, speaking behind me, passed through the wide casement, to vanish outside in a chill and sumptuous stillness.

". . . The relations of shipwrecks in the olden time tell us of much suffering. Often the castaways were only saved from drowning to die miserably from starvation on a barren coast; others suffered violent death or else slavery, passing through years of precarious existence with people to whom their strangeness was an object of suspicion, dislike or fear. We read about these things, and they are very pitiful. It is indeed hard upon a man to find himself a lost stranger, helpless, incomprehensible, and of a mysterious origin, in some obscure corner of the earth. Yet amongst all the adventurers shipwrecked in all the wild parts of the world, there is not one, it seems to me, that ever had to suffer a fate so simply tragic as the man I am speaking of, the most innocent of adventurers cast out by the sea in the bight of this bay, almost within sight from this very window.

"He did not know the name of his ship. Indeed in the course of time we discovered he did not even know that ships had names—'like Christian people'; and when, one day, from the top of Talfourd Hill, he beheld the sea lying open to his view, his eyes roamed afar, lost in an air of wild surprise, as though he had never seen such a sight before. And probably he had not. As far as I could make out, he had been hustled together with many others on board an emigrant ship at the mouth of the Elbe, too bewildered to take note of his surroundings, too weary to see anything, too anxious to care. They were driven below into the 'tween-deck and battened down from the very start. It was a low timber dwelling—he would say—with wooden beams overhead, like the houses in his country, but you went into it down a ladder. It was very large, very cold, damp and sombre, with places in the manner of wooden boxes where people had to sleep one above another, and it kept on rocking all ways at once all the time. He crept into one of these boxes and lay down there in the clothes in which he had left his home many days before, keeping his bundle and his stick by his side. People groaned, children cried, water dripped, the lights went out, the walls of the place creaked, and everything was being shaken so that in one's little box one dared not lift one's head. He had lost touch with his only companion (a young man from the same valley, he said), and all the time a great noise of wind went on outside and heavy blows fell—boom! boom! An awful sickness overcame him, even to the point of making him neglect his prayers. Besides, one could not tell whether it was morning or evening. It seemed always to be night in that place.

"Before that he had been travelling a long, long time on the iron track. He looked out of the window, which had a wonderfully clear glass in it, and the trees, the houses, the fields, and the long roads seemed to fly round and round about him till his head swam. He gave me to understand that he had on his passage beheld uncounted multitudes of people—whole nations—all dressed in such clothes as the rich wear. Once he was made to get out of the carriage, and slept through a night on a bench in a house of bricks with his bundle under his head; and once for many hours he had to sit on a floor of flat stones, dozing, with his knees up and with his bundle between his feet. There was a roof over him, which seemed made of glass, and was so high that the tallest mountain-pine he had ever seen would have had room to grow under it. Steam-machines rolled in at one end and out at the other. People swarmed more than you can see on a feast-day round the miraculous Holy Image in the yard of the Carmelite Convent down in the plains where, before he left his home, he drove his mother in a wooden cart:—a pious old woman who wanted to offer prayers and make a vow for his safety. He could not give me an idea of how large and lofty and full of noise and smoke and gloom, and clang of iron, the place was, but someone had told him it was called Berlin. Then they rang a bell, and another steam-machine came in, and again he was taken on and on through a land that wearied his eyes by its flatness without a single bit of a hill to be seen anywhere. One more night he spent shut up in a building like a good stable with a litter of straw on the floor, guarding his bundle amongst a lot of men, of whom not one could understand a single word he said. In the morning they were all led down to the stony shores of an extremely broad muddy river, flowing not between hills but between houses that seemed immense. There was a steam-machine that went on the water, and they all stood upon it packed tight, only now there were with them many women and children who made much noise. A cold rain fell, the wind blew in his face; he was wet through, and his teeth chattered. He and the young man from the same valley took each other by the hand.

"They thought they were being taken to America straight away, but suddenly the steam-machine bumped against the side of a thing like a great house on the water. The walls were smooth and black, and there uprose, growing from the roof as it were, bare trees in the shape of crosses, extremely high. That's how it appeared to him then, for he had never seen a ship before. This was the ship that was going to swim all the way to America. Voices shouted, everything swayed; there was a ladder dipping up and down. He went up on his hands and knees in mortal fear of falling into the water below, which made a great splashing. He got separated from his companion, and when he descended into the bottom of that ship his heart seemed to melt suddenly within him.

"It was then also, as he told me, that he lost contact for good and all with one of those three men who the summer before had been going about through all the little towns in the foothills of his country. They would arrive on market-days driving in a peasant's cart, and would set up an office in an inn or some other Jew's house. There were three of them, of whom one with a long beard looked venerable; and they had red cloth collars round their necks and gold lace on their sleeves like Government officials. They sat proudly behind a long table; and in the next room, so that the common people shouldn't hear, they kept a cunning telegraph machine, through which they could talk to the Emperor of America. The fathers hung about the door, but the young men of the mountains would crowd up to the table asking many questions, for there was work to be got all the year round at three dollars a day in America, and no military service to do.

"But the American Kaiser would not take everybody. Oh, no! He himself had a great difficulty in getting accepted, and the venerable man in uniform had to go out of the room several times to work the telegraph on his behalf. The American Kaiser engaged him at last at three dollars, he being young and strong. However, many able young men backed out, afraid of the great distance; besides, those only who had some money could be taken. There were some who sold their huts and their land because it cost a lot of money to get to America; but then, once there, you had three dollars a day, and if you were clever you could find places where true gold could be picked up on the ground. His father's house was getting over full. Two of his brothers were married and had children. He promised to send money home from America by post twice a year. His father sold an old cow, a pair of piebald mountain ponies of his own raising, and a cleared plot of fair pasture land on the sunny slope of a pine-clad pass to a Jew inn-keeper, in order to pay the people of the ship that took men to America to get rich in a short time.

"He must have been a real adventurer at heart, for how many of the greatest enterprises in the conquest of the earth had for their beginning just such a bargaining away of the paternal cow for the mirage of true gold far away! I have been telling you more or less in my own words what I learned fragmentarily in the course of two or three years, during which I seldom missed an opportunity of a friendly chat with him. He told me this story of his adventure with many flashes of white teeth and lively glances of black eyes, at first in a sort of anxious baby-talk, then, as he acquired the language, with great fluency, but always with that singing, soft, and at the same time vibrating intonation that instilled a strangely penetrating power into the sound of the most familiar English words, as if they had been the words of an unearthly language. And he always would come to an end, with many emphatic shakes of his head, upon that awful sensation of his heart melting within him directly he set foot on board that ship. Afterwards there seemed to come for him a period of blank ignorance, at any rate as to facts. No doubt he must have been abominably seasick and abominably unhappy—this soft and passionate adventurer, taken thus out of his knowledge, and feeling bitterly as he lay in his emigrant bunk his utter loneliness; for his was a highly sensitive nature. The next thing we know of him for certain is that he had been hiding in Hammond's pig-pound by the side of the road to Norton, six miles, as the crow flies, from the sea. Of these experiences he was unwilling to speak: they seemed to have seared into his soul a sombre sort of wonder and indignation. Through the rumours of the country-side, which lasted for a good many days after his arrival, we know that the fishermen of West Colebrook had been disturbed and startled by heavy knocks against the walls of weatherboard cottages, and by a voice crying piercingly strange words in the night. Several of them turned out even, but, no doubt, he had fled in sudden alarm at their rough angry tones hailing each other in the darkness. A sort of frenzy must have helped him up the steep Norton hill. It was he, no doubt, who early the following morning had been seen lying (in a swoon, I should say) on the roadside grass by the Brenzett carrier, who actually got down to have a nearer look, but drew back, intimidated by the perfect immobility, and by something queer in the aspect of that tramp, sleeping so still under the showers. As the day advanced, some children came dashing into school at Norton in such a fright that the schoolmistress went out and spoke indignantly to a 'horrid-looking man' on the road. He edged away, hanging his head, for a few steps, and then suddenly ran off with extraordinary fleetness. The driver of Mr. Bradley's milk-cart made no secret of it that he had lashed with his whip at a hairy sort of gipsy fellow who, jumping up at a turn of the road by the Vents, made a snatch at the pony's bridle. And he caught him a good one, too, right over the face, he said, that made him drop down in the mud a jolly sight quicker than he had jumped up; but it was a good half a mile before he could stop the pony. Maybe that in his desperate endeavours to get help, and in his need to get in touch with someone, the poor devil had tried to stop the cart. Also three boys confessed afterwards to throwing stones at a funny tramp, knocking about all wet and muddy, and, it seemed, very drunk, in the narrow deep lane by the limekilns. All this was the talk of three villages for days; but we have Mrs. Finn's (the wife of Smith's waggoner) unimpeachable testimony that she saw him get over the low wall of Hammond's pig-pound and lurch straight at her, babbling aloud in a voice that was enough to make one die of fright. Having the baby with her in a perambulator, Mrs. Finn called out to him to go away, and as he persisted in coming nearer, she hit him courageously with her umbrella over the head, and, without once looking back, ran like the wind with the perambulator as far as the first house in the village. She stopped then, out of breath, and spoke to old Lewis, hammering there at a heap of stones; and the old chap, taking off his immense black wire goggles, got up on his shaky legs to look where she pointed. Together they followed with their eyes the figure of the man running over a field; they saw him fall down, pick himself up, and run on again, staggering and waving his long arms above his head, in the direction of the New Barns Farm. From that moment he is plainly in the toils of his obscure and touching destiny. There is no doubt after this of what happened to him. All is certain now: Mrs. Smith's intense terror; Amy Foster's stolid conviction held against the other's nervous attack, that the man 'meant no harm': Smith's exasperation (on his return from Darnford Market) at finding the dog barking himself into a fit, the back-door locked, his wife in hysterics; and all for an unfortunate dirty tramp, supposed to be even then lurking in his stackyard. Was he? He would teach him to frighten women.

"Smith is notoriously hot-tempered, but the sight of some nondescript and miry creature sitting cross-legged amongst a lot of loose straw, and swinging itself to and fro like a bear in a cage, made him pause. Then this tramp stood up silently before him, one mass of mud and filth from head to foot. Smith, alone amongst his stacks with this apparition, in the stormy twilight ringing with the infuriated barking of the dog, felt the dread of an inexplicable strangeness. But when that being, parting with his black hands the long matted locks that hung before his face, as you part the two halves of a curtain, looked out at him with glistening, wild, black-and-white eyes, the weirdness of this silent encounter fairly staggered him. He has admitted since (for the story has been a legitimate subject of conversation about here for years) that he made more than one step backwards. Then a sudden burst of rapid, senseless speech persuaded him at once that he had to do with an escaped lunatic. In fact, that impression never wore off completely. Smith has not in his heart given up his secret conviction of the man's essential insanity to this very day.

"As the creature approached him, jabbering in a most discomposing manner, Smith (unaware that he was being addressed as 'gracious lord,' and adjured in God's name to afford food and shelter) kept on speaking firmly but gently to it, and retreating all the time into the other yard. At last, watching his chance, by a sudden charge he bundled him headlong into the wood-lodge, and instantly shot the bolt. Thereupon he wiped his brow, though the day was cold. He had done his duty to the community by shutting up a wandering and probably dangerous maniac. Smith isn't a hard man at all, but he had room in his brain only for that one idea of lunacy. He was not imaginative enough to ask himself whether the man might not be perishing with cold and hunger. Meantime, at first, the maniac made a great deal of noise in the lodge. Mrs. Smith was screaming upstairs, where she had locked herself in her bedroom; but Amy Foster sobbed piteously at the kitchen-door, wringing her hands and muttering, 'Don't! don't!' I daresay Smith had a rough time of it that evening with one noise and another, and this insane, disturbing voice crying obstinately through the door only added to his irritation. He couldn't possibly have connected this troublesome lunatic with the sinking of a ship in Eastbay, of which there had been a rumour in the Darnford market place. And I daresay the man inside had been very near to insanity on that night. Before his excitement collapsed and he became unconscious he was throwing himself violently about in the dark, rolling on some dirty sacks, and biting his fists with rage, cold, hunger, amazement, and despair.

"He was a mountaineer of the eastern range of the Carpathians, and the vessel sunk the night before in Eastbay was the Hamburg emigrant-ship *Herzogin Sophia-Dorothea,* of appalling memory.

"A few months later we could read in the papers the accounts of the bogus 'Emigration Agencies' among the Sclavonian peasantry in the more remote provinces of Austria. The object of these scoundrels was to get hold of the poor ignorant people's homesteads, and they were in league with the local usurers. They exported their victims through Hamburg mostly. As to the ship, I had watched her out of this very window, reaching close-hauled under short canvas into the bay on a dark, threatening afternoon. She came to an anchor, correctly by the chart, off the Brenzett Coastguard station. I remember before the night fell looking out again at the outlines of her spars and rigging that stood out dark and pointed on a background of ragged, slaty clouds like another and a slighter spire to the left of the Brenzett church-tower. In the evening the wind rose. At midnight I could hear in my bed the terrific gusts and the sounds of a driving deluge.

"About that time the Coastguardmen thought they saw the lights of a steamer over the anchoring-ground. In a moment they vanished; but it is clear that another vessel of some sort had tried for shelter in the bay on that awful, blind night, had rammed the German ship amidships (a breach—as one of the divers told me afterwards—'that you could sail a Thames barge through'), and then had gone out either scathless or damaged, who shall say; but had gone out, unknown, unseen, and fatal, to perish mysteriously at sea. Of her nothing ever came to light, and yet the hue and cry that was raised all over the world would have found her out if she had been in existence anywhere on the face of the waters.

"A completeness without a clue, and a stealthy silence as of a neatly executed crime, characterize this murderous disaster, which, as you may remember, had its gruesome celebrity. The wind would have prevented the loudest outcries from reaching the shore; there had been evidently no time for signals of distress. It was death without any sort of fuss. The Hamburg ship, filling all at once, capsized as she sank, and at daylight there was not even the end of a spar to be seen above water. She was missed, of course, and at first the Coastguardmen surmised that she had either dragged her anchor or parted her cable some time during the night, and had been blown out to sea. Then, after the tide turned, the wreck must have shifted a little and released some of the bodies, because a child—a little fair-haired child in a red frock—came ashore abreast of the Martello tower. By the afternoon you could see along three miles of beach dark figures with bare legs dashing in and out of the tumbling foam, and rough-looking men, women with hard faces, children, mostly fair-haired, were being carried, stiff and dripping, on stretchers, on wattles, on ladders, in a long procession past the door of the "Ship Inn," to be laid out in a row under the north wall of the Brenzett Church.

"Officially, the body of the little girl in the red frock is the first thing that came ashore from that ship. But I have patients amongst the seafaring population of West Colebrook, and, unofficially, I am informed that very early that morning two brothers, who went down to look after their cobble hauled up on the beach, found a good way from Brenzett, an ordinary ship's hencoop, lying high and dry on the shore, with eleven drowned ducks inside. Their families ate the birds, and the hencoop was split into firewood with a hatchet. It is possible that a man (supposing he happened to be on deck at the time of the accident) might have floated ashore on that hencoop. He might. I admit it is improbable, but there was the man—and for days, nay, for weeks—it didn't enter our heads that we had amongst us the only living soul that had escaped from that disaster. The man himself, even when he learned to speak intelligibly, could tell us very little. He remembered he had felt better (after the ship had anchored, I suppose), and that the darkness, the wind, and the rain took his breath away. This looks as if he had been on deck some time during that night. But we mustn't forget he had been taken out of his knowledge, that he had been sea-sick and battened down below for four days, that he had no general notion of a ship or of the sea, and therefore could have no definite idea of what was happening to him. The rain, the wind, the darkness he knew; he understood the bleating of the sheep, and he remembered the pain of his wretchedness and misery, his heartbroken astonishment that it was neither seen nor understood, his dismay at finding all the men angry and all the women fierce. He had approached them as a beggar, it is true, he said; but in his country, even if they gave nothing, they spoke gently to beggars. The children in his country were not taught to throw stones at those who asked for compassion. Smith's strategy overcame him completely. The wood-lodge presented the horrible aspect of a dungeon. What would be done to him next? . . . No wonder that Amy Foster appeared to his eyes with the aureole of an angel of light. The girl had not been able to sleep for thinking of the poor man, and in the morning, before the Smiths were up, she slipped out across the back yard. Holding the door of the wood-lodge ajar, she looked in and extended to him half a loaf of white bread—'such bread as the rich eat in my country,' he used to say.

"At this he got up slowly from amongst all sorts of rubbish, stiff, hungry, trembling, miserable, and doubtful. 'Can you eat this?' she asked in her soft and timid voice. He must have taken her for a 'gracious lady.' He devoured ferociously, and tears were falling on the crust. Suddenly he dropped the bread, seized her wrist, and imprinted a kiss on her hand. She was not frightened. Through his forlorn condition she had observed that he was good-looking. She shut the door and walked back slowly to the kitchen. Much later on, she told Mrs. Smith, who shuddered at the bare idea of being touched by that creature.

"Through this act of impulsive pity he was brought back again within the pale of human relations with his new surroundings. He never forgot it—never.

"That very same morning old Mr. Swaffer (Smith's nearest neighbour) came over to give his advice, and ended by carrying him off. He stood, unsteady on his legs, meek, and caked over in half-dried mud, while the two men talked around him in an incomprehensible tongue. Mrs. Smith had refused to come downstairs till the madman was off the premises; Amy Foster, far from within the dark kitchen, watched through the open back-door; and he obeyed the signs that were made to him to the best of his ability. But Smith was full of mistrust. 'Mind, sir! It may be all his cunning,' he cried repeatedly in a tone of warning. When Mr. Swaffer started the mare, the deplorable being sitting humbly by his side, through weakness, nearly fell out over the back of the high two-wheeled cart. Swaffer took him straight home. And it is then that I come upon the scene.

"I was called in by the simple process of the old man beckoning to me with his forefinger over the gate of his house as I happened to be driving past. I got down, of course.

" 'I've got something here,' he mumbled, leading the way to an out-house at a little distance from his other farm-buildings.

"It was there that I saw him first, in a long, low room taken upon the space of that sort of coach-house. It was bare and whitewashed, with a small square aperture glazed with one cracked, dusty pane at its further end. He was lying on his back upon a straw pallet; they had given him a couple of horse-blankets, and he seemed to have spent the remainder of his strength in the exertion of cleaning himself. He was almost speechless; his quick breathing under the blankets pulled up to his chin, his glittering, restless black eyes reminded me of a wild bird caught in a snare. While I was examining him, old Swaffer stood silently by the door, passing the tips of his fingers along his shaven upper lip. I gave some directions, promised to send a bottle of medicine, and naturally made some inquiries.

" 'Smith caught him in the stackyard at New Barns,' said the old chap in his deliberate, unmoved manner, and as if the other had been indeed a sort of wild animal. 'That's how I came by him. Quite a curiosity, isn't he? Now tell me, doctor—you've been all over the world—don't you think that's a bit of a Hindoo we've got hold of here?'

"I was greatly surprised. His long black hair scattered over the straw bolster contrasted with the olive pallor of his face. It occurred to me he might be a Basque. It didn't necessarily follow that he should understand

Spanish; but I tried him with the few words I know, and also with some French. The whispered sounds I caught by bending my ear to his lips puzzled me utterly. That afternoon the young ladies from the Rectory (one of them read Goethe with a dictionary, and the other had struggled with Dante for years), coming to see Miss Swaffer, tried their German and Italian on him from the doorway. They retreated, just the least bit scared by the flood of passionate speech which, turning on his pallet, he let out at them. They admitted that the sound was pleasant, soft, musical—but, in conjunction with his looks perhaps, it was startling—so excitable, so utterly unlike anything one had ever heard. The village boys climbed up the bank to have a peep through the little square aperture. Everybody was wondering what Mr. Swaffer would do with him.

"He simply kept him.

"Swaffer would be called eccentric were he not so much respected. They will tell you that Mr. Swaffer sits up as late as ten o'clock at night to read books, and they will tell you also that he can write a cheque for two hundred pounds without thinking twice about it. He himself would tell you that the Swaffers had owned land between this and Darnford for these three hundred years. He must be eighty-five to-day, but he does not look a bit older than when I first came here. He is a great breeder of sheep, and deals extensively in cattle. He attends market days for miles around in every sort of weather, and drives sitting bowed low over the reins, his lank gray hair curling over the collar of his warm coat, and with a green plaid rug round his legs. The calmness of advanced age gives a solemnity to his manner. He is clean-shaved; his lips are thin and sensitive; something rigid and monachal in the set of his features lends a certain elevation to the character of his face. He has been known to drive miles in the rain to see a new kind of rose in somebody's garden, or a monstrous cabbage grown by a cottager. He loves to hear tell of or to be shown something what he calls 'outlandish.' Perhaps it was just that outlandishness of the man which influenced old Swaffer. Perhaps it was only an inexplicable caprice. All I know is that at the end of three weeks I caught sight of Smith's lunatic digging in Swaffer's kitchen garden. They had found out he could use a spade. He dug barefooted.

"His black hair flowed over his shoulders. I suppose it was Swaffer who had given him the striped old cotton shirt; but he wore still the national brown cloth trousers (in which he had been washed ashore) fitting to the legs almost like tights; was belted with a broad leather belt studded with little brass discs; and had never yet ventured into the village. The land he looked upon seemed to him kept neatly, like the grounds round a landowner's house; the size of the cart-horses struck him with astonishment; the roads resembled garden walks, and the aspect of the people, especially on Sundays, spoke of opulence. He wondered what made them so hardhearted and their children so bold. He got his food at the back-door, carried it in both hands, carefully, to his outhouse, and, sitting alone on his pallet, would make the sign of the cross before he began. Beside the same pallet, kneeling in the early darkness of the short days, he recited aloud the Lord's Prayer before he slept. Whenever he saw old Swaffer he would bow with veneration from the waist, and stand erect while the old man, with his fingers over his upper lip, surveyed him silently. He bowed also to Miss Swaffer, who kept house frugally for her father—a broad-shouldered, big-boned woman of forty-five, with the pocket of her dress full of keys, and a gray, steady eye. She was Church—as people said (while her father was one of the trustees of the Baptist Chapel)—and wore a little steel cross at her waist. She dressed severely in black, in memory of one of the innumerable Bradleys of the neighbourhood, to whom she had been engaged some twenty-five years ago—a young farmer who broke his neck out hunting on the eve of the wedding-day. She had the unmoved countenance of the deaf, spoke very seldom, and her lips, thin like her father's, astonished one sometimes by a mysteriously ironic curl.

"These were the people to whom he owed allegiance, and an overwhelming loneliness seemed to fall from the leaden sky of that winter without sunshine. All the faces were sad. He could talk to no one, and had no hope of ever understanding anybody. It was as if these had been the faces of people from the other world—dead people—he used to tell me years afterwards. Upon my word, I wonder he did not go mad. He didn't know where he was. Somewhere very far from his mountains—somewhere over the water. Was this America, he wondered?

"If it hadn't been for the steel cross at Miss Swaffer's belt he would not, he confessed, have known whether he was in a Christian country at all. He used to cast stealthy glances at it, and feel comforted. There was nothing here the same as in his country! The earth and the water were different; there were no images of the Redeemer by the road-side. The very grass was different, and the trees. All the trees but the three old Norway pines on the bit of lawn before Swaffer's house, and these reminded him of his country. He had been detected once, after dusk, with his forehead against the trunk of one of them, sobbing, and talking to himself. They had been like brothers to him at that time, he affirmed. Everything else was strange. Conceive you the kind of an existence over-shadowed, oppressed, by the everyday material appearances, as if by the visions of a nightmare. At night, when he could not sleep, he kept on thinking of the girl who gave him the first piece of bread he had eaten in this foreign land. She had been neither fierce nor angry, nor frightened. Her face he remembered as the only comprehensible face amongst all these faces that were as closed, as mysterious, and as mute as the faces of the dead who are possessed of a knowledge beyond the comprehension of the living. I wonder whether the memory of her compassion prevented him from cutting his throat. But there! I suppose I am an old sentimentalist, and forget the instinctive love of life which it takes all the strength of an uncommon despair to overcome.

"He did the work which was given him with an intelligence which surprised old Swaffer. By-and-by it was discovered that he could help at the ploughing, could milk the cows, feed the bullocks in the cattle-yard, and was of some use with the sheep. He began to pick up words, too, very fast; and suddenly, one fine morning in spring, he rescued from an untimely death a grandchild of old Swaffer.

"Swaffer's younger daughter is married to Willcox, a solicitor and the Town Clerk of Colebrook. Regularly twice a year they come to stay with the old man for a few days. Their only child, a little girl not three years old at the time, ran out of the house alone in her little white pinafore, and, toddling across the grass of a terraced garden, pitched herself over a low wall head first into the horsepond in the yard below.

"Our man was out with the waggoner and the plough in the field nearest to the house, and as he was leading the team round to begin a fresh furrow, he saw, through the gap of a gate, what for anybody else would have been a mere flutter of something white. But he had straight-glancing, quick, far-reaching eyes, that only seemed to flinch and lose their amazing power before the immenisity of the sea. He was bare-footed and looking as outlandish as the heart of Swaffer could desire. Leaving the horses on the turn, to the inexpressible disgust of the waggoner he bounded off, going over the ploughed ground in long leaps, and suddenly appeared before the mother, thrust the child into her arms, and strode away.

"The pond was not very deep; but still, if he had not had such good eyes, the child would have perished—miserably suffocated in the foot or so of sticky mud at the bottom. Old Swaffer walked out slowly into the field, waited till the plough came over to his side, had a good look at him, and without saying a word went back to the house. But from that time they laid out his meals on the kitchen table; and at first, Miss Swaffer, all in black and with an inscrutable face, would come and stand in the doorway of the living-room to see him make a big sign of the cross before he fell to. I believe that from that day, too, Swaffer began to pay him regular wages.

"I can't follow step by step his development. He cut his hair short, was seen in the village and along the road going to and fro to his work like any other man. Children ceased to shout after him. He became aware of social differences, but remained for a long time surprised at the bare poverty of the churches among so much wealth. He couldn't understand either why they were kept shut up on weekdays. There was nothing to steal in them. Was it to keep people from praying too often? The rectory took much notice of him about that time, and I believe the young ladies attempted to prepare the ground for his conversion. They could not, however, break him of his habit of crossing himself, but he went so far as to take off the string with a couple of brass medals the size of a sixpence, a tiny metal cross, and a square sort of scapulary which he wore round his neck. He hung them on the wall by the side of his bed, and he was still to be heard every evening reciting the Lord's Prayer, in incomprehensible words and in a slow, fervent tone, as he had heard his old father do at the head of all the kneeling family, big and little, on every evening of his life. And though he wore corduroys at work, and a slop-made pepper-and-salt suit on Sundays, strangers would turn round to look after him on the road. His foreignness had a peculiar and indelible stamp. At last people became used to seeing him. But they never became used to him. His rapid, skimming walk; his swarthy complexion; his hat cocked on the left ear; his habit, on warm evenings, of wearing his coat over one shoulder, like a hussar's dolman; his manner of leaping over the stiles, not as a feat of agility, but in the ordinary course of progression—all these peculiarities were, as one may say, so many causes of scorn and offence to the inhabitants of the village. *They* wouldn't in their dinner hour lie flat on their backs on the grass to stare at the sky. Neither did they go about the fields screaming dismal tunes. Many times have I heard his high-pitched voice from behind the ridge of some sloping sheep-walk, a voice light and soaring, like a lark's, but with a melancholy human note, over our fields that hear only the song of birds. And I would be startled myself. Ah! He was different; innocent of heart, and full of good will, which nobody wanted, this castaway, that, like a man transplanted into another planet, was separated by an immense space from his past and by an immense ignorance from his future. His quick, fervent utterance positively shocked everybody. 'An excitable devil,' they called him. One evening, in the tap-room of the Coach and Horses, (having drunk some whisky), he upset them all by singing a love-song of his country. They hooted him down, and he was pained; but Preble, the lame wheelwright, and Vincent, the fat blacksmith, and the other notables, too, wanted to drink their evening beer in peace. On another occasion he tried to show them how to dance. The dust rose in clouds from the sanded floor; he leaped straight up amongst the deal tables, struck his heels together, squatted on one heel in front of old Preble, shooting out the other leg, uttered wild and exulting cries, jumped up to whirl on one foot, snapping his fingers above his head—and a strange carter who was having a drink in there began to swear, and cleared out with his half-pint in his hand into the bar. But when suddenly he sprang upon a table and continued to dance among the glasses, the landlord interfered. He didn't want any 'acrobat tricks in the tap-room.' They laid their hands on him. Having had a glass or two, Mr. Swaffer's foreigner tried to expostulate: was ejected forcibly: got a black eye.

"I believe he felt the hostility of his human surroundings. But he was tough—tough in spirit, too, as well as in body. Only the memory of the sea frightened him, with that vague terror that is left by a bad dream. His home was far away; and he did not want now to go to America. I had often explained to him that there is no place on earth where true gold can be found lying ready and to be got for the trouble of the picking up. How, then, he asked, could he ever return home with empty hands when there had been sold a cow, two ponies, and a bit of land to pay for his going? His eyes would fill with tears, and, averting them from the immense shimmer of the sea, he would throw himself face down on the grass. But sometimes, cocking his hat with a little conquering air, he would defy my wisdom. He had found his bit of true gold. That was Amy Foster's heart; which was 'a golden heart, and soft to people's misery,' he would say in the accents of overwhelming conviction.

"He was called Yanko. He had explained that this meant Little John; but as he would also repeat very often that he was a mountaineer (some word sounding in the dialect of his country like Goorall) he got it for his surname. And this is the only trace of him that the succeeding ages may find in the marriage register of the parish. There it stands—Yanko Goorall—in the rector's handwriting. The crooked cross made by the castaway, a cross whose tracing no doubt seemed to him the most solemn part of the whole ceremony, is all that remains now to perpetuate the memory of his name.

"His courtship had lasted some time—ever since he got his precarious footing in the community. It began by his buying for Amy Foster a green satin ribbon in Darnford. This was what you did in his country. You bought a ribbon at a Jew's stall on a fair-day. I don't suppose the girl knew what to do with it, but he seemed to think that his honourable intentions could not be mistaken.

"It was only when he declared his purpose to get married that I fully understood how, for a hundred futile and inappreciable reasons, how—shall I say odious?—he was to all the countryside. Every old woman in the village was up in arms. Smith, coming upon him near the farm, promised to break his head for him if he found him about again. But he twisted his little black moustache with such a bellicose air and rolled such big, black fierce eyes at Smith that this promise came to nothing. Smith, however, told the girl that she must be mad to take up with a man who was surely wrong in his head. All the same, when she heard him in the gloaming whistle from beyond the orchard a couple of bars of a weird and mournful tune, she would drop whatever she had in her hand—she would leave Mrs. Smith in the middle of a sentence—and she would run out to his call. Mrs. Smith called her a shameless hussy. She answered nothing. She said nothing at all to anybody, and went on her way as if she had been deaf. She and I alone in all the land, I fancy, could see his very real beauty. He was very good-looking, and most graceful in his bearing, with that something wild as of a woodland creature in his aspect. Her mother moaned over her dismally whenever the girl came to see her on her day out. The father was surly, but pretended not to know; and Mrs. Finn once told her plainly that 'this man, my dear, will do you some harm some day yet.' And so it went on. They could be seen on the roads, she tramping stolidly in her finery—gray dress, black feather, stout boots, prominent white cotton gloves that caught your eye a hundred yards away; and he, his coat slung picturesquely over one shoulder, pacing by her side, gallant of bearing and casting tender glances upon the girl with the golden heart. I wonder whether he saw how plain she was. Perhaps among types so different from what he had ever seen, he had not the power to judge; or perhaps he was seduced by the divine quality of her pity.

"Yanko was in great trouble meantime. In his country you get an old man for an ambassador in marriage affairs. He did not know how to proceed. However, one day in the midst of sheep in a field (he was now Swaffer's under-shepherd with Foster) he took off his hat to the father and declared himself humbly. 'I daresay she's fool enough to marry you,' was all Foster said. 'And then,' he used to relate, 'he puts his hat on his head, looks black at me as if he wanted to cut my throat, whistles the dog, and off he goes, leaving me to do the work.' The Fosters, of course, didn't like to lose the wages the girl earned: Amy used to give all her money to her mother. But there was in Foster a very genuine aversion to that match. He contended that the fellow was very good with sheep, but was not fit for any girl to marry. For one thing, he used to go along the hedges muttering to himself like a dam' fool; and then, these foreigners behave very queerly to women sometimes. And perhaps he would want to carry her off somewhere—or run off himself. It was not safe. He preached it to his daughter that the fellow might ill-use her in some way. She made no answer. It was, they said in the village, as if the man had done something to her. People discussed the matter. It was quite an excitement, and the two went on 'walking out' together in the face of opposition. Then something unexpected happened.

"I don't know whether old Swaffer ever understood how much he was regarded in the light of a father by his foreign retainer. Anyway the relation was curiously feudal. So when Yanko asked formally for an interview—'and the Miss, too' (he called the severe, deaf Miss Swaffer simply *Miss*)—it was to obtain their permission to marry. Swaffer heard him unmoved, dismissed him by a nod, and then shouted the intelligence into Miss Swaffer's best ear. She showed no surprise, and only remarked grimly, in a veiled blank voice, 'He certainly won't get any other girl to marry him.'

"It is Miss Swaffer who has all the credit of the munificence: but in a very few days it came out that Mr. Swaffer had presented Yanko with a cottage (the cottage you've seen this morning) and something like an acre of ground—had made it over to him in absolute property. Willcox expedited the deed, and I remember him telling me he had a great pleasure in making it ready. It recited: 'In consideration of saving the life of my beloved grandchild, Bertha Willcox.'

"Of course, after that no power on earth could prevent them from getting married.

"Her infatuation endured. People saw her going out to meet him in the evening. She stared with unblinking, fascinated eyes up the road where he was expected to appear, walking freely, with a swing from the hip, and humming one of the love-tunes of his country. When the boy was born, he got elevated at the 'Coach and Horses,' essayed again a song and a dance, and was again ejected. People expressed their commiseration for a woman married to that Jack-in-the-box. He didn't care. There was a man now (he told me boastfully) to whom he could sing and talk in the language of his country, and show how to dance by-and-by.

"But I don't know. To me he appeared to have grown less springy of step, heavier in body, less keen of eye. Imagination, no doubt; but it seems to me now as if the net of fate had been drawn closer round him already.

"One day I met him on the footpath over the Talfourd Hill. He told me that 'women were funny.' I had heard already of domestic differences. People were saying that Amy Foster was beginning to find out what sort of man she had married. He looked upon the sea with indifferent, unseeing eyes. His wife had snatched the child out of his arms one day as he sat on the doorstep crooning to it a song such as the mothers sing to babies in his mountains. She seemed to think he was doing it some harm. Women are funny. And she had objected to him praying aloud in the evening. Why? He expected the boy to repeat the prayer aloud after him by-and-by, as he used to do after his old father when he was a child—in his own country. And I discovered he longed for their boy to grow up so that he could have a man to talk with in that language that to our ears sounded so disturbing, so passionate, and so bizarre. Why his wife should dislike the idea he couldn't tell. But that would pass, he said. And tilting his head knowingly, he tapped his breastbone to indicate that she had a good heart: not hard, not fierce, open to compassion, charitable to the poor!

"I walked away thoughtfully; I wondered whether his difference, his strangeness, were not penetrating with repulsion that dull nature they had begun by irresistibly attracting. I wondered. . . ."

The Doctor came to the window and looked out at the frigid splendour of the sea, immense in the haze, as if enclosing all the earth with all the hearts lost among the passions of love and fear.

"Physiologically, now," he said, turning away abruptly, "it was possible. It was possible."

He remained silent. Then went on—

"At all events, the next time I saw him he was ill—lung trouble. He was tough, but I daresay he was not acclimatized as well as I had supposed. It was a bad winter; and, of course, these mountaineers do get fits of home sickness; and a state of depression would make him vulnerable. He was lying half dressed on a couch downstairs.

"A table covered with a dark oilcloth took up all the middle of the little room. There was a wicker cradle on the floor, a kettle spouting steam on the hob, and some child's linen lay drying on the fender. The room was warm, but the door opens right into the garden, as you noticed perhaps.

"He was very feverish, and kept on muttering to himself. She sat on a chair and looked at him fixedly across the table with her brown, blurred eyes. 'Why don't you have him upstairs?' I asked. With a start and a confused stammer she said, 'Oh! ah! I couldn't sit with him upstairs, sir.'

"I gave her certain directions; and going outside, I said again that he ought to be in bed upstairs. She wrung her hands. 'I couldn't. I couldn't. He keeps on saying something—I don't know what.' With the memory of all the talk against the man that had been dinned into her ears, I looked at her narrowly. I looked into her short-sighted eyes, at her dumb eyes that once in her life had seen an enticing shape, but seemed, staring at me, to see nothing at all now. But I saw she was uneasy.

" 'What's the matter with him?' she asked in a sort of vacant trepidation. 'He doesn't look very ill. I never did see anybody look like this before. . . .'

" 'Do you think,' I asked indignantly, 'he is shamming?'

" 'I can't help it, sir,' she said, stolidly. And suddenly she clapped her hands and looked right and left. 'And there's the baby. I am so frightened. He wanted me just now to give him the baby. I can't understand what he says to it.'

" 'Can't you ask a neighbour to come in to-night?' I asked.

" 'Please, sir, nobody seems to care to come,' she muttered, dully resigned all at once.

"I impressed upon her the necessity of the greatest care, and then had to go. There was a good deal of sickness that winter. 'Oh, I hope he won't talk!' she exclaimed softly just as I was going away.

"I don't know how it is I did not see—but I didn't. And yet, turning in my trap, I saw her lingering before the door, very still, as if meditating a flight up the miry road.

"Towards the night his fever increased.

"He tossed, moaned, and now and then muttered a complaint. And she sat with the table between her and the couch, watching every movement and every sound, with the terror, the unreasonable terror, of that man she could not understand creeping over her. She had drawn the wicker cradle close to her feet. There was nothing in her now but the maternal instinct and that unaccountable fear.

"Suddenly coming to himself, parched, he demanded a drink of water. She did not move. She had not understood, though he may have thought he was speaking in English. He waited, looking at her, burning with fever, amazed at her silence and immobility, and then he shouted impatiently, 'Water! Give me water!'

"She jumped to her feet, snatched up the child, and stood still. He spoke to her, and his passionate remonstrances only increased her fear of that strange man. I believe he spoke to her for a long time, entreating, wondering, pleading, ordering, I suppose. She says she bore it as long as she could. And then a gust of rage came over him.

"He sat up and called out terribly one word—some word. Then he got up as though he hadn't been ill at all, she says. And as in fevered dismay, indignation, and wonder he tried to get to her round the table, she simply opened the door and ran out with the child in her arms. She heard him call twice after her down the road in a terrible voice—and fled. . . . Ah! but you should have seen stirring behind the dull, blurred glance of those eyes the spectre of the fear which had haunted her on that night three miles and a half to the door of Foster's cottage! I did the next day.

"And it was I who found him lying face down and his body in a puddle, just outside the little wicker-gate.

"I had been called out that night to an urgent case in the village, and on my way home at daybreak passed by the cottage. The door stood open. My man helped me to carry him in. We laid him on the couch. The lamp smoked, the fire was out, the chill of the stormy night oozed from the cheerless yellow paper on the wall. 'Amy!' I called aloud, and my voice seemed to lose itself in the emptiness of this tiny house as if I had cried in a desert. He opened his eyes. 'Gone!' he said, distinctly. 'I had only asked for water—only for a little water. . . .'

"He was muddy. I covered him up and stood waiting in silence, catching a painfully gasped word now and then. They were no longer in his own language. The fever had left him, taking with it the heat of life. And with his panting breast and lustrous eyes he reminded me again of a wild creature under the net, of a bird caught in a snare. She had left him. She had left him—sick—helpless—thirsty. The spear of the hunter had entered his very soul. 'Why?' he cried, in the penetrating and indignant voice of a man calling to a responsible Maker. A gust of wind and a swish of rain answered.

"And as I turned away to shut the door he pronounced the word 'Merciful!' and expired.

"Eventually I certified heart-failure as the immediate cause of death. His heart must have indeed failed him, or else he might have stood this night of storm and exposure, too. I closed his eyes and drove away. Not very far from the cottage I met Foster walking sturdily between the dripping hedges with his collie at his heels.

" 'Do you know where your daughter is?' I asked.

" 'Don't I!' he cried. 'I am going to talk to him a bit. Frightening a poor woman like this.'

" 'He won't frighten her any more,' I said. 'He is dead.'

"He struck with his stick at the mud.

" 'And there's the child.'

"Then, after thinking deeply for a while—

" 'I don't know that it isn't for the best.'

"That's what he said. And she says nothing at all now. Not a word of him. Never. Is his image as utterly gone from her mind as his lithe and striding figure, his carolling voice are gone from our fields? He is no longer before her eyes to excite her imagination into a passion of love or fear; and his memory seems to have vanished from her dull brain as a shadow passes away upon a white screen. She lives in the cottage and works for Miss Swaffer. She is Amy Foster for everybody, and the child is 'Amy Foster's boy.' She calls him Johnny—which means Little John.

"It is impossible to say whether this name recalls anything to her. Does she ever think of the past? I have seen her hanging over the boy's cot in a very passion of maternal tenderness. The little fellow was lying on his back, a little frighened at me, but very still, with his big black eyes, with his fluttered air of a bird in a snare. And looking at him I seemed to see again the other one—the father, cast out mysteriously by the sea to perish in the supreme disaster of loneliness and despair."

THE LESSON

by Max Wiseman

"Did you find the dollar and a half?" she asked.

His mother was sitting across the room from him, removing her stockings. She had just come from the store.

"What dollar and a half?"

"What dollar and a half!" She looked up with a sudden, sharp sorrow

---

in her eyes. "I put a dollar and a half in your bag yesterday, I wanted you to have a good supper."

"Well for *that,*" he said, "I'm not going to eat supper here tonight."

"Because I put a dollar and a half in your bag?"

"Because you put it in the bag without my asking. All you did, Ma, was to throw away a dollar and a half."

"Throw away? I put it in the bag with your socks; I put it in a special envelope in the bag!"

"I took out the socks and threw away the bag without looking."

"But how could you! I only put coins in, to make it heavy; didn't you feel it? How could you throw it away?" Her face was twisted because of what he had told her.

He hadn't even opened the bag. It had been on the tip of his tongue to tell her that it was safe. The money meant almost three hours of standing behind the counter in the huge department store and saying to all manner of people, "Yes sir, can I help you?"

But it had gone too far; it was a great amorphous mass; a limitless sea that was drowning him.

"Oh you're lost—you're a lost sheep! To throw away a bag without looking!"

He rose. "I've told you again and again that I don't want you to force money on me when I don't ask for it. I want there to be some meaning in my words. I'm not staying for supper tonight. I'm going back to my room. All that you have done is to throw away a dollar and a half and send me away from supper."

"If you don't stay for supper," she said, looking passionately into his eyes, "you'll never set foot in this house again!"

"I mean what I say; can't you get that through your head? I'm doing this as a lesson." He put on his jacket. She still thought that he was bluffing. He had threatened thus many times and always he had given in to her deep-suffering tears and screams.

"Stay here," she said, sensing suddenly that he really intended leaving. "Take off your jacket. I only wanted you to eat. I can spare the extra money—what do you eat on?"

"This time it sticks. This is a lesson. It means that you've got to stop running around with money in your hands, pushing it into mine; you mustn't give without my asking. I would ask. I was going to ask on Wednesday. You force it and force it—as if I were a child; can't you understand that I *mean* what I say? You've got to believe, Mama, that I will be strong. I'll be here for supper in two days, but if you try any of that business with the money again I'm not coming back." He walked to the door and opened it. She ran after him.

"I'll yell in the hall," she said, seizing him by the arm. "I'll yell in the hall if you walk out now. I will come to your room tonight and make a scene."

"So what if you make a scene? I'm over age."

She pulled him back toward the house. He wrenched free and started down the stairs.

"Joseph," she yelled into the hall, "come back, or I will go down to your room tonight!"

He came back into the house and she closed the door behind him. "Ma, you're just making it worse. I'm not starving—I still have some money—and if I were so desperately hungry I'd pick up any job. I just want a chance to get one where I can respect myself."

"You're starving," she breathed in a low, husky voice, staring into his eyes. "Look at your face, you're starving." Her voice was compassionate and pleading. Her face was flushed, tragically and tenderly drawn. He had to turn his head away.

"I'm not starving, Mama. Why can't it be an intelligent thing? When I need money I'll ask you. Rely on me. I'm a man and I'm strong. Why do you degrade me by these childish methods? You'd make a hypocrite of me. The words have no meaning for you. I argue with you and say 'No, Ma, I don't want any money,' and then you stick some in my pocket or in my bag and I've taken it anyway; it's not clean. There is no dignity—"

"Dig-*nity!*" With contempt and despair she almost sobbed the word. "Stop it! Stop that word!" Her face was tired and sweating. She barred the way to the door. "Dignity with your mother? Not with your mother? Not with your mother!"

"God damn you!" he said. He turned and walked back toward the kitchen. "I'll give you ten minutes to let me out of here. If you don't I won't come back here at all."

Her eyes widened. "I won't let you come back if you leave now."

Then she again looked into his eyes, and she shook her head wearily. "Stay—stay: look at all this food!" She grabbed a basket of strawberries that she had bought for him on her way home. She held it up to him to tempt him. "Look at this—and you're starving—why shouldn't you eat?"

"Oh Mama—you don't understand."

He took out his wallet. "See, I have three dollars here. That's enough for meals for the next two days. I'll come for supper on Wednesday and I'll ask you for five dollars to finish out the week. I'll get a job tomorrow and I'll get paid on Friday."

"Hero! Hero! A martyr! What can you do with three dollars?"

"Now this? Let me get out and I'll come back in two days when perhaps you've learned a lesson."

"No!" she shouted and she seized a knife from the table. "You'll stay here!" She stood before the door with the knife in her hand.

"Don't you leave me any pride?"

"Pride," she hissed. "You have no money, you're starving!" It was not true, but she was staring at his neat, clean suit and his proud face. The woman with the fending arms of a mother saw his pride before life very clearly and it only hurt her more; the woman felt: what are pride and dignity without power?

"You exaggerate. I eat well. I can take care of myself."

"Take care of yourself! I had to help you pay for that suit! Stubborn! Stubborn! Why won't you stay for dinner? Why can't I give you money? That's your sickness—you're stubborn! You'll kill somebody. I know you will, and then you'll die alone in your room; you'll starve in the middle of the city and no one will know. They'll break down the door and find you in your room. You'll go picking garbage cans on the East Side, your fingers yellow from nicotine and shaking! I dreamed it, I dreamed it!"

There were tears in his eyes, and never had he felt so close to her as now. Yet it was atavistic and there was the dark, terrible loneliness and fear that only she could make him feel with her deep-suffering images. He felt his strength going from him; her fearful passion was like a nightmare.

"Ma—I'm going now. Put down that knife! Are you really mad? I'm a man!"

"A man with your mother?" she asked sadly, contemptuously, bitterly, tenderly.

"No, no, what are you doing?" She dropped the knife and caught at him as he moved past her. She charged at him. Her large, flabby, tired, sweating body was gripping him and her face looked insane. Her face was contorted with suffering and her eyes bulged. "Oh, what are you doing to me?" she asked weakly. "You've made me sick—stop this. All right, it's a lesson—let the lesson begin and end now—and then eat—I'll never do it again—but stay and eat—stay and eat!" And all of it had become that meal; the meal was everything; the meal was her strength and her protection of him. The meal was her love and her bounty for her proud son who was so good to look at with his dignity but had no strength or power.

He pushed at her and started down the stairs. She held him and yelled loudly into the hall: "Stop, Joseph! If you go I shall come down." But he was back in the house again. He had a newspaper rolled into a stiff club in his hand. "Mama—Mama," he said, sobbing, "what are you going to make me do to you?"

"Stay, Joseph—stay—please!" Her voice was tired and crying. "Never again—but stay! Why are you so stubborn?" She was holding his arms. Her heavy, sweating arms, with the lumpy flesh hanging thickly above the elbows, were smothering him.

He smashed the paper against her head. "Mama—Mama—what are you making me do to you? What are you making me do to you?" He swung again and again. "Mama, you selfish bitch!" he sobbed.

"You've murdered me," she cried. "You've murdered me and night and day I worry for you."

"That's it! Why must you be tortured for me? I'm happy," he lied, "and I like the life I lead. Only your suffering makes me unhappy."

"So stay, Joseph," she pleaded, "stay!" She was holding her head, and as she spoke she moved to the bathroom sink and dipped her handkerchief in water and put the wet cloth over her forehead.

He loved her hands that had worked for him. He loved her face; her now clumsy feet that foolishly stood there ready to leap for the door. He loved her for the few extra dollars that she tried to give him.

And he found himself shaking with repulsion at her physical nearness. He could not bear her hands upon him. He felt that her flesh was ugly. Tenderly and bitterly he looked into her face.

"Mama, what have you made me do? Let us forget this terrible day. But I must go, or there will be no change."

She sobbed brokenly and held him. He hit her again and again on the head. She tried to shield herself, now like a hunted, timid animal, as she crouched against the wall with her hands over her.

"Mama, what are you making me do?" He hit her until the paper was in shreds and was loose and fluttering in his hand.

But she rose, and crying, seized him as he left off beating her. She hit him with her hands to keep him from going.

He pushed her against the wall, the image of her bent head, shielded against his blows, graven on his mind. He threw the paper at her and ran to the door.

"I'll yell in the hall," she sobbed; "I'll yell in the hall and tonight I will come down to your room."

As he ran from the house, he cried freely, not noticing the passers-by.

Later he would see the money in his room. At that moment he felt that he would have died for her.

He hurried faster and faster, away from the house.

YANDA

by Isaac Bashevis Singer

The Peacock's Tail stood on a side street not far from the ruins of a Greek Orthodox church and cemetery. It was a two-story brick building with a weather vane on its crooked roof, and a battered sign over its entrance depicting a peacock with a faded gold tail. The front of the inn housed a windowless tavern, dark as dusk on the sunniest mornings. No peasants were served there even on market days. The owner, Shalom Pintchever, had no patience with the peasants, their dances and wild songs. Neither he nor Shaindel, his wife, had the strength to wait on these ruffians, or later when they got drunk, to throw them out into the gutter. The Peacock's Tail was a stopping place for squires, military men who were on their way to the Russian-Austrian border, and for salesmen who came to town to sell farm implements and goods from Russia. There was never any lack of guests. Occasionally a group of strolling players stayed the night. Once in a while the inn was visited by a magician, or a bear trainer. Sometimes a preacher stopped there, or

---

one of those travelers about whom the Lord alone knows what brought them there. The town coachman understood what kind of customers to bring to The Peacock's Tail.

When Shalom Pintchever, a stranger, bought the hotel, and with his wife came to live in the town, they brought with them a peasant woman called Yanda. Yanda would have been a beauty but for a face as pock-marked as a potato grater. She had black hair which she wore in a braid, white skin, a short nose, red cheeks, and eyes as black as cherries. Her bosom was high, her waist narrow, her hips rounded. She was a woman of great physical strength. She did all the work in the hotel: made the beds, washed the linen, cooked, dumped the chamber pots, and, in addition, visited the male guests when requested. The moment a visitor registered, Shalom Pintchever would ask, slyly winking an eye under his bushy brows, "With or without?" The traveler understood and almost always answered, "With." Shalom added the price to the bill.

There were guests who invited Yanda to drink with them, or go for a walk, but she never accepted. Shalom Pintchever was not going to have them taking up her time, or turning her into a drunk. He had once and for all forbidden her to drink liquor, and she never touched a drop, not even a glass of beer on a hot summer day. Shalom had rescued her from a drunkard father and a stepmother. In return she served him without asking for pay. Every few months he would give her pocket money. Yanda would grab Shalom's hand, kiss it, and hide the money in her stocking without counting it. From time to time she would order a dress, a pair of high-buttoned shoes, or buy herself a shawl, a kerchief, a comb. Sunday, when she went to church, she invariably threw a coin into the alms box. Sometimes she brought a present for the priest, or a candle to be lit for her patron saint. The old women objected to her entering a holy place, but she stood inside the door anyway. There was gossip that the priest was carrying on with her, even though he had a pretty house-keeper.

The Jews accused Shalom Pintchever of keeping a bawdy house. When the women quarreled with Shaindel, they called her Yanda. But without Yanda Shalom would have been out of business. Three maids could not have done her work. Besides, most servants stole and had to be watched. Neither Shalom nor Shaindel could be bothered with that. Husband and wife were mourning an only daughter who had died in a fire in the town in which they had previously lived. Shaindel suffered from asthma, Shalom had sick kidneys. Yanda carried the burden of the hotel. Summertime she got up at daybreak, in the winter she left her bed two hours before sunrise. She scrubbed floors, patched quilts and sheets, carried water from the well, even chopped wood when a woodchopper was not available. Shaindel was convinced Yanda would collapse from overwork. Husband and wife also feared that she might contract a contagious disease. But some devil or other impure power watched over her. Years passed, and she did not get sick, never even caught cold. Her employers did not stint on her food, but she preferred to eat the left-overs: cold soups, scraps of meat, stale bread. Shalom and Shaindel both suffered from toothaches, but Yanda had a mouth full of strong white teeth like a dog. She could crack peach pits with them.

"She is not a human being," Shaindel would say, "she's a beast."

The women spat when Yanda passed by, cursing her vehemently. Boys called her names and threw stones and mud at her. Young girls giggled, dropped their eyes, and blushed when they met her on the street. More than once the police called her in for questioning. But years passed and Yanda remained in Shalom Pintchever's service. With time the clientele of the inn changed. As long as the town belonged to Russia, its guests were mainly Russians. Later, when the Austrians took over, they were Germans, Magyars, Czechs, and Bosnians. Then, when Poland gained independence, it served the Polish officials who arrived from Warsaw and Lublin. What didn't the town live through—epidemics of typhoid and dysentery; the Austrian soldiers brought cholera with them and six hundred townspeople perished. For a short time, under Bolshevik rule, the inn was taken over by a Communist County Committee, and some commissar or other was put in charge. Yanda remained through it all. Somebody had to work, to wash, scour, serve the guests beer, vodka, snacks. Whatever their titles, at night the men wanted Yanda in their beds. There were some who kissed her and some who beat her. There were those who cursed her and called her names and those who wept before her and confessed to her as if she were a priest. One officer placed a glass of cognac on her head and shot it down with his revolver. Another bit into her shoulder and like a leech sucked her blood. Still, in the morning she washed, combed her hair, and everything began anew. There was no end to the dirty dishes. The floors were full of holes and cracks, the walls were peeling. No matter how often Yanda poured scalding water over cockroaches and bedbugs, and used all kinds of poison, the vermin continued to multiply. Each day the hotel was in danger of falling apart. It was Yanda who kept it together.

The owners themselves began to resemble the hotel. Shaindel grew bent and her face became as white and brittle as plaster. Her speech was unintelligible. She no longer walked, but shuffled. She would find a discarded caftan in a trunk and would try to patch it. Shalom protested that he didn't need the rag, but half-blind as she was, she would sit for days, with her glasses on the tip of her nose, trying to mend it. Again and again, she would ask Yanda to thread the needle, muttering. "It isn't thread, it's cobweb. These needles have no eyes."

Shalom Pintchever's face began to grow a kind of mold. His brows became even shaggier. Under his eyes there were bags and from them hung other bags. Between his wrinkles there was a black excrescence which no water could remove. His head shook from side to side. Nevertheless, when a guest arrived, Shalom would reach for his hotel register with a trembling hand and ask, "With or without?" And the guest would almost invariably reply, "With."

II

It all happened quickly. First Shaindel lay down and breathed her last. It occurred on the first day of Rosh Hashanah. The following day, the oldest woman in the town gave up her shroud, since it is forbidden to sew on the Holy days. The women of the burial society treated themselves to cake and brandy at the cemetery. Shalom, confused by grief, forgot the text of the Kaddish and had to be prompted. Those who attended the funeral said that his legs were so shaky, he almost fell into the grave. After Shaindel's death Shalom Pintchever became senile. He took money from the cashbox and didn't remember what he did with it. He became so deaf that even screaming into his ears did not help. The Feast of Tabernacles was followed by such a rain spell that even the oldest townspeople could not recall its like. The river overflowed. The wheel of the water mill had to be stopped. The roof of the inn sprang a leak. The guests who had rooms on the top floor came down in the middle of the night, complaining that water was pouring into their beds. Shalom lay helpless in his own bedroom. It was Yanda who apologized to the guests and made up beds for them downstairs. She even climbed a ladder up to the roof and tried to plug the leaks. But the shingles crumbled as soon as she touched them. In the morning, the guests left without paying their bills. Early Saturday as Shalom Pintchever picked up his prayer shawl and was about to leave for the synagogue, he began to sway and fell down. "Yanda, I am finished," he cried out. Yanda ran to get some brandy, but it was already too late. Shalom lay stretched out on the floor, dead. There was an uproar in the town. Shalom had left no children. Irreverent people, for whom the sacredness of the Sabbath had little meaning, began to search for a will and tried to force his strongbox. Officials from the City Hall made a list of his belongings and sealed the drawer in which he kept his money. Yanda had begun to weep the moment Shalom had fallen down and did not stop until after the funeral. She had worked in the inn for over twenty years, but was left with barely sixty zlotys. The authorities immediately ordered her to get out. Yanda packed her belongings in a sack, put on a pair of shoes, which she usually wore only to church, wrapped herself in a shawl, and walked the long way to the railroad station. There was nobody to say goodbye. At the station, she approached the ticket window and said,

"Kind sir, please give me a ticket to Skibica."

"There is no such station."

Yanda began to wail, "What am I to do, I am a forsaken orphan!"

The peasants at the station jeered at her. The women spat on her. A Jewish traveling salesman began to question her about Skibica. Is it a village, or a town? In what county, or district is it? At first Yanda remembered nothing. But the Jew in his torn coat and sheepskin hat persisted until Yanda finally remembered that the village was somewhere near Kielce, between Checzyn and Sobkow. The salesman told Yanda to take out the bank notes that she kept wrapped in a handkerchief and helped her to count the money. He talked it over with the ticket seller. There was no direct train to that area. The best way to go was by horse and buggy to Rozwadow, and from there on to Sandomierz, then to Opola, where she could either get a ride in another cart or go on foot to Skibica.

Just hearing the names of these familiar places made Yanda weep. In Skibica, she had once had a father, a mother, a sister, relatives. Her mother had died and her father, not long before he died, had married another woman. Yanda had been about to become engaged to Wojciech, a peasant boy, but the blacksmith's daughter, a girl called Zocha, had taken him away. During the years Yanda had worked for Shalom Pintchever she had seldom thought of the past. It all seemed so far away, at the end of the earth. But now that her employer was dead, there was nothing left for her but to return home. Who knew, perhaps some of her close ones were still alive. Perhaps somebody there still remembered her name.

Thank God, good people helped. No sooner had Yanda left the town where she had lived in shame, than they stopped laughing at her, making grimaces, spitting. The coachmen did not overcharge her. Jews with beards and sidelocks seemed to know the whole of Poland as well as they knew the palms of their hands. They mentioned names of places which Yanda had already forgotten, and looked for shortcuts. In one tavern, someone took out a map to find the shortest way home for her. Yanda marveled at the cleverness of men; how much knowledge they carried in their heads and how eager they were to help a homeless woman. But despite all the good advice, Yanda walked more than she rode. Rains soaked her, there was snow and hail. She waded through ditches of water as deep as streams. She had grown accustomed to sleeping on pillows with clean pillowcases, between white sheets, under a warm eiderdown, but now she was forced to stretch out on the floors of granaries and barns. Her clothes were wet through. Somehow she managed to keep her paper money dry. As Yanda walked she thought about her life. Once in a while Shalom Pintchever had given her money but it had dwindled away. The Russians had counted in rubles and kopecks. When the Austrians came the ruble lost its value, and everything was exchanged for kronen and hellers. The Bolsheviks used chervontzi; the Poles, zlotys. How was someone like Yanda, uneducated as she was, to keep track of such changes? It was a miracle that she had anything left with which to get home.

God in heaven, men were still chasing her! Wherever she slept, peasants came to her and had their way with her. In a wagon, at night, somebody seized her silently. What do they see in me? Yanda asked herself. It's my bad luck. Yanda remembered that she had never been able to refuse anyone. Her father had beaten her for her submissiveness. Her stepmother had torn Yanda's hair. Even as a child when she played with the other children, they had smeared her face with mud, given her a broom and made her take the part of Baba-Yaga. With the guests in Shalom's hotel, she had had such savage and foolish experiences that she sometimes hadn't known whether to laugh or cry. But to say no was not in her nature. When she was young, while still in her father's village, she had twice given birth to babies, but they had both died. Several times heavy work had caused her to miscarry. She could never really forget Wojciech, the peasant boy to whom she had almost been engaged, but who at the last moment had thrown her over. Yanda also had desired Shalom Pintchever, perhaps because he had always sent her to others and had never taken her himself. He would say, "Yanda, go to number three —Yanda, knock at the door of number seven." He himself had remained faithful to his old wife, Shaindel. Perhaps he had been disgusted by Yanda, but she had yearned for him. One kind word from him pleased her more than all the wild games of the others. Even when he scolded her, she waited for more. As for the guests, there were so many of them, that Yanda had forgotten all but a few who stuck in her memory. One Russian had demanded that Yanda spit on him, tear at his beard, and call him ugly names. Another, a schoolboy with red cheeks, had kissed her and called her mother. He had slept on her breast until dawn, although guests in other rooms had been waiting for her.

Now Yanda was old. But how old? She did not know herself—certainly in her forties, or perhaps fifty? Other women her age were grandmothers but she was returning to her village, alone, abandoned by God and man. Yanda made a resolution: once home, she would allow no man to approach her. In a village, there was always gossip and it usually ended in a quarrel. What did she need it for? The truth was that all this whoring had never given her any pleasure.

III

The Jews who showed Yanda the way had not fooled her. She reached Skibica in the morning, and even though it had changed considerably, she recognized her home. In a chapel at the outskirts of the village God's mother still stood with a halo around her head and the Christ child in her arms. The figure had become dingy with the years and a piece of the Holy Mother's shoulder was chipped off. A wreath of wilted flowers hung around her neck. Yanda's eyes filled with tears. She knelt in the snow and crossed herself. She walked into the village, and a smell she had long forgotten came to her nostrils: an odor of soggy potatoes, burned feathers, earth, and something else that had no name, but that her nose recognized. The huts were half-sunk into the ground, with tiny windows and low doors. The thatched roofs were mossy and rotting. Crows were cawing; smoke rose from the chimneys. Yanda looked for the hut where her parents had lived but it had disappeared and in its place was a smithy. She put down the sack she was carrying on her back. Dogs sniffed at her and barked. Women emerged from the dwellings. The younger ones did not know her, but the old ones clapped their hands and pinched their cheeks, calling,

"Oh, Father, Mother, Jesu Maria."

"Yes, it's Yanda, as I love God."

Men, too, came to look at her, some from behind the stoves where they had been sleeping, others from the tavern. One peasant woman invited Yanda into her hut. She gave her a piece of black bread and a cup of milk. On the dirt floor stood bins filled with potatoes, beets, black radishes, and cranberries. Chickens were cackling in a coop. The oven had a built-in kettle for hot water. At a spinning wheel sat an old woman with a balding head from which hung tufts of hair as white as flax. Someone screamed into her ear:

"Grandma, this is Yanda. Pawel Kuchma's daughter."

The old woman crossed herself. "Jesu Maria."

The peasant women all spoke together. Pawel Kuchma's home had burned down. Yanda's brother, Bolek, had gone to war and never returned. Her sister, Stasia, had married a man from Biczew and died there in childbirth. They also told Yanda what had happened to

Wojciech, her former bridegroom-to-be. He had married Zocha and she had borne him fourteen children. Nine of them were still alive, but their mother had died of typhoid fever. As for Wojciech, he had been drinking all these years. Zocha had worked for others to support the family. After her death three years before, he had become a complete derelict. Everything went for drink and he was half crazy. His boys ran around, wild. The girls washed clothes for the Jews of the town. His hut was practically in ruins. As the women spoke to Yanda somebody opened the door and pushed a tall man inside. He was as lean as a stick, barefoot, with holes in his pants. He wore an open jacket without a shirt, his hair was long and disheveled—a living scarecrow. He did not walk, but staggered along as though on stilts. He had mad eyes, a dripping nose, and his crooked mouth showed one long tooth. Somebody said,

"Wojciech, do you recognize this woman?"

"Pockmarked Yanda."

There was laughter and clapping. For the first time in years Yanda blushed.

"See how you look."

"I heard you are a whore."

There was laughter again.

"Don't listen to him, Yanda, he's drunk."

"What am I drunk on? Nobody gives me a drop of vodka."

Yanda gaped at him. Could this be Wojciech? Some similarity remained. She wanted to cry. She remembered an expression of Shaindel's, "There are some in their graves who look better than he does." Yanda regretted that she had come back to Skibica. A woman said,

"Why don't you have a look at his children?"

Yanda immediately lifted up her sack. She offered to pay for the bread and milk but the peasant woman rebuked her, "This is not the city. Here, you don't pay for a piece of bread." Wojciech's hut stood nearby. The roof almost touched the ground. Elflocks of straw hung from its edges. The windows had no panes. They were stuffed with rags or boarded up. One entered it like a cave. The floor had rotted away. The walls were as black as the inside of a chimney. In the semidarkness Yanda saw boys, girls. The place stank of dirty linen, rot, and something rancid. Yanda clutched her nose. Two girls stood at the tub. Half-naked children, smeared with mud, crawled on the floor. One child was pulling the tail of a kitten. A boy with a blind eye was mending a trap. Yanda blinked. She was no longer accustomed to such squalor. At the inn, the sheets had been changed each week. Every third day the guests got fresh towels. The leftover food had been enough to feed a whole family. Well, dirt has to be removed. It won't disappear by itself.

Yanda rolled up her sleeves. She still had a few zlotys and she sent one of the girls to buy food. A Jew had a store in the village where one could get bagels, herring, chickory. God in heaven, how the children devoured those stale bagels! Yanda began to sweep and scrub. She went to the well for water. At first the girls ignored her. Then they told her not to meddle in their affairs. But Yanda said, "I will take nothing from you. Your mother, peace be with her, was my friend."

Yanda worked until evening. She heated water and washed the

children. She sent an older child to buy soap, a fine comb, and kerosene which kills lice. Every few minutes she poured out the slops. Neighbors came to look and shook their heads. They all said the same thing, Yanda's work was in vain. The vermin could not be removed from that hut. In the evening, there was no lamp to light and Yanda bought a small kerosene lamp. The whole family slept on one wooden platform, and there were few blankets. Yanda covered the children with her own clothes. Late in the evening, the door opened and Wojciech intruded a leg. The girls began to giggle. Stefan, the boy with the blind eye, had already made friends with Yanda. He said,

"Here he comes—the skunk."

"You must not talk like that about your father."

Stefan replied with a village proverb, "When your father is a dog, you say 'git' to him."

Yanda had saved a bagel and a piece of herring for Wojciech, but he was too drunk to eat. He fell down like a log, muttering and drooling. The girls stepped over him. Stefan mentioned that there was a straw mat in the shed behind the hut that Yanda could use to sleep on. He offered to show her where it was. As soon as she opened the door of the shed, the boy pushed her and she fell. He threw himself on her. She tried to tell him that it was a sin, but he stopped her mouth with his hand. She struggled but he beat her with a heavy fist. She lay in the dark on wood-shavings, garbage, rotting rope, and the boy satisfied himself. Yanda closed her eyes. Well, I'm lost anyhow, she thought. Out loud, she muttered, "Woe is me, I might have been your mother."

The Scapegoat

THE universality and the timelessness of the Scapegoat archetype are confirmed by the religion and folklore of numerous cultures. We read in Leviticus:

> Aaron shall lay both his hands upon the head of the live goat, and confess over him all the iniquities of the children of Israel, and all their transgressions in all their sins, putting them upon the head of the goat, and shall send him away by the hand of a fit man into the wilderness.
>
> And the goat shall bear upon him all their iniquities unto a land not inhabited; and he shall let go the goat into the wilderness.

This practice as described in the Old Testament follows a pattern that is surprisingly constant in places as far apart as South Africa and the Carpathians, Morocco and Sumatra. Behind it lies the notion that an individual or a community can divest itself of guilt or illness by magically transferring it to another object—sometimes an animal, sometimes an inanimate object, sometimes a human being. This is the anthropological meaning of Scapegoatism, and in this sense the practice often acquires the aspect of a ritual that enjoys group sanction. The best discussion of the subject from this point of view is "The Scapegoat" by Sir James Frazer, published as Part IV of his monumental study, *The Golden Bough*. Frazer cites Dudley Kidd to the effect that among the Kafirs of South Africa, when a man is believed to be the victim of evil spirits:

> Natives sometimes adopt the custom of taking a goat into the presence of a sick man, and confess the sins of the kraal[1] over the animal. Sometimes a few drops of blood from the sick man are allowed to fall on the head of the goat, which is turned out into an uninhabited part of the veldt. The sickness

[1] South African village.

> is supposed to be transferred to the animal, and to become lost in the desert.

The similarity of this expedient to that recommended to Aaron is very striking.

Sacrifice of human scapegoats was equally universal. Frazer tells us that the Athenians maintained a group of "degraded and useless beings" at the public expense for this purpose, and that when the city was threatened by plague, drought, or famine, they sacrificed two of these, a man and a woman, by leading them outside the city and stoning them to death. Human scapegoats, however, were by no means invariably outcasts: the Yorubas of West Africa chose as their victim "either a free-born or a slave, a person of noble or wealthy parentage, or one of humble birth." Their term for him was *Oluwo*, and, like the woman in Lawrence's story, he "was always well fed and nourished and supplied with whatever he should desire."[2] Indeed in some cultures the victim was so far from being an inferior that he was often thought to possess divine powers and was considered either a man-god or a woman-goddess.

The custom of killing a god may be as ancient as that of employing a human scapegoat and had its source, according to Frazer, in the desire of the group "to save his divine life from being weakened by the inroads of age." It was therefore easy for the two customs to combine:

> He was killed, not originally to take away sin, but to save the divine life from the degeneracy of old age; but, since he had to be killed at any rate, people may have thought that they might as well seize the opportunity to lay upon him the burden of their sufferings and sins, in order that he might bear it away with him to the world beyond the grave.[3]

It is impossible not to see, in this tradition of slaying a god for the spiritual salvation of mankind, a resemblance to the crucifixion of Christ, who was in fact the most illustrious scapegoat of which history affords us an example.

Christ's trial and execution as a common criminal parallel other elements of the Scapegoat tradition commented on by Frazer:

> When a nation becomes civilized, if it does not drop human sacrifices altogether, it at least selects as victims only such wretches as would be put to death at any rate. Thus the killing of a god may sometimes come to be confounded with the execution of a criminal.[4]

Faulkner uses this aspect of Scapegoatism in *Light in August*, when he skillfully suggests an analogy between his character Joe Christmas,

---

[2] Sir James G. Frazer, *The Golden Bough* (New York: Macmillan, 1935), Vol. I, Part IV, p. 211.

[3] *Ibid.* p. 227.

[4] *Ibid.*

a criminal, and Christ, and when he symbolically confounds the execution of Christmas by Percy Grimm into the agony of Christ.

Besides its anthropological meaning, Scapegoatism denotes in psychology the process by which another person, or group, is blamed for one's own shortcomings, or the shortcomings of one's own group. In this sense it involves a kind of projection, which in its subtler forms, because of censorship from the conscious mind, may direct itself not at an individual or a group but rather, by the process known in psychology as displacement, at some object associated with him or them: thus, hatred of one's father may take the form of hating his pipe or his walking stick, which are synecdochic representations of the person, so that one may come to dislike these objects in themselves, often without knowing why. In its overt form Scapegoatism may lead to discrimination of various kinds; to active persecution; and even, as in Germany under the Third Reich, to genocide.

An interesting variety of psychological Scapegoatism is the tendency to blame others for moral offenses, real or imaginary, that a person would like to commit himself: in these cases his unconscious envy may lead him to punish the offender, who may be innocent, with unnatural severity. This is the situation in Denton Welch's brilliant story, "When I Was Thirteen."

The psychological phenomenon of Scapegoatism is undoubtedly an essential element in the anthropological phenomenon, which represents the formulation of the pattern on a grand scale, through repetition fixing the archetype permanently into the collective unconscious in the form of a racial memory. The anthropological Scapegoater, however, is usually conscious of his role; as is his victim, though his is a passive role and though he may not always act voluntarily. On the other hand, the psychological Scapegoater may or may not realize his role, and the victim is frequently unaware that he is one—as in "When I Was Thirteen."

In Greek mythology, the Scapegoat archetype frequently tends to combine with that of the Hero who offers himself as a sacrifice in order to save the community from some evil that threatens it. In the Middle Ages, the literature of martyrology abounds in Scapegoat figures, and the archetype is also found in the fiction and drama of the Renaissance. In Shakespeare's famous tragedy it is Othello, rather than Desdemona, who is the true Scapegoat, and in this connection the fact of his race is by no means irrelevant, since minority groups are traditionally a common source of supply.

Romantic literature in nineteenth-century America provides two outstanding Scapegoat characters: Hawthorne's Hester Prynne, in *The Scarlet Letter,* and Billy Budd, of whom Melville makes a Christ figure in the short novel of that name. Random examples from contemporary British and American literature might include the youth in Joyce's story, "Counterparts"; Aziz, in Forster's *A Passage to India;* Tessie Hutchinson, the stoning victim in Shirley Jackson's famous story, "The Lottery"; and Will Mayes, whom Minnie Cooper falsely accuses of molesting her, in Faulkner's "Dry September." Though the fact hardly needs to be pointed out, the experience of the Jew in Nazi Germany and of the Negro in the Deep South and Northern ghetto has been productive recently of a massive literature of psychological Scapegoatism.

The five stories chosen for this category represent various aspects of Scapegoatism. "October Island," "Red Leaves," and "The Woman Who Rode Away" represent the anthropological type, while the psychological is exemplified in "The Pair" and "When I Was Thirteen." In "October Island" the victim is unconscious of the role she plays, giving to the story an ironical dimension which is heightened by the circumstance that consciously she proselytizes for a very different faith from that to which she is destined to be a living sacrifice. "The Woman Who Rode Away" is complicated by the fact that the victim possesses two levels of awareness: on the unconscious level she knows almost from the beginning what her fate will be, and seems actually to be seeking it; while on the conscious level she realizes her situation only gradually, by a kind of dawning process.

It might be argued that "Red Leaves" is not a true case of Scapegoatism, since the Indians' avowed motive in burying the slave with his dead master is to provide for his wants in the hereafter. In this sense the ritual might be thought to resemble *suttee* [5] rather than a Scapegoat ceremony, but there is some evidence for thinking that the two customs, perhaps equally ancient, were often confused in actual practice. Since the victim was destined to die in any case, it would have been convenient for the group that he serve a double purpose, as in the case cited earlier from Frazer. There may also have existed the belief that the new leader should begin his career without being inhibited or impeded by the presence of someone whose loyalty belonged to the dead. Since it is suggested that Moketubbe may have slain his predecessor, there would in the case of the Faulkner story have been a practical reason why Issetibbeha's slave would have been unwelcome to him. Many ritualistic practices, incidentally, have their origin in expediency.

---

[5] A former Hindu practice according to which a widow is cremated with her husband's remains.

OCTOBER ISLAND

by William March

After so long a time in residence, Sam Barnfield and his wife Irma had come to think of October Island as their own, something which they themselves had visualized and moulded into its tapering, gourd-like shape, had colored theatrically with reds and yellows and greens, and had set down, at length, in the cobalt and sapphire waters of the vast Pacific Ocean.

On that first day when they had landed from a schooner, their goods piled helter-skelter on the stone mole that ran out into the lagoon, Sam had turned to his wife and said, "Here is a field awaiting the plough of the Lord." Irma nodded absently, but she did not speak at once, for her eyes at that instant were fixed with disbelief on a delegation of natives —a welcoming group who stood with an alert and graceful unconcern among a grove of wind-curved palms and watched their visitors in silence. She saw at once that they were entirely naked, except for their jewelry and the rather inadequate breech-clouts they wore; then, since the truest function of nudity is to make the clothed aware of their own more specialized immodesty, Irma tried the buttons of her shirtwaist, to assure herself that they were securely fastened, blushed, and settled her skirts more evenly about her shoetops.

The nakedness of the men, she felt, since there was nothing to corrupt the muscular, impersonal line of their bodies, was unremarkable and in no way offensive to her; it was the more focalized nudity of the women that had made her eyes widen in astonishment, for their stuffed, satiny breasts hung arrogantly from shoulder to waist, lifting in rhythm to the breath of their owners, or vibrating and swaying from side to side as the women yawned or laughed softly among themselves. Never in all her life—never at any time, or in any of the strange places of the world, had she seen such a brazen, fleshy opulence, and she lowered her eyes in confusion, thinking, "We must get clothes on them. That is clearly our first duty."

She turned back to the mole, and to the schooner anchored there, and in the pure, shallow water of the harbor, the fragile hull of the ship was outlined clearly. She could see the thin anchor-chain as it cut through the water, and the three flattened, brilliantly colored fish that swam untiringly around it in an exact and idiotic pattern; she saw the anchor itself as it lay, like the abandoned toy of a child, atop the yellow sand and the

---

pink, monotonous coral. The schooner had seemed neither frail nor small while she had been aboard it, and only yesterday she had thought of the anchor and its chain as things capable of holding any object firmly, under any stress or condition; but seeing them now at this angle, in this light, she was suddenly filled with anxiety. For a moment her life seemed senseless and of no importance to herself or to others; she doubted her mission, and in that terrifying interval, she was amazed at herself for having abandoned so many things that others set store by to embark on her life of thankless sacrifice and deprivation.

She reached out to touch the familiar flesh of her husband, but he had already moved away from her in the direction of the watching natives. When he was a courteous distance from them, he paused and said: "I am the Reverend Samuel Barnfield, and this is my wife Irma. We want to live here and share your lives, if that is agreeable to you. Do not be afraid of us. We are missionaries, and we have come to bring you peace and the Word of God."

When he had finished, the natives began to laugh and chatter among themselves, finding the seriousness of this spare, graying old man both stimulating and amusing; then, recognizing some signal unheard by others, they turned and ran through the palm trees, toward the beach at the far side of the harbor; and as the women balanced themselves and moved forward, each in turn, raised her left arm in a ritualistic, supporting gesture, lifting her breasts up, and holding them outward, as if she displayed a basket of ripe, tropical fruit for others to view and admire. The men, being unimpeded, ran more easily, and with a greater grace, their splayed, prehensile toes curling a little and grasping the sand for support. They outdistanced the women easily, but at intervals, when they saw their companions were falling too far behind, they would pause on the crumbling sand, pivot, and extend their arms to the brown, laughing women.

Almost at once the headman of the island appeared among the trees. Since he considered the greeting of visitors not a public occasion, but an affair of the deepest intimacy, he wore his heavy headdress of clam shells, and his ceremonial robe of yellow and green feathers; and in a long, rather tiresome speech, he welcomed the strangers to October Island. When he had finished, one of the sailors from the schooner, a young half-breed named Hansen, who inappropriately combined the flaxen hair and gray eyes of his father with the barely modified features, the slightly diluted skin of his mother's people, stepped forward and translated the headman's words:

It appeared that the white visitors who had preceded the present ones had been scientists of one sort or another, and had spent their time spading up the dry beds of old streams, digging in the hills, or searching through the interior jungle; but whatever it was they looked for, they had not found it, and, in disappointment, they had quit the island some years before, leaving behind them the house they had built, many books, and a few broken pieces of furniture. The house was still intact, and the Reverend Barnfield and his wife were welcome to live there, if they wanted to. He would show them the way in person, and, later on, when the young people had recovered from their nervous amusement, they would see that the strangers' belongings were properly transported from the stone mole to their new home.

The house was situated on a high, green plateau. It commanded an almost perfect view of Min-Raybaat, the great, twin-coned volcano for which October Island was celebrated, and after her new house had been repaired, scoured, and decorated with bright, native mats and blue-calico cushions and curtains, Irma would often stand outside, one hand shielding her eyes from the quivering, tropical sun, and stare upward at the twin cones with a sort of rapt disapprobation.

The volcano was the first thing you saw as you approached the island, and on that memorable day when it had appeared suddenly in the distance, seemingly without support above the curving horizon of the sea, Irma had caught her breath and had moved back from the rail of the schooner, alarmed at the menace implicit in its towering, austere magnificence; but the captain of the schooner had reassured her, telling her that Min-Raybaat had not been active for hundreds of years, and that for all purposes of reality, it could be considered extinct. It was true, on occasion, that senile, echoing rumbles were heard from its depths, and at times streams of smoke and ineffectual jets of steam issued from its craters, but that was about all. In fact, she need not concern herself further about the volcano, for she would be as safe in its shadow as she was on the deck of his fragile, straining ship. . . . Now, remembering the captain's words, Irma lowered her eyes and said aloud, "I am God's creature, and I am in His hands. What he has destined for me, I will accept."

She sighed, turned and went back to her tasks, finding a certain just appropriateness in her laborious, unimaginative toil. She left the spiritual side of their mission to her husband, feeling that while he was a preacher whose eloquence could move others to repentance and repudiation, her own usefulness was that of ministering to the dull, everyday wants of the congregation. In her heart, she knew herself to be a woman of little sense and of only the slightest moral worth—a restless, aggressive old charwoman of God whose duties were the menial ones of keeping the temple sweet and unprofaned, of seeing that the long, difficult road to salvation was swept and unimpeded.

Later, when she and her husband had made friends with the islanders, and Sam had already begun his first efforts at conversion, Irma would often take walks along the seashore, picking up dry wood for her oven, or shells for the borders of the flowerbeds she was setting against her porch. Once, while deep in the interior, not far from the base of Min-Raybaat itself, she saw a plant growing from the side of one of the small, rocky hills. From a distance it seemed to be a violet, and yet, from another angle, it was plainly too large, too brightly colored for any violet she had ever seen; nevertheless, it was as close to a violet as any plant in this land of brilliance, immodesty and ridiculous size could reasonably be expected to be, and at once she wanted it for her garden.

The roots of the plant went deeper than she had thought. They were laced about a small, elliptical stone, and she dug out both stone and roots together; but when the plant was safely in her hands, the stone fell away from the dirt and lay obscenely in the sunlight, beside her feet. She stared at it in disbelief, being unable at that instant to credit its shocking, hermaphroditic frankness. She would not touch the stone with her hands again, but she turned it over with the toe of her boot, got down on her knees, and examined its flat, smooth sides; then, shrouding one hand in her skirt, she grasped the stone by the end which represented a breast, and reburied it in its original place. She dusted her hands and hurried away, saying indignantly, "Who would have thought such nastiness could be hidden behind a violet?"

The unpleasant incident, which ordinarily she would have dismissed from her mind at once, made an odd impression on her, and that night as she lay beside her sleeping husband, she saw the image again in all its lewd significance. The surfaces of the stone were even and highly polished, and they were covered with faint, but quite legible characters. She told herself that these characters were merely the accidental markings of time and erosion, or, at best, the meaningless scribbling of an ancient native; but she could not make herself believe these things, for in her heart she knew that the markings on the stone were the written words of thousands of years ago, and that they had been put there for a purpose by some patient and highly skilled hand.

There was a set of encyclopedias among the books which the archeologists had left behind, and since she knew she could not sleep that night, she got up, lit a candle, and turned to *October Island,* not really expecting to find a place as obscure as it was mentioned at all. To her surprise, the island was not only mentioned by name, but there were many columns of fine print devoted to its remote and most remarkable history.

She read on and on, discovering that the island's name, which she had taken for granted as being the identifying month of its discovery, was, in reality, a corruption of the far older title, Ok-tur-baat, which was believed by Professor Hans Axel Hansen to mean, "Garden of the Living Breast," or, alternatively, "Garden of the Final Redemption"; or even, according to the dissenting reading of Reginald Sykes, "Place of the Beginning and Ending."

But regardless of the scientific battles which had been fought over its name, October Island was universally accepted as being the site of the world's first important culture—a sort of pagan Garden of Eden where Shurabast, that cult dedicated to the worship of the hermaphroditic god Raybaat, had originated some six to ten thousand years before the birth of Christ. At its peak, Shurabast had been world-wide in scope. Then, gradually, its power had abated, until, at length, its rituals were observed only on the island of its origin, and even there, according to Professor Hansen, who had studied the natives at first hand, in only a rudimentary and inconclusive form.

Some scientists, notably Professor Johannes Katz and Dr. Clement Higgs, were of opinion that the priests of Raybaat had perfected the first alphabet, and had passed it on to the budding civilizations of the mainland. There was little evidence to support this contention, since no example of Ok-tur-baat writing had so far come to light, although several expeditions, notably the one of Wayland Yates in 1900, had gone to October Island to seek it out; but if these claims could be supported in time, if October Island had actually possessed an alphabet, and had preserved a written record of its civilization, then it was plain that many of the sciences, and much of the history of man's eternal struggle upward, would have to be rewritten, or rejected in part.

The article ended with a description of Min-Raybaat: It was situated near the island's one harbor, a few miles back of the coastal-plain. It was once considered the home of Raybaat himself, the god occupying the larger cone, his enormous, top-heavy wife inappropriately dwelling in the smaller. . . .

When she had finished her reading, Irma went back to the bedroom and stared thoughtfully at her husband. He was deeply asleep, his mouth opened a little, his stringy, graying legs exposed as high as his thighs. She sighed patiently and pulled down his nightshirt, blew out her candle, and lay primly beside him. The article had both disturbed and frightened her, and she was glad now that she had not told her husband about the stone she had found that afternoon. His temperament was different from her own, and he would have insisted, in his patient yet stubborn voice, that the stone be sent to a museum for study, and perhaps eventual deciphering.

She turned on her side, wondering if, by any possible stretch of imagination, the stone contained matter at variance with her individual, specialized belief. She got up and walked about the room restlessly. It was not that her own faith was too weak to withstand some foolish, heathen doctrine, she thought scornfully. That was not the issue at all. She was sure of herself, and what she stood for—but were the faiths of others equally strong?

She sat by her window, her head lowered, her hands pressing against her cheeks; then, in a moment of commonplace revelation, she understood the purpose of the obscene, polished tablet she had found: It was a sort of prayer-stone, she thought—something prepared by the priests of Raybaat, and sold to their followers; and if this assumption was correct, then the hill itself was a priestly post office, a place where the worshippers had buried their petitions with the native trust of children sending letters to Santa Claus up a chimney.

She considered these matters for a long time, wondering where her truest duty lay, and then as the land breeze freshened, and the tropical daybreak was unbearable with the clangor and screaming of the harsh-voiced, beautiful birds, she dedicated herself to the performance of new acts of faith: to the destruction of the idolatrous writing.

That morning after her housework was done she dug up the stone she had reburied, broke it, and threw its fragments into the sea. In the years that followed, she could be seen daily as she scurried about the island on her quest. She dug patiently in the hills, she balanced herself on the slippery ledges beneath waterfalls, she lowered herself through crevices in the cliffs to investigate the existence of caves. Her passion was successful, and she found many specimens of the writing she sought, although her major find did not come until the twelfth year of her search.

It consisted of a few items of religious paraphernalia, and many tablets of baked clay, each tablet being covered with legible, minute writing. The objects were wrapped in thin, beautifully worked kidskin. They rested together in a carved stone box, and while she did not understand their significance, she knew that once they had been of overwhelming importance to others, since they were concealed so cleverly, in such a remote and unexpected place. She examined the tablets for a long time, one hand resting in indecision against her cheek, but she broke them all at last, just as she had done the others.

She found the last specimen of writing during her twentieth year of residence on the island. At the end of the twenty-third, she concluded that there was no writing left to be found; but by that time the natives had been saved in a sudden, mass conversion, and both she and her husband were content, feeling their tasks were accomplished at last.

It was in the years which followed that they first began thinking of home again, and wishing they could return there. Irma would often speak of the friends she had once known, wondering which of them were living, and which were now dead, and as she moved about her house, or sat rocking on her porch, she sometimes visualized her return, and she smiled gently, seeing a great gathering of her loved ones, all those that she had once cherished and held so dear, there at the station to welcome her.

Her husband's desire for his homeland was more focused in its aim, more intense in its origin; and sometimes at night when he knelt to say his prayers, he would find his lips saying instead, "Dear Lord, if I could only be cold once more! If I could only hear sleigh bells again, or see snow!" Then, to his astonishment, he would find himself weeping, his face pressed flat against the mattress of his bed. It was almost as if he were passing through some delayed and inappropriate change-of-life, and that the object of his fading desire was not the conventional, warm-bodied young girl, but the granite contours, the cold, spinsterish charm of his native Vermont.

Their actual departure from the island came suddenly and quite simply: It happened when Samuel was sixty-four, and his wife sixty-one, and the board of missions which had supported them so long merely wrote that their treasury was in a poor condition, and that they could no longer underwrite the good work being done on October Island. The letter came on the regular, autumn trip of the *Mattie B. Powell,* and after Samuel had read it aloud to his wife, she sat quietly for a moment, nodded, and began packing their possessions with her eyes.

Samuel said: "Do you remember that helpful young half-breed in the crew of the vessel that brought us here? He's the new mate on the *Powell.* He remembers you very well, and asked how you were getting along."

"His name is Hansen," said Irma. "We had long talks together on the voyage out. His mother was a native woman, I remember, and he was born right here on the island."

Sam nodded, and then continued: "The schooner can return for us in about two weeks. I think we'd better leave on it."

"Yes," said Irma. "I suppose we must."

The words became a sort of refrain for her during the days that followed, and she moved about in a world of indecision and operatic unreality, surrounded by the lamenting friends she must leave behind her forever; but once aboard the schooner, on her way to Honolulu, her vigor returned, and she felt herself again.

But she was unhappy in her idleness, for years ago, when she was a small girl and lived in Vermont, her grandmother had once told her that each new day was like a treasure-box of hours and minutes and seconds. These powerful gifts were not granted us to be wasted, she said; instead, they were to be used thriftily, and with thoughtful kindness, and they were to be lived up with such an undeviating earnestness, that none of them was frittered away, or remained unexpended at nightfall. She had long since forgotten both her grandmother and the parable she had heard, but the effect of the story was to remain with her forever—a part of her character, a pattern in her mind—so that even now, where others might have relaxed and enjoyed a holiday at sea, she had only a feeling of uneasiness, a sense of guilt in her indolence.

And so she asked Mate Hansen to bring her his clothes and the clothes of the other members of the crew that needed repairing; and seated placidly on the small deck of the ship, she worked methodically. Often, when he was off duty, Mate Hansen would come and talk with her. Before coming aboard, she had thought of him as being young, as he had been when she saw him last, but in the twenty-six years which had passed since that time, his hair had whitened at the sides, and there were now deep lines in his pensive, dark-skinned face. He regarded people warily, his gray eyes narrowed and on guard. He was familiar with every vice; he had participated in every depravity known to man; and he had rejected them all at length; not because he considered them wrong, but because he found them tiresome, so that now, as he approached his middle-age, he had achieved not corruption, but a kind of impervious and monstrous purity.

He leaned against the rail, watching the green, running water. The day was so calm, the schooner moved so imperceptibly, that for a moment he had a sense of danger, thinking himself on land again; then Irma bit off a thread, looked up from her work, and began talking once more of the things that interested her.

On this particular morning, she said rather plaintively that since the islanders were obviously simple people, one had a right to expect them to have simple minds, simple customs, and a simple language with which to express their needs. At first, she had reasonably assumed these things to be true, and had been taken in as a result of her trusting nature, for she had soon found out that the minds of the natives were not artless at all, but quite cunning in a harmless, captivating way; that their customs, instead of being simple, were, in reality, so complex, so dictated by tradition, that one despaired of understanding them at all; and insofar as language was concerned, there was not one to master, but four: the language men used in speaking to men; the language women used in speaking to women; the language men and women used in common, and the courtesy language for public occasions and for addressing strangers.

Mate Hansen nodded, took out his pocketknife and began whittling a soft board. There was another language on October Island—the language that the natives used in communicating with their god and his consort, but since Irma did not know of it, after her years of residence there, he felt it would be discourteous to mention it now, and he remained silent.

Later, she tried to draw him out, to induce him to discuss his religious convictions, his purpose in life, his plans for making the most of the years that remained; but he was embarrassed at her sentimental fervor, and to escape her, to divert her missionary zeal onto less personal things, he uttered the first thought that came into his mind. The one thing that he wanted now, was to own and command his own schooner, he said, although he realized there was little chance of his achieving such an ambitious goal. She chided him for his lack of faith. She would join her prayers with his, she promised, and perhaps God would see fit to grant his wish—particularly if they could convince Him that the schooner, if given, would be used somehow in a furtherance of His own Power and Glory. The mate did not answer, and, as she sewed busily, she talked on and on—affirming, defining, and arranging the articles of her belief.

He paused in his whittling at length, and glanced at her with his long, light gray eyes, impressed anew with her relentless kindness, feeling once more the shallowness of her inbred faith. He wondered, at that moment, if the identifying mark of adolescence was not the easiness of its definitions, its garrulous intimacy with concepts which awe the imaginative and mature and leave them silent. He sighed and lowered his head, since his was the melancholy of those who are neither one thing nor the other. Once, long ago, he had lived with assurance; but as the years receded, and the cleavage in his nature became more and more apparent, he saw nothing about him but sadness, as if a deep pathos, for his kind, was the essence of life itself, the background against which we are born, and struggle, and live out our lives to their ends.

He turned at the sound of footsteps, but it was only Sam Barnfield coming across the deck. He walked slowly, with little, mincing steps, putting down each foot as though it were precious to him, for this continent, saintly old man who neither drank, smoked, nor indulged in rich foods, suffered the punishments which are promised the drunkard, the glutton and the lecher as an atonement for their pleasures.

When he had seated himself on the covered hatchway beside Mate Hansen, Irma held up a pair of dungarees and examined their seams in the sunlight. She said, "There's still one question I'd like to ask you, Mate Hansen, and it's this: The women of October Island have a certain—well, a certain physical *peculiarity,* if you ever noticed what I have in mind. Both my husband and I have often wondered what the cause of it was, and if you know, perhaps you'll tell us."

Mate Hansen raised his head and stared at the unsteady rim of the sea, a far-away look in his melancholy eyes. He explained that, in the legendary past, when Shurabast had been all-powerful, the whole Pacific had been searched for young girls of such an overpowering attractiveness, that they were thought worthy to serve at the altar of Raybaat himself. When found, each novice was oiled, decked with flowers, and sent to October Island, where, in an elaborate ceremony of dedication, she became the spiritual bride of Raybaat, and the physical bride of his priests. The present people of the island were the random descendants of those voluptuous, carefully selected priestesses and their prurient, but sacred partners; and no doubt the specialized beauty, the freakish proportion which had been the sole factor in determining the vocation of the mother, had been passed on with such persistence by her, that, in time, Nature had sanctioned the variation from average, and had fixed it forever in the daughter.

Irma put down the dungarees, picked up a faded workshirt, and studied the condition of its cuffs. "Well!" she said. "Well, of all *things!*"

For a moment, Mate Hansen worked on the figure he was carving, his thin, brown fingers plying his knife with confident skill; but after a short silence, he turned his head and stared at Irma Barnfield with such thoughtful intensity that she became self-conscious, and fidgeted a little in her chair. Her hair had been admired all her life, she recalled. It was auburn, silky, and abundant; and there was no gray in it at all.—Even Samuel, although he had never been an ardent man, had once told her that it was her hair which had first attracted him to her; and so, remembering these things, this aged, wrinkled old woman arranged her scarf more modestly about her head, and tucked in the small, damp tendrils of floss which curled on the nape of her neck, as she did not want to be the instrument of Mate Hansen's undoing, or to tempt him to lust after her in his heart.

But she had misread the import of the mate's steady, inquiring glance. Actually, he was not thinking of her as a woman at all, but merely as one of the principals in the mass conversion of the people of October Island. Already the affair was famous in the neighboring port. He had even heard of it in places as far distant as Singapore, for once, in a waterfront brothel there, a plump, sedate young woman had entertained her patrons with an interminable song about it—a song which she called, "Condensed Milk Salvation." The woman sang softly, to the swishing accompaniment of the two small, sand-filled gourds that she held in her hands, and when she finished, her audience made kissing sounds with their lips, laughed gently and leaned back against their mats once more.

Mate Hansen, recalling the scene, now wanted to determine the facts, to discover, if he could, which of the song's allegations were fanciful, and which true. Then, as if the thought had just come to mind, he tossed his carving over the side of the schooner and asked his question casually; but some unconscious delicacy, connected perhaps with a memory of the singing woman and her rustling gourds, impelled him to speak not to Irma, whom he knew well, but to her husband, who had always alarmed him a little.

Sam looked up slowly, a rather vacant expression on his face. He suffered an enlargement of the liver, but he had known that for a long time, and, in a sense, he had come to accept his affliction as average and to be expected; but of late, he had also been plagued by days of dull, almost unbearable prostatic pain. He suffered such pain at this moment, and it was difficult for him to concentrate on anything outside his own misery, but hearing himself addressed personally, he summoned his will power, pressed one hand against his side, and said:

"When we first went to October Island, my wife and I knew that many missionaries had been there before us, and that they'd accomplished nothing at all. For many years the natives resisted us too. Oh, they were courteous and considerate enough; they were kind, gentle, and unassuming on all occasions; but when I tried to preach to them, to show them the way to happiness and divine peace, they would laugh, nudge one another, and then run off through the trees.

"Now, one of the old women of the village came down with a most peculiar sickness. She wouldn't move off her mats, and she wouldn't take food, except a little coconut milk at night and in the morning. We thought she'd die in a short time—from starvation, if nothing else; and it was at this point that my wife suggested we try giving condensed milk to the unfortunate woman. It was easy to take, and it was very nourishing; and there were a number of cans left over from our last consignment of supplies from the mainland; so when my wife and I concluded that condensed milk could do the poor creature no possible harm, and might even help sustain life a little longer in her, Irma went back to the house to fetch some of it."

His voice faltered, and he passed his hands roughly across his face, as if to brush something away from him. Irma, seeing his distress, took up the story, and finished in her quick, nasal voice: "When I got home, I opened a fresh can of milk; but I didn't want to serve the sick woman out of the tin itself, as that wouldn't look very polite, I thought; so I emptied the milk into an ornamental cup which I'd found on the island one day, and went back to the place where Sam was waiting for me."

She hesitated guiltily, for she had found the cup and the clay tablets together in the same box. At first she had meant to destroy the cup too, but the practical side of her nature had prevented so petulant an act, for she felt that, divorced of its heathen associations, and washed well with soap and hot water, she could easily put it to some Christian, everyday use of her own choosing.

"It was really less a cup than a ceremonial vessel of one kind or another," she said presently. "It was made out of polished stone, and there was a milky translucence about it. Perhaps it was alabaster, perhaps a variety of white jade. . . . Anyway, there was a decorated lid for the vessel, with a piece cut out where the spoon came through." She went on talking about the cup, describing it in circumstantial detail, but when she paused for breath, Mate Hansen bent forward excitedly and said, "Will you tell me what happened next, please?"

"What happened next was sudden, and almost incredible," said Irma. "You see, when I came back to the sick woman, Sam held up her head, and I offered her a spoonful of the milk. She took it willingly enough, but when she caught sight of the cup and the spoon, she got up from her bed and ran outside shouting, Manoa-el-rubo-aam! Manoa-el-rubo-aam!' "

Mate Hansen rolled a cigarette, lit it, and stared at Mrs. Barnfield, a disbelieving look in his eyes, but he did not speak. Irma said: "Almost at once, the other residents of the village came rushing out of their houses; and when they heard the sick woman's story, and saw the cup still in my hands, they gathered in groups and talked in a language I'd never heard before. Then they approached me slowly, as if they were in awe of me all of a sudden, and when they were a little way off, they knelt down and bowed their heads. I didn't know what was expected of me, but I gave them all a taste of the milk that remained in the cup, and after each had taken the milk, he fell on his face before me and kissed my shoes. Neither Sam nor I knew why they were behaving in such an odd manner —in fact, we don't know to this very day—but we did realize that God had somehow placed a great instrument for good in our hands, and we meant to make the most of it. Afterwards, the islanders made a confession of belief, as Sam instructed them to. Later, we baptized them all, and led them finally into the church of God."

She turned to Sam for confirmation, but he only sighed and inclined his head. He raised his face to the sunlight, and suddenly he knew that death stood there beside him. He trembled at his knowledge, closed his eyes and spoke soundlessly. "Dear Lord!" he said. "Do not let me die at sea! Let me see my mother's grave once more! Let me be buried among the hills where I was born!" He lowered his head, wondering if the faith of Shurabast was as ridiculous as he had once thought it; that if, after all, it was not the first and the final religion of all who live. He stared outward at the serene, deceptive sea, and in that interval he experienced a moment of clarity and resignation. It seemed to him, then, that when everything else had gone, hope sometimes remained; but when hope had gone too, then dignity must somehow take its place. . . .

Irma said: "Administering the milk became a bit of a nuisance later on. There were a number of ceremonials which the natives expected me to participate in, some of them quite original indeed. For instance, the milk must be given at sunset, and then only in that little grove of trees at the base of Min-Raybaat. I must stand in just such a way at the time, and I must hold the cup and spoon in the correct hands, at the right distance from the altar. Luckily, Sam and I were never ones to bother much about religious precedent, so we agreed to all the reasonable demands our congregation made on us."

Mate Hansen excused himself and went below to think out the things he had just heard, for the vessel which Irma had described in such detail seemed identical with the legendary communion cup of Raybaat. The story, which he had heard as a boy, and which he did not now believe, was concerned with the history of thousands of years ago; with the days when October Island had been attacked by savages from the mainland, and its civilization destroyed. It seemed, on that terrible, remote day, that the high priest had hidden the emblems of the temple in a place which only he knew. Later that morning, he had died in the general slaughter without revealing the place of concealment, and the holy communion cup, which Raybaat had fashioned with his own hands from the skull of his divine, cannibal mother, had never been seen again.

The loss of the cup had inevitably meant a loss of the power of Shurabast, which had drawn its strength from the holiness of the vessel; but there was comfort in the legend too, for it was prophesied that when the prestige of Raybaat was lowest, when his religion was discredited everywhere in the outside world, then he would return his cup to the faithful through the medium of a great priestess, a priestess who would restore Oktur-baat to its old power, and bring with her a thousand years of peace and glory.

Mate Hansen kicked off his shoes and stretched out on his bunk, his arms folded beneath his head. The words the sick woman had used when she ran out of her hut were in the fifth, or sacred language of the island. Translated freely, they were: "She is here! The Great Breast Mother of the Universe is here!" . . .

All at once he turned on his belly and laughed for the first time in months. He laughed hysterically, his mouth pressed flat against his pillow, for he wondered at that moment if the missionaries had actually converted the people of October Island to Christianity, as they imagined, or if they, themselves, had not unwittingly embraced Shurabast. Later, when he was calm once more, he washed his face and hands and went on deck about his duties.

Irma and her husband were still sitting in the sun. She had finished her mending for that morning, and as it was now close to lunch time, she folded the garments she had worked on, piled them on the deck, and patted them lightly with her hand. The gesture made her think of the islanders and the difficulties she had met with in clothing them. In a way, she felt that she had *succeeded* in her efforts; and yet, in another way, she had not succeeded at all, for although the women were now clad modestly from ankle to throat, they had cut holes in the waists of their frocks and let their long, ripe breasts hang outward against the calico. She had tried every means in her power to induce her daughters to cover themselves all over, but the women, who as a rule were so docile, so pathetically anxious to please her, had only smiled and shaken their heads, pretending that they did not understand her scoldings.

"I keep thinking about the natives and remembering how much they esteem us," said Irma after a moment. "Perhaps we were wrong to leave them, Sam." Her husband did not answer, and she went on: "We've been gone only a week, but already I miss them, and wonder if they miss us a little too." She got up from her chair, smoothed down her dress and continued quickly, "But of course they miss us too! They must miss us dreadfully, after all the things we *did* for them!"

She was correct in her surmise, for the people of October Island missed them a great deal indeed, and at the very moment she spoke, they were taking the most practical means at their command to bring their benefactors back again. They had missed them even on that first day, when the gray, dirty little schooner had receded slowly into the immensity of the Pacific Ocean, and they had stood in desolation among the palm trees, singing hymns and praying the prayers they had been taught; but to their surprise, the disappearing vessel, with only the tips of her masts now visible against the sky, did not miraculously turn in her course and speed back to them.

When there was no sign of the schooner at all, they turned and went back to their villages, but not without hope, for no matter how ineffectual the religion of the missionaries was in their unskilled hands, they still had the ceremonials of Raybaat to aid them in resolving their calamity.

Raybaat, as everyone knew, was fond of the flesh of fat young children. If such a child was delivered to him at sunrise each morning, he would in time, when his social debt became too embarrassing to be ignored further, see that the accompanying prayer of his donors was granted. . . . But the people did not want to sacrifice their greatly loved children if a milder solution could be found. They discussed the problem with sighs and shakes of their heads, and then one of the villagers pointed out that since Raybaat was so old, the chances were that he could no longer distinguish between the flesh of a child and that of any other young animal —a pig for example.

At once, the islanders began discussing this new way out of their dilemma. Pigs and children were identical both in appearance and in their disregard of all habits of ordinary daintiness, they said eagerly. Both were stubborn and unreasonable; both ate their food without manners, making loud, gulping noises as they did so; both cried all day long, and screamed with rage the instant their wishes were thwarted. They debated the question at length, coming to the conclusion that the most noticeable difference between a pig and a child was the fact that a pig was covered with hair, and a child was not—but that distinction, they said slyly, nudging one another with their elbows, was one which could be remedied.

So, early the next morning, they shaved a young pig with a sharp clam shell, and uttering their prayers for the return of the missionaries, they dropped the pig down the crater of the volcano. That day they waited nervously to see if Raybaat had been taken in by their cleverness, but just when they were convinced they had fooled him, a jet of steam and a few stones rose indignantly out of the crater, followed by grumbles from the depths of the cone, and a short, cynical belch of derision.

It was then they knew there was no hope of deceiving their god, and next morning, and each morning thereafter at sunrise, a living child, washed, oiled and perfumed with spices, was dropped into the crater; but at the end of the ninetieth day, the day when Raybaat should have granted their prayers, nothing had happened at all. Some time afterwards, when they were becoming desperate, teams of islanders would station themselves on either side of the volcano and hold pointed conversations across the crater.

One team would shout loudly: "It seems that when people do a certain favor for a person of high position, that that other person, no matter how exalted he happens to be, should, in common fairness, do something in return for the people we're speaking of at this instant."

Then the answer from the other side of the crater would be: "That's the way it seems to us, too. The laws of politeness advocate a prompt return of favors, as everybody knows; but some, whose names we would not dream of repeating, for fear they might hear us, and hold it against us, seem to be so old and discourteous that they've lost all the common decencies that others observe."

They continued these conversations through the sixth, the seventh, and the eighth months of their prayers, apparently neither arousing Raybaat, nor goading him into action; then, toward the end of the ninth month, when they had almost lost all hope, one of their number looked toward the harbor at the moment the sun freed itself from the sea, and lifted above it. He turned to the others and pointed in triumph, for there, coming toward them, was the schooner *Mattie B. Powell* under full sail.

At the sight, the people embraced one another and wept with a sort of nervous joy. Then, when their first emotions were expended, they hurried down the side of the volcano, some of them going to the home of the missionaries to clean it and decorate it with flowers and tropical fruits, others racing to the harbor, to stand there and chatter together shrilly. One of the group at the end of the mole shielded his eyes and called out suddenly, "Look! Somebody is standing at the bow of the vessel! Perhaps it's the missionary. Perhaps it's his wife!"

It was neither. It was Captain Hansen himself. He had called his passenger, Mrs. Barnfield, a little before sunrise, as she had asked him to do, and he now awaited her on deck. He lifted his binoculars and watched the natives as they waved their arms and scurried up and down the narrow beach. Listening, he could hear their voices when they shouted, and even the sound of their distant flutes and finger-drums; and he lowered his glasses and sighed, for the very warmth of this welcome, which so plainly was not for himself, reminded him inevitably of an event in his own past, and saddened him a little. . . .

His father was Professor Hans Axel Hansen, the famous antiquarian who had once lived on October Island to investigate the customs of its people, and who, obviously enough, had done so with some success. He had left the island, never to return, when his son was two years old, and, naturally, the boy had not remembered him at all. Later, when he was growing up, he thought of his father a great deal. He had visions of meeting him again, visions in which they were alone together in a quiet room. At first, they would stand looking at each other, neither quite knowing what to do next; then, at the same instant, they would raise their arms and walk toward each other blindly, and embrace, their cheeks pressed together. Perhaps the old man would weep a little, laugh with embarrassment and turn his head away so that his son could not see him; perhaps the boy himself would weep a little, too. . . . Then his father would give him his blessing, and the boy would kneel, kiss his father's hand, and walk out of the room satisfied, without looking back.

This fantasy had so haunted his youth, that, later on when he was a seaman, and in a port near his father's home, he had written him an affectionate but rather illiterate note, in which he expressed his intention of visiting him on a certain day at a certain hour. On that particular day, he walked down the quiet, European street where his father lived, stopped before the correct house, and rapped on the door. At once two policemen came out of the vestibule and confronted him. They thought it was only fair to advise him of the punishment that awaits the extortioner, they said. He must write no more threatening letters, and he must make no further effort to see Professor Hansen. If he disregarded this warning, he would be arrested and jailed immediately.

In those days, Captain Hansen had been a boy of nineteen, and he had listened to the policemen with a sort of shamed amazement. He kept saying, "But what you say is not true at all. He is my father. How could I possibly want to harm my own father?"

Then he had bowed gravely, and walked down the steps; but when he was on the sidewalk once more, something impelled him to turn and look at one of the upstairs windows. The curtain there was pulled to one side, and for a moment he stared into the cold, wary eyes of his father; then suddenly the face was gone, and the curtain had fallen back into place, and he was entirely alone once more.

The memory of that bitter day had remained with him all his life. When it was fresh, he would often stop what he was doing, stand still, and shudder; but now, so many years afterwards, he merely felt shame and a little regret as he recalled the senseless, unnecessary humiliation, and he sighed and moved his hand slowly across the rail.

Mrs. Barnfield joined him a minute or so later, and he handed her the binoculars without comment. The sounds from the island were clearer now, more definable in their purpose, and Irma, watching the natives, said quickly, "But how did they know I would be on this particular ship, at this particular time? How did they know I was coming back at all?"

Her one regret was that Sam was not present to share her triumph. Thus far, she had not been able to speak of his death, not even to Captain Hansen during the days they had spent together in Honolulu; but now, seeing the warmth of the welcome that awaited her, she felt as though she were released at last; and standing there in the early light, she explained that the Vermont winter had been too much for her husband, and that he had died a short time after their arrival.

She said: "When he was dying, and knew it, he asked me to bury him at the old Barnfield farm, where he was born. I promised I would, and did what I promised. He died when it was below zero, with the earth frozen solid. The farm was several miles from town. Nobody lived there any more, and the family burial-ground where he wanted to lie was on one side of a flinty hill. I went there with the grave diggers to see that everything was the way he wanted it. It was snowing lightly at the time, and as the men dug among the rocks, their picks struck sparks which sprang outward, and were quenched by the snow; but at last the grave was wide and deep enough, and that afternoon, we put him in it. Those in the village who remembered him stood there beside me in the cold; but during the long prayer, it began to snow once more, and before the men could fill the grave with earth, it had filled up first with snow."

She turned resolutely and smiled, knowing that this was no time for grief, but a time for joy. The schooner was nearing the lagoon itself, and the welcome from the beach was increasing in intensity. She pressed forward against the rail, waved her hand, and then blew a kiss to her worshippers. At once they began to scream louder, and to dance about the beach. Some of them plunged into the water and swam toward the vessel. When they reached it, they frolicked like welcoming porpoises, diving, turning, and coming to the surface to laugh and shake water from their hair, their teeth shining in the sunlight; but at last, when the schooner was abreast of the mole, and the people had moored it there, Irma came to the rail once more, while the natives, in an ecstasy of exhilaration, capered, cried out, and pelted her gently with flowers.

It was then she noticed that in her absence her converts had discarded the clothes she had made for them, and that they were now as naked as they had been on the day she first landed on the island. She made a mild, clucking sound of disapproval, then, collecting her thoughts, she held up her hand for silence, and began her official speech of return.

She explained that she had not once been happy after she had left the island, for it appeared that the land which she had always thought of as being her home, was not, in reality, her true home at all. October Island was her true home, she said, and not the foolish, terrifying world outside it; and now that her husband was dead, and no longer needed her, she had returned as quickly as she could to those she loved, and who loved her in return. She was deeply moved by the welcome she had received, and she promised she would never leave the island again. . . .

She paused, and at once the islanders began one of the hymns she had taught them, accompanying themselves with their pebble-gourds, their drums, and their native marimba-like instruments. Irma tilted her head and listened thoughtfully. There was something *wrong* with the hymn, she thought, although she could not say precisely what it was. The words seemed accurate enough, and the tune itself was reasonably true; but there was an excitement about it, a certain sensuousness which no hymn should have, and she shook her head in disapproval, and listened critically. When the hymn was finished, she continued her speech in her quick, positive voice saying:

"My return is the result of a miracle worked by the Lord. You see, I prayed diligently that I could somehow come back to you, and at last my prayers were answered, for a cousin of mine whom I'd not seen since childhood—a certain Miss Amelia Goodpasture—died without making a will, and the court decided that I was her next of kin, and sole heir. I was completely astonished, particularly when I was told the net estate was substantially more than a half million dollars."

She paused significantly and then said: "Now, at the finish of my prayers to be returned to October Island, I invariably appended a prayer on Captain Hansen's behalf: a prayer that he be granted a schooner of his own, since I knew that that was his dearest wish; so, since both prayers were linked together, I concluded, naturally enough, that both had been answered, and I arranged to meet him in Honolulu three weeks ago. He demurred at first, but finally he accepted the *Mattie B. Powell,* which I assured him was not a gift from me in any sense, but a gift from the Lord."

She motioned to Captain Hansen, and when he stood beside her, she finished her speech, stating that the remainder of her inheritance had been put into a trust fund for the benefit of the island, and that her agents on the mainland had been instructed to see that quantities of condensed milk were purchased, and transported to the inhabitants there at regular intervals.

She paused, shook hands with Captain Hansen, and began descending the ladder briskly, while the natives rushed toward her shouting, "Manoa-el-rubo-aam! Manoa-el-rubo-aam!" At once they lifted her in their arms and carried her to a sort of flower-decked throne, which they had prepared in anticipation of her return. They seated her on it, took the pins from her hair, and allowed it to fall loosely about her shoulders. They put a headdress of feathers and shells about her forehead, and anointed her brows, her lips, her hands, and her feet, with an ointment of a particular fragrance. She laughed at them with a sort of apologetic pleasure, protested the silliness of their activities, and tapped them indulgently with her fan; then, as the ceremonial neared its completion, she understood at last the real motive which had urged her to destroy the tablets: Their discovery would have meant a prompt emigration of scientists to the island, and that she did not want at all. The island was particularly her own, she felt. That was a thing she had known from the beginning, and she could do very well without the company of Mr. Reginald Sykes, Dr. Clement Higgs, Mr. Wayland Yates, or even Professor Johannes Katz, whose name had always fascinated her.

Seeing these things so clearly, she smiled, nodded her head, and looked languidly about her; and at once she knew what had bothered her since her return: There were almost no children at all in the welcoming crowd, and sitting up straight on her throne, she said in surprise: "But where are the children? What has become of all the children?" . . .

Captain Hansen, observing the last ceremonies of Mrs. Barnfield's deification—the final rites which were making her not only a goddess, but the divine concubine of Raybaat, as well, was suddenly filled with a sense of impotent horror. These goddess-concubines—although there had not been one on October Island since ancient times—were worshipped by the people for a year, and for a year only. During the period of their reign, they knew an adoration without limits; at the end of their year, they were dropped into the crater of the volcano in order that they might rejoin Raybaat, and lying intimately beside him, explain the human frailties of his followers, and intercede with him to forgive them all.

He wanted to call out to the old woman, to tell her of her danger; but he realized that she would not believe him if he warned her, or, if she did believe him, that she would only lift her chin and say in her nasal voice, "I've looked after myself all these years without your help, young man! If you'll mind your own business now, I'll continue to do so!"

When the ceremony was over, the natives made a sort of sedan chair of the throne, and riding there so high above her people, Mrs. Barnfield put the pins back in her hair, laughed easily, and called out: "But where are the children? Really, you must tell me where the children are!"

Suddenly, Captain Hansen was sick of this kind, opinionated, generous, stupid, courageous old woman; and as she disappeared with her worshippers around a curve in the beach, he knew that he never wanted to see her again, that he was through with her forever. In a short time, he must go below and see to the unloading of the condensed milk, but for the time being, he wanted only to stand here in the morning sunlight and think of Mrs. Barnfield, and her works. . . .

Once, a long time ago, when he had first left October Island, and his ship was on drydock in San Francisco, he had passed a theater at which a musical piece was playing. He had never been to the theater, and hoping that the experience would give him a better understanding of the lives and customs of others, he bought his ticket timidly, and went inside.

Even after all these years, he still remembered that wonderful evening, for the principals had been in good voice, the music tuneful, the costumes new and elaborate, and the girls beautiful. As the evening advanced, the plot of the piece became more and more involved, until, at length, there seemed no way out at all; but sitting alone in the darkened theater, in a strange land he had not seen before that morning, he accepted the play as real in every detail, until, at length, a stranger appeared in the final scene to set matters right for everyone: to clear the overseer of the forgery charge; to pay off the mortgage on the pineapple farm; to end the misunderstanding which kept the secondary lovers apart; to reveal that the handsome but penniless tenor was actually a prince, and, as such, worthy to marry an American girl.

It was at this point that he doubted the play's validity, and he had shaken his head in disbelief, saying, "Things don't happen that way. It's not true to life." But now, remembering what Mrs. Barnfield had accomplished for others, he wondered if his judgment had not been a little hasty. Certainly it was true that, through her efforts, he now owned a splendid schooner; that Sam had his cold grave on a bleak hillside, precisely as he had desired it; that the islanders had their great goddess and her cup filled with condensed milk; that Irma, herself, had the inexhaustible adoration she craved, and, later on, would have her quick unanticipated death in the volcano. . . .

When he said the play was untrue to life, did he not really mean it was untrue to his experience, to the special logic which gave his own life consequence, and made it tolerable? He moved his hands slowly along the rail, thinking that if we desire greatly enough, if we seek with a proper diligence, everything becomes true to life at the end. Perhaps that was the meaning which the divided ones like himself, who have peace nowhere in the world, seek with such desperation, and rarely find.

RED LEAVES
by William Faulkner

I

The two Indians crossed the plantation toward the slave quarters. Neat with whitewash, of baked soft brick, the two rows of houses in which lived the slaves belonging to the clan, faced one another across the mild shade of the lane marked and scored with naked feet and with a few homemade toys mute in the dust. There was no sign of life.

"I know what we will find," the first Indian said.

"What we will not find," the second said. Although it was noon, the lane was vacant, the doors of the cabins empty and quiet; no cooking smoke rose from any of the chinked and plastered chimneys.

"Yes. It happened like this when the father of him who is now the Man, died."

"You mean, of him who was the Man."

"Yao."

The first Indian's name was Three Basket. He was perhaps sixty. They were both squat men, a little solid, burgher-like; paunchy, with big heads, big, broad, dust-colored faces of a certain blurred serenity like carved heads on a ruined wall in Siam or Sumatra, looming out of a mist. The sun had done it, the violent sun, the violent shade. Their hair looked like sedge grass on burnt-over land. Clamped through one ear Three Basket wore an enameled snuffbox.

"I have said all the time that this is not the good way. In the old days there were no quarters, no Negroes. A man's time was his own then. He had time. Now he must spend most of it finding work for them who prefer sweating to do."

"They are like horses and dogs."

"They are like nothing in this sensible world. Nothing contents them save sweat. They are worse then the white people."

"It is not as though the Man himself had to find work for them to do."

"You said it. I do not like slavery. It is not the good way. In the old days, there was the good way. But not now."

"You do not remember the old way either."

"I have listened to them who do. And I have tried this way. Man was not made to sweat."

"That's so. See what it has done to their flesh."

"Yes. Black. It has a bitter taste, too."

"You have eaten of it?"

"Once. I was young then, and more hardy in the appetite than now. Now it is different with me."

"Yes. They are too valuable to eat now."

"There is a bitter taste to the flesh which I do not like."

"They are too valuable to eat, anyway, when the white men will give horses for them."

They entered the lane. The mute, meager toys—the fetish-shaped objects made of wood and rags and feathers—lay in the dust about the patinaed doorsteps, among bones and broken gourd dishes. But there was no sound from any cabin, no face in any door; had not been since yesterday, when Issetibbeha died. But they already knew what they would find.

It was in the central cabin, a house a little larger than the others, where at certain phases of the moon the Negroes would gather to begin their ceremonies before removing after nightfall to the creek bottom, where they kept the drums. In this room they kept the minor accessories, the cryptic ornaments, the ceremonial records which consisted of sticks daubed with red clay in symbols. It had a hearth in the center of the floor, beneath a hole in the roof, with a few cold wood ashes and a suspended iron pot. The window shutters were closed; when the two Indians entered, after the abashless sunlight they could distinguish nothing with the eyes save a movement, shadow, out of which eyeballs rolled, so that the place appeared to be full of Negroes. The two Indians stood in the doorway.

"Yao," Basket said. "I said this is not the good way."

"I don't think I want to be here," the second said.

"That is black man's fear which you smell. It does not smell as ours does."

"I don't think I want to be here."

"Your fear has an odor too."

"Maybe it is Issetibbeha which we smell."

"Yao. He knows. He knows what we will find here. He knew when he died what we should find here today." Out of the rank twilight of the room the eyes, the smell, of Negroes rolled about them. "I am Three Basket, whom you know," Basket said into the room. "We are come from the Man. He whom we seek is gone?" The Negroes said nothing. The smell of them, of their bodies, seemed to ebb and flux in the still hot air. They seemed to be musing as one upon something remote, inscrutable. They were like a single octopus. They were like the roots of a huge tree uncovered, the earth broken momentarily upon the writhen, thick, fetid tangle of its lightless and outraged life. "Come," Basket said. "You know our errand. Is he whom we seek gone?"

"They are thinking something," the second said. "I do not want to be here."

"They are knowing something," Basket said.

"They are hiding him, you think?"

"No. He is gone. He has been gone since last night. It happened like this before, when the grandfather of him who is now the Man died. It took us three days to catch him. For three days Doom lay above the ground, saying 'I see my horse and my dog. But I do not see my slave. What have you done with him that you will not permit me to lie quiet?' "

"They do not like to die."

"Yao. They cling. It makes trouble for us, always. A people without honor and without decorum. Always a trouble."

"I do not like it here."

"Nor do I. But then, they are savages; they cannot be expected to regard usage. That is why I say that this way is a bad way."

"Yao. They cling. They would even rather work in the sun than to enter the earth with a chief. But he is gone."

The Negroes had said nothing, made no sound. The white eyeballs rolled, wild, subdued; the smell was rank, violent. "Yes, they fear," the second said. "What shall we do now?"

"Let us go and talk with the Man."

"Will Moketubbe listen?"

"What can he do? He will not like to. But he has the Man now."

"Yao. He is the Man. He can wear the shoes with the red heels all the time now." They turned and went out. There was no door in the door frame. There were no doors in any of the cabins.

"He did that anyway," Basket said.

"Behind Issetibbeha's back. But now they are his shoes, since he is the Man."

"Yao. Issetibbeha did not like it. I have heard. I know that he said to Moketubbe: 'When you are the Man, the shoes will be yours. But until then, they are my shoes.' But now Moketubbe is the Man; he can wear them."

"Yao," the second said. "He is the Man now. He used to wear the shoes behind Issetibbeha's back, and it was not known if Issetibbeha knew this or not. And then Issetibbeha became dead, who was not old, and the shoes are Moketubbe's, since he is the Man now. What do you think of that?"

"I don't think about it," Basket said. "Do you?"

"No," the second said.

"Good," Basket said. 'You are wise."

II

The house sat on a knoll, surrounded by oak trees. The front of it was one story in height, composed of the deck house of a steamboat which had gone ashore and which Doom, Issetibbeha's father, had dismantled with his slaves and hauled on cypress rollers twelve miles home overland. It took them five months. His house consisted at the time of one brick wall. He set the steamboat broadside on to the wall, where now the chipped and flaked gilding of the rococo cornices arched in faint splendor above the gilt lettering of the stateroom names above the jalousied doors.

Doom had been born merely a subchief, a Mingo, one of three children on the mother's side of the family. He made a journey—he was a young man then and New Orleans was a European city—from north Mississippi to New Orleans by keel boat, where he met the Chevalier Sœur Blonde de Vitry, a man whose social position, on its face, was as equivocal as Doom's own. In New Orleans, among the gamblers and cutthroats of the river front, Doom, under the tutelage of his patron, passed as the chief, the Man, the hereditary owner of that land which belonged to the male side of the family; it was the Chevalier de Vitry who called him *du homme*, and hence Doom.

They were seen everywhere together—the Indian, the squat man with a bold, inscrutable, underbred face, and the Parisian, the expatriate, the friend, it was said, of Carondelet and the intimate of General Wilkinson. Then they disappeared, the two of them, vanishing from their old equivocal haunts and leaving behind them the legend of the sums which Doom was believed to have won, and some tale about a young woman, daughter of a fairly well-to-do West Indian family, the son and brother of whom sought Doom with a pistol about his old haunts for some time after his disappearance.

Six months later the young woman herself disappeared, boarding the St. Louis packet, which put in one night at a wood landing on the north Mississippi side, where the woman, accompanied by a Negro maid, got off. Four Indians met her with a horse and wagon, and they traveled for three days, slowly, since she was already big with child, to the plantation, where she found that Doom was now chief. He never told her how he accomplished it, save that his uncle and his cousin had died suddenly. At that time the house consisted of a brick wall built by shiftless slaves, against which was propped a thatched lean-to divided into rooms and littered with bones and refuse, set in the center of ten thousand acres of matchless parklike forest where deer grazed like domestic cattle. Doom and the woman were married there a short time before Issetibbeha was born, by a combination itinerant minister and slave trader who arrived on a mule, to the saddle of which was lashed a cotton umbrella and a three-gallon demijohn of whisky. After that, Doom began to acquire more slaves and to cultivate some of his land, as the white people did. But he never had enough for them to do. In utter idleness the majority of them led lives transplanted whole out of African jungles, save on the occasions when, entertaining guests, Doom coursed them with dogs.

When Doom died, Issetibbeha, his son, was nineteen. He became proprietor of the land and of the quintupled herd of blacks for which he had no use at all. Though the title of Man rested with him, there was a hierarchy of cousins and uncles who ruled the clan and who finally gathered in squatting conclave over the Negro question, squatting profoundly beneath the golden names above the doors of the steamboat.

"We cannot eat them," one said.

"Why not?"

"There are too many of them."

"That's true," a third said. "Once we started, we should have to eat them all. And that much flesh diet is not good for man."

"Perhaps they will be like deer flesh. That cannot hurt you."

"We might kill a few of them and not eat them," Issetibbeha said.

They looked at him for a while. "What for?" one said.

"That is true," a second said. "We cannot do that. They are too valuable; remember all the bother they have caused us, finding things for them to do. We must do as the white men do."

"How is that?" Issetibbeha said.

"Raise more Negroes by clearing more land to make corn to feed them, then sell them. We will clear the land and plant it with food and raise Negroes and sell them to the white men for money."

"But what will we do with this money?" a third said.

They thought for a while.

"We will see," the first said. They squatted, profound, grave.

"It means work," the third said.

"Let the Negroes do it," the first said.

"Yao. Let them. To sweat is bad. It is damp. It opens the pores."

"And then the night air enters."

"Yao. Let the Negroes do it. They appear to like sweating."

So they cleared the land with the Negroes and planted it in grain. Up to that time the slaves had lived in a huge pen with a lean-to roof over one corner, like a pen for pigs. But now they began to build quarters, cabins, putting the young Negroes in the cabins in pairs to mate; five years later Issetibbeha sold forty head to a Memphis trader, and he took the money and went abroad upon it, his maternal uncle from New Orleans conducting the trip. At that time the Chevalier Sœur Blonde de Vitry was an old man in Paris, in a toupee and a corset, with a careful toothless old face fixed in a grimace quizzical and profoundly tragic. He borrowed three hundred dollars from Issetibbeha and in return he introduced him into certain circles; a year later Issetibbeha returned home with a gilt bed, a pair of girandoles by whose light it was said that Pompadour arranged her hair while Louis smirked at his mirrored face across her powdered shoulder, and a pair of slippers with red heels. They were too small for him, since he had not worn shoes at all until he reached New Orleans on his way abroad.

He brought the slippers home in tissue paper and kept them in the remaining pocket of a pair of saddlebags filled with cedar shavings, save when he took them out on occasion for his son, Moketubbe, to play with. At three years of age Moketubbe had a broad, flat, Mongolian face that appeared to exist in a complete and unfathomable lethargy, until confronted by the slippers.

Moketubbe's mother was a comely girl whom Issetibbeha had seen one day working in her shift in a melon patch. He stopped and watched her for a while—the broad, solid thighs, the sound back, the serene face. He was on his way to the creek to fish that day, but he didn't go any farther; perhaps while he stood there watching the unaware girl he may have remembered his own mother, the city woman, the fugitive with her fans and laces and her Negro blood, and all the tawdry shabbiness of that sorry affair. Within the year Moketubbe was born; even at three he could not get his feet into the slippers. Watching him in the still, hot afternoons as he struggled with the slippers with a certain monstrous repudiation of fact, Issetibbeha laughed quietly to himself. He laughed at Moketubbe and the shoes for several years, because Moketubbe did not give up trying to put them on until he was sixteen. Then he quit. Or Issetibbeha thought he had. But he had merely quit trying in Issetibbeha's presence. Issetibbeha's newest wife told him that Moketubbe had stolen and hidden the shoes. Issetibbeha quit laughing then, and he sent the woman away, so that he was alone. "Yao," he said. "I too like being alive, it seems." He sent for Moketubbe. "I give them to you," he said.

Moketubbe was twenty-five then, unmarried. Issetibbeha was not tall, but he was taller by six inches than his son and almost a hundred pounds lighter. Moketubbe was already diseased with flesh, with a pale, broad, inert face and dropsical hands and feet. "They are yours now," Issetibbeha said, watching him. Moketubbe had looked at him once when he entered, a glance brief, discreet, veiled.

"Thanks," he said.

Issetibbeha looked at him. He could never tell if Moketubbe saw anything, looked at anything. "Why will it not be the same if I give the slippers to you?"

"Thanks," Moketubbe said. Issetibbeha was using snuff at the time; a white man had shown him how to put the powder into his lip and scour it against his teeth with a twig of gum or of alphea.

"Well," he said, "a man cannot live forever." He looked at his son, then his gaze went blank in turn, unseeing, and he mused for an instant. You could not tell what he was thinking, save that he said half aloud: "Yao. But Doom's uncle had no shoes with red heels." He looked at his son again, fat, inert. "Beneath all that, a man might think of doing anything and it not be known until too late." He sat in a splint chair hammocked with deer thongs. "He cannot even get them on; he and I are both frustrated by the same gross meat which he wears. He cannot even get them on. But is that my fault?"

He lived for five years longer, then he died. He was sick one night, and though the doctor came in a skunk-skin vest and burned sticks, he died before noon.

That was yesterday; the grave was dug, and for twelve hours now the

People had been coming in wagons and carriages and on horseback and afoot, to eat the baked dog and the succotash and the yams cooked in ashes and to attend the funeral.

III

"It will be three days," Basket said, as he and the other Indian returned to the house. "It will be three days and the food will not be enough; I have seen it before."

The second Indian's name was Louis Berry. "He will smell too, in this weather."

"Yao. They are nothing but a trouble and a care."

"Maybe it will not take three days."

"They run far. Yao. We will smell this Man before he enters the earth. You watch and see if I am not right."

They approached the house.

"He can wear the shoes now," Berry said. "He can wear them now in man's sight."

"He cannot wear them for a while yet," Basket said. Berry looked at him. "He will lead the hunt."

"Moketubbe?" Berry said. "Do you think he will? A man to whom even talking is travail?"

"What else can he do? It is his own father who will soon begin to smell."

"That is true," Berry said. "There is even yet a price he must pay for the shoes. Yao. He has truly bought them. What do you think?"

"What do you think?"

"What do you think?"

"I think nothing."

"Nor do I. Issetibbeha will not need the shoes now. Let Moketubbe have them; Issetibbeha will not care."

"Yao. Man must die."

"Yao. Let him; there is still the Man."

The bark roof of the porch was supported by peeled cypress poles, high above the texas of the steamboat, shading an unfloored banquette where on the trodden earth mules and horses were tethered in bad weather. On the forward end of the steamboat's deck sat an old man and two women. One of the women was dressing a fowl, the other was shelling corn. The old man was talking. He was barefoot, in a long linen frock coat and a beaver hat.

"This world is going to the dogs," he said. "It is being ruined by white men. We got along fine for years and years, before the white men foisted their Negroes upon us. In the old days the old men sat in the shade and ate stewed deer's flesh and corn and smoked tobacco and talked of honor and grave affairs; now what do we do? Even the old wear themselves into the grave taking care of them that like sweating." When Basket and Berry crossed the deck he ceased and looked up at them. His eyes were querulous, bleared; his face was myriad with tiny wrinkles. "He is fled also," he said.

"Yes," Berry said, "he is gone."

"I knew it. I told them so. It will take three weeks, like when Doom died. You watch and see."

"It was three days, not three weeks," Berry said.

"Were you there?"

"No," Berry said. "But I have heard."

"Well, I was there," the old man said. "For three whole weeks, through the swamps and the briers—" They went on and left him talking.

What had been the saloon of the steamboat was now a shell, rotting slowly; the polished mahogany, the carving glinting momentarily and fading through the mold in figures cabalistic and profound; the gutted windows were like cataracted eyes. It contained a few sacks of seed or grain, and the fore part of the running gear of a barouche, to the axle of which two C-springs rusted in graceful curves, supporting nothing. In one corner a fox cub ran steadily and soundlessly up and down a willow cage; three scrawny gamecocks moved in the dust, and the place was pocked and marked with their dried droppings.

They passed through the brick wall and entered a big room of chinked logs. It contained the hinder part of the barouche, and the dismantled body lying on its side, the window slatted over with willow withes, through which protruded the heads, the still, beady, outraged eyes and frayed combs of still more game chickens. It was floored with packed clay; in one corner leaned a crude plow and two hand-hewn boat paddles. From the ceiling, suspended by four deer thongs, hung the gilt bed which Issetibbeha had fetched from Paris. It had neither mattress nor springs, the frame crisscrossed now by a neat hammocking of thongs.

Issetibbeha had tried to have his newest wife, the young one, sleep in the bed. He was congenitally short of breath himself, and he passed the nights half reclining in his splint chair. He would see her to bed and, later, wakeful, sleeping as he did but three or four hours a night, he would sit in the darkness and simulate slumber and listen to her sneak infinitesimally from the gilt and ribboned bed, to lie on a quilt pallet on the floor until just before daylight. Then she would enter the bed quietly again and in turn simulate slumber, while in the darkness beside her Issetibbeha quietly laughed and laughed.

The girandoles were lashed by thongs to two sticks propped in a corner where a ten-gallon whisky keg lay also. There was a clay hearth; facing it, in the splint chair, Moketubbe sat. He was maybe an inch better than five feet tall, and he weighed two hundred and fifty pounds. He wore a broadcloth coat and no shirt, his round, smooth copper balloon of belly swelling above the bottom piece of a suit of linen underwear. On his feet were the slippers with the red heels. Behind his chair stood a stripling with a punkah-like fan made of fringed paper. Moketubbe sat motionless, with his broad, yellow face with its closed eyes and flat nostrils, his flipperlike arms extended. On his face was an expression profound, tragic, and inert. He did not open his eyes when Basket and Berry came in.

"He has worn them since daylight?" Basket said.

"Since daylight," the stripling said. The fan did not cease. "You can see."

"Yao," Basket said. "We can see." Moketubbe did not move. He looked like an effigy, like a Malay god in frock coat, drawers, naked chest, the trivial scarlet-heeled shoes.

"I wouldn't disturb him, if I were you," the stripling said.

"Not if I were you," Basket said. He and Berry squatted. The stripling moved the fan steadily. "O Man," Basket said, "listen." Moketubbe did not move. "He is gone," Basket said.

"I told you so," the stripling said. "I knew he would flee. I told you."

"Yao," Basket said. "You are not the first to tell us afterward what we should have known before. Why is it that some of you wise men took no steps yesterday to prevent this?"

"He does not wish to die," Berry said.

"Why should he not wish it?" Basket said.

"Because he must die some day is no reason," the stripling said. "That would not convince me either, old man."

"Hold your tongue," Berry said.

"For twenty years," Basket said, "while others of his race sweat in the fields, he served the Man in the shade. Why should he not wish to die, since he did not wish to sweat?"

"And it will be quick," Berry said. "It will not take long."

"Catch him and tell him that," the stripling said.

"Hush," Berry said. They squatted, watching Moketubbe's face. He might have been dead himself. It was as though he were cased so in flesh that even breathing took place too deep within him to show.

"Listen, O Man," Basket said. "Issetibbeha is dead. He waits. His dog and his horse we have. But his slave has fled. The one who held the pot for him, who ate of his food, from his dish, is fled. Issetibbeha waits."

"Yao," Berry said.

"This is not the first time," Basket said. "This happened when Doom, thy grandfather, lay waiting at the door of the earth. He lay waiting three days, saying, 'Where is my Negro?' And Issetibbeha, thy father, answered, 'I will find him. Rest; I will bring him to you so that you may begin the journey.'"

"Yao," Berry said.

Moketubbe had not moved, had not opened his eyes.

"For three days Issetibbeha hunted in the bottom," Basket said. "He did not even return home for food, until the Negro was with him; then he said to Doom, his father, 'Here is thy dog, thy horse, thy Negro; rest.' Issetibbeha, who is dead since yesterday, said it. And now Issetibbeha's Negro is fled. His horse and his dog wait with him, but his Negro is fled."

"Yao," Berry said.

Moketubbe had not moved. His eyes were closed; upon his supine monstrous shape there was a colossal inertia, something profoundly immobile, beyond and impervious to flesh. They watched his face, squatting.

"When thy father was newly the Man, this happened," Basket said. "And it was Issetibbeha who brought back the slave to where his father waited to enter the earth." Moketubbe's face had not moved, his eyes had not moved. After a while Basket said, "Remove the shoes."

The stripling removed the shoes. Moketubbe began to pant, his bare chest moving deep, as though he were rising from beyond his unfathomed flesh back into life, like up from the water, the sea. But his eyes had not opened yet.

Berry said, "He will lead the hunt."

"Yao," Basket said. "He is the Man. He will lead the hunt."

IV

All that day the Negro, Issetibbeha's body servant, hidden in the barn, watched Issetibbeha's dying. He was forty, a Guinea man. He had a flat nose, a close, small head; the inside corners of his eyes showed red a little, and his prominent gums were a pale bluish red above his square, broad teeth. He had been taken at fourteen by a trader off Kamerun, before his teeth had been filed. He had been Issetibbeha's body servant for twenty-three years.

On the day before, the day on which Issetibbeha lay sick, he returned to the quarters at dusk. In that unhurried hour the smoke of the cooking fires blew slowly across the street from door to door, carrying into the opposite one the smell of the identical meat and bread. The women tended them; the men were gathered at the head of the lane, watching him as he came down the slope from the house, putting his naked feet down carefully in a strange dusk. To the waiting men his eyeballs were a little luminous.

"Issetibbeha is not dead yet," the headman said.

"Not dead," the body servant said. "Who not dead?"

In the dusk they had faces like his, the different ages, the thoughts sealed inscrutable behind faces like the death masks of apes. The smell of the fires, the cooking, blew sharp and slow across the strange dusk, as from another world, above the lane and the pickaninnies naked in the dust.

"If he lives past sundown, he will live until daybreak," one said.

"Who says?"

"Talk says."

"Yao. Talk says. We know but one thing." They looked at the body servant as he stood among them, his eyeballs a little luminous. He was breathing slow and deep. His chest was bare, he was sweating a little. "He knows. He knows it."

"Let us let the drums talk."

"Yao. Let the drums tell it."

The drums began after dark. They kept them hidden in the creek bottom. They were made of hollowed cypress knees, and the Negroes kept them hidden; why, none knew. They were buried in the mud on the bank of a slough; a lad of fourteen guarded them. He was undersized, and a mute; he squatted in the mud there all day, clouded over with mosquitoes, naked save for the mud with which he coated himself against the mosquitoes, and about his neck a fiber bag containing a pig's rib to which black shreds of flesh still adhered, and two scaly barks on a wire. He slobbered onto his clutched knees, drooling; now and then Indians came noiselessly out of the bushes behind him and stood there and contemplated him for a while and went away, and he never knew it.

From the loft of the stable where he lay hidden until dark and after, the Negro could hear the drums. They were three miles away, but he could hear them as though they were in the barn itself below him, thudding and thudding. It was as though he could see the fire too, and the black limbs turning into and out of the flames in copper gleams. Only there would be no fire. There would be no more light there than where he lay in the dusty loft, with the whispering arpeggios of rat feet along the warm and immemorial ax-squared rafters. The only fire there would be the smudge against mosquitoes where the women with nursing children crouched, their heavy sluggish breasts nippled full and smooth into the mouths of men children; contemplative, oblivious of the drumming, since a fire would signify life.

There was a fire in the steamboat, where Issetibbeha lay dying among his wives, beneath the lashed girandoles and the suspended bed. He could see the smoke, and just before sunset he saw the doctor come out, in a waistcoat made of skunk skins, and set fire to two clay-daubed sticks at the bows of the boat deck. "So he is not dead yet," the Negro said into the whispering gloom of the loft, answering himself; he could hear the two voices, himself and himself:

"Who not dead?"

"You are dead."

"Yao, I am dead," he said quietly. He wished to be where the drums were. He imagined himself springing out of the bushes, leaping among the drums on his bare, lean, greasy, invisible limbs. But he could not do that, because man leaped past life, into where death was; he dashed into death and did not die, because when death took a man, it took him just this side of the end of living. It was when death overran him from behind, still in life. The thin whisper of rat feet died in fainting gusts along the rafters. Once he had eaten rat. He was a boy then, but just come to America. They had lived ninety days in a three-foot-high 'tween-deck in tropic latitudes, hearing from topside the drunken New England captain intoning aloud from a book which he did not recognize for ten years afterward to be the Bible. Squatting in the stable so, he had watched the rat, civilized, by association with man reft of its inherent cunning of limb and eye; he had caught it without difficulty, with scarce a movement of his hand, and he ate it slowly, wondering how any of the rats had escaped so long. At that time he was still wearing the single white garment which the trader, a deacon in the Unitarian church, had given him, and he spoke then only his native tongue.

He was naked now, save for a pair of dungaree pants bought by Indians from white men, and an amulet slung on a thong about his hips. The amulet consisted of one half of a mother-of-pearl lorgnon which Issetibbeha had brought back from Paris, and the skull of a cottonmouth moccasin. He had killed the snake himself and eaten it, save the poison head. He lay in the loft, watching the house, the steamboat, listening to the drums, thinking of himself among the drums.

He lay there all night. The next morning he saw the doctor come out, in his skunk vest, and get on his mule and ride away, and he became quite still and watched the final dust from beneath the mule's delicate feet die away, and then he found that he was still breathing and it seemed strange to him that he still breathed air, still needed air. Then he lay and watched quietly, waiting to move, his eyeballs a little luminous, but with a quiet light, and his breathing light and regular, and saw Louis Berry come out and look at the sky. It was good light then, and already five Indians squatted in their Sunday clothes along the steamboat deck; by noon there were twenty-five there. That afternoon they dug the trench in which the meat would be baked, and the yams; by that time there were almost a hundred guests—decorous, quiet, patient in their stiff European finery—and he watched Berry lead Issetibbeha's mare from the stable and tie her to a tree, and then he watched Berry emerge from the house with the old hound which lay beside Issetibbeha's chair. He tied the hound to the tree too, and it sat there, looking gravely about at the faces. Then it began to howl. It was still howling at sundown, when the Negro climbed down the back wall of the barn and entered the spring branch, where it was already dusk. He began to run then. He could hear the hound howling behind him, and near the spring, already running, he passed another Negro. The two men, the one motionless and the other running, looked for an instant at each other as though across an actual boundary between two different worlds. He ran on into full darkness, mouth closed, fists doubled, his broad nostrils bellowing steadily.

He ran on in the darkness. He knew the country well, because he had hunted it often with Issetibbeha, following on his mule the course of the fox or the cat beside Issetibbeha's mare; he knew it as well as did the men who would pursue him. He saw them for the first time shortly before sunset of the second day. He had run thirty miles then, up the creek bottom, before doubling back; lying in a pawpaw thicket he saw the pursuit for the first time. There were two of them, in shirts and straw hats, carrying their neatly rolled trousers under their arms, and they had no weapons. They were middle-aged, paunchy, and they could not have moved very fast anyway; it would be twelve hours before they could return to where he lay watching them. "So I will have until midnight to rest," he said. He was near enough to the plantation to smell the cooking fires, and he thought how he ought to be hungry, since he had not eaten in thirty hours. "But it is more important to rest," he told himself. He continued to tell himself that, lying in the pawpaw thicket, because the effort of resting, the need and the haste to rest, made his heart thud the same as the running had done. It was as though he had forgot how to rest, as though the six hours were not long enough to do it in, to remember again how to do it.

As soon as dark came he moved again. He had thought to keep going steadily and quietly through the night, since there was nowhere for him to go, but as soon as he moved he began to run at top speed, breasting his panting chest, his broad-flaring nostrils through the choked and whipping darkness. He ran for an hour, lost by then, without direction, when suddenly he stopped, and after a time his thudding heart unraveled from the sound of the drums. By the sound they were not two miles away; he followed the sound until he could smell the smudge fire and taste the acrid smoke. When he stood among them the drums did not cease; only the headman came to him where he stood in the drifting smudge, panting, his nostrils flaring and pulsing, the hushed glare of his ceaseless eyeballs in his mud-daubed face as though they were worked from lungs.

"We have expected thee," the headman said. "Go, now."

"Go?"

"Eat, and go. The dead may not consort with the living; thou knowest that."

"Yao. I know that." They did not look at one another. The drums had not ceased.

"Wilt thou eat?" the headman said.

"I am not hungry. I caught a rabbit this afternoon, and ate while I lay hidden."

"Take some cooked meat with thee, then."

He accepted the cooked meat, wrapped in leaves, and entered the creek bottom again; after a while the sound of the drums ceased. He walked steadily until daybreak. "I have twelve hours," he said. "Maybe more, since the trail was followed by night." He squatted and ate the meat and wiped his hands on his thighs. Then he rose and removed the dungaree pants and squatted again beside a slough and coated himself with mud—face, arms, body and legs—and squatted again, clasping his knees, his head bowed. When it was light enough to see, he moved back into the swamp and squatted again and went to sleep so. He did not dream at all. It was well that he moved, for, waking suddenly in broad daylight and the high sun, he saw the two Indians. They still carried their neatly rolled trousers; they stood opposite the place where he lay hidden, paunchy, thick, soft-looking, a little ludicrous in their straw hats and shirt tails.

"This is wearying work," one said.

"I'd rather be at home in the shade myself," the other said. "But there is the Man waiting at the door to the earth."

"Yao." They looked quietly about; stooping, one of them removed from his shirt tail a clot of cockleburs. "Damn that Negro," he said.

"Yao. When have they ever been anything but a trial and a care to us?"

In the early afternoon, from the top of a tree, the Negro looked down into the plantation. He could see Issetibbeha's body in a hammock between the two trees where the horse and the dog were tethered, and the concourse about the steamboat was filled with wagons and horses and mules, with carts and saddle-horses, while in bright clumps the women and the smaller children and the old men squatted about the long trench where the smoke from the barbecuing meat blew slow and thick. The men and the big boys would all be down there in the creek bottom behind him, on the trail, their Sunday clothes rolled carefully up and wedged into tree crotches. There was a clump of men near the door to the house, to the saloon of the steamboat, though, and he watched them, and after a while he saw them bring Moketubbe out in a litter made of buckskin and persimmon poles; high hidden in his leafed nook the Negro, the quarry, looked quietly down upon his irrevocable doom with an expression as profound as Moketubbe's own. "Yao," he said quietly. "He will go then. That man whose body has been dead for fifteen years, he will go also."

In the middle of the afternoon he came face to face with an Indian. They were both on a footlog across a slough—the Negro gaunt, lean, hard, tireless and desperate; the Indian thick, soft-looking, the apparent embodiment of the ultimate and the supreme reluctance and inertia. The

Indian made no move, no sound; he stood on the log and watched the Negro plunge into the slough and swim ashore and crash away into the undergrowth.

Just before sunset he lay behind a down log. Up the log in slow procession moved a line of ants. He caught them and ate them slowly, with a kind of detachment, like that of a dinner guest eating salted nuts from a dish. They too had a salt taste, engendering a salivary reaction out of all proportion. He ate them slowly, watching the unbroken line move up the log and into oblivious doom with a steady and terrific undeviation. He had eaten nothing else all day; in his caked mud mask his eyes rolled in reddened rims. At sunset, creeping along the creek bank toward where he had spotted a frog, a cottonmouth moccasin slashed him suddenly across the forearm with a thick, sluggish blow. It struck clumsily, leaving two long slashes across his arm like two razor slashes, and half sprawled with its own momentum and rage, it appeared for the moment utterly helpless with its own awkwardness and choleric anger. "Olé, grandfather," the Negro said. He touched its head and watched it slash him again across his arm, and again, with thick, raking, awkward blows. "It's that I do not wish to die," he said. Then he said it again—"It's that I do not wish to die"—in a quiet tone, of slow and low amaze, as though it were something that, until the words had said themselves, he found that he had not known, or had not known the depth and extent of his desire.

V

Moketubbe took the slippers with him. He could not wear them very long while in motion, not even in the litter where he was slung reclining, so they rested upon a square of fawnskin upon his lap—the cracked, frail slippers a little shapeless now, with their scaled patent-leather surfaces and buckleless tongues and scarlet heels, lying upon the supine obese shape just barely alive, carried through swamp and brier by swinging relays of men who bore steadily all day long the crime and its object, on the business of the slain. To Moketubbe it must have been as though, himself immortal, he were being carried rapidly through hell by doomed spirits which, alive, had contemplated his disaster, and, dead, were oblivious partners to his damnation.

After resting for a while, the litter propped in the center of the squatting circle and Moketubbe motionless in it, with closed eyes and his face at once peaceful for the instant and filled with inescapable foreknowledge, he could wear the slippers for a while. The stripling put them on him, forcing his big, tender, dropsical feet into them; whereupon into his face came again that expression tragic, passive and profoundly attentive, which dyspeptics wear. Then they went on. He made no move, no sound, inert in the rhythmic litter out of some reserve of inertia, or maybe of some kingly virtue such as courage or fortitude. After a time they set the litter down and looked at him, at the yellow face like that of an idol, beaded over with sweat. Then Three Basket or Had-Two-Fathers would say: "Take them off. Honor has been served." They would remove the shoes. Moketubbe's face would not alter, but only then would his breathing become perceptible, going in and out of his pale lips with a faint ah-ah-ah sound, and they would squat again while the couriers and the runners came up.

"Not yet?"

"Not yet. He is going east. By sunset he will reach Mouth of Tippah. Then he will turn back. We may take him tomorrow."

"Let us hope so. It will not be too soon."

"Yao. It has been three days now."

"When Doom died, it took only three days."

"But that was an old man. This one is young."

"Yao. A good race. If he is taken tomorrow, I will win a horse."

"May you win it."

"Yao. This work is not pleasant."

That was the day on which the food gave out at the plantation. The guests returned home and came back the next day with more food, enough for a week longer. On that day Issetibbeha began to smell; they could smell him for a long way up and down the bottom when it got hot toward noon and the wind blew. But they didn't capture the Negro on that day, nor on the next. It was about dusk on the sixth day when the couriers came up to the litter; they had found blood. "He has injured himself."

"Not bad, I hope," Basket said. "We cannot send with Issetibbeha one who will be of no service to him."

"Nor whom Issetibbeha himself will have to nurse and care for," Berry said.

"We do not know," the courier said. "He has hidden himself. He has crept back into the swamp. We have left pickets."

They trotted with the litter now. The place where the Negro had crept into the swamp was an hour away. In the hurry and excitement they had forgotten that Moketubbe still wore the slippers; when they reached the place Moketubbe had fainted. They removed the slippers and brought him to.

With dark, they formed a circle about the swamp. They squatted, clouded over with gnats and mosquitoes; the evening star burned low and close down the west, and the constellations began to wheel overhead. "We will give him time," they said. "Tomorrow is just another name for today."

"Yao. Let him have time." Then they ceased, and gazed as one into the darkness where the swamp lay. After a while the noise ceased, and soon the courier came out of the darkness.

"He tried to break out."

"But you turned him back?"

"He turned back. We feared for a moment, the three of us. We could smell him creeping in the darkness, and we could smell something else, which we did not know. That was why we feared, until he told us. He said to slay him there, since it would be dark and he would not have to see the face when it came. But it was not that which we smelled; he told us what it was. A snake had struck him. That was two days ago. The arm swelled, and it smelled bad. But it was not that which we smelled then, because the swelling had gone down and his arm was no larger than that of a child. He showed us. We felt the arm, all of us did; it was no larger than that of a child. He said to give him a hatchet so he could chop the arm off. But tomorrow is today also."

"Yao. Tomorrow is today."

"We feared for a while. Then he went back into the swamp."

"That is good."

"Yao. We feared. Shall I tell the Man?"

"I will see," Basket said. He went away. The courier squatted, telling again about the Negro. Basket returned. "The Man says that it is good. Return to your post."

The courier crept away. They squatted about the litter; now and then they slept. Sometime after midnight the Negro waked them. He began to shout and talk to himself, his voice coming sharp and sudden out of the darkness, then he fell silent. Dawn came; a white crane flapped slowly across the jonquil sky. Basket was awake. "Let us go now," he said. "It is today."

Two Indians entered the swamp, their movements noisy. Before they reached the Negro they stopped, because he began to sing. They could see him, naked and mud-caked, sitting on a log, singing. They squatted silently a short distance away, until he finished. He was chanting something in his own language, his face lifted to the rising sun. His voice was clear, full, with a quality wild and sad. "Let him have time," the Indians said, squatting, patient, waiting. He ceased and they approached. He looked back and up at them through the cracked mud mask. His eyes were bloodshot, his lips cracked upon his square short teeth. The mask of mud appeared to be loose on his face, as if he might have lost flesh since he put it there; he held his left arm close to his breast. From the elbow down it was caked and shapeless with black mud. They could smell him, a rank smell. He watched them quietly until one touched him on the arm. "Come," the Indian said. "You ran well. Do not be ashamed."

VI

As they neared the plantation in the tainted bright morning, the Negro's eyes began to roll a little, like those of a horse. The smoke from the cooking pit blew low along the earth and upon the squatting and waiting guests about the yard and upon the steamboat deck, in their bright, stiff, harsh finery; the women, the children, the old men. They had sent couriers along the bottom, and another on ahead, and Issetibbeha's body had already been removed to where the grave waited, along with the horse and the dog, though they could still smell him in death about the house where he had lived in life. The guests were beginning to move toward the grave when the bearers of Moketubbe's litter mounted the slope.

The Negro was the tallest there, his high, close, mud-caked head looming above them all. He was breathing hard, as though the desperate effort of the six suspended and desperate days had catapulted upon him at once; although they walked slowly, his naked scarred chest rose and fell above the close-clutched left arm. He looked this way and that continuously, as if he were not seeing, as though sight never quite caught up with the looking. His mouth was open a little upon his big white teeth;

he began to pant. The already moving guests halted, pausing, looking back, some with pieces of meat in their hands, as the Negro looked about at their faces with his wild, restrained, unceasing eyes.

"Will you eat first?" Basket said. He had to say it twice.

"Yes," the Negro said. "That's it. I want to eat."

The throng had begun to press back toward the center; the word passed to the outermost: "He will eat first."

They reached the steamboat. "Sit down," Basket said. The Negro sat on the edge of the deck. He was still panting, his chest rising and falling, his head ceaseless with its white eyeballs, turning from side to side. It was as if the inability to see came from within, from hopelessness, not from absence of vision. They brought food and watched quietly as he tried to eat it. He put the food into his mouth and chewed it, but chewing, the half-masticated matter began to emerge from the corners of his mouth and to drool down his chin, onto his chest, and after a while he stopped chewing and sat there, naked, covered with dried mud, the plate on his knees, and his mouth filled with a mass of chewed food, open, his eyes wide and unceasing, panting and panting. They watched him, patient, implacable, waiting.

"Come," Basket said at last.

"It's water I want," the Negro said. "I want water."

The well was a little way down the slope toward the quarters. The slope lay dappled with the shadows of noon, of that peaceful hour when, Issetibbeha napping in his chair and waiting for the noon meal and the long afternoon to sleep in, the Negro, the body servant, would be free. He would sit in the kitchen door then, talking with the women who prepared the food. Beyond the kitchen the lane between the quarters would be quiet, peaceful, with the women talking to one another across the lane and the smoke of the dinner fires blowing upon the pickaninnies like ebony toys in the dust.

"Come," Basket said.

The Negro walked among them, taller than any. The guests were moving on toward where Issetibbeha and the horse and the dog waited. The Negro walked with his high ceaseless head, his panting chest. "Come," Basket said. "You wanted water."

"Yes," the Negro said. "Yes." He looked back at the house, then down to the quarters, where today no fire burned, no face showed in any door, no pickaninny in the dust, panting. "It struck me here, raking me across this arm; once, twice, three times. I said, 'Olé, Grandfather.' "

"Come now," Basket said. The Negro was still going through the motion of walking, his knee action high, his head high, as though he were on a treadmill. His eyeballs had a wild, restrained glare, like those of a horse. "You wanted water," Basket said. "Here it is."

There was a gourd in the well. They dipped it full and gave it to the Negro, and they watched him try to drink. His eyes had not ceased as he tilted the gourd slowly against his caked face. They could watch his throat working and the bright water cascading from either side of the gourd, down his chin and breast. Then the water stopped. "Come," Basket said.

"Wait," the Negro said. He dipped the gourd again and tilted it against his face, beneath his ceaseless eyes. Again they watched his throat working and the unswallowed water sheathing broken and myriad down his chin, channeling his caked chest. They waited, patient, grave, decorous, implacable; clansman and guest and kin. Then the water ceased, though still the empty gourd tilted higher and higher, and still his black throat aped the vain motion of his frustrated swallowing. A piece of water-loosened mud carried away from his chest and broke at his muddy feet, and in the empty gourd they could hear his breath: ah-ah-ah.

"Come," Basket said, taking the gourd from the Negro and hanging it back in the well.

THE WOMAN WHO RODE AWAY

by D. H. Lawrence

I

She had thought that this marriage, of all marriages, would be an adventure. Not that the man himself was exactly magical to her. A little, wiry, twisted fellow, twenty years older than herself, with brown eyes and greying hair, who had come to America a scrap of a wastrel, from Holland, years ago, as a tiny boy, and from the gold-mines of the west had been kicked south into Mexico, and now was more or less rich, owning silver-mines in the wilds of the Sierra Madre: it was obvious that the adventure lay in his circumstances, rather than his person. But he was still a little dynamo of energy, in spite of accidents survived, and what he had accomplished he had accomplished alone. One of those human oddments there is no accounting for.

When she actually *saw* what he had accomplished, her heart quailed. Great green-covered, unbroken mountain-hills, and in the midst of the lifeless isolation, the sharp pinkish mounds of the dried mud from the silver-works. Under the nakedness of the works, the walled-in, one-storey adobe house, with its garden inside, and its deep inner veranda with tropical climbers on the sides. And when you looked up from this shut-in flowered patio, you saw the huge pink cone of the silver-mud refuse, and the machinery of the extracting plant against heaven above. No more.

To be sure, the great wooden doors were often open. And then she could stand outside, in the vast open world. And see great, void, tree-clad hills piling behind one another, from nowhere into nowhere. They were green in autumn-time. For the rest, pinkish, stark dry and abstract.

And in his battered Ford car her husband would take her into the dead, thrice-dead little Spanish town forgotten among the mountains. The great, sun-dried dead church, the dead portales, the hopeless covered market-place, where, the first time she went, she saw a dead dog lying between the meat-stalls and the vegetable array, stretched out as if for ever, nobody troubling to throw it away. Deadness within deadness.

Everybody feebly talking silver, and showing bits of ore. But silver was at a standstill. The great war came and went. Silver was a dead market. Her husband's mines were closed down. But she and he lived on in the adobe house under the works, among the flowers that were never very flowery to her.

She had two children, a boy and a girl. And her eldest, the boy, was nearly ten years old before she aroused from her stupor of subjected amazement. She was now thirty-three, a large, blue-eyed, dazed woman, beginning to grow stout. Her little, wiry, tough, twisted, brown-eyed husband was fifty-three, a man as tough as wire, tenacious as wire, still full of energy, but dimmed by the lapse of silver from the market, and by some curious inaccessibility on his wife's part.

He was a man of principles, and a good husband. In a way, he doted on her. He never quite got over his dazzled admiration of her. But essentially, he was still a bachelor. He had been thrown out on the world, a little bachelor, at the age of ten. When he married he was over forty, and had enough money to marry on. But his capital was all a bachelor's. He was boss of his own works, and marriage was the last and most intimate bit of his own works.

He admired his wife to extinction, he admired her body, all her points. And she was to him always the rather dazzling Californian girl from Berkeley, whom he had first known. Like any sheikh, he kept her guarded among those mountains of Chihuahua. He was jealous of her as he was of his silver-mine: and that is saying a lot.

At thirty-three she really was still the girl from Berkeley, in all but physique. Her conscious development had stopped mysteriously with her marriage, completely arrested. Her husband had never become real to her, neither mentally nor physically. In spite of his late sort of passion for her, he never meant anything to her, physically. Only morally he swayed her, downed her, kept her in an invincible slavery.

So the years went by, in the adobe house strung round the sunny patio, with the silver-works overhead. Her husband was never still. When the silver went dead, he ran a ranch lower down, some twenty miles away, and raised pure-bred hogs, splendid creatures. At the same time, he hated pigs. He was a squeamish waif of an idealist, and really hated the physical side of life. He loved work, work, work, and making things. His marriage, his children, were something he was making, part of his business, but with a sentimental income this time.

Gradually her nerves began to go wrong: she must get out. She must get out. So he took her to El Paso for three months. And at least it was the United States.

But he kept his spell over her. The three months ended: back she was, just the same, in her adobe house among those eternal green or pinky-brown hills, void as only the undiscovered is void. She taught her children, she supervised the Mexican boys who were her servants. And sometimes her husband brought visitors, Spaniards or Mexicans or occasionally white men.

He really loved to have white men staying on the place. Yet he had not a moment's peace when they were there. It was as if his wife were some peculiar secret vein of ore in his mines, which no one must be aware of except himself. And she was fascinated by the young gentlemen, mining engineers, who were his guests at times. He, too, was fascinated by a real gentleman. But he was an old-timer miner with a wife, and if a gentleman looked at his wife, he felt as if his mine were being looted, the secrets of it pried out.

It was one of these young gentlemen who put the idea into her mind. They were all standing outside the great wooden doors of the patio, looking at the outer world. The eternal, motionless hills were all green, it was September, after the rains. There was no sign of anything, save the deserted mine, the deserted works, and a bunch of half-deserted miners' dwellings.

"I wonder," said the young man, "what there is behind those great blank hills."

"More hills," said Lederman. "If you go that way, Sonora and the coast. This way is the desert—you came from there—and the other way, hills and mountains."

"Yes, but what *lives* in the hills and the mountains? *Surely* there is something wonderful? It looks *so* like nowhere on earth: like being on the moon."

"There's plenty of game, if you want to shoot. And Indians, if you call *them* wonderful."

"Wild ones?"

"Wild enough."

"But friendly?"

"It depends. Some of them are quite wild, and they don't let anybody near. They kill a missionary at sight. And where a missionary can't get, nobody can."

"But what does the government say?"

"They're so far from everywhere, the government leaves 'em alone. And they're wily; if they think there'll be trouble, they send a delegation to Chihuahua and make a formal submission. The government is glad to leave it at that."

"And do they live quite wild, with their own savage customs and religion?"

"Oh yes. They use nothing but bows and arrows. I've seen them in town, in the Plaza, with funny sort of hats with flowers round them, and a bow in one hand, quite naked except for a sort of shirt, even in cold weather—striding round with their savage's bare legs."

"But don't you suppose it's wonderful, up there in their secret villages?"

"No. What would there be wonderful about it? Savages are savages, and all savages behave more or less alike: rather low-down and dirty, unsanitary, with a few cunning tricks, and struggling to get enough to eat."

"But surely they have old, old religions and mysteries—it *must* be wonderful, surely it must."

"I don't know about mysteries—howling and heathen practices, more or less indecent. No, I see nothing wonderful in that kind of stuff. And I wonder that you should, when you have lived in London or Paris or New York—"

"Ah, *everybody* lives in London or Paris or New York"—said the young man, as if this were an argument.

And this particular vague enthusiasm for unknown Indians found a full echo in the woman's heart. She was overcome by a foolish romanticism more unreal than a girl's. She felt it was her destiny to wander into the secret haunts of these timeless, mysterious, marvellous Indians of the mountains.

She kept her secret. The young man was departing, her husband was going with him down to Torreon, on business: would be away for some days. But before the departure, she made her husband talk about the Indians: about the wandering tribes, resembling the Navajo, who were still wandering free; and the Yaquis of Sonora: and the different groups in the different valleys of Chihuahua State.

There was supposed to be one tribe, the Chilchuis, living in a high valley to the south, who were the sacred tribe of all the Indians. The descendants of Montezuma and the old Aztec or Totonac kings still lived among them, and the old priests still kept up the ancient religion, and offered human sacrifices—so it was said. Some scientists had been to the Chilchui country, and had come back gaunt and exhausted with hunger and bitter privation, bringing various curious, barbaric objects of worship, but having seen nothing extraordinary in the hungry, stark village of savages.

Though Lederman talked in this off-hand way, it was obvious he felt some of the vulgar excitement at the idea of ancient and mysterious savages.

"How far away are they?" she asked.

"Oh—three days on horseback—past Cuchitee and a little lake there is up there."

Her husband and the young man departed. The woman made her crazy plans. Of late, to break the monotony of her life, she had harassed her husband into letting her go riding with him, occasionally, on horseback. She was never allowed to go out alone. The country truly was not safe, lawless and crude.

But she had her own horse, and she dreamed of being free as she had been as a girl, among the hills of California.

Her daughter, nine years old, was now in a tiny convent in the little half-deserted Spanish mining-town five miles away.

"Manuel," said the woman to her house-servant, "I'm going to ride to the convent to see Margarita, and take her a few things. Perhaps I shall stay the night in the convent. You look after Freddy and see everything is all right till I come back."

"Shall I ride with you on the master's horse, or shall Juan?" asked the servant.

"Neither of you. I shall go alone."

The young man looked her in the eyes, in protest. Absolutely impossible that the woman should ride alone!

"I shall go alone," repeated the large, placid-seeming, fair-complexioned woman, with peculiar overbearing emphasis. And the man silently, unhappily yielded.

"Why are you going alone, mother?" asked her son, as she made up parcels of food.

"Am I *never* to be let alone? Not one moment of my life?" she cried, with sudden explosion of energy. And the child, like the servant, shrank into silence.

She set off without a qualm, riding astride on her strong roan horse, and wearing a riding-suit of coarse linen, a riding-skirt over her linen breeches, a scarlet neck-tie over her white blouse, and a black felt hat on her head. She had food in her saddle-bags, an army canteen with water, and a large, native blanket tied on behind the saddle. Peering into the distance, she set off from her home. Manuel and the little boy stood in the gateway to watch her go. She did not even turn to wave them farewell.

But when she had ridden about a mile, she left the wild road and took a small trail to the right, that led into another valley, over steep places and past great trees, and through another deserted mining settlement. It was September, the water was running freely in the little stream that had fed the now-abandoned mine. She got down to drink, and let the horse drink too.

She saw natives coming through the trees, away up the slope. They had seen her, and were watching her closely. She watched in turn. The three people, two women and a youth, were making a wide detour, so as not to come too close to her. She did not care. Mounting, she trotted ahead up the silent valley, beyond the silver-works, beyond any trace of mining. There was still a rough trail that led over rocks and loose stones into the valley beyond. This trail she had already ridden, with her husband. Beyond that she knew she must go south.

Curiously she was not afraid, although it was a frightening country, the silent, fatal-seeming mountains slopes, the occasional distant, suspicious, elusive natives among the trees, the great carrion birds occasionally hovering, like great flies, in the distance, over some carrion or some ranch-house or some group of huts.

As she climbed, the trees shrank and the trail ran through a thorny scrub, that was trailed over with blue convolvulus and an occasional pink creeper. Then these flowers lapsed. She was nearing the pine trees.

She was over the crest, and before her another silent, void, green-clad valley. It was past midday. Her horse turned to a little runlet of water, so she got down to eat her midday meal. She sat in silence looking at the motionless unliving valley, and at the sharp-peaked hills, rising higher to rock and pine trees, southwards. She rested two hours in the heat of the day, while the horse cropped around her.

Curious that she was neither afraid nor lonely. Indeed, the loneliness was like a drink of cold water to one who is very thirsty. And a strange elation sustained her from within.

She travelled on, and camped at night in a valley beside a stream, deep among the bushes. She had seen cattle and had crossed several trails. There must be a ranch not far off. She heard the strange wailing shriek of a mountain-lion, and the answer of dogs. But she sat by her small camp-fire in a secret hollow place and was not really afraid. She was buoyed up always by the curious, bubbling elation within her.

It was very cold before dawn. She lay wrapped in her blanket looking at the stars, listening to her horse shivering, and feeling like a woman who has died and passed beyond. She was not sure that she had not heard, during the night, a great crash at the centre of herself, which was the crash of her own death. Or else it was a crash at the centre of the earth, and meant something big and mysterious.

With the first peep of light she got up, numb with cold, and made a fire. She ate hastily, gave her horse some pieces of oil-seed cake, and set off again. She avoided any meeting—and since she met nobody, it was evident that she in turn was avoided. She came at last in sight of the village of Cuchitee, with its black houses with their reddish roofs, a sombre, dreary little cluster below another silent, long-abandoned mine. And beyond, a long, great mountain-side, rising up green and light to the darker, shaggier green of pine trees. And beyond the pine trees stretches of naked rock against the sky, rock slashed already and brindled with white stripes of snow. High up, the new snow had already begun to fall.

And now, as she neared, more or less, her destination, she began to go vague and disheartened. She had passed the little lake among yellowing aspen trees whose white trunks were round and suave like the white round arms of some woman. What a lovely place! In California she would have raved about it. But here she looked and saw that it was lovely, but she didn't care. She was weary and spent with her two nights in the open, afraid of the coming night. She didn't know where she was going, or what she was going for. Her horse plodded dejectedly on, towards that immense and forbidding mountain-slope, following a stony little trail. And if she had had any will of her own left, she would have turned back, to the village, to be protected and sent home to her husband.

But she had no will of her own. Her horse splashed through a brook, and turned up a valley, under immense yellowing cottonwood trees. She must have been near nine thousand feet above sea-level, and her head was light with the altitude and with weariness. Beyond the cottonwood trees she could see, on each side, the steep sides of mountain-slopes hemming her in, sharp-plumaged with overlapping aspen, and, higher up, with sprouting, pointed spruce and pine tree. Her horse went on automatically. In this tight valley, on this slight trail, there was nowhere to go but ahead, climbing.

Suddenly her horse jumped, and three men in dark blankets were on the trail before her.

"Adios!" came the greeting, in the full, restrained Indian voice.

"Adios!" she replied, in her assured, American woman's voice.

"Where are you going?" came the quiet question, in Spanish.

The men in the dark sarapes had come closer, and were looking up at her.

"On ahead," she replied coolly, in her hard, Saxon Spanish.

These were just natives to her: dark-faced, strongly-built men in dark sarapes and straw hats. They would have been the same as the men who worked for her husband, except, strangely, for the long black hair that fell over their shoulders. She noted this long black hair with a certain distaste. These must be the wild Indians she had come to see.

"Where do you come from?" the same man asked. It was always the one man who spoke. He was young, with quick, large, bright black eyes that glanced sideways at her. He had a soft black moustache on his dark face, and a sparse tuft of beard, loose hairs on his chin. His long black hair, full of life, hung unrestrained on his shoulders. Dark as he was, he did not look as if he had washed lately.

His two companions were the same, but older men, powerful and silent. One had a thin black line of moustache, but was beardless. The other had the smooth cheeks and the sparse dark hairs marking the lines of his chin with the beard characteristic of the Indians.

"I come from far away," she replied, with half-jocular evasion.

This was received in silence.

"But where do you live?" asked the young man, with that same quiet insistence.

"In the north," she replied airily.

Again there was a moment's silence. The young man conversed quietly, in Indian, with his two companions.

"Where do you want to go, up this way?" he asked suddenly, with challenge and authority, pointing briefly up the trail.

"To the Chilchui Indians," answered the woman laconically.

The young man looked at her. His eyes were quick and black, and inhuman. He saw, in the full evening light, the faint sub-smile of assurance on her rather large, calm, fresh-complexioned face; the weary, bluish lines under her large blue eyes; and in her eyes, as she looked down at him, a half-childish, half-arrogant confidence in her own female power. But in her eyes also, a curious look of trance.

"*Usted es Señora*? You are a lady?" the Indian asked her.

"Yes, I am a lady," she replied complacently.

"With a family?"

"With a husband and two children, boy and girl," she said.

The Indian turned to his companions and translated, in the low, gurgling speech, like hidden water running. They were evidently at a loss.

"Where is your husband?" asked the young man.

"Who knows?" she replied airily. "He has gone away on business for a week."

The black eyes watched her shrewdly. She, for all her weariness, smiled faintly in the pride of her own adventure and the assurance of her own womanhood, and the spell of the madness that was on her.

"And what do *you* want to do?" the Indian asked her.

"I want to visit the Chilchui Indians—to see their houses and to know their gods," she replied.

The young man turned and translated quickly, and there was a silence almost of consternation. The grave elder men were glancing at her sideways, with strange looks, from under their decorated hats. And they said something to the young man, in deep chest voices.

The latter still hesitated. Then he turned to the woman.

"Good!" he said. "Let us go. But we cannot arrive until to-morrow. We shall have to make a camp to-night."

"Good!" she said. "I can make a camp."

Without more ado, they set off at a good speed up the stony trail. The young Indian ran alongside her horse's head, the other two ran behind. One of them had taken a thick stick, and occasionally he struck her horse a resounding blow on the haunch, to urge him forward. This made the horse jump, and threw her back in the saddle, which, tired as she was, made her angry.

"Don't do that!" she cried, looking round angrily at the fellow. She met his black, large, bright eyes, and for the first time her spirit really quailed. The man's eyes were not human to her, and they did not see her as a beautiful white woman. He looked at her with a black, bright inhuman look, and saw no woman in her at all. As if she were some strange, unaccountable *thing,* incomprehensible to him, but inimical. She sat in her saddle in wonder, feeling once more as if she had died. And again he struck her horse, and jerked her badly in the saddle.

All the passionate anger of the spoilt white woman rose in her. She pulled her horse to a standstill, and turned with blazing eyes to the man at her bridle.

"Tell that fellow not to touch my horse again," she cried.

She met the eyes of the young man, and in their bright black inscrutability she saw a fine spark, as in a snake's eye, of derision. He spoke to his companion in the rear, in the low tones of the Indian. The man with the stick listened without looking. Then, giving a strange low cry to the horse, he struck it again on the rear, so that it leaped forward spasmodically up the stony trail, scattering the stones, pitching the weary woman in her seat.

The anger flew like a madness into her eyes, she went white at the gills. Fiercely she reined in her horse. But before she could turn, the young Indian had caught the reins under the horse's throat, jerked them forward, and was trotting ahead rapidly, leading the horse.

The woman was powerless. And along with her supreme anger there came a slight thrill of exultation. She knew she was dead.

The sun was setting, a great yellow light flooded the last of the aspens, flared on the trunks of the pine trees, the pine needles bristled and stood out with dark lustre, the rocks glowed with unearthly glamour. And through the effulgence the Indian at her horse's head trotted unweariedly on, his dark blanket swinging, his bare legs glowing with a strange transfigured ruddiness in the powerful light, and his straw hat with its half-absurd decorations of flowers and feathers shining showily above his river of long black hair. At times he would utter a low call to the horse, and then the other Indian, behind, would fetch the beast a whack with the stick.

The wonder-light faded off the mountains, the world began to grow dark, a cold air breathed down. In the sky, half a moon was struggling against the glow in the west. Huge shadows came down from steep rocky slopes. Water was rushing. The woman was conscious only of her fatigue, her unspeakable fatigue, and the cold wind from the heights. She was not aware how moonlight replaced daylight. It happened while she travelled unconscious with weariness.

For some hours they travelled by moonlight. Then suddenly they came to a standstill. The men conversed in low tones for a moment.

"We camp here," said the young man.

She waited for him to help her down. He merely stood holding the horse's bridle. She almost fell from the saddle, so fatigued.

They had chosen a place at the foot of rocks that still gave off a little warmth of the sun. One man cut pine boughs, another erected little screens of pine boughs against the rock for shelter, and put boughs of balsam pine for beds. The third made a small fire, to heat tortillas. They worked in silence.

The woman drank water. She did not want to eat—only to lie down.

"Where do I sleep?" she asked.

The young man pointed to one of the shelters. She crept in and lay inert. She did not care what happened to her, she was so weary, and so beyond everything. Through the twigs of spruce she could see the three men squatting round the fire on their hams, chewing the tortillas they picked from the ashes with their dark fingers, and drinking water from a gourd. They talked in low, muttering tones, with long intervals of silence. Her saddle and saddle-bags lay not far from the fire, unopened, untouched. The men were not interested in her nor her belongings. There they squatted with their hats on their heads, eating, eating mechanically, like animals, the dark sarape with its fringe falling to the ground before and behind, the powerful dark legs naked and squatting like an animal's showing the dirty white shirt and the sort of loin-cloth which was the only other garment, underneath. And they showed no more sign of interest in her than if she had been a piece of venison they were bringing home from the hunt, and had hung inside a shelter.

After a while they carefully extinguished the fire, and went inside their own shelter. Watching through the screen of boughs, she had a moment's thrill of fear and anxiety, seeing the dark forms cross and pass silently in the moonlight. Would they attack her now?

But no! They were as if oblivious to her. Her horse was hobbled; she could hear it hopping wearily. All was silent, mountain-silent, cold, deathly. She slept and woke and slept in a semi-conscious numbness of cold and fatigue. A long, long night, icy and eternal, and she aware that she had died.

II

Yet when there was a stirring, and a clink of flint and steel, and the form of a man crouching like a dog over a bone, at a red splutter of fire, and she knew it was morning coming, it seemed to her the night had passed too soon.

When the fire was going, she came out of her shelter with one real desire left: for coffee. The men were warming more tortillas.

"Can we make coffee?" she asked.

The young man looked at her, and she imagined the same faint spark of derision in his eyes. He shook his head.

"We don't take it," he said. "There is no time."

And the elder men, squatting on their haunches, looked up at her in the terrible paling dawn, and there was not even derision in their eyes. Only that intense, yet remote, inhuman glitter which was terrible to her. They were inaccessible. They could not see her as a woman at all. As if she *were* not a woman. As if, perhaps, her whiteness took away all her womanhood, and left her as some giant, female white ant. That was all they could see in her.

Before the sun was up, she was in the saddle again, and they were climbing steeply, in the icy air. The sun came, and soon she was very hot, exposed to the glare in the bare places. It seemed to her they were climbing to the roof of the world. Beyond against heaven were slashes of snow.

During the course of the morning, they came to a place where the horse could not go farther. They rested for a time with a great slant of living rock in front of them, like the glossy breast of some earth-beast. Across this rock, along a wavering crack, they had to go. It seemed to her that for hours she went in torment, on her hands and knees, from crack to crevice, along the slanting face of this pure rock-mountain. An Indian in front and an Indian behind walked slowly erect, shod with sandals of braided leather. But she in her riding-boots dared not stand erect.

Yet what she wondered, all the time, was why she persisted in clinging and crawling along these mile-long sheets of rock. Why she did not hurl herself down, and have done! The world was below her.

When they emerged at last on a stony slope, she looked back, and saw the third Indian coming carrying her saddle and saddle-bags on his back, the whole hung from a band across his forehead. And he had his hat in his hand, as he stepped slowly, with the slow, soft, heavy tread of the Indian, unwavering in the chinks of rock, as if along a scratch in the mountain's iron shield.

The stony slope led downwards. The Indians seemed to grow excited. One ran ahead at a slow trot, disappearing round the curve of stones. And the track curved round and down, till at last in the full blaze of the mid-morning sun, they could see a valley below them, between walls of rock, as in a great wide chasm let in the mountains. A green valley, with a river, and trees, and clusters of low flat sparkling houses. It was all tiny and perfect, three thousand feet below. Even the flat bridge over the stream, and the square with the houses around it, the bigger buildings piled up at opposite ends of the square, the tall cottonwood trees, the pastures and stretches of yellow-sere maize, the patches of brown sheep or goats in the distance, on the slopes, the railed enclosures by the streamside. There it was, all small and perfect, looking magical, as any place will look magical, seen from the mountains above. The unusual thing was that the low houses glittered white, white-washed, looking like crystals of salt, or silver. This frightened her.

They began the long, winding descent at the head of the barranca following the stream that rushed and fell. At first it was all rocks; then the pine trees began, and soon, the silver-limbed aspens. The flowers of autumn, big daisy-like flowers, and white ones, and many yellow flowers, were in profusion. But she had to sit down and rest, she was so weary. And she saw the bright flowers shadowily, as pale shadows hovering, as one who is dead must see them.

At length came grass and pasture-slopes between mingled aspen and pine trees. A shepherd, naked in the sun save for his hat and his cotton loin-cloth, was driving his brown sheep away. In a grove of trees they sat and waited, she and the young Indian. The one with the saddle had also gone forward.

They heard a sound of someone coming. It was three men, in fine sarapes of red and orange and yellow and black, and with brilliant feather head-dresses. The oldest had his grey hair braided with fur, and his red and orange-yellow sarape was covered with curious black markings, like a leopard-skin. The other two were not grey-haired, but they were elders too. Their blankets were in stripes, and their head-dresses not so elaborate.

The young Indian addressed the elders in a few quiet words. They listened without answering or looking at him or at the woman, keeping their faces averted and their eyes turned to the ground, only listening. And at length they turned and looked at the woman.

The old chief, or medicine-man, whatever he was, had a deeply wrinkled and lined face of dark bronze, with a few sparse grey hairs round the mouth. Two long braids of grey hair, braided with fur and coloured feather, hung on his shoulders. And yet, it was only his eyes that mattered. They were black and of extraordinary piercing strength, without a qualm of misgiving in their demonish, dauntless power. He looked into the eyes of the white woman with a long piercing look, seeking she knew not what. She summoned all her strength to meet his eyes and keep up her guard. But it was no good. He was not looking at her as one human being looks at another. He never even perceived her resistance or her challenge, but looked past them both, into she knew not what.

She could see it was hopeless to expect an human communication with this old being.

He turned and said a few words to the young Indian.

"He asks what do you seek here?" said the young man in Spanish.

"I? Nothing! I only came to see what it was like."

This was again translated, and the old man turned his eyes on her once more. Then he spoke again, in his low muttering tone, to the young Indian.

"He says, why does she leave her house with the white men? Does she want to bring the white man's God to the Chilchui?"

"No," she replied, foolhardy. "I came away from the white man's God myself. I came to look for the God of the Chilchui."

Profound silence followed, when this was translated. Then the old man spoke again, in a small voice almost of weariness.

"Does the white woman seek the gods of the Chilchui because she is weary of her own God?" came the question.

"Yes, she does. She is tired of the white man's God," she replied, thinking that was what they wanted her to say. She would like to serve the gods of the Chilchui.

She was aware of an extraordinary thrill of triumph and exultance passing through the Indians, in the tense silence that followed when this was translated. Then they all looked at her with piercing black eyes, in which a steely covetous intent glittered incomprehensible. She was the more puzzled, as there was nothing sensual or sexual in the look. It had a terrible glittering purity that was beyond her. She was afraid, she would have been paralysed with fear, had not something died within her, leaving her with a cold, watchful wonder only.

The elders talked a little while, then the two went away, leaving her with the young man and the oldest chief. The old man now looked at her with a certain solicitude.

"He says are you tired?" asked the young man.

"Very tired," she said.

"The men will bring you a carriage," said the young Indian.

The carriage, when it came, proved to be a litter consisting of a sort of hammock of dark woollen frieze, slung on to a pole which was borne on the shoulders of two long-haired Indians. The woollen hammock was spread on the ground, she sat down on it, and the two men raised the pole to their shoulders. Swinging rather as if she were in a sack, she was carried out of the grove of trees, following the old chief, whose leopard-spotted blanket moved curiously in the sunlight.

They had emerged in the valley-head. Just in front were the maize-fields, with ripe ears of maize. The corn was not very tall, in this high altitude. The well-worn path went between it, and all she could see was the erect form of the old chief, in the flame and black sarape, stepping soft and heavy and swift, his head forward, looking neither to right nor left. Her bearers followed, stepping rhythmically, the long blue-black hair glistening like a river down the naked shoulders of the man in front.

They passed the maize, and came to a big wall or earth-work made of earth and adobe bricks. The wooden doors were open. Passing on, they were in a network of small gardens, full of flowers and herbs and fruit trees, each garden watered by a tiny ditch of running water. Among each cluster of trees and flowers was a small, glittering white house, windowless, and with closed door. The place was a network of little paths, small streams, and little bridges among square, flowering gardens.

Following the broadest path—a soft narrow track between leaves and grass, a path worn smooth by centuries of human feet, no hoof of horse nor any wheel to disfigure it—they came to the little river of swift bright water, and crossed on a log bridge. Everything was silent—there was not a human being anywhere. The road went on under magnificent cottonwood trees. It emerged suddenly outside the central plaza or square of the village.

This was a long oblong of low white houses with flat roofs, and two bigger buildings, having as it were little square huts piled on top of bigger long huts, stood at either end of the oblong, facing each other rather askew. Every little house was a dazzling white, save for the great round beam-ends which projected under the flat eaves, and for the flat roofs. Round each of the bigger buildings, on the outside of the square, was a stockyard fence, inside which was garden with trees and flowers, and various small houses.

Not a soul was in sight. They passed silently between the houses into the central square. This was quite bare and arid, the earth trodden smooth by endless generations of passing feet, passing across from door to door. All the doors of the windowless houses gave on to this blank square, but all doors were closed. The firewood lay near the threshold, a clay oven was still smoking, but there was no sign of moving life.

The old man walked straight across the square to the big house at the end, where the two upper storeys, as in a house of toy bricks, stood each one smaller than the lower one. A stone staircase, outside, led up to the roof of the first storey.

At the foot of this staircase the litter-bearers stood still, and lowered the woman to the ground.

"You will come up," said the young Indian who spoke Spanish.

She mounted the stone stairs to the earthen roof of the first house, which formed a platform round the wall of the second storey. She followed around this platform to the back of the big house. There they descended again, into the garden at the rear.

So far they had seen no one. But now two men appeared, bareheaded, with long braided hair, and wearing a sort of white shirt gathered into a loin-cloth. These went along with the three newcomers, across the garden where red flowers and yellow flowers were blooming, to a long, low white house. There they entered without knocking.

It was dark inside. There was a low murmur of men's voices. Several men were present, their white shirts showing in the gloom, their dark faces invisible. They were sitting on a great log of smooth old wood, that lay along the far wall. And save for this log, the room seemed empty. But no, in the dark at one end was a couch, a sort of bed, and someone lying there, covered with furs.

The old Indian in the spotted sarape, who had accompanied the woman, now took off his hat and his blanket and his sandals. Laying them aside, he approached the couch, and spoke in a low voice. For some moments there was no answer. Then an old man with the snow-white hair hanging round his darkly-visible face, roused himself like a vision, and leaned on one elbow, looking vaguely at the company, in tense silence.

The grey-haired Indian spoke again, and then the young Indian, taking the woman's hand, led her forward. In her linen riding-habit, and black boots and hat, and her pathetic bit of a red tie, she stood there beside the fur-covered bed of the old, old man, who sat reared up, leaning on one elbow, remote as a ghost, his white hair streaming in disorder, his face almost black, yet with a far-off intentness, not of this world, leaning forward to look at her.

His face was so old, it was like dark glass, and the few curling hairs that sprang white from his lips and chin were quite incredible. The long white locks fell unbraided and disorderly on either side of the glassy dark face. And under a faint powder of white eyebrows, the black eyes of the old chief looked at her as if from the far, far dead, seeing something that was never to be seen.

At last he spoke a few deep, hollow words, as if to the dark air.

"He says, do you bring your heart to the god of the Chilchui?" translated the young Indian.

"Tell him yes," she said, automatically.

There was a pause. The old Indian spoke again, as if to the air. One of the men present went out. There was a silence as if of eternity in the dim room that was lighted only through the open door.

The woman looked round. Four old men with grey hair sat on the log by the wall facing the door. Two other men, powerful and impassive, stood near the door. They all had long hair, and wore white shirts gathered into a loin-cloth. Their powerful legs were naked and dark. There was a silence like eternity.

At length the man returned, with white and dark clothing on his arm. The young Indian took them, and holding them in front of the woman, said:

"You must take off your clothes, and put these on."

"If all you men will go out," she said.

"No one will hurt you," he said quietly.

"Not while you men are here," she said.

He looked at the two men by the door. They came quickly forward, and suddenly gripped her arms as she stood, without hurting her, but with great power. Then two of the old men came, and with curious skill slit her boots down with keen knives, and drew them off, and slit her clothing so that it came away from her. In a few moments she stood there white and uncovered. The old man on the bed spoke, and they turned her round for him to see. He spoke again, and the young Indian deftly took the pins and comb from her fair hair, so that it fell over her shoulders in a bunchy tangle.

Then the old man spoke again. The Indian led her to the bedside. The white-haired, glassy-dark old man moistened his finger-tips at his mouth, and most delicately touched her on the breasts and on the body, then on the back. And she winced strangely each time, as the finger-tips drew along her skin, as if Death itself were touching her.

And she wondered, almost sadly, why she did not feel shamed in her nakedness. She only felt sad and lost. Because nobody felt ashamed. The elder men were all dark and tense with some other deep, gloomy, incomprehensible emotion, which suspended all her agitation, while the young Indian had a strange look of ecstasy on his face. And she, she was only utterly strange and beyond herself, as if her body were not her own.

They gave her the new clothing: a long white cotton shift, that came to her knees: then a tunic of thick blue woollen stuff, embroidered with scarlet and green flowers. It was fastened over one shoulder only, and belted with a braid sash of scarlet and black wool.

When she was thus dressed, they took her away, barefoot, to a little house in the stockaded garden. The young Indian told her she might have what she wanted. She asked for water to wash herself. He brought it in a jar, together with a long wooden bowl. Then he fastened the gate-door of her house, and left her a prisoner. She could see through the bars of the gate-door of her house, the red flowers of the garden, and a humming-bird. Then from the roof of the big house she heard the long, heavy sound of a drum, unearthly to her in its summons, and an uplifted voice calling from the house-top in a strange language, with a far-away emotionless intonation, delivering some speech or message. And she listened as if from the dead.

But she was very tired. She lay down on a couch of skins, pulling over her the blanket of dark wool, and she slept, giving up everything.

When she woke it was late afternoon, and the young Indian was entering with a basket-tray containing food, tortillas, and corn-mush with bits of meat, probably mutton, and a drink made of honey, and some fresh plums. He brought her also a long garland of red and yellow flowers with knots of blue buds at the end. He sprinkled the garland with water from a jar, then offered it to her, with a smile. He seemed very gentle and thoughtful, and on his face and in his dark eyes was a curious look of triumph and ecstasy, that frightened her a little. The glitter had gone from the black eyes, with their curving dark lashes, and he would look at her with this strange soft glow of ecstasy that was not quite human, and terribly impersonal, and which made her uneasy.

"Is there anything you want?" he said, in his low, slow, melodious voice, that always seemed withheld, as if he were speaking aside to somebody else, or as if he did not want to let the sound come out to her.

"Am I going to be kept a prisoner here?" she asked.

"No, you can walk in the garden to-morrow," he said softly. Always this curious solicitude.

"Do you like that drink?" he said, offering her a little earthenware cup. "It is very refreshing."

She sipped the liquor curiously. It was made with herbs and sweetened with honey, and had a strange, lingering flavour. The young man watched her with gratification.

"It has a peculiar taste," she said.

"It is very refreshing," he replied, his black eyes resting on her always with that look of gratified ecstasy. Then he went away. And presently she began to be sick, and to vomit violently, as if she had no control over herself.

Afterwards she felt a great soothing languor steal over her, her limbs felt strong and loose and full of languor, and she lay on her couch listening to the sounds of the village, watching the yellowing sky, smelling the scent of burning cedar wood, or pine wood. So distinctly she heard the yapping of tiny dogs, the shuffle of far-off feet, the murmur of voices, so keenly she detected the smell of smoke, and flowers, and evening falling, so vividly she saw the one bright star infinitely remote, stirring above the sunset, that she felt as if all her senses were diffused on the air, that she could distinguish the sound of evening flowers unfolding, and the actual crystal sound of the heavens, as the vast belts of the world-atmosphere slid past one another, and as if the moisture ascending and the moisture descending in the air resounded like some harp in the cosmos.

She was a prisoner in her house, and in the stockaded garden, but she scarcely minded. And it was days before she realised that she never saw another woman. Only the men, the elderly men of the big house, that she imagined must be some sort of temple, and the men priests of some sort. For they always had the same colours, red, orange, yellow, and black, and the same grave, abstracted demeanour.

Sometimes an old man would come and sit in her room with her, in absolute silence. None spoke any language but Indian, save the one younger man. The older men would smile at her, and sit with her for an hour at a time, sometimes smiling at her when she spoke in Spanish, but never answering save with this slow, benevolent-seeming smile. And they gave off a feeling of almost fatherly solicitude. Yet their dark eyes, brooding over her, had something away in their depths that was awesomely ferocious and relentless. They would cover it with a smile, at once, if they felt her looking. But she had seen it.

Always they treated her with this curious impersonal solicitude, this utterly impersonal gentleness, as an old man treats a child. But underneath it she felt there was something else, something terrible. When her old visitor had gone away, in his silent, insidious, fatherly fashion, a shock of fear would come over her; though of what she knew not.

The young Indian would sit and talk with her freely, as if with great candour. But with him, too, she felt that everything real was unsaid. Perhaps it was unspeakable. His big dark eyes would rest on her almost cherishingly, touched with ecstasy, and his beautiful, slow, languorous voice would trail out its simple, ungrammatical Spanish. He told her he was the grandson of the old, old man, son of the man in the spotted sarape: and they were caciques, kings from the old, old days, before even the Spaniards came. But he himself had been in Mexico City, and also in the United States. He had worked as a labourer, building the roads in Los Angeles. He had travelled as far as Chicago.

"Don't you speak English, then?" she asked.

His eyes rested on her with a curious look of duplicity and conflict, and he mutely shook his head.

"What did you do with your long hair, when you were in the United States?" she asked. "Did you cut it off?"

Again, with the look of torment in his eyes, he shook his head.

"No," he said, in a low, subdued voice, "I wore a hat, and a handkerchief tied round my head."

And he relapsed into silence, as if of tormented memories.

"Are you the only man of your people who has been to the United States?" she asked him.

"Yes. I am the only one who has been away from here for a long time. The others come back soon, in one week. They don't stay away. The old men don't let them."

"And why did you go?"

"The old men want me to go—because I shall be the cacique—"

He talked always with the same naïveté, and almost childish candour. But she felt that this was perhaps just the effect of his Spanish.

Or perhaps speech altogether was unreal to him. Anyhow, she felt that all the real things were kept back.

He came and sat with her a good deal—sometimes more than she wished—as if he wanted to be near her. She asked him if he was married. He said he was—with two children.

"I should like to see your children," she said.

But he answered only with that smile, a sweet, almost ecstatic smile, above which the dark eyes hardly changed from their enigmatic abstraction.

It was curious, he would sit with her by the hour, without ever making her self-conscious, or sex-conscious. He seemed to have no sex, as he sat there so still and gentle and apparently submissive with his head bent a little forward, and the river of glistening black hair streaming maidenly over his shoulders.

Yet when she looked again, she saw his shoulders broad and powerful, his eyebrows black and level, the short, curved, obstinate black lashes over his lowered eyes, the small, fur-like line of moustache above his blackish, heavy lips, and the strong chin, and she knew that in some other mysterious way he was darkly and powerfully male. And he, feeling her watching him, would glance up at her swiftly with a dark lurking look in his eyes, which immediately he veiled with that half-sad smile.

The days and the weeks went by, in a vague kind of contentment. She was uneasy sometimes, feeling she had lost the power over herself. She was not in her own power, she was under the spell of some other control. And at times she had moments of terror and horror. But then these Indians would come and sit with her, casting their insidious spell over her by their very silent presence, their silent, sexless, powerful physical presence. As they sat they seemed to take her will away, and leaving her will-less and victim to her own indifference. And the young man would bring her sweetened drink, often the same emetic drink, but sometimes other kinds. And after drinking, the languor filled her heavy limbs, her senses seemed to float in the air, listening, hearing. They had brought her a little female dog, which she called Flora. And once, in the trance of her senses, she felt she *heard* the little dog conceive, in her tiny womb, and begin to be complex, with young. And another day she could hear the vast sound of the earth going round, like some immense arrow-string booming.

But as the days grew shorter and colder, when she was cold, she would get a sudden revival of her will, and a desire to go out, to go away. And she insisted to the young man, she wanted to go out.

So one day, they let her climb to the topmost roof of the big house where she was, and look down the square. It was the day of the big dance, but not everybody was dancing. Women with babies in their arms stood in their doorways, watching. Opposite, at the other end of the square, there was a throng before the other big house, and a small, brilliant group on the terrace roof of the first storey, in front of wide open doors of the upper storey. Through these wide open doors she could see fire glinting in darkness and priests in head-dresses of black and yellow and scarlet feathers, wearing robe-like blankets of black and red and yellow, with long green fringes, were moving about. A big drum was beating slowly and regularly, in the dense, Indian silence. The crowd below waited.

Then a drum started on a high beat, and there came the deep, powerful burst of men singing a heavy, savage music, like a wind roaring in some timeless forest, many mature men singing in one breath, like the wind; and long lines of dancers walked out from under the big house. Men with naked, golden-bronze bodies and streaming black hair, tufts of red and yellow feathers on their arms, and kilts of white frieze with a bar of heavy red and black and green embroidery round their waists, bending slightly forward and stamping the earth in their absorbed, monotonous stamp of the dance, a fox-fur, hung by the nose from their belt behind, swaying with the sumptuous swaying of a beautiful fox-fur, the tip of the tail writhing above the dancer's heels. And after each man, a woman with a strange elaborate head-dress of feathers and sea-shells, and wearing a short black tunic, moving erect, holding up tufts of feathers in each hand, swaying her wrists rythmically and subtly beating the earth with her bare feet.

So, the long line of the dance unfurling from the big house opposite. And from the big house beneath her, strange scent of incense, strange tense silence, then the answering burst of inhuman male singing, and the long line of the dance unfurling.

It went on all day, the insistence of the drum, the cavernous, roaring storm-like sound of male singing, the incessant swinging of the fox-skins behind the powerful, gold-bronze, stamping legs of the men, the autumn sun from a perfect blue heaven pouring on the rivers of black hair, men's and women's, the valley all still, the walls of rock beyond, the awful huge bulking of the mountain against the pure sky, its snow seething with sheer whiteness.

For hours and hours she watched, spellbound, and as if drugged. And in all the terrible persistence of the drumming and the primeval, rushing deep singing, and the endless stamping of the dance of fox-tailed men, the tread of heavy, bird-erect women in their black tunics, she seemed at last to feel her own death; her own obliteration. As if she were to be obliterated from the field of life again. In the strange towering symbols on the heads of the changeless, absorbed women she seemed to read once more the *Mene Mene Tekel Upharsin.* Her kind of womanhood, intensely personal and individual, was to be obliterated again, and the great primeval symbols were to tower once more over the fallen individual independence of woman. The sharpness and the quivering nervous consciousness of the highly-bred white woman was to be destroyed again, womanhood was to be cast once more into the great stream of impersonal sex and impersonal passion. Strangely, as if clairvoyant, she saw the immense sacrifice prepared. And she went back to her little house in a trance of agony.

After this, there was always a certain agony when she heard the drums at evening, and the strange uplifted savage sound of men singing round the drum, like wild creatures howling to the invisible gods of the moon and the vanished sun. Something of the chuckling, sobbing cry of the coyote, something of the exultant bark of the fox, the far-off wild melancholy exultance of the howling wolf, the torment of the puma's scream, and the insistence of the ancient fierce human male, with his lapses of tenderness and his abiding ferocity.

Sometimes she would climb the high roof after nightfall, and listen to the dim cluster of young men round the drum on the bridge just beyond the square, singing by the hour. Sometimes there would be a fire, and in the fire-glow, men in their white shirts or naked save for a loin-cloth, would be dancing and stamping like spectres, hour after hour in the dark cold air, within the fire-glow, forever dancing and stamping like turkeys, or dropping squatting by the fire to rest, throwing their blankets round them.

"Why do you all have the same colours?" she asked the young Indian. "Why do you all have red and yellow and black, over your white shirts? And the women have black tunics?"

He looked into her eyes, curiously, and the faint, evasive smile came on to his face. Behind the smile lay a soft, strange malignancy.

"Because our men are the fire and the day-time, and our women are the spaces between the stars at night," he said.

"Aren't the women even stars?" she said.

"No. We say they are the spaces between the stars, that keep the stars apart."

"White people," he said, "they know nothing. They are like children, always with toys. We know the sun, and we know the moon. And we say, when a white woman sacrifice herself to our gods, then our gods will begin to make the world again, and the white man's gods will fall to pieces."

"How sacrifice herself?" she asked quickly.

And he, as quickly covered, covered himself with a subtle smile. "She sacrifice her own gods and come to our gods, I mean that," he said soothingly.

But she was not reassured. An icy pang of fear and certainty was at her heart.

"The sun he is alive at one end of the sky," he continued, "and the moon lives at the other end. And the man all the time have to keep the sun happy in his side of the sky, and the woman have to keep the moon quiet at her side of the sky. All the time she have to work at this. And the sun can't ever go into the house of the moon, and the moon can't ever go into the house of the sun, in the sky. So the woman, she asks the moon to come into her cave, inside her. And the man, he draws the sun down till he has the power of the sun. All the time he do this. Then when the man gets a woman, the sun goes into the cave of the moon, and that is how everything in the world starts."

She listened, watching him closely, as one enemy watches another who is speaking with double meaning.

"Then," she said, "why aren't you Indians masters of the white men?"

"Because," he said, "the Indian got weak, and lost his power with the sun, so the white men stole the sun. But they can't keep him—they don't know how. They got him, but they don't know what to do with him, like a boy who catch a big grizzly bear, and can't kill him, and can't run away from him. The grizzly bear eats the boy that catch him, when he want to run away from him. White men don't know what they are doing with the sun, and white women don't know what they do with the moon. The moon she got angry with white women, like a puma when someone kills her little ones. The moon, she bites white women—here inside," and he pressed his side. "The moon, she is angry in a white woman's cave. The Indian can see it. And soon," he added, "the Indian women get the moon back and keep her quiet in their house. And the Indian men get the sun, and the power over all the world. White men don't know what the sun is. They never know."

He subsided into a curious exultant silence.

"But," she faltered, "why do you hate us so? Why do you hate me?"

He looked up suddenly with a light on his face, and a startling flame of a smile.

"No, we don't hate," he said softly, looking with a curious glitter into her face.

"You do," she said, forlorn and hopeless.

And after a moment's silence, he rose and went away.

III

Winter had now come, in the high valley, with snow that melted in the day's sun, and nights that were bitter cold. She lived on, in a kind of daze, feeling her power ebbing more and more away from her, as if her will were leaving her. She felt always in the same relaxed, confused, victimised state, unless the sweetened herb drink would numb her mind altogether, and release her senses into a sort of heightened, mystic acuteness and a feeling as if she were diffusing out deliciously into the harmony of things. This at length became the only state of consciousness she really recognised: this exquisite sense of bleeding out into the higher beauty and harmony of things. Then she could actually hear the great stars in heaven, which she saw through her door, speaking from their motion and brightness, saying things perfectly to the cosmos, as they trod in perfect ripples, like bells on the floor of heaven, passing one another and grouping in the timeless dance, with the spaces of dark between. And she could hear the snow on a cold, cloudy day twittering and faintly whistling in the sky, like birds that flock and fly away in autumn, suddenly calling farewell to the invisible moon, and slipping out of the plains of the air, releasing peaceful warmth. She herself would call to the arrested snow to fall from the upper air. She would call to the unseen moon to cease to be angry, to make peace again with the unseen sun like a woman who ceases to be angry in her house. And she would smell the sweetness of the moon relaxing to the sun in the wintry heaven, when the snow fell in a faint, cold-perfumed relaxation, as the peace of the sun mingled again in a sort of unison with the peace of the moon.

She was aware too of the sort of shadow that was on the Indians of the valley, a deep stoical disconsolation, almost religious in its depth.

"We have lost our power over the sun, and we are trying to get him back. But he is wild with us, and shy like a horse that has got away. We have to go through a lot." So the young Indian said to her, looking into her eyes with a strained meaning. And she, as if bewitched, replied:

"I hope you will get him back."

The smile of triumph flew over his face.

"Do you hope it?" he said.

"I do," she answered fatally.

"Then all right," he said. "We shall get him."

And he went away in exultance.

She felt she was drifting on some consummation, which she had no will to avoid, yet which seemed heavy and finally terrible to her.

It must have been almost December, for the days were short when she was taken again before the aged man, and stripped of her clothing, and touched with the old finger-tips.

The aged cacique looked her in the eyes, with his eyes of lonely, far-off, black intentness, and murmured something to her.

"He wants you to make the sign of peace," the young man translated, showing her the gesture. "Peace and farewell to him."

She was fascinated by the black, glass-like, intent eyes of the old cacique, that watched her without blinking, like a basilisk's, overpowering her. In their depths also she saw a certain fatherly compassion, and pleading. She put her hand before her face, in the required manner, making the sign of peace and farewell. He made the sign of peace back again to her, then sank among his furs. She thought he was going to die, and that he knew it.

There followed a day of ceremonial, when she was brought out before all the people, in a blue blanket with white fringe, and holding blue feathers in her hands. Before an altar of one house she was perfumed with incense and sprinkled with ash. Before the altar of the opposite house she was fumigated again with incense by the gorgeous, terrifying priests in yellow and scarlet and black, their faces painted with scarlet paint. And then they threw water on her. Meanwhile she was faintly aware of the fire on the altar, the heavy, heavy sound of a drum, the heavy sound of men beginning powerfully, deeply, savagely to sing, the swaying of the crowd of faces in the plaza below, and the formation for a sacred dance.

But at this time her commonplace consciousness was numb, she was aware of her immediate surroundings as shadows, almost immaterial. With refined and heightened senses she could hear the sound of the earth winging on its journey, like a shot arrow, the ripple-rustling of the air, and the boom of the great arrow-string. And it seemed to her there were two great influences in the upper air, one golden towards the sun, and one invisible silver; the first travelling like rain ascending to the gold presence sunwards, the second like rain silverily descending the ladders of space towards the hovering, lurking clouds over the snowy mountain-top. Then between them, another presence, waiting to shake himself free of moisture, of heavy white snow that had mysteriously collected about him. And in summer, like a scorched eagle, he would wait to shake himself clear of the weight of heavy sunbeams. And he was coloured like fire. And he was always shaking himself clear, of snow or of heavy heat, like an eagle rustling.

Then there was a still stranger presence, standing watching from the blue distance, always watching. Sometimes running in upon the wind, or shimmering in the heat-waves. The blue wind itself, rushing, as it were, out of the holes into the sky, rushing out of the sky down upon the earth. The blue wind, the go-between, the invisible ghost that belonged to two worlds, that played upon the ascending and the descending chords of the rains.

More and more her ordinary personal consciousness had left her, she had gone into that other state of passional cosmic consciousness, like one who is drugged. The Indians, with their heavily religious natures, had made her succumb to their vision.

Only one personal question she asked the young Indian:

"Why am I the only one that wears blue?"

"It is the colour of the wind. It is the colour of what goes away and is never coming back, but which is always here, waiting like death among us. It is the colour of the dead. And it is the colour that stands away off, looking at us from the distance, that cannot come near to us. When we go near, it goes farther. It can't be near. We are all brown and yellow and black hair, and white teeth and red blood. We are the ones that are here. You with blue eyes, you are the messengers from the far-away, you cannot stay, and now it is time for you to go back."

"Where to?" she asked.

"To the way-off things like the sun and the blue mother of rain, and tell them that we are the people on the world again, and we can bring the sun to the moon again, like a red horse to a blue mare; we are the people. The white women have driven back the moon in the sky, won't let her come to the sun. So the sun is angry. And the Indian must give the moon to the sun."

"How?" she said.

"The white woman got to die and go like a wind to the sun, tell him the Indians will open the gate to him. And the Indian women will open the gate to the moon. The white women don't let the moon come down out of the blue coral. The moon used to come down among the Indian women, like a white goat among the flowers. And the sun want to come down to the Indian men, like an eagle to the pine trees. The sun, he is shut out behind the white man, and the moon she is shut out behind the white woman, and they can't get away. They are angry, everything in the world gets angrier. The Indian says he will give the white woman to the sun, so the sun will leap over the white man and come to the Indian again. And the moon will be surprised, she will see the gate open, and she not know which way to go. But the Indian woman will call to the moon: *Come! Come! Come back into my grasslands. The wicked white woman can't harm you any more.* Then the sun will look over the heads of the white men, and see the moon in the pastures of our women, with the Red Men standing around like pine trees. Then he will leap over the heads of the white men, and come running past to the Indians through the spruce trees. And we, who are red and black and yellow, we who stay, we shall have the sun on our right hand and the moon on our left. So we can bring the rain down out of the blue meadows, and up out of the black; and we can call the wind that tells the corn to grow, when we ask him, and we shall make the clouds to break, and the sheep to have twin lambs. And we shall be full of power, like a spring day. But the white people will be a hard winter, without snow—"

"But," said the white woman, "I don't shut out the moon—how can I?"

"Yes," he said, "you shut the gate, and then laugh, think you have it all your own way."

She could never quite understand the way he looked at her. He was always so curiously gentle, and his smile was so soft. Yet there was such a glitter in his eyes, and an unrelenting sort of hate came out of his words, a strange, profound impersonal hate. Personally he liked her, she was sure. He was gentle with her, attracted by her in some strange, soft, passionless way. But impersonally he hated her with a mystic hatred. He would smile at her, winningly. Yet if, the next moment, she glanced round at him unawares, she would catch that gleam of pure after-hate in his eyes.

"Have I got to die and be given to the sun?" she asked.

"Some time," he said, laughing evasively. "Some time we all die."

They were gentle with her, and very considerate with her. Strange men, the old priests and the young cacique alike, they watched over her and cared for her like women. In their soft, insidious understanding, there was something womanly. Yet their eyes, with that strange glitter, and their dark, shut mouths that would open to the broad jaw, the small, strong, white teeth, had something very primitively male and cruel.

One wintry day, when snow was falling, they took her to a great dark chamber in the big house. The fire was burning in a corner on a high raised dais under a sort of hood or canopy of adobe-work. She saw in the fire-glow the glowing bodies of the almost naked priests, and strange symbols on the roof and walls of the chamber. There was no door or window in the chamber, they had descended by a ladder, from the roof. And the fire of pinewood danced continually, showing walls painted with strange devices, which she could not understand, and a ceiling of poles making a curious pattern of black and red and yellow, and alcoves or niches in which were curious objects she could not discern.

The older priests were going through some ceremony near the fire, in silence, intense Indian silence. She was seated on a low projection of the wall, opposite the fire, two men seated beside her. Presently they gave her a drink from a cup, which she took gladly, because of the semi-trance it would induce.

In the darkness and in the silence she was accurately aware of everything that happened to her: how they took off her clothes, and, standing her before a great, weird device on the wall, coloured blue and white and black, washed her all over with water and the amole infusion; washed even her hair, softly, carefully, and dried it on white cloths, till it was soft and glistening. Then they laid her on a couch under another great indecipherable image of red and black and yellow, and now rubbed all her body with sweet-scented oil, and massaged all her limbs, and her back, and her sides, with a long, strange, hypnotic massage. Their dark hands were incredibly powerful, yet soft with a watery softness she could not understand. And the dark faces, leaning near her white body, she saw were darkened with red pigment, with lines of yellow round the cheeks.

And the dark eyes glittered absorbed, as the hands worked upon the soft white body of the woman.

They were so impersonal, absorbed in something that was beyond her. They never saw her as a personal woman: she could tell that. She was some mystic object to them, some vehicle of passions too remote for her to grasp. Herself in a state of trance, she watched their faces bending over her, dark, strangely glistening with the transparent red paint, and lined with bars of yellow. And in this weird, luminous-dark mask of living face, the eyes were fixed with an unchanging steadfast gleam, and the purplish-pigmented lips were closed in a full, sinister, sad grimness. The immense fundamental sadness, the grimness of ultimate decision, the fixity of revenge, and the nascent exultance of those that are going to triumph—these things she could read in their faces, as she lay and was rubbed into a misty glow by their uncanny dark hands. Her limbs, her flesh, her very bones at last seemed to be diffusing into a roseate sort of mist, in which her consciousness hovered like some sun-gleam in a flushed cloud.

She knew the gleam would fade, the cloud would go grey. But at present she did not believe it. She knew she was a victim; that all this elaborate work upon her was the work of victimising her. But she did not mind. She wanted it.

Later, they put a short blue tunic on her and took her to the upper terrace, and presented her to the people. She saw the plaza below her full of dark faces and of glittering eyes. There was no pity: only the curious hard exultance. The people gave a subdued cry when they saw her, and she shuddered. But she hardly cared.

Next day was the last. She slept in a chamber of the big house. At dawn they put on her a big blue blanket with a fringe, and led her out into the plaza, among the throng of silent, dark-blanketed people. There was pure white snow on the ground, and the dark people in their dark-brown blankets looked like inhabitants of another world.

A large drum was slowly pounding, and an old priest was declaiming from a house-top. But it was not till noon that a litter came forth, and the people gave that low, animal cry which was so moving. In the sack-like litter sat the old, old cacique, his white hair braided with black braid and large turquoise stones. His face was like a piece of obsidian. He lifted his hand in token, and the litter stopped in front of her. Fixing her with his old eyes, he spoke to her for a few moments, in his hollow voice. No one translated.

Another litter came, and she was placed in it. Four priests moved ahead, in their scarlet and yellow and black, with plumed head-dresses. Then came the litter of the old cacique. Then the light drums began, and two groups of singers burst simultaneously into song, male and wild. And the golden-red, almost naked men, adorned with ceremonial feathers and kilts, the rivers of black hair down their backs, formed into two files and began to tread the dance. So they threaded out of the snowy plaza, in two long, sumptuous lines of dark red-gold and black and fur, swaying with a faint tinkle of bits of shell and flint, winding over the snow between the two bee-clusters of men who sang around the drums.

Slowly they moved out, and her litter, with its attendance of feathered, lurid dancing priests, moved after. Everybody danced the tread of the dance-step, even, subtly, the litter-bearers. And out of the plaza they went, past smoking ovens, on the trail to the great cottonwood trees, that stood like grey-silver lace against the blue sky, bare and exquisite above the snow. The river, diminished, rushed among fangs of ice. The chequer-squares of gardens within fences were all snowy, and the white houses now looked yellowish.

The whole valley glittered intolerably with pure snow, away to the walls of the standing rock. And across the flat cradle of snow-bed wound the long thread of the dance, shaking slowly and sumptuously in its orange and black motion. The high drums thudded quickly, and on the crystalline frozen air the swell and roar of the chant of savages was like an obsession.

She sat looking out of her litter with big, transfixed blue eyes, under which were the wan markings of her drugged weariness. She knew she was going to die, among the glisten of this snow, at the hands of this savage, sumptuous people. And as she stared at the blaze of the blue sky above the slashed and ponderous mountain, she thought: "I am dead already. What difference does it make, the transition from the dead I am to the dead I shall be, very soon!" Yet her soul sickened and felt wan.

The strange procession trailed on, in perpetual dance, slowly across the plain of snow, and then entered the slopes between the pine trees. She saw the copper-dark men dancing the dance-tread, onwards, between the copper-pale tree trunks. And at last, she, too, in her swaying litter, entered the pine trees.

They were travelling on and on, upwards, across the snow under the trees, past superb shafts of pale, flaked copper, the rustle and shake and tread of the threading dance, penetrating into the forest, into the mountain. They were following a stream-bed: but the stream was dry, like summer, dried up by the frozenness of the head-waters. There were dark, red-bronze willow bushes with wattles like wild hair, and pallid aspen trees looking cold flesh against the snow. Then jutting dark rocks.

At last she could tell that the dancers were moving forward no more. Nearer and nearer she came upon the drums, as to a lair of mysterious animals. Then through the bushes she emerged into a strange amphitheatre. Facing was a great wall of hollow rock, down the front of which hung a great, dripping, fang-like spoke of ice. The ice came pouring over the rock from the precipice above, and then stood arrested, dripping out of high heaven, almost down to the hollow stones where the stream-pool should be below. But the pool was dry.

On either side the dry pool the lines of dancers had formed, and the dance was continuing without intermission, against a background of bushes.

But what she felt was that fanged inverted pinnacle of ice, hanging from the lip of the dark precipice above. And behind the great rope of ice she saw the leopard-like figures of priests climbing the hollow cliff face, to the cave that like a dark socket bored a cavity, an orifice, half-way up the crag.

Before she could realise, her litter-bearers were staggering in the footholds, climbing the rock. She, too, was behind the ice. There it hung, like a curtain that is not spread, but hangs like a great fang. And near above her was the orifice of the cave sinking dark into the rock. She watched it as she swayed upwards.

On the platform of the cave stood the priests, waiting in all their gorgeousness of feathers and fringed robes, watching her ascent. Two of them stooped to help her litter-bearer. And at length she was on the platform of the cave, far in behind the shaft of ice, above the hollow amphitheatre among the bushes below, where men were dancing, and the whole populace of the village was clustered in silence.

The sun was sloping down the afternoon sky, on the left. She knew that this was the shortest day of the year, and the last day of her life. They stood her facing the iridescent column of ice, which fell down marvellously arrested, away in front of her.

Some signal was given, and the dance below stopped. There was now absolute silence. She was given a little to drink, then two priests took off her mantle and her tunic, and in her strange pallor she stood there, between the lurid robes of the priests, beyond the pillar of ice, beyond and above the dark-faced people. The throng below gave the low, wild cry. Then the priest turned her round, so she stood with her back to the open world, her long blonde hair to the people below. And they cried again.

She was facing the cave, inwards. A fire was burning and flickering in the depths. Four priests had taken off their robes, and were almost as naked as she was. They were powerful men in the prime of life, and they kept their dark, painted faces lowered.

From the fire came the old, old priest, with an incense-pan. He was naked and in a state of barbaric esctasy. He fumigated his victim, reciting at the same time in a hollow voice. Behind him came another robeless priest, with two flint knives.

When she was fumigated, they laid her on a large flat stone, the four powerful men holding her by the outstretched arms and legs. Behind stood the aged man, like a skeleton covered with dark glass, holding a knife and transfixedly watching the sun; and behind him again was another naked priest, with a knife.

She felt little sensation, though she knew all that was happening. Turning to the sky, she looked at the yellow sun. It was sinking. The shaft of ice was like a shadow between her and it. And she realised that the yellow rays were filling half the cave, though they had not reached the altar where the fire was, at the far end of the funnel-shaped cavity.

Yes, the rays were creeping round slowly. As they grew ruddier, they penetrated farther. When the red sun was about to sink, he would shine full through the shaft of ice deep into the hollow of the cave, to the innermost.

She understood now that this was what the men were waiting for. Even those that held her down were bent and twisted round, their black eyes watching the sun with a glittering eagerness, and awe, and craving. The black eyes of the aged cacique were fixed like black mirrors on the sun, as if sightless, yet containing some terrible answer to the reddening winter planet. And all the eyes of the priests were fixed and glittering on the sinking orb, in the reddening, icy silence of the winter afternoon.

They were anxious, terribly anxious, and fierce. Their ferocity wanted something, and they were waiting the moment. And their ferocity was ready to leap out into a mystic exultance, of triumph. But they were anxious.

Only the eyes of the oldest man were not anxious. Black, and fixed, and as if sightless, they watched the sun, seeing beyond the sun. And in their black, empty concentration there was power, power intensely abstract and remote, but deep, deep to the heart of the earth, and the heart of the sun. In absolute motionlessness he watched till the red sun should send his ray through the column of ice. Then the old man would strike, and strike home, accomplish the sacrifice and achieve the power.

The mastery that man must hold, and that passes from race to race.

THE PAIR

by Sholom Aleichem

It was a damp and dreary spring night. The world slept in darkness and in silence. It was a night for weird dreams.

The dreams that troubled our hero were violent. All night long his mind was disturbed by chickens, geese, and ducks. And in his dream one rooster figured with special prominence, a red bird, young and insolent, who refused to fade away. Persistently he remained in the foreground and provokingly chanted a nonsensical ditty:

Cockadoodledo-o-o-o . . .
They will catch you too-oo;
They will beat you,
They will eat you,
They will slit your throat too-oo-oo.

And each time the red rooster concluded his chant, all the chickens, geese, and ducks would make an unbearable noise.

From *A Treasury of Yiddish Stories*, edited by Irving Howe and Eliezer Greenberg (New York: Viking Press) and also from *Selected Stories* of Sholem Aleichem, with an introduction by Alfred Kazin, pp. 12–27. Reprinted by permission of The Viking Press, Inc., and André Deutsch Ltd., publishers.

Our hero was preparing to teach this audacious young rooster a lesson when suddenly there was heard a stamping of feet. A light appeared. Wild unfamiliar voices shouted in unearthly tones, "Not this one—the other—grab him—don't let him get away—tie him—careful with his legs, don't break them—ready?—get a move on—into the wagon with him—"

A pair of powerful hands seized our hero, bound him, twisted his legs, and thrust him into a roomy wagon. In the dark he could discern another creature, apparently female, crouching in the corner and trembling. Two people were puttering about the wagon. One was a savage-looking individual with head bare, the other equally savage but with his head covered by a fur cap. The bareheaded one carefully examined the wagon and the horses. The one with the fur cap leaped savagely onto the wagon and landed on the feet of the prisoners with such force that their heads reeled.

"Be careful now that they don't get untied and escape. Hear me?"

The admonition came from the bareheaded one, but the other did not trouble to answer. He merely lashed the horses and they were off.

II

That they survived the night was itself a miracle. They had no idea where they were, to whom they were being taken, or why.

Because of the darkness they could not see each other very well. Only after dawn could they make each other out and converse quietly.

"Good morning, madam."

"Good morning."

"I could swear you're one of our kind—"

"There's no need to swear. You'll be believed without an oath."

"I recognized you at once, by your beads."

"That shows you have a good eye."

Some minutes passed and he spoke again. "How do you feel?"

"I could wish my feelings on my worst enemies."

Another pause, and then he whispered into her ear, "I want to ask you something."

"Yes."

"What are you accused of?"

"The same as you."

"I mean, what have you done wrong?"

"The same as you."

"It strikes me that you're annoyed about something."

"Annoyed! The boor! He plants himself on my feet and then complains that I'm annoyed."

"What are you saying? I, on your feet?"

"Who else?"

"It's he, that savage with the fur cap, may the devil take him!"

"Really? And I thought it was you. Forgive me if I hurt your feelings."

They could say no more, for the man in the fur cap roused himself and began whipping the horse furiously. The wagon leaped forward. The two prisoners listened to the quivering of their vitals. Suddenly the wagon came to a halt, and they beheld something they had never seen before.

III

For the first time in their lives they saw a tremendous gathering of horses, cows, calves, pigs, and people. There were wagons with hoods raised, filled with goods, loaves of bread, and living creatures—chickens, geese, and ducks piled on top of one another. To one side a bound pig lay on a wagon, and his screeches of protest were deafening, yet no one paid any attention to him. Everyone was excited, everyone talked at once, everyone bustled about—it was a regular fair.

It was to this place that the fur-capped savage brought them. He lowered himself from the wagon and began puttering around with his prisoners. They awoke, strangely excited. What would be done with them now? Would they be untied? Or would he free them and let them go at will?

But their joy was short-lived. He merely moved them somewhat higher on the wagon, probably so that they could be seen better. A terrible humiliation! And yet one could think of it in another way. Perhaps it would be better if everyone could see them. Let the world see! Some kind soul might take their part and demand an explanation from the savage: Why? For what?

Thus the innocent prisoners reasoned, and it seemed that they reasoned well, for a kind soul did appear, a thickset woman in a Turkish shawl. She approached, felt around in the wagon, and asked the fur cap, "Your pair?"

"Any of your business?"

"How much do you want?"

"Where will you get so much money?"

"If I had no money would I talk to a lout like you?"

Such was the conversation between the Turkish shawl and the fur cap. They haggled for a long time. The savage in the fur cap remained cold and indifferent. The woman in the Turkish shawl grew excited. She turned away as if to leave, but came back at once and the bargaining resumed. This went on so long that the fur cap grew angry and the two started cursing each other. Meanwhile the prisoners exchanged a few words.

"Do you hear, madam?"

"Of course. Why shouldn't I?"

"Is it likely we are about to be ransomed?"

"It certainly looks that way."

"Then why does she bargain over us as if we were geese?"

"The humiliation!"

"Well, let them quarrel, just as long as we go free."

"Amen! I hope so."

The Lord be praised! The Turkish shawl dipped her hand into her pocket and took out the money.

"You won't let the price down?"

"No."

"Perhaps—all right, all right, just look at him rage. Here's your money."

And the pair passed from the savage in the fur cap to the fat woman in the Turkish shawl—that is, from one bondage to another.

IV

At the new place the prisoners were untied. Joyfully they felt the ground beneath them. They stretched and paced back and forth to make sure their feet still served them. In their happiness, however, they neglected to notice they were still far from free. Indeed, it took them a while to realize that they remained prisoners. They found themselves in a dark corner, with a warm oven on one side, a cold wall on the other, and an overturned ladder barring the exit. Food and drink had been left for them, and they were now alone, at God's mercy, so to speak. After examining their new dwelling they stood eying each other for a long time, as strangers will, and then they turned each to his own corner, where each surrendered to his own thoughts.

But they were not allowed to think for long. The door of their prison opened, and a crowd of women headed by the Turkish shawl came in. The Turkish shawl led the women to the prisoners, pointed at them, and, her face aglow, asked, "How do you like these two?"

"How much did you pay for them?"

"Guess."

All of them guessed and all were wrong. When the Turkish shawl named the price they clapped their hands in amazement.

Envy crept into their faces. Their cheeks grew flushed, their eyes gleamed, but from their mouths flowed a stream of well wishing.

"Use them in good health! May you enjoy them! May you be as lucky all year! Together with your husband and children!"

"Amen! The same to you. The same to you."

The women left, and a moment later the Turkish shawl returned, leading in tow a man, a strange creature whose face was matted with red hair. Her face beamed with pride as she led him up to the prisoners.

"Now, *you* are a man of understanding, what do *you* think of this pair?"

The hairy person stared wildly. "I, an expert? What do I know of such things?"

"You're a scholar, and where there is learning there must be wisdom. Shouldn't God grant us a kosher Passover? Isn't it all for the sake of His precious name?"

The hairy person passed his hand over his beard, gazed heavenward, and intoned piously, "May the Almighty grant a kosher Passover to all Jews!"

The Turkish shawl and the hairy man departed, leaving the pair alone. For a moment they stood speechless, still wary of each other. Then she uttered a strange cry that was a cross between a cough and a scream.

He turned toward her. "What ails you, madam?"

"Nothing. I was thinking of home."

"Nonsense. You must forget that. We'd do better to get our bearings and consider what to do."

"Get our bearings? It's clear enough. We're in trouble, great trouble."

"For instance?"

"Don't you see we've been sold to savages just as one sells domestic beasts?"

"What will they do to us?"

"Plenty. When I was still a little bit of a thing I heard a lot of stories about what these savages do to those of our kind who fall into their hands."

"Nonsense! You mustn't believe in fairy tales."

"These aren't fairy tales. I heard it from my own sister. She said they are worse than wild beasts. When one of us is caught by a beast he is devoured, and that's all there is to it, but if—"

"There, there, my friend, it seems to me that you take too pessimistic a view of the world."

"Too which?"

"Too pessimistic."

"What does that mean, pessimistic?"

"It means, well, that you look through dark glasses."

"I don't wear glasses."

"Ha-ha."

"Why do you laugh?"

"Madam, you are a—"

"A what?"

He wanted to tell her, but the door suddenly opened and—

Better read on.

V

The door opened wide, and a mob of small fry charged in like a whirlwind. Their cheeks flushed and their black eyes eager, they dashed toward the oven.

"Where are they? Where? Here they are, right here. Yankel! Berel! Velvel! Elie! Getzel! Quick! Over here!"

Only now did the pair discover what hell really meant: torment, suffering, endless humiliation. The small fry fell upon them like savages in the jungle. They skipped around them, examining them from all sides and loudly ridiculing them.

"Yosel, just look at that nose!"

"A schnozzle, Berel, a real schnozzola."

"Velvel! Pull his nose."

"No, by the mouth, Elie, like this!"

"Pull harder, Getzel! Make him holler!"

"You're all crazy. They holler only when you whistle at them. They can't stand whistling. Want to see? I'll whistle: Pheeeeeeee."

Ruffled, the prisoners blushed, lowered their heads, and exclaimed in unison, *Halder! Halder! Halder!*

The small fry picked it up and savagely mocked them. "Hold him! Hold her! Hold 'em."

Further enraged, the prisoners shouted louder. The youngsters were delighted. Convulsed with laughter, they mocked still louder. "Hold him! Hold her! Hold 'em!"

This competition resulted in such a racket that the Turkish shawl, God bless her, came charging in, grabbed the small fry, and tossed them out one by one, giving each a few sound slaps. This procedure she concluded with an all-round curse. "May a stroke descend on you, O Lord of the World, a fire and a plague and a cholera. May it seize you and shake you one by one, together with all the apostates, dear God, and may not one of you remain to see the Passover, dear merciful God."

Once rid of this torment, the prisoners did not regain their composure for some time. The savage outcries, the whistling, the laughter of the little barbarians rang in their ears. Later our hero came gradually to realize that it was pointless to continue grieving on an empty stomach, and he slowly approached the food.

"Madam," he said to his companion, "how long will you keep worrying? It's time to eat. The heavens haven't caved in, believe me, and we haven't had a bite all day."

"Eat well. I don't care for any."

"Why not? Are you fasting?"

"No. It's just that I don't care for any."

"Perhaps you want to teach them a lesson? Go on a hunger strike? You'll only succeed in doing yourself harm—that's all the good it will do."

"I don't see how one can possibly eat anything. It just won't go down."

"It'll go down, it'll go down. The first bite acts like a drill."

"A what?"

"A drill."

"You do use such strange words."

"Ha-ha!"

"Laughing again? What's the occasion?"

"I remembered the small fry."

"That's no laughing matter."

"What do you want me to do? Cry?"

"Why didn't you laugh when they were here?"

"What did I do?"

"It seemed to me you screamed."

"I screamed? I?"

"Who else? Maybe I did?"

"You were the first to start crying *halder, halder, halder.*"

"Excuse me, but it was you who first cried *halder, halder.*"

"So what is there to be ashamed of if I was the first?"

"And why should I feel ashamed if I was the first?"

"If there is nothing to be ashamed of, why have you lowered your nose?"

"I lowered my nose?"

"Who else?"

"Oh, it's so easy to notice someone else's nose!"

It was a pity that this interesting conversation could not be continued, but they were interrupted by the Turkish shawl, the mistress of their prison—as will be related in the next chapter.

VI

The Turkish shawl, as it turned out, was not their only mistress. They were fated to make the acquaintance of still another strange creature, a girl with a greenish complexion and a red kerchief. The two entered with arms full of good things: a bowl of rice mixed with beans and peas, a plate of boiled potatoes, chopped eggs, and an apronful of sliced apples and nuts.

As soon as they came in the greenish maid with the red kerchief pointed to the pair and addressed the Turkish shawl. "Look, they haven't even touched the food."

"Let's feed them now. I'll hold them and you put it in their mouths. Well? Why are you standing there like a dummy, with your teeth hanging out?"

"Why do they scream so when they look at me?"

"Silly girl! Take off that kerchief—they can't stand red."

"May all my troubles descend on their heads!"

"On your own head, silly—you come first. Why don't you put some rice and beans into his mouth?"

"Mistress dear, may you live long! I don't like the way he stares. Be careful that he shouldn't, God forbid, choke."

"You choke—you come first! All of a sudden she talks of choking, as if it were the first time I've done this. Stuff it down his throat—this way! I've been a housekeeper for twenty-one years, thank God. Now put a piece of apple and a nut in his mouth. More, more, don't be stingy!"

"I begrudge him? Why should I? It isn't mine. It's simply a pity, the way he suffers!"

"What do you say to this girl! A pity, she says. Am I doing him any harm? I'm only feeding him. And for whose sake? For the sake of God! For the sake of the holy Passover! The Almighty help me, I have fattened more than one pair for Passover. Let's have another nut and make an end of it. He's had enough for now. Now her. Begin with rice and beans."

"Good health to you, mistress, but how can you tell which is he and which is she?"

"May all my evil dreams descend on your head! She's asked to do one thing and her mind is the devil knows where! Wait till you get married, silly girl, and become a housekeeper, then you'll ask. Meantime do as you are told. More, more, don't be stingy! It's for the sake of nobody, except His Precious Name. For Passover! For Passover!"

Finished with their task, the women went off and the tortured prisoners remained alone. They staggered into a corner, rested their mournful heads upon each other, and surrendered themselves to thoughts of sadness, such as come very rarely, perhaps only a few minutes before death.

VII

Nothing begets friendship so readily as trouble. The two unfortunate prisoners are the best proof of this. During the brief term of their imprisonment they became as one, they began to understand each other at a mere hint, they were no longer bashful before each other, and they gave up addressing each other with the formal "you." They became, indeed, like one soul. She would address him as "My dear," and he would counter with "My soul."

Whenever the Turkish shawl and the red kerchief came with the food they could not admire the pair enough.

"What do you say to my pair?"

"A delight."

"Just feel them. Now what do you say? Some flesh, eh? Now shouldn't God help me because of the pair I fattened for Passover?"

When their work was done the wild women left, and the couple pondered the meaning of the Turkish shawl's remarks that she "fattens them for Passover" and that God should help her. Why should He? They thought hard and discussed the matter.

"Dearest, what is Passover?"

"Passover, my soul, is a sort of holiday among them, a holiday of freedom, of liberation."

"What does that mean—liberation?"

"Let me explain it to you. They consider it a great good deed to catch one of our kind and fatten him until this holiday Passover comes around, and then they let him free. Now do you understand?"

"Is it long till this Passover?"

"According to what I overheard the Turkish shawl say, it shouldn't be more than about three days."

"Three days!"

"What scared you so, you silly? The three days will pass like a dream, and when the dear Passover comes, they will open the doors for us and, 'Out you go, back where you came from.' Will we make tracks!"

"Dearest, you say such wonderful things. If only it were as you say, but I am afraid of one thing—"

"Sweetheart, you are always afraid."

"My dear, you don't know these savages."

"And where did you learn about them?"

"I heard plenty about them, dearest; when still at home I heard tell such stories about them! My sister told me she saw it herself."

"Again your sister's stories? Forget them."

"I would gladly forget them, but I can't. I can't get them out of my head by day or out of my dreams by night."

"And what are these stories that bother you day and night?"

"Darling, you won't laugh at me?"

"Why should I laugh?"

"Because you are like that. Whenever I tell you something you laugh and call me a silly goose or a foolish turkey or some other name."

"I promise not to laugh. Now tell me what you heard from your sister."

"My sister told me that people are worse than beasts. When a wild beast catches one of us it devours him and that's all, but when people catch one of us they imprison him and feed him well until he gets fat."

"And then?"

"And then they slaughter him and skin him and cut him to pieces and sprinkle salt on him and soak him."

"And then?"

"And then they make a fire and fry him in his own fat and eat him, meat, bones, and everything."

"Fairy tales, nothing to it, a cow flew over the moon. And you, you silly, you believe all this? Ha-ha-ha!"

"Well? What did I say? Didn't I say you'd laugh at me?"

"What else did you expect me to do, when you don't understand anything at all? It seems to me you must have heard a hundred times that the Turkish shawl said she was feeding us for the sake of no one but God."

"So what of it?"

"Just this, darling, that you are a silly goose."

"That is your nature! Right away you become insulting."

"Who do you mean by 'you'?"

"I mean all of you men!"

"All men? I am curious to know how many men you have known."

"I know only one, and that's quite enough for me."

"Oh no, you said 'men,' and that means you knew others besides me."

"What will you think of next?"

"Now you are angry again. Come here, I want to whisper something to you."

This loving scene was suddenly interrupted by the gang of small fry outside the window. They were not permitted inside, so they came each day to the window, and there they made strange gestures, stuck out their tongues, and shouted *halder, halder, halder*. The two would naturally respond, not as angrily as they had the first time, but more in the way of a greeting.

There is nothing in the world to which God's creatures can't become accustomed. Our prisoners had grown so used to their troubles that they now thought things were as they should be, just like the proverbial worm that has made its home in horseradish and thinks it sweet.

VIII

There came a foggy morning. Inside it was still dark. The pair was immersed in deep sleep. They dreamed of their old home—a broad, unfenced out-of-doors, a blue sky, green grass, a shining brook, a mill that turned around, made noise, and splashed water. Ducks and geese splashed near the bank. Hens scratched, roosters crowed, birds flew about. What a beautiful world God had made for them. For them? Of course. For whom else were the tall, broad-branched trees under which one could stroll? For whom else was the mill where their entire family fed without letting anyone else near? For whom the round light in the sky that dipped into the river each evening? What wouldn't they give now for just one more look at the beautiful warm sun! at the big, free, light out-of-doors! at the mill and everything near it!

In the very midst of these sweet dreams they were seized and carried out. The fresh air of the foggy morning hit them full force. Another instant and they would take off and fly away over roofs and gardens and forests to where their home had been. There they would meet their own kind. "Welcome home, where have you been?" "Among wild people." "What did they do with you?" "They fed us for Passover." "What is Passover?" "It's a sort of holiday among people, a fine, dear holiday of freedom and liberation."

This is how they dreamed as they were taken to a narrow, dank alley where they were dropped in the mud. The wall was spattered with blood and many bound fowl lay on the ground in pairs and even in threes. Alongside stood young women and girls chatting and giggling. The pair looked about. Why had they been brought there? What were all the bound fowl doing there? What were the women and girls giggling about? And what was the meaning of the bloodstained wall? Was this the dear, good holiday of Passover? And what about freedom? And liberation?

Thus did the pair reason as they examined the bound fowl that lay quietly without asking any questions, as if this were the natural order of events. Only one loud-mouthed hen did not rest. Straining with all her strength, she flapped her wings in the mud and raved insanely. "Let me go! Let me go! I don't want to lie here! I want to run! Let me go!"

"Cockadoodledooo," a red rooster bound to two hens responded. "What do you say to this smarty? She doesn't want to lie here! She wants to go, she wants to run. Ha-ha!"

Our hero raised his head, carefully examined the insolent red rooster, and felt the blood rushing to his head. He could have sworn that he knew the fellow; he had seen him somewhere, had heard him before, but where? He couldn't remember. Yet wasn't there something hauntingly familiar about him? In heaven's name, where had he seen him? He raised his head a little higher, and the rooster noticed him and intoned in his high soprano:

Cockadoodledooo . . .
You were led
And you were fed,
Now you're tied,
Soon you'll be fried—

The red poet had no chance to finish. Someone's hand grabbed him with such force and so unexpectedly that he suddenly lost his voice.

The one who grabbed the rooster was an uncouth fellow with sleepy eyes, tall, thin, with long earlocks, his sleeves rolled up and his coat tails tucked in. In his hand he held a black shiny knife. Without delay he drew the rooster to himself, pulled up his head, looked briefly into his eyes, plucked three small feathers from his neck, and, *fft,* he passed the knife over his throat and tossed him back into the mud. For a moment the rooster lay motionless, as if stunned, then he got up and started running and turning his head back and forth as if looking for someone, or as if he had lost something. Our hero looked at the rooster and recognized him; it was the same one he had seen in his dream, and he recalled the song the rooster had sung. Now he could not say a word to his beloved, who lay close to him, trembling in all her limbs.

Meanwhile the savage with the shining knife proceeded with his work, unconcerned, like a true executioner. One after another the fowl flew from his hands, each first being tickled on the throat with the knife before being tossed into the mud. Some stretched out their legs, trembled, and kicked as they lost blood. Others flapped their wings. And every minute more victims joined them with cut throats. The women and girls observed all this yet did not seem to mind. On the contrary, some of them seized upon the still living fowl and started plucking their feathers, meantime chatting and joking and giggling as if it were water that flowed instead of the blood of living creatures. Where were their eyes? Where were their ears? And their hearts? And their sense of justice? And their God?

Our two bound prisoners watched the terrible scene, the horrible carnage at daybreak. Could it be that they too had been brought here for the same purpose as the chickens, ducks, and geese? Could it be that aristocrats, who hailed from among the Indians, would share this terrible end with ordinary beings? Was it really true, what they had been told about these savages? And the prophecy of the red rooster, was that also true?

They began to understand the cold, bare truth and to comprehend everything they had seen and heard. One thing only they could not fathom. Why had the Turkish shawl boasted that God would reward her for fattening such a pair for Passover? Was that what their God wanted?

A few minutes later our loving pair, the prisoners, lay on the ground. Their still warm throats rested on each other, and from a distance it might have seemed they were asleep and dreaming beautiful dreams.

WHEN I WAS THIRTEEN

by Denton Welch

When I was thirteen, I went to Switzerland for the Christmas holidays in the charge of my eldest brother, who was at that time still up at Oxford.

In the hotel we found another undergraduate whom my brother knew.

From *Horizon*, April 1944, Vol. 4, No. 52, pp. 250–65. Reprinted by permission of David Higham Associates Ltd.

His name was Archer. They were not at the same college, but they had met and evidently had not agreed with each other. At first my brother William would say nothing about Archer; then one day, in answer to a question of mine, he said: 'He's not very much liked; although he's a very good swimmer.' As he spoke, William held his lips in a very firm, almost pursed, line which was most damaging to Archer.

After this I began to look at Archer with a certain amount of interest. He had broad shoulders but was not tall. He had a look of strength and solidity which I admired and envied. He had rather a nice pug face with insignificant nose and broad cheeks. Sometimes, when he was animated, a tassel of fair, almost colourless, hair would fall across his forehead, half covering one eye. He had a thick beautiful neck, rather meaty barbarian hands, and a skin as smooth and evenly coloured as a pink fondant.

His whole body appeared to be suffused with this gentle pink colour. He never wore proper ski-ing clothes of waterproof material like the rest of us. Usually he came out in nothing but a pair of grey flannels and a white cotton shirt with all the buttons left undone. When the sun grew very hot, he would even discard this thin shirt, and ski up and down the slopes behind the hotel in nothing but his trousers. I had often seen him fall down in this half-naked state and get buried in snow. The next moment he would jerk himself to his feet again, laughing and swearing.

After William's curt nod to him on our first evening at the hotel, we had hardly exchanged any remarks. We sometimes passed one another on the way to the basement to get our skis in the morning, and often we found ourselves sitting near Archer on the glassed-in terrace; but some Oxford snobbery I knew nothing of, or some more profound reason, always made William throw off waves of hostility. Archer never showed any signs of wishing to approach. He was content to look at me sometimes with a mild inoffensive curiosity, but he seemed to ignore William completely. This pleased me more than I would have admitted at that time. I was so used to being passed over myself by all William's friends, that it was pleasant when someone who knew him seemed to take a sort of interest, however slight and amused, in me.

William was often away from the hotel for days and nights together, going for expeditions with guides and other friends. He would never take me because he said I was too young and had not enough stamina. He said that I would fall down a crevasse or get my nose frost-bitten, or hang up the party by lagging behind.

In consequence I was often alone at the hotel; but I did not mind this; I enjoyed it. I was slightly afraid of my brother William and found life very much easier and less exacting when he was not there. I think other people in the hotel thought that I looked lonely. Strangers would often come up and talk to me and smile, and once a nice absurd Belgian woman, dressed from head to foot in a babyish suit of fluffy orange knitted wool, held out a bright five-franc piece to me and told me to go and buy chocolate caramels with it. I think she must have taken me for a much younger child.

On one of these afternoons when I had come in from the Nursery Slopes and was sitting alone over my tea on the sun-terrace, I noticed that

Archer was sitting in the corner huddled over a book and munching greedily and absent-mindedly.

I, too, was reading a book, while I ate delicious rhum-babas and little tarts filled with worm-castles of chestnut purée topped with caps of whipped cream. I have called the meal tea, but what I was drinking was not tea but chocolate. When I poured out, I held the pot high in the air, so that my cup, when filled, should be covered in a rich froth of bubbles.

The book I was reading was Tolstoy's *Resurrection*. Although I did not quite understand some parts of it, it gave me intense pleasure to read it while I ate the rich cakes and drank the frothy chocolate. I thought it a noble and terrible story, but I was worried and mystified by the words 'illegitimate child' which had occurred several times lately. What sort of child could this be? Clearly a child that brought trouble and difficulty. Could it have some terrible disease, or was it a special sort of imbecile? I looked up from my book, still wondering about this phrase 'illegitimate child,' and saw that Archer had turned in his creaking wicker chair and was gazing blankly in my direction. The orchestra was playing 'The Birth of the Blues' in a rather remarkable Swiss arrangement, and it was clear that Archer had been distracted from his book by the music, only to be lulled into a daydream, as he gazed into space.

Suddenly his eyes lost their blank look and focused on my face. 'Your brother off up to the Jungfrau Joch again, or somewhere?' he called out.

I nodded my head, saying nothing, becoming slightly confused.

Archer grinned. He seemed to find me amusing.

'What are you reading?' he asked.

'This,' I said, taking my book over to him. I did not want to call out either the word 'Resurrection' or 'Tolstoy.' But Archer did not make fun of me for reading a 'classic,' as most of William's friends would have done. He only said: 'I should think it's rather good. Mine's frightful; it's called *The Story of My Life,* by Queen Marie of Roumania.' He held the book up and I saw an extraordinary photograph of a lady who looked like a snake-charmer in full regalia. The head-dress seemed to be made of white satin, embroidered with beads, stretched over cardboard. There were tassels and trailing things hanging down everywhere.

I laughed at the amusing picture and Archer went on: 'I always read books like this when I can get them. Last week I had Lady Oxford's autobiography, and before that I found a perfectly wonderful book called *Flaming Sex.* It was by a French woman who married an English knight and then went back to France to shoot a French doctor. She didn't kill him, of course, but she was sent to prison, where she had a very interesting time with the nuns who looked after her in the hospital. I also lately found an old book by a Crown Princess of Saxony who ended up picnicking on a haystack with a simple Italian gentleman in a straw hat. I love these "real life" stories, don't you?'

I again nodded my head, not altogether daring to venture on a spoken answer. I wondered whether to go back to my own table or whether to pluck up courage and ask Archer what an 'illegitimate child' was. He solved the problem by saying 'Sit down' rather abruptly.

I subsided next to him with 'Tolstoy' on my knee. I waited for a moment and then plunged.

'What exactly does "illegitimate child" mean?' I asked rather breathlessly.

'Outside the law—when two people have a child although they're not married.'

'Oh.' I went bright pink. I thought Archer must be wrong. I still believed that it was quite impossible to have a child unless one was married. The very fact of being married produced the child. I had a vague idea that some particularly reckless people attempted, without being married, to have children in places called 'night clubs,' but they were always unsuccessful, and this made them drink, and plunge into the most hectic gaiety.

I did not tell Archer that I thought he had made a mistake, for I did not want to hurt his feelings. I went on sitting at his table and, although he turned his eyes back to his book and went on reading, I knew that he was friendly.

After some time he looked up again and said: 'Would you like to come out with me tomorrow? We could take our lunch, go up the mountain and then ski down in the afternoon.'

I was delighted at the suggestion, but also a little alarmed at my own shortcomings. I thought it my duty to explain that I was not a very good skier, only a moderate one, and that I could only do stem turns. I hated the thought of being a drag on Archer.

'I expect you're much better than I am. I'm always falling down or crashing into something,' he answered.

It was all arranged. We were to meet early, soon after six, as Archer wanted to go to the highest station on the mountain railway and then climb on skis to a nearby peak which had a small rest-house of logs.

I went to bed very excited, thankful that William was away on a long expedition. I lay under my enormous feather-bed eiderdown, felt the freezing mountain air on my face, and saw the stars sparkling through the open window.

I got up very early in the morning and put on my most sober ski socks and woollen shirt, for I felt that Archer disliked any suspicion of bright colours or dressing-up. I made my appearance as workmanlike as possible, and then went down to breakfast.

I ate several crackly rolls, which I spread thickly with dewy slivers of butter and gobbets of rich black cherry jam; then I drank my last cup of coffee and went to wax my skis. As I passed through the hall I picked up my picnic lunch in its neat grease-proof paper packet.

The nails in my boots slid and then caught on the snow, trodden hard down to the basement door. I found my skis in their rack, took them down and then heated the iron and the wax. I loved spreading the hot black wax smoothly on the white wood. Soon they were both done beautifully.

I will go like a bird, I thought.

I looked up and saw Archer standing in the doorway.

'I hope you haven't put too much on, else you'll be sitting on your arse all day,' he said gaily.

How fresh and pink he looked! I was excited.

He started to wax his own skis. When they were finished, we went outside and strapped them on. Archer carried a rucksack and he told me to put my lunch and my spare sweater into it.

We started off down the gentle slopes to the station. The sun was shining prickingly. The lovely snow had rainbow colours in it. I was so happy I swung my sticks with their steel points and basket ends. I even tried to show off, and jumped a little terrace which I knew well. Nevertheless it nearly brought me down. I just regained my balance in time. I would have hated at that moment to have fallen down in front of Archer.

When we got to the station we found a compartment to ourselves. It was still early. Gently we were pulled up the mountain, past the water station stop and the other three halts.

We got out at the very top where the railway ended. A huge unused snow-plough stood by the side of the track, with its vicious shark's nose pointed at me. We ran to the van to get out our skis. Archer found mine as well as his own and slung both pairs across his shoulders. He looked like a very tough Jesus carrying two crosses, I thought.

We stood by the old snow-plough and slipped on our skis; then we began to climb laboriously up the ridge to the wooden rest-house. We hardly talked at all, for we needed all our breath, and also, I was still shy of Archer. Sometimes he helped me, telling me where to place my skis, and, if I slipped backwards, hauling on the rope which he had half playfully tied round my waist.

In spite of growing tired, I enjoyed the grim plodding. It gave me a sense of work and purpose. When Archer looked round to smile at me, his pink face was slippery with sweat. His white shirt above the small rucksack was plastered to his shoulder-blades. On my own face I could feel the drops of sweat just being held back by my eyebrows. I would wipe my hand across my upper lip and break all the tiny beads that had formed there.

Every now and then Archer would stop. We would put our skis sideways on the track and rest, leaning forward on our sticks. The sun struck down on our necks with a steady seeping heat and the light striking up from the snow was as bright as the fiery dazzle of a mirror. From the ridge we could see down into two valleys; and standing all round us were the other peaks, black rock and white snow, tangling and mixing until the mountains looked like vast teeth which had begun to decay.

I was so tired when we reached the long gentle incline to the rest-house that I was afraid of falling down. The rope was still round my waist, and so the slightest lagging would have been perceptible to Archer. I think he must have slackened his pace for my benefit, for I somehow managed to reach the iron seats in front of the hut. I sank down, still with my skis on. I half shut my eyes. From walking so long with my feet turned out, my ankles felt almost broken.

The next thing I knew was that Archer had disappeared into the rest-house. He came out carrying a steaming cup.

'You must drink this,' he said, holding out black coffee to me, which I hated. He unwrapped four lumps of sugar and dropped them in the cup.

'I don't like it black,' I said.

'Never mind,' he answered sharply, 'drink it.'

Rather surprised, I began to drink the syrupy coffee. 'The sugar and the strong coffee will be good for you,' said Archer. He went back into the rest-house and brought out a glass of what looked like hot water with a piece of lemon floating in it. The mountain of sugar at the bottom was melting into thin Arabian Nights wreaths and spirals, smoke-rings of syrup.

'What else has it got in it?' I asked, with an attempt at worldliness.

'Rum!' said Archer.

We sat there on the terrace and unwrapped our picnic lunches. We both had two rolls, one with tongue in it, and one with ham, a hard-boiled egg, sweet biscuits, and a bar of delicious bitter chocolate; tangerine oranges were our dessert.

We began to take huge bites out of our rolls. We could not talk for some time. The food brought out a thousand times more clearly the beauty of the mountain peaks and sun. My tiredness made me thrillingly conscious of delight and satisfaction. I wanted to sit there with Archer for a long time.

At the end of the meal Archer gave me a piece of his own bar of chocolate, and then began to skin pigs of tangerine very skilfully and hand them to me on his outstretched palm, as one offers a lump of sugar to a horse. I thought for one moment of bending down my head and licking the pigs up in imitation of a horse; then I saw how mad it would look.

We threw the brilliant tangerine peel into the snow, which immediately seemed to dim and darken its colour.

Archer felt in his hip pocket and brought out black, cheap Swiss cigarettes, wrapped in leaf. They were out of a slot machine. He put one between my lips and lighted it. I felt extremely conscious of the thing jutting out from my lips. I wondered if I would betray my ignorance by not breathing the smoke in and out correctly. I turned my head a little away from Archer and experimented. It seemed easy if one did not breathe too deeply. It was wonderful to be really smoking with Archer. He treated me just like a man.

'Come on, let's get cracking,' he said, 'or, if anything happens, we'll be out all night.'

I scrambled to my feet at once and snapped the clips of the skis round my boot heels. Archer was in high spirits from the rum. He ran on his skis along the flat ridge in front of the rest-house and then fell down.

'Serves me right,' he said. He shook the snow off and we started properly. In five minutes we had swooped down the ridge we had climbed so painfully all morning. The snow was perfect; new and dry with no crust. We followed a new way which Archer had discovered. The ground was uneven with dips and curves. Often we were out of sight of each other. When we came to the icy path through a wood, my courage failed me.

'Stem like hell and don't get out of control,' Archer yelled back at me. I pointed my skis together, praying that they would not cross. I leant on my sticks, digging their metal points into the compressed snow. Twice I fell, though not badly.

'Well done, well done!' shouted Archer, as I shot past him and out of the wood into a thick snowdrift. He hauled me out of the snow and stood me on my feet, beating me all over hastily to get off the snow, then we began the descent of a field called the 'Bumps.' Little hillocks, if manoevered successfully, gave one that thrilling sinking and rising feeling experienced on a scenic railway at a fun fair.

Archer went before me, dipping and rising, shouting and yelling in his exuberance. I followed more sedately. We both fell several times, but in that not unpleasant, bouncing way which brings you to your feet again almost at once.

Archer was roaring now and trying to yodel in an absurd, rich contralto. I had never enjoyed myself quite so much before. I thought him the most wonderful companion, not a bit intimidating, in spite of being rather a hero.

When at last we swooped down to the village street, it was nearly evening. Early orange lights were shining in the shop windows. We planked our skis down on the hard, iced road, trying not to slip.

I looked in at the *patisserie, confiserie* window, where all the electric bulbs had fluffy pink shades like powder-puffs. Archer saw my look.

'Let's go in,' he said. He ordered me hot chocolate with whipped cream, and *croissant* rolls. Afterwards we both went up to the little counter and chose cakes. I had one shaped like a little log. It was made of soft chocolate, and had green moss trimmings made in pistachio nut. When Archer went to pay the bill he bought me some chocolate caramels, in a little birds-eye maple box, and a bar labelled *'Chocolat Polychrome.'* Each finger was a different-coloured cream: mauve, pink, green, yellow, orange, brown, white, even blue.

We went out into the village street and began to climb up the path to the hotel. About half-way up Archer stopped outside a little wooden chalet and said: 'This is where I hang out.'

'But you're staying at the hotel,' I said incredulously.

'Oh yes, I have all my meals there, but I sleep here. It's a sort of little annex when there aren't any rooms left in the hotel. It's only got two rooms; I've paid just a bit more and got it all to myself. Someone comes every morning and makes the bed and stokes the boiler and the stove. Come in and see it.'

I followed Archer up the outside wooden staircase and stood with him on the little landing outside the two rooms. The place seemed wonderfully warm and dry. The walls were unpainted wood; there were double windows. There was a gentle creaking in all the joints of the wood when one moved. Archer pushed open one of the doors and ushered me in. I saw in one corner a huge white porcelain stove, the sort I had only before seen in pictures. Some of Archer's ski-ing gloves and socks were drying round it on a ledge. Against another wall were two beds, like wooden troughs built into the wall. The balloon-like quilts bulged up above the wood.

'I hardly use the other room,' said Archer. 'I just throw my muck into it and leave my trunks there.' He opened the connecting door and I saw a smaller room with dirty clothes strewn on the floor; white shirts, hard evening collars, some very short pants, and many pairs of thick grey socks. The room smelt mildly of Archer's old sweat. I didn't mind at all.

Archer shut the door and said: 'I'm going to run the bath.'

'Have you a bathroom too—all your own?' I exclaimed enviously. 'Every time anyone has a bath at the hotel, he has to pay two francs fifty to the fraulein before she unlocks the door. I've only had two proper baths since I've been here. I don't think it matters though. It seems almost impossible to get really dirty in Switzerland, and you can always wash all over in your bedroom basin.'

'Why don't you have a bath here after me? The water's lovely and hot, although there's not much of it. If you went back first and got your evening clothes, you could change straight into them.'

I looked at Archer a little uncertainly. I longed to soak in hot water after my wonderful but gruelling day.

'Could I really bath here?' I asked.

'If you don't mind using my water. I'll promise not to pee in it. I'm not really filthy you know.'

Archer laughed and chuckled, because he saw me turning red at his coarseness. He lit another of his peasant cigarettes and began to unlace his boots. He got me to pull them off. I knelt down, bowed my head and pulled. When the ski boot suddenly flew off, my nose dipped forward and I smelt Archer's foot in its woolly, hairy, humid casing of sock.

'Would you just rub my foot and leg?' Archer said urgently, a look of pain suddenly shooting across his face. 'I've got cramp. It often comes on at the end of the day.'

He shot his leg out rigidly and told me where to rub and massage. I felt each of his curled toes separately and the hard tendons in his leg. His calf was like a firm sponge ball. His thigh, swelling out, amazed me. I likened it in my mind to the trumpet of some musical instrument. I went on rubbing methodically. I was able to feel his pain melting away.

When the tense look had quite left his face, he said, 'Thanks,' and stood up. He unbuttoned his trousers, let them fall to the ground, and pulled his shirt up. Speaking to me with his head imprisoned in it, he said: 'You go and get your clothes and I'll begin bathing.'

I left him and hurried up to the hotel, carrying my skis on my shoulder. I ran up to my room and pulled my evening clothes out of the wardrobe. The dinner jacket and trousers had belonged to my brother William six years before, when he was my age. I was secretly ashamed of this fact, and had taken my brother's name from the inside of the breast pocket and had written my own in elaborate lettering.

I took my comb, face flannel and soap, and getting out my toboggan slid back to Archer's chalet in a few minutes. I let myself in and heard Archer splashing. The little hall was full of steam and I saw Archer's shoulders and arms like a pink smudge through the open bathroom door.

'Come and scrub my back,' he yelled; 'it gives me a lovely feeling.' He thrust a large stiff nailbrush into my hands and told me to scrub as hard as I could.

I ran it up and down his back until I'd made harsh red tramlines. Delicious tremors seemed to be passing through Archer.

'Ah! go on!' said Archer in a dream, like a purring cat. 'When I'm rich I'll have a special back-scratcher slave.' I went on industriously scrubbing his back till I was afraid that I would rub the skin off. I liked to give him pleasure.

At last he stood up all dripping and said: 'Now it's your turn.'

I undressed and got into Archer's opaque, soapy water. I lay back and wallowed. Archer poured some very smelly salts on to my stomach. One crystal stuck in my naval and tickled and grated against me.

'This whiff ought to cover up all remaining traces of me!' Archer laughed.

'What's the smell supposed to be?' I asked, brushing the crystals off my stomach into the water, and playing with the one that lodged so snugly in my naval.

'Russian pine,' said Archer, shutting his eyes ecstatically and making inbreathing dreamy noises. He rubbed himself roughly with the towel and made his hair stand up on end.

I wanted to soak in the bath for hours, but it was already getting late, and so I had to hurry.

Archer saw what difficulty I had in tying my tie. He came up to me and said: 'Let me do it.' I turned round relieved, but slightly ashamed of being incompetent.

I kept very still, and he tied it tightly and rapidly with his ham-like hands. He gave the bows a little expert jerk and pat. His eyes had a very concentrated, almost crossed look and I felt him breathing down on my face. All down the front our bodies touched featherily; little points of warmth came together. The hard boiled shirts were like slightly warmed dinner-plates.

When I had brushed my hair, we left the chalet and began to walk up the path to the hotel. The beaten snow was so slippery, now that we were shod only in patent leather slippers, that we kept sliding backwards. I threw out my arms, laughing, and shouting to Archer to rescue me; then, when he grabbed me and started to haul me to him, he too would begin to slip. It was a still, Prussian-blue night with rather weak stars. Our laughter seemed to ring across the valley, to hit the mountains and then to travel on and on and on.

We reached the hotel a little the worse for wear. The soles of my patent-leather shoes had become soaked, and there was snow on my trousers. Through bending forward, the studs in Archer's shirt had burst undone, and the slab of hair hung over one of his eyes as I had noticed before. We went into the cloak-room to readjust ourselves; then we entered the dining-room.

'Come and sit at my table,' Archer said; then he added:

'No, we'll sit at yours, as there are two places there already.'

We sat down and began to eat Roman *gnocchi.* (The proprietor of the hotel was Italian-Swiss.) I did not like mine very much and was glad when I could go on to *oeufs au beurre noir.* Now that my brother was away I could pick and choose in this way, leaving out the meat course, if I chose to, without causing any comment.

Archer drank Pilsner and suggested that I should too. Not wanting to disagree with him, I nodded my head, although I hated the pale, yellow, bitter water.

After the meal Archer ordered me *crème de menthe* with my coffee; I had seen a nearby lady drinking this pretty liquid and asked him about it. To be ordered a liqueur in all seriousness was a thrilling moment for me. I sipped the fumy peppermint, which left such an artificial heat in my throat and chest, and thought that apart from my mother who was dead, I had never liked anyone so much as I liked Archer. He didn't try to interfere with me at all. He just took me as I was and yet seemed to like me.

Archer was now smoking a proper cigar, not the leaf-rolled cigarettes we had had at lunch-time. He offered me one too, but I had the sense to realize that he did not mean me to take one and smoke it there before the eyes of all the hotel. I knew also that it would have made me sick, for my father had given me a cigar when I was eleven, in an attempt to put me off smoking for ever.

I always associated cigars with middle-aged men, and I watched Archer interestedly, thinking how funny the stiff fat thing looked sticking out of his young mouth.

We were sitting on the uncurtained sun-terrace, looking out on to the snow in the night; the moon was just beginning to rise. It made the snow glitter suddenly, like fish-scales. Behind us people were dancing in the salon and adjoining rooms. The music came to us in angry snatches, some notes distorted, others quite obliterated. Archer did not seem to want to dance. He seemed content to sit with me in silence.

Near me on a what-not stand stood a high-heeled slipper made of china. I took it down and slipped my hand into it. How hideously ugly the china pom-poms were down the front! The painted centipede climbing up the red heel wore a knowing, human expression. I moved my fingers in the china shoe, pretending they were toes.

'I love monstrosities, too,' said Archer, as I put the shoe back beside the fern in its crinkly paper-covered pot.

Later we wandered to the buffet bar and stood there drinking many glasses of the *limonade* which was made with white wine. I took the tinkly pieces of ice into my mouth and sucked them, trying to cool myself a little. Blood seemed to rise in my face; my head buzzed.

Suddenly I felt full of *limonade* and lager. I left Archer to go to the cloak-room, but he followed and stood beside me in the next china niche, while the water flushed and gushed importantly in the polished copper tubes, and an interesting, curious smell came from the wire basket which held some strange disinfectant crystals. Archer stood so quietly and guardingly beside me there that I had to say:

'Do I look queer?'

'No, you don't look queer; you look nice,' he said simply.

A rush of surprise and pleasure made me hotter still. We clanked over the tiles and left the cloak-room.

In the hall, I remembered that I had left all my ski-ing clothes at the chalet.

'I shall need them in the morning,' I said to Archer.

'Let's go down there now, then I can make cocoa on my spirit-lamp, and you can bring the clothes back with you.'

We set out in the moonlight; Archer soon took my arm, for he saw that

I was drunk, and the path was more slippery than ever. Archer sang *Stille Nacht* in German, and I began to cry. I could not stop myself. It was such a delight to cry in the moonlight with Archer singing my favourite song; and William far away up the mountain.

Suddenly we both sat down on our behinds with a thump. There was a jarring pain at the bottom of my spine but I began to laugh wildly; so did Archer. We lay there laughing, the snow melting under us and soaking through the seats of our trousers and the shoulders of our jackets.

Archer pulled me to my feet and dusted me down with hard slaps. My teeth grated together each time he slapped me. He saw that I was becoming more and more drunk in the freezing air. He propelled me along to the chalet, more or less frog-marching me in an expert fashion. I was quite content to leave myself in his hands.

When he got me upstairs, he put me into one of the bunks and told me to rest. The feathers ballooned out round me. I sank down deliciously. I felt as if I were floating down some magic staircase for ever.

Archer got his little meta-stove out and made coffee—not cocoa as he had said. He brought me over a strong cup and held it to my lips. I drank it unthinkingly and not tasting it, doing it only because he told me to.

When he took the cup away, my head fell back on the pillow, and I felt myself sinking and floating away again. I was on skis this time, but they were liquid skis, made of melted glass, and the snow was glass too, but a sort of glass that was springy, like gelatine, and flowing like water.

I felt a change in the light, and knew that Archer was bending over me. Very quietly he took off my shoes, undid my tie, loosened the collar and unbuttoned my braces in front. I remembered thinking, before I finally fell asleep, how clever he was to know about undoing the braces; they had begun to feel so tight pulling down on my shoulders and dragging the trousers up between my legs. Archer covered me with several blankets and another quilt.

When I woke in the morning, Archer was already up. He had made me some tea and had put it on the stove to keep warm. He brought it over to me and I sat up. I felt ill, rather sick. I remembered what a glorious day yesterday had been, and thought how extraordinary it was that I had not slept in my own bed at the hotel, but in Archer's room, in my clothes.

I looked at him shamefacedly. 'What happened last night? I felt peculiar,' I said.

'The lager and the lemonade, and the *crème de menthe* made you a bit tight, I'm afraid,' Archer said, laughing.

'Do you feel better now? We'll go up to the hotel and have breakfast soon.'

I got up and washed and changed into my ski-ing clothes. I still felt rather sick. I made my evening clothes into a neat bundle and tied them on to my toboggan. I had the sweets Archer had given me in my pocket.

We went up to the hotel, dragging the toboggan behind us.

And there on the doorstep we met William with one of the guides. They had had to return early, because someone in the party had broken a ski.

William was in a temper. He looked at us and then said to me: 'What have you been doing?'

I was at a loss to know what to answer. The very sight of William had so troubled me that this added difficulty of explaining my actions was too much for me.

I looked at him miserably and mouthed something about going in to have breakfast.

William turned to Archer fiercely, but said nothing.

Archer explained: 'Your brother's just been down to my place. We went ski-ing together yesterday and he left some clothes at the chalet.'

'It's very early,' was all William said; then he swept me on into the hotel before him, without another word to the guide or to Archer.

He went with me up to my room and saw that the bed had not been slept in.

I said clumsily: 'The maid must have been in and done my room early.' I could not bear to explain to William about my wonderful day, or why I had slept at the chalet.

William was so furious that he took no more notice of my weak explanations and lies.

When I suddenly said in desperation, 'I feel sick,' he seized me, took me to the basin, forced his fingers down my throat and struck me on the back till a yellow cascade of vomit gushed out of my mouth. My eyes were filled with stinging water; I was trembling. I ran the water in the basin madly, to wash away this sign of shame.

Gradually I grew a little more composed. I felt better, after being sick, and William had stopped swearing at me. I filled the basin with freezing water and dipped my face into it. The icy feel seemed to bite round my eye-sockets and make the flesh round my nose firm again. I waited, holding my breath for as long as possible.

Suddenly my head was pushed down and held. I felt William's hard fingers digging into my neck. He was hitting me now with a slipper, beating my buttocks and my back with slashing strokes, hitting a different place each time, as he had been taught as a prefect at school, so that the flesh should not be numbed from a previous blow.

I felt that I was going to choke. I could not breathe under the water, and realized that I would die. I was seized with such a panic that I wrenched myself free from William and darted round the room, with him after me. Water dripped on the bed, the carpet, the chest of drawers. Splashes of it spat against the mirror in the wardrobe door. William aimed vicious blows at me until he had driven me into a corner. There he beat against my uplifted arms, yelling in a hoarse, mad, religious voice: 'Bastard, Devil, Harlot, Sod!'

As I cowered under his blows, I remember thinking that my brother had suddenly become a lunatic and was talking gibberish in his madness, for, of the words he was using, I had not heard any before, except 'Devil.'

The Alter Ego

LIKE the Scapegoat archetype, that of the Alter Ego has two aspects, the anthropological and the psychological, and exactly the same relationship exists between them; that is, the first represents a collective manifestation in religion and folklore of the second.

The belief in a multiple soul is found in many primitive societies. In one form of this belief, a man is thought to have a "bush soul" incarnate in a wild animal or tree, with which he has a kind of psychic identity. In another form, the individual soul is thought to consist of several parts, separate but linked: Since primitive man also believes that he is surrounded by spirits, some good and some evil, it becomes difficult to distinguish between cases in which an individual is thought to be dominated by one part of his soul at the expense of the others and cases in which he is believed to be the victim of influences from without.

Perhaps the commonest form of the Alter Ego archetype is that in which an individual is believed to have a counterpart, or double. Ralph Tymms, in what is the most thorough study of the Alter Ego in literature,[1] distinguishes between doubles-by-duplication and doubles-by-division, but rightly observes that in practice the two are constantly mingling. The belief in doubles, he suggests, may have arisen as an attempt to explain dreams or hallucinations in which the individual seemed to perceive himself as a separate being. A rational explanation for this, he suggests, may be a visual memory on the part of the dreamer of his own shadow or reflection, and he cites Lévy-Bruhl to the effect that primitive man often believes that his shadow "is his spiritual double, and forms an extension, and vital part of him." Sir James Frazer notes that in some cultures it is believed that one can inflict harm upon an enemy by striking at his shadow, so that in primitive thought the latter comes to be identified with the soul, which when separated from the body results in death. The belief that the soul can be duplicated magically by fashioning an image of the individual is universal; one sees a modern example of it in the reluctance with

[1] Ralph Tymms, *Doubles in Literary Psychology* (Cambridge: Bowes and Bowes, 1949).

which certain Moslems will permit themselves to be photographed.

Frazer explains another widespread theory of the soul that visualizes it as being neither shadow nor reflection but as a creature "with the same features, the same gait, even the same dress as the man himself." This being may roam about independently of the owner when the latter is asleep, ill, or dead, though if violence is done to the owner's body or corpse the double is affected correspondingly. (Note that the girl in "The Disembodied Soul" has been sick in her room during the five years that her double has been happily married.) If the owner is dead and the spirit haunts living people, the only way in which it may be exorcised is through destruction of the corpse. The belief in vampires and werewolves is proof of the persistence of this theory.

Psychologically, the splitting of the human psyche is a well-recognized phenomenon that can in extreme cases result in neurosis or even insanity. Psychology has also tended to identify the concept of the Alter Ego with that of the unconscious itself. In the seventeenth century Locke reasoned that, since a man cannot think without being conscious that he does, the soul, conversely, could, while the body slept, have its own "thinking, enjoyments, and concerns, its pleasures or its pains" of which the individual is unconscious; so that it could be said of a man that he had two identities. This idea was later popularized by Mesmer, who showed that an individual under hypnosis sometimes reveals hitherto unsuspected traits of character. Since it is natural to fear the unknown, writers like Hoffmann and Dostoyevsky tended to connect the unconscious personality with evil; and this onus was not lifted until the researches of Freud were publicized—and then only partially.[2] It is interesting to note that Jung identifies the negative aspect of the Alter Ego with the Shadow archetype, which may, as was mentioned in the Introduction, manifest itself in the form of "daemonic possession." For practical purposes we may say of the Alter Ego that, like other archetypes we have examined, it has both the usual negative and positive aspects and tends to combine frequently the archetype of Transformation.

In Greek mythology, the gods frequently assumed, often for ulterior motives, the form either of animals or of human beings. One of the commonest of these exploits was the impersonation by Jupiter of Amphitryon for the purpose of seducing the latter's wife. Medieval literature, both Western and Oriental, abounds in Alter Ego motifs, of which we have selected three examples: "How the Proud Emperor Was Humbled," from the *Gesta Romanorum;* [3] "The Sixth Captain's Tale," from *The Book of the Thousand Nights and One Night;* and "The Disembodied Soul," from the classical fiction of early China. Chinese literature, indeed, is bewilderingly rich in such projections; one lengthy narrative, *Monkey,*[4] by Wu Ch'eng-en (sixteenth century) contains no fewer than seven examples.

---

[2] *Ibid.*, p. 42.

[3] A Latin collection of anecdotes and tales compiled by monks early in the fourteenth century and containing material from classical history and legend as well as from Oriental sources.

[4] An abridged version of this tale is available in English translation by Arthur Waley.

Elizabethan poetry contains numerous allusions to a good and a bad angel (Shakespeare's sonnets are an example), nor was the Alter Ego archetype lacking in the drama of the period. This notion of good and bad angels is expressive of Christianity's conception of man's dual nature: his immortal soul and corrupt body, good and evil struggling within his person for possession of his soul. It is illuminating, if somewhat unorthodox, to consider *Hamlet* from this point of view, for in the ghost of the murdered father we have an example of the unsatisfied spirit which roams in search of revenge; and Hamlet's irresolution, perhaps the central problem of the play, involves a dialogue between the hero and his Alter Ego, which functions in the play as his conscience—exactly as William Wilson's does in Poe's story of that name which appears in this collection. Self-division and the concept of the double furnished seventeenth-century poets, especially in England and Italy, with material for the exercise of their wit in the productions of the so-called Metaphysical School (*Concettismo* in Italy). Eighteenth-century examples are rarer, and it is in the romanticism of the nineteenth century, which was influenced by Mesmer's experiments, that we find the purest and most emphatic manifestations of the archetype in narratives such as Hoffmann's *Die Doppelgänger* and *Mademoiselle de Scudéry*, Stevenson's "Markheim" and *The Strange Case of Doctor Jekyll and Mister Hyde*, Hawthorne's *The Blithedale Romance*, Poe's "A Tale of the Ragged Mountains," Dostoyevsky's "The Double," Maupassant's *Les Deux Âmes de Rudolf Hafner*, Wilde's "The Fisherman and His Soul," Hans Andersen's "The Shadow," Kipling's "The Dream of Duncan Parrenness," and H. G. Wells's "The Story of the Late Mr. Elvesham"; in plays such as Strindberg's *Road to Damascus;* and in poems such as Heine's *Stille ist die Nacht*. The tradition persisted well into the present century, with Conrad's "The Secret Sharer," James's "The Jolly Corner," Huxley's "The Farcical History of Richard Greenow," and Mann's *The Transposed Heads;* and plays such as Franz Werfel's *Spiegelmensch*. The special form of Alter Ego in which a connection exists between an individual and an artistic representation of him is illustrated in nineteenth-century British literature by Wilde's *The Picture of Dorian Gray* and in this country by Poe's "The Oval Portrait" and Hawthorne's "The Prophetic Pictures."

However, as in the case of other genuine archetypes, it is unnecessary to search in literature for examples of the Alter Ego. We need only to look about us, to reflect upon our own experience, or to read the newspapers, in order to recognize the pattern: the successful housewife who, like Madame Curie, simultaneously pursues a career in physics; the insurance executive or the statesman who, like Wallace Stevens or Dag Hammarskjöld, has a double identity as a poet; the glamour girl who, like Susan Sontag, can discuss academic philosophy on a professional level. And, on the darker side, there is the apparently happily married husband and father with a long record of sexual deviation, or the clean-cut all-American boy, honor graduate of his high school and pride of his college fraternity, who is suddenly and dramatically revealed to be a rapist or murderer on the grand scale.

WILLIAM WILSON
by Edgar Allan Poe

What say of it? what say CONSCIENCE grim,
That spectre in my path?
—CHAMBERLAIN'S *Pharronida*

Let me call myself, for the present, William Wilson. The fair page now lying before me need not be sullied with my real appellation. This has been already too much an object for the scorn—for the horror—for the detestation of my race. To the uttermost regions of the globe have not the indignant winds bruited its unparalleled infamy? Oh, outcast of all outcasts most abandoned!—to the earth art thou not for ever dead? to its honors, to its flowers, to its golden aspirations?—and a cloud, dense, dismal, and limitless, does it not hang eternally between thy hopes and heaven?

I would not, if I could, here or to-day, embody a record of my later years of unspeakable misery, and unpardonable crime. This epoch—these later years—took unto themselves a sudden elevation in turpitude, whose origin alone it is my present purpose to assign. Men usually grow base by degrees. From me, in an instant, all virtue dropped bodily as a mantle. From comparatively trivial wickedness I passed, with the stride of a giant, into more than the enormities of an Elah-Gabalus. What chance—what one event brought this evil thing to pass, bear with me while I relate. Death approaches; and the shadow which foreruns him has thrown a softening influence over my spirit. I long, in passing through the dim valley, for the sympathy—I had nearly said for the pity —of my fellow men. I would fain have them believe that I have been, in some measure, the slave of circumstances beyond human control. I would wish them to seek out for me, in the details I am about to give, some little oasis of *fatality* amid a wilderness of error, I would have them allow—what they cannot refrain from allowing—that, although temptation may have erewhile existed as great, man was never *thus,* at least, tempted before—certainly, never *thus* fell. And is it therefore that he has never thus suffered? Have I not indeed been living in a dream? And am I not now dying a victim to the horror and the mystery of the wildest of all sublunary visions?

I am the descendant of a race whose imaginative and easily excitable temperament has at all times rendered them remarkable; and, in my earliest infancy, I gave evidence of having fully inherited the family character. As I advanced in years it was more strongly developed; becoming,

---

From *The Complete Tales & Poems of Edgar Allan Poe,* with an Introduction by Harvey Allen (New York: Random House, 1938), pp. 626–41.

for many reasons, a cause of serious disquietude to my friends, and of positive injury to myself. I grew self-willed, addicted to the wildest caprices, and a prey to the most ungovernable passions. Weak-minded, and beset with constitutional infirmities akin to my own, my parents could do but little to check the evil propensities which distinguished me. Some feeble and ill-directed efforts resulted in complete failure on their part, and, of course, in total triumph on mine. Thenceforward my voice was a household law; and at an age when few children have abandoned their leading-strings, I was left to the guidance of my own will, and became, in all but name, the master of my own actions.

My earliest recollections of a school-life, are connected with a large, rambling, Elizabethan house, in a misty-looking village of England, where were a vast number of gigantic and gnarled trees, and where all the houses were excessively ancient. In truth, it was a dream-like and spirit-soothing place, that venerable old town. At this moment, in fancy, I feel the refreshing chilliness of its deeply-shadowed avenues, inhale the fragrance of its thousand shrubberies, and thrill anew with undefinable delight, at the deep hollow note of the church-bell, breaking, each hour, with sullen and sudden roar, upon the stillness of the dusky atmosphere in which the fretted Gothic steeple lay imbedded and asleep.

It gives me, perhaps, as much of pleasure as I can now in any manner experience, to dwell upon minute recollections of the school and its concerns. Steeped in misery as I am—misery, alas! only too real—I shall be pardoned for seeking relief, however slight and temporary, in the weakness of a few rambling details. These, moreover, utterly trivial, and even ridiculous in themselves, assume, to my fancy, adventitious importance, as connected with a period and a locality when and where I recognize the first ambiguous monitions of the destiny which afterward so fully overshadowed me. Let me then remember.

The house, I have said, was old and irregular. The grounds were extensive, and a high and solid brick wall, topped with a bed of mortar and broken glass, encompassed the whole. This prison-like rampart formed the limit of our domain; beyond it we saw but thrice a week—once every Saturday afternoon, when, attended by two ushers, we were permitted to take brief walks in a body through some of the neighboring fields—and twice during Sunday, when we were paraded in the same formal manner to the morning and evening service in the one church of the village. Of this church the principal of our school was pastor. With how deep a spirit of wonder and perplexity was I wont to regard him from our remote pew in the gallery, as, with step solemn and slow, he ascended the pulpit! This reverend man, with countenance so demurely benign, with robes so glossy and so clerically flowing, with wig so minutely powdered, so rigid and so vast,—could this be he who, of late, with sour visage, and in snuffy habiliments, administered, ferule in hand, the Draconian Laws of the academy? Oh, gigantic paradox, too utterly monstrous for solution!

At an angle of the ponderous wall frowned a more ponderous gate. It was riveted and studded with iron bolts, and surmounted with jagged iron spikes. What impressions of deep awe did it inspire! It was never opened save for the three periodical egressions and ingressions already mentioned; then, in every creak of its mighty hinges, we found a plenitude of mystery—a world of matter for solemn remark, or for more solemn meditation.

The extensive enclosure was irregular in form, having many capacious recesses. Of these, three or four of the largest constituted the playground. It was level, and covered with fine hard gravel. I well remember it had no trees, nor benches, nor any thing similar within it. Of course it was in the rear of the house. In front lay a small parterre, planted with box and other shrubs, but through this sacred division we passed only upon rare occasions indeed—such as a first advent to school or final departure thence, or perhaps, when a parent or friend having called for us, we joyfully took our way home for the Christmas or Midsummer holidays.

But the house!—how quaint an old building was this!—to me how veritably a palace of enchantment! There was really no end to its windings—to its incomprehensible subdivisions. It was difficult, at any given time, to say with certainty upon which of its two stories one happened to be. From each room to every other there were sure to be found three or four steps either in ascent or descent. Then the lateral branches were innumerable—inconceivable—and so returning in upon themselves, that our most exact ideas in regard to the whole mansion were not very far different from those with which we pondered upon infinity. During the five years of my residence here, I was never able to ascertain with precision, in what remote locality lay the little sleeping apartment assigned to myself and some eighteen or twenty other scholars.

The school-room was the largest in the house—I could not help thinking, in the world. It was very long, narrow, and dismally low, with pointed Gothic windows and a ceiling of oak. In a remote and terror-inspiring angle was a square enclosure of eight or ten feet, comprising the *sanctum*, "during hours," of our principal, the Reverend Dr. Bransby, It was a solid structure, with massy door, sooner than open which in the absence of the "Dominie," we would all have willingly perished by the *peine forte et dure*. In other angles were two other similar boxes, far less reverenced, indeed, but still greatly matters of awe. One of these was the pulpit of the "classical" usher, one of the "English amd mathematical." Interspersed about the room, crossing and recrossing in endless irregularity, were innumerable benches and desks, black, ancient, and time-worn, piled desperately with much bethumbed books, and so beseamed with initial letters, names at full length, grotesque figures, and other multiplied efforts of the knife, as to have entirely lost what little of original form might have been their portion in days long departed. A huge bucket with water stood at one extremity of the room, and a clock of stupendous dimensions at the other.

Encompassed by the massy walls of this venerable academy, I passed, yet not in tedium or disgust, the years of the third lustrum of my life. The teeming brain of childhood requires no external world of incident to occupy or amuse it; and the apparently dismal monotony of a school was replete with more intense excitement than my riper youth has derived from luxury, or my full manhood from crime. Yet I must believe that my first mental development had in it much of the uncommon—even much of the *outré*. Upon mankind at large the events of very early existence rarely leave in mature age any definite impression. All is gray shadow —a weak and irregular remembrance—an indistinct regathering of feeble pleasures and phantasmagoric pains. With me this is not so. In childhood I must have felt with the energy of a man what I now find stamped upon memory in lines as vivid, as deep, and as durable as the *exergues* of the Carthaginian medals.

Yet in fact—in the fact of the world's view—how little was there to remember! The morning's awakening, the nightly summons to bed; the connings, the recitations; the periodical half-holidays, and perambulations; the play-ground, with its broils, its pastimes, its intrigues;—these, by a mental sorcery long forgotten, were made to involve a wilderness of sensation, a world of rich incident, an universe of varied emotion, of excitement the most passionate and spirit-stirring. *"Oh, le bon temps, que ce siècle de fer!"*

In truth, the ardor, the enthusiasm, and the imperiousness of my disposition, soon rendered me a marked character among my schoolmates, and by slow, but natural gradations, gave me an ascendency over all not greatly older than myself;—over all with a single exception. This exception was found in the person of a scholar, who, although no relation, bore the same Christian and surname as myself;—a circumstance, in fact, little remarkable; for, notwithstanding a noble descent, mine was one of those everyday appellations which seem, by prescriptive right, to have been, time out of mind, the common property of the mob. In this narrative I have therefore designated myself as William Wilson,—a fictitious title not very dissimilar to the real. My namesake alone, of those who in school phraseology constituted "our set," presumed to compete with me in the studies of the class—in the sports and broils of the play-ground—to refuse implicit belief in my assertions, and submission to my will—indeed, to interfere with my arbitrary dictation in any respect whatsoever. If there is on earth a supreme and unqualified despotism, it is the despotism of a mastermind in boyhood over the less energetic spirits of its companions.

Wilson's rebellion was to me a source of the greatest embarrassment; the more so as, in spite of the bravado with which in public I made a point of treating him and his pretensions, I secretly felt that I feared him, and could not help thinking the equality which he maintained so easily with myself, a proof of his true superiority; since not to be overcome, cost me a perpetual struggle. Yet this superiority—even this equality —was in truth acknowledged by no one but myself; our associates, by some unaccountable blindness, seemed not even to suspect it. Indeed, his competition, his resistance, and especially his impertinent and dogged interference with my purposes, were not more pointed than private. He appeared to be destitute alike of the ambition which urged, and of the passionate energy of mind which enabled me to excel. In his rivalry he might have been supposed actuated solely by a whimsical desire to thwart, astonish, or mortify myself; although there were times when I could not help observing, with a feeling made up of wonder, abasement, and pique, that he mingled with his injuries, his insults, or his contradictions, a certain most inappropriate, and assuredly most unwelcome *affection-*

ateness of manner. I could only conceive this singular behavior to arise from a consummate self-conceit assuming the vulgar airs of patronage and protection.

Perhaps it was this latter trait in Wilson's conduct, conjoined with our identity of name, and the mere accident of our having entered the school upon the same day, which set afloat the notion that we were brothers, among the senior classes in the academy. These do not usually inquire with much strictness into the affairs of their juniors. I have before said, or should have said, that Wilson was not, in a most remote degree, connected with my family. But assuredly if we *had* been brothers we must have been twins; for, after leaving Dr. Bransby's, I casually learned that my namesake was born on the nineteenth of January, 1813—and this is a somewhat remarkable coincidence; for the day is precisely that of my own nativity.

It may seem strange that in spite of the continual anxiety occasioned me by the rivalry of Wilson, and his intolerable spirit of contradiction, I could not bring myself to hate him altogether. We had, to be sure, nearly every day a quarrel in which, yielding me publicly the palm of victory, he, in some manner, contrived to make me feel that it was he who had deserved it; yet a sense of pride on my part, and a veritable dignity on his own, kept us always upon what are called "speaking terms," while there were many points of strong congeniality in our tempers, operating to awake in me a sentiment which out position alone, perhaps, prevented from ripening into friendship. It is difficult, indeed, to define, or even to describe, my real feelings toward him. They formed a motley and heterogeneous admixture—some petulant animosity, which was not yet hatred, some esteem, more respect, much fear, with a world of uneasy curiosity. To the moralist it will be necessary to say, in addition, that Wilson and myself were the most inseparable of companions.

It was no doubt the anomalous state of affairs existing between us, which turned all my attacks upon him (and there were many, either open or covert) into the channel of banter or practical joke (giving pain while assuming the aspect of mere fun) rather than into a more serious and determined hostility. But my endeavors on this head were by no means uniformly successful, even when my plans were the most wittily concocted; for my namesake had much about him, in character, of that unassuming and quiet austerity which, while enjoying the poignancy of its own jokes, has no heel of Achilles in itself, and absolutely refuses to be laughed at. I could find, indeed, but one vulnerable point, and that, lying in a personal peculiarity, arising, perhaps, from constitutional disease, would have been spared by an antagonist less at his wit's end than myself;—my rival had a weakness in the faucial or guttural organs, which precluded him from raising his voice at any time *above a very low whisper*. Of this defect I did not fail to take what poor advantage lay in my power.

Wilson's retaliations in kind were many; and there was one form of his practical wit that disturbed me beyond measure. How his sagacity first discovered at all that so petty a thing would vex me, is a question I never could solve; but having discovered, he habitually practised the annoyance. I had always felt aversion to my uncourtly patronymic, and its very common, if not plebeian praenomen. The words were venom in my ears; and when, upon the day of my arrival, a second William Wilson came also to the academy, I felt angry with him for bearing the name, and doubly disgusted with the name because a stranger bore it, who would be the cause of its twofold repetition, who would be constantly in my presence, and whose concerns, in the ordinary routine of the school business, must inevitably, on account of the detestable coincidence, be often confounded with my own.

The feeling of vexation thus engendered grew stronger with every circumstance tending to show resemblance, moral or physical, between my rival and myself. I had not then discovered the remarkable fact that we were of the same age; but I saw that we were of the same height, and I perceived that we were even singularly alike in general contour of person and outline of feature. I was galled, too, by the rumor touching a relationship, which had grown current in the upper forms. In a word, nothing could more seriously disturb me (although I scrupulously concealed such disturbance) than any allusion to a similarity of mind, person, or condition existing between us. But, in truth, I had no reason to believe that (with the exception of the matter of relationship, and in the case of Wilson himself) this similarity had ever been made a subject of comment, or even observed at all by our schoolfellows. That *he* observed it in all its bearings, and as fixedly as I, was apparent; but that he could discover in such circumstances so fruitful a field of annoyance, can only be attributed, as I said before, to his more than ordinary penetration.

His cue, which was to perfect an imitation of myself, lay both in words and in actions; and most admirably did he play his part. My dress it was an easy matter to copy; my gait and general manner were without difficulty, appropriated; in spite of his constitutional defect, even my voice did not escape him. My louder tones were, of course, unattempted, but then the key,—it was identical; *and his singular whisper, it grew the very echo of my own.*

How greatly this most exquisite portraiture harassed me (for it could not justly be termed a caricature), I will not now venture to describe. I had but one consolation—in the fact that the imitation, apparently, was noticed by myself alone, and that I had to endure only the knowing and strangely sarcastic smiles of my namesake himself. Satisfied with having produced in my bosom the intended effect, he seemed to chuckle in secret over the sting he had inflicted, and was characteristically disregardful of the public applause which the success of his witty endeavors might have so easily elicited. That the school, indeed, did not feel his design, perceive its accomplishment, and participate in his sneer, was, for many anxious months, a riddle I could not resolve. Perhaps the *gradation* of his copy rendered it not readily perceptible; or, more possibly, I owed my security to the masterly air of the copyist, who, disdaining the letter (which in a painting is all the obtuse can see), gave but the full spirit of his original for my individual contemplation and chagrin.

I have already more than once spoken of the disgusting air of patronage which he assumed toward me, and of his frequent officious interference with my will. This interference often took the ungracious character of advice; advice not openly given, but hinted or insinuated. I received it with a repugnance which gained strength as I grew in years. Yet, at this distant day, let me do him the simple justice to acknowledge that I can recall no occasion when the suggestions of my rival were on the side of those errors or follies so usual to his immature age and seeming inexperience; that his moral sense, at least, if not his general talents and worldly wisdom, was far keener than my own; and that I might, to-day, have been a better and thus a happier man, had I less frequently rejected the counsels embodied in those meaning whispers which I then but too cordially hated and too bitterly despised.

As it was I at length grew restive in the extreme under his distasteful supervision, and daily resented more and more openly, what I considered his intolerable arrogance. I have said that, in the first years of our connection as schoolmates, my feelings in regard to him might have been easily ripened into friendship; but, in the latter months of my residence at the academy, although the intrusion of his ordinary manner had, beyond doubt, in some measure, abated, my sentiments, in nearly similar proportion, partook very much of positive hatred. Upon one occasion he saw this, I think, and afterward avoided, or made a show of avoiding me.

It was about the same period, if I remember aright, that, in an altercation of violence with him, in which he was more than usually thrown off his guard, and spoke and acted with an openness of demeanor rather foreign to his nature, I discovered, or fancied I discovered, in his accent, in his air, and general appearance, a something which first startled, and then deeply interested me, by bringing to mind dim visions of my earliest infancy—wild, confused, and thronging memories of a time when memory herself was yet unborn. I cannot better describe the sensation which oppressed me, than by saying that I could with difficulty shake off the belief of my having been acquainted with the being who stood before me, at some epoch very long ago—some point of the past even infinitely remote. The delusion, however, faded rapidly as it came; and I mention it at all but to define the day of the last conversation I there held with my singular namesake.

The huge old house, with its countless subdivisions, had several large chambers communicating with each other, where slept the greater number of the students. There were, however (as must necessarily happen in a building so awkwardly planned), many little nooks or recesses, the odds and ends of the structure; and these the economic ingenuity of Dr. Bransby had also fitted up as dormitories; although, being the merest closets, they were capable of accommodating but a single individual. One of these small apartments was occupied by Wilson.

One night, about the close of my fifth year at the school, and immediately after the altercation just mentioned, finding every one wrapped in sleep, I arose from bed, and, lamp in hand, stole through a wilderness of narrow passages, from my own bedroom to that of my rival. I had long been plotting one of these ill-natured pieces of practical wit at his expense in which I had hitherto been so uniformly unsuccessful. It was my intention, now, to put my scheme in operation and I resolved to make him feel the whole extent of the malice with which I was imbued. Having reached his closet, I noiselessly entered, leaving the lamp, with a shade over it, on the outside. I advanced a step and listened to the sound of his tranquil breathing. Assured of his being asleep, I returned, took the light, and with it again approached the bed. Close curtains were around it, which, in the prosecution of my plan, I slowly and quietly withdrew, when the bright rays fell vividly upon the sleeper, and my eyes at the same moment, upon his countenance. I looked;—and a numbness, an iciness of feeling instantly pervaded my frame. My breast heaved, my knees tottered, my whole spirit became possessed with an objectless yet intolerable horror. Gasping for breath, I lowered the lamp in still nearer proximity to the face. Were these—*these* the lineaments of William Wilson? I saw, indeed, that they were his, but I shook as if with a fit of the ague, in fancying they were not. What *was* there about them to confound me in this manner? I gazed;—while my brain reeled with a multitude of incoherent thoughts. Not thus he appeared—assuredly not *thus*—in the vivacity of his waking hours. The same name! the same contour of person! the same day of arrival at the academy! And then his dogged and meaningless imitation of my gait, my voice, my habits, and my manner! Was it, in truth, within the bounds of human possibility, that *what I now saw* was the result, merely, of the habitual practice of this sarcastic imitation? Awe-stricken, and with a creeping shudder, I extinguished the lamp, passed silently from the chamber, and left, at once, the halls of that old academy, never to enter them again.

After a lapse of some months, spent at home in mere idleness, I found myself a student at Eton. The brief interval had been sufficient to enfeeble my remembrance of the events at Dr. Bransby's, or at least to effect a material change in the nature of the feelings with which I remembered them. The truth—the tragedy—of the drama was no more. I could now find room to doubt the evidence of my senses; and seldom called up the subject at all but with wonder at the extent of human credulity, and a smile at the vivid force of the imagination which I hereditarily possessed. Neither was this species of skepticism likely to be diminished by the character of the life I led at Eton. The vortex of thoughtless folly into which I there so immediately and so recklessly plunged, washed away all but the froth of my past hours, ingulfed at once every solid or serious impression, and left to memory only the veriest levities of a former existence.

I do not wish, however, to trace the course of my miserable profligacy here—a profligacy which set at defiance the laws, while it eluded the vigilance of the institution. Three years of folly, passed without profit, had but given me rooted habits of vice, and added, in a somewhat unusual degree, to my bodily stature, when, after a week of soulless dissipation, I invited a small party of the most dissolute students to a secret carousal in my chambers. We met at a late hour of the night; for our debaucheries were to be faithfully protracted until morning. The wine flowed freely, and there were not wanting other and perhaps more dangerous seductions; so that the gray dawn had already faintly appeared in the east while our delirious extravagance was at its height. Madly flushed with cards and intoxication, I was in the act of insisting upon a toast of more than wonted profanity, when my attention was suddenly diverted by the violent, although partial, unclosing of the door of the apartment, and by the eager voice of a servant from without. He said that some person, apparently in great haste, demanded to speak with me in the hall.

Wildly excited with wine, the unexpected interruption rather delighted than surprised me. I staggered forward at once, and a few steps brought me to the vestibule of the building. In this low and small room there hung no lamp; and now no light at all was admitted, save that of the exceedingly feeble dawn which made its way through the semi-circular window. As I put my foot over the threshold, I became aware of the figure of a youth about my own height, and habited in a white kerseymere morning frock, cut in the novel fashion of the one I myself wore at the moment. This the faint light enabled me to perceive; but the features of his face I could not distinguish. Upon my entering, he strode hurriedly up to me, and, seizing me by the arm with a gesture of petulant impatience, whispered the words "William Wilson" in my ear.

I grew perfectly sober in an instant.

There was that in the manner of the stranger, and in the tremulous shake of his uplifted finger, as he held it between my eyes and the light, which filled me with unqualified amazement; but it was not this which had so violently moved me. It was the pregnancy of solemn admonition in the singular, low, hissing utterance; and, above all, it was the character, the tone, *the key,* of those few, simple, and familiar, yet *whispered* syllables, which came with a thousand thronging memories of by-gone days, and struck upon my soul with the shock of a galvanic battery. Ere I could recover the use of my senses he was gone.

Although this event failed not of a vivid effect upon my disordered imagination, yet was it evanescent as vivid. For some weeks, indeed, I busied myself in earnest enquiry, or was wrapped in a cloud of morbid speculation. I did not pretend to disguise from my perception the identity of the singular individual who thus perseveringly interfered with my affairs, and harassed me with his insinuated counsel. But who and what was this Wilson?—and whence came he?—and what were his purposes? Upon neither of these points could I be satisfied—merely ascertaining, in regard to him, that a sudden accident in his family had caused his removal from Dr. Bransby's academy on the afternoon of the day in which I myself had eloped. But in a brief period I ceased to think upon the subject, my attention being all absorbed in a contemplated departure for Oxford. Thither I soon went, the uncalculating vanity of my parents furnishing me with an outfit and annual establishment, which would enable me to indulge at will in the luxury already so dear to my heart—to vie in profuseness of expenditure with the haughtiest heirs of the wealthiest earldoms in Great Britain.

Excited by such appliances to vice, my constitutional temperament broke forth with redoubled ardor, and I spurned even the common restraints of decency in the mad infatuation of my revels. But it were absurd to pause in the detail of my extravagance. Let it suffice, that among spend-thrifts I out-Heroded Herod, and that, giving name to a multitude of novel follies, I added no brief appendix to the long catalogue of vices then usual in the most dissolute university of Europe.

It could hardly be credited, however, that I had, even here, so utterly fallen from the gentlemanly estate, as to seek acquaintance with the vilest arts of the gambler by profession, and, having become an adept in his despicable science, to practice it habitually as a means of increasing my already enormous income at the expense of the weak-minded among my fellow-collegians. Such, nevertheless, was the fact. And the very enormity of this offence against all manly and honorable sentiment proved, beyond doubt, the main if not the sole reason of the impunity with which it was committed. Who, indeed, among my most abandoned associates, would not rather have disputed the clearest evidence of his senses, than have suspected of such courses, the gay, the frank, the generous William Wilson—the noblest and most liberal commoner at Oxford—him whose follies (said his parasites) were but the follies of youth and unbridled fancy—whose errors but inimitable whim—whose darkest vice but a careless and dashing extravagance?

I had been now two years successfully busied in this way, when there came to the university a young *parvenu* nobleman, Glendinning—rich, said report, as Herodes Atticus—his riches, too, as easily acquired. I soon found him of weak intellect, and, of course, marked him as a fitting subject for my skill. I frequently engaged him in play, and contrived, with the gambler's usual art, to let him win considerable sums, the more effectually to entangle him in my snares. At length, my schemes being ripe, I met him (with the full intention that this meeting should be final and decisive) at the chambers of a fellow-commoner (Mr. Preston), equally intimate with both, but who, to do him justice, entertained not even a remote suspicion of my design. To give to this a better coloring, I had contrived to have assembled a party of some eight or ten, and was solicitously careful that the introduction of cards should appear accidental, and originate in the proposal of my contemplated dupe himself. To be brief upon a vile topic, none of the low finesse was omitted, so customary upon similar occasions, that it is a just matter for wonder how any are still found so besotted as to fall its victim.

We had protracted our sitting far into the night, and I had at length effected the manoeuvre of getting Glendinning as my sole antagonist. The game, too, was my favorite *écarté*. The rest of the company, interested in the extent of our play, had abandoned their own cards, and were standing around us as spectators. The *parvenu*, who had been induced by my artifices in the early part of the evening, to drink deeply, now shuffled, dealt, or played, with a wild nervousness of manner for which his intoxication, I thought, might partially, but could not altogether account. In a very short period he had become my debtor to a large amount, when, having taken a long draught of port, he did precisely what I had been coolly anticipating—he proposed to double our already extravagant stakes. With a well-feigned show of reluctance, and not until after my repeated refusal had seduced him into some angry words which gave a color of *pique* to my compliance, did I finally comply. The result, of course, did but prove how entirely the prey was in my toils: in less than an hour he had quadrupled his debt. For some time his countenance had been losing the florid tinge lent it by the wine; but now, to my astonishment, I perceived that it had grown to a pallor truly fearful. I say, to my astonishment. Glendinning had been represented to my eager inquiries as immeasurably wealthy; and the sums which he had as yet lost, although in themselves vast, could not, I supposed, very seriously annoy, much less so violently affect him. That he was overcome by the wine just swallowed, was the idea which most readily presented itself; and, rather with a view to the preservation of my own character in the eyes of my associates, than from any less interested motive, I was about to insist, peremptorily, upon a discontinuance of the play, when some expressions at my elbow from among the company, and an ejaculation evincing utter despair on the part of Glendinning, gave me to understand that I had effected his total ruin under circumstances which, rendering him an object for the pity of all, should have protected him from the ill offices even of a fiend.

What now might have been my conduct it is difficult to say. The pitiable condition of my dupe had thrown an air of embarrassed gloom over all; and, for some moments, a profound silence was maintained, during which I could not help feeling my cheeks tingle with the many burning glances of scorn or reproach cast upon me by the less abandoned of the party. I will even own that an intolerable weight of anxiety was for a brief instant lifted from my bosom by the sudden and extraordinary interruption which ensued. The wide, heavy folding doors of the apartment were all at once thrown open, to their full extent, with a vigorous and rushing impetuosity that extinguished, as if by magic, every candle in the room. Their light, in dying, enabled us just to perceive that a stranger had entered, about my own height, and closely muffled in a cloak. The darkness, however, was not total; and we could only *feel* that he was standing in our midst. Before any one of us could recover from the extreme astonishment into which this rudeness had thrown all, we heard the voice of the intruder.

"Gentlemen," he said, in a low, distinct, and never-to-be-forgotten *whisper* which thrilled to the very marrow of my bones, "Gentlemen, I make an apology for this behavior, because in thus behaving, I am fulfilling a duty. You are, beyond doubt, uninformed of the true character of the person who has to-night won at *écarté* a large sum of money from Lord Glendinning. I will therefore put you upon an expeditious and decisive plan of obtaining this very necessary information. Please to examine, at your leisure, the inner linings of the cuff of his left sleeve, and the several little packages which may be found in the somewhat capacious pockets of his embroidered morning wrapper."

While he spoke, so profound was the stillness that one might have heard a pin drop upon the floor. In ceasing, he departed at once, and as abruptly as he had entered. Can I—shall I describe my sensations? Must I say that I felt all the horrors of the damned? Most assuredly I had little time for reflection. Many hands roughly seized me upon the spot, and lights were immediately reprocured. A search ensued. In the lining of my sleeve were found all the court cards essential in *écarté,* and, in the pockets of my wrapper, a number of packs, fac-similes of those used at our sittings, with the single exception that mine were of the species called, technically, *arrondees;* the honors being slightly convex at the ends, the lower cards slightly convex at the sides. In this disposition, the dupe who cuts, as customary, at the length of the pack, will invariably find that he cuts his antagonist an honor; while the gambler, cutting at the breadth, will as certainly, cut nothing for his victim which may count in the records of the game.

Any burst of indignation upon this discovery would have affected me less than the silent contempt, or the sarcastic composure, with which it was received.

"Mr. Wilson," said our host, stooping to remove from beneath his feet an exceedingly luxurious cloak of rare furs, "Mr. Wilson, this is your property." (The weather was cold; and, upon quitting my own room, I had thrown a cloak over my dressing wrapper, putting it off upon reaching the scene of play.) "I presume it is supererogatory to seek here (eyeing the folds of the garment with a bitter smile) for any farther evidence of your skill. Indeed, we have had enough. You will see the necessity, I hope, of quitting Oxford—at all events, of quitting instantly my chambers."

Abased, humbled to the dust as I then was, it is probable that I should have resented this galling language by immediate personal voilence, had not my whole attention been at the moment arrested by a fact of the most startling character. The cloak which I had worn was of a rare description of fur; how rare, how extravagantly costly, I shall not venture to say. Its fashion, too, was of my own fantastic invention; for I was fastidious to an absurd degree of coxcombry, in matters of this frivolous nature. When, therefore, Mr. Preston reached me that which he had picked up upon the floor, and near the folding-doors of the apartment, it was with an astonishment nearly bordering upon terror, that I perceived my own already hanging on my arm (where I had no doubt unwittingly placed it), and that the one presented me was but its exact counterpart in every, in even the minutest possible particular. The singular being who had so disastrously exposed me, had been muffled, I remembered, in a cloak; and none had been worn at all by any of the members of our party, with the exception of myself. Retaining some presence of mind, I took the one offered me by Preston; placed it, unnoticed, over my own; left the apartment with a resolute scowl of defiance; and, next morning ere dawn of day, commenced a hurried journey from Oxford to the continent, in a perfect agony of horror and of shame.

I fled in vain. My evil destiny pursued me as if in exultation, and proved, indeed, that the exercise of its mysterious dominion had as yet only begun. Scarcely had I set foot in Paris, ere I had fresh evidence of the detestable interest taken by this Wilson in my concerns. Years flew, while I experienced no relief. Villain!—at Rome, with how untimely, yet with how spectral an officiousness, stepped he in between me and my ambition! at Vienna, too—at Berlin—and at Moscow! Where, in truth, had I *not* bitter cause to curse him within my heart? From his inscrutable tyranny did I at length flee, panic-stricken, as from a pestilence; and to the very ends of the earth *I fled in vain.*

And again, and again, in secret communion with my own spirit, would I demand the questions "Who is he?—whence came he?—and what are his objects?" But no answer was there found. And now I scrutinized, with a minute scrutiny, the forms, and the methods, and the leading traits of his impertinent supervision. But even here there was very little upon which to base a conjecture. It was noticeable, indeed, that, in no one of the multiplied instances in which he had of late crossed my path, had he so crossed it except to frustrate those schemes, or to disturb those actions, which, if fully carried out, might have resulted in bitter mischief. Poor justification this, in truth, for an authority so imperiously assumed! Poor indemnity for natural rights of self-agency so pertinaciously, so insultingly denied!

I had also been forced to notice that my tormentor, for a very long period of time (while scrupulously and with miraculous dexterity maintaining his whim of an identity of apparel with myself) had so contrived it, in the execution of his varied interference with my will, that I saw not, at any moment, the features of his face. Be Wilson what he might, *this*, at least, was but the veriest of affectation, or of folly. Could he, for an instant, have supposed that, in my admonisher at Eton—in the destroyer of my honor at Oxford,—in him who thwarted my ambition at Rome, my revenge at Paris, my passionate love at Naples, or what he falsely termed my avarice in Egypt,—that in this, my arch-enemy and evil genius, I could fail to recognize the William Wilson of my school-boy days,—the namesake, the companion, the rival,—the hated and dreaded rival at Dr. Bransby's? Impossible!—But let me hasten to the last eventful scene of the drama.

Thus far I had succumbed supinely to this imperious domination. The sentiment of deep awe with which I habitually regarded the elevated character, the majestic wisdom, the apparent omnipresence and omnipotence of Wilson, added to a feeling of even terror, with which certain other traits in his nature and assumptions inspired me, had operated, hitherto, to impress me with an idea of my own utter weakness and helplessness, and to suggest an implicit, although bitterly reluctant submission to his arbitrary will. But, of late days, I had given myself up entirely to wine; and its maddening influence upon my hereditary temper rendered me more and more impatient of control. I began to murmur,—to hesitate,—to resist. And was it only fancy which induced me to believe that, with the increase of my own firmness, that of my tormentor underwent a proportional diminution? Be this as it may, I now began to feel the inspiration of a burning hope, and at length nurtured in my secret thoughts a stern and desperate resolution that I would submit no longer to be enslaved.

It was at Rome, during the Carnival of 18—, that I attended a masquerade in the palazzo of the Neapolitan Duke Di Broglio. I had indulged more freely than usual in the excesses of the wine-table; and now the suffocating atmosphere of the crowded rooms irritated me beyond endurance. The difficulty, too, of forcing my way through the mazes of the company contributed not a little to the ruffling of my temper; for I was anxiously seeking (let me not say with what unworthy motive) the young, the gay, the beautiful wife of the aged and doting Di Broglio. With a too unscrupulous confidence she had previously communicated to me the secret of the costume in which she would be habited, and now, having caught a glimpse of her person, I was hurrying to make my way into her presence. At this moment I felt a light hand placed upon my shoulder, and that ever-remembered, low, damnable *whisper* within my ear.

In an absolute frenzy of wrath, I turned at once upon him who had thus interrupted me, and seized him violently by the collar. He was attired, as I had expected, in a costume altogether similar to my own; wearing a Spanish cloak of blue velvet, begirt about the waist with a crimson belt sustaining a rapier. A mask of black silk entirely covered his face.

"Scoundrel!" I said, in a voice husky with rage, while every syllable I uttered seemed as new fuel to my fury; "scoundrel! impostor! accursed villain! you shall not—you *shall not* dog me unto death! Follow me, or I stab you where you stand!"—and I broke my way from the ballroom into a small antechamber adjoining, dragging him unresistingly with me as I went.

Upon entering, I thrust him furiously from me. He staggered against the wall, while I closed the door with an oath, and commanded him to draw. He hesitated but for an instant; then, with a slight sigh, drew in silence, and put himself upon his defence.

The contest was brief indeed. I was frantic with every species of wild excitement, and felt within my single arm the energy and power of a multitude. In a few seconds I forced him by sheer strength against the wainscotting, and thus, getting him at mercy, plunged my sword, with brute ferocity, repeatedly through and through his bosom.

At that instant some person tried the latch of the door. I hastened to prevent an intrusion, and then immediately returned to my dying antagonist. But what human language can adequately portray *that* astonishment, *that* horror which possessed me at the spectacle then presented to view? The brief moment in which I averted my eyes had been sufficient to produce, apparently, a material change in the arrangements at the upper or farther end of the room. A large mirror,—so at first it seemed to me in my confusion—now stood where none had been perceptible before; and as I stepped up to it in extremity of terror, mine own image, but with features all pale and dabbled in blood, advanced to meet with a feeble and tottering gait.

Thus it appeared, I say, but was not. It was my antagonist—it was Wilson, who then stood before me in the agônies of his dissolution. His mask and cloak lay, where he had thrown them, upon the floor. Not a thread in all his raiment—not a line in all the marked and singular lineaments of his face which was not, even in the most absolute identity, *mine own!*

It was Wilson; but he spoke no longer in a whisper, and I could have fancied that I myself was speaking while he said:

"You have conquered, and I yield. Yet henceforward art thou also dead—dead to the World, to Heaven, and to Hope! In me didst thou exist—and, in my death, see by this image, which is thine own, how utterly thou hast murdered thyself."

THE SIXTH CAPTAIN'S TALE
from *The Book of the Thousand Nights and One Night*

There was once a Sultān who had a very beautiful daughter, well-loved and petted and most elegant. Therefore she was called Dalāl.

One day, as she sat scratching her head, she caught a little louse; she looked at it for a long time and then carried it in her fingers to the provision cellar, which was filled with large jars of oil, butter and honey. Opening a big oil jar, she set the louse down gently upon the surface of its contents and then, replacing the lid, went her way.

Days and years passed by, and Princess Dalāl reached her fifteenth year, with no memory at all of the louse and its imprisonment.

But one day the louse broke the jar by its great bulk and came forth with the appearance of a Nile buffalo. The cellar guard fled in terror, calling loudly to the servants for help; and at length the louse was caught by the horns and led into the presence of the King.

"What is this?" cried the astonished monarch; and Dalāl, who was standing near, exclaimed: "Yeh, yeh! It is my louse! When I was little, I found it in my head and fastened it in an oil jar. Now it has become so big that it has broken its prison."

"My daughter," answered the King, "it is high time that you were married. The louse has broken his jar, and to-morrow we shall have you breaking your wall and going to men. Allāh protect us from such breakages!"

Then he turned to his wazīr, and said: "Cut the thing's throat, flay it, and hang its skin to the palace gate. Then go forth, with my executioner and chief scribe, for I intend to marry my daughter to the man who can recognise the skin for what it is. Those suitors who fail shall have their heads cut off and their hides hung beside the louse."

The wazīr cut the throat of the louse in that same hour and, after flaying it, hung its skin to the palace gate. Then he sent a herald about the city to proclaim: "He who can recognise the skin upon the palace door for what it is shall marry the Lady Dalāl, daughter of our King; but he who fails to recognise it shall have his head cut off." Many of the young men of the city defiled before the dubious hide; some said that it had belonged to a buffalo, some that it had been taken from a wild goat; and thus forty lost their heads and had their skins hung up beside the louse.

From *The Book of the Thousand Nights and One Night,* translated by Powys and Mardrus Mathers (London: Routledge & Sons Ltd., 1951), Vol. 4, pp. 520–32.

At this point Shahrazād saw the approach of morning and discretely fell silent.

BUT WHEN
THE NINE-HUNDRED-AND-FORTY-SIXTH NIGHT
HAD COME

SHE said:

Then there passed a youth who was as fair as the star Canopus shining upon the sea. When he was informed that the suitor who recognised the skin for what it was might marry the King's daughter, he went up to the wazīr, the executioner and the chief scribe, saying: "It is the skin of a louse which has grown great in oil."

"True, true, O excellent young man!" they cried, and led him into the presence of the King. When he stood before the throne, he said: "It is the skin of a louse grown great in oil." And the King exclaimed: "True, true! Let the marriage contract be written out at once."

The wedding took place on the same day, and that night the star-like youth rejoiced in the virgin Dalāl, who learned all the beauty of love in his arms, for he was like the star Canopus shining upon the sea.

They stayed together for forty days in the palace, and then the youth sought out his father-in-law, saying: "I am a King's son, and would take my princess to abide in my father's kingdom." After trying to dissuade him from this course, the Sultān gave his consent, and said: "Tomorrow, my son, we will collect gifts for you, together with slaves and eunuchs." But the youth replied: "We have a sufficiency of such things, and I desire naught save Dalāl." "Take her, then, and depart in Allāh's name!" said the King. "But take her mother also, that she may learn the way to your father's palace and afterwards visit our daughter from time to time." But the youth replied: "Why should we uselessly fatigue your queen, who is far on in years? I undertake to send my wife back once a month, to rejoice your eyes and tell you of her doings." "So be it," answered the King, and forthwith the youth departed with Dalāl for his own country.

Now this handsome youth was none other than a ghoul of the most dangerous kind. He installed Dalāl in his house on the top of a lonely mountain and then went forth to beat the country, to lie in wait about the roads, to make pregnant women miscarry, to frighten old dames, to terrify children, to howl in the wind, to whine at doors, to bark in the night, to haunt ruins, to cast spells, to grin in the shadows, to visit tombs, to sniff at the dead, to commit a thousand assaults and provoke a thousand calamities. Worn out at length, however, he became a youth again and carried back a man's head to his wife, saying: "O Dalāl, cook this in the oven and carve it so that we may eat." But Dalāl answered: "It is a man's head and I eat nothing except mutton." So the ghoul brought her a sheep, and she was fed.

They lived together alone in this solitude, and Dalāl was defenceless against her horrible husband, who would come back to her with traces of murder and rape upon his body.

After eight days of such existence, the ghoul went out and changed himself into the appearance of his mother-in-law. He dressed in woman's clothes, knocked at his own door, and, when Dalāl asked from her window who was there, answered in the old woman's voice. Dalāl ran down and opened the doors, and behold! in those eight days she had become pale and thin and languishing. The false mother kissed her daughter, and said: "My dear, I have come to see you in spite of all opposition, for we have learnt that your husband is a ghoul and makes you eat human flesh. Oh, how is it with you, my daughter? Alas, I fear that a time may come when he will be tempted to eat you also; so flee with me now, my dear!" But the loyal Dalāl answered: "Be quiet, mother! There is no ghoul here, no trace or smell of a ghoul. Oh, my calamity, you must not say such things! My husband is a King's son and as beautiful as the star Canopus shining upon the sea. He gives me a fat sheep every day."

The ghoul departed, rejoicing at his wife's discretion, and, when he returned in his male form, carrying a sheep, Dalāl said to him: "My mother came to visit me; it was not my fault. She bade me salute you." "I am sorry that I did not hurry home," answered the ghoul, "for I should have rejoiced to greet so solicitous a lady. Would you like to see your aunt, your mother's sister?" "O yes," she cried, and he promised to send the old woman to her on the morrow.

Next morning, at dawn, he took on the appearance of Dalāl's aunt, and, when he came into her presence, kissed her upon the cheeks, weeping and sobbing as if his heart would break. Dalāl asked what was the matter, and the false aunt replied: "Ay! ay! ay! Alas, alas! It is not for myself but for you that I lament! We have found out that you have married a ghoul." But Dalāl cried: "Be quiet! I will not listen to such wicked words! My husband is a King's son, even as I am a King's daughter; his treasures are greater than my father's treasures, and he is as handsome as the little star Canopus shining upon the sea."

At this point Shahrazād saw the approach of morning and discreetly fell silent.

BUT WHEN
THE NINE-HUNDRED-AND-FORTY-SEVENTH-NIGHT
HAD COME

SHE said:

Then Dalāl fed the false aunt on sheep's head, to show her that mutton and not man was eaten there; and the ghoul departed in high good humour.

When he returned with a sheep for Dalāl and a freshly-severed head for himself, his wife said to him: "My aunt has been to visit me, and sends you greeting." "Praise be to Allāh!" he answered. "I take it kindly that your family do not forget you. Would you like to see your other aunt, your father's sister?" "O yes," she cried; and he continued: "I will send her to-morrow and, after that, you shall see no more of your relations, for I fear their blabbing tongues."

Next morning he presented himself before Dalāl in the form of her other aunt, and wept long upon her neck. "Alas, what desolation upon our heads and upon you, O daughter of my brother!" she sobbed at length. "We have found out that you have married a ghoul. Tell me the truth, my daughter, I conjure you by the virtues of our lord Muhammad (upon whom be prayer and peace!)" Then Dalāl, who could hold her terrible secret no longer, answered in a low voice: "Be quiet, good aunt, be quiet, or he will destroy us both. He brings me human heads, think of it! When I refuse, he eats them all himself. I fear that soon he will make a meal of me."

As she said these last words, the ghoul took on his own terrible shape and ground his teeth at her in fury. As she fell back, trembling for yellow terror, he spoke gently to her, saying: "So you have already told my secret, Dalāl?" She threw herself at his feet, crying: "Pardon me this time, spare me this time!" "And did you spare my character before your aunt?" he asked. "Where shall I begin to eat you?" "If it is in my Destiny, then you must eat me," she answered, "but to-day I am dirty and would not taste at all pleasant. It will be well for you to take me to the hammām where I can wash myself for your table. After the bath, I shall be white and sweet, and my flesh a delicious savour in your mouth. Also I give you leave to start with any part you please."

At once the ghoul collected suitable linens and a large gold basin. Then he changed one of his evil friends into a white ass and, after transforming himself into a donkey-boy, led the ass, with Dalāl upon its back, towards the hammām of the nearest village.

When he came to the hammām, carrying the gold basin upon his head, he said to the female guard: "Here are three dīnārs for you. Give this King's daughter a good bath and return her safely to me." Then he sat down outside the door to wait.

Dalāl entered the vestibule and seated herself sadly upon a marble bench, with the basin and the rare linens beside her. The young girls went into the bath and bathed, and were rubbed, and came out jesting happily with each other; but Dalāl wept silently in her corner. At length a troop of maidens came to her, saying: "Why do you weep? Rather undress and take a bath with us." But though she thanked them, she answered: "Is there any bath which can wash away grief, or cure the hopeless sorrows of the world? There will be time enough to bathe, my sisters."

As the girls turned away, an old woman entered the hammām, bearing a bowl upon her head, filled with fried earth-nuts and roast lupins. Some of the young women bought her goods for a penny, a half-penny, or two pence; and Dalāl, wishing to forget her trouble, called to her, saying: "Give me a pennyworth of lupins, good aunt." The old woman sat down by the bench and filled a horn measure with lupins; but, instead of giving her a penny, Dalāl handed her a necklace of pearls, saying: "Take this for your children." Then, as the seller confounded herself in thanks and kissings of the hand, she said again: "Will you give me your bowl and your ragged clothes in exchange for this gold basin, these linens, and all my jewelry and garments?" "Why mock a poor old woman, my daughter?" asked the incredulous seller; but, when Dalāl had reassured her, she hastily stripped off her rags. Dalāl dressed herself hastily in them, balanced the bowl of lupins upon her head, muffled herself in the old woman's filthy blue veil, blackened her hands with the mud of the vestibule pavement, and went out by the door near which the ghoul was sitting.

Her whole body was one stupendous fright, but she schooled herself to cry: "Lupins, roast lupins, pleasant distractions! Earth-nuts, delightful earth-nuts, piping hot!"

Though the ghoul had not recognised her, he smelt her smell after she had gone by, and said to himself: "How can this old lupin-seller have my Dalāl's smell? As Allāh lives, I must look into this!" Then he cried aloud: "Hi, lupin-seller! Earth-nuts, earth-nuts, come here!" But, as the woman did not turn her head, he said again to himself: "It will be safer to make enquiry at the hammām." He approached the guard, and asked: "Why is the woman whom I gave into your charge so long?" "She will come out later with the other women," answered the guard. "They do not leave till nightfall; for they have much to do, what with depilating themselves and tinting their fingers in henna, what with scenting themselves and tressing their hair."

The ghoul was reassured and sat down again; but, when all the women had left and the guard came out to shut the door, he cried: "What are you doing? Do you mean to shut my lady in?" "There is no one left in the hammām," she answered, "except the old lupin-seller whom we always allow to sleep there, because she has no home." The ghoul took the woman by the neck and shook her and made as if to strangle her, shouting in her face: "O bawd, you are responsible for her! I gave her into your hands!" "I am here to look after slippers," she answered, "I am no keeper of foul men's wives." Then, as he increased the grip of his fingers about her neck, she cried: "Help, help, good Mussulmāns!" The men of that village ran up from all sides; but the ogre took no heed of them and began to beat the slipper-guard. "You shall give her back to me," he bawled, "even if she be in the seventh planet, O property of ancient whores!" So much for him.

Dalāl walked on across the country in the direction of her father's kingdom, until she came to a running stream, where she bathed her hands and face and feet. Then she made her way to a King's palace which stood near and sat down by the wall.

A negress slave, who came down for some purpose, saw her and returned to her mistress, saying: "Dear mistress, were it not for the terror which I have of you, I would make bold to say that there is a woman below more beautiful even than yourself." "Bring her up here," answered her mistress. So the negress went down, and said to Dalāl: "My mistress bids you come and have speech with her." "Was my mother a black slave," replied Dalāl, "was my father a black slave, that I should walk with slaves?" The woman carried this answer to her mistress, who sent down a white slave with the same message. But when she had spoken, Dalāl answered: "Was my mother a white slave, was my father a white slave, that I should walk with slaves?" When she heard of this, the Queen of that palace called her son to her and bade him go down to Dalāl.

The young prince, who was as handsome as the little star Canopus shining upon the sea, went down to the girl, and said to her: "Dear lady, have the great goodness to visit the Queen, my mother, in her harīm." And this time Dalāl answered: "I will go up with you; for you are a King's son, even as I am a King's daughter." So saying, she began to walk up the stairs before him.

At this point Shahrazād saw the approach of morning and discreetly fell silent.

BUT WHEN
THE NINE-HUNDRED-AND-FORTY-EIGHTH NIGHT
HAD COME

SHE said:

When the prince saw Dalāl mounting the stairs in her beauty, a great love for her descended upon his heart. Also Dalāl opened her soul to the beauty of his regal youth. Also the Queen, the wife of the King of that palace, said to herself when she looked upon the girl: "The slave was right. She is more beautiful than I."

After greeting and salutation, the prince said to his mother: "I would marry this lady. The royalty of her line shines clearly forth from her." "That is your business, my son," answered his mother. "You are old enough to know what you are doing."

The young prince called the kādī to write out a marriage contract, and the wedding was celebrated on that day. At night he went up into the bridal chamber.

But what, in the meanwhile, had happened to the ghoul?

You shall hear.

On the wedding day a man came to the palace, leading a fat white ram, and gave it to the King, saying: "My lord, I am one of your farmers and have brought this as a gift for your son's marriage. We fattened him ourselves. But I must beg you to fasten him at the door of the harīm, for he was born and raised among women and, if you leave him below, he will bleat all night and trouble the sleep of your palace." The King accepted this present and sent the farmer on his way with a robe of honour; then he handed over the ram to the āgah of the harīm, saying: "Tie him at the door of the harīm, for he is only quiet and happy when he is among women."

When the prince had entered the marriage chamber that night and accomplished that which there was to accomplish, he fell into a deep sleep at Dalāl's side. Then the white ram broke his cord and entered the room. He lifted Dalāl and carried her out into the courtyard, saying gently: "Have you left me much of my honour, Dalāl?" "Do not eat me," she begged; but he replied: "This time there is no help for it." Then she prayed him to wait, before eating her, until she had satisfied a need in the privy; so the ghoul carried her to the courtyard privy and waited outside until she should have finished.

As soon as she was alone in the privy, Dalāl lifted her two hands on high, praying: "O our Lady Zainab, O daughter of the blessed Prophet, come to my aid!" The saint heard her and sent down one of her following, a daughter of the Jinn, who came through the wall and asked: "What is your desire, O Dalāl?" "The ghoul is outside," answered the princess, "and he will eat me when I go forth." Then said the Jinnīyah: "If I save you from him, will you let me kiss you?" and, when Dalāl consented to this condition, she passed through the wall into the courtyard, threw herself upon the ghoul, and kicked him so violently in the testicles that he fell dead.

Then the Jinnīyah went back to the privy and led out Dalāl to see the body of the fat white ram. The two dragged him away from the courtyard and threw him into the ditch. So much, definitively, for him.

"Now I wish to ask a service of you," said the Jinnīyah, as she kissed Dalāl upon the cheek. "I am your humble servant, dear," answered the princess. "Come with me then," urged the Jinnīyah, "for one little hour, to the Emerald Sea. My son is ill, and the doctor has said that the only cure for him is a porringer of the water of the Emerald Sea. But none save a human can fill a porringer at the Emerald Sea, my darling, and I ask your help in return for the trifling service which I have done you." "I will go willingly," answered Dalāl, "as long as I can return before my husband wakes."

The Jinnīyah took up Dalāl upon her shoulders and carried her to the shores of the Emerald Sea, where she gave her a gold porringer; and Dalāl filled the porringer with that water of marvel, but, as she lifted the vessel, a little wave, which had been thus commanded, lapped over her hand so that it became as green as clover. Then the Jinnīyah took up Dalāl again and soon laid her upon her bride bed at the prince's side. So much for the servant of the Lady Zainab (upon whom be prayer and peace!)

Now there is a weigher of the Emerald Sea, who comes to measure and weigh it every morning, for he is responsible and wishes to know if any of the water has been stolen. Next day, when he had weighed and measured the sea, he found that there was a porringer missing. "Who can have been the thief?" he cried. "I will voyage the world until I catch him. If I can find a man, or more likely a woman, with a green hand, our Sultān will know the proper punishment."

He provided himself with a tray of green glass rings and bracelets, and wandered over the world, crying under the windows of kings' palaces: "Green glass bracelets, O princesses! O young ladies, emerald rings!"

After ten years of fruitless searching in all lands, he came to the palace where Dalāl dwelt in her content. As soon as he began to cry beneath the windows: "Green glass bracelets, O princesses! O young ladies, emerald rings!", the princess came down to him and stretched forth her left hand, saying: "Try some of your fairest bracelets." But the weigher of the Emerald Sea recoiled, and cried: "Lady, are you not ashamed to give me your left hand? I only try my bracelets on the right." "My right hand hurts," answered Dalāl; but the weigher insisted, saying: "I will only look and take the measure with my eye. I will not touch." So the princess showed her right hand, and lo! it was as green as clover.

At once the weigher of the Emerald Sea lifted her in his arms and carried her, with the speed of light, into the presence of his King, saying: "O Sultān of the Sea, she has stolen a porringer of your water. My lord knows the penalty." The Sultān of the Emerald Sea prepared to look angrily upon Dalāl, but, as soon as his eyes beheld her, he was troubled by her beauty, and said: "O young girl, I wish to marry you." "That is a pity," she answered, "for I am already lawfully married to a youth as fair as the little star Canopus shining upon the sea." "Have you a sister who at all resembles you?" asked the King, "or a daughter, or even a son?" "I have a daughter, ten years old," answered Dalāl. "To-day she has become ripe for marriage, and she is as beautiful as her father." "That is excellent," said the Sultān of the Emerald Sea.

He took Dalāl's hand in his, and the weigher carried them both to the spot from which he had ravished the princess.

Dalāl led the King into the presence of her husband and, when the demand for their daughter's hand had been made in due form, the prince requested the stranger to name a dowry. Then said the lord of the miraculous water: "I will give forty camels loaded with emeralds and hyacinths."

Thus it came about that the Sultān of the Emerald Sea married the daughter of Dalāl and the starry prince. It is not recorded whether the four lived together in perfect harmony. But glory be to Allāh in any case!

THE DISEMBODIED SOUL

by Ch'en Hsüan-yu

In the third year of the T'ien Shou period [692] Chang Yi of Ching-ho settled in Hengchow, where he served as an official. He was of a quiet disposition and had few friends. He had no son, only two daughters; the older of these died in her childhood, while Chien-niang, the younger daughter, grew up to be without equal in virtue and beauty. Yi had living with him his sister's son, Wang Chu, a talented and handsome youth, and he so esteemed this nephew that he said more than once that he would some day give Chien-niang to him in marriage. On their part, Chu and Chien-niang had a secret passion, of which Chien-niang's parents had no knowledge, so that when Yi later promised Chien-niang in marriage to the son of one of his colleagues, the maiden became saddened and the youth, too, quite unhappy. On the pretext that he must go to the capital to attend the civil service test, Chu begged leave to go thither, and Yi, after trying in vain to detain him, gave in to his wishes and sent him off with handsome presents.

Nursing a secret sorrow in his heart, Chu took leave of his hosts and embarked on his journey. By the end of the day he had covered a distance of some li and found himself among the mountains. At mid-

---

From *Traditional Chinese Tales*, translated by Chi-Chen Wang (New York: Columbia University Press, 1944), pp. 17–19.

night, still unable to fall asleep, he suddenly heard rapid footsteps on the bank and, investigating, found Chien-niang running barefooted after his boat. Chu was beside himself with surprise and happiness. He took her hands in his and asked how she came to be there.

"I cannot forget you even in my dreams," she said, weeping. "But now they are about to force me to marry someone else. As I know that you too have not changed, I have resolved to give up my very life to repay your faithfulness. I have therefore fled from my parents' house and come to you."

Chu was overcome with joy by his unexpected good fortune. He hid her in the boat and resumed his journey that very night, traveling thereafter by double stages until he reached Szechwan a few months later. There they lived for five years, during which she gave birth to two sons. Though she had not sent word to her parents, she was always thinking of them. "I have come to you against the wishes of my parents," she said weeping to him one day, "because I cannot be unfaithful to you. Now it is five years since I have beheld the loving faces of my parents. There can be no place in the universe for such an unfilial daughter as I." Touched by her piety, Chu said to her, "Do not fret, I shall take you there," and set out with her for Hengchow in fulfillment of his promise.

When they arrived at their destination, Chu went ahead to Yi's house to make his apologies but Yi said, "What preposterous talk is this! for has not my daughter been sick in her room these last five years?" "But she is now in the boat," Chu said. Yi was greatly astonished and sent one of his domestics to the boat to see if it was true. There indeed was Chien-niang in the boat looking well and contented. When she saw the servant she asked him how her parents were. The servant was perplexed and hastened back to report to his master.

Now when the girl lying sick in her room heard of the extraordinary occurrence, she rose from her bed, did her toilet, and changed her clothes. There was a smile on her face as she went out to meet the other Chien-niang, but never a word did she speak. Then before the very eyes of all those present, the two girls joined and became one, wearing the two sets of garments that the separate forms had worn.

Because of the bizarre nature of the event, Yi's family kept it secret, but it got to be known among some of his relatives. The couple lived forty years longer. Both their sons passed the examinations and became assistant magistrates.

I, Hsüan-yu, used to hear of the story in my youth. There were many versions of it, and some held it to be fictitious. Toward the end of the Ta Li period [766–791] I happened to meet Chang Chung-hsien, the magistrate of Laiwu, and learned from him the strange circumstances which I have related. Chung-hsien is Yi's cousin and is acquainted with all the details of that strange story.

THE JOLLY CORNER
by Henry James

I

"Every one asks me what I 'think' of everything," said Spencer Brydon; "and I make answer as I can—begging or dodging the question, putting them off with any nonsense. It wouldn't matter to any of them really," he went on, "for, even were it possible to meet in that stand-and-deliver way so silly a demand on so big a subject, my 'thoughts' would still be almost altogether about something that concerns only myself." He was talking to Miss Staverton, with whom for a couple of months now he had availed himself of every possible occasion to talk; this disposition and this resource, this comfort and support, as the situation in fact presented itself, having promptly enough taken the first place in the considerable array of rather unattenuated surprises attending his so strangely belated return to America. Everything was somehow a surprise; and that might be natural when one had so long and so consistently neglected everything, taken pains to give surprises so much margin for play. He had given them more than thirty years—thirty-three, to be exact; and they now seemed to him to have organised their performance quite on the scale of that licence. He had been twenty-three on leaving New York—he was fifty-six to-day: unless indeed he were to reckon as he had sometimes, since his repatriation, found himself feeling; in which case he would have lived longer than is often allotted to man. It would have taken a century, he repeatedly said to himself, and said also to Alice Staverton, it would have taken a longer absence and a more averted mind than those even of which he had been guilty, to pile up the differences, the newnesses, the queernesses, above all the bignessses, for the better or the worse, that at present assaulted his vision wherever he looked.

The great fact all the while however had been the incalculability; since he *had* supposed himself, from decade to decade, to be allowing, and in the most liberal and intelligent manner, for brilliancy of change. He actually saw that he had allowed for nothing; he missed what he would have been sure of finding, he found what he would never have imagined. Proportions and values were upside-down; the ugly things he had expected, the ugly things of his far-away youth, when he had too promptly waked up to a sense of the ugly—these uncanny phenomena placed him rather, as it happened, under the charm; whereas the "swagger" things, the modern, the monstrous, the famous things, those he had more par-

From *The Novels and Tales of Henry James*, Vol. 17 (New York: Charles Scribner's Sons, 1909). Reprinted by permission.

ticularly, like thousands of ingenuous enquirers every year, come over to see, were exactly his sources of dismay. They were as so many set traps for displeasure, above all for reaction, of which his restless tread was constantly pressing the spring. It was interesting, doubtless, the whole show, but it would have been too disconcerting hadn't a certain finer truth saved the situation. He had distinctly not, in this steadier light, come over *all* for the monstrosities; he had come, not only in the last analysis but quite on the face of the act, under an impulse with which they had nothing to do. He had come—putting the thing pompously—to look at his "property," which he had thus for a third of a century not been within four thousand miles of; or, expressing it less sordidly, he had yielded to the humour of seeing again his house on the jolly corner, as he usually, and quite fondly, described it—the one in which he had first seen the light, in which various members of his family had lived and had died, in which the holidays of his overschooled boyhood had been passed and the few social flowers of his chilled adolescence gathered, and which, alienated then for so long a period, had, through the successive deaths of his two brothers and the termination of old arrangements, come wholly into his hands. He was the owner of another, not quite so "good"—the jolly corner having been, from far back, superlatively extended and consecrated; and the value of the pair represented his main capital, with an income consisting, in these later years, of their respective rents which (thanks precisely to their original excellent type) had never been depressingly low. He could live in "Europe," as he had been in the habit of living, on the product of these flourishing New York leases, and all the better since, that of the second structure, the mere number in its long row, having within a twelvemonth fallen in, renovation at a high advance had proved beautifully possible.

These were items of property indeed, but he had found himself since his arrival distinguishing more than ever between them. The house within the street, two bristling blocks westward, was already in course of reconstruction as a tall mass of flats; he had acceded, some time before, to overtures for this conversion—in which, now that it was going forward, it had been not the least of his astonishments to find himself able, on the spot, and though without a previous ounce of such experience, to participate with a certain intelligence, almost with a certain authority. He had lived his life with his back so turned to such concerns and his face addressed to those of so different an order that he scarce knew what to make of this lively stir, in a compartment of his mind never yet penetrated, of a capacity for business and a sense for construction. These virtues, so common all round him now, had been dormant in his own organism—where it might be said of them perhaps that they had slept the sleep of the just. At present, in the splendid autumn weather—the autumn at least was a pure boon in the terrible place—he loafed about his "work" undeterred, secretly agitated; not in the least "minding" that the whole proposition, as they said, was vulgar and sordid, and ready to climb ladders, to walk the plank, to handle materials and look wise about them, to ask questions, in fine, and challenge explanations and really "go into" figures.

It amused, it verily quite charmed him; and, by the same stroke, it amused, and even more, Alice Staverton, though perhaps charming her perceptibly less. She wasn't however going to be better-off for it, as *he* was—and so astonishingly much: nothing was now likely, he knew, ever to make her better-off than she found herself, in the afternoon of life, as the delicately frugal possessor and tenant of the small house in Irving Place to which she had subtly managed to cling through her almost unbroken New York career. If he knew the way to it now better than to any other address among the dreadful multiplied numberings which seemed to him to reduce the whole place to some vast ledger-page, overgrown, fantastic, of ruled and criss-crossed lines and figures—if he had formed, for his consolation, that habit, it was really not a little because of the charm of his having encountered and recognised, in the vast wilderness of the wholesale, breaking through the mere gross generalisation of wealth and force and success, a small still scene where items and shades, all delicate things, kept the sharpness of the notes of a high voice perfectly trained, and where economy hung about like the scent of a garden. His old friend lived with one maid and herself dusted her relics and trimmed her lamps and polished her silver; she stood off, in the awful modern crush, when she could, but she sallied forth and did battle when the challenge was really to "spirit," the spirit she after all confessed to, proudly and a little shyly, as to that of the better time, that of *their* common, their quite far-away and antediluvian social period and order. She made use of the street-cars when need be, the terrible things that people scrambled for as the panic-stricken at sea scramble for the boats; she affronted, inscrutably, under stress, all the public concussions and ordeals; and yet, with that slim mystifying grace of her appearance, which defied you to say if she were a fair young woman who looked older through trouble, or a fine smooth older one who looked young through successful indifference; with her precious reference, above all, to memories and histories into which he could enter, she was as exquisite for him as some pale pressed flower (a rarity to begin with), and, failing other sweetnesses, she was a sufficient reward of his effort. They had communities of knowledge, "their" knowledge (this discriminating possessive was always on her lips) of presences of the other age, presences all overlaid, in his case, by the experience of a man and the freedom of a wanderer, overlaid by pleasure, by infidelity, by passages of life that were strange and dim to her, just by "Europe" in short, but still unobscured, still exposed and cherished, under that pious visitation of the spirit from which she had never been diverted.

She had come with him one day to see how his "apartment-house" was rising; he had helped her over gaps and explained to her plans, and while they were there had happened to have, before her, a brief but lively discussion with the man in charge, the representative of the building-firm that had undertaken his work. He had found himself quite "standing-up" to this personage over a failure on the latter's part to observe some detail of one of their noted conditions, and had so lucidly argued his case that, besides ever so prettily flushing, at the time, for sympathy in his triumph, she had afterwards said to him (though to a slightly greater effect of irony) that he had clearly for too many years neglected a real gift. If he had but stayed at home he would have anticipated the inventor of the sky-scraper. If he had but stayed at home he would have discovered his genius in time really to start some new variety of awful architectural hare and run it till it burrowed in a gold-mine. He was to remember these words, while the weeks elapsed, for the small silver ring they had sounded over the queerest and deepest of his own lately most disguised and most muffled vibrations.

It had begun to be present to him after the first fortnight, it had broken out with the oddest abruptness, this particular wanton wonderment: it met him there—and this was the image under which he himself judged the matter, or at least, not a little, thrilled and flushed with it—very much as he might have been met by some strange figure, some unexpected occupant, at a turn of one of the dim passages of an empty house. The quaint analogy quite hauntingly remained with him, when he didn't indeed rather improve it by a still intenser form: that of his opening a door behind which he would have made sure of finding nothing, a door into a room shuttered and void, and yet so coming, with a great suppressed start, on some quite erect confronting presence, something planted in the middle of the place and facing him through the dusk. After that visit to the house in construction he walked with his companion to see the other and always so much the better one, which in the eastward direction formed one of the corners, the "jolly" one precisely, of the street now so generally dishonoured and disfigured in its westward reaches, and of the comparatively conservative Avenue. The Avenue still had pretensions, as Miss Staverton said, to decency; the old people had mostly gone, the old names were unknown, and here and there an old association seemed to stray, all vaguely, like some very aged person, out too late, whom you might meet and feel the impulse to watch or follow, in kindness, for safe restoration to shelter.

They went in together, our friends; he admitted himself with his key, as he kept no one there, he explained, preferring, for his reasons, to leave the place empty, under a simple arrangement with a good woman living in the neighbourhood and who came for a daily hour to open windows and dust and sweep. Spencer Brydon had his reasons and was growingly aware of them; they seemed to him better each time he was there, though he didn't name them all to his companion, any more than he told her as yet how often, how quite absurdly often, he himself came. He only let her see for the present, while they walked through the great blank rooms, that absolute vacancy reigned and that, from top to bottom, there was nothing but Mrs Muldoon's broomstick, in a corner, to tempt the burglar. Mrs Muldoon was then on the premises, and she loquaciously attended the visitors, preceding them from room to room and pushing back shutters and throwing up sashes—all to show them, as she remarked, how little there was to see. There was little indeed to see in the great gaunt shell where the main dispositions and the general apportionment of space, the style of an age of ampler allowances, had nevertheless for its master their honest pleading message, affecting him as some good old servant's, some lifelong retainer's appeal for a character, or even for a retiring-pension; yet it was also a remark of Mrs Muldoon's that, glad as she was to oblige him by her noonday round, there was a request she greatly hoped he would never make of her. If he should wish her for any reason to come in after dark she would just tell him, if he "plased," that he must ask it of somebody else.

The fact that there was nothing to see didn't militate for the worthy woman against what one *might* see, and she put it frankly to Miss Staverton that no lady could be expected to like, could she? "craping up to thim top storeys in the ayvil hours." The gas and the electric light were off the house, and she fairly evoked a gruesome vision of her march through the great grey rooms—so many of them as there were too!—with her glimmering taper. Miss Staverton met her honest glare with a smile and the profession that she herself certainly would recoil from such an adventure. Spencer Brydon meanwhile held his peace—for the moment; the question of the "evil" hours in his old home had already become too grave for him. He had begun some time since to "crape," and he knew just why a packet of candles addressed to that pursuit had been stowed by his own hand, three weeks before, at the back of a drawer of the fine old sideboard that occupied, as a "fixture," the deep recess in the dining-room. Just now he laughed at his companions—quickly however changing the subject; for the reason that, in the first place, his laugh struck him even at that moment as starting the odd echo, the conscious human resonance (he scarce knew how to qualify it) that sounds made while he was there alone sent back to his ear or his fancy; and that, in the second, he imagined Alice Staverton for the instant on the point of asking him, with a divination, if he ever so prowled. There were divinations he was unprepared for, and he had at all events averted enquiry by the time Mrs Muldoon had left them, passing on to other parts.

There was happily enough to say, on so consecrated a spot, that could be said freely and fairly; so that a whole train of declarations was precipitated by his friend's having herself broken out, after a yearning look round: "But I hope you don't mean they want you to pull *this* to pieces!" His answer came, promptly, with his re-awakened wrath: it was of course exactly what they wanted, and what they were "at" him for, daily, with the iteration of people who couldn't for their life understand a man's liability to decent feelings. He had found the place, just as it stood and beyond what he could express, an interest and a joy. There were values other than the beastly rent-values, and in short, in short—! But it was thus Miss Staverton took him up. "In short you're to make so good a thing of your sky-scraper that, living in luxury on *those* ill-gotten gains, you can afford for a while to be sentimental here!" Her smile had for him, with the words, the particular mild irony with which he found half her talk suffused; an irony without bitterness and that came, exactly, from her having so much imagination—not, like the cheap sarcasms with which one heard most people, about the world of "society," bid for the reputation of cleverness, from nobody's really having any. It was agreeable to him at this very moment to be sure that when he had answered, after a brief demur, "Well yes: so, precisely, you may put it!" her imagination would still do him justice. He explained that even if never a dollar were to come to him from the other house he would nevertheless cherish this one; and he dwelt, further, while they lingered and wandered, on the fact of the stupefaction he was already exciting, the positive mystification he felt himself create.

He spoke of the value of all he read into it, into the mere sight of the walls, mere shapes of the rooms, mere sound of the floors, mere feel, in his hand, of the old silver-plated knobs of the several mahogany doors, which suggested the pressure of the palms of the dead; the seventy years of the past in fine that these things represented, the annals of nearly three generations, counting his grandfather's, the one that had ended there, and the impalpable ashes of his long-extinct youth, afloat in the very air like microscopic motes. She listened to everything; she was a woman who answered intimately but who utterly didn't chatter. She scattered abroad therefore no cloud of words; she could assent, she could agree, above all she could encourage, without doing that. Only at the last she went a little further than he had done himself. "And then how do you know? You may still, after all, want to live here." It rather indeed pulled him up, for it wasn't what he had been thinking, at least in her sense of the words. "You mean I may decide to stay on for the sake of it?"

"Well, *with* such a home—!" But, quite beautifully, she had too much tact to dot so monstrous an *i*, and it was precisely an illustration of the way she didn't rattle. How could any one—of any wit—insist on any one else's "wanting" to live in New York?

"Oh," he said, "I *might* have lived here (since I had my opportunity early in life); I might have put in here all these years. Then everything would have been different enough—and, I dare say, 'funny' enough. But that's another matter. And then the beauty of it—I mean of my perversity, of my refusal to agree to a 'deal'—is just in the total absence of a reason. Don't you see that if I had a reason about the matter at all it would *have* to be the other way, and would then be inevitably a reason of dollars? There are no reasons here *but* of dollars. Let us therefore have none whatever—not the ghost of one."

They were back in the hall then for departure, but from where they stood the vista was large, through an open door, into the great square main saloon, with its almost antique felicity of brave spaces between windows. Her eyes came back from that reach and met his own a moment. "Are you very sure the 'ghost' of one doesn't, much rather, serve—?"

He had a positive sense of turning pale. But it was as near as they were then to come. For he made answer, he believed, between a glare and a grin: "Oh ghosts—of course the place must swarm with them! I should be ashamed of it if it didn't. Poor Mrs Muldoon's right, and it's why I haven't asked her to do more than look in."

Miss Staverton's gaze again lost itself, and things she didn't utter, it was clear, came and went in her mind. She might even for the minute, off there in the fine room, have imagined some element dimly gathering. Simplified like the death-mask of a handsome face, it perhaps produced for her just then an effect akin to the stir of an expression in the "set" commemorative plaster. Yet whatever her impression may have been she produced instead a vague platitude. "Well, if it were only furnished and lived in—!"

She appeared to imply that in case of its being still furnished he might have been a little less opposed to the idea of a return. But she passed straight into the vestibule, as if to leave her words behind her, and the next moment he had opened the house-door and was standing with her on the steps. He closed the door and, while he re-pocketed his key, looking up and down, they took in the comparatively harsh actuality of the Avenue, which reminded him of the assault of the outer light of the Desert on the traveller emerging from an Egyptian tomb. But he risked before they stepped into the street his gathered answer to her speech. "For me it *is* lived in. For me it *is* furnished." At which it was easy for her to sigh "Ah yes—!" all vaguely and discreetly; since his parents and his favourite sister, to say nothing of other kin, in numbers, had run their course and met their end there. That represented, within the walls, ineffaceable life.

It was a few days after this that, during an hour passed with her again, he had expressed his impatience of the too flattering curiosity—among the people he met—about his appreciation of New York. He had arrived at none at all that was socially producible, and as for that matter of his "thinking" (thinking the better or the worse of anything there) he was wholly taken up with one subject of thought. It was mere vain egoism, and it was moreover, if she liked, a morbid obsession. He found all things come back to the question of what he personally might have been, how he might have led his life and "turned out," if he had not so, at the outset, given it up. And confessing for the first time to the intensity within him of this absurd speculation—which but proved also, no doubt, the habit of too selfishly thinking—he affirmed the impotence there of any other source of interest, any other native appeal. "What would it have made of me, what would it have made of me? I keep for ever wondering, all idiotically; as if I could possibly know! I see what it has made of dozens of others, those I meet, and it positively aches within me, to the point of exasperation, that it would have made something of me as well. Only I can't make out *what*, and the worry of it, the small rage of curiosity never to be satisfied, brings back what I remember to have felt, once or twice, after judging best, for reasons, to burn some important letter unopened. I've been sorry, I've hated it—I've never known what was in the letter. You may of course say it's a trifle—!"

"I don't say it's a trifle," Miss Staverton gravely interrupted.

She was seated by her fire, and before her, on his feet and restless, he turned to and fro between this intensity of his idea and a fitful and unseeing inspection, through his single eye-glass, of the dear little old objects on her chimney-piece. Her interruption made him for an instant look at her harder. "I shouldn't care if you did!" he laughed, however; "and it's only a figure, at any rate, for the way I now feel. *Not* to have followed my perverse young course—and almost in the teeth of my father's curse, as I may say; not to have kept it up, so, 'over there,' from that day to this, without a doubt or a pang; not, above all, to have liked it, to have loved it, so much, loved it, no doubt, with such an abysmal conceit of my own preference: some variation from *that*, I say, must have produced some different effect for my life and for my 'form.' I should have stuck here—if it had been possible; and I was too young, at twenty-three, to judge, *pour deux sous*, whether it *were* possible. If I had waited I might have seen it was, and then I might have been, by staying here, something nearer to one of these types who have been hammered so hard and made so keen by their conditions. It isn't that I admire them so much—the question of any charm in them, or of any charm, beyond that of the rank money-passion, exerted by their conditions *for* them, has nothing to do with the matter: it's only a question of what fantastic, yet perfectly possible, development of my own nature I mayn't have missed. It comes over me that I had then a strange *alter ego* deep down somewhere within me, as the full-blown flower is in the small tight bud, and that I just took the course, I just transferred him to the climate, that blighted him for once and for ever."

"And you wonder about the flower," Miss Staverton said. "So do I, if you want to know; and so I've been wondering these several weeks. I believe in the flower," she continued, "I feel it would have been quite splendid, quite huge and monstrous."

"Monstrous above all!" her visitor echoed; "and I imagine, by the same stroke, quite hideous and offensive."

"You don't believe that," she returned; "if you did you wouldn't wonder. You'd know, and that would be enough for you. What you feel—and what I feel *for* you—is that you'd have had power."

"You'd have liked me that way?" he asked.

She barely hung fire. "How should I not have liked you?"

"I see. You'd have liked me, have preferred me, a billionaire!"

"How should I not have liked you?" she simply again asked.

He stood before her still—her question kept him motionless. He took it in, so much there was of it; and indeed his not otherwise meeting it testified to that. "I know at least what I am," he simply went on; "the other side of the medal's clear enough. I've not been edifying—I believe I'm thought in a hundred quarters to have been barely decent. I've followed strange paths and worshipped strange gods; it must have come to you again and again—in fact you've admitted to me as much—that I was leading, at any time these thirty years, a selfish frivolous scandalous life. And you see what it has made of me."

She just waited, smiling at him. "You see what it has made of *me*."

"Oh you're a person whom nothing can have altered. You were born to be what you are, anywhere, anyway: you've the perfection nothing else could have blighted. And don't you see how, without my exile, I shouldn't have been waiting till now—?" But he pulled up for the strange pang.

"The great thing to see," she presently said, "seems to me to be that it has spoiled nothing. It hasn't spoiled your being here at last. It hasn't spoiled this. It hasn't spoiled your speaking—" She also however faltered.

He wondered at everything her controlled emotion might mean. "Do you believe then—too dreadfully!—that I *am* as good as I might ever have been?"

"Oh no! Far from it!" With which she got up from her chair and was nearer to him. "But I don't care," she smiled.

"You mean I'm good enough?"

She considered a little. "Will you believe it if I say so? I mean will you let that settle your question for you?" And then as if making out in his face that he drew back from this, that he had some idea which, however absurd, he couldn't yet bargain away: "Oh you don't care either—but very differently: you don't care for anything but yourself."

Spencer Brydon recognised it—it was in fact what he had absolutely professed. Yet he importantly qualified. "*He* isn't myself. He's the just so totally other person. But I do want to see him," he added. "And I can. And I shall."

Their eyes met for a minute while he guessed from something in hers that she divined his strange sense. But neither of them otherwise expressed it, and her apparent understanding, with no protesting shock, no easy derision, touched him more deeply than anything yet, constituting for his stifled perversity, on the spot, an element that was like breathable air. What she said however was unexpected. "Well, *I've* seen him."

"You—?"

"I've seen him in a dream."

"Oh a 'dream'—!" It let him down.

"But twice over," she continued. "I saw him as I see you now."

"You've dreamed the same dream—?"

"Twice over," she repeated. "The very same."

This did somehow a little speak to him, as it also gratified him. "You dream about me at that rate?"

"Ah about *him!*" she smiled.

His eyes again sounded her. "Then you know all about him." And as she said nothing more: "What's the wretch like?"

She hesitated, and it was as if he were pressing her so hard that, resisting for reasons of her own, she had to turn away.

"I'll tell you some other time!"

II

It was after this that there was most of a virtue for him, most of a cultivated charm, most of a preposterous secret thrill, in the particular form of surrender to his obsession and of address to what he more and more believed to be his privilege. It was what in these weeks he was living for—since he really felt life to begin but after Mrs Muldoon had retired from the scene and, visiting the ample house from attic to cellar, making sure he was alone, he knew himself in safe possession and, as he tacitly expressed it, let himself go. He sometimes came twice in the twenty-four hours; the moments he liked best were those of gathering dusk, of the short autumn twilight; this was the time of which, again and again, he found himself hoping most. Then he could, as seemed to him, most intimately wander and wait, linger and listen, feel his fine attention, never in his life before so fine, on the pulse of the great vague place: he preferred the lampless hour and only wished he might have prolonged each day the deep crepuscular spell. Later—rarely much before midnight, but then for a considerable vigil—he watched with his glimmering light; moving slowly, holding it high, playing it far, rejoicing above all, as much as he might, in open vistas, reaches of communication between rooms and by passages; the long straight chance or show, as he would have called it, for the revelation he pretended to invite. It was a practice he found he could perfectly "work" without exciting remark; no one was in the least the wiser for it; even Alice Staverton, who was moreover a well of discretion, didn't quite fully imagine.

He let himself in and let himself out with the assurance of calm proprietorship; and accident so far favoured him that, if a fat Avenue "officer" had happened on occasion to see him entering at eleven-thirty, he had never yet, to the best of his belief, been noticed as emerging at two. He walked there on the crisp November nights, arrived regularly at the evening's end; it was as easy to do this after dining out as to take his way to a club or to his hotel. When he left his club, if he hadn't been dining out, it was ostensibly to go to his hotel; and when he left his hotel, if he had spent a part of the evening there, it was ostensibly to go to his club. Everything was easy in fine; everything conspired and promoted: there was truly even in the strain of his experience something that glossed over, something that salved and simplified, all the rest of consciousness. He circulated, talked, renewed, loosely and pleasantly, old relations—met indeed, so far as he could, new expectations and seemed to make out on the whole that in spite of the career, of such different contacts, which he had spoken of to Miss Staverton as ministering so little, for those who might have watched it, to edification, he was positively rather liked than not. He was a dim secondary social success—and all with people who had truly not an idea of him. It was all mere surface sound, this murmur of their welcome, this popping of their corks—just as his gestures of response were the extravagant shadows, emphatic in proportion as they meant little, of some game of *ombres chinoises*. He projected himself all day, in thought, straight over the bristling line of hard unconscious heads and into the other, the real, the waiting life; the life that, as soon as he had heard behind him the click of his great house-door, began for him, on the jolly corner, as beguilingly as the slow opening bars of some rich music follows the tap of the conductor's wand.

He always caught the first effect of the steel point of his stick on the old marble of the hall pavement, large black-and-white squares that he remembered as the admiration of his childhood and that had then made in him, as he now saw, for the growth of an early conception of style. This effect was the dim reverberating tinkle as of some far-off bell hung who should say where?—in the depths of the house, of the past, of that mystical other world that might have flourished for him had he not, for weal or woe, abandoned it. On this impression he did ever the same thing; he put his stick noiselessly away in a corner—feeling the place once more in the likeness of some great glass bowl, all precious concave crystal, set delicately humming by the play of a moist finger round its edge. The concave crystal held, as it were, this mystical other world, and the indescribably fine murmur of its rim was the sigh there, the scarce audible pathetic wail to his strained ear, of all the old baffled forsworn possibilities. What he did therefore by this appeal of his hushed presence was to wake them into such measure of ghostly life as they might still enjoy. They were shy, all but unappeasably shy, but they weren't really sinister; at least they weren't as he had hitherto felt them—before they had taken the Form he so yearned to make them take, the Form he at moments saw himself in the light of fairly hunting on tiptoe, the points of his evening-shoes, from room to room and from storey to storey.

That was the essence of his vision—which was all rank folly, if one would, while he was out of the house and otherwise occupied, but which took on the last verisimilitude as soon as he was placed and posted. He knew what he meant and what he wanted; it was as clear as the figure on a cheque presented in demand for cash. His *alter ego* "walked"—that was the note of his image of him, while his image of his motive for his own odd pastime was the desire to waylay him and meet him. He roamed, slowly, warily, but all restlessly, he himself did—Mrs Muldoon had been right, absolutely, with her figure of their "craping"; and the presence he watched for would roam restlessly too. But it would be as cautious and as shifty; the conviction of its probable, in fact its already quite sensible, quite audible evasion of pursuit grew for him from night to night, laying on him finally a rigour to which nothing in his life had been comparable. It had been the theory of many superficially-judging persons, he knew, that he was wasting that life in a surrender to sensations, but he had tasted of no pleasure so fine as his actual tension, had been introduced to no sport that demanded at once the patience and the nerve of this stalking of a creature more subtle, yet at bay perhaps more formidable, than any beast of the forest. The terms, the comparisons, the very practices of the chase positively came again into play; there were even moments when passages of his occasional experience as a sportsman, stirred memories, from his younger time, of moor and mountain and desert, revived for him—and to the increase of his keenness—by the tremendous force of analogy. He found himself at moments—once he had placed his single light on some mantel-shelf or in some recess—stepping back into shelter or shade, effacing himself behind a door or in an embrasure, as he had sought of old the vantage of rock and tree; he found himself holding his breath and living in the joy of the instant, the supreme suspense created by big game alone.

He wasn't afraid (though putting himself the question as he believed gentlemen on Bengal tiger-shoots or in close quarters with the great bear of the Rockies had been known to confess to having put it); and this indeed—since here at least he might be frank!—because of the impression, so intimate and so strange, that he himself produced as yet a dread, produced certainly a strain, beyond the liveliest he was likely to feel. They fell for him into categories, they fairly became familiar, the signs, for his own perception, of the alarm his presence and his vigilance created; though leaving him always to remark, portentously, on his probably having formed a relation, his probably enjoying a consciousness, unique in the experience of man. People enough, first and last, had been in terror of apparitions, but who had ever before so turned the tables and become himself, in the apparitional world, an incalculable terror? He might have found this sublime had he quite dared to think of it; but he didn't too much insist, truly, on that side of his privilege. With habit and repetition he gained to an extraordinary degree the power to penetrate the dusk of distances and the darkness of corners, to resolve back into their innocence the treacheries of uncertain light, the evil-looking forms taken in the gloom by mere shadows, by accidents of the air, by shifting effects of perspective; putting down his dim luminary he could still wander on without it, pass into other rooms and, only knowing it was there behind him in case of need, see his way about, visually project for his purpose a comparative clearness. It made him feel, this acquired faculty, like some monstrous stealthy cat; he wondered if he would have glared at these moments with large shining yellow eyes, and what it mightn't verily be, for the poor hard-pressed *alter ego,* to be confronted with such a type.

He liked however the open shutters; he opened everywhere those Mrs Muldoon had closed, closing them as carefully afterwards, so that she shouldn't notice: he liked—oh this he did like, and above all in the upper rooms!—the sense of the hard silver of the autumn stars through the window-panes, and scarcely less the flare of the street-lamps below, the white electric lustre which it would have taken curtains to keep out. This was human actual social; this was of the world he had lived in, and he was more at his ease certainly for the countenance, coldly general and impersonal, that all the while and in spite of his detachment it seemed to give him. He had support of course mostly in the rooms at the wide front and the prolonged side; it failed him considerably in the central shades and the parts at the back. But if he sometimes, on his rounds, was glad of his optical reach, so none the less often the rear of the house affected him as the very jungle of his prey. The place was there more subdivided; a large "extension" in particular, where small rooms for servants had been multiplied, abounded in nooks and corners, in closets and passages, in the ramifications especially of an ample back staircase over which he leaned, many a time, to look far down—not deterred from his gravity even while aware that he might, for a spectator, have figured some solemn simpleton playing at hide-and-seek. Outside in fact he might himself make that ironic *rapprochement;* but within the walls, and in spite of the clear windows, his consistency was proof against the cynical light of New York.

It had belonged to that idea of the exasperated consciousness of his victim to become a real test for him; since he had quite put it to himself from the first that, oh distinctly! he could "cultivate" his whole perception. He had felt it as above all open to cultivation—which indeed was but another name for his manner of spending his time. He was bringing it on, bringing it to perfection, by practice; in consequence of which it had grown so fine that he was now aware of impressions, attestations of his general postulate, that couldn't have broken upon him at once. This was the case more specifically with a phenomenon at last quite frequent for him in the upper rooms, the recognition—absolutely unmistakable, and by a turn dating from a particular hour, his resumption of his campaign after a diplomatic drop, a calculated absence of three nights—of his being definitely followed, tracked at a distance carefully taken and to the express end that he should the less confidently, less arrogantly, appear to himself merely to pursue. It worried, it finally quite broke him up, for it proved, of all the conceivable impressions, the one least suited to his book. He was kept in sight while remaining himself—as regards the essence of his position—sightless, and his only recourse then was in abrupt turns, rapid recoveries of ground. He wheeled about, retracing his steps, as if he might so catch in his face at least the stirred air of some other quick revolution. It was indeed true that his fully dislocalised thought of these manoeuvres recalled to him Pantaloon, at the Christmas farce, buffeted and tricked from behind by ubiquitous Harlequin; but it left intact the influence of the conditions themselves each time he was re-exposed to them, so that in fact this association, had he suffered it to become constant, would on a certain side have but ministered to his intenser gravity. He had made, as I have said, to create on the premises the baseless sense of a reprieve, his three absences; and the result of the third was to confirm the after-effect of the second.

On his return, that night—the night succeeding his last intermission—he stood in the hall and looked up the staircase with a certainty more intimate than any he had yet known. "He's *there,* at the top, and waiting—not, as in general, falling back for disappearance. He's holding his ground, and it's the first time—which is a proof, isn't it? that something has happened for him." So Brydon argued with his hand on the banister and his foot on the lowest stair; in which position he felt as never before the air chilled by his logic. He himself turned cold in it, for he seemed of a sudden to know what now was involved. "Harder pressed?—yes, he takes it in, with its thus making clear to him that I've come, as they say, 'to stay.' He finally doesn't like and can't bear it, in the sense, I mean, that his wrath, his menaced interest, now balances with his dread. I've hunted him till he has 'turned': that, up there, is what has happened—he's the fanged or the antlered animal brought at last to bay." There came to him, as I say—but determined by an influence beyond my notation!—the acuteness of this certainty; under which however the next moment he had broken into a sweat that he would as little have consented to attribute to fear as he would have dared immediately to act upon it for enterprise. It marked none the less a prodigious thrill, a thrill that represented sudden dismay, no doubt, but also represented, and with the self-same throb, the strangest, the most joyous, possibly the next minute almost the proudest, duplication of consciousness.

"He has been dodging, retreating, hiding, but now, worked up to anger, he'll fight!"—this intense impression made a single mouthful, as it were, of terror and applause. But what was wondrous was that the applause, for the felt fact, was so eager, since, if it was his other self he was running to earth, this ineffable identity was thus in the last resort not unworthy of him. It bristled there—somewhere near at hand, however unseen still—as the hunted thing, even as the trodden worm of the adage *must* at last bristle; and Brydon at this instant tasted probably of a sensation more complex than had ever before found itself consistent with sanity. It was as if it would have shamed him that a character so associated with his own should triumphantly succeed in just skulking, should to the end not risk the open; so that the drop of this danger was, on the spot, a great lift of the whole situation. Yet with another rare shift of the same subtlety he was already trying to measure by how much more he himself might now be in peril of fear; so rejoicing that he could, in another form, actively inspire that fear, and simultaneously quaking for the form in which he might passively know it.

The apprehension of knowing it must after a little have grown in him, and the strangest moment of his adventure perhaps, the most memorable or really most interesting, afterwards, of his crisis, was the lapse of certain instants of concentrated conscious *combat,* the sense of a need to hold on to something, even after the manner of a man slipping and slipping on some awful incline; the vivid impulse, above all, to move, to act, to charge, somehow and upon something—to show himself, in a word, that he wasn't afraid. The state of "holding-on" was thus the state to which he was momentarily reduced; if there had been anything, in the great vacancy, to seize, he would presently have been aware of having clutched it as he might under a shock at home have clutched the nearest chair-back. He had been surprised at any rate—of this he *was* aware—into something unprecedented since his original appropriation of the place; he had closed his eyes, held them tight, for a long minute, as with that instinct of dismay and that terror of vision. When he opened them the room, the other contiguous rooms, extraordinarily, seemed lighter—so light, almost, that at first he took the change for day. He stood firm, however that might be, just where he had paused; his resistance had helped him—it was as if there were something he had tided over. He knew after a little what this was—it had been in the imminent danger of flight. He had stiffened his will against going; without this he would have made for the stairs, and it seemed to him that, still with his eyes closed, he would have descended them, would have known how, straight and swiftly, to the bottom.

Well, as he had held out, here he was—still at the top, among the more intricate upper rooms and with the gauntlet of the others, of all the rest of the house, still to run when it should be his time to go. He would go at his time—only at his time: didn't he go every night very much at the same hour? He took out his watch—there was light for that: it was scarcely a quarter past one, and he had never withdrawn so soon. He reached his lodgings for the most part at two—with his walk of a quarter of an hour. He would wait for the last quarter—he wouldn't stir till then; and he kept his watch there with his eyes on it, reflecting while he held it that this deliberate wait, a wait with an effort, which he recognised, would serve perfectly for the attestation he desired to make. It would prove his courage—unless indeed the latter might most be proved by his budging at last from his place. What he mainly felt now was that, since he hadn't originally scuttled, he had his dignities—which had never in his life seemed so many—all to preserve and to carry aloft. This was before him in truth as a physical image, an image almost worthy of an age of greater romance. That remark indeed glimmered for him only to glow the next instant with a finer light; since what age of romance, after all, could have matched either the state of his mind or, "objectively," as they said, the wonder of his situation? The only difference would have been that, brandishing his dignities over his head as in a parchment scroll, he might then—that is in the heroic time—have proceeded downstairs with a drawn sword in his other grasp.

At present, really, the light he had set down on the mantel of the next room would have to figure his sword; which utensil, in the course of a minute, he had taken the requisite number of steps to possess himself of. The door between the rooms was open, and from the second another door opened to a third. These rooms, as he remembered, gave all three upon a common corridor as well, but there was a fourth, beyond them, without issue save through the preceding. To have moved, to have heard his step again, was appreciably a help; though even in recognising this he lingered once more a little by the chimney-piece on which his light had rested. When he next moved, just hesitating where to turn, he found himself considering a circumstance that, after his first and comparatively vague apprehension of it, produced in him the start that often attends some pang of recollection, the violent shock of having ceased happily to forget. He had come into sight of the door in which the brief chain of communication ended and which he now surveyed from the nearer threshold, the one not directly facing it. Placed at some distance to the left of this point, it would have admitted him to the last room of the four, the room without other approach or egress, had it not, to his intimate conviction, been closed *since* his former visitation, the matter probably of a quarter of an hour before. He stared with all his eyes at the wonder of the fact, arrested again where he stood and again holding his breath while he sounded its sense. Surely it had been *subsequently* closed—that is it had been on his previous passage indubitably open!

He took it full in the face that something had happened between—that he couldn't have noticed before (by which he meant on his original tour of all the rooms that evening) that such a barrier had exceptionally presented itself. He had indeed since that moment undergone an agitation so extraordinary that it might have muddled for him any earlier view; and he tried to convince himself that he might perhaps then have gone into the room and, inadvertently, automatically, on coming out, have drawn the door after him. The difficulty was that this exactly was what he never did; it was against his whole policy, as he might have said, the essence of which was to keep vistas clear. He had them from the first, as he was well aware, quite on the brain: the strange apparition, at the far end of one of them, of his baffled "prey" (which had become by so sharp an irony so little the term now to apply!) was the form of success his imagination had most cherished, projecting into it always a refinement of beauty. He had known fifty times the start of perception that had afterwards dropped; had fifty times gasped to himself "There!" under some fond brief hallucination. The house, as the case stood, admirably lent itself; he might wonder at the taste, the native architecture of the particular time, which could rejoice so in the multiplication of doors—the opposite extreme to the modern, the actual almost complete proscription of them; but it had fairly contributed to provoke this obsession of the presence encountered telescopically, as he might say, focussed and studied in diminishing perspective and as by a rest for the elbow.

It was with these considerations that his present attention was charged—they perfectly availed to make what he saw portentous. He *couldn't,* by any lapse, have blocked that aperture; and if he hadn't, if it was unthinkable, why what else was clear but that there had been another agent? Another agent?—he had been catching, as he felt, a moment back, the very breath of him; but when had he been so close as in this simple, this logical, this completely personal act? It was so logical, that is, that one might have *taken* it for personal; yet for what did Brydon take it, he asked himself, while, softly panting, he felt his eyes almost leave their sockets. Ah this time at last they *were*, the two, the opposed projections of him, in presence; and this time, as much as one would, the question of danger loomed. With it rose, as not before, the question of courage—for what he knew the blank face of the door to say to him was "Show us how much you have!" It stared, it glared back at him with that challenge; it put to him the two alternatives: should he just push it open or not? Oh to have this consciousness was to *think*—and to think, Brydon knew, as he stood there, was, with the lapsing moments, not to have acted! Not to have acted—that was the misery and the pang—was even still not to act; was in fact *all* to feel the thing in another, in a new and terrible way. How long did he pause and how long did he debate? There was presently nothing to measure it; for his vibration had already changed—as just by the effect of its intensity. Shut up there, at bay, defiant, and with the prodigy of the thing palpably provably *done*, thus giving notice like some stark signboard—under that accession of accent the situation itself had turned; and Brydon at last remarkably made up his mind on what it had turned to.

It had turned altogether to a different admonition; to a supreme hint, for him, of the value of Discretion! This slowly dawned, no doubt—for it could take its time; so perfectly, on his threshold, had he been stayed, so little as yet had he either advanced or retreated. It was the strangest of all things that now when, by his taking ten steps and applying his hand to a latch, or even his shoulder and his knee, if necessary, to a panel, all the hunger of his prime need might have been met, his high curiosity crowned, his unrest assuaged—it was amazing, but it was also exquisite and rare, that insistence should have, at a touch, quite dropped from him. Discretion—he jumped at that; and yet not, verily, at such a pitch, because it saved his nerves or his skin, but because, much more valuably, it saved the situation. When I say he "jumped" at it I feel the consonance of this term with the fact that—at the end indeed of I know not how long—he did move again, he crossed straight to the door. He wouldn't touch it—it seemed now that he might *if* he would: he would only just wait there a little, to show, to prove, that he wouldn't. He had thus another station, close to the thin partition by which revelation was denied him; but with his eyes bent and his hands held off in a mere intensity of stillness. He listened as if there had been something to hear, but this attitude, while it lasted, was his own communication. "If you won't then—good: I spare you and I give up. You affect me as by the appeal positively for pity: you convince me that for reasons rigid and sublime—what do I know?—we both of us should have suffered. I respect them then, and, though moved and privileged as, I believe, it has never been given to man, I retire, I renounce—never, on my honour, to try again. So rest for ever—and let *me!*"

That, for Brydon was the deep sense of this last demonstration—solemn, measured, directed, as he felt it to be. He brought it to a close, he turned away; and now verily he knew how deeply he had been stirred. He retraced his steps, taking up his candle, burnt, he observed, well-nigh to the socket, and marking again, lighten it as he would, the distinctness of his footfall; after which, in a moment, he knew himself at the other side of the house. He did here what he had not yet done at these hours—he opened half a casement, one of those in the front, and let in the air of the night; a thing he would have taken at any time previous for a sharp rupture of his spell. His spell was broken now, and it didn't matter—broken by his concession and his surrender, which made it idle henceforth that he should ever come back. The empty street—its other life so marked even by the great lamplit vacancy—was within call, within touch; he stayed there as to be in it again, high above it though he was still perched; he watched as for some comforting common fact, some vulgar human note, the passage of a scavenger or a thief, some night-bird however base. He would have blessed that sign of life; he would have welcomed positively the slow approach of his friend the policeman, whom he had hitherto only sought to avoid, and was not sure that if the patrol had come into sight he mightn't have felt the impulse to get into relation with it, to hail it, on some pretext, from his fourth floor.

The pretext that wouldn't have been too silly or too compromising, the explanation that would have saved his dignity and kept his name, in such a case, out of the papers, was not definite to him: he was so occupied with the thought of recording his Discretion—as an effect of the vow he had just uttered to his intimate adversary—that the importance of this loomed large and something had overtaken all ironically his sense of proportion. If there had been a ladder applied to the front of the house, even one of the vertiginous perpendiculars employed by painters and roofers and sometimes left standing overnight, he would have managed somehow, astride of the window-sill, to compass by outstretched leg and arm that mode of descent. If there had been some such uncanny thing as he had found in his room at hotels, a workable fire-escape in the form of notched cable or a canvas shoot, he would have availed himself of it as a proof—well, of his present delicacy. He nursed that sentiment, as the question stood, a little in vain, and even—at the end of he scarce knew, once more, how long—found it, as by the action on his mind of the failure of response of the outer world, sinking back to vague anguish. It seemed to him he had waited an age for some stir of the great grim hush; the life of the town was itself under a spell—so unnaturally, up and down the whole prospect of known and rather ugly objects, the blankness and the silence lasted. Had they ever, he asked himself, the hard-faced houses, which had begun to look livid in the dim dawn, had they ever spoken so little to any need of his spirit? Great builded voids, great crowded stillnesses put on, often, in the heart of cities, for the small hours, a sort of sinister mask, and it was of this large collective negation that Brydon presently became conscious—all the more that the break of day was, almost incredibly, now at hand, proving to him what a night he had made of it.

He looked again at his watch, saw what had become of his time-values (he had taken hours for minutes—not, as in other tense situations, minutes for hours) and the strange air of the streets was but the weak, the sullen flush of a dawn in which everything was still locked up. His choked appeal from his own open window had been the sole note of life, and he could but break off at last as for a worse despair. Yet while so deeply demoralised he was capable again of an impulse denoting—at least by his present measure—extraordinary resolution; of retracing his steps to the spot where he had turned cold with the extinction of his last pulse of doubt as to there being in the place another presence than his own. This required an effort strong enough to sicken him; but he had his reason, which overmastered for the moment everything else. There was the whole of the rest of the house to traverse, and how should he screw himself to that if the door he had seen closed were at present open? He could hold to the idea that the closing had practically been for him an act of mercy, a chance offered him to descend, depart, get off the ground and never again profane it. This conception held together, it worked; but what it meant for him depended now clearly on the amount of forbearance his recent action, or rather his recent inaction, had engendered. The image of the "presence," whatever it was, waiting there for him to go—this image had not yet been so concrete for his nerves as when he stopped short of the point at which certainty would have come to him. For, with all his resolution, or more exactly with all his dread, he did stop short—he hung back from really seeing. The risk was too great and his fear too definite: it took at this moment an awful specific form.

He knew—yes, as he had never known anything—that, *should* he see the door open, it would all too abjectly be the end of him. It would mean that the agent of his shame—for his shame was the deep abjection—was once more at large and in general possession; and what glared him thus in the face was the act that this would determine for him. It would send him straight about to the window he had left open, and by that window, be long ladder and dangling rope as absent as they would, he saw himself uncontrollably insanely fatally take his way to the street. The hideous chance of this he at least could avert; but he could only avert it by recoiling in time from assurance. He had the whole house to deal with, this fact was still there; only he now knew that uncertainty alone could start him. He stole back from where he had checked himself—merely to do so was suddenly like safety—and, making blindly for the greater staircase, left gaping rooms and sounding passages behind. Here was the top of the stairs, with a fine large dim descent and three spacious landings to mark off. His instinct was all for mildness, but his feet were harsh on the floors, and, strangely, when he had in a couple of minutes become aware of this, it counted somehow for help. He couldn't have spoken, the tone of his voice would have scared him, and the common conceit or resource of "whistling in the dark" (whether literally or figuratively) have appeared basely vulgar; yet he liked none the less to hear himself go, and when he had reached his first landing—taking it all with no rush, but quite steadily—that stage of success drew from him a gasp of relief.

The house, withal, seemed immense, the scale of space again inordinate; the open rooms, to no one of which his eyes deflected, gloomed in their shuttered state like mouths of caverns; only the high skylight that formed the crown of the deep well created for him a medium in which he could advance, but which might have been, for queerness of colour, some watery under-world. He tried to think of something noble, as that his property was really grand, a splendid possession; but this nobleness took the form too of the clear delight with which he was finally to sacrifice it. They might come in now, the builders, the destroyers—they might come as soon as they would. At the end of two flights he had dropped to another zone, and from the middle of the third, with only one more left, he recognised the influence of the lower windows, of half-drawn blinds, of the occasional gleam of street-lamps, of the glazed spaces of the vestibule. This was the bottom of the sea, which showed an illumination of its own and which he even saw paved—when at a given moment he drew up to sink a long look over the banisters—with the marble squares of his childhood. By that time indubitably he felt, as he might have said in a commoner cause, better; it had allowed him to stop and draw breath, and the ease increased with the sight of the old black-and-white slabs. But what he most felt was that now surely, with the element of impunity pulling him as by hard firm hands, the case was settled for what he might have seen above had he dared that last look. The closed door, blessedly remote now, was still closed—and he had only in short to reach that of the house.

He came down further, he crossed the passage forming the access to the last flight; and if here again he stopped an instant it was almost for the sharpness of the thrill of assured escape. It made him shut his eyes—which opened again to the straight slope of the remainder of the stairs. Here was impunity still, but impunity almost excessive; inasmuch as the side-lights and the high fan-tracery of the entrance were glimmering straight into the hall; an appearance produced, he the next instant saw, by the fact that the vestibule gaped wide, that the hinged halves of the inner door had been thrown far back. Out of that again the *question* sprang at him, making his eyes, as he felt, half-start from his head, as they had done, at the top of the house, before the sign of the other door. If he had left that one open, hadn't he left this one closed, and wasn't he now in *most* immediate presence of some inconceivable occult activity? It was as sharp, the question, as a knife in his side, but the answer hung fire still and seemed to lose itself in the vague darkness to which the thin admitted dawn, glimmering archwise over the whole outer door, made a semicircular margin, a cold silvery nimbus that seemed to play a little as he looked—to shift and expand and contract.

It was as if there had been something within it, protected by indistinctness and corresponding in extent with the opaque surface behind, the painted panels of the last barrier to his escape, of which the key was in his pocket. The indistinctness mocked him even while he stared, affected him as somehow shrouding or challenging certitude, so that after faltering an instant on his step he let himself go with the sense that here *was* at last something to meet, to touch, to take, to know—something all unnatural and dreadful, but to advance upon which was the condition for him either of liberation or of supreme defeat. The penumbra, dense and dark, was the virtual screen of a figure which stood in it as still as some image erect in a niche or as some black-vizored sentinel guarding a treasure. Brydon was to know afterwards, was to recall and make out, the particular thing he had believed during the rest of his descent. He saw, in its great grey glimmering margin, the central vagueness diminish, and he felt it to be taking the very form toward which, for so many days, the passion of his curiosity had yearned. It gloomed, it loomed, it was something, it was somebody, the prodigy of a personal presence.

Rigid and conscious, spectral yet human, a man of his own substance and stature waited there to measure himself with his power to dismay. This only could it be—this only till he recognised, with his advance, that what made the face dim was the pair of raised hands that covered it and in which, so far from being offered in defiance, it was buried as for dark deprecation. So Brydon, before him, took him in; with every fact of him now, in the higher light, hard and acute—his planted stillness, his vivid truth, his grizzled bent head and white masking hands, his queer actuality of evening-dress, of dangling double eye-glass, of gleaming silk lappet and white linen, of pearl button and gold watch-guard and polished shoe. No portrait by a great modern master could have presented him with more intensity, thrust him out of his frame with more art, as if there had been "treatment," of the consummate sort, in his every shade and salience. The revulsion, for our friend, had become, before he knew it, immense—this drop, in the act of apprehension, to the sense of his adversary's inscrutable manoeuvre. That meaning at least, while he gaped, it offered him; for he could but gape at his other self in this other anguish, gape as a proof that *he*, standing there for the achieved, the enjoyed, the triumphant life, couldn't be faced in his triumph. Wasn't the proof in the splendid covering hands, strong and completely spread?—so spread and so intentional that, in spite of a special verity that surpassed every other, the fact that one of these hands had lost two fingers, which were reduced to stumps, as if accidentally shot away, the face was effectually guarded and saved.

"Saved," though, *would* it be?—Brydon breathed his wonder till the very impunity of his attitude and the very insistence of his eyes produced, as he felt, a sudden stir which showed the next instant as a deeper portent, while the head raised itself, the betrayal of a braver purpose. The hands, as he looked, began to move, to open; then, as if deciding in a flash, dropped from the face and left it uncovered and presented. Horror, with the sight, had leaped into Brydon's throat, gasping there in a sound he couldn't utter; for the bared identity was too hideous as *his*, and his glare was the passion of his protest. The face, *that* face, Spencer Brydon's?—he searched it still, but looking away from it in dismay and denial, falling straight from his height of sublimity. It was unknown, inconceivable, awful, disconnected from any possibility—! He had been "sold," he inwardly moaned, stalking such game as this: the presence before him was a presence, the horror within him a horror, but the waste of his nights had been only grotesque and the success of his adventure an irony. Such an identity fitted his at *no* point, made its alternative monstrous. A thousand times yes, as it came upon him nearer now—the face was the face of a stranger. It came upon him nearer now, quite as one of those expanding fantastic images projected by the magic lantern of childhood; for the stranger, whoever he might be, evil, odious, blatant, vulgar, had advanced as for aggression, and he knew himself give ground. Then harder pressed still, sick with the force of his shock, and falling back as under the hot breath and the roused passion of a life larger than his own, a rage of personality before which his own collapsed, he felt the whole vision turn to darkness and his very feet give way. His head went round; he was going; he had gone.

III

What had next brought him back, clearly—though after how long?—was Mrs Muldoon's voice, coming to him from quite near, from so near that he seemed presently to see her as kneeling on the ground before him while he lay looking up at her; himself not wholly on the ground, but half-raised and upheld—conscious, yes, of tenderness of support and, more particularly, of a head pillowed in extraordinary softness and faintly refreshing fragrance. He considered, he wondered, his wit but half at his service; then another face intervened, bending more directly over him, and he finally knew that Alice Staverton had made her lap an ample and perfect cushion to him, and that she had to this end seated herself on the lowest degree of the staircase, the rest of his long person remaining stretched on his old black-and-white slabs. They were cold, these marble squares of his youth; but *he* somehow was not, in this rich return of consciousness—the most wonderful hour, little by little, that he had ever known, leaving him, as it did, so gratefully, so abysmally passive, and yet as with a treasure of intelligence waiting all round him for quiet appropriation; dissolved, he might call it, in the air of the place and producing the golden glow of a late autumn afternoon. He had come back, yes—come back from further away than any man but himself had ever travelled; but it was strange how with this sense what he had come back *to* seemed really the great thing, and as if his prodigious journey had been all for the sake of it. Slowly but surely his consciousness grew, his vision of his state thus completing itself: he had been miraculously *carried* back—lifted and carefully borne as from where he had been picked up, the uttermost end of an interminable grey passage. Even with this he was suffered to rest, and what had now brought him to knowledge was the break in the long mild motion.

It had brought him to knowledge, to knowledge—yes, this was the beauty of his state; which came to resemble more and more that of a man who has gone to sleep on some news of a great inheritance, and then, after dreaming it way, after profaning it with matters strange to it, has waked up again to serenity of certitude and has only to lie and watch it grow. This was the drift of his patience—that he had only to let it shine on him. He must moreover, with intermissions, still have been lifted and borne; since why and how else should he have known himself, later on, with the afternoon glow intenser, no longer at the foot of his stairs—situated as these now seemed at that dark other end of his tunnel—but on a deep window-bench of his high saloon, over which had been spread, couch-fashion, a mantle of soft stuff lined with grey fur that was familiar to his eyes and that one of his hands kept fondly feeling as for its pledge of truth. Mrs Muldoon's face had gone, but the other, the second he had recognised, hung over him in a way that showed how he was still propped and pillowed. He took it all in, and the more he took it the more it seemed to suffice: he was as much at peace as if he had had food and drink. It was the two women who had found him, on Mrs Muldoon's having plied, at her usual hour, her latch-key—and on her having above all arrived while Miss Staverton still lingered near the house. She had been turning away, all anxiety, from worrying the vain bell-handle—her calculation having been of the hour of the good woman's visit; but the latter, blessedly, had come up while she was still there, and they had entered together. He had then lain, beyond the vestibule, very much as he was lying now—quite, that is, as he appeared to have fallen, but all so wondrously without bruise or gash; only in a depth of stupor. What he most took in, however, at present, with the steadier clearance, was that Alice Staverton had for a long unspeakable moment not doubted he was dead.

"It must have been that I *was*." He made it out as she held him. "Yes—I can only have died. You brought me literally to life. Only," he wondered, his eyes rising to her, "only, in the name of all the benedictions, how?"

It took her but an instant to bend her face and kiss him, and something in the manner of it, and in the way her hands clasped and locked his head while he felt the cool charity and virtue of her lips, something in all this beatitude somehow answered everything. "And now I keep you," she said.

"Oh keep me, keep me!" he pleaded while her face still hung over him: in response to which it dropped again and stayed close, clingingly close. It was the seal of their situation—of which he tasted the impress for a long blissful moment in silence. But he came back. "Yet how did you know—?"

"I was uneasy. You were to have come, you remember—and you had sent no word."

"Yes, I remember—I was to have gone to you at one to-day." It caught on to their "old" life and relation—which were so near and so far. "I was still out there in my strange darkness—where was it, what was it? I must have stayed there so long." He could but wonder at the depth and the duration of his swoon.

"Since last night?" she asked with a shade of fear for her possible indiscretion.

"Since this morning—it must have been: the cold dim dawn of to-day. Where have I been," he vaguely wailed, "where have I been?" He felt her hold him close, and it was as if this helped him now to make in all security his mild moan. "What a long dark day!"

All in her tenderness she had waited a moment. "In the cold dim dawn?" she quavered.

But he had already gone on piecing together the parts of the whole prodigy. "As I didn't turn up you came straight—?"

She barely cast about. "I went first to your hotel—where they told me of your absence. You had dined out last evening and hadn't been back since. But they appeared to know you had been at your club."

"So you had the idea of *this*—?"

"Of what?" she asked in a moment.

"Well—of what has happened."

"I believed at least you'd have been here. I've known, all along," she said, "that you've been coming."

" 'Known' it—?"

"Well, I've believed it. I said nothing to you after that talk we had a month ago—but I felt sure. I knew you *would*," she declared.

"That I'd persist, you mean?"

"That you'd see him."

"Ah but I didn't!" cried Brydon with his long wail. "There's somebody—an awful beast; whom I brought, too horribly, to bay. But it's not me."

At this she bent over him again, and her eyes were in his eyes. "No—it's not you." And it was as if, while her face hovered, he might have made out in it, hadn't it been so near, some particular meaning blurred by a smile. "No, thank heaven," she repeated—"it's not you! Of course it wasn't to have been."

"Ah but it *was*," he gently insisted. And he stared before him now as he had been staring for so many weeks. "I was to have known myself."

"You couldn't!" she returned consolingly. And then reverting, and as if to account further for what she had herself done, "But it wasn't only *that*, that you hadn't been at home," she went on. "I waited till the hour at which we had found Mrs Muldoon that day of my going with you; and she arrived, as I've told you, while, failing to bring any one to the door, I lingered in my despair on the steps. After a little, if she hadn't come, by such a mercy, I should have found means to hunt her up. But it wasn't," said Alice Staverton, as if once more with her fine intention—"it wasn't only that."

His eyes, as he lay, turned back to her. "What more then?"

She met it, the wonder she had stirred. "In the cold dim dawn, you say? Well, in the cold dim dawn of this morning I too saw you."

"Saw *me*—?"

"Saw *him*," said Alice Staverton. "It must have been at the same moment."

He lay an instant taking it in—as if he wished to be quite reasonable. "At the same moment?"

"Yes—in my dream again, the same one I've named to you. He came back to me. Then I knew it for a sign. He had come to you."

At this Brydon raised himself; he had to see her better. She helped him when she understood his movement, and he sat up, steadying himself beside her there on the window-bench and with his right hand grasping her left. "*He* didn't come to me."

"You came to yourself," she beautifully smiled.

"Ah I've come to myself now—thanks to you, dearest. But this brute, with his awful face—this brute's a black stranger. He's none of *me*, even as I *might* have been," Brydon sturdily declared.

But she kept the clearness that was like the breath of infallibility. "Isn't the whole point that you'd have been different?"

He almost scowled for it. "As different as *that*—?"

Her look again was more beautiful to him than the things of this world. "Haven't you exactly wanted to know *how* different? So this morning," she said, "you appeared to me."

"Like *him?*"

"A black stranger!"

"Then how did you know it was I?"

"Because, as I told you weeks ago, my mind, my imagination, had worked so over what you might, what you mightn't have been—to show you, you see, how I've thought of you. In the midst of that you came to me—that my wonder might be answered. So I knew," she went on; "and believed that, since the question held you too so fast, as you told me that day, you too would see for yourself. And when this morning I again saw I knew it would be because you had—and also then, from the first moment, because you somehow wanted me. *He* seemed to tell me of that. So why," she strangely smiled, "shouldn't I like him?"

It brought Spencer Brydon to his feet. "You 'like' that horror—?"

"I *could* have liked him. And to me," she said, "he was no horror. I had accepted him."

" 'Accepted'—?" Brydon oddly sounded.

"Before, for the interest of his difference—yes. And as *I* didn't disown him, as *I* knew him—which you at last, confronted with him in his difference, so cruelly didn't, my dear—well, he must have been, you see, less dreadful to me. And it may have pleased him that I pitied him."

She was beside him on her feet, but still holding his hand—still with her arm supporting him. But though it all brought for him thus a dim light, "You 'pitied' him?" he grudgingly, resentfully asked.

"He has been unhappy, he has been ravaged," she said.

"And haven't I been unhappy? Am not I—you've only to look at me!—ravaged?"

"Ah I don't say I like him *better,*" she granted after a thought. "But he's grim, he's worn—and things have happened to him. He doesn't make shift, for sight, with your charming monocle."

"No"—it struck Brydon: "I couldn't have sported mine 'downtown.' They'd have guyed me there."

"His great convex pince-nez—I saw it, I recognised the kind—is for his poor ruined sight. And his poor right hand—!"

"Ah!" Brydon winced—whether for his proved identity or for his lost fingers. Then, "He has a million a year," he lucidly added. "But he hasn't you."

"And he isn't—no, he isn't—*you!*" she murmured as he drew her to his breast.

HOW THE PROUD EMPEROR WAS HUMBLED

from *Tales of the Monks*

When Jovinian was emperor, he possessed very great power; and as he lay in bed reflecting upon the extent of his dominions, his heart was elated to an extraordinary degree. "Is there," he impiously asked, "is there any other god than me?" Amid such thoughts he fell asleep.

In the morning he reviewed his troops, and said, "My friends, after breakfast we will hunt." Preparations being made accordingly, he set out with a large retinue. During the chase, the emperor felt such extreme oppression from the heat, that he believed his very existence depended upon a cold bath. As he anxiously looked around, he discovered a sheet of water at no great distance. "Remain here," said he to his guard, "until I have refreshed myself in yonder stream."

Then spurring his steed, he rode hastily to the edge of the water. Alighting, he divested himself of his apparel, and experienced the greatest pleasure from its invigorating freshness and coolness. But whilst he was thus employed, a person similar to him in every respect—in countenance and gesture—arrayed himself unperceived in the emperor's dress, and then mounting his horse, rode off to the attendants. The resemblance to the sovereign was such, that no doubt was entertained of the reality; and when the sport was over command was issued for their return to the palace.

Jovinian, however, have quitted the water, sought in every possible direction for his horse and clothes, and to his utter astonishment could find neither. Vexed beyond measure at the circumstance, for he was completely naked, and saw no one near to assist him, he began to reflect upon what course he should pursue. "Miserable man that I am," said he, "to what a strait am I reduced! There is, I remember, a knight residing close by, whom I have promoted to a military post; I will go to him and command his attendance and service. I will then ride on to the palace and strictly investigate the cause of this extraordinary conduct."

Jovinian proceeded, naked and ashamed, to the castle of the aforesaid knight, and beat loudly at the gate. The porter inquired the cause of the knocking. "Open the gate," said the enraged emperor, "and you will see whom I am."

The gate was opened; and the porter, struck with the strange appear-

---

From *Tales of the Monks,* from the *Gesta Romanorum,* edited by Manuel Komroff (New York: Tudor Publishing Co., 1939), pp. 80–7. Reprinted by permission.

ance he exhibited, replied, "In the name of all that is marvellous, what are you?"

"I am," said he, "Jovinian, your emperor; go to your lord, and command him from me to supply the wants of his sovereign. I have lost both horse and clothes."

"Thou liest, infamous ribald!" shouted the porter; "just before thy approach, the Emperor Jovinian, accompanied by the officers of his household, entered the palace. My lord both went and returned with him; and but even now sat with him at meat. But because thou hast called thyself the emperor, my lord shall know of thy presumption."

The porter entered, and related what had passed. Jovinian was introduced, but the knight retained not the slightest recollection of his master, although the emperor remembered him.

"Who are you?" said the former, "and what is your name?"

"I am the Emperor Jovinian," rejoined he; "canst thou have forgotten me? At such a time I promoted thee to a military command."

"Why, thou most audacious scoundrel," said the knight, "darest thou call thyself the emperor? I rode with him myself to the palace, from whence I am this moment returned. But they impudence shall not go without its reward. Flog him," said he, turning to his servants, "flog him soundly, and drive him away."

This sentence was immediately executed, and the poor emperor, bursting into a convulsion of tears, exclaimed, "Oh, my God, is it possible that one whom I have so much honoured and exalted should do this? Not content with pretending ignorance of my person, he orders these merciless villains to abuse me!"

He next thought within himself, "There is a certain duke, one of my privy councillors, to whom I will make known my calamity. At least, he will enable me to return decently to the palace." To him, therefore, Jovinian proceeded, and the gate was opened at his knock.

But the porter, beholding a naked man, exclaimed in the greatest amaze, "Friend, who are you, and why come you here in such a guise?"

He replied, "I am your emperor; I have accidentally lost my clothes and my horse, and I have come for succour to your lord. I beg you, therefore, to do me this errand to the duke." The porter, more and more astonished, entered the hall, and communicated the strange intelligence which he had received.

"Bring him in," said the duke. He was brought in, but neither did he recognize the person of the emperor.

"What art thou?" he asked.

"I am the emperor," replied Jovinian, "and I have promoted thee to riches and honour, since I made thee a duke and one of my councillors."

"Poor mad wretch," said the duke, "a short time since I returned from the palace, where I left the very emperor thou assumest to be. But since thou hast claimed such rank, thou shalt not escape unpunished. Carry him to prison, and feed him with bread and water."

The command was no sooner delivered than obeyed; and the following day his naked body was submitted to the lash, and he was again cast into the dungeon.

Thus afflicted, he gave himself up to the wretchedness of his undeserved condition. In the agony of his heart, he said, "What shall I do? Oh, what will be my destiny? I am loaded with the coarsest insolence, and exposed to the malicious observation of my people. It were better to hasten immediately to my palace, and there discover myself—my servants will know me; and even if they do not my wife will know me!" Escaping, therefore, from his confinement, he approached the palace and beat upon the gate.

"Who art thou?" said the porter.

"It is strange," replied the aggrieved emperor, "it is strange that thou shouldst not know me; thou, who hast served me so long!"

"Served *thee!*" returned the porter indignantly, "thou liest abominably. I have served none but the emperor."

"Why," said the other, "thou knowest that I am he. Yet, though you disregard my words, go, I implore you, to the empress; communicate what I will tell thee, and by these signs bid her send the imperial robes, of which some rogue has deprived me. The signs I tell thee of are known to none but to ourselves."

"In verity," said the porter, "thou art mad: at this very moment my lord sits at table with the empress herself. Nevertheless, out of regard for thy singular merits, I will intimate thy declaration within; and rest assured, thou wilt presently find thyself most royally beaten."

The porter went accordingly, and related what he had heard. But the empress became very sorrowful, and said, "Oh, my Lord, what am I to think? The most hidden passages of our lives are revealed by an obscene fellow at the gate, and repeated to me by the porter, on the strength of which he declares himself the emperor and my espoused lord!"

When the fictitious monarch was apprized of this, he commanded him to be brought in. He had no sooner entered than a large dog, which couched upon the hearth, and had been much cherished by him, flew at his throat, and, but for timely prevention, would have killed him. A falcon, also, seated upon her perch, no sooner beheld him, than she broke her leather straps and flew out of the hall.

Then the pretended emperor, addressing those who stood about him, said, "My friends, hear what I will ask of yon ribald. Who are you? and what do you want?"

"These questions," said the suffering man, "are very strange. You know I am the emperor and master of this place."

The other, turning to the nobles who sat or stood at the table, continued, "Tell me, on your allegiance, which of us two is your lord and master?"

"Your majesty asks us an easy thing," replied they, "and need not to remind us of our allegiance. That obscene wretch we have never before seen. You alone are he, whom we have known from childhood; and we entreat that this fellow may be severely punished, as a warning to others how they give scope to their mad presumption."

Then turning to the empress, the usurper said, "Tell me, my lady, on the faith you have sworn, do you know this man who calls himself thy lord and emperor?"

She answered, "My lord, how can you ask such a question? Have I not known thee more than thirty years, and borne thee many children? Yet, at one thing I do admire. How can this fellow have acquired so intimate a knowledge of what has passed between us?"

The pretended emperor made no reply, but addressing the real one, said, "Friend, how darest thou to call thyself emperor? We sentence thee, for this unexampled impudence, to be drawn, without loss of time, at the tail of a horse. And if thou utterest the same words again, thou shalt be doomed to an ignominious death." He then commanded his guards to see the sentence put in force, but to preserve his life. The unfortunate emperor was now almost distracted; and urged by his despair, wished vehemently for death.

"Why was I born?" he exclaimed. "My friends shun me; and my wife and children will not acknowledge me. But there is my confessor, still. To him will I go; perhaps he will recollect me, because he has often received my confessions." He went accordingly, and knocked at the window of his cell.

"Who is there?" said the confessor.

"The emperor Jovinian," was the reply; "open the window, and I will speak to thee." The window was opened; but no sooner had he looked out than he closed it again in great haste.

"Depart from me," said he "accursed thing; thou art not the emperor, but the devil incarnate."

This completed the miseries of the persecuted man; and he tore his hair, and plucked up his beard by the roots. "Woe is me!" he cried, "for what strange doom am I reserved?"

At this crisis, the impious words which, in the arrogance of his heart, he had uttered, crossed his recollection. Immediately he beat again at the window of the confessor's cell, and exclaimed, "For the love of Him who was suspended from the cross, hear my confession with the window closed."

The recluse said, "I will do this with pleasure"; and then Jovinian acquainted him with every particular of his past life; and principally how he had lifted himself up against his Maker, saying that he believed there was no other god but himself.

The confession made, and absolution given, the recluse opened the window, and directly knew him. "Blessed be the most high God," said he, "now do I know thee. I have here a few garments: clothe thyself, and go to the palace. I trust that they also will recognize thee."

The emperor did as the confessor directed. The porter opened the gate, and made a low obeisance to him. "Dost thou know me?" said he. "Very well, my lord!" replied the menial; "but I marvel that I did not observe you go out."

Entering the hall of his mansion, Jovinian was received by all with a profound reverence. The strange emperor was at that time in another apartment with the queen; and a certain knight came out of the chamber, looked narrowly at Jovinian, and returning to the supposed emperor, said, "My lord, there is one in the hall to whom everybody bends; he so much resembles you, that we know not which is the emperor."

Hearing this, the usurper said to the empress, "Go and see if you know him." She went, and returned greatly surprised at what she saw.

"Oh, my lord," said she, "I declare to you that I know not whom to trust."

"Then," returned he, "I will go and convince you." When he had entered the hall, he took Jovinian by the hand and placed him near him. Addressing the assembly, he said, "By the oaths you have taken, declare which of us is your emperor."

The empress answered, "It is my duty to speak first; but Heaven is my witness that I am unable to determine which is he."

And so said all.

Then the feigned emperor spoke thus, "My friends, hearken! That man is your king and your lord. He exalted himself to the disparagement of his Maker; and God, therefore, scourged and hid him from your knowledge. I am the angel that watches over his soul, and I have guarded his kingdom while he was undergoing his penance. But his repentance removes the rod; he has now made ample satisfaction, and again let your obedience wait upon him. Commend yourselves to the protection of Heaven."

So saying, he disappeared. The emperor gave thanks to God, and lived happily, and finished his days in peace.

A MOMENT OF GREEN LAUREL
by Gore Vidal

My absent-mindedness seems to have only to do with places. I have little difficulty in recalling either names or faces and I usually get to appointments on time, although even in this I have become a bit careless lately.

Last week I arrived for an appointment not only at the wrong hour but at the wrong address, a somewhat disturbing experience. But now the Treasury Building was straight ahead and I was relieved that I could still find my way so easily through the streets of Washington, a city I had not lived in for many years.

Thousands of people crowded the sidewalks, for this was Inauguration Day and all were eager to watch the new President ride in state to the Capitol for the Inaugural ceremony. The crowd was in a gala mood though the sky was dull, threatening rain.

With difficulty, I crossed the street to the Willard Hotel. At the curb I was stopped by the pillar of some Midwestern community, a pillar now wreathed in alcohol. In one hand he carried a small banner and in the other a bottle of whiskey with no label (I did not then guess the significance of this detail). "Things going change in this town. Take it from me." Gracefully, I took it from him and, avoiding the bottle proffered, moved as quickly as I could to the hotel entrance and went inside.

The Willard has two lobbies: one on the "F" Street side and one on the Pennsylvania Avenue side, parallel to it. The lobbies are connected by a carpeted, mirrored, marbled corridor where I was able to find a sofa to sit on as I observed the hundreds of people who now passed from street to avenue, all hurrying, all delighted.

Out of loyalty to our elegant Washington society, I decided these noisy passers-by must be from out of town: thick businessmen with rimless glasses, Southwesterners with stetsons and boots, New York ladies in silver fox . . . all political and all, for one reason or another, well pleased with the new President. Some carried whiskey flasks, I noticed: the first I had seen since I was a child and Prohibition was, in theory, law. Now, apparently, flashs had come back, as the advertisers would say.

A political personage sat down beside me, his right buttock, a bony one, glancing off my thigh as he squeezed a place for himself on the sofa. He wiggled about, making more room for himself. I scowled, unnoticed.

"You sure get mighty tired standing around," he said at large, stumbling on truth. I agreed. He was Southern and he talked to me and from time to time I nodded with discreet half-attention, pretending to look for someone, hoping to excuse thereby my inattention. I even squinted nearsightedly as though a familiar face had suddenly appeared among strangers. Then one did. I saw my grandfather, white-haired and ruddy-faced, approach with a political colleague. He was smiling at something the other was saying. As they passed in front of me, I heard my grandfather say: "He knows as well as you do what I think of gold . . ."

By the time I had got to my feet, upsetting the Southerner, the ghost was gone. My stomach contracted nervously; it had been someone else, of course. I have always had a habit of looking for likenesses. I will often notice a young boy and think: why, there's so-and-so! He was in school with me. Then I'd recall that my acquaintance would be a grown man by now, no longer fourteen. Nevertheless, disturbed by this vision of my dead grandfather, I got to my feet and went into the Pennsylvania Avenue lobby. Here, among palms and portraits of the new President, more politicians and hangers-on celebrated the great moment with noise, whiskey and thunderous good will.

"Come on up," said a woman beside me. She was blonde, well dressed, a little drunk and in a friendly mood. "We've got a suite upstairs. We're having a party. We're going to watch the parade. . . . Emily!" And Emily joined us too and we all went up in the elevator together.

The suite was two rooms hired weeks in advance for this day. The party had already begun: thirty or forty men and women, young office-holders for the most part, although there were, I soon discovered, some native Washingtonians, too.

I was given a glass of champagne and left alone. My hostess and Emily, arm in arm, broke through circle after circle, penetrating to the center of the party. I could hear their laughter long after they had vanished.

I moved slowly about the room. It was like a dance and I wished for the sake of appearances that I had a partner. There is something profoundly negative about standing alone on the outskirts of a group where everyone has arrived in twos, like animals in a Noah's Ark, and departs in twos. I thought of floods.

I finished the champagne, wondering idly why I knew no one in the room. The city has changed, I thought; I had been away ten years, a long time. I crossed the room to the window and looked out at the parade which had begun. Loudspeakers at each street corner made the Inaugural Address audible but unintelligible. Something had gone wrong with the synchronization and the loudspeakers echoed one another dismally, confusing the Presidential voice. The woman next to me remarked, "It doesn't make any sense."

I looked at her and saw to my surprise that it was my mother who had spoken. "What're you doing here?" I asked.

"What am I . . . ?" She looked puzzled. "Dorothy—you know Dorothy, don't you?—asked me."

There was a sudden burst of noise, as I said: "But I thought you were going to stay home today."

She looked at me oddly and I realized that she had not heard me. Conversation was now impossible. People shoved us, gave us drinks, greeted her enthusiastically. As I watched her, I wondered, as I often do, at all the people she knows. It was apparent that during the many years I have been away from Washington, a whole new group had come to town and she knew them all.

"How long've you been here?" she asked brightly.

"I got here just a few minutes ago."

"No, I meant how long . . ." But a large cavalry officer came between us. Isolated by his enormous, uniformed back I looked out the window.

The sky was pale. Night loitered behind the dome of the Capitol where the President, with unusual resonance for him, had just finished his address. Below my window, soldiers were marching and the mob that lined both sides of the Avenue murmured at their ordered progress.

"How do you like it?" my mother asked, pitching her voice above the noise of the room; the cavalry officer had gone.

"Just like all the others we've seen."

"I meant Washington."

I paused. We had been through this so many times before. "Well, you know what I think. . . ."

"I know . . . ?"

"I meant it's just as dull as it always was." Then I thought she said: "How long did you live here before?" But since there was now so much confusion in the room I was not positive. I cleared my throat; men separated us. She was looking, I thought, extremely handsome. I had not seen her look so fine in years.

But now something unusual was happening outside. The noise of the crowd increased its volume like a radio being turned up or like an approaching earthquake which, in earthquake countries, can always be heard minutes in advance: a distant rumbling as the ground ripples in ever-widening circles from some disturbed and hidden center. Responding to this urgent sound, the people in the room pushed against the windows and looked out just as the President passed beneath us in an open car. He lifted his top hat and waved it. Then he was gone and the shouting died away.

"Are you going back to the house?" I asked, turning to my mother. We were together again, circled by Air Corps officers.

She frowned vaguely. "I suppose I'll see you later . . . some time," she added and before I could answer, a squad of women, wearing paper hats and blowing horns, divided the room with the fury of their passage and I took that wise moment to leave the party, narrowly avoiding the gift of a paper hat.

I wondered, as I walked back to the hotel, why my mother had been at that party. I realize that she knows a good many people nowadays that I don't know: people who have come to town in the years I have been away, traveling farther and farther from Washington, without regret or longing, always conscious, however, that nostalgia for place may yet occur in time. My family is a sentimental one and more and more I tend to believe in the heredity of behavior. I shall probably be very moved one day at the thought of spring (or autumn) in Rock Creek Park where most of my childhood was spent, in a gray stone house on a hill, bordered by a steep lawn, by maple and oak trees, among hills evenly crossed by the rock-littered, iron-brown Rock Creek whose bright course winds through those green woods.

As I walked, I contemplated the election and the Inauguration, which meant much less to me than I publicly pretended. I have a conviction that individuals have little to do with state affairs, that governments are essentially filing systems that in time break down for lack of cabinet space, clerks, typewriters, paper and, perhaps, faith in order. More and more I find it difficult to take public matters seriously: a definite schizoid tendency, as a psychologist friend of mine would say, placing me figuratively in a gray rubber sack where, cut off from the world outside, I am able to regard with neither pleasure nor dismay the interior of my private realm, complacent at having escaped so neatly, so thoroughly.

I was now on the outskirts of Rock Creek Park. Obeying an impulse, I turned into the park and walked down to Broad Branch Road, past Pierce's Mill . . . named for that good President who gave Hawthorne a consulate.

As I walked, day ended. The planet Venus, a circle of silver in a green sky, pierced the edge of the evening while the wintry woods darkened about me, and in the stillness the regular sound of my footsteps striking the pavement was like the rhythmic beating of a giant's stone heart.

At last I came to the hill where, at the top of a serpentine drive, our old house stood, a solid gray house, owned now by strangers. I was about to continue on when a young boy crossed the road, coming from the creek.

He was half-grown, with silver-blond hair and dark eyes. In his arms he carried several branches of laurel. When he saw me he stopped. Then, magically, the street lamps went on, ending twilight, shadowing our faces.

"You live up there?"

"Yes." His voice was light, not yet changed. He moved the green branches from one arm to another, tentatively, as though undecided whether to stay and talk or to go home. "It's my grandfather's house."

"Have you lived there long?"

"Most of my life. You know my grandfather?"

I said I did not. "But I used to live in that house, too . . . when I was about your age. *My* grandfather built it thirty years ago."

"No, I don't think so. *Mine* built it a long time ago: when I was born."

I smiled, not questioning this. "How old are you?" I asked.

"Twelve," he said, embarrassed he was not older. In the unshaded white light, his hair glittered like metal.

Then I asked the traditional questions about school: adults and children meet always as foreigners with a limited common vocabulary and mutual distrust. I should have liked to talk to him as an equal, I thought: my eyes on the green only, not on silver or on brown skin. There was a directness about him which is rare among children, who usually are not only careful but often downright politic in their dealings with the larger people. I asked questions by rote: "What do you like best in school?"

"Reading. My grandfather has a big library . . ."

"In the attic," I said, remembering my own childhood.

"Yes, in the attic," he said, wonderingly. "How did you know?"

"We kept books there, too, thousands of them."

"So do we. I like the history ones."

"And the Arabian Nights."

He looked surprised. "Yes. How did you know?"

I nodded, looking at him directly for the first time: a square brown face between silver hair and green laurel, a beardless, smooth face, uncomplicated by lines or dry skin or broken veins or by character that, once formed, like a poison in the blood, corrupts the face. The street lamp was directly overhead revealing the line and shape of that familiar skull. We looked at one another and I knew that I should say something, ask yet another question but I could not and so we stood until at last, to stop this silence, I repeated: "Do you like school?"

"No. You live in Washington?"

"I used to . . . when I lived up there." I indicated the hill. "Before the war."

"That was a long time ago," said the boy, frowning, and time, I remembered, depends on how old one is; ten years, nothing to me now, was all his life.

"Yes, a long time ago."

He shifted his weight from one foot to another. "Where do you live?"

"In New York . . . sometimes. Have you been there?"

"Oh, yes. I don't like it."

I smiled, remembering as a child the prejudice Washington people had against New York. "What are you going to do with these?" I asked, touching a branch of laurel. "Make wreaths the way the Romans did?"

I remembered an illustrated Victorian edition of Livy in which all the heroes wore Apollo's laurel.

He looked at me with surprise; then he smiled. "Yes, I do that sometimes."

Nothing has changed, I thought, and the terror began.

"I have to go," he said, stepping out of the circle of electric light.

"Yes, it's time for dinner."

From the top of the hill a woman's voice called a name which made us both start.

"I have to go," he said again. "Good-bye."

"Good-bye."

I watched him as he clambered straight up the hill and across the lawn, not following the paved driveway. I continued to watch until the front door opened and he stepped into the yellow light. Then, as I walked away, down the road between the dark evening hills, I wondered if I should ever recall an old encounter with a stranger who had asked me odd questions about our house, and about the green laurel that I carried in my arms.

1949

Part Two

SOME ARCHETYPAL THEMES

The Search

So far as we know, man is the only creature which, even when his material needs are satisfied, and he is not suffering physical discomfort, seems always to be seeking something, something that he is often unable to define. Or, if he thinks himself perfectly conscious of what he seeks, the attainment of it is frequently disillusioning, for he finds that he has deceived himself—that this, after all, is not what he was really looking for. If he longs for forbidden fruit, involving the violation of a taboo, he must choose either to be a hypocrite or criminal; for he may eat of it in secret, in which case he must lead a double life, or in public, in which case he suffers ostracism or confinement. There is yet a third choice: to go hungry. The picture is really not that gloomy, even for those who seek the fruit that is forbidden, for man unconsciously, and as it were instinctively, tends to protect himself in advance by making symbolic substitutions: thus, an incest-drive with a mother-object (to take a common example) will satisfy itself—or at least relieve itself—when the individual finds a mate who resembles the mother that, without realizing it, he is, unconsciously, actually seeking.

But even when the object of his search is socially acceptable, even when the individual has defined it quite accurately for himself in his conscious mind, so that he feels on attaining it a strong sense of satisfaction—even then, as often as not, he will not rest content with his achievement, but, like the speaker in Tennyson's dramatic monologue "Ulysses," will conceive another object and proceed to pursue *it*. To seek is, in other words, to be human, though the objects of the search may be as numerous as the persons who seek them. A man who was not seeking for something—even if that something were death—would truly be a monster; but, since he does not exist, we need not feel sorry for him. Or, if he exists, he does so in body only, for he is lacking one of the elements that give him human definition. The search for death itself (of which we have seen an example, subtly disguised as a search for life, in the story by D. H. Lawrence in the Scapegoat category) may well be a human monopoly. Even naturalistic writers like Zola and Dreiser, who were impressed, or rather depressed, by the implications—which seemed to them wholly negative—of nineteenth-century science, and who insisted with a kind of unholy glee on the innate depravity of man, were forced to concede the uniqueness of that aspect of man which yet enabled him, while fettered biologically and environmentally to the fact, to indulge in the spiritual consolation and the luxury of the dream.

If the theory of archetypes has any validity whatever, it is only to be expected that so universal a drive as the Search would provide the collective unconscious with a number of related archetypes; and this indeed seems to be the case. We have chosen seven such archetypes, with no pretense at exhaustiveness and in the realization that they do not necessarily exclude one another. Thus, while "The Mines of Falun" is essentially a story of the Adventure-Treasure Search (referred to variously by the archetypal critics as "the Quest" and "the Voyage"), it may also be viewed as an example of the Mother-Search. And there is one rather important respect in which it is *not* typical of the Quest: the hero does not overcome an obstacle and return victorious. We have the feeling, as we do in "The Woman Who Rode Away," that he is doomed and that he is being propelled toward his destruction by a force over which he has no control—that, even unconsciously, he may be seeking his own destruction, so that there is yet a third way of classifying the story: as an example of the Return to the Womb. Nor must we overlook the existence of an Alter-Ego motif, for, especially toward the end, Elis Frobom has two allegiances: one to air, sunlight, life, and his fiancée; the other to sulphur fumes, darkness, death, and his mother, who appears transfigured as a death-deity. The truth is that Hoffmann is a writer who is extraordinarily rich in archetypal meanings and that these combine with complete harmony to make "The Mines of Falun" one of the most remarkable stories in the whole repertory of German romanticism.

The death-wish may also be present in two other stories in this section: "A Hunger Artist" and "The Lily's Quest." The tendency of archetypes to combine and overlap has been noted before, and in any case classification is secondary to comprehension: so long as we are able to recognize the archetypal content of the story and to understand how it functions, it matters little how we label it. That is, whether it is more proper to view Theseus [1] as a Search figure or as a voluntary Scapegoat is, in the last analysis, an academic question, for he possesses some of the characteristics of each.

Classical mythology furnishes us with numerous examples of Search archetypes, of which perhaps the commonest are the Mother-Search, dramatized in the tragic career of Oedipus,[2] and the Quest or Voyage, illustrated in the adventures of Theseus, of Jason,[3] and of Odysseus

---

[1] Athenian prince who delivers his city from the yearly sacrifice of seven youths and seven maidens to the Minotaur by volunteering to go to Crete as one of the youths and by killing the monster in the famous maze.

[2] King of Thebes, of whom it was prophesied that he would slay his father and marry his mother. The prophecy was fulfilled. This myth formed the plot of *Oedipus Rex*, regarded by many as Sophocles' masterpiece.

[3] Leader of the Argonauts, a group of fifty heroes who voyaged to Colchis and obtained the treasure of the Golden Fleece.

(Ulysses).[4] The Quest theme is closely related to that of the Hero, but is not identical with it. Joseph Campbell, in *The Hero With a Thousand Faces,* distinguishes several stages in myths exhibiting the Quest pattern: the call to adventure, which may occur in a very casual and undramatic way, but which the Hero refuses to answer at his peril; the initiation stage, which involves the triumph over obstacles; and the return.

Obeying the call to adventure traditionally involves the severance, real or symbolic, of whatever ties may serve to connect one with the past. This was the function, in primitive cultures, of those ceremonies known in anthropology as the "rites of passage." Campbell notes:

> The so-called rites of passage, which occupy such a prominent place in the life of a primitive society (ceremonials of birth, naming, puberty, marriage, burial, etc.) are distinguished by formal, and usually very severe, exercises of severance, whereby the mind is radically cut away from the attitudes, attachments, and life patterns of the stage being left behind.[5]

In "The Mines of Falun," the umbilical cord is symbolically severed for Elis Frobom when his mother dies, and it is only after this event, in his case particularly traumatic, that he is free to begin his adventure.

Few themes are more universal than that of the Quest: a Germanic version of it is seen in the epic poem of the *Nibelungenlied,* where Siegfried succeeds in acquiring the treasure hoard of the Nibelungs; and a Norman French version is found in the Arthurian romances, in one of which (by Chrétien de Troyes) Percival seeks unsuccessfully for the Holy Grail, and in another of which (by Thomas Malory) Sir Galahad actually attains it.

Psychologists believe that myths were devised in order to satisfy man's psychic needs, and they have interpreted them in various ways. Thus, the Oedipus story gratifies the male's concealed wish for union with his mother,[6] while some psychologists see in Theseus' penetration of the labyrinth to slay the Minotaur a symbolic enactment of the desire for self-knowledge. What he slays, according to this interpretation, is the enemy that each man carries within himself—that part of him which limits his freedom and makes of him only half a man.

Some of the symbols through which myths communicate their meanings are, of course, easier to recognize than others. It is easy and

---

[4] Prince of Ithaca, whose return home after participating in the ten year siege of Troy took another ten years, during which he triumphed over a number of obstacles in various far-flung places. The story of his wanderings is the subject of Homer's epic *The Odyssey.* Ulysses is the Latin name for Odysseus.

[5] Joseph Campbell, *The Hero With a Thousand Faces* (New York: Bollingen Foundation, 1961), p. 10.

[6] Freud writes: "King Oedipus, who slew his father Laius and married his mother Jocasta, is nothing more than a wish fulfilment—the fulfilment of the wish of our childhood. But we, more fortunate than he, in so far as we have not become psychoneurotics, have since our childhood succeeded in withdrawing our sexual impulses from our mothers, and in forgetting our jealousy of our fathers." Sigmund Freud, *The Basic Writings of Sigmund Freud* (New York: Modern Library, 1938), p. 308.

natural, for example, to connect the Golden Apples of the Hesperides [7] with the idea of happiness; and the Search for Happiness is a theme which is also very familiar from the morality plays of the Middle Ages, where it took a form very similar to that in "The Lily's Quest," with its melancholy moral that happiness is not of this world. Early in the present century this archetype found literary expression in Maurice Maeterlinck's popular play *The Bluebird* and in Henry James's story "The Great Good Place." Because of the divine nature of the Grail, the cup from which Christ is said to have drunk at the Last Supper, it is also easy and natural to connect the search for it with the Search for God.

Besides the Hero, another archetypal character likely to figure importantly in the Search pattern is one whom Jung designates as the Wise Old Man—a character generally beneficent, whose function is to act as a kind of guide to whatever the Hero is seeking. Jung writes: "The old man . . . represents knowledge, reflection, insight, wisdom, cleverness and intuition on the one hand, and, on the other, moral qualities such as good will and readiness to help." [8] Given this positive function of the archetype, it is not difficult to identify the mysterious master in Hesse's story "The Poet" and the tramp in McCullers' "A Tree. A Rock. A Cloud." In Greek mythology Daedalus, the architect who masterminded the construction of the Minotaur's labyrinth and who has symbolized the artist-scientist for centuries, performs this function when he suggests to Ariadne that Theseus use a thread to retrace his steps through the maze. In Arthurian legend Merlin, the King's magician and counsellor, renders him innumerable helpful services; and in Dante's medieval epic, *The Divine Comedy,* Virgil acts as the poet's guide and mentor.

However, Jung also states: "Just as all archetypes have a positive, favorable, bright side that points upwards, so also they have one that points downwards, partly negative and unfavorable, partly chthonic, but for the rest merely neutral." [9] This sinister function is seen in the character of Mephistopheles in Goethe's poem *Faust*. In the Oedipus story Tiresias is obliged as a prophet to utter truths that are unwelcome, but in reality he is, in Jung's phrase, "merely neutral." In our stories the negative aspect of the archetype is seen in the characters of Walter Gascoigne in "The Lily's Quest" and old Torbern in "The Mines of Falun." It might be pointed out, however, that though these characters *seem* sinister, when viewed through the eyes of the Hero, we might argue that they too are "merely neutral." For Walter Gascoigne, like Tiresias, is nothing if not honest; and though it is tempting to cast Torbern, or rather his ghost, in the role of murderer, there is another way of looking

---

[7] Gaea's wedding gift to Juno, guarded over by a dragon. Hercules' successful search for them constituted one of the Twelve Labors, a series of desperate adventures that hero undertook at the command of Eurystheus.

[8] C. G. Jung, *The Archetypes and the Collective Unconscious* in *The Collected Works of C. G. Jung,* ed. by Sir Herbert Read, *et al.,* and trans, by R. F. C. Hull, Bollingen Series XX (Princeton: Princeton Univ. Press, 1959), Vol. 9, Part I, p. 226.

[9] *Ibid.*

at him: as the agent by means of whom Elis Frobom fulfills his destiny. The latter interpretation seems especially valid if we honor the view which has already been mentioned—that a death-wish, or a Mother-Search, is also involved in the story.

A HUNGER ARTIST

by Franz Kafka

During these last decades the interest in professional fasting has markedly diminished. It used to pay very well to stage such great performances under one's own management, but today that is quite impossible. We live in a different world now. At one time the whole town took a lively interest in the hunger artist; from day to day of his fast the excitement mounted; everybody wanted to see him at least once a day; there were people who bought season tickets for the last few days and sat from morning till night in front of his small barred cage; even in the nighttime there were visiting hours, when the whole effect was heightened by torch flares; on fine days the cage was set out in the open air, and then it was the children's special treat to see the hunger artist; for their elders he was often just a joke that happened to be in fashion, but the children stood open-mouthed, holding each other's hands for greater security, marveling at him as he sat there pallid in black tights, with his ribs sticking out so prominently, not even on a seat but down among straw on the ground, sometimes giving a courteous nod, answering questions with a constrained smile, or perhaps stretching an arm through the bars so that one might feel how thin it was, and then again withdrawing deep into himself, paying no attention to anyone or anything, not even to the all-important striking of the clock that was the only piece of furniture in his cage, but merely staring into vacancy with half-shut eyes, now and then taking a sip from a tiny glass of water to moisten his lips.

Besides casual onlookers there were also relays of permanent watchers selected by the public, usually butchers, strangely enough, and it was their task to watch the hunger artist day and night, three of them at a time, in case he should have some secret recourse to nourishment. This was nothing but a formality, instituted to reassure the masses, for the initiates knew well enough that during his fast the artist would never in

---

any circumstances, not even under forcible compulsion, swallow the smallest morsel of food; the honor of his profession forbade it. Not every watcher, of course, was capable of understanding this, there were often groups of night watchers who were very lax in carrying out their duties and deliberately huddled together in a retired corner to play cards with great absorption, obviously intending to give the hunger artist the chance of a little refreshment, which they supposed he could draw from some private hoard. Nothing annoyed the artist more than such watchers; they made him miserable; they made his fast seem unendurable; sometimes he mastered his feebleness sufficiently to sing during their watch for as long as he could keep going, to show them how unjust their suspicions were. But that was of little use; they only wondered at his cleverness in being able to fill his mouth even while singing. Much more to his taste were the watchers who sat close up to the bars, who were not content with the dim night lighting of the hall but focused him in the full glare of the electric pocket torch given them by the impresario. The harsh light did not trouble him at all. In any case he could never sleep properly, and he could always drowse a little, whatever the light, at any hour, even when the hall was thronged with noisy onlookers. He was quite happy at the prospect of spending a sleepless night with such watchers; he was ready to exchange jokes with them, to tell them stories out of his nomadic life, anything at all to keep them awake and demonstrate to them again that he had no eatables in his cage and that he was fasting as not one of them could fast. But his happiest moment was when the morning came and an enormous breakfast was brought them, at his expense, on which they flung themselves with the keen appetite of healthy men after a weary night of wakefulness. Of course there were people who argued that this breakfast was an unfair attempt to bribe the watchers, but that was going rather too far, and when they were invited to take on a night's vigil without a breakfast, merely for the sake of the cause, they made themselves scarce, although they stuck stubbornly to their suspicions.

Such suspicions, anyhow, were a necessary accompaniment to the profession of fasting. No one could possibly watch the hunger artist continuously, day and night, and so no one could produce first-hand evidence that the fast had really been rigorous and continuous; only the artist himself could know that; he was therefore bound to be the sole completely satisfied spectator of his own fast. Yet for other reasons he was never satisfied; it was not perhaps mere fasting that had brought him to such skeleton thinness that many people had regretfully to keep away from his exhibitions, because the sight of him was too much for them, perhaps it was dissatisfaction with himself that had worn him down. For he alone knew, what no other initiate knew, how easy it was to fast. It was the easiest thing in the world. He made no secret of this, yet people did not believe him; at the best they set him down as modest, most of them, however, thought he was out for publicity or else was some kind of cheat who found it easy to fast because he had discovered a way of making it easy, and then had the impudence to admit the fact, more or less. He had to put up with all that, and in the course of time had got used to it, but his inner dissatisfaction always rankled, and never yet, after any term of fasting—this must be granted to his credit—had he left the cage of his own free will. The longest period of fasting was fixed by his impresario at forty days, beyond that term he was not allowed to go, not even in great cities, and there was good reason for it, too. Experience had proved that for about forty days the interest of the public could be stimulated by a steadily increasing pressure of advertisement, but after that the town began to lose interest, sympathetic support began notably to fall off; there were of course local variations as between one town and another or one country and another, but as a general rule forty days marked the limit. So on the fortieth day the flower-bedecked cage was opened, enthusiastic spectators filled the hall, a military band played, two doctors entered the cage to measure the results of the fast, which were announced through a megaphone, and finally two young ladies appeared, blissful at having been selected for the honor, to help the hunger artist down the few steps leading to a small table on which was spread a carefully chosen invalid repast. And at this very moment the artist always turned stubborn. True, he would entrust his bony arms to the outstretched helping hands of the ladies bending over him, but stand up he would not. Why stop fasting at this particular moment, after forty days of it? He had held out for a long time, an illimitably long time; why stop now, when he was in his best fasting form, or rather, not yet quite in his best fasting form? Why should he be cheated of the fame he would get for fasting longer, for being not only the record hunger artist of all time, which presumably he was already, but for beating his own record by a performance beyond human imagination, since he felt that there were no limits to his capacity for fasting? His public pretended to admire him so much, why should it have so little patience with him; if he could endure fasting longer, why shouldn't the public endure it? Besides, he was tired, he was comfortable sitting in the straw, and now he was supposed to lift himself to his full height and go down to a meal the very thought of which gave him a nausea that only the presence of the ladies kept him for betraying, and even that with an effort. And he looked up into the eyes of the ladies who were apparently so friendly and in reality so cruel, and shook his head, which felt too heavy on its strengthless neck. But then there happened yet again what always happened. The impresario came forward, without a word—for the band made speech impossible—lifted his arms in the air above the artist, as if inviting Heaven to look down upon its creature here in the straw, this suffering martyr, which indeed he was, although in quite another sense; grasped him round the emaciated waist, with exaggerated caution, so that the frail condition he was in might be appreciated; and committed him to the care of the blenching ladies, not without secretly giving him a shaking so that his legs and body tottered and swayed. The artist now submitted completely; his head lolled on his breast as if it had landed there by chance; his body was hollowed out; his legs in a spasm of self-preservation clung close to each other at the knees, yet scraped on the ground as if it were not really solid ground, as if they were only trying to find solid ground; and the whole weight of his body, a featherweight after all, relapsed onto one of the ladies, who, looking round for help and panting a little—this post of honor was not at all what she had expected it to be—first stretched her neck as far as she could to keep her face at least free from contact with the artist, then finding this impossible, and her more fortunate companion not coming to her aid but merely holding extended on her own trembling hand the little bunch of knucklebones that was the artist's, to the great delight of the spectators burst into tears and had to be replaced by an attendant who had long been stationed in readiness. Then came the food, a little of which the impresario managed to get between the artist's lips, while he sat in a kind of half-fainting trance, to the accompaniment of cheerful patter designed to distract the public's attention from the artist's condition; after that, a toast was drunk to the public, supposedly prompted by a whisper from the artist in the impresario's ear; the band confirmed it with a mighty flourish, the spectators melted away, and no one had any cause to be dissatisfied with the proceedings, no one except the hunger artist himself, he only, as always.

So he lived for many years, with small regular intervals of recuperation, in visible glory, honored by the world, yet in spite of that troubled in spirit, and all the more troubled because no one would take his trouble seriously. What comfort could he possibly need? What more could he possibly wish for? And if some good-natured person, feeling sorry for him, tried to console him by pointing out that his melancholy was probably caused by fasting, it could happen, especially when he had been fasting for some time, that he reacted with an outburst of fury and to the general alarm began to shake the bars of his cage like a wild animal. Yet the impresario had a way of punishing these outbreaks which he rather enjoyed putting into operation. He would apologize publicly for the artist's behavior, which was only to be excused, he admitted, because of the irritability caused by fasting; a condition hardly to be understood by well-fed people; then by natural transition he went on to mention the artist's equally incomprehensible boast that he could fast for much longer than he was doing; he praised the high ambition, the good will, the great self-denial undoubtedly implicit in such a statement; and then quite simply countered it by bringing out photographs, which were also on sale to the public, showing the artist on the fortieth day of a fast lying in bed almost dead from exhaustion. This perversion of the truth, familiar to the artist though it was, always unnerved him afresh and proved too much for him. What was a consequence of the premature ending of his fast was here presented as the cause of it! To fight against this lack of understanding, against a whole world of non-understanding, was impossible. Time and again in good faith he stood by the bars listening to the impresario, but as soon as the photographs appeared he always let go and sank with a groan back on to his straw, and the reassured public could once more come close and gaze at him.

A few years later when the witnesses of such scenes called them to mind, they often failed to understand themselves at all. For meanwhile the aforementioned change in public interest had set in; it seemed to happen almost overnight; there may have been profound causes for it, but who was going to bother about that; at any rate the pampered hunger artist suddenly found himself deserted one fine day by the amusement seekers, who went streaming past him to other more favored attractions. For the last time the impresario hurried him over half Europe to discover whether the old interest might still survive here and there; all in vain; everywhere, as if by secret agreement, a positive revulsion from professional fasting was in evidence. Of course it could not really have sprung up so suddenly as all that, and many premonitory symptoms which had not been sufficiently remarked or suppressed during the rush and glitter of success now came retrospectively to mind, but it was now too late to take any countermeasures. Fasting would surely come into fashion again at some future date, yet that was no comfort for those living in the present. What, then, was the hunger artist to do? He had been applauded by thousands in his time and could hardly come down to showing himself in a street booth at village fairs, and as for adopting another profession, he was not only too old for that but too fanatically devoted to fasting. So he took leave of the impresario, his partner in an unparalleled career, and hired himself to a large circus; in order to spare his own feelings he avoided reading the conditions of his contract.

A large circus with its enormous traffic in replacing and recruiting men, animals and apparatus can always find a use for people at any time, even for a hunger artist, provided of course that he does not ask too much, and in this particular case anyhow it was not only the artist who was taken on but his famous and long-known name as well; indeed considering the peculiar nature of his performance, which was not impaired by advancing age, it could not be objected that here was an artist past his prime, no longer at the height of his professional skill, seeking a refuge in some quiet corner of a circus; on the contrary, the hunger artist averred that he could fast as well as ever, which was entirely credible; he even alleged that if he were allowed to fast as he liked, and this was at once promised him without more ado, he could astound the world by establishing a record never yet achieved, a statement which certainly provoked a smile among the other professionals, since it left out of account the change in public opinion, which the hunger artist in his zeal conveniently forgot.

He had not, however, actually lost his sense of the real situation and took it as a matter of course that he and his cage should be stationed, not in the middle of the ring as a main attraction, but outside, near the animal cages, on a site that was after all easily accessible. Large and gaily painted placards made a frame for the cage and announced what was to be seen inside it. When the public came thronging out in the intervals to see the animals, they could hardly avoid passing the hunger artist's cage and stopping there for a moment, perhaps they might even have stayed longer had not those pressing behind them in the narrow gangway, who did not understand why they should be held up on their way towards the excitements of the menagerie, made it impossible for anyone to stand gazing quietly for any length of time. And that was the reason why the hunger artist, who had of course been looking forward to these visiting hours as the main achievement of his life, began instead to shrink from them. At first he could hardly wait for the intervals; it was exhilarating to watch the crowds come streaming his way, until only too soon—not even the most obstinate self-deception, clung to almost consciously, could hold out against the fact—the conviction was borne in upon him that these people, most of them, to judge from their actions, again and again, without exception, were all on their way to the menagerie. And the first sight of them from the distance remained the best. For when they reached his cage he was at once deafened by the storm of shouting and abuse that arose from the two contending factions, which renewed themselves continuously, of those who wanted to stop and stare at him—he soon began to dislike them more than the others—not out of real interest but only out of obstinate self-assertiveness, and those who wanted to go straight on to the animals. When the first great rush was past, the stragglers came along, and these, whom nothing could have prevented from stopping to look at him as long as they had breath, raced past with long strides, hardly even glancing at him, in their haste to get to the menagerie in time. And all too rarely did it happen that he had a stroke of luck, when some father of a family fetched up before him with his children, pointed a finger at the hunger artist and explained at length what the phenomenon meant, telling stories of earlier years when he himself had watched similar but much more thrilling performances, and the children, still rather uncomprehending, since neither inside nor outside school had they been sufficiently prepared for this lesson—what did they care about fasting?—yet showed by the brightness of their intent eyes that new and better times might be coming. Perhaps, said the hunger artist to himself many a time, things would be a little better if his cage were set not quite so near the menagerie. That made it too easy for people to make their choice, to say nothing of what he suffered from the stench of the menagerie, the animals' restlessness by night, the carrying past of raw lumps of flesh for the beasts of prey, the roaring at feeding times, which depressed him continually. But he did not dare to lodge a complaint with the management; after all, he had the animals to thank for the troops of people who passed his cage, among whom there might always be one here and there to take an interest in him, and who could tell where they might seclude him if he called attention to his existence and thereby to the fact that, strictly speaking, he was only an impediment on the way to the menagerie.

A small impediment, to be sure, one that grew steadily less. People grew familiar with the strange idea that they could be expected, in times like these, to take an interest in a hunger artist, and with this familiarity the verdict went out against him. He might fast as much as he could, and he did so; but nothing could save him now, people passed him by. Just try to explain to anyone the art of fasting! Anyone who has no feeling for it cannot be made to understand it. The fine placards grew dirty and illegible, they were torn down; the little notice board telling the number of fast days achieved, which at first was changed carefully every day, had long stayed at the same figure, for after the first few weeks even this small task seemed pointless to the staff; and so the artist simply fasted on and on, as he had once dreamed of doing, and it was no trouble to him, just as he had always foretold, but no one counted the days, no one, not even the artist himself, knew what records he was already breaking, and his heart grew heavy. And when once in a time some leisurely passer-by stopped, made merry over the old figure on the board and spoke of swindling, that was in its way the stupidest lie ever invented by indifference and inborn malice, since it was not the hunger artist who was cheating; he was working honestly, but the world was cheating him of his reward.

Many more days went by, however, and that too came to an end. An overseer's eye fell on the cage one day and he asked the attendants why this perfectly good stage should be left standing there unused with dirty straw inside it; nobody knew, until one man, helped out by the notice board, remembered about the hunger artist. They poked into the straw with sticks and found him in it. "Are you still fasting?" asked the overseer. "When on earth do you mean to stop?" "Forgive me, everybody," whispered the hunger artist; only the overseer, who had his ear to the bars, understood him. "Of course," said the overseer, and tapped his forehead with a finger to let the attendants know what state the man was in, "we forgive you." "I always wanted you to admire my fasting," said the hunger artist. "We do admire it," said the overseer, affably. "But you shouldn't admire it," said the hunger artist. "Well, then we don't admire it," said the overseer, "but why shouldn't we admire it?" "Because I have to fast, I can't help it," said the hunger artist. "What a fellow you are," said the overseer, "and why can't you help it?" "Because," said the hunger artist, lifting his head a little and speaking, with his lips pursed, as if for a kiss, right into the overseer's ear, so that no syllable might be lost, "because I couldn't find the food I liked. If I had found it, believe me, I should have made no fuss and stuffed myself like you or anyone else." These were his last words, but in his dimming eyes remained the firm though no longer proud persuasion that he was still continuing to fast.

"Well, clear this out now!" said the overseer, and they buried the hunger artist, straw and all. Into the cage they put a young panther. Even the most insensitive felt it refreshing to see this wild creature leaping around the cage that had so long been dreary. The panther was all right. The food he liked was brought him without hesitation by the attendants; he seemed not even to miss his freedom; his noble body, furnished almost to the bursting point with all that it needed, seemed to carry freedom around with it too; somewhere in his jaws it seemed to lurk; and the joy of life streamed with such ardent passion from his throat that for the onlookers it was not easy to stand the shock of it. But they braced themselves, crowded round the cage, and did not want ever to move away.

AUTUMN MOUNTAIN

by Ryūnosuké Akutagawa

"And speaking of Ta Ch'ih, have you ever seen his Autumn Mountain painting?"

One evening, Wang Shih-ku, who was visiting his friend Yün Nan-t'ien, asked this question.

"No, I have never seen it. And you?"

Ta Ch'ih, together with Mei-tao-jen and Huang-hao-shan-ch'iao, had been one of the great painters of the Mongol dynasty. As Yün Nan-t'ien replied, there passed before his eyes images of the artist's famous works, the Sandy Shore painting and the Joyful Spring picture scroll.

"Well, strange to say," said Wang Shih-ku, "I'm really not sure whether or not I have seen it. In fact. . . ."

"You don't know whether you have seen it or you haven't?" said Yün Nan-t'ien, looking curiously at his guest. "Do you mean that you've seen an imitation?"

"No, not an imitation. I saw the original. And it is not I alone who have seen it. The great critics Yen-k'o and Lien-chou both became involved with the Autumn Mountain." Wang Shih-ku sipped his tea and smiled thoughtfully. "Would it bore you to hear about it?"

"Quite the contrary," said Yün Nan-t'ien, bowing his head politely. He stirred the flame in the copper lamp.

At that time [began Wang Shih-ku] the old master Yüan Tsai was still alive. One evening while he was discussing paintings with Yen-k'o, he asked him whether he had ever seen Ta Ch'ih's Autumn Mountain. As you know, Yen-k'o made a veritable religion of Ta Ch'ih's painting and was certainly not likely to have missed any of his works. But he had never set eyes on his Autumn Mountain.

"No, I haven't seen it," he answered shamefacedly, "and I've never even heard of its existence."

"In that case," said Yüan Tsai, "please don't miss the first opportunity you have of seeing it. As a work of art it's on an even higher level than his Summer Mountain or Wandering Storm. In fact, I'm not sure that it isn't the finest of all Ta Ch'ih's paintings."

"Is it really such a masterpiece? Then I must do my best to see it. May I ask who owns this painting?"

"It's in the house of a Mr. Chang in the County of Jun. If you ever have

---

From *Modern Japanese Stories*, edited by Ivan Morris (Rutland, Vermont: Charles E. Tuttle, 1962), pp. 175–84. Reprinted by permission.

occasion to visit the Chin-shan Temple, you should call on him and see the picture. Allow me to give you a letter of introduction."

As soon as Yen-k'o received Yüan Tsai's letter, he made plans to set out for the County of Jun. A house which harbored so precious a painting as this would, he thought, be bound to have other great works of different periods. Yen-k'o was quite giddy with anticipation as he started out.

When he reached the County of Jun, however, he was surprised to find that Mr. Chang's house, though imposing in structure, was dilapidated. Ivy was coiled about the walls, and in the garden grass and weeds grew rank. As the old man approached, chickens, ducks, and other barnyard fowl looked up, as if surprised to see any stranger enter here. For a moment he could not help doubting Yüan Tsai's words and wondering how a masterpiece of Ta Ch'ih's could possibly have found its way into such a house. Upon a servant's answering his knock, he handed over the letter, explaining that he had come from far in the hope of seeing the Autumn Mountain.

He was led almost immediately into the great hall. Here again, though the divans and tables of red sandalwood stood in perfect order, a moldy smell hung over everything and an atmosphere of desolation had settled even on the tiles. The owner of the house, who now appeared, was an unhealthy-looking man; but he had a pleasant air about him and his pale face and delicate hands bore signs of nobility. Yen-k'o, after briefly introducing himself, lost no time in telling his host how grateful he would be if he might be shown the famous Ta Ch'ih painting. There was an urgency in the master's words, as if he feared that were he not to see the great painting at once, it might somehow vanish like a mist.

Mr. Chang assented without hesitation and had the painting hung on the bare wall of the great hall.

"This," he said, "is the Autumn Mountain to which you refer."

At the first glance Yen-k'o let out a gasp of admiration. The dominant color was a dark green. From one end to the other a river ran its twisting course; bridges crossed the river at various places and along its banks were little hamlets. Dominating it all rose the main peak of the mountain range, before which floated peaceful wisps of autumn cloud. The mountain and its neighboring hills were fresh green, as if newly washed by rain, and there was an uncanny beauty in the red leaves of the bushes and thickets scattered along their slopes. This was no ordinary painting, but one in which both design and color had reached an apex of perfection. It was a work of art instinct with the classical sense of beauty.

"Well, what do you think of it? Does it please you?" said Mr. Chang, peering at Yen-k'o with a smile.

"Oh, it is truly of godlike quality!" cried Yen-k'o, while he stared at the picture in awe. "Yüan Tsai's lavish praise was more than merited. Compared to this painting, everything I have seen until now seems second-rate."

"Really? You find it such a masterpiece?"

Yen-k'o could not help turning a surprised look at his host. "Can you doubt it?"

"Oh no, it isn't that I have any doubts," said Mr. Chang, and he blushed with confusion like a schoolboy. Looking almost timidly at the painting, he continued: "The fact is that each time I look at this picture I have the feeling that I am dreaming, though my eyes are wide open. I cannot help feeling that it is I alone who see its beauty, which is somehow too intense for this world of ours. What you just said brought back these strange feelings."

But Yen-k'o was not much impressed by his host's evident attempt at self-vindication. His attention was absorbed by the painting, and Mr. Chang's speech seemed to him merely designed to hide a deficiency in critical judgment.

Soon after, Yen-k'o left the desolate house.

As the weeks passed, the vivid image of the Autumn Mountain remained fresh in Yen-k'o's mind [continued Wang Shih-ku after accepting another cup of tea]. Now that he had seen Ta Ch'ih's masterpiece, he felt ready to give up anything whatsoever to possess it. Inveterate collector that he was, he knew that not one of the great works that hung in his own house—not even Li Ying-ch'iu's Floating Snowflakes, for which he had paid five hundred taels of silver—could stand comparison with that transcendent Autumn Mountain.

While still sojourning in the County of Jun, he sent an agent to the Chang house to negotiate for the sale of the painting. Despite repeated overtures, he was unable to persuade Mr. Chang to enter into any arrangement. On each occasion that pallid gentleman would reply that while he deeply appreciated the master's admiration of the Autumn Mountain and while he would be quite willing to lend the painting, he must ask to be excused from actually parting with it.

These refusals only served to strengthen the impetuous Yen-k'o's resolve. "One day," he promised himself, "that great picture will hang in my own hall." Confident of the eventual outcome, he finally resigned himself to returning home and temporarily abandoning the Autumn Mountain.

About a year later, in the course of a further visit to the County of Jun, he tried calling once more at the house of Mr. Chang. Nothing had changed: the ivy was still coiled in disorder about the walls and fences, and the garden was covered with weeds. But when the servant answered his knock, Yen-k'o was told that Chang was not in residence. The old man asked if he might have another look at the Autumn Mountain despite the owner's absence, but his importunacy was of no avail: the servant repeated that he had no authority to admit anyone until his master returned. As Yen-k'o persisted, the man finally shut the door in his face. Overcome with chagrin, Yen-k'o had to leave the house and the great painting that lay somewhere in one of the dilapidated rooms.

Wang Shih-ku paused for a moment.

"All that I have related so far," he said, "I heard from the master Yen-k'o himself."

"But tell me," said Yün Nan-t'ien, stroking his white beard, "did Yen-k'o ever really see the Autumn Mountain?"

"He said that he saw it. Whether or not he did, I cannot know for certain. Let me tell you the sequel, and then you can judge for yourself."

Wang Shih-ku continued his story with a concentrated air, and now he was no longer sipping his tea.

When Yen-k'o told me all this [said Wang Shih-ku] almost fifty years had passed since his visits to the County of Jun. The master Yüan Tsai was long since dead and Mr. Chang's large house had already passed into the hands of two successive generations of his family. There was no telling where the Autumn Mountain might be—nor if the best parts of the scroll might not have suffered hopeless deterioration. In the course of our talk old Yen-k'o described that mysterious painting so vividly that I was almost convinced I could see it before my eyes. It was not the details that had impressed the master but the indefinable beauty of the picture as a whole. Through the words of Yen-k'o, that beauty had entered into my heart as well as his.

It happened that, about a month after my meeting with Yen-k'o, I had myself to make a journey to the southern provinces, including the County of Jun. When I mentioned this to the old man, he suggested that I go and see if I could not find the Autumn Mountain. "If that painting ever comes to light again," he said, "it will indeed be a great day for the world of art."

Needless to say, by this time I also was anxious to see the painting, but my journey was crowded and it soon became clear that I would not find time to visit Mr. Chang's house. Meanwhile, however, I happened to hear a report that the Autumn Mountain had come into the hands of a certain nobleman by the name of Wang. Having learned of the painting, Mr. Wang had despatched a messenger with greetings to Chang's grandson. The latter was said to have sent back with the messenger not only the ancient family documents and the great ceremonial cauldron which had been in the family for countless generations, but also a painting which fitted the description of Ta Ch'ih's Autumn Mountain. Delighted with these gifts, Mr. Wang had arranged a great banquet for Chang's grandson, at which he had placed the young man in the seat of honor and regaled him with the choicest delicacies, gay music, and lovely girls; in addition he had given him one thousand pieces of gold.

On hearing this report I almost leaped with joy. Despite the vicissitudes of half a century, it seemed that the Autumn Mountain was still safe! Not only that, but it actually had come within my range. Taking along only the barest necessities, I set out at once to see the painting.

I still vividly remember the day. It was a clear, calm afternoon in early summer and the peonies were proudly in bloom in Mr. Wang's garden. On meeting Mr. Wang, my face broke into a smile of delight even before I had completed my ceremonial bow. "To think that the Autumn Mountain is in this very house!" I cried. "Yen-k'o spent all those years in vain attempts to see it again—and now I am to satisfy my own ambition without the slightest effort. . . ."

"You come at an auspicious time," replied Mr. Wang. "It happens that today I am expecting Yen-k'o himself, as well as the great critic Lien-chou. Please come inside, and since you are the first to arrive you shall be the first to see the painting."

Mr. Wang at once gave instructions for the Autumn Mountain to be hung on the wall. And then it all leaped forth before my eyes: the little villages on the river, the flocks of white cloud floating over the valley, the green of the towering mountain range which extended into the distance like a succession of folding-screens—the whole world, in fact, that Ta Ch'ih had created, a world far more wonderful than our own. My heart seemed to beat faster as I gazed intently at the scroll on the wall.

These clouds and mists and hills and valleys were unmistakably the work of Ta Ch'ih. Who but Ta Ch'ih could carry the art of drawing to such perfection that every brush-stroke became a thing alive? Who but he could produce colors of such depth and richness, and at the same time hide all mechanical trace of brush and paint? And yet . . . and yet I felt at once that this was not the same painting that Yen-k'o had seen once long ago. No, no, a magnificent painting it surely was, yet just as surely not the unique painting which he had described with such religious awe!

Mr. Wang and his entourage had gathered around me and were watching my expression, so I hastened to express my enthusiasm. Naturally I did not want him to doubt the authenticity of his picture, yet it was clear that my words of praise failed to satisfy him. Just then Yen-k'o himself was announced—he who had first spoken to me of this Autumn Mountain. As the old man bowed to Mr. Wang, I could sense the excitement inside him, but no sooner had his eyes settled on the scroll than a cloud seemed to pass before his face.

"What do you think of it, Master?" asked Mr. Wang, who had been carefully observing him. "We have just heard the teacher Wang Shih-ku's enthusiastic praise, but . . ."

"Oh, you are, sir, a very fortunate man to have acquired this painting," answered Yen-k'o promptly. "Its presence in your house will add luster to all your other treasures."

Yen-k'o's courteous words only seemed to deepen Mr. Wang's anxiety; he, like me, must have heard in them a note of insincerity. I think we were all a bit relieved when Lien-chou, the famous critic, made his appearance at this juncture. After bowing to us, he turned to the scroll and stood looking at it silently, chewing his long mustaches.

"This, apparently, is the same painting that the master Yen-k'o last saw half a century ago," Mr. Wang explained to him. "Now I would much like to hear your opinion of the work. Your candid opinion," Mr. Wang added, forcing a smile.

Lien-chou sighed and continued to look at the picture. Then he took a deep breath and, turning to Mr. Wang, said: "This, sir, is probably Ta Ch'ih's greatest work. Just see how the artist has shaded those clouds. What power there was in his brush! Note also the color of his trees. And then that distant peak which brings the whole composition to life." As he spoke, Lien-chou pointed to various outstanding features of the painting, and needless to say, a look of relief, then of delight, spread over Mr. Wang's face.

Meanwhile I secretly exchanged glances with Yen-k'o. "Master," I whispered, "is that the real Autumn Mountain?" Almost imperceptibly the old man shook his head, and there was a twinkle in his eyes.

"It's all like a dream," he murmured. "I really can't help wondering if that Mr. Chang wasn't some sort of hobgoblin."

"So that is the story of the Autumn Mountain," said Wang Shih-ku after a pause, and took a sip of his tea. "Later on it appears that Mr. Wang made all sorts of exhaustive enquiries. He visited Mr. Chang, but when he mentioned to him the Autumn Mountain, the young man denied all knowledge of any other version. So one cannot tell if that Autumn Mountain which Yen-k'o saw all those years ago is not even now hidden away somewhere. Or perhaps the whole thing was just a case of faulty memory on an old man's part. It would seem unlikely, though, that Yen-k'o's story about visiting Mr. Chang's house to see the Autumn Mountain was not based on solid fact."

"Well, in any case the image of that strange painting is no doubt engraved forever on Yen-k'o's mind. And on yours too."

"Yes," said Wang Shih-ku, "I still see the dark green of the mountain rock, as Yen-k'o described it all those years ago. I can see the red leaves of the bushes as if the painting were before my eyes this very moment."

"So even if it never existed, there is not really much cause for regret!"

The two men laughed and clapped their hands with delight.

---

for Wisdom

THE POET

by Hermann Hesse

It is told that, in his youth, the Chinese poet Han Fook was inspired with a wonderful urge to learn everything and to perfect himself in everything that in any way pertained to the art of poetry. At that time, when he still lived in his native city by the Yellow River, he had become engaged to a young lady of good family, at his own request and with the help of his parents who loved him tenderly. The wedding was soon to

---

From *German Stories*, by Herman Hesse, edited and translated by H. Steinhauser (New York: Farrar, Straus & Giroux, 1961).

be fixed for an auspicious day. At that time Han Fook was about twenty years old, a handsome youth, modest and with pleasant manners, well informed in the sciences and, in spite of his youth, already known for some excellent poems among the literati of his native city. Without being exactly rich, he could nevertheless expect an adequate fortune which was to be further increased by his bride's dowry; and since this bride was very beautiful and virtuous besides, the youth's happiness seemed to lack absolutely nothing. And yet he was not altogether contented, for his heart was filled with the ambition to become a perfect poet.

Then it happened one evening, when a lantern feast was being celebrated on the river, that Han Fook was walking alone on the opposite bank of the river. He leaned against the trunk of a tree that bent over into the water, and saw a thousand lights swimming and trembling on the surface of the river; he saw men and women and young girls greet each other on the boats and rafts, resplendent like beautiful flowers in their festive clothes; he heard the faint murmur of the illumined waters, the songs of the girl singers, the vibration of the zithers and the sweet tones of the flutists; and above all this he saw the bluish night suspended like the vault of a temple. The youth's heart beat fast when, as a lonely spectator following his whim, he contemplated all this beauty. But, however much he wanted to cross over, to participate, and to enjoy the festival in the company of his bride and his friends, he yet desired far more ardently to absorb all this as a sensitive spectator and to reflect it in a quite perfect poem: the blue of the night and the play of lights on the water as well as the pleasure of the festival guests and the yearning of the silent spectator who leans against the trunk of the tree above the bank. He felt that, despite all the festivals and pleasures of this earth, his heart could never feel quite comfortable and serene, that even in the midst of life he would remain a lonely man and to a certain extent a spectator and a stranger. And he felt that his soul, alone among many others, was so constituted that he must at the same time feel the beauty of the earth and the secret yearning of the stranger. This saddened him and he pondered on it, and the goal of his thoughts was this: that true happiness and a deep satisfaction could only be his if he once succeeded in mirroring the world so perfectly in a poem that he would possess the world itself, purified and perpetuated in these mirror images.

Han Fook scarcely knew whether he was still awake or had fallen asleep, when he heard a slight rustle and saw an unknown man standing near the tree trunk, an old man of venerable mien, dressed in a violet cloak. Han Fook drew himself up and saluted him with the greeting that is fitting for old and distinguished men. But the stranger smiled and spoke some verses which contained everything that the young man had just felt, expressed so perfectly and beautifully and according to the rules of the great poets that the youth's heart stood still in astonishment.

"Oh, who are you," he cried, bowing deeply, "you who can see into my soul and speak more beautiful verses than I have ever heard from all my teachers?"

The stranger smiled again, the smile of the accomplished, and said:

"If you want to become a poet, come to me. You will find my hut by the source of the great river in the northwestern mountains. My name is Master of the Perfect Word."

With that the old man stepped into the narrow shadow of the tree and had soon vanished; and Han Fook, who looked for him in vain and found no trace of him, now firmly believed that it had all been a dream born of his weariness. He hurried over to the boats and took part in the feast, but between the conversation and the flute playing he constantly heard the mysterious voice of the stranger; and his soul seemed to have left with the other, for he sat, a stranger and dreamy-eyed, among the cheerful guests who teased him about his lovesickness.

A few days later Han Fook's father wanted to summon his friends and relatives to set the date of the wedding. But the bridegroom objected and said: "Forgive me if I seem to offend against the obedience which the son owes his father. But you know how very much it is my desire to distinguish myself in the art of the poets; and even though some of my friends praise my poems, I know quite well that I am still only a beginner and only on the first steps of the road. Therefore I beg you, let me first go into solitude for a while and pursue my studies, for it seems to me that once I have a wife and a house to manage, they will keep me away from those things. But now I am still young and without other duties and would like to live a little while longer just for my poetry, from which I hope to gain happiness and fame."

This speech astonished his father and he said: "This art must surely be dear to you above everything else, since you even want to postpone your wedding because of it. Or if something has come between your bride and you, tell me about it, so that I may help you to appease her or to find you another."

But the son swore that he loved his bride no less than yesterday and always, and that not even the shadow of a quarrel had fallen between him and her. And at the same time he told his father that, in a dream which he had had on the day of the lantern feast, a master had been revealed to him; and that he yearned more ardently to become his pupil than to possess all the happiness of the world.

"Very well," said his father, "then I will give you a year. During this time you may pursue your dream, which was perhaps sent to you by a god."

"It may well be two years," said Han Fook hesitatingly, "who can know?"

So his father let him go and was saddened; but the youth wrote his bride a letter, said good-bye and left.

When he had walked for a very long time, he reached the source of the river and found a bamboo hut standing there in great solitude; and before the hut the old man whom he had seen by the bank near the tree trunk sat on a woven mat. He sat there playing the lute, and when he saw his guest approaching reverently, he did not rise nor did he greet him, but only smiled and let his delicate fingers run over the strings, and an enchanting music floated like a silver cloud through the valley, so that the youth stood and marveled, and in his sweet wonderment he forgot everything else until the Master of the Perfect Word laid his little lute aside and went into the hut. Han Fook followed him in reverence and stayed with him as his servant and pupil.

A month passed and he had learned to despise all the songs which he had composed till now, and he obliterated them from his memory. And after several more months, he also removed from his mind those songs which he had learned from his teachers at home. The master scarcely spoke a word to him; he silently taught him the art of lute playing, until the soul of the pupil was completely saturated with music. Once Han Fook made a little poem in which he described the flight of two birds in the autumnal sky and which he liked well. He did not dare to show it to the master, but he sang it one evening at a little distance from the hut, and the master must have heard it. But he did not say a word. He merely played softly on his lute, and soon the air grew cool and the twilight dimmer; a sharp wind arose although it was midsummer, and across the sky, which had turned gray, two herons flew, driven by a powerful wanderlust; and all this was so much more beautiful and more perfect than the pupil's verses that he became sad and fell silent and felt himself to be worthless. And the old man did this every time; and when a year had passed, Han Fook had almost completely learned the art of lute playing; but the art of poetry stood before him more and more difficult and sublime.

When two years had passed, the youth felt an intense nostalgia for his family, his native city and his bride, and he asked the master to let him journey.

The master smiled and nodded. "You are free," he said, "and may go wherever you will. You may come back, you may stay away, just as you please."

So the pupil set out on his journey and walked without resting, until one morning at dawn he stood on his native shore and looked across the arched bridge toward his home town. He crept stealthily into his father's garden and heard his father's breathing through the window of his bedroom, for he was still sleeping; and he crept into the orchard beside his bride's house and, from the top of a pear tree which he climbed, he saw his bride standing in her room, combing her hair. And when he compared all this that he saw with his eyes with the picture he had painted of it in his homesickness, it became clear to him that he was destined, after all, to be a poet; and he realized that in the dreams of poets there dwells a beauty and grace which one seeks in vain in the things of reality. And he climbed down from the tree and fled from the garden, over the bridge and from his native city, and returned to the high valley in the mountains. There the old master sat, as before, in front of his hut on the modest mat, plucking the lute with his fingers. Instead of a greeting he spoke two verses on the joys of art, whose depth and euphony caused the youth's eyes to fill with tears.

Again Han Fook stayed with the Master of the Perfect Word, who now instructed him on the zither, since he had mastered the lute, and the months vanished away like snow in the west wind. Twice more it happened that he was overcome by homesickness. One time he ran away secretly at night; but even before he had reached the last bend of the valley, the night wind rustled over the zither which hung in the door of the hut, and the tones sped after him and called him back, so that he was unable to resist. The other time, however, he dreamed that he was planting a sapling in his garden, and his wife stood beside him and his children watered the tree with wine and milk. When he awakened, the moon was shining into his room, and he arose in a disturbed state and saw the master lying in slumber nearby, his ancient beard quivering gently. A bitter hatred arose in him against this man who, as it seemed to him, had destroyed his life and cheated him of his future. He wanted to fall upon him and murder him; at that moment the old man opened his eyes and soon began to smile with a subtle, sad gentleness, which disarmed the pupil.

"Remember, Han Fook," the old man said softly, "you are free to do as you please. You may go to your native city and plant trees, or you may hate and slay me, it matters little."

"Ah, how could I hate you," cried the poet deeply moved, "that would be like hating Heaven itself."

And he stayed and learned to play the zither, and then the flute, and later on he began, under the direction of the master, to make poems; and he slowly learned the secret art of saying what seems uncomplicated and simple, yet stirs the listener's soul as the wind stirs the surface of the water. He described the coming of the sun, how it hesitates at the ridge of the mountains, and the noiseless gliding of the fish when they flit by like shadows under the water, or the swaying of a young willow in the spring wind; and when one heard it, it was not merely the sun and the play of the fish and the whispering of the willow, but the sky and the world seemed each time to harmonize for a moment in perfect music; and every listener thought, as he listened with pleasure or pain, of what he loved or hated: the boy thought of his games, the youth of his beloved and the old man of death.

Han Fook no longer knew how many years he had spent with the master at the source of the great river. Often it seemed to him as if he had entered this valley only last night and had been received by the old man's music. Often, too, he felt as if all human generations and ages had fallen away behind him and become insubstantial.

Then one morning he awoke alone in the hut, and no matter where he looked and called, the master had vanished. Autumn seemed to have come suddenly over night; a raw wind shook the old hut, and over the ridge of the mountains great flocks of migratory birds were flying, although their time had not come yet.

Then Han Fook took his little lute with him and descended into the land of his native city, and wherever he met people they gave him the greeting which is fitting for old and distinguished men. And when he came to his native city, his father and his bride and his relatives had died and other people lived in their houses. In the evening the lantern festival was celebrated on the river, and the poet Han Fook stood on the far side, on the darker shore, leaning against the trunk of an old tree; and when he began to play on his small lute, the women sighed and looked in rapture and uneasiness into the night, and the young men called for the lute player, whom they could find nowhere, and shouted that not one of them had ever heard such lute tones before. But Han Fook smiled. He looked into the river where the mirrored images of the thousand lanterns swam. And just as he was no longer able to distinguish the mirrored images from the real ones, he found no difference in his soul between this feast and that first one, when he had stood here as a youth and had heard the words of the strange master.

for Happiness

THE LILY'S QUEST

by Nathaniel Hawthorne

Two lovers, once upon a time, had planned a little summer-house, in the form of an antique temple, which it was their purpose to consecrate to all manner of refined and innocent enjoyments. There they would hold pleasant intercourse with one another and the circle of their familiar friends; there they would give festivals of delicious fruit; there they would hear lightsome music, intermingled with the strains of pathos which make joy more sweet; there they would read poetry and fiction, and permit their own minds to flit away in day-dreams and romance; there, in short—for why should we shape out the vague sunshine of their hopes?—there all pure delights were to cluster like roses among the pillars of the edifice, and blossom ever new and spontaneously. So, one breezy and cloudless afternoon, Adam Forrester and Lilias Fay set out upon a ramble over the wide estate which they were to possess together, seeking a proper site for their Temple of Happiness. They were themselves a fair and happy spectacle, fit priest and priestess for such a shrine; al-

From *The Complete Works of Nathaniel Hawthorne,* Riverside Edition, Vol. 1, with introduction by George Parsons Lathrop (Boston and New York: Houghton Mifflin Co., 1886), pp. 495–503.

though, making poetry of the pretty name of Lilias, Adam Forrester was wont to call her LILY, because her form was as fragile, and her cheek almost as pale.

As they passed hand in hand down the avenue of drooping elms that led from the portal of Lilias Fay's paternal mansion, they seemed to glance like winged creatures through the strips of sunshine, and to scatter brightness where the deep shadows fell. But setting forth at the same time with this youthful pair, there was a dismal figure, wrapped in a black velvet cloak that might have been made of a coffin pall, and with a sombre hat such as mourners wear drooping its broad brim over his heavy brows. Glancing behind them, the lovers well knew who it was that followed, but wished from their hearts that he had been elsewhere, as being a companion so strangely unsuited to their joyous errand. It was a near relative of Lilias Fay, an old man by the name of Walter Gascoigne, who had long labored under the burden of a melancholy spirit, which was sometimes maddened into absolute insanity, and always had a tinge of it. What a contrast between the young pilgrims of bliss and their unbidden associate! They looked as if moulded of heaven's sunshine, and he of earth's gloomiest shade; they flitted along like Hope and Joy roaming hand in hand through life; while his darksome figure stalked behind, a type of all the woful influences which life could fling upon them. But the three had not gone far when they reached a spot that pleased the gentle Lily, and she paused.

"What sweeter place shall we find than this?" said she. "Why should we seek farther for the site of our Temple?"

It was indeed a delightful spot of earth, though undistinguished by any very prominent beauties, being merely a nook in the shelter of a hill, with the prospect of a distant lake in one direction, and of a church spire in another. There were vistas and pathways leading onward and onward into the green woodlands, and vanishing away in the glimmering shade. The Temple, if erected here, would look towards the west: so that the lovers could shape all sorts of magnificent dreams out of the purple, violet, and gold of the sunset sky; and few of their anticipated pleasures were dearer than this sport of fantasy.

"Yes," said Adam Forrester, "we might seek all day and find no lovelier spot. We will build our Temple here."

But their sad old companion, who had taken his stand on the very site which they proposed to cover with a marble floor, shook his head and frowned; and the young man and the Lily deemed it almost enough to blight the spot, and desecrate it for their airy Temple, that his dismal figure had thrown its shadow there. He pointed to some scattered stones, the remnants of a former structure, and to flowers such as young girls delight to nurse in their gardens, but which had now relapsed into the wild simplicity of nature.

"Not here!" cried old Walter Gascoigne. "Here, long ago, other mortals built their Temple of Happiness. Seek another site for yours!"

"What!" exclaimed Lilias Fay. "Have any ever planned such a Temple save ourselves?"

"Poor child!" said her gloomy kinsman. "In one shape or other, every mortal has dreamed your dream."

Then he told the lovers how, not, indeed, an antique Temple, but a dwelling, had once stood there, and that a dark-clad guest had dwelt among its inmates, sitting forever at the fireside, and poisoning all their household mirth. Under this type, Adam Forrester and Lilias saw that the old man spake of Sorrow. He told of nothing that might not be recorded in the history of almost every household; and yet his hearers felt as if no sunshine ought to fall upon a spot where human grief had left so deep a stain; or, at least, that no joyous Temple should be built there.

"This is very sad," said the Lily, sighing.

"Well, there are lovelier spots than this," said Adam Forrester, soothingly,—"spots which sorrow has not blighted."

So they hastened away, and the melancholy Gascoigne followed them, looking as if he had gathered up all the gloom of the deserted spot, and was bearing it as a burden of inestimable treasure. But still they rambled on, and soon found themselves in a rocky dell through the midst of which ran a streamlet with ripple and foam, and a continual voice of inarticulate joy. It was a wild retreat, walled on either side with gray precipices, which would have frowned somewhat too sternly, had not a profusion of green shrubbery rooted itself into their crevices, and wreathed gladsome foliage around their solemn brows. But the chief joy of the dell was in the little stream, which seemed like the presence of a blissful child, with nothing earthly to do save to babble merrily and disport itself, and make every living soul its playfellow, and throw the sunny gleams of its spirit upon all.

"Here, here is the spot!" cried the two lovers with one voice as they reached a level space on the brink of a small cascade. "This glen was made on purpose for our Temple!"

"And the glad song of the brook will be always in our ears," said Lilias Fay.

"And its long melody shall sing the bliss of our lifetime," said Adam Forrester.

"Ye must build no Temple here!" murmured their dismal companion.

And there again was the old lunatic, standing just on the spot where they meant to rear their lightsome dome, and looking like the embodied symbol of some great woe, that, in forgotten days, had happened there. And, alas! there had been woe, nor that alone. A young man, more than a hundred years before, had lured hither a girl that loved him, and on this spot had murdered her, and washed his bloody hands in the stream which sung so merrily. And ever since the victim's death shrieks were often heard to echo between the cliffs.

"And see!" cried old Gascoigne, "is the stream yet pure from the stain of the murderer's hands?"

"Methinks it has a tinge of blood," faintly answered the Lily; and being as slight as the gossamer, she trembled and clung to her lover's arm, whispering, "Let us flee from this dreadful vale!"

"Come, then," said Adam Forrester, as cheerily as he could, "we shall soon find a happier spot."

They set forth again, young Pilgrims on that quest which millions—which every child of Earth—has tried in turn. And were the Lily and her lover to be more fortunate than all those millions? For a long time it seemed not so. The dismal shape of the old lunatic still glided behind them; and for every spot that looked lovely in their eyes, he had some legend of human wrong or suffering, so miserably sad that his auditors could never afterwards connect the idea of joy with the place where it had happened. Here, a heart-broken woman, kneeling to her child, had been spurned from his feet; here, a desolate old creature had prayed to the evil one, and had received a fiendish malignity of soul in answer to her prayer; here, a new-born infant, sweet blossom of life, had been found dead, with the impress of its mother's fingers round its throat; and here, under a shattered oak, two lovers had been stricken by lightning, and fell blackened corpses in each other's arms. The dreary Gascoigne had a gift to know whatever evil and lamentable thing had stained the bosom of Mother Earth; and when his funereal voice had told the tale, it appeared like a prophecy of future woe as well as a tradition of the past. And now, by their sad demeanor, you would have fancied that the pilgrim lovers were seeking, not a temple of earthly joy, but a tomb for themselves and their posterity.

"Where in this world," exclaimed Adam Forrester, despondingly, "shall we build our Temple of Happiness?"

"Where in this world, indeed!" repeated Lilias Fay; and being faint and weary, the more so by the heaviness of her heart, the Lily drooped her head and sat down on the summit of a knoll, repeating, "Where in this world shall we build our Temple?"

"Ah! have you already asked yourselves that question?" said their companion, his shaded features growing even gloomier with the smile that dwelt on them; "yet there is a place, even in this world, where ye may build it."

While the old man spoke, Adam Forrester and Lilias had carelessly thrown their eyes around, and perceived that the spot where they had chanced to pause possessed a quiet charm, which was well enough adapted to their present mood of mind. It was a small rise of ground, with a certain regularity of shape, that had perhaps been bestowed by art; and a group of trees, which almost surrounded it, threw their pensive shadows across and far beyond, although some softened glory of the sunshine found its way there. The ancestral mansion, wherein the lovers would dwell together, appeared on one side, and the ivied church, where they were to worship, on another. Happening to cast their eyes on the ground they smiled, yet with a sense of wonder, to see that a pale lily was growing at their feet.

"We will build our Temple here," said they, simultaneously, and with an indescribable conviction that they had at last found the very spot.

Yet, while they uttered this exclamation, the young man and the Lily turned an apprehensive glance at their dreary associate, deeming it hardly possible that some tale of earthly affliction should not make those precincts loathsome, as in every former case. The old man stood just behind them, so as to form the chief figure in the group, with his sable cloak muffling the lower part of his visage, and his sombre hat overshadowing his brows. But he gave no word of dissent from their purpose; and an inscrutable smile was accepted by the lovers as a token that here had been no footprint of guilt or sorrow to desecrate the site of their Temple of Happiness.

In a little time longer, while summer was still in its prime, the fairy structure of the Temple arose on the summit of the knoll, amid the solemn shadows of the trees, yet often gladdened with bright sunshine. It was built of white marble, with slender and graceful pillars supporting a vaulted dome; and beneath the centre of this dome, upon a pedestal, was a slab of dark-veined marble, on which books and music might be strewn. But there was a fantasy among the people of the neighborhood that the edifice was planned after an ancient mausoleum and was intended for a tomb, and that the central slab of dark-veined marble was to be inscribed with the names of buried ones. They doubted, too, whether the form of Lilias Fay could appertain to a creature of this earth, being so very delicate, and growing every day more fragile, so that she looked as if the summer breeze should snatch her up and waft her heavenward. But still she watched the daily growth of the Temple; and so did old Walter Gascoigne, who now made that spot his continual haunt, leaning whole hours together on his staff, and giving as deep attention to the work as though it had been indeed a tomb. In due time it was finished, and a day appointed for a simple rite of dedication.

On the preceding evening, after Adam Forrester had taken leave of his mistress, he looked back towards the portal of her dwelling, and felt a strange thrill of fear; for he imagined that, as the setting sunbeams faded from her figure, she was exhaling away, and that something of her ethereal substance was withdrawn with each lessening gleam of light. With his farewell glance a shadow had fallen over the portal and Lilias was invisible. His foreboding spirit deemed it an omen at the time, and so it proved; for the sweet earthly form, by which the Lily had been manifested to the world, was found lifeless the next morning in the Temple, with her head resting on her arms, which were folded upon the slab of dark-veined marble. The chill winds of the earth had long since breathed a blight into this beautiful flower, so that a loving hand had now transplanted it, to blossom brightly in the garden of Paradise.

But alas, for the Temple of Happiness! In his unutterable grief, Adam Forrester had no purpose more at heart than to covert this Temple of many delightful hopes into a tomb, and bury his dead mistress there. And lo! a wonder! Digging a grave beneath the Temple's marble floor, the sexton found no virgin earth, such as was meet to receive the maiden's dust, but an ancient sepulchre, in which were treasured up the bones of generations that had died long ago. Among those forgotten ancestors was the Lily to be laid. And when the funeral procession brought Lilias thither in her coffin, they beheld old Walter Gascoigne standing beneath the dome of the Temple, with his cloak of pall and face of darkest gloom; and wherever that figure might take its stand the spot would seem a sepulchre. He watched the mourners as they lowered the coffin down.

"And so," said he to Adam Forrester, with the strange smile in which his insanity was wont to gleam forth, "you have found no better foundation for your happiness than on a grave!"

But as the Shadow of Affliction spoke, a vision of Hope and Joy had its birth in Adam's mind, even from the old man's taunting words; for then he knew what was betokened by the parable in which the Lily and himself had acted; and the mystery of Life and Death was opened to him.

"Joy! joy!" he cried, throwing his arms towards heaven, "on a grave be the site of our Temple; and now our happiness is for Eternity!"

With those words, a ray of sunshine broke through the dismal sky, and glimmered down into the sepulchre; while, at the same moment, the shape of old Walter Gascoigne stalked drearily away, because his gloom, symbolic of all earthly sorrow, might no longer abide there, now that the darkest riddle of humanity was read.

---

for Adventure and Treasure

THE MINES OF FALUN
by E. T. A. Hoffmann

On a hot sunny July day all the people of Gothaborg were assembled by the waterside. A rich East Indiaman, safely returned from distant lands, lay at anchor in the rocky harbor, the long pennant, the Swedish flag, waving gaily in the clear, warm air, while hundreds of boats of all kind, filled with jubilant sailors, floated on the mirror-like surface of the Goathaelf, and the cannon on Masthuggetorg sent its resounding greeting far across the open sea. The gentlemen of the East India Company wandered up and down by the harbor and with smiling faces counted up their gains, delighted with the way in which their undertakings improved year by year and dear Gothaborg bloomed ever more fresh and lovely as trade grew more flourishing. And therefore everybody looked with pleasure on these good gentlemen, and rejoiced with them, for with their earnings came strength and energy into the brisk life of the whole town.

The crew of the East Indiaman, about a hundred and fifty strong, landed from many boats and started off to keep the Honsung. That is the

---

From *Tales of Hoffman, Stories by E. T. A. Hoffman* (New York: Heritage Press, 1943), pp. 36–56. Reprinted by permission of the George Macy Companies.

name of the feast which the sailors celebrate on such occasions, and which often lasts several days. Musicians in marvelously colored garments went ahead, with fiddles, pipes, oboes, and trumpets which they played upon valiantly, while others sang merry songs to their accompaniment. These were followed by the sailors, two by two. Some with coats and hats decorated with gaily colored ribbons were waving flags, others danced and jumped, and all shouted and made merry so that the gay noise could be heard a great distance.

Thus the joyous procession went through the docks, through the suburbs to Haga, there to drink and make merry to their hearts' desire.

The finest beer flowed there in streams, and tankard after tankard was emptied. As is always the case when sailors return from a long voyage, a number of smart young women were soon there to greet them. Dancing began, the festivities got wilder and wilder, the rejoicings louder and more exciting.

One single sailor, a slim good-looking youth, scarcely twenty years of age, had slipped away from the turmoil and seated himself on a bench beside the door of the inn.

A few sailors came out to him, and one of them, laughing loudly, cried out: "Elis Frobom! Elis Frobom! Are you being a miserable fool again and wasting this good time in silly brooding? Listen here, Elis, if you are going to stay away from our Honsung, you had better stay away from the ship as well. At this rate you will never become a decent, hard-working sailor. You have courage and are brave in face of danger, but you can't drink, and you would rather keep your ducats in your pockets than throw them to the landlubbers here! Drink, fellow, or may the sea devils, the whole pack of them, fall upon you!"

Elis Frobom jumped up from the bench, stared at the sailors with glowing eyes, took up a brimming cup of spirits and emptied it at one draught. Then he said, "There, Joens, now you see that I can drink as well as any of you, and the captain can decide what sort of sailor I am. But now hold your tongue and get away from here. I hate your wild merriment. What I am doing out here is no concern of yours."

"Now, now," replied Joens, "I know you have always been a Neriker and they are all gloomy and sad, and don't really enjoy a sailor's life. Wait a bit, Elis, I will send someone out to you who'll soon get you away from that bench to which you seem to have been nailed."

In a very short time a smart young girl came out of the door of the inn and sat beside the gloomy Elis, who was again seated, dumb and brooding, on the bench. The girl's profession was obvious from her clothes and her manner, but she was still young enough to have retained freshness and charm in her yet pleasing features. There was no sign of repellent shamelessness about her, rather an expression of yearning sorrow lay in her dark eyes.

"Elis! aren't you going to take any part in the gaieties of your comrades? Don't you feel any pleasure in having once again escaped the threatening dangers of the treacherous sea, and being back again in your own country?"

Thus spoke the girl in a gentle, quiet voice, putting her arm round the youth's shoulders. Elis Frobom, as though waking from a dream, gazed into the girl's eyes, took her hand and pressed it tightly. It was obvious that her soft whisper had sunk deep into his heart.

"Ah," he said at last, "happiness and pleasure are not for me. At least, I cannot take part in the orgies of my companions. Go in, my dear child, dance and make merry with the others if it gives you pleasure, but leave sad, miserable Elis out here alone; he will only spoil all your pleasure. But wait—I like you, and you must think well of me when I have gone to sea again."

So saying, he took two shining ducats from his pocket, drew a fine East Indian shawl from under his coat, and gave both to the girl. Tears came into her eyes. She stood up, laid the money on the bench, and said, "Oh, keep your ducats, they only make me unhappy, but this beautiful shawl, I will keep it to wear in memory of you, and next year when you keep Honsung here you won't find me."

With that, she went, not back into the inn, but, both hands before her face, away down the road.

Once again Elis Frobom sank back into his gloomy meditations, until, when the merrymaking in the inn had reached its loudest, he called out, "Oh, would that I were lying at the bottom of the deepest sea, for there is nobody left alive with whom I could be happy."

A deep, gruff voice behind him replied, "You must have suffered a very great unhappiness, young man, if already, with life just opening before you, you wish yourself dead."

Elis looked around and saw an old miner leaning with folded arms against the wall of the inn and looking down on him with eager, searching eyes.

Looking up at him, Elis felt like a man who, thinking himself lost in a lonely place, suddenly sees a well-known figure coming towards him, offering a welcoming hand. He pulled himself together and explained that his father had been a skillful pilot but had been lost at sea in a storm from which he himself had been rescued in a marvelous manner. Both his brothers had been soldiers and had fallen in battle. He had been keeping his poor, lonely mother on the splendid earnings of his East Indian voyages. Destined from childhood for a sailor's life, a sailor he had remained, thinking himself very lucky to get into the service of the East India Company.

This voyage had been even more prosperous than usual, and every member of the crew had received a good sum of money apart from his wages, so that with his pockets full of ducats he had gone joyfully off to the cottage where his mother lived. But strange faces had gazed at him from the windows, and the young woman who had finally opened the door to him, and to whom he explained who he was, told him coldly that his mother had died three months before, and that the few rags left over when the funeral expenses were paid were lying at the town hall waiting for him to claim them. His mother's death was breaking his heart; he felt himself forsaken by everyone—lonely as one wrecked on a desert island, helpless, miserable. His whole life at sea appeared to him as a useless, purposeless activity. Yes, when he considered that his mother had probably been wretchedly cared for by strangers, it seemed to him even infamous and horrible that he ever went to sea and did not rather stay at home to look after and care for her. His comrades had brought him forcibly to the Honsung, and he had himself thought that perhaps the merriment around him and the strong drink would deaden his sorrow, but instead of that he felt as though his heart must break.

"Yes," said the old miner, "you will soon be at sea again, Elis, and then your sorrow will be forgotten in a short time. Old people die. That is only natural, and you yourself have said that your mother's was but a poor, miserable existence."

"Ah," sighed Elis, "nobody believes in my unhappiness; most people chide me for being silly and foolish, and that is what makes me feel so forsaken. I do not want to go to sea again. I have a horror of the life. And it used to be my greatest joy when the sails were unfurled like stately wings, and the ship glided over the water, and the waves rippled or blustered, making merry music, and the wind whistled through the rigging. Then I shouted gaily with my comrades on the deck, and if I had the watch on a still, dark night, I thought of the happiness of returning home, and how my good old mother would rejoice when Elis returned! Ah, yes! then I could make merry at the Honsung, when I had poured my ducats into my mother's lap, when I had given her the lovely shawls and the other gifts I had brought her from distant lands.

"How her eyes would light up with pleasure when she folded her arms, quite overcome with happiness and excitement, when she tripped busily about, and brought out the finest beer which she had stored up for Elis's return. And when I sat with her in the evenings I used to tell her about all the queer people I met, about their customs and habits, about anything strange I had seen during my long voyages. She loved to hear it, and in return told me about my father's wonderful voyages to the Far North, interspersed with many a terrifying seaman's legend which I had heard hundreds of times but could not hear too often. Ah! who can give that happiness back to me! No, never again will I go to sea! What should I do among my comrades who would only laugh me to scorn, and how should I enjoy work which would seem but a wearisome expense of energy for nothing!"

"I have listened to you gladly, young man," said the old miner as Elis ceased speaking, "just as I have watched you during the last few hours without your noticing it, and felt pleased with your behavior. Everything which you have done or spoken is a sign that yours is a retiring, pious, childlike disposition, and high heaven could not give you a more precious gift. But you have never been suited for a sailor's life. How should so quiet, almost somber a Neriker (for that you are one, your features, your whole bearing, show) fit into the wild, restless life at sea? You are wise to forsake such a life. But you don't want to fold your arms and sit back yet? Take my advice, Elis Frobom, go to Falun and become a miner. You are young, strong, certainly you would soon be a good apprentice, then a hewer, master miner, and always higher up the ladder. You have useful money in your pockets; invest that, add your earnings, and you will soon own a miner's license and a share in the mine. Take my advice, become a miner."

Elis Frobom was startled by the old man's words. "What?" he cried, "what are you advising me to do? I am to leave the beautiful, free earth, the bright, sunny heavens which surround me, reviving, refreshing. I am to leave all that and go down into the terrifying depths of the underworld to dig and bore like a mole for minerals and metals just for the sake of vile profit?"

"You are all alike," cried the old man angrily, "you are all scornful of anything you do not understand. Vile profit! As though all the horrible torments which are part of commerce above ground were nobler than the work of a miner, to whose knowledge, to whose unwearying toil Nature opens her most secret treasure hoards. And you talk of vile profit, Elis Frobom! This is a matter of something much higher. If the blind mole bores into the earth following blind instinct, it may well be that in the deepest shafts by the faint light of the lantern the human eye becomes more clear-sighted, yes, that at last, growing stronger and stronger, it may see in the marvelous metals a reflection of that which is hidden above the clouds. You know nothing of mining, Elis Frobom, let me explain it to you."

With these words the old man seated himself on the bench beside Elis and began to describe in great detail the workings of a mine, and took great trouble to paint it in the most living colors to make it real to one who knew nothing of it. He spoke of the mines of Falun, in which, he said, he had worked since his boyhood; he described the great pit head with its dark-brown walls through which one passed; he spoke of the immeasurable richness in lovely metals of the principal shaft. He grew more and more vivacious, his eyes more glowing. He wandered among the shafts as in a magic garden. The minerals came to life, the fossils moved, the wonderful pyrope, the almandine, blazed in the light of the lanterns, the rock crystal caught the light and sparkled.

Elis listened eagerly; he was completely enthralled by the old man's strange manner of speaking of the underground wonders as though he were among them at the moment. Oppression seized him; he felt as though he were already in the pits with the old man, and a powerful magic was keeping him there so that he should never again see the friendly light of day. And yet he felt as though the old man had opened to him a new, unknown world to which he belonged, and the magic of that new world had really been his in secret since his childhood.

"I have shown you, Elis Frobom," said the old man at last, "all the glories of a realm for which Nature really designed you. Go and think it over and then do as your feelings dictate."

With that the old man jumped hastily up from the bench and strode away without speaking another word to Elis or turning for another glance. He was soon out of sight.

In the meantime, the noise in the inn had ceased. The strong beer and spirits had exerted their power. Many of the sailors had slipped away with their sweethearts, others lay about in corners and snored. Elis, who had now no home, rented a tiny attic in the inn, in which to sleep.

Hardly had he lain down, tired and weary as he was, than dreams began to weave their spell over him. He thought he was on a beautiful ship under full sail on a sea smooth as glass, under a sky overcast with dark clouds. But when he looked down into the water, he soon realized that what he had imagined to be sea was really a solid, transparent, glittering mass, in which in some strange manner the whole ship melted away, so that he was left standing on a floor of crystal, and could see over him a vault of shining black stone. For what he had thought were clouds was stone. He hurried forward, urged by an unknown power, but at the same moment everything around him began to move, and, like ruffled waves, marvelous flowers and plants of shining metal rose from the floor, the flowers and leaves creeping out of the depths and intertwining in the most charming manner. The floor was so transparent that Elis could see quite clearly the roots of the plants; but searching ever deeper he saw, far down, innumerable beautiful young female figures, their white arms encircling one another; and in their hearts were the roots of those plants which were growing up around him. When the girls laughed a sweet harmony filled the great vault, and the wonderful metal flowers grew taller and more lovely.

An indescribable feeling of mingled pain and pleasure seized the youth, a world of love, longing, and ardent desire flooded his heart. "Down, down to you," he cried, and threw himself with outstretched arms on the crystal floor. But it gave under him and he was left to swim in shimmering ether. "Well, Elis Frobom, how do you like this glorious place?" cried a powerful voice, and Elis found at his side the old miner, but as he looked at him he appeared to turn into a gigantic figure in glowing bronze. The chill of terror began to spread over Elis, but in that instant there was a flash as of lightning in the depths, and the earnest face of a majestic woman appeared. Elis felt the delight in his heart growing and growing until it became almost a crushing dread. The old man had thrown his arm round him, and cried: "Take care, Elis Frobom, that is the Queen, you can still look up."

Involuntarily he turned his head and realized that the stars in the night sky were shining through a crack in the vault. A soft voice called his name as though in inconsolable sorrow. It was the voice of his mother. He thought he saw her figure through the crack overhead. But it was a lovely young woman who thrust her hand down through the crack and called his name. "Carry me above," he cried to the old man, "I belong to the upper world with its friendly sky." "Take care," muttered the old man, "Frobom, be true to the Queen to whom you have surrendered."

When the youth looked down again into the calm face of the majestic woman, he felt his whole being melting into the glittering stone. He screamed aloud in nameless terror, and woke from the wonderful dream whose beauty and horror found an echo deep in his soul.

"It had to be, I suppose," said Elis to himself, when he had pulled himself together, "I had to have such a curious dream. The old miner told me so much about the wonders of the underworld that my whole being is full of it, and in all my life I never had such strange feelings as now. Perhaps I am still dreaming. No, no—I must be ill. I will go out into the open, the fresh sea breezes will cure me."

He got up quickly and hurried down to the harbor where the merriment of the Honsung was just beginning again. But he soon noticed that he had no pleasure in anything, that he could not keep his mind on anything, that ideas, wishes, he was unable to put into words, kept going through his head. He thought with deep sorrow about his dead mother; then it seemed to him that his one desire was to meet the girl who had spoken so kindly to him yesterday. Then he feared that if the girl came out of one of the lanes towards him it would prove to be the old miner of whom, in spite of himself, he was in dread. And yet he would gladly have heard from the old man more about the wonders of the mines.

He stood looking down into the water, these thoughts driving backwards and forwards through his head. It seemed as though the silvery waves froze into a glittering glimmer in which the lovely great ships melted away, as though the dark clouds which were just gathering in the bright sky were sinking and turning into a vault of stone. He was back in the midst of his dream again, looking again into the earnest face of the majestic woman, and the disturbing anxiety and longing took hold of him anew.

His comrades shook him out of his dream to follow in their procession. But now he felt that an unknown voice was whispering ceaselessly in his ear: "What, are you still here?—away—away—your home is in the mines of Falun. There you shall see all the glory of which you have dreamed—go, go to Falun!"

For three days Elis Frobom wandered about the streets of Gothaborg, followed the whole time by the marvelous figures of his dream, exhorted all the time by the unknown voice.

On the fourth day Elis stood at the gate leading out of the town on the way to Gefle. A big man went through just ahead of him. Elis thought he recognized the old miner and was impelled to hurry after him, but he could not catch up with him.

Disquieted, he followed him.

Elis knew quite well that he was on the road to Falun, and that pacified him strangely, for he was certain that Fate had spoken to him through the voice of the old miner, and was now leading him to his destiny.

Certainly he noticed often that, when he was not quite sure which road to take, the old man suddenly appeared from behind rocks or bushes and walked ahead of him for a while without looking round, disappearing again quickly when the way became plain.

At last, after days of hard walking, Elis saw in the distance two large lakes, between which arose thick columns of steam. As he climbed higher and higher towards the west, he was able to make out in the smoke a few towers and black roofs. The old man stood gigantic before him, pointed with outstretched arm at this smoke and disappeared again among the rocks.

"This is Falun," cried Elis, "the goal of my journey." He was right, for people who came up with him at that moment confirmed the fact that the town of Falun lay there between the two lakes, Runn and Warpann, and that he was then climbing Guffris Hill on which was the great pit head of the mine.

Elis went cheerfully on, but when he reached the monstrous abyss leading to the underworld, the blood froze in his veins, and he remained rooted to the ground at the sight of the terrible destruction.

As is well known, the great entrance to the mine of Falun is twelve hundred feet long, six hundred feet wide and one hundred and eighty feet deep. The dark-brown walls are vertical at first, then they slope away owing to enormous heaps of rubble and fragments. Both here and in the walls remains of the woodwork of old shafts are visible, strong, closely packed tree trunks grooved together at one end in the same way as the walls of log cabins. No tree, no blade of grass grew among the bare, crumbling, stony chasms and the jagged cliffs which were formed into strange shapes, sometimes like enormous stone beasts, sometimes like human forms of gigantic proportions. At the bottom lay in wild disorder stones, dross, burnt-out ore; and stupefying sulphur fumes rose eternally as though an infernal brew was always being prepared there, whose steam destroyed all the green things in Nature. One could believe that here Dante descended into the Inferno with all its desperate torments, all its horrors.

As Elis Frobom looked down into the chasm he remembered what an old helmsman on his ship had told him long ago. As he lay in a fever, he said, he felt suddenly that the sea had rolled away and left him looking down into a measureless pit in which he could see all the fearful creatures which live on the floor of the ocean writhing horribly among strange shellfish and corals and wonderful stones, until with wide-open jaws they lay motionless in death. Such a sight, declared the old sailor, was a sign of a speedy death in the waves, and shortly afterwards he did fall accidentally from the deck into the sea and was not seen again. It was brought back to Elis's mind by the sight of the pit, which reminded him of the old helmsman's description of the pit into which he looked when the waters rolled back. The black stones and blue and red dross of the metal looked to him like horrible creatures stretching out their ugly polypus arms towards him. Just at that time some of the miners were climbing out of the depths, and in their dark working clothes, with their black faces, they looked like hateful monsters trying laboriously to make themselves a road to the surface.

Elis felt himself shaken with horror, and, what had never happened to him at sea, a feeling of giddiness overcame him; it seemed to him that unseen hands were drawing him down into the abyss.

With closed eyes he stumbled away, and only when he was far from the pit head, descending Guffris Hill, and looked up to the bright, sunny sky, did all his fear leave him. He breathed freely again, and cried from the depths of his soul: "Oh, God, what are all the terrors of the ocean compared to the horror which inhabits that rocky chasm! Let the gale rage, let the black clouds sink to meet the raging waves, the beautiful, kindly sun very soon conquers them, and beneath his friendly rays the storm soon calms down; but those rays never pierce that black pit, and no soft spring breeze ever refreshes the air down there. No, I do not want to join you, you black earthworms, I could never accustom myself to your gloomy life!"

Elis decided to spend the night in Falun, and early the next morning to set out on his return to Gothaborg.

When he reached the market place, the Helsingtorget, he found a great crowd of people assembled.

A long procession of miners in festal attire, led by musicians, had just come to a halt in front of a stately house. A tall, slim, middle-aged man came out and looked round with a friendly smile. One could recognize the true Dalecarlian from his upright carriage, open brow, and dark-blue, beaming eyes. The miners encircled him, to each one he gave a hearty handshake and a friendly word.

Elis made inquiries and found that this man was Pehrson Dahlsjo, engineer and owner of a fine Bergsfralse near Stora-Kopparberg. "Bergsfralse" is the Swedish word for land granted for copper and silver mines. The owners of such Fralsen have shares in the mines for the workings of which they are responsible.

Elis was also told that it was the last day of the sitting of the court, and on that day it was usual for the miners to go in procession to the surveyor, the overseer, and the owners, and at each place to be entertained.

Looking at these fine, stately men with their open, friendly faces, he forgot the earthworms he had seen at the pit head.

The evident happiness of these people, which seemed to break out afresh through the crowd when Pehrson Dahlsjo came out, was evidently something very different from the wild, mad merrymaking of the sailors at the Honsung.

The heart of the quiet youth was deeply touched by the manner in which the miners took their pleasure. He felt undescribably happy, but he could hardly keep back his tears when some of the younger men began to sing an old song, a very simple but deeply moving melody in praise of mining.

When the song ended, Pehrson Dahlsjo threw open the doors of his house and all the miners went in. Involuntarily Elis followed and stood on the threshold so that he could overlook the whole hall in which the miners were taking their places on benches. A large meal was spread out before them.

The door opposite Elis opened, and a lovely girl in festal attire entered the hall. Tall and slim, with dark hair wound in many plaits round her head, her lovely dress fastened with rich clasps, she moved with the charm and grace of blooming youth. All the miners stood up and a quiet murmur ran through the rows: "Ulla Dahlsjo—how God's blessing has descended on our excellent manager in that beautiful and good child." The eyes of even the oldest miners sparkled as Ulla shook hands with them one after another and gave them friendly greeting. Then she fetched beautiful silver jugs and poured out such excellent beer as was at that time only to be found in Falun, and handed it to the guests, her face all the time beaming with innocent pleasure.

As Elis Frobom caught sight of the girl, it seemed to him that a flash of lightning went through him and awakened again all the love, the joy, the ardor which he had thought dead. It was Ulla Dahlsjo who in that ominous dream had held out to him a helping hand; he thought now that he could understand the deeper meaning of that dream, and, forgetting the old miner, thanked the fate which had brought him to Falun.

But standing there on the threshold, he felt that he was an unnoticed stranger, miserable, disconsolate and alone, and he wished that he had died before he saw Ulla Dahlsjo, for now he must perish miserably of love and longing. He could not bring himself to take his eyes off the girl, and as she passed quite close to him, he spoke her name in a shaky undertone.

Ulla looked round and noticed poor Elis, who stood there with burning cheeks and downcast eyes, motionless, unable to utter a word.

Ulla went up to him and said with a sweet smile, "Ah, you must be a stranger, dear friend! I can tell that by your sailor's clothes. But why are you standing there on the threshold? Come along in and enjoy yourself with us." And she took him by the hand, drew him into the hall and, handing him a tankard of beer, said, "Drink, dear friend, to your welcome."

It seemed to Elis as though he were in the paradise of a glorious dream, from which he must awake to indescribable misery. He emptied the tankard mechanically. At that moment Pehrson Dahlsjo came up to him, shook him by the hand in friendly greeting and inquired whence he came and what had brought him to Falun.

The warmth of the noble liquor spread through Elis's veins. He grew courageous and cheerful as he gazed into the eyes of the gallant Pehrson, and explained how he, the son of a sailor, brought up to the sea from childhood, had just returned from the East Indies to find that his mother, whom he had kept in comfort with his wages, had died during his last voyage, so that he was now alone in the world, how repugnant the wild life of a sailor had become to him, that his greatest longing was to become a miner and that he should try to get taken on as a miner at Falun. This last wish, so contrary to what he had felt but a few moments previously, was drawn from him involuntarily as though he had not been able to help saying it, almost as though he had expressed his deepest desires, desires in which he himself had not previously believed.

Pehrson Dahlsjo looked earnestly at the young man as though he wanted to read his inmost thoughts; then he said: "I do not imagine, Elis Frobom, that sheer frivolity is driving you away from your previous occupation, or that you have not weighed carefully all the hardships and difficulties of a miner's life before making your decision. It is an old belief that the powerful elements in which a miner works destroy him unless he puts forth his whole strength to gain the mastery over them, and puts aside all other thoughts which might weaken the wholehearted devotion he owes to his work in earth and fire. If you have really given careful thought to your desire and really wish to devote yourself to mining, then you have come at the right moment. I am short of workmen. You can, if you like, stay here now, and tomorrow morning go down the mine with the mine inspector who will show you your duties."

The heart of Elis beat high at these words. He thought no more of the fear he had felt looking down into that horrible abyss of hell. He was filled with joy and delight at the thought of seeing the lovely Ulla every day, of living under the same roof with her; the sweetest hopes were his.

Pehrson Dahlsjo informed the assembled miners that a young man had just arrived who wished to apprentice himself to mining, and introduced Elis to them.

They all looked with pleasure on the vigorous youth, and said that he was a born miner with his fine, strong limbs, and that they doubted not that he had his share of diligence and piety.

One of the miners, an elderly man, approached Elis, and shaking him by the hand said that he was the chief inspector of Pehrson Dahlsjo's mine, and that he would make it his care to see that Elis was instructed in everything necessary. Elis had to sit by him, and over a tankard of beer the old man began to explain the work.

Elis suddenly remembered the old miner of Gothaborg, and was able to repeat almost everything the old man had said to him. "Oh," cried the inspector in astonishment, "Elis Frobom, where did you learn all that? Why! there can be no doubt that in a short time you will be the best apprentice in the mine."

The lovely Ulla, moving about among the guests and waiting on them, gave many friendly nods to Elis, and disposed him to be really happy. "Now," she said, "you are no longer a stranger but belong here and not on the treacherous sea. Falun with its rich hills is your home." Heaven itself opened before the young man's eyes at Ulla's words. It was noticed that Ulla liked to be near him, and that even Pehrson Dahlsjo in his quiet, earnest way looked on him with pleasure.

Elis's heart beat fast when he stood once more by the smoking abyss, and, clothed in his miner's outfit, the heavy iron-shod Dalecarlian shoes on his feet, went down for the first time into the mine with the inspector. At first the hot steam nearly suffocated him, then a cutting wind nearly extinguished the lamps they carried. Deeper and deeper they went, at last down a narrow iron ladder, and Elis Frobom discovered that all his dexterity in climbing, learned in the rigging of ships, was of no use to him here.

At last they reached the deepest shaft, and the inspector showed Elis what he was to do.

Elis thought of the lovely Ulla; like a beautiful angel her form floated over him and he forgot all his horror of the depths, and all the difficulties of his work. He was certain that his dearest hopes could only be realized if he worked with all his might, with all the strength of which his body was capable, and so it happened that in a remarkably short time he was as good a worker as any in the mine.

Each day Pehrson Dahlsjo grew fonder of the hard-working quiet youth and often told him that he had found in him not only a good workman but also a well-loved son. Ulla also showed her feelings more and more openly. Often when Elis was going to his work and there was anything dangerous to be done, she begged him with tears in her eyes to guard himself against accident. And when he came back, she ran joyfully to meet him and was always ready with the finest beer or some good thing to refresh him.

Elis's heart beat high with joy when one day Pehrson Dahlsjo said to him that, though he had brought no money with him, yet, because of his activity and his economy, he would certainly one day own a share in a mine or even become a mine owner; and then no owner in Falun would refuse his request if he begged for his daughter's hand. He longed to say how deeply he loved Ulla and that all his hopes were fixed on gaining her, but an unconquerable shyness and, even more, a doubt whether Ulla really loved him kept him from speaking.

One day Elis was working in the deepest shaft, the sulphur fumes so thick around him that his lamp gave out only a tiny glimmer and he could hardly distinguish the different strata in the rock. Suddenly he heard, as though from an even deeper shaft, a knocking as though somebody was using a pick. As such work is not possible in the depths, and Elis knew for certain that he was the only person who had come down that day, the inspector having sent the other men to work in another direction, there seemed to him something sinister in the sounds. He put down his tools and listened to the hollow sounds which seemed to come nearer and nearer. Then he noticed a dark shadow, and as a blast of cold air blew aside the sulphur fumes, he saw the old miner of Gothaborg beside him. "Good luck!" cried the old man, "good luck, Elis Frobom, down here in the earth! Well—how do you like the work, comrade?"

Elis wanted to ask him how he got into the shaft; but hitting the rock with his hammer with such force that sparks flew and the echo went through the shaft like thunder, the old man shouted in a terrible voice: "This is a wonderful trap-vein, but to you, you worthless, rascally good-for-nothing, it is only a Trumm, not worth a blade of grass. Down here you are nothing but a blind mole, to whom the prince of metals will always be unfriendly, and up on the surface you dare attempt nothing. So you want to win Pehrson Dahlsjo's daughter as your wife, and for that reason work down here, neither caring for your work nor thinking about it? Take care, false creature, that the prince of metals, whom you scorn, does not take you and throw you against the rocks until all your bones are broken. And Ulla shall never be your wife, I warn you!"

A furious anger rose in Elis at the insolent words of the old man. "What are you doing here in my master's mine, where I work with all my strength, as is my duty? Go away as you came, or we'll see down here which of us will manage to brain the other." With these words Elis took his stand in front of the old man and swung the iron hammer with which he had been working. The old man gave a mocking laugh, and a feeling of terror went through Elis as he watched him climb the narrow ladder like a squirrel and disappear into the darkness.

Elis felt paralyzed, he could not work any longer, and so he followed the other out of the shaft. The old inspector, just then returning from the other shaft, noticed him, and cried: "In heaven's name, what has happened to you, Elis, you are so deathly pale! Have the sulphur fumes, to which you are not yet accustomed, upset you? Drink this, young man, that will help." Elis took a long pull at the brandy bottle which the inspector held out to him, and, thus strengthened, related what had happened to him in the mine, also how he had made the acquaintance of the sinister old man in Gothaborg.

The inspector listened quietly, then he shook his head and said: "Elis Frobom, that was old Torbern, and now I know that the story which is told about him is more than a fairy tale. More than a hundred years ago there was here in Falun a miner named Torbern. He is said to have been one of the first to make a success of mining in Falun, and in his day the output was far richer than it is now. Nobody understood mining as Torbern did, his knowledge was so great that he was head of all the mining in Falun. He seemed to possess greater strength than anybody else, to know exactly where to find the richest veins, added to which he was a gloomy, serious man, without wife or child, even without a home in Falun, rarely coming up from the mine into the light of day, but always working in the depths. And so naturally the story soon began to get about that he was in alliance with the secret power which rules the underworld and makes the metals. In spite of Torbern's stern warnings that misfortune would follow unless the miners went to their work only from a feeling of real love for the wonderful minerals and metals, the mines were enlarged for the sake of gain, until at last on the Feast of St. John, in the year 1687, the terrible disaster occurred which opened the enormous chasm and wrecked the mines so completely that only through great labor and much skill have some of the shafts been made workable again. Torbern was never seen again; it was thought that he was buried under the ruins. Soon afterwards, as the work improved, many of the diggers swore that they had seen old Torbern down the mines and that he had given them much good advice and pointed out to them some rich veins. Others had seen the old man wandering about the pit head, sometimes lamenting, sometimes shouting angrily. Other youths have come here, as you have done, saying that an old miner had advised them to work in the mines and to come to Falun. That always happened when there was a shortage of labor, and was probably old Torbern's way of helping. If it was really old Torbern with whom you quarreled in the mine, and if he spoke of a wonderful trap-vein, then there is certainly a rich vein of iron there, and tomorrow we will search for it. You know that here the iron veins are called trap-veins, and that the 'Trumm' is a vein of that kind that splits into many pieces."

When Elis, deep in thought, entered Pehrson Dahlsjo's house that day, Ulla did not come as usual to meet him. With lowered gaze, and, as Elis thought, eyes red with weeping, Ulla sat there, and by her side a handsome young man who held her hand fast in his was trying to cheer her up by his merry talk of which Ulla did not appear to be taking much notice. Elis stared at the couple, a horrid fear taking hold of him, till Pehrson Dahlsjo drew him aside into another room and said: "Now, Elis Frobom, you will soon be able to show your love to me, and your faithfulness, for I have always looked upon you as a son, and soon you will be that completely. That man is the rich merchant, Eric Olawsen, of Gothaborg. He has my consent to marry my daughter; they will go to Gothaborg and you will then be alone here with me, my only support in my old age. Why, Elis, have you nothing to say? You blench. I hope my plans do not upset you, and that you will not wish to leave me as well! but I hear Eric Olawsen calling me. I must go!"

And Pehrson went back into the other room.

Elis felt as though thousands of sharp knives were being driven into his heart. He could not speak; tears would not come. In wild despair he rushed out of the house—away—away—to the pit head. If the enormous chasm was terrifying by daylight, how much more awful was it now that night had fallen and the moon was just rising to look down upon the rocks, which seemed more than ever like a restless crowd of horrible monsters, ghastly fiends moving about on the smoking floor, their terrible eyes flashing upwards and their gigantic claws stretching ever towards the world of man.

"Torbern—Torbern," called Elis with a dreadful voice which echoed through the desolate chasm, "Torbern—here I am! You were right, I have been a rascally sort of worker, and given myself over to stupid hopes in the world above ground. Down there lies my treasure, my life, my all! Torbern! come down with me, show me the richest trap-veins, there I will work and dig, and never more see the light of day. Torbern! Torbern! come down with me!"

Elis took steel and flint out of his pocket, lit his lamp and descended to the shaft where he had been working, but the old man did not appear. But how surprised he was in the deepest shaft to see the trap-vein, clear and distinct, so that he could even distinguish the streaks and faults in it.

As he looked more and more closely at the wonderful vein in the rock, it seemed as though a blinding light lit up the whole shaft and its walls became as transparent as pure crystal. The ominous dream which he had dreamed in Gothaborg came back to him. He looked again into the heavenly regions where grew lovely metal trees and plants whose fruit and flowers were precious stones. He saw the maidens; he gazed again into the noble face of the mighty Queen. She caught hold of him, drew him down, pressed him to her breast; a thrill of wonder went through him and he was conscious only of feeling that he was swimming in a blue, transparent, sparkling mist.

"Elis Frobom, Elis Frobom!" cried a strong voice from above, and the light of torches flooded the shaft. Pehrson Dahlsjo himself had come with the inspector who had seen Elis rushing like one possessed towards the pit head.

They found him standing motionless, his face pressed to the cold stone.

"What are you doing here by night, you rash young man?" cried Pehrson. "Pull yourself together, and come up with us; who knows what good news you will hear up there!"

In deep silence Elis followed Pehrson Dahlsjo, who continued to scold him for running into such danger.

It was already broad daylight when they reached the house. With a loud cry Ulla threw herself into Elis's arms, and called him by the sweetest names. But Pehrson spoke to Elis: "You fool! do you suppose that I have not known for a long time that you love Ulla, and that all your work for me was for her sake? Have I not also known for a long time that Ulla loves you from the bottom of her heart? Could I wish for a better son-in-law, a more hard-working, honest miner than you, my brave Elis? But your silence angered me, hurt me."

"But did we know," Ulla interrupted her father, "how much we loved each other?"

"Let that be as it will," went on Pehrson, "it annoyed me that Elis was not open and honest with me about his love for you, and because I wanted to try you also, I invented the fairy tale about Eric Olawsen yesterday, which soon brought you to your senses. You foolish man! Eric Olawsen has long been married, and to you, Elis Frobom, I give my daughter, for, I repeat, I could not wish a better son-in-law."

Tears of joy ran down Elis's cheeks. So much happiness had come so unexpectedly upon him that it seemed to him he was again in the midst of a wonderful dream.

By Pehrson Dahlsjo's orders the miners assembled at midday for a feast. Ulla had put on her finest attire and looked more lovely than ever, so that everybody exclaimed: "Ah, what a lovely bride our brave Elis Frobom has won! Now may heaven bless them both!"

The horror of the previous night was still to be seen on Elis's pale face, and he often stood staring straight before him as though far removed from what was going on around him.

"What is the matter, my Elis?" asked Ulla. Elis held her tight in his arms and said, "Yes, yes! you are really mine, and now everything will be right."

Yet in the midst of his joy it sometimes seemed to Elis as though an ice-cold hand were laid on him and a dark voice said: "Have you everything you desire now that you have won Ulla? Poor fool! Have you not looked on the face of the Queen?"

He was nearly overcome by an unspeakable dread. The thought was ever with him that one of the miners would rise before him, a gigantic figure, and he would recognize Torbern, come to remind him in terrible form of that underground kingdom of stone and metal to which he had made his submission.

And yet he had no idea why the ghostly old man was so hostile to him, or what, indeed, mining had to do with his love for Ulla.

Pehrson noticed Elis's strange behavior and put it down to the pain he had suffered and to the night in the mine. Not so Ulla who, filled with secret dread, pressed her lover to tell her what horrible experience it was that he had suffered, which cut her off so completely. Elis felt that his heart would break. In vain he tried to tell his loved one of the marvelous sight he had seen in the mine. It was as though an unknown power was forcibly shutting his mouth, as though the terrible face of the Queen was looking at him, and if he spoke her name, then, as at the sight of the head of Medusa, everything around would turn to stone. All that loveliness, which down the mine had filled him with the deepest ecstasy, seemed now to be a hell of desperate misery tricked out for his temptation.

Pehrson Dahlsjo ordered Elis to stay at home for a few days in order to recover from the illness from which he seemed to be suffering. During this time the love which shone forth bright and clear from Ulla's childlike and pure heart overcame any remembrance of that ominous adventure in the mine. Elis revived completely in this atmosphere of love and happiness, and believed firmly that no evil power had any further influence over him.

When next he went down the mine, everything seemed different to him. The most wonderful seams lay opened before his eyes, he worked with redoubled vigor, he forgot everything; when he reached the surface again he had to force himself to remember Pehrson Dahlsjo and even his Ulla; he felt as though he were divided in two, as though his real, his better, self remained down in the depths of the earth, resting in the arms of the Queen, while the rest of him sought his unhappy couch in Falun. If Ulla spoke to him of their love and how happily they would live together, he began to talk about the wonders of the mine, the priceless treasures which lay hidden there, and became so involved in such marvelous and unintelligible descriptions that the poor girl was overcome with fear and anxiety and could not understand how Elis had suddenly changed so completely.

Elis often told the mine inspector of the wonderful seams he had found, and when the miners could find nothing but barren rock, he laughed ironically and said that of course he alone understood the secret signs, the momentous writing which the Queen herself engraved on the stone, and it was really sufficient to understand these signs without making clear what the meaning was.

The old inspector looked sadly at the young man talking, with wild, glittering eyes, of the wonderful paradise buried deep in the earth.

"Oh, sir," he whispered softly into Pehrson Dahlsjo's ear, "the wicked Torbern has bewitched the young man."

"Don't believe such old miner's yarns, old man," answered Pehrson Dahlsjo. "Love has turned his head, that is all. Wait till the wedding is over, then there will be an end of these stories of rich seams and treasures and underground paradises."

The day Pehrson Dahlsjo had appointed for the wedding came round at last. Days beforehand, Elis Frobom was quieter, graver, more retiring than ever, but more in love with Ulla. He could not bear to be parted from her for an instant and for that reason he did not go to the mines; he appeared to have forgotten his strange behavior and no word of the underground kingdom crossed his lips. Ulla was full of joy. She had lost her fear that the threatening powers of the underworld, of which she had heard old miners speak, should lure her Elis to destruction. And Pehrson Dahlsjo said laughingly to the old inspector, "There, you see, it was only love for Ulla which turned Elis Frobom's head."

Early on the wedding morning—it was midsummer day—Elis knocked on his bride's door. She opened it and started back in terror when she saw Elis already dressed for the wedding, but deathly pale and with dark flaming eyes. "I only want," he said in a light, unsteady voice, "to tell you, my beloved Ulla, that we are standing on the brink of the greatest happiness which human beings can experience on earth. It has all been revealed to me tonight. Down at the bottom of the mine, buried in chloride and mica, lies the cherry-red, sparkling almandine on which our life lines are engraved. I must fetch that to give you as a wedding present. It is more lovely than the finest blood-red carbuncle; and when, knit together by our great love, we look into its beaming light, we shall be able to see clearly how our inner life is bound up with that wonderful branch which grows out of the heart of the Queen at the center of the world. It is only necessary for me to bring this stone up to the light of day, and that I will do now. Take care of yourself in the meantime, my beloved Ulla! I shall soon be back."

With tears in her eyes, Ulla begged her lover to refrain from this chimerical undertaking, for she had a foreboding of great misfortune; but Elis assured her that without the stone he would never again have peace, and that there could be no question of danger. He embraced her fervently and left her.

The guests had assembled to accompany the bride and bridegroom to the Kopparberg church where the wedding was to take place. A crowd of gaily dressed girls who, according to the custom of the country, were to lead the bride to the church, were laughing and joking round Ulla. The musicians finished tuning up and began a gay wedding march. It was nearly midday, and there was still no sign of Elis. Suddenly a crowd of miners rushed in, anxiety and horror in their pale faces, and announced that a terrible landslide had destroyed Dahlsjo's mine completely.

"Elis—my Elis—dead—dead!" Ulla shrieked and fell unconscious. Now, for the first time, Pehrson heard from the inspector that in the early morning Elis had gone to the pit head and descended the mine, where he was quite alone, for all the others had been invited to the wedding. The miners hurried out, but all search was hopeless. No trace of Elis Frobom was found. It was certain that he was buried under the fall: and so misery and sorrow entered the house of Pehrson Dahlsjo in that moment when he had thought to assure himself peace and quiet for his old age.

The brave mine owner Pehrson Dahlsjo had long been dead, his daughter Ulla long vanished, nobody in Falun knew anything of them any more, for more than fifty years had elapsed since Elis Frobom's unlucky wedding day. Then it happened one day that miners trying a crosscut between two shafts deep down found the body of a young miner in vitriolic water. When they brought it to the surface, it appeared to have been turned to stone.

To the onlookers the youth seemed to be in a deep sleep, the features were so well preserved; there was no sign of decay about the festal attire which he wore, even the flowers in his buttonhole seemed quite fresh. Everybody in the neighborhood gathered at the pit head where the youth had been carried, but nobody recognized his face and none of the miners remembered one of their number having disappeared. They were just about to carry the corpse to Falun when there appeared in the distance an old woman hobbling along on crutches. "Here comes the old midsummer woman!" cried some of the miners. The old crone had received this name from the fact that for many years on midsummer day she had appeared out of nowhere, gazed down the mine shaft, and, wringing her hands, crept sighing and moaning round the pit head before disappearing again.

Hardly had the old woman caught sight of the youth than she let fall both her crutches and, raising her arms to heaven, cried in tones of heart-rending sorrow: "Oh, Elis Frobom—oh, my dear love." And kneeling beside the corpse she seized the stiff hands and pressed them to her breast in which, like a holy flame under a covering of ice, there beat a heart full of passionate love. "Ah," she said at last, "none, none of you remember poor Ulla Dahlsjo who, fifty years ago, was the happy bride of this youth. When in misery and sorrow I left Falun and went to Ornas, old Torbern comforted me and promised me that I should see my Elis, who was buried by a fall of stone on our wedding day, again on this earth, and so, year after year, filled with longing and true love, I have come and gazed down into the pit. And today I have seen him! Oh, my Elis—my beloved!"

And she threw her thin arms round the youth and held him as though she would never let him go, while the people stood, deeply moved, around her.

Fainter and fainter came the old woman's sobs and moans until at last they ceased altogether.

The miners drew near; they wanted to lift her away, but she had breathed her last over the corpse of her bridegroom. Then the onlookers noticed that the corpse that they had thought turned to stone was beginning to turn to dust.

In the Kopparberg church where, fifty years before, the couple should have been married, his dust was laid to rest beside the body of his faithful bride.

for the Mother

THE BRIDGE OF DREAMS

by Junichiro Tanizaki

On reading the last chapter of The Tale of Genji:
Today when the summer thrush
Came to sing at Heron's Nest
I crossed the Bridge of Dreams.

This poem was written by my mother. But I have had two mothers—the second was a stepmother—and although I am inclined to think my real mother wrote it, I cannot be sure. The reasons for this uncertainty will become clear later: one of them is that both women went by the name of Chinu. I remember hearing as a child that Mother was named after the Bay of Chinu, since she was born nearby at Hamadera, where her family, who were Kyoto people, had a seaside villa. She is listed as Chinu in the official city records. My second mother was also called Chinu from the time she came to our house. She never used her real name,

---

Tsuneko, again. Even my father's letters to her were invariably addressed to "Chinu"; you can't tell by the name which of the two he meant. And the "Bridge of Dreams" poem is simply signed "Chinu."

Anyway, I know of no other poems by either woman. I happen to be acquainted with this one because the square slip of wave-patterned paper on which it is written was reverently mounted in a hanging scroll to be kept as a family heirloom. According to my old nurse, who is now in her sixties, this kind of handmade paper was decorated by the ancient "flowing ink" process (that is, by dipping it in water and letting it absorb a swirl of ink) and had to be ordered all the way from Echizen. My mother must have gone to a great deal of trouble to get it. For years I puzzled over the Konoé-style calligraphy of the poem, and the many unusual Chinese characters that even an adult—let alone a child—would find hard to read. No one uses such characters nowadays. I am reminded that we have a set of poem cards which seem to have been written by one of my mothers in that same esoteric style.

As for the quality of the hand, I am not really able to judge. "They tell me nobody else wrote such a beautiful Konoé style," my nurse used to say; and to my own amateur taste, for whatever that is worth, it appears to be the work of quite an accomplished calligrapher. But you would expect a woman to choose the slender, graceful style of the Kozei school. It seems odd that she preferred the thick, fleshy Konoé line, with its heavy sprinkling of Chinese characters. Probably that reveals something of her personality.

When it comes to poetry I am even less qualified to speak, but I hardly think this verse has any special merit. The line "I crossed the Bridge of Dreams" must mean "Today I read 'The Bridge of Dreams'—the last chapter of *The Tale of Genji.*" Since that is only a short chapter, one that would take very little time to read, no doubt she is saying that today she at last finished the whole of *Genji.* "Heron's Nest" is the name by which our house has been known ever since my grandfather's time, a name given to it because night herons often alighted in its garden. Even now, herons occasionally come swooping down. Although I have seldom actually seen them, I have often heard their long, strident cry.

Heron's Nest is on a lane running eastward through the woods below the Shimogamo Shrine in Kyoto. When you go into the woods a little way, with the main building of the shrine on your left, you come to a narrow stone bridge over a stream: our gate is just beyond it. People who live in the neighborhood say that the stream flowing under this bridge is the subject of the famous poem by Chomei:

The stony Shallow Stream—
So pure that even the moon
Seeks it out to dwell in it.

But this seems doubtful. Yoshida Togo's gazetteer describes our "Shallow Stream" as "the brook that flows southward, east of the Shimogamo Shrine, into the Kamo River." Then it adds: "However, the 'Shallow Stream' mentioned in ancient topographical writings was the Kamo River itself, of which the brook in question is merely a tributary having its source in Matsugasaki." That is probably right, since Chomei is quoted elsewhere as saying that "Shallow Stream" is the old name of the Kamo River. The Kamo is also mentioned by that name in a poem by Jozan, which I will cite later, and the poet's prefatory note explains: "On refusing to cross the Kamo River into Kyoto." Of course our little stream is no longer especially pure and limpid, but until my childhood it was as clear as Chomei's poem might suggest. I remember that in mid-June, during the ceremony of purification, people bathed in its shallow waters.

The garden pond at Heron's Nest was linked to this stream by earthen drainage pipes to prevent it from overflowing. Once inside our main gate, with its two thick cedar pillars, you went down a flagstone walk to an inner gate. Dwarf bamboo were planted along both sides of the walk, and a pair of stone figures of Korean court officials (apparently of the Yi Dynasty) stood face to face on either side of it. The inner gate, which was always kept closed, had a roof thatched with cypress bark in an elegant rustic style. Each gate pillar bore a narrow bamboo tablet inscribed with one line of a Chinese couplet:

Deep in the grove the many birds are gay.
Far from the dust the pine and bamboo are clean.

But my father said he had no idea whose poem or whose calligraphy it was.

When you rang the doorbell (the button was beside one of the poem tablets) someone came out to open the gate for you. Then you went along under the shade of a large chestnut tree to the front door; in the main entrance hall, you saw mounted over the transom a piece of calligraphy from the brush of the scholar-poet Rai Sanyo:

The hawk soars, the fish dives.

What gave Heron's Nest its value was its landscape garden of almost an acre; the house itself was low and rambling but not particularly large. There were only some eight rooms, including the maids' room and the smaller entrance hall; but the kitchen was a spacious one, big enough for an average restaurant, and there was an artesian well next to the sink. Originally my grandfather lived on Muromachi Street near the Bukko Temple, and used Heron's Nest as his villa. Later, though, he sold the Muromachi Street house and made this his home, adding a sizable storehouse at its northwest corner. Going back and forth to the storehouse for a scroll or vase was quite inconvenient, since you had to go through the kitchen.

Our household consisted of seven persons—my parents and me, my nurse Okane, and three maids—and we found the house comfortable enough. Father liked a quiet life. He put in an appearance at his bank now and then, but spent most of his time at home, seldom inviting guests. It seems that my grandfather enjoyed the tea ceremony and led an active social life: he had a fine old teahouse brought in by the side of the pond, and built another small place for entertaining, which he called the Silk-Tree Pavilion, in the southeast corner of the garden. But after his death his prized teahouse and pavilion were no longer used, except as a place to take an afternoon nap or read or practice calligraphy.

All of my father's love was concentrated on my mother. With this house, this garden, and this wife, he seemed perfectly happy. Sometimes he would have her play the koto for him, and he would listen intently, but that was almost his only amusement at home. A garden of less than an acre seems a little cramped to be called a true landscape garden, but it had been laid out with the greatest care and gave the impression of being far deeper and more secluded than it actually was.

When you went through the sliding doors on the other side of the main entrance hall you found yourself in an average-sized room of eight mats, beyond which was a wide, twelve-mat chamber, the largest room in the house. The twelve-mat room was somewhat after the fashion of the Palace style, with a veranda along the eastern and southern sides, enclosed by a formal balustrade. On the south, in order to screen out the sun, the wide eaves were extended by latticework with a luxuriant growth of wild akebia vine hanging out over the pond; the water came lapping up under the vine leaves to the edge of the veranda. If you leaned on the rail and gazed across the pond you saw a waterfall plunging out of a densely wooded hill, its waters flowing under double globeflowers in the spring or begonias in autumn, emerging as a rippling stream for a little way, and then dropping into the pond. Just at the point where the stream entered the pond a bamboo device called a "water mortar" was set up: as soon as the water filled its bamboo tube, which was pivoted off-center, the tube would drop with a hollow clack against a block of wood set below it and the water would run out. Since the tube was supposed to be of fresh green bamboo, with a cleanly cut open end, the gardener had to replace it often. This sort of device is mentioned in a fourteenth-century poem:

Has the water upstream
Become a lazy current?
The sound of the mortar is rarely heard.

Even today, the sound of a water mortar echoes through the garden of the well-known Hall of Poets, the home of the early Edo poet Ishikawa Jozan in the northern suburbs of Kyoto. There, too, is displayed an explanatory text written in Chinese by Jozan. I suppose the reason why we had a water mortar is that my grandfather went there, read the description, and got the impulse to copy the device for his own house. It is said that Jozan's poem about not wishing to cross the Kamo River was written as a polite way of declining an invitation from the Emperor:

Alas, I am ashamed to cross it—
Though only a Shallow Stream
It would mirror my wrinkled age.

A rubbing of the poem hangs in an alcove in the Hall of Poets, and we had one at our house too.

When I was about three or four, I was enchanted by the clack, clack of our water mortar.

"Tadasu!" Mother would call. "Don't go over there or you'll fall in the pond!" But no matter how often she stopped me, I would run out into the garden and make my way through the tall bamboo grass of the artificial hill, trying to get to the edge of the stream.

"Wait! It's dangerous! You mustn't go there alone!" Mother or Okane would hurry after me in alarm and seize me by the back of my sash. Squirming forward while one of them held fast to me, I would peer down into the stream. As I watched, the green bamboo tube of the mortar slowly filled, dropped with a sharp rap against the block of wood, spilling its water into the pond, and then sprang back into place. After a few minutes it was full again, repeating the process. I suppose this clacking noise is my earliest memory of our house. Day and night it echoed in my ears, all the while that I was growing up.

Okane was always on her guard with me, hardly daring to let me out of her sight. Yet my mother often scolded her. "Do be careful, Okane!" she would say. There was an earth-covered footbridge over the pond, and whenever I tried to cross it Okane was sure to stop me. Sometimes Mother came running after me too. Most of the pond was shallow, but it was over six feet deep at one place, where a hole had been sunk so that the fish could survive if the rest of the water dried up. The hole was near the bridge, and Mother warned me about it time and again. "It would be dreadful if you fell in there," she used to say. "Even a grownup couldn't get out."

On the other side of the bridge was an arbor, and next to it the teahouse, my favorite playroom.

"Wait outside, Okane!" I would tell my nurse. "You mustn't come in after me." I was delighted with the low-roofed, narrow little building because it seemed exactly like a toy house for a child. I would play there for hours: sprawling out on its straw-matted floor, going through the tiny doorways, turning the water on and off in the pantry, untying the braided cords of the wooden boxes I found and taking out the tea objects, or putting on one of the wide rush hats the guests wore when coming to the tea ceremony in the rain.

Okane, who was standing outside, would begin to worry. "Tadasu!" she would call. "Don't stay any longer—your mother won't like it." Or again: "Look! There's a great big centipede here! It's terrible if a centipede bites you!" I actually did see large centipedes in the teahouse a few times, but I was never bitten.

I was far more afraid of the half dozen stone figures of Buddhist saints which stood here and there on the hill and around the pond. These were only three or four feet high, considerably smaller than the Korean statues before the inner gate, but their ugly, grotesque faces seemed somehow very Japanese. Some of them had hideously distorted noses and seemed to be staring at you out of the corners of their eyes; others seemed on the verge of a sly, malicious laugh. I never went near them after sunset.

Now and then Mother called me over to the veranda when she fed crumbs to the fish.

"Here, little fish," she said, scattering crumbs out into the pond as the carp and crucian came swimming up from their hiding place in that deep hollow. Sometimes I sat close to her on the edge of the veranda, leaning against the low rail and tossing crumbs to them too; or else I sat on her lap, feeling the warm, resilient touch of her rather full thighs as she held me snugly in her embrace.

In the summer my parents and I used to have supper by the pond, and sit there to enjoy the cool of evening. Occasionally we ordered food from a restaurant or had a man come in from a caterer, bringing all the ingredients and cooking them in our huge kitchen. Father would put a bottle of beer under the spout of the bamboo mortar. Mother would sit at the edge of the pond and dangle her feet in the water, where they looked more beautiful than ever. She was a small, delicately built woman, with plump, white little dumpling-like feet which she held quite motionless as she soaked them in the water, letting the coolness seep through her body. Years later, after I was grown up, I came across this line of Chinese verse:

When she washes the inkstone,
the fish come to swallow ink.

Even as a young child I thought how pleasant it would be if the fish in our pond came gliding playfully around her beautiful feet, instead of coming only when we fed them.

I remember that on one of those summer evenings I noticed some long, thin, slippery-looking leaves in my soup, and asked Mother what they were.

"That's called *nenunawa,*" she said.

"Oh? What's *that*?"

"A kind of water plant, like a lotus—they gather it at Mizoro Pond," she explained in her soft, well-bred voice.

Father laughed. "If you say it's *nenunawa* people won't know what you're talking about," he told her. "They call it *junsai* nowadays."

"But doesn't *nenunawa* sound long and slippery, just the way it is? That's the name for it in all the old poems, you know." And she began reciting one of them. From that time on it was always called *nenunawa* at our house, even by the maids and by the men who came to cook for us.

At nine o'clock I would be told that it was bedtime, and be taken away by my nurse. I don't know how late my parents stayed up; they slept in the room with the veranda around it, while Okane and I were in a small room of six mats on the north side, across the corridor from them. Sometimes I fretted and lay awake a long time, pleading: "Let me sleep with Mama!"

Then Mother would come to look in at me. "My, what a little baby I have tonight," she would say, taking me up in her arms and carrying me to her bedroom. Even though the bed had already been prepared for sleeping, father would not be in it—perhaps he was still out in the pavilion. Mother herself had yet to dress for bed. She lay down beside me just as she was, not taking off her sash, and held me so that my head nestled under her chin. The light was on, but I buried my face inside the neck opening of her kimono and had a blurred impression of being swathed in darkness. The faint scent of her hair, which was done up in a chignon, wafted into my nostrils. Seeking out her nipples with my mouth, I played with them like an infant, took them between my lips, ran my tongue over them. She always let me do that as long as I wanted, without a word of reproach. I believe I used to suckle at her breasts until I was a fairly large child, perhaps because in those days people were not at all strict about weaning their children. When I used my tongue as hard as I could, licking her nipples and pressing around them, the milk flowed out nicely. The mingled scents of her hair and milk hovered there in her bosom, around my face. As dark as it was, I could still dimly see her white breasts.

"Go to sleep now," she would murmur; and as she comforted me, patting me on the head and stroking my back, she began to sing her usual lullaby:

"Go to sleep, go to sleep.
Don't cry, there's a good child, go to sleep.
It's Mother cuddling you,
Mother cradling you,
Don't cry, there's a good child, go to sleep."

She would sing it over and over while I drifted off into a peaceful sleep, still clutching her breasts and running my tongue around her nipples. Often my dreams were penetrated by the distant clack of the water mortar, far beyond my shuttered windows.

Okane also knew a number of lullabies, such as this one:

When I asked the pillow, "Is he asleep?"
The honest pillow said, "He is!"

She sang many others for me too, but I was never easily lulled asleep by her songs. (Nor, in the room I shared with her, could I hear the sound of the water mortar.) Mother's voice had a seductive rhythm all its own, a rhythm that filled my mind with pleasant fancies and quickly put me to sleep.

Although I have thus far written "mother" without specifying which of the two I meant, my intention has been to relate only memories of my true mother. Yet it occurs to me that these recollections seem a little too detailed for a child of three or four. Seeing her dangle her feet in the pond, or hearing her talk about *nenunawa,* for instance—would such things, if they had really happened when I was a child of that age, have left any impression whatever? Possibly impressions of the first mother were overlaid by those of the second, confusing my memory. For early one autumn, just as the chestnut tree at our doorway was beginning to shed its leaves, my twenty-two-year-old mother, who was with child, contracted an infection of the womb and died. I was five at the time. A few years later I had a stepmother.

I cannot recall my first mother's features distinctly. According to Okane, she was very beautiful, but all that I can summon to my mind's eye is the vague image of a full, round face. Since I often looked up at her as she held me in her arms, I could see her nostrils clearly. The lamplight gave a pink luminosity to her lovely nose: seen from that angle, it appeared to be all the more exquisitely proportioned—not in the least like Okane's nose, or anyone else's. But when I try to remember her other features—her eyes, her mouth—I can only visualize them in a very general way. Here too I am perhaps being misled by the superimposed image of my second mother. After my real mother's death Father used to read the sutras and say prayers for her every morning and evening before her memorial tablet, and I often sat beside him praying too. But as hard as I stared at her photograph, which stood beside the tablet on our Buddhist altar, I never had the sudden poignant feeling that this was my own mother—the woman who had suckled me at her breasts.

All I could tell from the picture was that she wore her hair in an old-fashioned style, and that she seemed even plumper than I had remembered. It was too faded to re-create in my mind the way she actually looked.

"Papa," I asked, "is that really Mama's picture?"

"Yes, of course it is," he said. "It was taken before we were married, when she was about sixteen."

"But it doesn't look like her, does it? Why don't you put up something better? Don't you have another one?"

"Your mother didn't like to be photographed, so this is the only one I could find of her by herself. After we were married we had some pictures taken together, but the man did such a bad job retouching them that she thought they spoiled her face. Now this one shows her when she was a very young girl, and she may seem different from the way you remember her. But that was how she really looked at the time."

I could see then that it did bear a certain resemblance to her, though by no means enough to bring the forgotten image of my mother back to life.

I would think of her wistfully as I leaned on the balustrade and watched the carp swimming in the pond, yearn for her as I listened to the clack of the bamboo mortar. But it was especially at night, when I was lying in bed in my nurse's arms, that I felt an indescribable longing for my dead mother. That sweet, dimly white dream world there in her warm bosom among the mingled scents of her hair and her milk—why had it disappeared? Was this what "death" meant? Where could she have gone? Okane tried to console me by singing Mother's lullabies, but that made my grief all the worse. "No, no!" I cried, thrashing about in bed. "I don't like you to sing for me! I want Mama!" Kicking off the covers, I howled and wept.

At last my father would come in to say: "Tadasu, you mustn't give Okane so much trouble. Now be a good boy and go to sleep." But I cried even harder.

"Your mother has died," he would tell me, his voice thickening and faltering. "It doesn't do any good to cry about it. I feel as much like crying as you do—maybe more—but I'm being brave. You try to be brave too."

Then Okane would say: "If you want to see your mama, you ought to pray as hard as you can. If you do, she'll come to you in a dream, and say: 'Tadasu, you're such a good little boy!' But if you cry she won't come!"

Sometimes Father would give up in despair at my incessant wailing and screaming, and say: "All right then, come sleep with me." Taking me along to his room, he would lie down with me in his arms. But I found his masculine smell so different from my mother's fragrance that I was inconsolable. Rather than sleep with him, I preferred to sleep with my nurse.

"Papa, you make me feel sick. I want to go back to Okane."

"Well, go sleep in the other room then."

But Okane would scold me for it when I got back into bed with her. "Even if your father *does* make you feel sick, why do you have to say such an awful thing?" She used to say I looked exactly like him, not like my mother. That made me unhappy too.

Father always spent an hour morning and evening reading aloud from the sutras before the memorial tablet. As soon as I thought he was going to stop I would steal up to the altar and sit beside him for the few remaining minutes, running my little string of prayer beads through my fingers. But sometimes he led me there by the hand, saying: "Come to pray for your mother"; and I had to sit still beside him for the whole hour.

The next spring, when I was six, I entered elementary school, and from that time on I seldom made a nuisance of myself at night. But I longed for Mother all the more. Even my unsociable father, who had never cared for any company except my mother's, seemed to feel lonely, and began going out occasionally for diversion. On Sundays he often took Okane and me along to dine at a riverside restaurant in Yamabana, or on an excursion to the hills west of the city.

One day he said to me: "When your mother was alive we often used to go out to Yamabana for dinner. Do you remember that, Tadasu?"

"I only remember once. Weren't some frogs croaking in the river behind us?"

"That's right. Do you remember hearing your mother sing a song there one evening?"

"I don't think so."

Then, as if it had suddenly occurred to him: "Tadasu, suppose there was someone just like your mother, and suppose she was willing to come and *be* your mother—how would you feel about that?"

"Do you really think there *is* such a person?" I asked dubiously. "Do you know anyone, Papa?"

"No," he replied hastily, "I only said 'suppose.'" He seemed anxious to drop the subject.

I am not sure exactly how old I was when Father and I had that conversation. Nor have I any way of knowing whether he already had someone in mind, or whether it was simply a chance remark. But when I was in the second grade—in the spring, when the double globeflowers at the mouth of the waterfall were in full bloom—I came home from school one day and was startled to hear the sound of a koto from the inner room. Who could be playing? My mother had been an accomplished musician of the Ikuta school, and I had often seen Father sitting beside her on the veranda, listening absorbedly as she played for him on her six-foot-long koto, which was decorated with a pine-tree pattern worked in gold lacquer. After her death, her beloved koto was wrapped in a cloth dyed with our family crest of paulownia leaves and flowers, placed in a black-lacquered box, and put away in the storehouse, where it had remained undisturbed ever since. Could that be her koto? I wondered, as I came in through the side entrance. Just then Okane appeared, and whispered into my ear. "Tadasu, be very quiet and peek in the other room. There's a pretty young lady here today!"

When I went through the eight-mat room to the other side, pushed open the sliding doors a little, and peered in, Father noticed me at once and beckoned. The strange lady was engrossed in her koto; even after I came up beside her she kept on playing without so much as turning her head. She sat where my mother used to sit, and in the very same pose, her instrument laid out at the same angle, her left hand stretched out in the same way as she pressed the strings. The koto was not Mother's—it was a plain one, completely unadorned. But Father's position and attitude as he sat there listening so attentively were exactly the same as in my mother's time. It was only after she finished and took off the ivory finger picks that the strange lady turned to smile at me.

"Are you Tadasu?" she inquired politely, in a well-bred Kyoto accent. "You look just like your father."

"Make a nice bow," Father said, putting his hand on my head.

"Did you just come home from school?" she asked. Then she slipped the picks back on her fingers and began to play again. I didn't recognize the piece, but it sounded extremely difficult. Meanwhile I sat obediently beside my father and watched her every movement, hardly daring to breathe. Even after she stopped playing for us, she made no attempt to shower me with compliments—all she did was smile when our eyes met. She talked to Father in a calm, relaxed way, and seemed to have an air of composure. Soon a ricksha came for her; she was gone before dusk. But she left her koto with us. We stood it up against the wall in the alcove of the eight-mat room.

I was sure that Father would ask me what I thought of her, whether I didn't agree that she looked like my mother. But he said nothing, nor did I try to find out how they happened to become acquainted. Somehow I hesitated to bring the matter up. To tell the truth, if I'd been asked whether or not she looked like my mother I would scarcely have known what to say. At least, my first glimpse of her had not given me the impression that here indeed was the reincarnation of my mother. And yet her soft, round face, her delicate body, her calm, unhurried speech, in particular her polite reserve and utter lack of flattery when we met, together with her indefinable attractiveness and charm—in all this she seemed to resemble my mother, and I felt friendly toward her.

"Who was that?" I asked Okane later.

"I really don't know," she said. Possibly she had been warned not to tell me.

"Is this the first time she's come here?"

"No, she was here about twice before. . . . It's the first time she's played the koto, though."

I saw the woman once more that summer, around the season when you begin to hear the song of the thrush. That time she seemed even more at ease, staying to feed crumbs to the fish with Father and me after playing the koto. But she left before supper. Again her koto was put in the alcove—maybe she came to the house more often than I knew.

One day in March, when I was eight years old, Father called me into the veranda room to talk to me. I think it was after supper, about eight o'clock in the evening, when no one else was around.

"I have something to discuss with you, Tadasu," he began, in an unusually solemn tone. "I don't know how you feel about the lady who's been coming to visit us, but for various reasons—reasons that concern you as well as me—I'm thinking of marrying her. You'll be in the third grade this year, so I want you to try to understand what I'm saying. As you know, I had the greatest love for your mother. If she were only alive today I wouldn't want anyone else. Her death was a terrible blow to me—I couldn't get over it. But then I happened to meet this lady. You say you don't remember your mother's face very clearly, but you'll soon find that this lady resembles her in all sorts of ways. Of course no two people are quite alike, unless they're twins. That isn't what I mean by resembling her. I mean the impressions she makes, the way she talks, the way she carries herself, her quiet, easygoing personality, sweet and gentle, and yet deep—that's why I say she's like your mother. If I hadn't met her I'd never have wanted to marry again. It's only because there *is* such a person that I've come to feel this way. Maybe your mother saw to it that I happened to find this lady, for your sake as well as mine. If she'll come and stay with us, she'll be a wonderful help to you as you grow up. And now that the second anniversary of your mother's death has passed, this seems like a proper time for marrying her. What do you think, Tadasu? You understand what I've been telling you, don't you?"

Curiously enough, I had already given my consent long before he finished what he intended to say. Seeing my face light up, he added: "There's one thing more I'd like you to remember. When she comes you mustn't think of her as your second mother. Think that your mother has been away somewhere for a while and has just come home. Even if I didn't tell you so, you'd soon begin to look at it that way. Your two mothers will become one, with no distinction between them. Your first mother's name was Chinu, and your new mother's name is Chinu too. And in everything she says and does, your new mother will behave the way the first one did."

After that, Father stopped taking me in to sit beside him during his morning and evening worship at the memorial tablet. The time he spent reading the sutras gradually became shorter. Then one evening in April the wedding ceremony was held in the veranda room. Maybe there was a reception afterward, in some restaurant, but I have no remembrance of that. The ceremony itself was a very quiet affair: only a few close relatives attended on either side. From that day on Father called his bride "Chinu," and I, having been told to call her "Mama," found that the word came to my lips with surprising ease.

For the past two or three years I had been accustomed to sleeping in the room next to Father's, but from the night my new mother arrived I went back to sharing the little room across the corridor with Okane. Father seemed to be truly happy, and began living the same kind of tranquil domestic life he had enjoyed with my first mother. Even Okane and the maids, who had been with us for years and who might have been expected to gossip and criticize their new mistress, were won over completely by her. Probably it was because of her natural kindness and warmth—anyway, they served her as faithfully as they had her predecessor.

Our household returned to its old routine. Father would sit listening attentively while Mother played the koto, just as he used to when my real mother was alive; and he always had the gold-lacquered koto brought out for the occasion. In summer the three of us would have supper beside the pond. Father would take his beer to cool under the spout of the bamboo mortar. Mother would dangle her feet in the pond. As I looked at her feet through the water I found myself remembering my real mother's feet. I felt as if they were the same; or rather, to put it more accurately, whenever I caught a glimpse of my new mother's feet I recalled that those of my own mother, the memory of which had long ago faded, had had the same lovely shape.

My stepmother also called the water plant we had in soup *nenunawa*, and told me how it was gathered at Mizoro Pond.

"I imagine that sooner or later you'll hear at school about the Court anthologies," she remarked one day. "Well, there's a poem in the earliest one that goes like this." And she recited a poem which had a pun on the word *nenunawa*.

As I have said before, I suspect that these incidents occurred during my real mother's lifetime and were only being repeated. No doubt Father had instructed my present mother how to behave, and was trying his best to confuse me about what my two mothers had said or done, so that I would identify them in my mind.

One evening—I believe it was that autumn—Mother came into my room just as I was about to go to sleep with Okane.

"Tadasu," she asked, "do you remember how your mama used to nurse you till you were about four years old?"

"Yes," I said.

"And do you remember how she always sang lullabies to you?"

"I remember."

"Wouldn't you still like to have your mama do those things?"

"I suppose so. . . ." I answered, flushing, aware that my heart had begun to pound.

"Then come and sleep with me tonight."

She took my hand and led me to the veranda room. The bed was ready for sleeping, but Father had not yet come in. Mother herself was still fully dressed, still wearing her usual sash. The light was shining overhead. I could hear the clack of the bamboo mortar. Everything was the way it used to be. Mother got into bed first, propped her head on the wooden pillow (her hair was done up in an old-fashioned chignon), and lifted the covers for me to crawl in after her. I was already too tall to bury myself easily under her chin, but being face to face with her made me feel so awkward that I shrank as far as I could under the covers. When I did, the neckline of her kimono was just at my nose.

Then I heard her whisper: "Tadasu, do you want some milk?" As she spoke, she bent her head down to look at me. Her cool hair brushed against my forehead.

"You must've been awfully lonely, with no one but Okane to sleep with for such a long time. If you wanted to sleep with Mama, why didn't you say so earlier? Were you feeling shy about it?"

I nodded.

"What a funny little boy you are! Now, hurry up and see if you can find the milk!"

I drew the top of her kimono open, pressed my face between her breasts, and played with her nipples with both hands. Because she was still looking down at me, a beam of light shone in over the edge of the bedclothes. I held one nipple and then the other in my mouth, sucking and using my tongue avidly to start the flow of milk. But as hard as I tried, it wouldn't come.

"Ooh, that tickles!" Mother exclaimed.

"I can't get a drop," I told her. "Maybe I've forgotten how."

"I'm sorry," she said. "Just be patient—I'll have a baby one of these days, and then there'll be lots of milk for you."

Even so, I wouldn't let go of her breasts, and kept sucking at them. I knew it was hopeless, but still I enjoyed the sensation of rolling around in my mouth those firm little buds at the tips of her soft, full breasts.

"I'm terribly sorry—and you've worked so hard at it! Do you want to go on trying anyway?"

Nodding my head, I kept on suckling. Once again, by some strange association, I seemed to drift among the mingled scents of hair oil and milk that had hovered in my mother's bosom so long ago. That warm, dimly white dream world—the world I thought had disappeared forever—had unexpectedly returned.

Then Mother began to sing the old lullaby, in the very rhythm that I knew so well:

> *"Go to sleep, go to sleep,*
> *Don't cry, there's a good child, go to sleep. . . ."*

But in spite of her singing I was too excited to relax that night, and I went on sucking away greedily at her nipples.

Within half a year, though I hadn't forgotten my real mother, I could no longer distinguish sharply between her and the present one. When I tried to remember my real mother's face, my stepmother's appeared before me; when I tried to remember her voice, my stepmother's echoed in my ears. Gradually the two images merged: I found it hard to believe that I had ever had a different mother. Everything turned out just as Father had planned.

When I reached the age of twelve or thirteen, I began sleeping alone at night. But even then I would sometimes long to be held in my mother's bosom. "Mama, let me sleep with you!" I would beg. Drawing open her kimono, I would suck at her milkless breasts, and listen to her lullabies. And after drifting peacefully asleep I would awaken the next morning to find that in the meantime—I had no idea when—someone had carried me back and put me to bed alone in my own small room.

Whenever I said: "Let me sleep with you!" Mother was glad to do as I wished, and Father made no objection.

For a long time I didn't know where this second mother was born, what her background was, or how she happened to marry my father; such subjects were never brought up in my presence. I knew I might have found some clue in the city records, but I obeyed my father's orders: "Think of her as your real mother. You mustn't take the attitude that she's a stepmother." Also, I had some qualms about what I might find. However, when I was about to enter higher school I had to get an abstract from the records, and at that time I learned that my stepmother's real name was not Chinu but Tsuneko.

The following year my nurse Okane, who was then fifty-seven, ended her long service with us and retired to her home town of Nagahama. One day in late October before she left I went along with her to visit the Shimogamo Shrine. She made an offering, prayed briefly before the main altar, and then said in a voice filled with emotion: "I don't know when I'll see this shrine again. . . ." After that she suggested we go for a little walk through the shrine forest, toward the Aoi Bridge.

As we were walking along she suddenly turned to me and said: "You know all about it, Tadasu, don't you?"

"Know about what?" I asked, surprised.

"If you haven't heard, I won't say any more. . . ."

"What are you talking about?"

"I wonder if I ought to tell you," she said, hesitating. Then, still strangely evasive: "Tadasu, do you know much about your stepmother?"

"No," I answered. "I know that her real name is Tsuneko."

"How did you find that out?"

"I had to get an abstract from the city records last year."

"Is that really all you know?"

"That's all. Father said I shouldn't be too inquisitive about her, and you didn't tell me anything either, so I decided not to ask."

"As long as I was working at your house I didn't want to mention it, but once I go back to the country I can't say when I'll set eyes on you again. So I think maybe I ought to tell you after all. You mustn't let your father hear about it, though."

"Never mind then," I said, without really meaning it. "Don't tell me—I think I ought to do what Father says."

But she insisted. "Anyway, you're bound to find out sooner or later. It's something you ought to know."

I couldn't help being fascinated by her long, rambling story, told to me bit by bit as we walked along the shrine road.

"I've only heard this at second hand, so I can't be sure," Okane began, and went on to give me a full account of my stepmother's past.

It seems that she was born into a Kyoto family that owned a large stationery shop in the Nijo district, specializing in decorative papers and writing brushes. But when she was about nine years old the family went bankrupt; by the time of Okane's story their shop no longer existed. At eleven, she was taken in as an apprentice geisha at one of the houses in Gion; from twelve to fifteen she entertained at parties as a dancer. You could probably have discovered the professional name she used at that time, the name of the geisha house, and so on; but Okane didn't know. Then, at fifteen, she is supposed to have had her debts paid off by the son of a wholesale cotton merchant, and to have been taken into the family as his bride. Opinions differ as to whether or not she was his legal wife, some declaring that her name was never entered in the official records.

Anyhow, she enjoyed all the privileges of a wife, and for about three years lived comfortably as the young mistress of a prosperous household. But at eighteen, for one reason or another, she was divorced. Some say that family pressure drove her out; others that her dissipated husband simply tired of her. No doubt she received a considerable sum of money at the time, but she went back to her parents' drab little house in Rokujo, turned the upstairs room into a studio, and made her living by teaching flower arrangement and the tea ceremony to the young women of the neighborhood.

Apparently it was during those days that my father became acquainted with her. But no one knew how he happened to meet her, or where they were seeing each other before she came to Heron's Nest as his bride. Two and a half years passed from the time of my mother's death until father's second marriage. As vividly as the girl may have reminded him of his lost wife, he could hardly have fallen in love with her less than a year after the death of the woman he had so much adored; probably he made his mind up only a few months before the wedding took place. His first wife had died at twenty-two; his second was twenty when she married him; father himself was thirty-three, thirteen years her senior; and I, at eight, was almost that much younger.

Learning about my stepmother's background aroused strong curiosity in me, along with all sorts of other feelings. I had never dreamed that she was once a professional entertainer in Gion. Of course she was very different from the ordinary girl of that kind: she came from a respectable family, and had left the gay quarter after only a few years to take up the life of the young mistress of a well-to-do household, during which time she seems to have acquired a number of polite feminine accomplishments. Yet I had to admire her for preserving her unaffected charm and graciousness, in spite of having been a Gion dancer. But what of the evident refinement of her voice, that soft speech in the tradition of the old Kyoto merchant class? Even if she had only spent two or three years in Gion one would expect to find some trace of it in her speech. Did her first husband and his parents make a point of correcting her?

I suppose it was natural for my father, at a time when he was sad and lonely, to be attracted by such a woman. And it was natural, too, for him to come to believe that a woman like her would have all the fine qualities of his former wife and could help me forget the sorrow of having lost my mother. I began to realize how much thought he had given to this, not merely for his own sake but for mine. Even if my stepmother shared his wish to make me think of my two mothers as a single woman, it was his own extraordinary effort that enabled him to mold her in the image of my real mother. I could see that the love he lavished on my stepmother and me only strengthened his love for his first wife all the more. And so, while it might seem that exposing the secrets of my new mother's earlier life had frustrated all of Father's patient efforts, the result was to deepen my gratitude to him and my respect for my stepmother.

After Okane left we added another maid, so that there were four in all. And in January of the following year I learned that Mother was pregnant. It was in the eleventh year of her marriage to my father. Since she had never had a child before, even by her former husband, both Father and she seemed to be surprised that such a thing could happen, after all these years.

"I feel ashamed to be getting big like this, at my age," she used to say. Or again: "When you're past thirty it's hard to give birth for the first time, I hear." Both Mother and Father had concentrated all their parental love on me, and perhaps they worried about my reaction to this event. If they did, they needn't have: I cannot describe how pleased I was to think that, after all these years as an only child, I was about to have a little brother or sister. I suppose, too, that Father's heart was darkened now and then by the ominous memory of my first mother's death in pregnancy. But what struck me as odd was that neither Father nor Mother seemed to want to bring up the matter; I began to notice that they looked strangely gloomy whenever the subject was mentioned.

"Since I have Tadasu I don't need another child," she would say, half-jokingly. "I'm too old to have a baby." Knowing her as I did, I thought it unlikely that she said such a thing merely to hide her embarrassment at being pregnant.

"What are you talking about, Mother?" I would object. "You mustn't say foolish things like that!" But somehow Father seemed to agree with her.

The doctor who examined her said that Mother's heart was rather weak, but that it was not bad enough to be a cause for concern—on the whole, she had a strong constitution. And in May of that year she gave birth to a baby boy. Her delivery took place at our house: the little six-mat room that I had been using was given over to her. The baby was a healthy one, and in due time Father gave it the name Takeshi. But when I came home from school one day—I believe it was about two weeks later—I was startled to find that Takeshi wasn't there.

"Father, where is Takeshi?" I asked.

"We've sent him out to Shizuichino for adoption," he told me. "Someday I think you'll understand, but for the present, please don't ask too many questions. I didn't plan this by myself—from the time we knew the child was coming your mother and I discussed it together every night. She wanted to do it even more than I did. Maybe we shouldn't have gone ahead without a word to you, but I was afraid that talking to you about it might do more harm than good."

For a moment I looked at him incredulously. Mother, who had left her bed only the day before, seemed to have deliberately slipped off somewhere, to leave us alone, "Where's Mother?" I asked.

"I think she may have gone out to the garden," he said, as if he didn't know.

I went out to look for her at once. She was in the middle of the bridge, clapping her hands and calling the fish, and scattering food to them.

When she saw me, she went over to the other side of the pond, sat down on a celadon porcelain drum beside one of those sinister-looking stone saints, and beckoned me to come and sit on the other drum, facing her.

"I was just talking to Father," I said. "What on earth is the meaning of this?"

"Were you surprised, Tadasu?" Her soft, round face dimpled in a smile. The expression in her eyes was far too serene for a mother struggling to hold back her grief at having just been robbed of her beloved newborn infant.

"Of course I was."

"But haven't I always said that Tadasu is the only child I need?" Her calm expression remained unchanged. "Your father and I both thought it was for the best. Let's talk about it another time."

That night the room I had given up to Mother and her baby was once again my bedroom. The more I thought about what had happened, the more puzzled I became. It was dawn before I fell asleep.

Here I should like to say a little about Shizuichino, the place to which Takeshi had been sent.

Shizuichino is the modern name for the Ichiharano district, where the legendary hero Raiko is supposed to have killed the two robber chiefs. Even now one of its villages is called Ichihara, and that is also the name of the local station on the electric-car line to Mount Kurama. However, it was only in recent years that the car line opened; before that, you had to make the six- or seven-mile trip from Kyoto to Shizuichino by ricksha, or go by carriage as far as Miyake-Hachiman and then walk about three and a half miles. For several generations we had had close ties with a family named Nosé who were prosperous farmers in this district—I suppose one of my ancestors had been sent out to nurse at their house. Even in Father's time, the head of the Nosé family and his wife would come to pay their respects to us at the Bon Festival and at New Year's, bringing with them a cartload of fresh vegetables. Their Kamo eggplants and green soybeans were unobtainable at the market; we were always delighted to see them coming with their little handcart. Since we often went to stay overnight with them in the fall, to go mushroom hunting, I had been familiar with that region since childhood.

The road from the Nosé house to the mushroom hill led along the Kurama River, one of the sources of the Kamo. We were already well above Kyoto: as we climbed still higher we could see the city lying below us. They say that the great scholar Fujiwara Seika retired here, after declining the invitation of the Shogun Ieyasu to come to Edo. The mountain villa Seika lived in has long since disappeared, but its site was in a wide bend of the meandering Kurama River. Not far away were the places he chose as the "Eight Scenic Beauties," to which he gave such names as Pillow-Stream Grotto and Flying-Bird Pool.

Another nearby point of interest was the Fudaraku Temple, popularly known as the Komachi Temple, where Ono no Komachi and her tormented suitor are said to lie buried. According to the *Illustrated Guide to the Capital,* this is also the temple which the Emperor Go-Shirakawa visited during his journey to Ohara, as related in *The Tale of the Heiké.*

There is a passage in one of the No plays about Komachi saying that many years ago a man who happened to be passing Ichiharano heard a voice from a clump of tall *susuki* grass recite this poem:

When the autumn wind blows,
Eyeless Komachi wails in pain.
But where is her lovely face
In this wilderness of susuki?

Whereupon the priest who recalls the poem decides to go to Ichiharano and pray for the repose of Komachi's soul. I have seen an old painting which shows *susuki* growing out of the eye sockets of what is presumably Komachi's skull; and in the Komachi Temple there was a "wailing stone" on which was carved the poem I have quoted. In my childhood, that whole area was a lonely waste covered with a rank growth of *susuki* grass.

A few days after I learned the astonishing news about Takeshi I decided that I had to make a secret visit to the Nosé family in Shizuichino. Not that I was determined to steal Takeshi away from them and bring him home again. I am not the sort of person to do a thing like that on my own initiative. It was simply that I felt an overpowering rush of pity for my poor little brother, taken from his mother's arms to a house far away in the country. At least I could make sure that he was well, I thought, and then go home and urge Father and Mother to reconsider. If they didn't listen to me at first, I meant to go on visiting Takeshi regularly, keeping our link with him intact. Sooner or later they would understand how I felt.

I set out early in the morning and reached the house a little before noon. Fortunately, Nosé and his wife had just returned from the fields, but when I asked to see Takeshi they seemed embarrassed.

"Takeshi isn't here," they told me.

"He isn't? Then where is he?"

"Well, now . . ." they began, exchanging worried glances as if they were at a loss for an answer.

But after I repeated my question several times, Nosé's wife broke down and said: "We left him with some people a little farther out." Then they explained that because there wasn't anyone in the house just then to nurse a baby, and because my parents wanted Takeshi further away, they took him out to live with some old friends of theirs, people you could trust.

When I asked where "a little farther out" was, Nosé seemed even more embarrassed. "Your parents know where it is," he said; "so please ask them. It wouldn't do for me to tell you myself."

His wife chimed in: "They said if you ever happened to ask us we shouldn't tell you!" But I was finally able to worm it out of them that the place in question was a village called Seriu.

There is a folk song with the line "Out beyond Kyoto, by Ohara and Seriu"; and the Kabuki play *The Village School* has a passage about "hiding their lord's child in the village of Seriu, nestled in the hills." But this Seriu is over the Ebumi Pass on the road from Shizuichino to Ohara, and now has a different name. The Seriu that Nosé and his wife were talking about is a mountain village in Tamba, even more remote and isolated. To go there, you take the electric car to Kibune, the second stop after Shizuichino, and cross the Seriu Pass into Tamba. The pass is a difficult one, more than twice as high as the Ebumi Pass, and there is not a single house in the five miles from Kibune to Seriu.

Why would my parents have sent my little brother to such a place? Even the Seriu in the play—the village "nestled in the hills" where a lord's child was kept in hiding—wasn't that far from Kyoto. Why had Takeshi been hidden away deep in the mountains of Tamba? I felt that I should try to find him that very day, but since all I knew was the name of the village I would have had to look for him from house to house. Anyway, there was hardly time for me to go on to Kibune and cross that steep mountain pass. Giving up for the time being, I went back home, thoroughly dejected, along the same road I had come that morning.

For the next two or three days my relations with my parents were strained; even at supper we seldom talked. Whether or not they had heard from the Nosé family, they never said a word about my trip to Shizuichino, nor did I mention having gone. Mother was bothered by the swelling of her breasts and often secluded herself in the teahouse to use a milking device to relieve the pressure, or call one of the maids to massage her. Around this time my father seemed to be in poor health, and began taking afternoon naps in the veranda room, his head on a Chinese pillow of crimson papier-mâché. He seemed feverish too; I often saw him with a thermometer in his mouth.

I intended to go to Seriu as soon as possible, and was trying to think of an excuse to be away from home overnight. But one afternoon—it must have been late spring, since the silk tree my grandfather had been so proud of was in blossom—I decided to spend a little time reading in the pavilion. Taking along a novel, I went through the garden, past the flowering tree, and up the pavilion steps. Suddenly I noticed that Mother was sitting there on a cushion before me, busily milking her breasts. That was something she did in the teahouse, I thought. I had never imagined I'd find her on the pavilion veranda in that state: leaning over in a languid pose, her kimono open so that her naked breasts were bared to my view. Startled, I turned to leave, but she called after me in her usual calm voice: "Don't go away, Tadasu."

"I'll come again later," I said. "I didn't mean to disturb you."

"It's stifling in the teahouse, so I thought I'd sit out here. Did you want to read?"

"I'll come later," I repeated, feeling very uncomfortable. But again she stopped me from leaving.

"You needn't go—I'll be done in a moment. Just stay where you are." And then: "Look! My breasts are so full they hurt!"

I said nothing, and she continued: "You must remember how you tried to nurse at them till you were twelve or thirteen. You used to fret because nothing would come out, no matter how hard you sucked."

Mother removed the milking device from her left nipple and placed it over the right one. Her breast swelled up inside the glass receptacle, almost filling it, and a number of tiny streams of milk spurted from her nipple. She emptied the milk into a drinking glass and held it up to show me.

"I told you I'd have a baby someday and there'd be lots of milk for you too, didn't I?" I had somewhat recovered from my initial shock and was watching her fixedly, though I hardly knew what to say.

"Do you remember how it tastes?" she asked. I lowered my gaze and shook my head.

"Then try a little," she said, holding the glass out to me. "Go on and try it!"

The next moment, before I realized what I was doing, my hand reached out for the glass, and I took a sip of the sweet white liquid.

"How is it? Does it remind you of how it used to taste? Your mother nursed you till you were four, I think." It was extraordinary for my stepmother to say "your mother" to me, distinguishing between herself and my father's first wife.

"I wonder if you remember how to nurse," she went on. "You can try, if you like." Mother held one of her breasts in her hand and offered me the nipple. "Just try it and see!"

I sat down before her so close that our knees were touching, bent my head toward her, and took one of her nipples between my lips. At first it was hard for me to get any milk, but as I kept on suckling, my tongue began to recover its old skill. I was several inches taller than she was, but I leaned down and buried my face in her bosom, greedily sucking up the milk that came gushing out. "Mama," I began murmuring instinctively, in a spoiled, childish voice.

I suppose Mother and I were in each other's embrace for about half an hour. At last she said: "That's enough for today, isn't it?" and drew her breast away from my mouth. I thrust her aside without a word, jumped down from the veranda, and ran off into the garden.

But what was the meaning of her behavior that afternoon? I knew she hadn't deliberately planned it, since we met in the pavilion by accident. Did our sudden encounter give her the impulse to embarrass and upset me? If our meeting was as much a surprise to her as it was to me, perhaps she merely yielded to a passing whim. Yet she had seemed far too cool to be playing such a mischievous trick: she had acted as if this were nothing out of the ordinary. Maybe she would have been just as calm even if someone had come upon us. Maybe, in spite of my having grown up, she still thought of me as a child. Mother's state of mind was a mystery to me, but my own actions had been equally abnormal. The moment I saw her breasts there before me, so unexpectedly revealed, I was back in the dream world that I had longed for, back in the power of the old memories that had haunted me for so many years. Then, because she lured me into it by having me drink her milk, I ended by doing the crazy thing I did. In an agony of shame, wondering how I could have harbored such insane feelings, I paced back and forth around the pond alone. But at the same time that I regretted my behavior, and tortured myself for it, I felt that I wanted to do it again—not once, but over and over. I knew that if I were placed in those circumstances again—if I were lured by her that way—I would not have the will power to resist.

After that I stayed away from the pavilion; and Mother, possibly aware of how I felt, seemed to be using only the teahouse. Somehow the desire that had occupied such a large place in my heart—the desire to go to

Seriu to see Takeshi—was no longer quite so strong. First of all, I wanted to find out why my parents had disposed of him in that way. Was it Father's idea or Mother's? As far as I could judge, it seemed likely that my stepmother—out of deference to my own mother—had decided that she ought not to keep her child here with us. And perhaps Father shared her scruples. Undoubtedly his love for his former wife was still intense, and he may well have thought it wrong for him to have any other child than the one she left him. Perhaps that is why my stepmother gave up her baby. For her, such an act would have shown self-sacrificing devotion to my father—and wasn't she more attached to me than to her own son? I could only suppose that they had come to their decision for reasons of this sort. But why hadn't they confided in me, or at least given me some hint of their intentions? Why had they kept Takeshi's whereabouts such a dark secret?

I have mentioned that Father's health seemed to be failing, and it occurred to me that that might have influenced his decision. Since about the end of the last year he had begun to look pale, and had become noticeably thinner. Although he seldom coughed or cleared his throat, he seemed to have a low fever, which made me suspect that he was suffering from some kind of chest trouble. Our family doctor was a man named Kato, whose office was on Teramachi at Imadegawa. During the early stages of his illness Father never had him come to the house. "I'm going for a walk," he would say, and then take the streetcar to visit Dr. Kato. It was not until after the episode in the pavilion that I managed to find out where he was going.

"Father," I asked, "is anything wrong with you?"

"No, not in particular," he answered vaguely.

"But why do you have a prescription from Dr. Kato?"

"It isn't serious. I'm just having a little trouble passing water."

"Then it's inflammation of the bladder?"

"Yes," he said. "Something like that."

At last it became obvious to everyone that Father had to urinate frequently. You could see that he was always going to relieve himself. Also, his coloring was worse than ever, and he had lost his appetite completely. That summer, after the rainy season, he began to spend most of the day resting, as if he felt exhausted; in the evening he sometimes came out to have dinner with us beside the pond, but even then he was listless and seemed to be making the effort out of consideration for Mother and me.

I felt suspicious because he was so evasive about his illness, even concealing his regular visits to his doctor. One day I made a visit of my own to Dr. Kato's office and asked him about it.

"Father tells me he has inflammation of the bladder," I said. "I wonder if that's really all it is."

"It's true that he has an inflamed bladder," said Dr. Kato, who had known me all my life. "But hasn't he told you any more than that?" He looked a little surprised.

"You know how retiring and secretive Father is. He doesn't like to talk about his illness."

"That puts me in a difficult position," Dr. Kato said. "Of course I haven't been too blunt with your father about it, but I've let him know his condition is serious. So I suppose that he and your mother are pretty well prepared for the worst—I can't understand why they've kept it from you. Probably they want to spare you any unnecessary grief. To my own way of thinking, I'm not sure it's wise to hide the truth from you, since you're already so worried. I've known your family for a good many years—your grandfather was a patient of mine—and so I don't think there should be any objection if I take it on myself to inform you." He paused a moment, and went on: "I'm sorry to have to say this, but as you must have gathered by now your father's condition is not at all hopeful." Then he told me the whole story.

It was last autumn that Father noticed a change in the state of his health and went to be examined by Dr. Kato. He complained of various symptoms—fever, blood in his urine, pain after urinating, a sensation of pressure in his lower abdomen—and Dr. Kato found immediately, by touch, that both of his kidneys were swollen. He also discovered tuberculous bacilli in the urine. This is very serious, he thought; and he urged Father to go to the urology department at the university hospital for a special examination, with X-rays. Father seems to have been reluctant. However, he finally went, after Dr. Kato urged him repeatedly and gave him a letter of introduction to a friend of his at the hospital.

Two days later Dr. Kato learned the results of the examination from his friend: just as he had feared, both the cystoscope and the X-rays showed clearly that the disease was tuberculosis of the kidneys, and that Father's condition was fatal. If only one of his kidneys had been attacked he could probably have been saved by its removal. Even in such cases, the prognosis was bad: thirty or forty per cent of the patients died. Unfortunately both of my father's kidneys were affected, so nothing could be done for him. Though he still didn't seem to be a very sick man, he would soon have to take to his bed—at the longest, he might live another year or two.

"This isn't the kind of thing you can afford to neglect," Dr. Kato had warned him at the time, in a roundabout way. "From now on I'll come to see you once or twice a week—you ought to stay at home and rest as much as possible." And he added: "I must ask you to refrain from sexual intercourse. There's no danger of respiratory contagion at present, so you needn't worry as far as the rest of the family is concerned. But your wife will have to be careful."

"Is it some kind of tuberculosis?"

"Well, yes. But it isn't tuberculosis of the lungs."

"Then what is it?"

"The bacilli have attacked the kidney. Since you have two kidneys, it's nothing to be so alarmed about."

Dr. Kato managed to gloss it over for the moment in that way, and Father quietly accepted his advice. "I understand," he said. "I'll do as you've told me. But I like going out for walks, and as long as I'm able to get around I'll come to your office."

Father continued to visit Dr. Kato as usual, apparently not wishing to have him call at our house. Most of the time he came alone, but now and then Mother accompanied him. Although Dr. Kato felt an obligation to inform her frankly of her husband's condition, he had not yet found an opportunity to do so.

Then one day Father surprised him by saying: "Doctor, how much longer do I have, the way things are going?"

"Why do you talk like that?" Dr. Kato asked him.

Father smiled faintly. "You needn't keep anything from me. I've had a premonition about it all along."

"But why?"

"I don't know . . . maybe you'd call it instinct. It's just a feeling I've had. How about it, Doctor? I know what to expect, so please tell me the truth."

Dr. Kato was well acquainted with Father's character and took him at his word. Father had always been an acutely perceptive man; possibly he had been able to guess the nature of his illness from the way the specialists at the university treated him. Sooner or later I'll have to tell him or tell someone in his family, Dr. Kato thought; if he's so well prepared for it maybe I'd better do it now and get it over with. Indirectly, but without trying to evade my father's questions any longer, he confirmed his fears.

This is what Dr. Kato reported to me. Then he warned me that, since the disease often ended by invading the lungs, all of us—not just my mother—had to be careful.

I come now to the part of my narrative that I find most difficult.

I have tentatively given this narrative the title of *The Bridge of Dreams,* and have written it, however amateurishly, in the form of a novel. But everything that I have set forth actually happened—there is not one falsehood in it. Still, if I were asked why I took it into my head to write at all, I should be unable to reply. I am not writing out of any desire to have others read this. At least, I don't intend to let anyone see it as long as I am alive. If someone happens across it after my death, there will be no harm in that; but even if it is lost in oblivion, if no one ever reads it, I shall have no regret. I write for the sake of writing, simply because I enjoy looking back at the events of the past and trying to remember them one by one. Of course, all that I record here is true: I do not allow myself the slightest falsehood or distortion. But there are limits even to telling the truth; there is a line one ought not to cross. And so, although I certainly never write anything untrue, neither do I write the whole of the truth. Perhaps I leave part of it unwritten out of consideration for my father, for my mother, for myself. . . . If anyone says that not to tell the whole truth is in fact to lie, that is his own interpretation. I shall not venture to deny it.

What Dr. Kato revealed to me about my father's physical condition filled my mind with wild, nightmarish fancies. If it was last fall that Father became aware of his unhappy fate, he was then forty-three years old, Mother was thirty, and I was eighteen. At thirty, however, Mother looked four or five years younger—people took her for my sister. Suddenly I recalled the story of her earlier life, which Okane had told me as we walked through the shrine forest before she left us last year. "You mustn't let your father hear about it," she had said, but might she not have done so on his instructions? Perhaps he had reason to want to sever the connection between my real mother and my stepmother, who had become so closely linked in my mind.

Also, I thought of what had happened not long ago in the Silk-Tree Pavilion. Perhaps Father had had something to do with *that*. I hardly think Mother would have tried to tantalize me so shamelessly without his permission. The fact is, although I stayed away from the pavilion for several weeks after that incident, I went there to suckle at Mother's breast more than once. Sometimes Father was away, sometimes at home: it seems unlikely that he didn't realize what she was doing, or that she concealed it from him. Possibly, knowing he hadn't long to live, he was trying to create a deeper intimacy between Mother and me, so that she would think of me as taking his place—and she made no objection. That is all I can bring myself to say. However, such a theory would explain why they sent Takeshi to Seriu. . . . It may seem that I have imagined the most preposterous things about my parents, but what Father told me on his deathbed, as I shall relate presently, appears to bear me out.

I don't know when Mother learned that Father's days were numbered; perhaps he told her as soon as he knew. But that afternoon in the pavilion when she used the phrase "your mother"—was it really by chance, as it seemed then, or had she intended to say that? Indeed, Father must have told her about his illness even before she gave birth to Takeshi in May. Once they anticipated what the future held in store for them they may have come to an understanding—even if they never discussed the matter openly—and sent Takeshi off for adoption.

What seemed strange was that, as far as I could tell, Mother showed no sign of gloom or depression at the impending separation from her husband. It would have been contrary to her nature to display her emotions plainly—but was there even a shadow of secret grief across that bland, lovely face? Was she forcibly suppressing her tears, thinking she must not let me see her lose control of herself? Whenever I looked at them, her eyes were dry and clear. Even now I cannot say that I really understand how she felt, the complex emotions that seem to have existed beneath her surface calm. Until Father was at his dying hour she never tried to talk to me about his death.

It was in August that Father lost the strength to get out of bed. By then his entire body was swollen. Dr. Kato came to see him almost every day. Father grew steadily weaker, losing even the will to sit up to eat. Mother hardly left his bedside.

"You ought to hire a nurse," Dr. Kato told her.

But Mother said: "I'll take care of him myself." She let no one else touch him. Evidently that was also my father's wish. All his meals—though he ate only a few bites—were carefully planned by her; she would order his favorite delicacies, such as sweetfish or sea eel, and serve them to him. As his urination became more and more frequent she had to be always ready to give him the bedpan. It was during the midsummer heat, and he suffered from bedsores, which she also cared for. Often, too, she had to wipe his body with a solution of alcohol. Mother never spared herself any pains at these tasks, all of which she did with her own hands. Father grumbled if anyone else tried to help him, but he never uttered a word of complaint about what she did. His nerves became so tense that the least sound seemed to bother him: even the bamboo mortar in the garden was too noisy, and he had us stop it. Toward the end he spoke only when he needed something, and then only to Mother. Occasionally friends or relatives came to visit him, but he didn't seem to want to see them. Mother was busy with him day and night; whenever she was too exhausted to go on, her place was taken by my old nurse, Okane, who had come back to help us. I was amazed to discover that Mother had so much stamina and perseverance.

It was one day in late September, the day after an unusually heavy rainstorm when the "Shallow Stream" overflowed its banks and backed up into our pond, clouding the water, that Mother and I were summoned to Father's bedside. He was lying on his back, but he had us turn him over on his side so that he could look into our faces more easily. Beckoning me to sit close to him, he said: "Come here, Tadasu. Your mother can listen from where she is." He kept his gaze fixed on me all the while he spoke, as if he were seeking something in the depths of my eyes.

"I haven't much longer," he said. "But this was meant to be, so I am resigned to it. When I go to the other world your mother will be waiting for me, and I'm happy at the thought of meeting her again after all these years. What worries me most is your poor stepmother. She still has a long life ahead of her, but once I'm gone she'll have only you to rely on. So please take good care of her—give her all your love. Everyone says you resemble me. I think so myself. As you get older you'll look even more like me. If she has you, she'll feel as if I am still alive. I want you to think of taking my place with her as your chief aim in life, as the only kind of happiness you need."

Never had he looked at me that way before, deep into my eyes. Though I felt I could not fully understand the meaning of his gaze, I nodded my consent; and he gave a sigh of relief. Then, after pausing a few minutes until he was breathing easily once more, he went on:

"In order to make her happy you'll have to marry, but instead of marrying for your own sake you must marry for your mother's, to have someone who will help you take care of her. I've been thinking of Kajikawa's daughter Sawako. . . ."

Kajikawa was a gardener who had come to our house regularly for many years. (His father had been an apprentice of the man who laid out the garden at Heron's Nest.) We saw him frequently, since he and his helpers still worked in our garden several days a week. And we knew his daughter Sawako too: ever since she had been in Girls' High School she used to call on us once a year, on the day of the Aoi Festival.

Sawako had a fair complexion and a slender, oval face of the classic melon-seed shape, the kind of face you see in ukiyoye woodblock prints. I suppose some people would consider her beautiful. After graduating from high school, she began wearing extremely heavy make-up, and was even more striking. It had seemed to me that a girl with a lovely white skin needn't paint herself so; but the year before last she stopped by during the midsummer festival, after viewing the great bonfire in the Eastern Hills from the Kamo riverbank, and since she said she was hot we invited her to have a bath, which she did, reappearing later and passing so near me that I noticed a few freckles on her cheeks. That explains why she wears so much make-up, I thought. After that I didn't see her for a long time, but about ten days ago she and Kajikawa had come to pay a sick call. I found their visit rather disturbing. Father, who usually refused to see any visitors, asked that they be brought to his room and spent over twenty minutes talking with them. Realizing that something was up, I half expected what he had to say to me.

"I dare say you know a good deal about the girl," Father continued; and he gave me a brief description of how Sawako had been brought up and what she was like. But there was nothing particularly new to me, since I had been hearing about her for years. She was nineteen, my own age, having also been born in 1906; she was intelligent and talented, and had been graduated from Girls' High School three years ago with an excellent record; after graduation she had kept busy taking lessons of one kind or another, acquiring a range of accomplishments far beyond what one might have expected of a gardener's daughter. Thus she had all the qualifications to make a fine bride for any family—except that 1906 was the Year of the Fiery Horse, by the old calendar, and she was a victim of the superstition that women born in that year are shrews. As a result, she had not yet received an attractive offer of marriage.

All this was long since familiar to me, and Father concluded by asking me to take her as my wife. Then he added that both the girl and her parents would be delighted to accept such a proposal. "If you'll only agree to it, everything will be settled," he said. "But in that case there's one thing more I'd like to ask of you. If you have a child, send it elsewhere, just as your mother gave up her own child for your sake. There's no need to say anything to Sawako or her parents right away—you might as well keep this to yourself until the time comes when you have to tell them. The earlier you're married, the better. Have the ceremony as soon as the year of mourning is over. I can't think of a suitable go-between at the moment, but you and your mother can discuss that with Kajikawa and decide on someone."

After having talked for such a long time, Father closed his eyes and drew a deep breath. He seemed suddenly reassured that I would obey his wishes. Mother and I turned him on his back again.

The next day Father began to show symptoms of uremia. He could eat nothing whatever, his mind was hazy, and now and then he talked deliriously. He lived about three more days, until the beginning of October; but all that we could catch of his incoherent speech was my mother's name, "Chinu," and the broken phrase "the bridge . . . of dreams," a phrase he repeated over and over. Those were the last words I heard my father utter.

Okane had come back from the country in August to help us, and as soon as the Buddhist service of the Seventh Day was over she went home. Relatives we hadn't seen for years gathered at the house even for the services of the Thirty-fifth and Forty-ninth Days; but their number gradually dwindled until, on the Hundredth Day, only two or three people made an appearance.

The following spring I was graduated from higher school and entered the law department of the university. After the death of my unsociable father the guests who called at Heron's Nest, never very many, became so rare that at last there was hardly anyone but Sawako and her parents, who came about once a week. Mother would spend the whole day indoors, worshipping before Father's memorial tablet or, if she needed diversion, taking out my first mother's koto and playing it for a while. Because our house seemed so lonely and quiet now, she decided to start the bamboo mortar up again after its long silence; and she had Kajikawa cut a piece of green bamboo for it. Once again I could hear the familiar clack, clack that I had always loved.

Mother had borne up well while she was nursing Father the year before; even throughout the long series of Buddhist services that followed his death she always received our guests with dignity and self-control, and looked as full-cheeked and glowing with health as ever. But lately she seemed to show signs of fatigue, and sometimes had one of the maids massage her. Sawako offered her services whenever she was there.

One day when the silk tree was beginning to blossom I went out to the pavilion, knowing that I would find Mother and Sawako. Mother was lying in her usual place, on two cushions, while Sawako was energetically rubbing her arms.

"Sawako's good at massaging, isn't she?" I said.

"She's really wonderful!" Mother replied. "I don't know anyone who can equal her. She makes me so drowsy I almost drop off to sleep—it's a delicious feeling!"

"She *does* seem to know how to use her hands. Sawako, did you ever take lessons at this?"

"No, no lessons," she answered; "but I'm used to massaging my parents every day."

"That's what I thought," Mother said. "No wonder she'd put even a professional to shame. Tadasu, let her try it on you."

"I don't need a massage. But maybe I'll be her pupil and learn how to do it."

"Why should you learn?" asked Mother.

"Then I can massage you too. I ought to be able to learn that much."

"But your hands are too rough—"

"They're not rough, for a man. Isn't that so, Sawako? Just feel them!"

"Let's see," Sawako said, clasping my fingers in her own, and then stroking my palms. "My, you really do have nice smooth hands! You'll be fine!"

"It's because I've never gone in much for sports."

"Once you get the knack of it you'll soon be an expert!"

For some weeks after that I had Sawako teach me the various massaging techniques, and practiced them on Mother. Sometimes she got so ticklish that she shrieked with laughter.

In July the three of us would sit by the pond together to enjoy the cool of evening. Like my father, I would take a few bottles of beer to put under the spout of the bamboo mortar. Mother drank too, several glasses if I urged her; but Sawako always refused.

Mother would dangle her bare feet in the water, saying: "Sawako, you ought to try this. It makes you delightfully cool!"

But Sawako would sit there primly in her rather formal summer dress, with a heavy silk sash bound tightly around her waist. "Your feet are so pretty!" she would say. "I couldn't possibly show ugly ones like mine beside them!"

It seemed to me that she was too reserved. She might have been a little freer and more intimate with someone who would eventually become her mother-in-law. But she seemed too solicitous, too eager to please; often her words had a tinge of insincerity. Even her attitude toward me was curiously old-fashioned, for a girl who had been graduated from high school. Perhaps marriage would change her, but at the moment I couldn't help feeling that our relations were those of master and servant. Of course, it may have been precisely that quality in her which appealed to my father, and no doubt Mother's strength and firmness made her seem retiring, by contrast. Yet she seemed inadequate, somehow, for a young girl who was to become the third member of our small family.

A month or two after the silk-tree and pomegranate blossoms had fallen, when the crape myrtle was beginning to bloom and the plantain ripening, I had become fairly skillful at massaging and often asked Mother to come out to the pavilion for a treatment.

"A few minutes then, if you like," she would reply.

Naturally I took Sawako's place whenever she wasn't there, but even when she was with us I would brush her aside and say: "Let me try it—you watch!" Unable to forget the days when Mother had given her breasts to me, I now found my sole pleasure in massaging her. It was around then that Sawako, who had always worn her hair in Western style, began having it done up in a traditional high-piled Shimada, a coiffure that set off beautifully her ukiyoye-like face. She appeared to be getting ready for the Buddhist service that would be held on the first anniversary of my father's death, a time which was drawing near. Mother herself ordered new clothes for the occasion: among them, a formal robe of dark purple figured satin with a hollyhock pattern on the skirt, and a broad sash of thick-woven white silk dyed with a pattern of the seven autumn flowers.

The anniversary service was held at a temple at Hyakumamben, and we had dinner served in the reception hall of its private quarters. Both Mother and I noticed how cold and distant my relatives were. Some of them left as soon as they had burned incense, without stopping to join us at dinner. Ever since Father had married a former entertainer my relatives had held an oddly hostile and disdainful attitude toward our family. And now, to make matters worse, I was engaged to marry the gardener's daughter: it was only to be expected that they would talk. Still, I hadn't thought they would treat us quite so brusquely. Mother carried it off with her usual aplomb; but Sawako, who had gone to great trouble to dress appropriately for the occasion, seemed so dejected that I had to feel sorry for her.

"I'm beginning to wonder how our wedding will turn out," I said to Mother. "Do you suppose those people will come?"

"Why should you worry? You're not getting married for *their* benefit—it's enough if you and I and Sawako are happy." Mother seemed unconcerned, but before long I discovered that the hostility of our relatives was even more bitter than I had imagined.

Okane, who had come from Nagahama for the service, stayed with us a few days before going home. On the morning of the day she left, she suggested we go for another walk through the shrine forest.

"Okane, do you have something to tell me?" I asked.

"Yes, I do."

"I think I know what it is. It's about my wedding, isn't it?"

"That's not the only thing."

"Then what is it?"

"Well . . . but you mustn't get angry, Tadasu."

"I won't. Go ahead and say it."

"Anyway, you're sure to hear about it from somebody, so I guess it ought to come from me." Then, little by little, she told me the following story.

Of course it was true that my relatives were opposed to my forthcoming marriage, but that wasn't the only reason why they disapproved of us. Mother and I were the objects of their criticism, more than the match with Kajikawa's daughter. To put it bluntly, they believed that we were committing incest. According to them, Okane said, Mother and I began carrying on that way while Father was still alive, and Father himself, once he knew he wouldn't recover, had tolerated it—even encouraged it. Some went so far as to ask whose baby had been smuggled out to Tamba, suggesting that Takeshi was my own child, not my father's.

I wondered how on earth these people, who had been avoiding us for years, could have heard anything that would make them spread such wild rumors. But Okane explained that everyone in our neighborhood had been gossiping this way about us for a long time. It seems they all knew that Mother and I spent many hours alone together in the Silk-Tree Pavilion, which is probably why the rumors began to circulate. My relatives thought that my dying father arranged for me to marry Sawako because only a girl with her disadvantages would accept such a match. Most scandalous of all, his reason for wanting me to keep up appearances by taking a wife was presumably to have me continue my immoral relationship with Mother. Kajikawa was well aware of these circumstances in giving his daughter, and Sawako was going to marry out of respect for her father's wishes—needless to say, they had their eyes on our property. And so my relatives were outraged first of all by my father's part in this, then by Mother's, by mine, by Kajikawa's, and by his daughter's, in that order.

"Tadasu, be careful!" Okane ended by warning me. "Everybody knows people will talk, but they can say terrible things!" And she gave me a strange look out of the corner of her eye.

"Let them say what they please," I answered. "Nasty rumors like that will soon be forgotten."

"Well, maybe they'll come to the wedding next month after all," she said doubtfully as we parted.

I have no interest in going into detail about later events. But perhaps I should summarize the important ones.

Our wedding ceremony was held on an auspicious day in November of that year. To please Mother, I wore a crested black silk kimono of Father's instead of a morning coat. Hardly any of my relatives appeared for the wedding; even the ones on Mother's side stayed away. Those who came were chiefly persons related to the Kajikawa family. Dr. Kato and his wife were kind enough to act as go-between. The doctor had been taking lessons in the No drama for many years, and he was more than happy to oblige by chanting the usual lines from *Takasago.* But as I listened to his sonorous voice my thoughts were far away.

After our marriage, Sawako's attitude toward Mother and me showed no particular change. We spent a few days in Nara and Isé for our honeymoon, but I was always careful to take precautions against having a child—that was one thing I never neglected. On the surface, Mother appeared to get along with her newly wed son and daughter-in-law in perfect harmony. After Father's death, she had continued to sleep in the twelve-mat veranda room, and she stayed there even after Sawako came; Sawako and I slept in my little six-mat room. That was as it should be, we felt, since I was still going to school and was still a dependent. For the same reason, Mother was in charge of all the household accounts.

As for Mother's life in those days, anyone would have taken it to be enviably carefree and leisurely. She amused herself by practicing Konoé-style calligraphy, reading classical Japanese literature, playing the koto, or strolling in the garden; and whenever she felt tired, day or night, she would have one of us give her a massage. During the day she had her massages in the pavilion, but at night she always called Sawako to her bedroom. Occasionally the three of us would go out to the theater, or on an excursion; but Mother was inclined to be frugal and paid close attention to even trivial sums of money, warning us to do our best to avoid needless expense. She was especially strict with Sawako and caused her a good deal of worry over the food bills. Mother was looking fresher and more youthful than ever, and so plump that she was beginning to get a double chin. Indeed, she was almost too plump—as if now that Father was dead her worries were over.

Our life went on in that way while I finished two more years at the university. Then about eleven o'clock one night in late June, shortly after I had gone to bed, I found myself being shaken by Sawako and told to get up.

"It's your mother!" she exclaimed, hurrying me off toward the other bedroom. "Something dreadful has happened!"

"Mother!" I called. "What's wrong?" There was no reply. She was lying there face down, moaning weakly and clutching her pillow with both hands.

"I'll show you what did it!" Sawako said, picking up a round fan from the floor near the head of the bed to reveal a large crushed centipede. Sawako explained that Mother had wanted a massage, and she had been giving her one for almost an hour. Mother was lying on her back asleep, breathing evenly, as Sawako rubbed her legs all the way down to her ankles. Suddenly she gave a scream of pain, and her feet arched convulsively. When Sawako looked up in alarm she saw a centipede crawling across Mother's breast, near the heart. Startled into action, she snatched up a nearby fan and brushed the insect away, luckily flicking it to the floor, where she covered it with the fan and then crushed it.

"If I'd only paid more attention . . ." Sawako said, looking deadly pale. "I was so busy massaging her . . ."

Dr. Kato came over immediately and took emergency measures, giving one injection after another; but Mother's suffering seemed to increase by the moment. All her symptoms—her color, breathing, pulse, and the rest—showed that her condition was more serious than we had thought. Dr. Kato stayed by her side, doing his best to save her; but around dawn she took a turn for the worse, and died soon afterward.

"It must have been shock," Dr. Kato told us.

Sawako was weeping aloud. "I'm to blame, I'm to blame," she kept repeating.

I have no intention of trying to describe the feelings of horror, grief, despair, dejection, which swept over me then; nor do I think it reflects credit on myself to be suspicious of anyone without a shred of evidence. Yet I cannot escape certain nagging doubts. . . .

It was some forty years since my grandfather had built the house he called Heron's Nest, which was by then at its most beautiful, well seasoned, with the patina of age that suits a Japanese-style building of this kind. In Grandfather's day the wood must have been too new to have such character, and as it grows older it will doubtless lose its satiny luster. The one really old building at Heron's Nest was the teahouse that Grandfather had brought there; and during my childhood, as I have said, it was infested by centipedes. But after that centipedes began to be seen frequently both in the pavilion and in the main house. There was nothing strange about finding one of them in the veranda room, where Mother was sleeping. Probably she had often seen centipedes in her room before, and Sawako, who was always going in to massage her, must have had the same experience. And so I wonder if Mother's death was entirely accidental. Might not someone have had a scheme in mind for using a centipede, if one of them appeared? Perhaps it was only a rather nasty joke, with no thought that a mere insect bite could be fatal. But supposing that her weak heart had been taken into account, that the possibility had seemed attractive. . . . Even if the scheme failed, no one could prove that the centipede had been deliberately caught and placed there.

Maybe the centipede did crawl onto her by accident. But Mother was a person who fell asleep very easily: whenever we massaged her she relaxed and dropped off into a sound sleep. She disliked a hard massage, preferring to have us stroke her so lightly and gently that her sleep was not disturbed. It would have been quite possible for someone to put a small object on her body without immediately awakening her. When I ran into her room, she was lying face-down writhing with pain; but Sawako said that earlier she had been lying on her back. I found it hard to believe that Sawako, who was massaging her legs, saw the centipede on Mother's breast the moment she looked up. Mother wasn't lying there naked; she was wearing her night kimono. It was odd that Sawako happened to see the insect—surely it would have been crawling under the kimono, out of sight. Perhaps she knew it was there.

I wish to emphasize that this is purely my own assumption, nothing more. But because this notion has become so firmly lodged in my mind, has haunted me for so long, I have at last tried to set it down in writing. After all, I intend to keep this record secret as long as I live.

Three more years have passed since then.

When I finished school two years ago, I was given a job as a clerk at the bank of which Father had been a director; and last spring, for reasons of my own, I divorced Sawako. A number of difficult conditions were proposed by her family, and in the end I had to agree to their terms. The whole complicated affair was so unpleasant that I have no desire to write about it. At the same time that I took steps to be divorced I sold Heron's Nest, so full of memories for me, both happy and sad, and built a small house for myself near the Honen Temple. I had Takeshi come to live with me, insisting on bringing him back from Seriu in spite of his own reluctance as well as that of his foster parents. And I asked Okane, who was quietly living out her days at Nagahama, to come and look after him, at least for a few years. Fortunately, she is still in good health, at sixty-four, and still able to take care of children. "If that's what you want, I'll help out with the little boy," she said, and left her comfortable retirement to come and live with us. Takeshi is six. At first he refused to be won over by Okane and me, but now we have become very close. Next year he will begin going to school. What makes me happiest is that he looks exactly like Mother. Not only that, he seems to have inherited something of her calm, open, generous temperament. I have no wish to marry again: I simply want to go on living as long as possible with Takeshi, my one link with Mother. Because my real mother died when I was a child, and my father and stepmother when I was some years older, I want to live for Takeshi until he is grown. I want to spare him the loneliness I knew.

June 27, 1931 (the anniversary of Mother's death)

Otokuni Tadasu

for Love

A TREE. A ROCK. A CLOUD

by Carson McCullers

It was raining that morning, and still very dark. When the boy reached the streetcar café he had almost finished his route and he went in for a cup of coffee. The place was an all-night café owned by a bitter and stingy man called Leo. After the raw, empty street the café seemed friendly and bright: along the counter there were a couple of soldiers, three spinners from the cotton mill, and in a corner a man who sat hunched over with his nose and half his face down in a beer mug. The boy wore a helmet such as aviators wear. When he went into the café he unbuckled the chin strap and raised the right flap up over his pink little ear; often as he drank his coffee someone would speak to him in a friendly way. But this morning Leo did not look into his face and none of the men were talking. He paid and was leaving the café when a voice called out to him:

"Son! Hey Son!"

He turned back and the man in the corner was crooking his finger and nodding to him. He had brought his face out of the beer mug and he seemed suddenly very happy. The man was long and pale, with a big nose and faded orange hair.

"Hey Son!"

The boy went toward him. He was an undersized boy of about twelve, with one shoulder drawn higher than the other because of the weight of the paper sack. His face was shallow, freckled, and his eyes were round child eyes.

"Yeah Mister?"

The man laid one hand on the paper boy's shoulders, then grasped the boy's chin and turned his face slowly from one side to the other. The boy shrank back uneasily.

"Say! What's the big idea?"

From *The Ballad of the Sad Café*, by Carson McCullers (Boston: Houghton Mifflin, 1955), pp. 129–39. Copyright 1955 by Carson McCullers. Reprinted by permission of the publisher, Houghton Mifflin Company, and the author.

The boy's voice was shrill; inside the café it was suddenly very quiet.

The man said slowly: "I love you."

All along the counter the men laughed. The boy, who had scowled and sidled away, did not know what to do. He looked over the counter at Leo, and Leo watched him with a weary, brittle jeer. The boy tried to laugh also. But the man was serious and sad.

"I did not mean to tease you, Son," he said. "Sit down and have a beer with me. There is something I have to explain."

Cautiously, out of the corner of his eye, the paper boy questioned the men along the counter to see what he should do. But they had gone back to their beer or their breakfast and did not notice him. Leo put a cup of coffee on the counter and a little jug of cream.

"He is a minor," Leo said.

The paper boy slid himself up onto the stool. His ear beneath the up-turned flap of the helmet was very small and red. The man was nodding at him soberly. "It is important," he said. Then he reached in his hip pocket and brought out something which he held up in the palm of his hand for the boy to see.

"Look very carefully," he said.

The boy stared, but there was nothing to look at very carefully. The man held in his big, grimy palm a photograph. It was the face of a woman, but blurred, so that only the hat and the dress she was wearing stood out clearly.

"See?" the man asked.

The boy nodded and the man placed another picture in his palm. The woman was standing on a beach in a bathing suit. The suit made her stomach very big, and that was the main thing you noticed.

"Got a good look?" He leaned over closer and finally asked: "You ever seen her before?"

The boy sat motionless, staring slantwise at the man. "Not so I know of."

"Very well." The man blew on the photographs and put them back into his pocket. "That was my wife."

"Dead?" the boy asked.

Slowly the man shook his head. He pursed his lips as though about to whistle and answered in a long-drawn way: "Nuuu—" he said. "I will explain."

The beer on the counter before the man was in a large brown mug. He did not pick it up to drink. Instead he bent down and, putting his face over the rim, he rested there for a moment. Then with both hands he tilted the mug and sipped.

"Some night you'll go to sleep with your big nose in a mug and drown," said Leo. "Prominent transient drowns in beer. That would be a cute death."

The paper boy tried to signal to Leo. While the man was not looking he screwed up his face and worked his mouth to question soundlessly: "Drunk?" But Leo only raised his eyebrows and turned away to put some pink strips of bacon on the grill. The man pushed the mug away from him, straightened himself, and folded his loose crooked hands on the counter. His face was sad as he looked at the paper boy. He did not blink, but from time to time the lids closed down with delicate gravity over his pale green eyes. It was nearing dawn and the boy shifted the weight of the paper sack.

"I am talking about love," the man said. "With me it is a science."

The boy half slid down from the stool. But the man raised his forefinger, and there was something about him that held the boy and would not let him go away.

"Twelve years ago I married the woman in the photograph. She was my wife for one year, nine months, three days, and two nights. I loved her. Yes . . ." He tightened his blurred, rambling voice and said again: "I loved her. I thought also that she loved me. I was a railroad engineer. She had all home comforts and luxuries. It never crept into my brain that she was not satisfied. But do you know what happened?"

"Mgneeow!" said Leo.

The man did not take his eyes from the boy's face. "She left me. I came in one night and the house was empty and she was gone. She left me."

"With a fellow?" the boy asked.

Gently the man placed his palm down on the counter. "Why naturally, Son. A woman does not run off like that alone."

The café was quiet, the soft rain black and endless in the street outside. Leo pressed down the frying bacon with the prongs of his long fork. "So you have been chasing the floozie for eleven years. You frazzled old rascal!"

For the first time the man glanced at Leo. "Please don't be vulgar. Besides, I was not speaking to you." He turned back to the boy and said in a trusting and secretive undertone: "Let's not pay any attention to him. O.K.?"

The paper boy nodded doubtfully.

"It was like this," the man continued. "I am a person who feels many things. All my life one thing after another has impressed me. Moonlight. The leg of a pretty girl. One thing after another. But the point is that when I had enjoyed anything there was a peculiar sensation as though it was laying around loose in me. Nothing seemed to finish itself up or fit in with the other things. Women? I had my portion of them. The same. Afterwards laying around loose in me. I was a man who had never loved."

Very slowly he closed his eyelids, and the gesture was like a curtain drawn at the end of a scene in a play. When he spoke again his voice was excited and the words came fast—the lobes of his large, loose ears seemed to tremble.

"Then I met this woman. I was fifty-one years old and she always said she was thirty. I met her at a filling station and we were married within three days. And do you know what it was like? I just can't tell you. All I had ever felt was gathered together around this woman. Nothing lay around loose in me any more but was finished up by her."

The man stopped suddenly and stroked his long nose. His voice sank down to a steady and reproachful undertone: "I'm not explaining this right. What happened was this. There were these beautiful feelings and loose little pleasures inside me. And this woman was something like an assembly line for my soul. I run these little pieces of myself through her and I come out complete. Now do you follow me?"

"What was her name?" the boy asked.

"Oh," he said. "I called her Dodo. But that is immaterial."

"Did you try to make her come back?"

The man did not seem to hear. "Under the circumstances you can imagine how I felt when she left me."

Leo took the bacon from the grill and folded two strips of it between a bun. He had a gray face, with slitted eyes, and a pinched nose saddled by faint blue shadows. One of the mill workers signaled for more coffee and Leo poured it. He did not give refills on coffee free. The spinner ate breakfast there every morning, but the better Leo knew his customers the stingier he treated them. He nibbled his own bun as though he grudged it to himself.

"And you never got hold of her again?"

The boy did not know what to think of the man, and his child's face was uncertain with mingled curiosity and doubt. He was new on the paper route; it was still strange to him to be out in the town in the black, queer early morning.

"Yes," the man said. "I took a number of steps to get her back. I went around trying to locate her. I went to Tulsa where she had folks. And to Mobile. I went to every town she had ever mentioned to me, and I hunted down every man she had formerly been connected with. Tulsa, Atlanta, Chicago, Cheehaw, Memphis. . . . For the better part of two years I chased around the country trying to lay hold of her."

"But the pair of them had vanished from the face of the earth!" said Leo.

"Don't listen to him," the man said confidentially. "And also just forget those two years. They are not important. What matters is that around the third year a curious thing begun to happen to me."

"What?" the boy asked.

The man leaned down and tilted his mug to take a sip of beer. But as he hovered over the mug his nostrils fluttered slightly; he sniffed the staleness of the beer and did not drink. "Love is a curious thing to begin with. At first I thought only of getting her back. It was a kind of mania. But then as time went on I tried to remember her. But do you know what happened?"

"No," the boy said.

"When I laid myself down on a bed and tried to think about her my mind became a blank. I couldn't see her. I would take out her pictures and look. No good. Nothing doing. A blank. Can you imagine it?"

"Say Mac!" Leo called down the counter. "Can you imagine this bozo's mind a blank!"

Slowly, as though fanning away flies, the man waved his hand. His green eyes were concentrated and fixed on the shallow little face of the paper boy.

"But a sudden piece of glass on a sidewalk. Or a nickel tune in a music box. A shadow on a wall at night. And I would remember. It might happen in a street and I would cry or bang my head against a lamppost. You follow me?"

"A piece of glass . . ." the boy said.

"Anything. I would walk around and I had no power of how and when to remember her. You think you can put up a kind of shield. But remembering don't come to a man face forward—it corners around sideways. I was at the mercy of everything I saw and heard. Suddenly instead of me combing the countryside to find her she began to chase me around in my very soul. *She* chasing *me,* mind you! And in my soul."

The boy asked finally: "What part of the country were you in then?"

"Ooh," the man groaned. "I was a sick mortal. It was like smallpox. I confess, Son, that I boozed. I fornicated. I committed any sin that suddenly appealed to me. I am loath to confess it but I will do so. When I recall that period it is all curdled in my mind, it was so terrible."

The man leaned his head down and tapped his forehead on the counter. For a few seconds he stayed bowed over in this position, the back of his stringy neck covered with orange furze, his hands with their long warped fingers held palm to palm in an attitude of prayer. Then the man straightened himself; he was smiling and suddenly his face was bright and tremulous and old.

"It was in the fifth year that it happened," he said. "And with it I started my science."

Leo's mouth jerked with a pale, quick grin. "Well none of we boys are getting any younger," he said. Then with sudden anger he balled up a dishcloth he was holding and threw it down hard on the floor. "You draggle-tailed old Romeo!"

"What happened?" the boy asked.

The old man's voice was high and clear: "Peace," he answered.

"Huh?"

"It is hard to explain scientifically, Son," he said. "I guess the logical explanation is that she and I had fleed around from each other for so long that finally we just got tangled up together and lay down and quit. Peace. A queer and beautiful blankness. It was spring in Portland and the rain came every afternoon. All evening I just stayed there on my bed in the dark. And that is how the science come to me."

The windows in the streetcar were pale blue with light. The two soldiers paid for their beers and opened the door—one of the soldiers combed his hair and wiped off his muddy puttees before they went outside. The three mill workers bent silently over their breakfasts. Leo's clock was ticking on the wall.

"It is this. And listen carefully. I meditated on love and reasoned it out. I realized what is wrong with us. Men fall in love for the first time. And what do they fall in love with?"

The boy's soft mouth was partly open and he did not answer.

"A woman," the old man said. "Without science, with nothing to go by, they undertake the most dangerous and sacred experience in God's earth. They fall in love with a woman. Is that correct, Son?"

"Yeah," the boy said faintly.

"They start at the wrong end of love. They begin at the climax. Can you wonder it is so miserable? Do you know how men should love?"

The old man reached over and grasped the boy by the collar of his leather jacket. He gave him a gentle little shake and his green eyes gazed down and unblinking and grave.

"Son, do you know how love should be begun?"

The boy sat small and listening and still. Slowly he shook his head. The old man leaned closer and whispered:

"A tree. A rock. A cloud!"

It was still raining outside in the street: a mild, gray, endless rain. The mill whistle blew for the six o'clock shift and the three spinners paid and went away. There was no one in the café but Leo, the old man, and the little paper boy.

"The weather was like this in Portland," he said. "At the time my science was begun. I meditated and I started very cautious. I would pick up something from the street and take it home with me. I bought a goldfish and I concentrated on the goldfish and I loved it. I graduated from one thing to another. Day by day I was getting this technique. On the road from Portland to San Diego—"

"Aw shut up!" screamed Leo suddenly. "Shut up! Shut up!"

The old man still held the collar of the boy's jacket; he was trembling and his face was earnest and bright and wild. "For six years now I have gone around by myself and built up my science. And now I am a master. Son, I can love anything. No longer do I have to think about it even. I see a street full of people and a beautiful light comes in me. I watch a bird in the sky. Or I meet a traveler on the road. Everything, Son. And anybody. All stranger and all loved! Do you realize what a science like mine can mean?"

The boy held himself stifly, his hands curled tight around the counter edge. Finally he asked: "Did you ever really find that lady?"

"What? What say, Son?"

"I mean," the boy asked timidly. "Have you fallen in love with a woman again?"

The old man loosened his grasp on the boy's collar. He turned away and for the first time his green eyes had a vague and scattered look. He lifted the mug from the counter, drank down the yellow beer. His head was shaking slowly from side to side. Then finally he answered: "No, Son. You see that is the last step in my science. I go cautious. And I am not quite ready yet."

"Well!" said Leo. "Well well well!"

The old man stood in the open doorway. "Remember," he said. Framed there in the gray damp light of the early morning he looked shrunken and seedy and frail. But his smile was bright. "Remember I love you," he said with a last nod. And the door closed quietly behind him.

The boy did not speak for a long time. He pulled down the bangs on his forehead and slid his grimy little forefinger around the rim of his empty cup. Then without looking at Leo he finally asked:

"Was he drunk?"

"No," said Leo shortly.

The boy raised his clear voice higher. "Then was he a dope fiend?"

"No."

The boy looked up at Leo, and his flat little face was desperate, his voice urgent and shrill. "Was he crazy? Do you think he was a lunatic?" The paper boy's voice dropped suddenly with doubt. "Leo? Or not?"

But Leo would not answer him. Leo had run a night café for fourteen years, and he held himself to be a critic of craziness. There were the town characters and also the transients who roamed in from the night. He knew the manias of all of them. But he did not want to satisfy the questions of the waiting child. He tightened his pale face and was silent.

So the boy pulled down the right flap of his helmet and as he turned to leave he made the only comment that seemed safe to him, the only remark that could not be laughed down and despised:

"He sure has done a lot of traveling."

Transformation

THE belief that gods have the power of assuming other forms is common to many mythologies and religions: the Greek deities, especially Zeus, frequently changed themselves into animals for particular purposes, and transformation is implicit in the Christian concept of the Trinity and the transfiguration and ascension of Christ. In one of the stories that follows, an eighteenth-century Chinese tale entitled "The Spirit of the River," a river-god assumes the form of a small child so as to enjoy the company of the fisherman to whom he has taken a liking. Nor was this power, in many cultures, the exclusive prerogative of Deity: Circe, though a mortal, filled her palace with beasts who had formerly been men and whom she had converted into animals by her magic; and she was able to change Odysseus' men into swine. The belief that certain individuals have the power of changing themselves or others into other human beings, animals, plants, and even inanimate objects, exists today among primitive people; even in so-called civilized society the belief in witches and their ability to assume animal forms enjoyed religious sanction in Europe and America as late as the seventeenth century.

The theme is obviously archetypal. J. A. MacCulloch writes:

> An examination of the enormous mass of evidence for the belief in metamorphosis suggests that man's idea of personality, or perhaps rather of the forms in which personality may lurk, is an extremely fluid one. There has everywhere been a stage of human thought when no clear distinction was drawn between man and the rest of the universe, between human and animal, between animate and inanimate. In this stage of thought animate and inanimate are equally believed to be alive; men, animals, and things have the same feelings and passions, or act and speak in the same manner. Or, when the idea of soul or spirit is attained, all are equally alive by virtue of the possession of such a soul or spirit . . . Where the idea of spirit or soul exists, and where it is thought that the spirit can leave

> its containing body, nothing is easier than to believe further that it can enter for a time into an animal or a tree.[1]

In folklore, perhaps the commonest manifestation of this belief in physical transformation is the universal superstition involving werewolves. Sir James Frazer writes:

> It is commonly supposed that certain men and women can transfer themselves by magic art into wolves or other animals, but that any wound inflicted on such a transformed beast (a were-wolf or other were-animal) is simultaneously inflicted on the human body of the witch or warlock who had transformed himself into the creature. This belief is widely diffused; it meets us in Europe, Asia, and Africa.[2]

Among the many cases he cites is the typical one wherein a werewolf is trapped in the streets of an Italian city; when his four paws are cut off, he changes into a man whose hands and feet have been amputated. Because of this vulnerability a man who transformed himself into an animal had to take great care, and the risk was apparently equal in the case of animals who transformed themselves into human beings. In Isaac Bashevis Singer's story "Blood" we thus have a contemporary treatment of one of the oldest of all folk themes when Risha finally becomes a werewolf.

Another contemporary treatment of the transformation theme is seen in "The Sailor-Boy's Tale," by Isak Dinesen. MacCulloch notes that while few men believe that they themselves possess the power of transformation, all who believe in it think that others may possess it: "Hence we have beliefs in the existence of distant tribes or groups possessing the power." It is understandable that some Scandinavians used to credit the isolated Lapps who clung to their own customs and beliefs with mysterious and magical powers. Speaking of the Lapp religion, U. Holmberg says:

> The mediators between mankind and the spiritual world were *noaide*. This spirit-company was called *noaide-gaddse* ("shaman retinue")—a name which is often given to certain animals who helped the shaman during his spirit journey. From the close connection in which such animals stand to their masters, it is probable that it was the shaman's own soul that, severed from the body, could put on different shapes: as a reindeer it hastened over hills, as a bird it flew through space.[3]

---

1 J. A. MacCulloch, "Bible in the Church: Textual Criticism," James Hastings (ed.), *The Encyclopaedia of Religion and Ethics* (New York: Scribner, 1928), Vol. XI, pp. 593–594.

2 Sir James G. Frazer, *The Golden Bough* (New York: Macmillan, 1935), Vol. I, Part 7, p. 317.

3 U. Holmberg, "Lapps: Nature Gods," *Encyclopaedia of Religion and Ethics*, *op. cit.*, Vol. VII, p. 799.

This comment may help to illuminate some of the strange events in Isak Dinesen's haunting tale.

Serpents, scarcely less than wolves and birds, are also frequently involved in transformation folklore. MacCulloch writes:

> In folk tales and myth, and occasionally in ritual, woman is brought into relation with the serpent, which is often her lover or husband. This is but one aspect of the world-wide myths in which an animal marries a woman, though frequently the animal is a god in disguise or a being now human, now animal, often as a result of enchantment.

Noting the similarity of this motif to that of Beauty and the Beast, he adds that often the serpent is "a youth bewitched to serpent form till a maiden releases him from the enchantment by kissing him or burning his snake-skin." [4] The reader will observe in the Sanskrit tale, "The Girl Who Married a Snake," that the Brahman is careful to burn the skin which his transformed son has left behind in the chest.

Whether physical transformation was believed to be accompanied by corresponding psychological changes—whether a man changing himself into an animal, for example, retained his human personality or exchanged it for the psychic identity of an animal—is a question that each culture apparently answered differently. Because physical transformation belongs to the realm of magic, it is not in itself the concern of psychology, but the belief in it, like the belief in supernatural occurrences generally, justifies itself on a symbolic level by gratifying a psychic need of some sort. Thus the idea of rebirth, a kind of transformation, is one that human beings generally find consoling, which is the reason why most of the mythologies and religions of the world have somehow made provision for it.

As for spiritual transformation, which does not require that we accept the supernatural—which is, in other words, unaccompanied by corresponding changes and which occurs within the lifetime of the individual—Jung distinguishes between two kinds: direct and indirect. In the direct type, the individual may experience renewal with or without any essential change of personality; an essential change (transmutation) is naturally more striking. In indirect transformation the individual participates in some rite that involves a transformation of substances, such as the Roman Catholic Mass, which represents a transformation of the Deity. Here the process takes place outside the individual and he participates in it indirectly.

Essential change of personality with spiritual transformation is dramatically illustrated in two stories in this section: March's "This Heavy Load" and Forster's "The Story of a Panic." The Forster story involves a case of spirit possession as well. In "Hejda," on the other hand, the transformation is temporary and the young woman undergoes

---

[4] MacCulloch, *op. cit.*, p. 409.

what Jung refers to as a "diminution of personality" [5] followed by an emphatic reversion to her original personality after her separation from her artist-husband.

Spiritual transformation is also possible on a collective scale, though Jung warns us that "a group experience takes place on a lower level of consciousness than the experience of an individual." He is generally pessimistic concerning collective psychic transformation,[6] but concedes that "there are also positive experiences, for instance a positive enthusiasm which spurs the individual to noble deeds, or an equally positive feeling of human solidarity." Such a positive experience is recorded in the strangely beautiful African story, "New Life at Kyerefaso." Stories on such themes, however, are by no means invariably successful: in "The Luck of Roaring Camp" by Bret Harte, a settlement of desperadoes is regenerated almost overnight because of the presence of an infant born illegitimately to one of the camp followers, but the story, which has a strong appeal for the sentimental reader, is something less than plausible.

It is probably no accident that examples of spiritual transformation occur more frequently in romantic than in realistic fiction. Hawthorne was particularly fond of this theme: one thinks of Donatello in *The Marble Faun,* of Chillingworth in *The Scarlet Letter,* and of Ethan Brand and Young Goodman Brown in the stories bearing those names as titles. In his "Rappaccini's Daughter," on the other hand, the evil doctor is unable to corrupt his daughter's soul but succeeds in poisoning her body. There is the famous case of Scrooge, in Dickens' *A Christmas Carol,* and the scarcely less famous one of Raskolnikov in Dostoyevsky's *Crime and Punishment*—and of Dmitri in *The Brothers Karamazov.* Tolstoy also treats the theme in his novel *Resurrection,* and in the short story "What Men Live By." Another very beautiful story of psychic transformation is "Japanese Quince," by John Galsworthy.

The archetypes of transformation frequently occur in combination with other archetypes. There is an obvious affinity with that of the Alter Ego (three of the five stories in that section involve cases of physical transformation), and March's "This Heavy Load," while essentially a story of spiritual transformation, also contains a Search theme.

---

[5] C. G. Jung, *The Archetypes and the Collective Unconscious* in *The Collected Works of C. G. Jung,* ed. by Sir Herbert Read *et al.* and trans. by R. F. C. Hull, Bollingen Series XX (Princeton: Princeton Univ. Press, 1959), Vol. 9, Part I, pp. 119–120.

[6] "If it is a very large group, the collective psyche will be more like the psyche of an animal, which is the reason why the ethical attitude of a large organization is always doubtful. The psychology of a large crowd inevitably sinks to the level of mob psychology." *Ibid.,* p. 125.

Physical

THE GIRL WHO MARRIED A SNAKE

from *The Panchatantra*

In Palace City lived a Brahman named Godly, whose childless wife wept bitterly when she saw the neighbors' youngsters. But one day the Brahman said: "Forget your sorrow, mother dear. See! When I was offering the sacrifice for birth of children, an invisible being said to me in the clearest words: 'Brahman, you shall have a son surpassing all mankind in beauty, character, and charm.' "

When she heard this, the wife felt her heart swell with supreme delight. "I only hope his promises come true," she said. Presently she conceived, and in course of time gave birth to a snake. When she saw him, she paid no attention to her companions, who all advised her to throw him away. Instead, she took him and bathed him, laid him with motherly tenderness in a large, clean box, and pampered him with milk, fresh butter, and other good things, so that before many days had passed, he grew to maturity.

But one day the Brahman's wife was watching the marriage festival of a neighbor's son, and the tears streamed down her face as she said to her husband: "I know that you despise me, because you do nothing about a marriage festival for my boy." "My good wife," answered he, "am I to go to the depths of the underworld and beseech Vasuki the serpent-king? Who else, you foolish woman, would give his own daughter to this snake?"

But when he had spoken, he was disturbed at seeing the utter woe in his wife's countenance. He therefore packed provisions for a long journey, and undertook foreign travel from love of his wife. In the course of some months he arrived at a spot called Kutkuta City in a distant land. There in the house of a kinsman whom he could visit with pleasure since each respected the other's character, he was hospitably received, was given a bath, food, and the like, and there he spent the night.

From *The Panchatantra*, translated by Arthur W. Ryder (Chicago: University of Chicago Press, 1956), pp. 177–81. Reprinted by permission of the University of Chicago Press.

Now at dawn, when he paid his respects to his Brahman host and made ready to depart, the other asked him: "What was your purpose in coming hither? And where will your errand lead you?"

To this he replied: "I have come in search of a fit wife for my son." "In that case," said his host, "I have a very beautiful daughter, and my own person is yours to command. Pray take her for your son." So the Brahman took the girl with her attendants and returned to his own place.

But when the people of the country beheld her incomparable opulence of beauty, her supreme loveliness and superhuman graces, their eyes popped out with pleasure, and they said to her attendants: "How can right-thinking persons bestow such a pearl of a girl upon a snake?" On hearing this, all her elderly relatives without exception were troubled at heart, and they said: "Let her be taken from this imp-ridden creature." But the girl said: "No more of this mockery! Remember the text:

> Do once, only once, these three things:
> Once spoken, stands the word of kings;
> The speech of saints has no miscarriage;
> A maid is given once in marriage.

And again:

> All fated happenings, derived
>   From any former state,
> Must changeless stand: the very gods
>   Endured poor Blossom's fate."

Whereupon they all asked in chorus: "Who was this Blossom person?" And the girl told the story of

POOR BLOSSOM

God Indra once had a parrot named Blossom. He enjoyed supreme beauty, loveliness, and various graces, while his intelligence was not blunted by his extensive scientific attainments.

One day he was resting on the palm of great Indra's hand, his body thrilling with delight at that contact, and was reciting a variety of authoritative formulas, when he caught sight of Yama, lord of death, who had come to pay his respects at the time appointed. Seeing the god, the parrot edged away. And all the thronging immortals asked him: "Why did you move away, sir, upon beholding that personage?" "But," said the parrot, "he brings harm to all living creatures. Why not move away from him?"

Upon hearing this, they all desired to calm his fears, so said to Yama: "As a favor to us, you must please not kill this parrot." And Yama replied: "I do not know about that. It is Time who determines these matters."

They therefore took Blossom with them, paid a visit to Time, and made the same request. To which Time replied: "It is Death who is posted in these affairs. Pray speak to him."

But when they did so, the parrot died at the mere sight of Death. And they were all distressed at seeing the occurrence, so that they said to Yama: "What does this mean?" And Yama said: "It was simply fated that he should die at the mere sight of Death." With this reply they went back to heaven.

"And that is why I say:

> All fated happenings, ...

and the rest of it. Furthermore, I do not wish my father reproached for double dealing on the part of his daughter." When she had said this, she married the snake, with the permission of her companions, and at once began devoted attendance upon him by offering milk to drink and performing other services.

One night the serpent issued from the generous chest which had been set for him in her chamber, and entered her bed. "Who is this?" she cried. "He has the form of a man." And thinking him a strange man, she started up, trembling in every limb, unlocked the door, and was about to dart away when she heard him say: "Stay, my dear wife. I am your husband." Then, in order to convince her, he reentered the body which he had left behind in the chest, issued from it again, and came to her.

When she beheld him flashing with lofty diadem, with earrings, bracelets, armbands, and rings, she fell at his feet, and then they sank into a glad embrace.

Now his father, the Brahman, rose betimes and discovered how matters stood. He therefore seized the serpent's skin that lay in the chest, and consumed it with fire, for he thought: "I do not want him to enter that again." And in the morning he and his wife, with the greatest possible joy, introduced to everybody as their own an extraordinarily handsome son, quite wrapped up in his love affair.

BLOOD

by Isaac Bashevis Singer

I

The cabalists know that the passion for blood and the passion for flesh have the same origin, and this is the reason "Thou shalt not kill" is followed by "Thou shalt not commit adultery."

Reb Falik Ehrlichman was the owner of a large estate not far from the town of Laskev. He was born Reb Falik but because of his honesty in business his neighbors had called him *ehrlichman* for so long that it had become a part of his name. By his first wife Reb Falik had had two children, a son and a daughter, who had both died young and without issue. His wife had died too. In later years he had married again, according to the Book of Ecclesiastes: "In the morning sow thy seed, and in the evening withhold not thy hand." Reb Falik's second wife was thirty years younger than he and his friends had tried to dissuade him from the match. For one thing Risha had been widowed twice and was considered a man-killer. For another, she came of a coarse family and had a bad name. It was said of her that she had beaten her first husband with a stick, and that during the two years her second husband had lain paralyzed she had never called in a doctor. There was other gossip as well. But Reb Falik was not frightened by warnings or whisperings. His first wife, peace be with her, had been ill for a long time before she died of consumption. Risha, corpulent and strong as a man, was a good housekeeper and knew how to manage a farm. Under her kerchief she had a full head of red hair and eyes as green as gooseberries. Her bosom was high and she had the broad hips of a childbearer. Though she had not had children by either of her first two husbands, she contended it was their fault. She had a loud voice and when she laughed one could hear her from far off. Soon after marrying Reb Falik, she began to take charge: she sent away the old bailiff who drank and hired in his place a young and diligent one; she supervised the sowing, the reaping, the cattle breeding; she kept an eye on the peasants to make sure they did not steal eggs, chickens, honey from the hives. Reb Falik hoped Risha would bear him a son to recite Kaddish after his death, but the years passed without her becoming pregnant. She said he was too old. One day she took him with her to Laskev to the notary public where he signed all his property over to her.

From *Short Friday*, by Isaac Bashevis Singer (New York: Farrar, Straus & Giroux, 1964).

Reb Falik gradually ceased to attend to the affairs of the estate at all. He was a man of moderate height with a snowy white beard and rosy cheeks flushed with that half-faded redness of winter apples characteristic of affluent and meek old men. He was friendly to rich and poor alike and never shouted at his servants or peasants. Every spring before Passover he sent a load of wheat to Laskev for the poor, and in the fall after the Feast of Tabernacles he supplied the poorhouse with firewood for the winter as well as sacks of potatoes, cabbages, and beets. On the estate was a small study house which Reb Falik had built and furnished with a bookcase and Holy Scroll. When there were ten Jews on the estate to provide a quorum, they could pray there. After he had signed over all his possessions to Risha, Reb Falik sat almost all day long in this study house, reciting psalms, or sometimes dozing on the sofa in a side room. His strength began to leave him; his hands trembled; and when he spoke his head shook sidewise. Nearly seventy, completely dependent on Risha, he was, so to speak, already eating the bread of mercy. Formerly, the peasants could come to him for relief when one of their cows or horses wandered into his fields and the bailiff demanded payment for damages. But now that Risha had the upper hand, the peasant had to pay to the last penny.

On the estate there lived for many years a ritual slaughterer named Reb Dan, an old man who acted as beadle in the study house, and who, together with Reb Falik, studied a chapter of the Mishnah every morning. When Reb Dan died, Risha began to look about for a new slaughterer. Reb Falik ate a piece of chicken every evening for supper; Risha herself liked meat. Laskev was too far to visit every time she wanted an animal killed. Moreover, in both fall and spring, the Laskev road was flooded. Asking around, Risha heard that among the Jews in the nearby village of Krowica there was a ritual slaughterer named Reuben whose wife had died giving birth to their first child and who, in addition to being a butcher, owned a small tavern where the peasants drank in the evenings.

One morning Risha ordered one of the peasants to harness the britska in order to take her to Krowica to talk to Reuben. She wanted him to come to the estate from time to time to do their slaughtering. She took along several chickens and a gander in a sack so tight it was a wonder the fowl did not choke.

When she reached the village, they pointed out Reuben's hut near the smithy. The britska stopped and Risha, followed by the driver carrying the bag of poultry, opened the front door and went in. Reuben was not there but looking out a window into the courtyard behind she saw him standing by a flat ditch. A barefooted woman handed him a chicken which he slaughtered. Unaware he was being watched from his own house, Reuben was being playful with the woman. Jokingly, he swung the slaughtered chicken as if about to toss it into her face. When she handed him the penny fee, he clasped her wrist and held it. Meanwhile the chicken, its throat slit, fell to the ground where it fluttered about, flapping its wings in its attempt to fly and spattering Reuben's boots with blood. Finally the little rooster gave a last start and then lay still, one glassy eye and its slit neck facing up to God's heaven. The creature seemed to say: "See, Father in Heaven, what they have done to me. And still they make merry."

II

Reuben, like most butchers, was fat with a big stomach and a red neck. His throat was short and fleshy. On his cheeks grew bunches of pitch-black hair. His dark eyes held the cold look of those born under the sign of Mars. When he caught sight of Risha, mistress of the large neighboring estate, he became confused and his face turned even redder than it was. Hurriedly, the woman with him picked up the slaughtered bird and scurried away. Risha went into the courtyard, directing the peasant to set the sack with the fowl near Reuben's feet. She could see that he did not stand on his dignity, and she spoke to him lightly, half-jokingly, and he answered her in kind. When she asked if he would slaughter the birds in the sack for her, he answered: "What else should I do? Revive dead ones?" And when she remarked how important it was to her husband that his food be strictly kosher, he said: "Tell him he shouldn't worry. My knife is as smooth as a fiddle!"—and to show her he drew the bluish edge of the blade across the nail of his index finger. The peasant untied the sack and handed Reuben a yellow chicken. He promptly turned back its head, pulled a tuft of down from the center of its throat and slit it. Soon he was ready for the white gander.

"He's a tough one," said Risha. "All the geese were afraid of him."

"He won't be tough much longer," Reuben answered.

"Don't you have any pity?" Risha teased. She had never seen a slaughterer who was so deft. His hands were thick with short fingers matted with dense black hair.

"With pity, one doesn't become a slaughterer," answered Reuben. A moment later, he added, "When you scale a fish on the Sabbath, do you think the fish enjoys it?"

Holding the fowl, Reuben looked at Risha intently, his gaze traveling up and down her and finally coming to rest on her bosom. Still staring at her, he slaughtered the gander. Its white feathers grew red with blood. It shook its neck menacingly and suddenly went up in the air and flew a few yards. Risha bit her lip.

"They say slaughterers are destined to be born murderers but become slaughterers instead," Risha said.

"If you're so soft-hearted, why did you bring me the birds?" Reuben asked.

"Why? One has to eat meat."

"If someone has to eat meat, someone has to do the slaughtering."

Risha told the peasant to take away the fowl. When she paid Reuben, he took her hand and held it for a moment in his. His hand was warm and her body shivered pleasurably. When she asked him if he would be willing to come to the estate to slaughter, he said yes if in addition to paying him she would send a cart for him.

"I won't have any herd of cattle for you," Risha joked.

"Why not?" Reuben countered. "I have slaughtered cattle before.

In Lublin I slaughtered more in one day than I do here in a month," he boasted.

Since Risha did not seem to be in any hurry, Reuben asked her to sit down on a box and he himself sat on a log. He told her of his studies in Lublin and explained how he had happened to come to this God-forsaken village where his wife, peace be with her, had died in childbirth due to the lack of an experienced midwife.

"Why haven't you remarried?" Risha questioned. "There's no shortage of women—widows, divorcees, or young girls."

Reuben told her the matchmakers were trying to find him a wife but the destined one had not yet appeared.

"How will you know the one who is destined for you?" Risha asked.

"My stomach will know. She will grab me right here"—and Reuben snapped his fingers and pointed at his navel. Risha would have stayed longer, except that a girl came in with a duck. Reuben arose. Risha returned to the britska.

On the way back Risha thought about the slaughterer Reuben, his levity and his jocular talk. Though she came to the conclusion that he was thick-skinned and his future wife would not lick honey all her life, still she could not get him out of her mind. That night, retiring to her canopied bed across the room from her husband's, she tossed and turned sleeplessly. When she finally dozed off, her dreams both frightened and excited her. She got up in the morning full of desire, wanting to see Reuben as quickly as possible, wondering how she might arrange it, and worried that he might find some woman and leave the village.

Three days later Risha went to Krowica again even though the larder was still full. This time she caught the birds herself, bound their legs, and shoved them into the sack. On the estate was a black rooster with a voice clear as a bell, a bird famous for its size, its red comb, and its crowing. There was also a hen that laid an egg every day and always at the same spot. Risha now caught both of these creatures, murmuring, "Come, children, you will soon taste Reuben's knife," and as she said these words a tremor ran down her spine. She did not order a peasant to drive the britska but, harnessing the horse herself, went off alone. She found Reuben standing at the threshold of his house as if he were waiting impatiently for her, as in fact he was. When a male and a female lust after each other, their thoughts meet and each can foresee what the other will do.

Reuben ushered Risha in with all the formality due a guest. He brought her a pitcher of water, offered her liqueur and a slice of honey cake. He did not go into the courtyard but untrussed the fowl indoors. When he took out the black rooster, he exclaimed, "What a fine cavalier!"

"Don't worry. You will soon take care of him," said Risha.

"No one can escape my knife," Reuben assured her. He slaughtered the rooster on the spot. The bird did not exhale its spirit immediately but finally, like an eagle caught by a bullet, it slumped to the floor. Then Reuben set the knife down on the whetstone, turned, and came over to Risha. His face was pale with passion and the fire in his dark eyes frightened her. She felt as if he were about to slaughter her. He put his arms around her without a word and pressed her against his body.

"What are you doing? Have you lost your mind?" she asked.

"I like you," Reuben said hoarsely.

"Let me go. Somebody might come in," she warned.

"Nobody will come," Reuben assured her. He put up the chain on the door and pulled Risha into a windowless alcove.

Risha wrangled, pretending to defend herself, and exclaimed, "Woe is me. I'm a married woman. And you—a pious man, a scholar. We'll roast in Gehenna for this . . ." But Reuben paid no attention. He forced Risha down on his bench-bed and she, thrice married, had never before felt desire as great as on that day. Though she called him murderer, robber, highwayman, and reproached him for bringing shame to an honest woman, yet at the same time she kissed him, fondled him, and responded to his masculine whims. In their amorous play, she asked him to slaughter her. Taking her head, he bent it back and fiddled with his finger across her throat. When Risha finally arose, she said to Reuben: "You certainly murdered me that time."

"And you, me," he answered.

III

Because Risha wanted Reuben all to herself and was afraid he might leave Krowica or marry some younger woman, she determined to find a way to have him live on the estate. She could not simply hire him to replace Reb Dan, for Reb Dan had been a relative whom Reb Falik would have had to provide for in any case. To keep a man just to slaughter a few chickens every week did not make sense and to propose it would arouse her husband's suspicions. After puzzling for a while, Risha found a solution.

She began to complain to her husband about how little profit the crops were bringing; how meagre the harvests were; if things went on this way, in a few years they would be ruined. Reb Falik tried to comfort his wife saying that God had not forsaken him hitherto and that one must have faith, to which Risha retorted that faith could not be eaten. She proposed that they stock the pastures with cattle and open a butcher shop in Laskev —that way there would be a double profit both from the dairy and from the meat sold at retail. Reb Falik opposed the plan as impractical and beneath his dignity. He argued that the butchers in Laskev would raise a commotion and that the community would never agree to him, Reb Falik, becoming a butcher. But Risha insisted. She went to Laskev, called a meeting of the community elders, and told them that she intended to open a butcher shop. Her meat would be sold at two cents a pound less than the meat in the other shops. The town was in an uproar. The rabbi warned her he would prohibit the meat from the estate. The butchers threatened to stab anyone who interfered with their livelihood. But Risha was not daunted. In the first place she had influence with the government, for the *starosta* of the neighborhood had received many fine gifts from her, often visited her estate and went hunting in her wood. Moreover, she soon found allies among the Laskev poor who could not afford to buy much meat at the usual high prices. Many took her side, coachmen, shoemakers, tailors, furriers, potters, and they announced that if the butchers did her any violence, they would retaliate by burning the butcher shops. Risha invited a mob of them to the estate, gave them bottles of homemade beer from her brewery, and got them to promise her their support. Soon afterwards she rented a store in Laskev and employed Wolf Bonder, a fearless man known as a horse-thief and brawler. Every other day, Wolf Bonder drove to the estate with his horse and buggy to cart meat to the city. Risha hired Reuben to do the slaughtering.

For many months the new business lost money, the rabbi having proscribed Risha's meat. Reb Falik was ashamed to look the townspeople in the face, but Risha had the means and strength to wait for victory. Since her meat was cheap, the number of her customers increased steadily, and soon because of competition several butchers were forced to close their shops and of the two Laskev slaughterers, one lost his job. Risha was cursed by many.

The new business provided the cover Risha needed to conceal the sins she was committing on Reb Falik's estate. From the beginning it was her custom to be present when Reuben slaughtered. Often she helped him bind an ox or a cow. And her thirst to watch the cutting of throats and the shedding of blood soon became so mixed with carnal desire that she hardly knew where one began and the other ended. As soon as the business became profitable, Risha built a slaughtering shed and gave Reuben an apartment in the main house. She bought him fine clothes and he ate his meals at Reb Falik's table. Reuben grew sleeker and fatter. During the day he seldom slaughtered but wandered about in a silken robe, soft slippers on his feet, skullcap on his head, watching the peasants working in the fields, the shepherds caring for the cattle. He enjoyed all the pleasures of the outdoors and, in the afternoons, often went swimming in the river. The aging Reb Falik retired early. Late in the evening Reuben, accompanied by Risha, went to the shed where she stood next to him as he slaughtered and while the animal was throwing itself about in the anguish of its death throes she would discuss with him their next act of lust. Sometimes she gave herself to him immediately after the slaughtering. By then all the peasants were in their huts asleep except for one old man, half deaf and nearly blind, who aided them at the shed. Sometimes Reuben lay with her on a pile of straw in the shed, sometimes on the grass just outside, and the thought of the dead and dying creatures near them whetted their enjoyment. Reb Falik disliked Reuben. The new business was repulsive to him but he seldom said a word in opposition. He accepted the annoyance with humility, thinking that he would soon be dead anyway and what was the point of starting a quarrel? Occasionally it occurred to him that his wife was overly familiar with Reuben, but he pushed the suspicion out of his mind since he was by nature honest and righteous, a man who gave everyone the benefit of the doubt.

One transgression begets another. One day Satan, the father of all lust and cunning, tempted Risha to take a hand in the slaughtering. Reuben was alarmed when she first suggested this. True, he was an adulterer, but nevertheless he was also a believer as many sinners are. He argued that for their sins they would be whipped, but why should they lead other people into iniquity, causing them to eat non-kosher carcasses? No, God forbid he and Risha should do anything like that. To becoma a slaughterer it was necessary to study the *Shulchan Aruch* and the Commentaries. A slaughterer was responsible for any blemish on the knife, no matter how small, and for any sin one of his customers incurred by eating impure meat. But Risha was adamant. What difference did it make? she asked. They would both toss on the bed of needles anyhow. If one committed sins, one should get as much enjoyment as possible out of them. Risha kept after Reuben constantly, alternating threats and bribes. She promised him new excitements, presents, money. She swore that if he would let her slaughter, immediately upon Reb Falik's death she would marry him and sign over all her property so that he could redeem some part of his iniquity through acts of charity. Finally Reuben gave in. Risha took such pleasure in killing that before long she was doing all the slaughtering herself, with Reuben acting merely as her assistant. She began to cheat, to sell tallow for kosher fat, and she stopped extracting the forbidden sinews in the thighs of the cows. She began a price war with the other Laskev butchers until those who remained became her hired employees. She got the contract to supply meat to the Polish army barracks, and since the officers took bribes, and the soldiers received only the worst meat, she earned vast sums. Risha became so rich that even she did not know how large her fortune was. Her malice grew. Once she slaughtered a horse and sold it as kosher beef. She killed some pigs too, scalding them in boiling water like the pork butchers. She managed never to be caught. She got so much satisfaction from deceiving the community that this soon became as powerful a passion with her as lechery and cruelty.

Like all those who devote themselves entirely to the pleasures of the flesh, Risha and Reuben grew prematurely old. Their bodies became so swollen they could barely meet. Their hearts floated in fat. Reuben took to drink. He lay all day long on his bed, and when he woke drank liquor from a carafe with a straw. Risha brought him refreshments and they passed their time in idle talk, chattering as do those who have sold their souls for the vanities of this world. They quarreled and kissed, teased and mocked, bemoaned the fact that time was passing and the grave coming nearer. Reb Falik was now sick most of the time but, though it often seemed his end was near, somehow his soul did not forsake his body. Risha toyed with ideas of death and even thought of poisoning Reb Falik. Another time, she said to Reuben: "Do you know, already I am satiated with life! If you want, slaughter me and marry a young woman."

After saying this, she transferred the straw from Reuben's lips to hers and sucked until the carafe was empty.

IV

There is a proverb: Heaven and earth have sworn together that no secret can remain undivulged. The sins of Reuben and Risha could not stay hidden forever. People began to murmur that the two lived too well together. They remarked how old and feeble Reb Falik had become, how much oftener he stayed in bed than on his feet, and they concluded that Reuben and Risha were having an affair. The butchers Risha had forced to close their businesses had been spreading all kinds of calumny about her every since. Some of the more scholarly housewives found sinews in Risha's meat which, according to the Law, should have been removed. The Gentile butcher to whom Risha had been accustomed to sell the forbidden flanken complained that she had not sold him anything for months. With this evidence, the former butchers went in a body to the rabbi and community leaders and demanded an investigation of Risha's meat. But the council of elders was hesitant to start a quarrel with her. The rabbi quoted the Talmud to the effect that one who suspects the righteous deserves to be lashed, and added that, as long as there were no witnesses to any of Risha's transgressions, it was wrong to shame her, for the one who shames his fellow man loses his portion in the world to come.

The butcher, thus rebuffed by the rabbi, decided to hire a spy and they chose a tough youth named Jechiel. This young man, a ruffian, set out from Laskev one night after dark, stole into the estate, managing to avoid the fierce dogs Risha kept, and took up his position behind the slaughtering shed. Putting his eye to a large crack, he saw Reuben and Risha inside and watched with astonishmenat as the old servant led in the hobbled animals and Risha, using a rope, threw them one by one to the ground. When the old man left, Jechiel was amazed in the torchlight to see Risha catch up a long knife and begin to cut the throats of the cattle one after the other. The streaming blood gurgled and flowed. While the beasts were bleeding, Risha threw off all her clothes and stretched out naked on a pile of straw. Reuben came to her and they were so fat their bodies could barely join. They puffed and panted. Their wheezing mixed with the death-rattles of the animals made an unearthly noise; contorted shadows fell on the walls; the shed was saturated with the heat of blood. Jechiel was a hoodlum, but even he was terrified because only devils could behave like this. Afraid that fiends would seize him, he fled.

At dawn, Jechiel knocked on the rabbi's shutter. Stammering, he blurted out what he had witnessed. The rabbi roused the beadle and sent him with his wooden hammer to knock at the windows of the elders and summon them at once. At first no one believed Jechiel could be telling the truth. They suspected he had been hired by the butchers to bear false witness and they threatened him with beating and excommunication. Jechiel, to prove he was not lying, ran to the Ark of the Holy Scroll which stood in the Judgment Chamber, opened the door, and before those present could stop him swore by the Scroll that his words were true.

His story threw the town into a turmoil. Women ran out into the streets, striking their heads with their fists, crying and wailing. According to the evidence, the townspeople had been eating non-kosher meat for years. The wealthy housewives carried their pottery into the market place and broke it into shards. Some of the sick and several pregnant women fainted. Many of the pious tore their lapels, strewed their heads with ashes, and sat down to mourn. A crowd formed and ran to the butcher shops to punish the men who sold Risha's meat. Refusing to listen to what the butchers said in their own defense, they beat up several of them, threw whatever carcasses were on hand outdoors, and overturned the butcher blocks. Soon voices arose suggesting they go to Reb Falik's estate and the mob began to arm itself with bludgeons, rope, and knives. The rabbi, fearing bloodshed, came out into the street to stop them, warning that punishment must wait until the sin had been proved intentional and a verdict had been passed. But the mob wouldn't listen. The rabbi decided to go with them, hoping to calm them down on the way. The elders followed. Women trailed after them, pinching their cheeks and weeping as if at a funeral. Schoolboys dashed alongside.

Wolf Bonder, to whom Risha had given gifts and whom she had always paid well to cart the meat from the estate to Laskev, remained loyal to her. Seeing how ugly the temper of the crowd was becoming, he went to his stable, saddled a fast horse, and galloped out toward the estate to warn Risha. As it happened, Reuben and Risha had stayed overnight in the shed and were still there. Hearing hoofbeats, they got up and came out and watched with surprise as Wolf Bonder rode up. He explained what had happened and warned them of the mob on its way. He advised them to flee, unless they could prove their innocence; otherwise the angry men would surely tear them to pieces. He himself was afraid to stay any longer lest before he could get back the mob turn against him. Mounting his horse, he rode away at a gallop.

Reuben and Risha stood frozen with shock. Reuben's face turned a fiery red, then a deadly white. His hands trembled and he had to clutch at the door behind him to remain on his feet. Risha smiled anxiously and her face turned yellow as if she had jaundice, but it was Risha who moved first. Approaching her lover, she stared into his eyes. "So, my love," she said, "the end of a thief is the gallows."

"Let's run away." Reuben was shaking so violently that he could hardly get the words out.

But Risha answered that it was not possible. The estate had only six horses and all of them had been taken early that morning by peasants going to the forest for wood. A yoke of oxen would move so slowly that the rabble could overtake them. Besides, she, Risha, had no intention of abandoning her property and wandering like a beggar. Reuben implored her to flee with him, since life is more precious than all possessions, but Risha remained stubborn. She would not go. Finally they went into the main house where Risha rolled some linen up into a bundle for Reuben, gave him a roast chicken, a loaf of bread, and a pouch with some money. Standing outdoors, she watched as he set out, swaying and wobbling across the wooden bridge that led into the pine woods. Once in the forest he would strike the path to the Lublin road. Several times Reuben turned about-face, muttered and waved his hand as if calling her, but Risha stood impassively. She had already learned he was a coward. He was only a hero against a weak chicken and a tethered ox.

V

As soon as Reuben was out of sight, Risha moved towards the fields to call in the peasants. She told them to pick up axes, scythes, shovels, explained to them that a mob was on its way from Laskev, and promised each man a gulden and a pitcher of beer if he would help defend her. Risha herself seized a long knife in one hand and brandished a meat cleaver in the other. Soon the noise of the crowd could be heard in the distance and before long the mob was visible. Surrounded by her peasant guard, Risha mounted a hill at the entrance to the estate. When those who were coming saw peasants with axes and scythes, they slowed down. A few even tried to retreat. Risha's fierce dogs ran among them snarling, barking, growling.

The rabbi, seeing that the situation could lead only to bloodshed, demanded of his flock that they return home, but the tougher of the men refused to obey him. Risha called out taunting them: "Come on, let's see what you can do! I'll cut your heads off with this knife—the same knife I used on the horses and pigs I made you eat." When a man shouted that no one in Laskev would buy her meat anymore and that she would be excommunicated, Risha shouted back: "I don't need your money. I don't need your God either. I'll convert. Immediately!" And she began to scream in Polish, calling the Jews cursed Christ-killers and crossing herself as if she were already a Gentile. Turning to one of the peasants beside her, she said: "What are you waiting for, Maciek? Run and summon the priest. I don't want to belong to this filthy sect anymore." The peasant went and the mob became silent. Everyone knew that converts soon became enemies of Israel and invented all kinds of accusations against their former brethren. They turned away and went home. The Jews were afraid to instigate the anger of the Christians.

Meanwhile Reb Falik sat in his study house and recided the Mishnah. Deaf and half-blind, he saw nothing and heard nothing. Suddenly Risha entered, knife in hand, screaming: "Go to your Jews. What do I need a synagogue here for?" When Reb Falik saw her with her head uncovered, a knife in her hand, her face contorted by abuse, he was seized by such anguish that he lost his tongue. In his prayer shawl and phylacteries, he rose to ask her what had happened, but his feet gave way and he collapsed to the floor dead. Risha ordered his body placed in an ox cart and she sent his corpse to the Jews in Laskev without even linen for a shroud. During the time the Laskev Burial Society cleansed and laid out Reb Falik's body, and while the burial was taking place and the rabbi speaking the eulogy, Risha prepared for her conversion. She sent men out to look for Reuben, for she wanted to persuade him to follow her example, but her lover had vanished.

Risha was now free to do as she pleased. After her conversion she reopened her shops and sold non-kosher meats to the Gentiles of Laskev and to the peasants who came in on market days. She no longer had to hide anything. She could slaughter openly and in whatever manner she pleased pigs, oxen, calves, sheep. She hired a Gentile slaughterer to replace Reuben and went hunting with him in the forest and shot deer, hares, rabbits. But she no longer took the same pleasure in torturing creatures; slaughtering no longer incited her lust; and she got little satisfaction from lying with the pig butcher. Fishing in the river, sometimes when a fish dangled on her hook or danced in her net, a moment of joy came to her heart imbedded in fat and she would mutter: "Well, fish, you are worse off than I am . . . !"

The truth was that she yearned for Reuben. She missed their lascivious talk, his scholarship, his dread of reincarnation, his terror of Gehenna. Now that Reb Falik was in his grave, she had no one to betray, to pity, to mock. She had bought a pew in the Christian church immediately upon conversion and for some months went every Sunday to listen to the priest's sermon. Going and coming, she had her driver take her past the synagogue. Teasing the Jews gave her some satisfaction for a while, but soon this too palled.

With time Risha became so lazy that she no longer went to the slaughtering shed. She left everything in the hands of the pork butcher and did not even care that he was stealing from her. Immediately upon getting up in the morning, she poured herself a glass of liqueur and crept on her heavy feet from room to room talking to herself. She would stop at a mirror and mutter: "Woe, woe, Risha. What has happened to you? If your saintly mother should rise from her grave and see you—she would lie down again!" Some mornings she tried to improve her appearance but her clothes would not hang straight, her hair could not be untangled. Frequently she sang for hours in Yiddish and in Polish. Her voice was harsh and cracked and she invented the songs as she went along, repeating meaningless phrases, uttering sounds that resembled the cackling of fowls, the grunting of pigs, the death-rattles of oxen. Falling onto her bed she hiccuped, belched, laughed, cried. At night in her dreams, phantoms tormented her: bulls gored her with their horns; pigs shoved their snouts into her face and bit her; roosters cut her flesh to ribbons with their spurs. Reb Falik appeared dressed in his shroud, covered with wounds, waving a bunch of palm leaves, screaming: "I cannot rest in my grave. You have defiled my house."

Then Risha, or Maria Pawlowska as she was now called, would start up in bed, her limbs numb, her body covered with a cold sweat. Reb Falik's ghost would vanish but she could still hear the rustle of the palm leaves, the echo of his outcry. Simultaneously she would cross herself and repeat a Hebrew incantation learned in childhood from her mother. She would force her bare feet down to the floor and would begin to stumble through the dark from one room to another. She had thrown out all Reb Falik's books, had burned his Holy Scroll. The study house was now a shed for drying hides. But in the dining room there still remained the table on which Reb Falik had eaten his Sabbath meals, and from the ceiling hung the candelabra where his Sabbath candles had once burned. Sometimes Risha remembered her first two husbands whom she had tortured with her wrath, her greed, her curses and shrewish tongue. She was far from repenting, but something inside her was mourning and filling her with bitterness. Opening a window, she would look out into the midnight sky full of stars and cry out: "God, come and punish me! Come Satan! Come Asmodeus! Show your might. Carry me to the burning desert behind the dark mountains!"

VI

One winter Laskev was terrified by a carnivorous animal lurking about at night and attacking people. Some who had seen the creature said it was a bear, others a wolf, others a demon. One woman, going outdoors to urinate, had her neck bitten. A yeshiva boy was chased through the streets. An elderly night-watchman had his face clawed. The women and children of Laskev were afraid to leave their houses after nightfall. Everywhere shutters were bolted tight. Many strange things were recounted about the beast: someone had heard it rave with a human voice; another had seen it rise on its hind legs and run. It had overturned a barrel of cabbage in a courtyard, had opened chicken coops, thrown out the dough set to rise in the wooden trough in the bakery, and it had defiled the butcher blocks in the kosher shops with excrement.

One dark night the butchers of Laskev gathered with axes and knives determined either to kill or capture the monster. Splitting up into small groups they waited, their eyes growing accustomed to the darkness. In the middle of the night there was a scream and running toward it they caught sight of the animal making for the outskirts of town. A man shouted that he had been bitten in the shoulder. Frightened, some of the men dropped back, but others continued to give chase. One of the hunters saw it and threw his axe. Apparently the animal was hit, for with a ghastly scream it wobbled and fell. A horrible howling filled the air. Then the beast began to curse in Polish and Yiddish and to wail in a high-pitched voice like a woman in labor. Convinced that they had wounded a she-devil, the men ran home.

All that night the animal groaned and babbled. It even dragged itself to a house and knocked at the shutters. Then it became silent and the dogs began to bark. When day dawned, the bolder people came out of their houses. They discovered to their amazement that the animal was Risha. She lay dead dressed in a skunk fur coat wet with blood. One felt boot was missing. The hatchet had buried itself in her back. The dogs had already partaken of her entrails. Nearby was the knife she had used to stab one of her pursuers. It was now clear that Risha had become a werewolf. Since the Jews refused to bury her in their cemetery and the Christians were unwilling to give her a plot in theirs, she was taken to the hill on the estate where she had fought off the mob, and a ditch was dug for her there. Her wealth was confiscated by the city.

Some years later a wandering stranger lodged in the poorhouse of Laskev became sick. Before his death, he summoned the rabbi and the seven elders of the town and divulged to them that he was Reuben the slaughterer, with whom Risha had sinned. For years he had wandered from town to town, eating no meat, fasting Mondays and Thursdays, wearing a shirt of sack cloth, and repenting his abominations. He had come to Laskev to die because it was here his parents were buried. The rabbi recited the confession with him and Reuben revealed many details of the past which the townspeople had not known.

Risha's grave on the hill soon became covered with refuse. Yet long afterwards it remained customary for the Laskev schoolboys on the thirty-third day of Omer, when they went out carrying bows and arrows and a provision of hard-boiled eggs, to stop there. They danced on the hill and sang:

"Risha slaughtered
Black horses
Now she's fallen
To evil forces.

A pig for an ox
Sold Risha the witch
Now she's roasting
In sulphur and pitch."

Before the children left, they spat on the grave and recited:

"Thou shalt not suffer a witch to live
A witch to live thou shalt not suffer
Suffer a witch to live thou shalt not."

THE SPIRIT OF THE RIVER

by P'ou Sung-ling

In a small village along the river Tsz lived a fisherman named Siu. He started every night with his nets, and took very great care not to forget to bring with him a small jar of spirits. Before throwing his cast-net, he drank a small cup of the fragrant liquor and poured some drops into the slow current, praying aloud:

"O Spirit-of-the-river, please accept these offerings and favour your humble servant. I am poor and I must take some of the fishes that live in your cold kingdom. Don't be angry against me and don't prevent the eels and trouts coming to me!"

When every fisherman on the river brought back only one basket of fishes, he always proudly bore home a heavy charge of two or three baskets full to the brim.

From *Strange Stories from the Lodge of Leisures,* translated from the Chinese by George Soulié (London: Constable & Co., Ltd., 1913), pp. 125–30. Reprinted by permission of Constable & Co. Ltd., publishers.

Once, on a rosy dawn of early spring, when the sun, still below the horizon, began to eat with its golden teeth the vanishing darkness, he said aloud:

"O Spirit-of-the-river! For many years, every night I have drunk with you a good number of wine-cups; but I never saw your face; won't you favour me with your presence? We could sit together, and the pleasure of drinking would be much greater."

Hardly had he finished these words when, from the middle of the stream, emerged a beautiful young man clothed in pink, who slowly walked on the smooth surface of the limpid water, and sat on the boat's end, saying:

"Here I am."

The fisherman, being half-drunk, was not troubled in any way; he bowed to the young man, offered him, with his two hands, a cup of the strong wine, and said:

"Well! I long wished to receive your instructions, and I am very glad to see you. You must be mighty tired of living in that water; the few drops of wine I pour every night are quite lost in such a quantity of tasteless liquid. You had better come up every night; we will drink together and enjoy each other's company."

From this day, when darkness closed in, the Spirit waited for the fisherman and partook of his provisions. As soon as the sun rose above the horizon he suddenly disappeared. The fisherman did not find that very convenient; he asked his companion if he could not arrange to stay with him sometimes in the daytime.

"Impossible; we can't do such a thing, we spirits and ghosts. We belong to the kingdom of shadows. When the shadows, fighting the daylight, bring with them the Night, we are free to go and wander about. But as soon as the herald of the morn, the cock, has proclaimed the daily victory of the sun, we are powerless and must disappear."

On the same day the fisherman was sitting on the bank, smoking a pipe before going home with his baskets, when he saw a woman holding a child in her arms and hastening along the river towards a ford some hundred yards up stream. She was already in the water, she missed her footing, fell into the river, and was rolled away by the stream. The child, by some happy chance, had fallen on the bank and lay there, crying.

The fisherman could easily have gone in his boat and saved the woman, who was still struggling to regain the bank, but he was a prudent man:

"This woman, whom I don't know, seems to be beautiful," thought he. "Maybe it is my friend The-Spirit-of-the-river who has arranged all this, and chosen the girl to be his wife. If I prevent her going down to his cold lodgings, he will be angry and ruin my fishing. All I could do is to adopt this boy until somebody comes and asks for him."

And he did not move, until the poor woman had disappeared in the yellow stream; then he took the child. Once back in the village, he inquired about the mother; nobody could tell who she was. The days passed and nobody asked for the boy. This was strange enough, but, stranger still, from this day the fisherman never saw The-Spirit-of-the-river again. He offered him many cups of wine, and his fishing was as good as ever, but though he prayed heartily, his companion of so many nights did not appear any more.

When the boy was three years old he insisted on accompanying his adopted father in his night fishing. Summer had come; the cold was no more to be feared. The man consented to take his adopted son with him; they started together in the twilight.

As soon as the darkness closed, the boy's voice changed; his appearance was different.

"What a silly man you are!" said he. "Don't you know me now? For more than two years I waited for an opportunity to tell you who I was. But you always went out at night and you never came back before the sun was high in the sky. You had never failed to present your offerings; so I could not resist your prayer when you asked me to stay with you in the daytime. Now, here I am, till your death; when the sun is up I shall only be your son, but when the night closes I shall be your companion, and we will enjoy together what longevity the Fate allows you."

THE ANKLET

from *The Book of The Thousand Nights and One Night*

Among other sayings, it is said that there were once in a city three sisters, daughters of the same father but not of the same mother, who lived together and earned their bread by spinning flax. All three were as beautiful as the moon, but the youngest was also the fairest and the most charming; she could spin more than the other two together, and her spinning was faultless. This superiority roused the jealousy of the two elder sisters, for they were born of a different mother.

One day, the youngest went to the market and, with the money of her spinning, bought a little alabaster pot to set before her with flowers in it as she worked; but, when she returned with her purchase, her two sisters mocked her for foolish extravagance. In her shame and grief she answered nothing, but set a rose in the pot and, placing it before her, went on spinning.

Now this little alabaster pot was a thing of magic; when its mistress

From *The Book of The Thousand Nights and One Night*, translated by Powys and Mardrus Mathers (London: Routledge & Sons Ltd., 1951), Vol. 4, pp. 268–72. Reprinted by permission of Routledge & Kegan Paul Ltd.

wished to eat, it brought her delicate food, and when she wished to dress, it gave her robes of marvel. But the child was careful to keep the secret of its virtue from her jealous sisters; while she was with them, she feigned to go on living as before and dressed even more modestly than they dressed. As soon as they went forth, however, she would shut herself up alone in her bedroom and caress the little alabaster pot, saying: "Little pot, little pot, I want such and such to-day." Then the little pot would bring her fair robes or sweetmeats, and, in her loneliness, she would put on garments of gold-embroidered silk, and deck herself with jewels, with rings on all her fingers, with bracelets and anklets, and would eat delicious sweetmeats by herself. When the sisters were due to return, the little pot would make the gifts of its magic providing disappear, and they ever found their youngest spinning flax, with the little pot in front of her holding a rose.

She lived in this way for many weeks, poor in the presence of her jealous sisters and rich when she was alone, until a day came when the King of that city gave a great feast in his palace and invited all his people to present themselves. The three sisters received an invitation and the two elder, bidding the youngest stay at home to mind the house, dressed themselves in their poor best and departed for the feast. As soon as they had gone, the youngest went to her own room, and said to the alabaster pot: "Little pot, I want a green silk robe, a red silk vest, and a white silk mantle, all of the most lovely quality. I want rings for my fingers, turquoise bracelets for my wrists, and little diamond anklets. O little pot, I want to be the fairest of all at the palace to-night." The alabaster pot provided these things, and the girl, dressing herself hastily, made her way to the palace and entered the harīm, where the women's side of the entertainment was taking place. Not even her sisters recognised her, so greatly had her magic apparelling enhanced her natural beauty. All the other women looked at her with moist eyes and went into an ecstasy before her. She received their homage like a sweet and gentle queen, and they fell in love with her.

When the feast was near its end, the girl took advantage of the chaining of the general attention by certain singers, to glide from the harīm and leave the palace. But in the haste of her flight she dropped one of her diamond anklets into the sunken trough where the King's horses were used to drink. She was not conscious of her loss, and her only care was to be waiting in the house when her sisters returned.

At this point Shahrazād saw the approach of morning and discreetly fell silent.

BUT WHEN
THE EIGHT-HUNDRED-AND-EIGHTY-THIRD NIGHT
HAD COME

SHE SAID:

Next morning the King's grooms took the horses out to drink, but they would not go near the water; their nostrils dilated in terror at the sight of something shining like a round of stars at the bottom of the trough and they backed away, panting and blowing. The grooms whistled them on and tugged at their halters in vain; then they let the beasts be and, looking down into the water, discovered the diamond anklet.

When the King's son, who always superintended the care of his own horses, had looked at the anklet and determined the wonderful slimness of the ankle which it must fit, he marvelled and cried: "By my life, surely no woman born could wear it!" He turned it about and, seeing that each of the stones was singly worth all the jewels in his father's crown, he thought: "By Allāh, I shall marry the girl whom this anklet fits and no other woman!" He went and woke the King, his father, and, showing him the anklet, said: "I wish to marry the owner of so slim an ankle." "I see no harm in that," answered the King, "but such things are in your mother's province, for she knows and I do not."

So the prince went to his mother and told her the story of the anklet. "I trust you to marry me to the owner of so slim an ankle," he said, "for my father says that you know about such things." "I hear and I obey!" answered the Queen, and she called her women together and went out with them from the palace to search for the owner of the anklet.

They entered all the harīms of the city and tried the ornament upon the ankles of every woman, young and old, but none were found slim enough to wear it. After two weeks of vain pilgrimage, they came to the house of the three sisters and, when the Queen tried the anklet upon the youngest, behold! it fitted to a marvel.

The Queen embraced the girl, and the women of the court embraced her; they took her by the hand and led her to the palace, where her marriage with the prince was at once arranged. Feasts and entertainments of great magnificence were given, and lasted for forty days and forty nights.

On the last day, after the bride had been conducted to the hammām, her sisters, whom she had brought with her to share the enjoyments of her royal state, began to dress her and arrange her hair. But she had trusted in their affection and told them the secret of the alabaster pot, in order that they might not be astonished at the magnificent robes and ornaments which she had been able to obtain for her marriage night. When they had coifed her hair, they fastened it with a series of diamond pins.

As soon as the last pin had gone into place, the sweet bride was changed into a dove with a large crest upon her head, and flew away in fright through the window.

For the pins were magic pins which could transform all girls to doves, and the two sisters had required them from the pot to ease their jealousy.

The wicked women had been alone with their sister at the time and, when question was made, they told the King's son that his bride had gone out only for a moment. When she did not return, the young man sent search parties throughout the city and about all his father's kingdom, but these came back with no news at all. His loss plunged him into a wasting bitterness.

The dove came every morning and every evening to her husband's window and crooned there long and sadly. Soon the prince began to find an answer to his misery in this crooning, and came to love the bird. One day, noticing that she did not fly away when he approached the window, he stretched forth his hand and caught her. She shook in his fingers and went on crooning; so he began to caress her gently and smooth her feathers and scratch her head. While he did this last, he felt several little hard objects beneath his finger-tips, as if they had been the heads of pins. He pulled them from the crest one by one, and, when the last pin had come forth, the dove shook herself and became his bride again.

The two lived together in great delight and Allāh granted them numberless children as beautiful as themselves; but the two wicked sisters died of jealousy and a flowing back of their poisoned blood upon their hearts.

THE SAILOR-BOY'S TALE

by Isak Dinesen

The barque *Charlotte* was on her way from Marseille to Athens, in grey weather, on a high sea, after three days' heavy gale. A small sailor-boy, named Simon, stood on the wet, swinging deck, held on to a shroud, and looked up towards the drifting clouds, and to the upper top-gallant yard of the main-mast.

A bird, that had sought refuge upon the mast, had got her feet entangled in some loose tackle-yarn of the halliard, and, high up there, struggled to get free. The boy on the deck could see her wings flapping and her head turning from side to side.

Through his own experience of life he had come to the conviction in this world everyone must look after himself, and expect no help from others. But the mute, deadly fight kept him fascinated for more than an hour. He wondered what kind of bird it would be. These last days a number of birds had come to settle in the barque's rigging: swallows, quails, and a pair of peregrine falcons; he believed that this bird was a peregrine falcon. He remembered how, many years ago, in his own country and near his home, he had once seen a peregrine falcon quite close, sitting on a stone and flying straight up from it. Perhaps this was the same bird. He thought: "That bird is like me. Then she was there, and now she is here."

At that a fellow-feeling rose in him, a sense of common tragedy; he

From *Winter's Tales* by Isak Dinesen (New York: Random House, 1942), pp. 91–103; and (London: Putnam & Co. Ltd., 1942).

stood looking at the bird with his heart in his mouth. There were none of the sailors about to make fun of him; he began to think out how he might go up by the shrouds to help the falcon out. He brushed his hair back and pulled up his sleeves, gave the deck round him a great glance, and climbed up. He had to stop a couple of times in the swaying rigging.

It was indeed, he found when he got to the top of the mast, a peregrine falcon. As his head was on a level with hers, she gave up her struggle, and looked at him with a pair of angry, desperate yellow eyes. He had to take hold of her with one hand while he got his knife out, and cut off the tackle-yarn. He was scared as he looked down, but at the same time he felt that he had been ordered up by nobody, but that this was his own venture, and this gave him a proud, steadying sensation, as if the sea and the sky, the ship, the bird and himself were all one. Just as he had freed the falcon, she hacked him in the thumb, so that the blood ran, and he nearly let her go. He grew angry with her, and gave her a clout on the head, then he put her inside his jacket, and climbed down again.

When he reached the deck the mate and the cook were standing there, looking up; they roared to him to ask what he had had to do in the mast. He was so tired that the tears were in his eyes. He took the falcon out and showed her to them, and she kept still within his hands. They laughed and walked off. Simon set the falcon down, stood back and watched her. After a while he reflected that she might not be able to get up from the slippery deck, so he caught her once more, walked away with her and placed her upon a bolt of canvas. A little after she began to trim her feathers, made two or three sharp jerks forward, and then suddenly flew off. The boy could follow her flight above the troughs of the grey sea. He thought: "There flies my falcon."

When the *Charlotte* came home, Simon signed aboard another ship, and two years later he was a light hand on the schooner *Hebe* lying at Bodø, high up on the coast of Norway, to buy herrings.

To the great herring-markets of Bodø ships came together from all corners of the world; here were Swedish, Finnish and Russian boats, a forest of masts, and on shore a turbulent, irregular display of life, with many languages spoken, and mighty fights. On the shore booths had been set up, and the Lapps, small yellow people, noiseless in their movements, with watchful eyes, whom Simon had never seen before, came down to sell bead-embroidered leather-goods. It was April, the sky and the sea were so clear that it was difficult to hold one's eyes up against them—salt, infinitely wide, and filled with bird-shrieks—as if someone were incessantly whetting invisible knives, on all sides, high up in Heaven.

Simon was amazed at the lightness of these April evenings. He knew no geography, and did not assign it to the latitude, but he took it as a sign of an unwonted good-will in the Universe, a favour. Simon had been small for his age all his life, but this last winter he had grown, and had become strong of limb. That good luck, he felt, must spring from the very same source as the sweetness of the weather, from a new benevolence in the world. He had been in need of such encouragement, for he was timid by nature; now he asked for no more. The rest he felt to be his own affair. He went about slowly, and proudly.

One evening he was ashore with land-leave, and walked up to the booth of a small Russian trader, a Jew who sold gold watches. All the sailors knew that his watches were made from bad metal, and would not go, still they bought them, and paraded them about. Simon looked at these watches for a long time, but did not buy. The old Jew had divers goods in his shop, and amongst others a case of oranges. Simon had tasted oranges on his journeys; he bought one and took it with him. He meant to go up on a hill, from where he could see the sea, and suck it there.

As he walked on, and had got to the outskirts of the place, he saw a little girl in a blue frock, standing at the other side of a fence and looking at him. She was thirteen or fourteen years old, as slim as an eel, but with a round, clear, freckled face, and a pair of long plaits. The two looked at one another.

"Who are you looking out for?" Simon asked, to say something. The girl's face broke into an ecstatic, presumptuous smile. "For the man I am going to marry, of course," she said. Something in her countenance made the boy confident and happy; he grinned a little at her. "That will perhaps be me," he said. "Ha, ha," said the girl, "he is a few years older than you, I can tell you." "Why," said Simon, "you are not grown up yourself." The little girl shook her head solemnly. "Nay," she said, "but when I grow up I will be exceedingly beautiful, and wear brown shoes with heels, and a hat." "Will you have an orange?" asked Simon, who could give her none of the things she had named. She looked at the orange and at him. "They are very good to eat," said he. "Why do you not eat it yourself then?" she asked. "I have eaten so many already," said he, "when I was in Athens. Here I had to pay a mark for it." "What is your name?" asked she. "My name is Simon," said he. "What is yours?" "Nora," said the girl. "What do you want for your orange now, Simon?"

When he heard his name in her mouth Simon grew bold. "Will you give me a kiss for the orange?" he asked. Nora looked at him gravely for a moment. "Yes," she said, "I should not mind giving you a kiss." He grew as warm as if he had been running quickly. When she stretched out her hand for the orange he took hold of it. At that moment somebody in the house called out for her. "That is my father," said she, and tried to give him back the orange, but he would not take it. "Then come again tomorrow," she said quickly, "then I will give you a kiss." At that she slipped off. He stood and looked after her, and a little later went back to his ship.

Simon was not in the habit of making plans for the future, and now he did not know whether he would be going back to her or not.

The following evening he had to stay aboard, as the other sailors were going ashore, and he did not mind that either. He meant to sit on the deck with the ship's dog, Balthasar, and to practise upon a concertina that he had purchased some time ago. The pale evening was all round him, the sky was faintly roseate, the sea was quite calm, like milk-and-water, only in the wake of the boats going inshore it broke into streaks of vivid indigo. Simon sat and played; after a while his own music began to speak to him so strongly that he stopped, got up and looked upwards. Then he saw that the full moon was sitting high on the sky.

The sky was so light that she hardly seemed needed there; it was as if she had turned up by a caprice of her own. She was round, demure and presumptuous. At that he knew that he must go ashore, whatever it was to cost him. But he did not know how to get away, since the others had taken the yawl with them. He stood on the deck for a long time, a small lonely figure of a sailor-boy on a boat, when he caught sight of a yawl coming in from a ship farther out, and hailed her. He found that it was the Russian crew from a boat named *Anna,* going ashore. When he could make himself understood to them, they took him with them; they first asked him for money for his fare, then, laughing, gave it back to him. He thought: "These people will be believing that I am going in to town, wenching." And then he felt, with some pride, that they were right, although at the same time they were infinitely wrong, and knew nothing about anything.

When they came ashore they invited him to come in and drink in their company, and he would not refuse, because they had helped him. One of the Russians was a giant, as big as a bear; he told Simon that his name was Ivan. He got drunk at once, and then fell upon the boy with a bear-like affection, pawed him, smiled and laughed into his face, made him a present of a gold watchchain, and kissed him on both cheeks. At that Simon reflected that he also ought to give Nora a present when they met again, and as soon as he could get away from the Russians he walked up to a booth that he knew of, and bought a small blue silk handkerchief, the same colour as her eyes.

It was Saturday evening, and there were many people amongst the houses; they came in long rows, some of them singing, all keen to have some fun that night. Simon, in the midst of this rich, bawling life under the clear moon, felt his head light with the flight from the ship and the strong drinks. He crammed the handkerchief in his pocket; it was silk, which he had never touched before, a present for his girl.

He could not remember the path up to Nora's house, lost his way, and came back to where he had started. Then he grew deadly afraid that he should be too late, and began to run. In a small passage between two wooden huts he ran straight into a big man, and found that it was Ivan once more. The Russian folded his arms round him and held him. "Good! Good!" he cried in high glee, "I have found you, my little chicken. I have looked for you everywhere, and poor Ivan has wept because he lost his friend." "Let me go, Ivan," cried Simon. "Oho," said Ivan, "I shall go with you and get you what you want. My heart and my money are all yours, all yours; I have been seventeen years old myself, a little lamb of God, and I want to be so again tonight." "Let me go," cried Simon, "I am in a hurry." Ivan held him so that it hurt, and patted him with his other hand. "I feel it, I feel it," he said. "Now trust to me, my little friend. Nothing shall part you and me. I hear the others coming; we will have such a night together as you will remember when you are an old grandpapa."

Suddenly he crushed the boy to him, like a bear that carries off a sheep. The odious sensation of male bodily warmth and the bulk of a man close to him made the lean boy mad. He thought of Nora waiting, like a slender ship in the dim air, and of himself, here, in the hot embrace of a hairy animal. He struck Ivan with all his might. "I shall kill you, Ivan," he cried out, "if you do not let me go." "Oh, you will be thankful to me later on," said Ivan, and began to sing. Simon fumbled in his pocket for his knife, and got it opened. He could not lift his hand, but he drove the knife, furiously, in under the big man's arm. Almost immediately he felt the blood spouting out, and running down in his sleeve. Ivan stopped short in the song, let go his hold of the boy and gave two long deep grunts. The next second he tumbled down on his knees. "Poor Ivan, poor Ivan," he groaned. He fell straight on his face. At that moment Simon heard the other sailors coming along, singing, in the by-street.

He stood still for a minute, wiped his knife, and watched the blood spread into a dark pool underneath the big body. Then he ran. As he stopped for a second to choose his way, he heard the sailors behind him scream out over their dead comrade. He thought: "I must get down to the sea, where I can wash my hand." But at the same time he ran the other way. After a little while he found himself on the path that he had walked on the day before, and it seemed as familiar to him, as if he had walked it many hundred times in his life.

He slackened his pace to look round, and suddenly saw Nora standing on the other side of the fence; she was quite close to him when he caught sight of her in the moonlight. Wavering and out of breath he sank down on his knees. For a moment he could not speak. The little girl looked down at him. "Good evening, Simon," she said in her small coy voice. "I have waited for you a long time," and after a moment she added: "I have eaten your orange."

"Oh, Nora," cried the boy. "I have killed a man." She stared at him, but did not move. "Why did you kill a man?" she asked after a moment. "To get here," said Simon. "Because he tried to stop me. But he was my friend." Slowly he got on to his feet. "He loved me!" the boy cried out, and at that burst into tears. "Yes," said she slowly and thoughtfully. "Yes, because you must be here in time." "Can you hide me?" he asked. "For they are after me." "Nay," said Nora, "I cannot hide you. For my father is the parson here at Bodø, and he would be sure to hand you over to them, if he knew that you had killed a man." "Then," said Simon, "give me something to wipe my hands on." "What is the matter with your hands?" she asked, and took a little step forward. He stretched out his hands to her. "Is that your own blood?" she asked. "No," said he, "it is his." She took the step back again. "Do you hate me now?" he asked. "No, I do not hate you," said she. "But do put your hands at your back."

As he did so she came up close to him, at the other side of the fence, and clasped her arms round his neck. She pressed her young body to his, and kissed him tenderly. He felt her face, cool as the moonlight, upon his own, and when she released him, his head swam, and he did not know if the kiss had lasted a second or an hour. Nora stood up straight, her eyes wide open. "Now," she said slowly and proudly, "I promise you that I will never marry anybody, as long as I live." The boy kept standing with his hands on his back, as if she had tied them there. "And now," she said, "you must run, for they are coming." They looked at one another. "Do not forget Nora," said she. He turned and ran.

He leapt over a fence, and when he was down amongst the houses he walked. He did not know at all where to go. As he came to a house, from where music and noise streamed out, he slowly went through the door. The room was full of people; they were dancing in here. A lamp hung from the ceiling, and shone down on them; the air was thick and brown with the dust rising from the floor. There were some women in the room, but many of the men danced with each other, and gravely or laughingly stamped the floor. A moment after Simon had come in the crowd withdrew to the walls to clear the floor for two sailors, who were showing a dance from their own country.

Simon thought: "Now, very soon, the men from the boat will come round to look for their comrade's murderer, and from my hands they will know that I have done it." These five minutes during which he stood by the wall of the dancing-room, in the midst of the gay, sweating dancers, were of great significance to the boy. He himself felt it, as if during this time he grew up, and became like other people. He did not entreat his destiny, nor complain. Here he was, he had killed a man, and had kissed a girl. He did not demand any more from life, nor did life now demand more from him. He was Simon, a man like the men round him, and going to die, as all men are going to die.

He only became aware of what was going on outside him, when he saw that a woman had come in, and was standing in the midst of the cleared floor, looking round her. She was a short, broad old woman, in the clothes of the Lapps, and she took her stand with such majesty and fierceness as if she owned the whole place. It was obvious that most of the people knew her, and were a little afraid of her, although a few laughed; the din of the dancing-room stopped when she spoke.

"Where is my son?" she asked in a high shrill voice, like a bird's. The next moment her eyes fell on Simon himself, and she steered through the crowd, which opened up before her, stretched out her old skinny, dark hand, and took him by the elbow. "Come home with me now," she said. "You need not dance here tonight. You may be dancing a high enough dance soon."

Simon drew back, for he thought that she was drunk. But as she looked him straight in the face with her yellow eyes, it seemed to him that he had met her before, and that he might do well in listening to her. The old woman pulled him with her across the floor, and he followed her without a word. "Do not birch your boy too badly, Sunniva," one of the men in the room cried to her. "He has done no harm, he only wanted to look at the dance."

At the same moment as they came out through the door, there was an alarm in the street, a flock of people came running down it, and one of them, as he turned into the house, knocked against Simon, looked at him and the old woman, and ran on.

While the two walked along the street, the old woman lifted up her skirt, and put the hem of it into the boy's hand. "Wipe your hand on my skirt," she said. They had not gone far before they came to a small wooden house, and stopped; the door to it was so low that they must bend to get through it. As the Lapp-woman went in before Simon, still holding on to his arm, the boy looked up for a moment. The night had grown misty; there was a wide ring round the moon.

The old woman's room was narrow and dark, with but one small window to it; a lantern stood on the floor and lighted it up dimly. It was all filled with reindeer skins and wolf skins, and with reindeer horn, such as the Lapps use to make their carved buttons and knife-handles, and the air in here was rank and stifling. As soon as they were in, the woman turned to Simon, took hold of his head, and with her crooked fingers parted his hair and combed it down in Lapp fashion. She clapped a Lapp cap on him and stood back to glance at him. "Sit down on my stool, now," she said. "But first take out your knife." She was so commanding in voice and manner that the boy could not but choose to do as she told him; he sat down on the stool, and he could not take his eyes off her face, which was flat and brown, and as if smeared with dirt in its net of fine wrinkles. As he sat there he heard many people come along outside, and stop by the house; then someone knocked at the door, waited a moment and knocked again. The old woman stood and listened, as still as a mouse.

"Nay," said the boy and got up. "This is no good, for it is me that they are after. It will be better for you to let me go out to them." "Give me your knife," said she. When he handed it to her, she stuck it straight into her thumb, so that the blood spouted out, and she let it drip all over her skirt. "Come in, then," she cried.

The door opened, and two of the Russian sailors came and stood in the opening; there were more people outside. "Has anybody come in here?" they asked. "We are after a man who has killed our mate, but he has run away from us. Have you seen or heard anybody this way?" The old Lapp-woman turned upon them, and her eyes shone like gold in the lamplight. "Have I seen or heard anyone?" she cried, "I have heard you shriek murder all over the town. You frightened me, and my poor silly boy there, so that I cut my thumb as I was ripping the skin-rug that I sew. The boy is too scared to help me, and the rug is all ruined. I shall make you pay me for that. If you are looking for a murderer, come in and search my house for me, and I shall know you when we meet again." She was so furious that she danced where she stood, and jerked her head like an angry bird of prey.

The Russian came in, looked round the room, and at her and her blood-stained hand and shirt. "Do not put a curse on us now, Sunniva," he said timidly. "We know that you can do many things when you like. Here is a mark to pay you for the blood you have spilled." She stretched out her hand, and he placed a piece of money in it. She spat on it. "Then go, and there shall be no bad blood between us," said Sunniva, and shut the door after them. She stuck her thumb in her mouth, and chuckled a little.

The boy got up from his stool, stood straight up before her and stared into her face. He felt as if he were swaying high up in the air, with but a small hold. "Why have you helped me?" he asked her. "Do you not know?" she answered. "Have you not recognised me yet? But you will remember the peregrine falcon which was caught in the tackle-yarn of your boat, the *Charlotte*, as she sailed in the Mediterranean. That day you climbed up by the shrouds of the top-gallantmast to help her out, in a stiff wind, and with a high sea. That falcon was me. We Lapps often fly in such a manner, to see the world. When I first met you I was on my way to Africa, to see my younger sister and her children. She is a falcon too, when she chooses. By that time she was living at Takaunga, within an old ruined tower, which down there they call a minaret." She swathed a corner of her skirt round her thumb, and bit at it. "We do not forget," she said. "I hacked your thumb, when you took hold of me; it is only fair that I should cut my thumb for you tonight."

She came close to him, and gently rubbed her two brown, claw-like fingers against his forehead. "So you are a boy," she said, "who will kill a man rather than be late to meet your sweetheart? We hold together, the females of this earth. I shall mark your forehead now, so that the girls will know of that, when they look at you, and they will like you for it." She played with the boy's hair, and twisted it round her finger.

"Listen now, my little bird," said she. "My great grandson's brother-in-law is lying with his boat by the landing-place at this moment; he is to take a consignment of skins out to a Danish boat. He will bring you back to your boat, in time, before your mate comes. The *Hebe* is sailing tomorrow morning, is it not so? But when you are aboard, give him back my cap for me." She took up his knife, wiped it in her skirt and handed it to him. "Here is your knife," she said. "You will stick it into no more men; you will not need to, for from now you will sail the seas like a faithful seaman. We have enough trouble with our sons as it is."

The bewildered boy began to stammer his thanks to her. "Wait," said she, "I shall make you a cup of coffee, to bring back your wits, while I wash your jacket." She went and rattled an old copper kettle upon the fireplace. After a while she handed him a hot, strong, black drink in a cup without a handle to it. "You have drunk with Sunniva now," she said; "you have drunk down a little wisdom, so that in the future all your thoughts shall not fall like raindrops into the salt sea."

When he had finished and set down the cup, she led him to the door and opened it for him. He was surprised to see that it was almost clear morning. The house was so high up that the boy could see the sea from it, and a milky mist about it. He gave her his hand to say good-bye.

She stared into his face. "We do not forget," she said. "And you, you knocked me on the head there, high up in the mast. I shall give you that blow back." With that she smacked him on the ear as hard as she could, so that his head swam. "Now we are quits," she said, gave him a great, mischievous, shining glance, and a little push down the doorstep, and nodded to him.

In this way the sailor-boy got back to his ship, which was to sail the next morning, and lived to tell the story.

Spiritual

THE STORY OF A PANIC

by E. M. Forster

Eustace's career—if career it can be called—certainly dates from that afternoon in the chestnut woods above Ravello. I confess at once that I am a plain, simple man, with no pretensions to literary style. Still, I do flatter myself that I can tell a story without exaggerating, and I have therefore decided to give an unbiassed account of the extraordinary events of eight years ago.

Ravello is a delightful place with a delightful little hotel in which we met some charming people. There were the two Miss Robinsons, who had been there for six weeks with Eustace, their nephew, then a boy of about fourteen. Mr. Sandbach had also been there some time. He had held a curacy in the north of England, which he had been compelled to resign on account of ill-health, and while he was recruiting at Ravello he had taken in hand Eustace's education—which was then sadly deficient—and was endeavouring to fit him for one of our great public schools. Then there was Mr. Leyland, a would-be artist, and, finally, there was the nice landlady, Signora Scafetti, and the nice English-speaking waiter, Emmanuele—though at the time of which I am speaking Emmanuele was away, visiting a sick father.

To this little circle, I, my wife, and my two daughters made, I venture to think, a not unwelcome addition. But though I liked most of the company well enough, there were two of them to whom I did not take at all. They were the artist, Leyland, and the Miss Robinsons' nephew, Eustace.

Leyland was simply conceited and odious, and, as those qualities will be amply illustrated in my narrative, I need not enlarge upon them here. But Eustace was something besides: he was indescribably repellent.

I am fond of boys as a rule, and was quite disposed to be friendly. I and my daughters offered to take him out—'No, walking was such a fag.' Then I asked him to come and bathe—'No, he could not swim.'

From *The Collected Tales of E. M. Forster* by E. M. Forster (New York: Alfred A. Knopf, 1947), pp. 3–38. Reprinted by permission of Sedgwick & Jackson Ltd. and the publisher.

"Every English boy should be able to swim," I said, "I will teach you myself."

"There, Eustace dear," said Miss Robinson; "here is a chance for you."

But he said he was afraid of the water!—a boy afraid!—and of course I said no more.

I would not have minded so much if he had been a really studious boy, but he neither played hard nor worked hard. His favourite occupations were lounging on the terrace in an easy chair and loafing along the high road, with his feet shuffling up the dust and his shoulders stooping forward. Naturally enough, his features were pale, his chest contracted, and his muscles undeveloped. His aunts thought him delicate; what he really needed was discipline.

That memorable day we all arranged to go for a picnic up in the chestnut woods—all, that is, except Janet, who stopped behind to finish her water-colour of the Cathedral—not a very successful attempt, I am afraid.

I wander off into these irrelevant details, because in my mind I cannot separate them from an account of the day; and it is the same with the conversation during the picnic: all is imprinted on my brain together. After a couple of hours' ascent, we left the donkeys that had carried the Miss Robinsons and my wife, and all proceeded on foot to the head of the valley—Vallone Fontana Caroso is its proper name, I find.

I have visited a good deal of fine scenery before and since, but have found little that has pleased me more. The valley ended in a vast hollow, shaped like a cup, into which radiated ravines from the precipitous hills around. Both the valley and the ravines and the ribs of hill that divided the ravines were covered with leafy chestnut, so that the general appearance was that of a many-fingered green hand, palm upwards, which was clutching convulsively to keep us in its grasp. Far down the valley we could see Ravello and the sea, but that was the only sign of another world.

"Oh, what a perfectly lovely place," said my daughter Rose. "What a picture it would make!"

"Yes," said Mr. Sandbach. "Many a famous European gallery would be proud to have a landscape a tithe as beautiful as this upon its walls."

"On the contrary," said Leyland, "it would make a very poor picture. Indeed, it is not paintable at all."

"And why is that?" said Rose, with far more deference than he deserved.

"Look, in the first place," he replied, "how intolerably straight against the sky is the line of the hill. It would need breaking up and diversifying. And where we are standing the whole thing is out of perspective. Besides, all the colouring is monotonous and crude."

"I do not know anything about pictures," I put in, "and I do not pretend to know: but I know what is beautiful when I see it, and I am thoroughly content with this."

"Indeed, who could help being contented!" said the elder Miss Robinson; and Mr. Sandbach said the same.

"Ah!" said Leyland, "you all confuse the artistic view of Nature with the photographic."

Poor Rose had brought her camera with her, so I thought this positively rude. I did not wish any unpleasantness; so I merely turned away and assisted my wife and Miss Mary Robinson to put out the lunch—not a very nice lunch.

"Eustace, dear," said his aunt, "come and help us here."

He was in a particularly bad temper that morning. He had, as usual, not wanted to come, and his aunts had nearly allowed him to stop at the hotel to vex Janet. But I, with their permission, spoke to him rather sharply on the subject of exercise; and the result was that he had come, but was even more taciturn and moody than usual.

Obedience was not his strong point. He invariably questioned every command, and only executed it grumbling. I should always insist on prompt and cheerful obedience, if I had a son.

"I'm—coming—Aunt—Mary," he at last replied, and dawdled to cut a piece of wood to make a whistle, taking care not to arrive till we had finished.

"Well, well, sir!" said I, "you stroll in at the end and profit by our labours." He sighed, for he could not endure being chaffed. Miss Mary, very unwisely, insisted on giving him the wing of the chicken, in spite of all my attempts to prevent her. I remember that I had a moment's vexation when I thought that, instead of enjoying the sun, and the air, and the woods, we were all engaged in wrangling over the diet of a spoilt boy.

But, after lunch, he was a little less in evidence. He withdrew to a tree trunk, and began to loosen the bark from his whistle. I was thankful to see him employed, for once in a way. We reclined, and took a *dolce far niente*.

Those sweet chestnuts of the South are puny striplings compared with our robust Northerners. But they clothed the contours of the hills and valleys in a most pleasing way, their veil being only broken by two clearings, in one of which we were sitting.

And because these few trees were cut down, Leyland burst into a petty indictment of the proprietor.

"All the poetry is going from Nature," he cried, "her lakes and marshes are drained, her seas banked up, her forests cut down. Everywhere we see the vulgarity of desolation spreading."

I have had some experience of estates, and answered that cutting was very necessary for the health of the larger trees. Besides, it was unreasonable to expect the proprietor to derive no income from his lands.

"If you take the commercial side of landscape, you may feel pleasure in the owner's activity. But to me the mere thought that a tree is convertible into cash is disgusting."

"I see no reason," I observed politely, "to despise the gifts of Nature because they are of value."

It did not stop him. "It is no matter," he went on, "we are all hopelessly steeped in vulgarity. I do not except myself. It is through us, and to our shame, that the Nereids have left the waters and the Oreads the mountains, that the woods no longer give shelter to Pan."

"Pan!" cried Mr. Sandbach, his mellow voice filling the valley as if it had been a great green church, "Pan is dead. That is why the woods do not shelter him." And he began to tell the striking story of the mariners who were sailing near the coast at the time of the birth of Christ, and three times heard a loud voice saying: "The great God Pan is dead."

"Yes. The great God Pan is dead," said Leyland. And he abandoned himself to that mock misery in which artistic people are so fond of indulging. His cigar went out, and he had to ask me for a match.

"How very interesting," said Rose. "I do wish I knew some ancient history."

"It is not worth your notice," said Mr. Sandbach. "Eh, Eustace?"

Eustace was finishing his whistle. He looked up, with the irritable frown in which his aunts allowed him to indulge, and made no reply.

The conversation turned to various topics and then died out. It was a cloudless afternoon in May, and the pale green of the young chestnut leaves made a pretty contrast with the dark blue of the sky. We were all sitting at the edge of the small clearing for the sake of the view, and the shade of the chestnut saplings behind us was manifestly insufficient. All sounds died away—at least that is my account: Miss Robinson says that the clamour of the birds was the first sign of uneasiness hat she discerned. All sounds died away, except that, far in the distance, I could hear two boughs of a great chestnut grinding together as the tree swayed. The grinds grew shorter and shorter, and finally that sound stopped also. As I looked over the green fingers of the valley, everything was absolutely motionless and still; and that feeling of suspense which one so often experiences when Nature is in repose, began to steal over me.

Suddenly, we were all electrified by the excruciating noise of Eustace's whistle. I never heard any instrument give forth so ear-splitting and discordant a sound.

"Eustace, dear," said Miss Mary Robinson, "you might have thought of your poor Aunt Julia's head."

Leyland who had apparently been asleep, sat up.

"It is astonishing how blind a boy is to anything that is elevating or beautiful," he observed. "I should not have thought he could have found the wherewithal out here to spoil our pleasure like this."

Then the terrible silence fell upon us again. I was now standing up and watching a catspaw of wind that was running down one of the ridges opposite, turning the light green to dark as it travelled. A fanciful feeling of foreboding came over me; so I turned away, to find to my amazement, that all the others were also on their feet, watching it too.

It is not possible to describe coherently what happened next: but I, for one, am not ashamed to confess that, though the fair blue sky was above me, and the green spring woods beneath me, and the kindest of friends around me, yet I became terribly frightened, more frightened than I ever wish to become again, frightened in a way I never have known either before or after. And in the eyes of the others, too, I saw blank, expressionless fear, while their mouths strove in vain to speak and their hands to gesticulate. Yet, all around us were prosperity, beauty, and peace, and all was motionless, save the catspaw of wind, now travelling up the ridge on which we stood.

Who moved first has never been settled. It is enough to say that in one second we were tearing away along the hill-side. Leyland was in front, then Mr. Sandbach, then my wife. But I only saw for a brief moment;

for I ran across the little clearing and through the woods and over the undergrowth and the rocks and down the dry torrent beds into the valley below. The sky might have been black as I ran, and the trees short grass, and the hillside a level road; for I saw nothing and heard nothing and felt nothing, since all the channels of sense and reason were blocked. It was not the spiritual fear that one has known at other times, but brutal overmastering physical fear, stopping up the ears, and dropping clouds before the eyes, and filling the mouth with foul tastes. And it was no ordinary humiliation that survived; for I had been afraid, not as a man, but as a beast.

II

I cannot describe our finish any better than our start; for our fear passed away as it had come, without cause. Suddenly I was able to see, and hear, and cough, and clear my mouth. Looking back, I saw that the others were stopping too; and, in a short time, we were all together, though it was long before we could speak, and longer before we dared to.

No one was seriously injured. My poor wife had sprained her ankle, Leyland had torn one of his nails on a tree trunk, and I myself had scraped and damaged my ear. I never noticed it till I had stopped.

We were all silent, searching one another's faces. Suddenly Miss Mary Robinson gave a terrible shriek. "Oh, merciful heavens! where is Eustace?" And then she would have fallen, if Mr. Sandbach had not caught her.

"We must go back, we must go back at once," said my Rose, who was quite the most collected of the party. "But I hope—I feel he is safe."

Such was the cowardice of Leyland, that he objected. But, finding himself in a minority, and being afraid of being left alone, he gave in. Rose and I supported my poor wife, Mr. Sandbach and Miss Robinson helped Miss Mary, and we returned slowly and silently, taking forty minutes to ascend the path that we had descended in ten.

Our conversation was naturally disjointed, as no one wished to offer an opinion on what had happened. Rose was the most talkative: she startled us all by saying that she had very nearly stopped where she was.

"Do you mean to say that you weren't—that you didn't feel compelled to go?" said Mr. Sandbach.

"Oh, of course, I did feel frightened"—she was the first to use the word—"but I somehow felt that if I could stop on it would be quite different, that I shouldn't be frightened at all, so to speak." Rose never did express herself clearly: still, it is greatly to her credit that she, the youngest of us, should have held on so long at that terrible time.

"I should have stopped, I do believe," she continued, "if I had not seen mamma go."

Rose's experience comforted us a little about Eustace. But a feeling of terrible foreboding was on us all, as we painfully climbed the chestnut-covered slopes and neared the little clearing. When we reached it our tongues broke loose. There, at the further side, were the remains of our lunch, and close to them, lying motionless on his back, was Eustace.

With some presence of mind I at once cried out: "Hey, you young monkey! jump up!" But he made no reply, nor did he answer when his poor aunts spoke to him. And, to my unspeakable horror, I saw one of those green lizards dart out from under his shirt-cuff as we approached.

We stood watching him as he lay there so silently, and my ears began to tingle in expectation of the outbursts of lamentations and tears.

Miss Mary fell on her knees beside him and touched his hand, which was convulsively entwined in the long grass.

As she did so, he opened his eyes and smiled.

I have often seen that peculiar smile since, both on the possessor's face and on the photographs of him that are beginning to get into the illustrated papers. But, till then, Eustace had always worn a peevish, discontented frown; and we were all unused to this disquieting smile, which always seemed to be without adequate reason.

His aunts showered kisses on him, which he did not reciprocate, and then there was an awkward pause. Eustace seemed so natural and undisturbed; yet, if he had not had astonishing experiences himself, he ought to have been all the more astonished at our extraordinary behaviour. My wife, with ready tact, endeavoured to behave as if nothing had happened.

"Well, Mr. Eustace," she said, sitting down as she spoke, to ease her foot, "how have you been amusing yourself since we have been away?"

"Thank you, Mrs. Tytler, I have been very happy."

"And where have you been?"

"Here."

"And lying down all the time, you idle boy?"

"No, not all the time."

"What were you doing before?"

"Oh; standing or sitting."

"Stood and sat doing nothing! Don't you know the poem 'Satan finds some mischief still for—' "

"Oh, my dear madam, hush! hush!" Mr. Sandbach's voice broke in; and my wife, naturally mortified by the interruption, said no more and moved away. I was surprised to see Rose immediately take her place, and, with more freedom than she generally displayed, run her fingers through the boy's tousled hair.

"Eustace! Eustace!" she said, hurriedly, "tell me everything—every single thing."

Slowly he sat up—till then he had lain on his back.

"Oh Rose—," he whispered, and, my curiosity being aroused, I moved nearer to hear what he was going to say. As I did so, I caught sight of some goats' footmarks in the moist earth beneath the trees.

"Apparently you have had a visit from some goats," I observed. "I had no idea they fed up here."

Eustace laboriously got on to his feet and came to see; and when he saw the footmarks he lay down and rolled on them, as a dog rolls in dirt.

After that there was a grave silence, broken at length by the solemn speech of Mr. Sandbach.

"My dear friends," he said, "it is best to confess the truth bravely. I know that what I am going to say now is what you are all now feeling. The Evil One has been very near us in bodily form. Time may yet discover some injury that he has wrought among us. But, at present, for myself at all events, I wish to offer up thanks for a merciful deliverance."

With that he knelt down, and, as the others knelt, I knelt too, though I do not believe in the Devil being allowed to assail us in visible form, as I told Mr. Sandbach afterwards. Eustace came too, and knelt quietly enough between his aunts after they had beckoned to him. But when it was over he at once got up, and began hunting for something.

"Why! Someone has cut my whistle in two," he said. (I had seen Leyland with an open knife in his hand—a superstitious act which I could hardly approve.)

"Well, it doesn't matter," he continued.

"And why doesn't it matter?" said Mr. Sandbach, who has ever since tried to entrap Eustace into an account of that mysterious hour.

"Because I don't want it any more."

"Why?"

At that he smiled; and, as no one seemed to have anything more to say, I set off as fast as I could through the wood, and hauled up a donkey to carry my poor wife home. Nothing occurred in my absence, except that Rose had again asked Eustace to tell her what had happened; and he, this time, had turned away his head, and had not answered her a single word.

As soon as I returned, we all set off. Eustace walked with difficulty, almost with pain, so that, when we reached the other donkeys, his aunts wished him to mount one of them and ride all the way home. I make it a rule never to interfere between relatives, but I put my foot down at this. As it turned out, I was perfectly right, for the healthy exercise, I suppose, began to thaw Eustace's sluggish blood and loosen his stiffened muscles. He stepped out manfully, for the first time in his life, holding his head up and taking deep draughts of air into his chest. I observed with satisfaction to Miss Mary Robinson, that Eustace was at last taking some pride in his personal appearance.

Mr. Sandbach sighed, and said that Eustace must be carefully watched, for we none of us understood him yet. Miss Mary Robinson being very much—over much, I think—guided by him, sighed too.

"Come, come, Miss Robinson," I said, "there's nothing wrong with Eustace. Our experiences are mysterious, not his. He was astonished at our sudden departure, that's why he was so strange when we returned. He's right enough—improved, if anything."

"And is the worship of athletics, the cult of insensate activity, to be counted as an improvement?" put in Leyland, fixing a large, sorrowful eye on Eustace, who had stopped to scramble on to a rock to pick some cyclamen. "The passionate desire to rend from Nature the few beauties that have been still left her—that is to be counted as an improvement too?"

It is mere waste of time to reply to such remarks, especially when they come from any unsuccessful artist, suffering from a damaged finger. I changed the conversation by asking what we should say at the hotel. After some discussion, it was agreed that we should say nothing, either there or in our letters home. Importunate truth-telling, which brings only bewilderment and discomfort to the hearers, is, in my opinion, a mistake; and, after a long discussion, I managed to make Mr. Sandbach acquiesce in my view.

Eustace did not share in our conversation. He was racing about, like a real boy, in the wood to the right. A strange feeling of shame prevented us from openly mentioning our fright to him. Indeed, it seemed almost reasonable to conclude that it had made but little impression on him. So it disconcerted us when he bounded back with an armful of flowering acanthus, calling out:

"Do you suppose Gennaro'll be there when we get back?"

Gennaro was the stop-gap waiter, a clumsy, impertinent fisher-lad, who had been had up from Minori in the absence of the nice English-speaking Emmanuele. It was to him that we owed our scrappy lunch; and I could not conceive why Eustace desired to see him, unless it was to make mock with him of our behaviour.

"Yes, of course he will be there," said Miss Robinson. "Why do you ask, dear?"

"Oh, thought I'd like to see him."

"And why?" snapped Mr. Sandbach.

"Because, because I do, I do; because, because I do." He danced away into the darkening wood to the rhythm of his words.

"This is very extraordinary," said Mr. Sandbach. "Did he like Gennaro before?"

"Gennaro has only been here two days," said Rose, "and I know that they haven't spoken to each other a dozen times."

Each time Eustace returned from the wood his spirits were higher. Once he came whooping down on us as a wild Indian, and another time he made believe to be a dog. The last time he came back with a poor dazed hare, too frightened to move, sitting on his arm. He was getting too uproarious, I thought; and we were all glad to leave the wood, and start upon the steep staircase path that leads down into Ravello. It was late and turning dark; and we made all the speed we could, Eustace scurrying in front of us like a goat.

Just where the staircase path debouches on the white high road, the next extraordinary incident of this extraordinary day occurred. Three old women were standing by the wayside. They, like ourselves, had come down from the woods, and they were resting their heavy bundles of fuel on the low parapet of the road. Eustace stopped in front of them, and, after a moment's deliberation, stepped forward and—kissed the left-hand one on the cheek!

"My good fellow!" exclaimed Mr. Sandbach, "are you quite crazy?"

Eustace said nothing, but offered the old woman some of his flowers, and then hurried on. I looked back; and the old woman's companions seemed as much astonished at the proceeding as we were. But she herself had put the flowers in her bosom, and was murmuring blessings.

This salutation of the old lady was the first example of Eustace's strange behaviour, and we were both surprised and alarmed. It was useless talking to him, for he either made silly replies, or else bounded away without replying at all.

He made no reference on the way home to Gennaro, and I hoped that

that was forgotten. But when we came to the Piazza, in front of the Cathedral, he screamed out: "Gennaro! Gennaro!" at the top of his voice, and began running up the little alley that led to the hotel. Sure enough, there was Gennaro at the end of it, with his arms and legs sticking out of the nice little English-speaking waiter's dress suit, and a dirty fisherman's cap on his head—for, as the poor landlady truly said, however much she superintended his toilette, he always managed to introduce something incongruous into it before he had done.

Eustace sprang to meet him, and leapt right up into his arms, and put his own arms round his neck. And this in the presence, not only of us, but also of the landlady, the chambermaid, the facchino, and of two American ladies who were coming for a few days' visit to the little hotel.

I always make a point of behaving pleasantly to Italians, however little they may deserve it; but this habit of promiscuous intimacy was perfectly intolerable, and could only lead to familiarity and mortification for all. Taking Miss Robinson aside, I asked her permission to speak seriously to Eustace on the subject of intercourse with social inferiors. She granted it; but I determined to wait till the absurd boy had calmed down a little from the excitement of the day. Meanwhile, Gennaro, instead of attending to the wants of the two new ladies, carried Eustace into the house, as if it was the most natural thing in the world.

"Ho capito," I heard him say as he passed me. 'Ho capito' is the Italian for 'I have understood'; but, as Eustace had not spoken to him, I could not see the force of the remark. It served to increase our bewilderment, and, by the time we sat down at the dinner-table, our imaginations and our tongues were alike exhausted.

I omit from this account the various comments that were made, as few of them seem worthy of being recorded. But, for three or four hours, seven of us were pouring forth our bewilderment in a stream of appropriate and inappropriate exclamations. Some traced a connection between our behaviour in the afternoon and the behaviour of Eustace now. Others saw no connection at all. Mr. Sandbach still held to the possibility of infernal influences, and also said that he ought to have a doctor. Leyland only saw the development of "that unspeakable Philistine, the boy." Rose maintained, to my surprise, that everything was excusable; while I began to see that the young gentleman wanted a sound thrashing. The poor Miss Robinsons swayed helplessly about between these diverse opinions; inclining now to careful supervision, now to acquiescence, now to corporal chastisement, now to Eno's Fruit Salt.

Dinner passed off fairly well, though Eustace was terribly fidgety, Gennaro as usual dropping the knives and spoons, and hawking and clearing his throat. He only knew a few words of English, and we were all reduced to Italian for making known our wants. Eustace, who had picked up a little somehow, asked for some oranges. To my annoyance, Gennaro, in his answer made use of the second person singular—a form only used when addressing those who are both intimates and equals. Eustace had brought it on himself; but an impertinence of this kind was an affront to us all, and I was determined to speak, and to speak at once.

When I heard him clearing the table I went in, and, summoning up my Italian, or rather Neapolitan—the Southern dialects are execrable—I said, "Gennaro! I heard you address Signor Eustace with 'Tu.' "

"It is true."

"You are not right. You must use 'Lei' or 'Voi'—more polite forms. And remember that, though Signor Eustace is sometimes silly and foolish—this afternoon for example—yet you must always behave respectfully to him; for he is a young English gentleman, and you are a poor Italian fisher-boy."

I know that speech sounds terribly snobbish, but in Italian one can say things that one would never dream of saying in English. Besides, it is no good speaking delicately to persons of that class. Unless you put things plainly, they take a vicious pleasure in misunderstanding you.

An honest English fisherman would have landed me one in the eye in a minute for such a remark, but the wretched down-trodden Italians have no pride. Gennaro only sighed, and said: "It is true."

"Quite so," I said, and turned to go. To my indignation I heard him add: "But sometimes it is not important."

"What do you mean?" I shouted.

He came close up to me with horrid gesticulating fingers.

"Signor Tytler, I wish to say this. If Eustazio asks me to call him 'Voi,' I will call him 'Voi.' Otherwise, no."

With that he seized up a tray of dinner things, and fled from the room with them; and I heard two more wine-glasses go on the courtyard floor.

I was now fairly angry, and strode out to interview Eustace. But he had gone to bed, and the landlady, to whom I also wished to speak, was engaged. After more vague wonderings, obscurely expressed owing to the presence of Janet and the two American ladies, we all went to bed, too, after a harassing and most extraordinary day.

III

But the day was nothing to the night.

I suppose I had slept for about four hours, when I woke suddenly thinking I heard a noise in the garden. And, immediately, before my eyes were open, cold terrible fear seized me—not fear of something that was happening, like the fear in the wood, but fear of something that might happen.

Our room was on the first floor, looking out on to the garden—or terrace, it was rather: a wedge-shaped block of ground covered with roses and vines, and intersected with little asphalt paths. It was bounded on the small side by the house; round the two long sides ran a wall, only three feet above the terrace level, but with a good twenty feet drop over it into the olive yards, for the ground fell very precipitously away.

Trembling all over I stole to the window. There, pattering up and down the asphalt paths, was something white. I was too much alarmed to see clearly; and in the uncertain light of the stars the thing took all manner of curious shapes. Now it was a great dog, now an enormous white bat, now a mass of quickly travelling cloud. It would bounce like a ball, or take short flights like a bird, or glide slowly like a wraith. It gave no sound—save the pattering sound of what, after all, must be human feet. And at last the obvious explanation forced itself upon my disordered mind; and I realized that Eustace had got out of bed, and that we were in for something more.

I hastily dressed myself, and went down into the dining-room which opened upon the terrace. The door was already unfastened. My terror had almost entirely passed away, but for quite five minutes I struggled with a curious cowardly feeling, which bade me not interfere with the poor strange boy, but leave him to his ghostly patterings, and merely watch him from the window, to see he took no harm.

But better impulses prevailed and, opening the door, I called out:

"Eustace! what on earth are you doing? Come in at once."

He stopped his antics, and said: "I hate my bedroom. I could not stop in it, it is too small."

"Come! come! I'm tired of affectation. You've never complained of it before."

"Besides I can't see anything—no flowers, no leaves, no sky: only a stone wall." The outlook of Eustace's room certainly was limited; but, as I told him, he had never complained of it before.

"Eustace, you talk like a child. Come in! Prompt obedience, if you please."

He did not move.

"Very well: I shall carry you in by force," I added, and made a few steps towards him. But I was soon convinced of the futility of pursuing a boy through a tangle of asphalt paths, and went in instead, to call Mr. Sandbach and Leyland to my aid.

When I returned with them he was worse than ever. He would not even answer us when we spoke, but began singing and chattering to himself in a most alarming way.

"It's a case for the doctor now," said Mr. Sandbach, gravely tapping his forehead.

He had stopped his running and was singing, first low, then loud—singing five-finger exercises, scales, hymn tunes, scraps of Wagner—anything that came into his head. His voice—a very untuneful voice—grew stronger and stronger, and he ended with a tremendous shout which boomed like a gun among the mountains, and awoke everyone who was still sleeping in the hotel. My poor wife and the two girls appeared at their respective windows, and the American ladies were heard violently ringing their bell.

"Eustace," we all cried, "stop! stop, dear boy, and come into the house."

He shook his head, and started off again—talking this time. Never have I listened to such an extraordinary speech. At any other time it would have been ludicrous, for here was a boy, with no sense of beauty and puerile command of words, attempting to tackle themes which the greatest poets have found almost beyond their power. Eustace Robinson, aged fourteen, was standing in his nightshirt saluting, praising, and blessing, the great forces and manifestations of Nature.

He spoke first of night and the stars and planets above his head, of the swarms of fire-flies below him, of the invisible sea below the fire-flies, of the great rocks covered with anemones and shells that were slumbering in the invisible sea. He spoke of the rivers and waterfalls, of the ripening bunches of grapes, of the smoking cone of Vesuvius and the hidden fire-channels that made the smoke, of the myriads of lizards who were lying curled up in the crannies of the sultry earth, of the showers of white rose-leaves that were tangled in his hair. And then he spoke of the rain and the wind by which all things are changed, of the air through which all things live, and of the woods in which all things can be hidden.

Of course, it was all absurdly high faluting: yet I could have kicked Leyland for audibly observing that it was 'a diabolical caricature of all that was most holy and beautiful in life.'

"And then,"—Eustace was going on in the pitiable conversational doggerel which was his only mode of expression—"and then there are men, but I can't make them out so well." He knelt down by the parapet, and rested his head on his arms.

"Now's the time," whispered Leyland. I hate stealth, but we darted forward and endeavoured to catch hold of him from behind. He was away in a twinkling, but turned round at once to look at us. As far as I could see in the starlight, he was crying. Leyland rushed at him again, and we tried to corner him among the asphalt paths, but without the slightest approach to success.

We returned, breathless and discomfited, leaving him at his madness in the further corner of the terrace. But my Rose had an inspiration.

"Papa," she called from the window, "if you get Gennaro, he might be able to catch him for you."

I had no wish to ask a favour of Gennaro, but, as the landlady had by now appeared on the scene, I begged her to summon him from the charcoal-bin in which he slept, and make him try what he could do.

She soon returned, and was shortly followed by Gennaro, attired in a dress coat, without either waistcoat, shirt, or vest, and a ragged pair of what had been trousers, cut short above the knees for purposes of wading. The landlady, who had quite picked up English ways, rebuked him for the incongruous and even indecent appearance which he presented.

"I have a coat and I have trousers. What more do you desire?"

"Never mind, Signora Scafetti," I put in. "As there are no ladies here, it is not of the slightest consequence." Then, turning to Gennaro, I said: "The aunts of Signor Eustace wish you to fetch him into the house."

He did not answer.

"Do you hear me? He is not well. I order you to fetch him into the house."

"Fetch! fetch!" said Signora Scafetti, and shook him roughly by the arm.

"Eustazio is well where he is."

"Fetch! fetch!" Signora Scafetti screamed, and let loose a flood of Italian, most of which, I am glad to say, I could not follow. I glanced up nervously at the girls' window, but they hardly know as much as I do, and I am thankful to say that none of us caught one word of Gennaro's answer.

The two yelled and shouted at each other for quite ten minutes, at the end of which Gennaro rushed back to his charcoal-bin and Signora Scafetti burst into tears, as well she might, for she greatly valued her English guests.

"He says," she sobbed, "that Signor Eustace is well where he is, and that he will not fetch him. I can do no more."

But I could, for, in my stupid British way, I have got some insight into the Italian character. I followed Mr. Gennaro to his place of repose, and found him wriggling down on to a dirty sack.

"I wish you to fetch Signor Eustace to me," I began.

He hurled at me an unintelligible reply.

"If you fetch him, I will give you this." And out of my pocket I took a new ten lira note.

This time he did not answer.

"This note is equal to ten lire in silver," I continued, for I knew that the poor-class Italian is unable to conceive of a single large sum.

"I know it."

"That is, two hundred soldi."

"I do not desire them. Eustazio is my friend."

I put the note into my pocket.

"Besides, you would not give it me."

"I am an Englishman. The English always do what they promise."

"That is true." It is astonishing how the most dishonest of nations trust us. Indeed they often trust us more than we trust one another. Gennaro knelt up on his sack. It was too dark to see his face, but I could feel his warm garlicky breath coming out in gasps, and I knew that the eternal avarice of the South had laid hold upon him.

"I could not fetch Eustazio to the house. He might die there."

"You need not do that," I replied patiently. "You need only bring him to me; and I will stand outside in the garden." And to this, as if it were something quite different, the pitiable youth consented.

"But give me first the ten lire."

"No"—for I knew the kind of person with whom I had to deal. Once faithless, always faithless.

We returned to the terrace, and Gennaro, without a single word, pattered off towards the pattering that could be heard at the remoter end. Mr. Sandbach, Leyland, and myself moved away a little from the house, and stood in the shadow of the white climbing roses, practically invisible.

We heard "Eustazio" called, followed by absurd cries of pleasure from the poor boy. The pattering ceased, and we heard them talking. Their voices got nearer, and presently I could discern them through the creepers, the grotesque figure of the young man, and the slim little white-robed boy. Gennaro had his arm round Eustace's neck, and Eustace was talking away in his fluent, slip-shod Italian.

"I understand almost everything," I heard him say. "The trees, hills, stars, water, I can see all. But isn't it odd! I can't make out men a bit. Do you know what I mean?"

"Ho capito," said Gennaro gravely, and took his arm off Eustace's shoulder. But I made the new note crackle in my pocket; and he heard it. He stuck his hand out with a jerk; and the unsuspecting Eustace gripped it in his own.

"It is odd!" Eustace went on—they were quite close now—"It almost seems as if—as if—"

I darted out and caught hold of his arm, and Leyland got hold of the other arm, and Mr. Sandbach hung on to his feet. He gave shrill heart-piercing screams; and the white roses, which were falling early that year, descended in showers on him as we dragged him into the house.

As soon as we entered the house he stopped shrieking; but floods of tears silently burst forth, and spread over his upturned face.

"Not to my room," he pleaded. "It is so small."

His infinitely dolorous look filled me with strange pity, but what could I do? Besides, his window was the only one that had bars to it.

"Never mind, dear boy," said kind Mr. Sandbach. "I will bear you company till the morning."

At this his convulsive struggles began again. "Oh, please, not that. Anything but that. I will promise to lie still and not to cry more than I can help, if I am left alone."

So we laid him on the bed, and drew the sheets over him, and left him sobbing bitterly, and saying: "I nearly saw everything, and now I can see nothing at all."

We informed the Miss Robinsons of all that had happened, and returned to the dining-room, where we found Signora Scafetti and Gennaro whispering together. Mr. Sandbach got pen and paper, and began writing to the English doctor at Naples. I at once drew out the note, and flung it down on the table to Gennaro.

"Here is your pay," I said sternly, for I was thinking of the Thirty Pieces of Silver.

"Thank you very much, sir," said Gennaro, and grabbed it.

He was going off, when Leyland, whose interest and indifference were always equally misplaced, asked him what Eustace had meant by saying 'he could not make out men a bit.'

"I cannot say. Signor Eustazio" (I was glad to observe a little deference at last) "has a subtle brain. He understands many things."

"But I heard you say you understood," Leyland persisted.

"I understand, but I cannot explain. I am a poor Italian fisher-lad. Yet, listen: I will try." I saw to my alarm that his manner was changing, and tried to stop him. But he sat down on the edge of the table and started off, with some absolutely incoherent remarks.

"It is sad," he observed at last. "What has happened is very sad. But what can I do? I am poor. It is not I."

I turned away in contempt. Leyland went on asking questions. He wanted to know who it was that Eustace had in his mind when he spoke.

"That is easy to say," Gennaro gravely answered. "It is you, it is I. It is all in this house, and many outside it. If he wishes for mirth, we discomfort him. If he asks to be alone, we disturb him. He longed for a friend, and found none for fifteen years. Then he found me, and the first night I—I who have been in the woods and understood things too—betray him to you, and send him in to die. But what could I do?"

"Gently, gently," said I.

"Oh, assuredly he will die. He will lie in the small room all night, and in the morning he will be dead. That I know for certain."

"There, that will do," said Mr. Sandbach. "I shall be sitting with him."

"Filomena Giusti sat all night with Caterina, but Caterina was dead in the morning. They would not let her out, though I begged, and prayed, and cursed, and beat the door, and climbed the wall. They were ignorant fools, and thought I wished to carry her away. And in the morning she was dead."

"What is all this?" I asked Signora Scafetti.

"All kinds of stories will get about," she replied, "and he, least of anyone, has reason to repeat them."

"And I am alive now," he went on, "because I had neither parents nor relatives nor friends, so that, when the first night came, I could run through the woods, and climb the rocks, and plunge into the water, until I had accomplished my desire!"

We heard a cry from Eustace's room—a faint but steady sound, like the sound of wind in a distant wood heard by one standing in tranquillity.

"That," said Gennaro, "was the last noise of Caterina. I was hanging on to her window then, and it blew out past me."

And, lifting up his hand, in which my ten lira note was safely packed, he solemnly cursed Mr. Sandbach, and Leyland, and myself, and Fate, because Eustace was dying in the upstairs room. Such is the working of the Southern mind; and I verily believe that he would not have moved even then, had not Leyland, that unspeakable idiot, upset the lamp with his elbow. It was a patent self-extinguishing lamp, bought by Signora Scafetti, at my special request, to replace the dangerous thing that she was using. The result was, that it went out; and the mere physical change from light to darkness had more power over the ignorant animal nature of Gennaro than the most obvious dictates of logic and reason.

I felt, rather than saw, that he had left the room and shouted out to Mr. Sandbach: "Have you got the key to Eustace's room in your pocket?" But Mr. Sandbach and Leyland were both on the floor, having mistaken each other for Gennaro, and some more precious time was wasted in finding a match. Mr. Sandbach had only just time to say that he had left the key in the door, in case the Miss Robinsons wished to pay Eustace a visit, when we heard a noise on the stairs, and there was Gennaro, carrying Eustace down.

We rushed out and blocked up the passage, and they lost heart and retreated to the upper landing.

"Now they are caught," cried Signora Scafetti. "There is no other way out."

We were cautiously ascending the staircase, when there was a terrific scream from my wife's room, followed by a heavy thud on the asphalt path. They had leapt out of her window.

I reached the terrace just in time to see Eustace jumping over the parapet of the garden wall. This time I knew for certain he would be killed. But he alighted in an olive tree, looking like a great white moth, and from the tree he slid on to the earth. And as soon as his bare feet touched the clods of earth he uttered a strange loud cry, such as I should not have thought the human voice could have produced, and disappeared among the trees below.

"He has understood and he is saved," cried Gennaro, who was still sitting on the asphalt path. "Now, instead of dying he will live!"

"And you, instead of keeping the ten lire, will give them up," I retorted, for at this theatrical remark I could contain myself no longer.

"The ten lire are mine," he hissed back, in a scarcely audible voice. He clasped his hand over his breast to protect his ill-gotten gains, and, as he did so, he swayed forward and fell upon his face on the path. He had not broken any limbs, and a leap like that would never have killed an Englishman, for the drop was not great. But those miserable Italians have no stamina. Something had gone wrong inside him, and he was dead.

The morning was still far off, but the morning breeze had begun, and more rose leaves fell on us as we carried him in. Signora Scafetti burst into screams at the sight of the dead body, and, far down the valley towards the sea, there still resounded the shouts and the laughter of the escaping boy.

THIS HEAVY LOAD

by William March

It was a dilapidated brick house, with sagging balconies and rusty, iron grill-work. Mrs. Southworth, the landlady, who was intended by nature to be a bos'n on some sailing vessel, but who, by mistake, had become a woman instead, showed me her vacant room and stood with her hands folded under her apron, her iron jaw clamped down. "All right, find fault with it, and see what happens to you, my fine sailor man!" I imagined her thinking. But when I told her the room would suit very well, and paid her for a week in advance, she became more cordial.

Later she invited me downstairs for a drink. We had three together, and by that time we were excellent friends. She began to tell me about the other people in the house: Across the hall from my room lived a man named Downey, and Mrs. Southworth didn't quite know what to do about him. He hadn't paid her a cent of rent for the past two weeks, since he

---

From *A William March Omnibus,* by William March (New York and Toronto: Rinehart & Company, 1956), pp. 216–26.

lost his job, and why she let him stay on was a mystery to her! Only there was something about him, something she couldn't quite understand. But what he ate, or how he managed to keep alive, was something she couldn't figure out. He spent all his time sitting by his window, carving on a block of wood, or looking at the river, deep in thought. "If it was *you,* now," she continued, "I'd have you out in the street, bag and baggage, before you knew it, but *this* fellow . . ." She paused and shook her head, as if puzzled.

That night I saw Downey for the first time. He came out of his room as I was coming up the stairs, a paper parcel in his hand from which minute shavings were spilling. His skin was porcelain-like in its dry brittleness, and his eyes were sunken. The lines in his cheeks and in his forehead were so deep they seemed cut there with a knife. When I passed him on the stairs, he stopped and held on to the banisters for support. Then I spoke to him, and he looked up quickly and stared into my eyes; and I understood why even a realist as hard and as unimaginative as Mrs. Southworth couldn't throw him out. There was the same eagerness in his eyes that you see occasionally in the eyes of a dog mourning for his lost master. I looked at the lined face and his full, sensuous mouth for a moment. I said: "I understand we are neighbors. I've just taken the room across the hall until my ship is ready. I'll be glad to have you come in and talk to me sometime."

"Thanks very much," he said gravely. That's all there was; he didn't commit himself one way or the other. As I went to my room, I saw him still standing there by the banisters watching me. A few nights later he did come to my room. He sat in my one chair, without movement. He seemed even frailer and more exhausted than when I first saw him. I took out a bottle of whiskey from my bag and offered him a drink. He shook his head. "There's no answer in that," he said; "there's no comfort there."

"Well, maybe not," I replied; "but it'll warm up your belly nicely."

Then, somehow, I began to talk to him about my early life. I talked simply, without pose or affectation. For some reason I put myself out to please him. He listened gravely, sympathetically. When I had finished, he in turn began to talk about himself. He came of well-to-do people, I think. At any rate he had gone to college and had got his degree. The next year he returned to his hometown and married the girl he had loved since boyhood. Then war had been declared and he wanted to enlist. There had been a scene with his wife when he signed up at the recruiting station: He was married with a wife and two babies to look out for; there was no reason for him going to France. Leave that to men without obligations! But he had gone anyway. He didn't know why; he simply knew that he must go. He had come through the fighting without injury; or rather he came through without bodily injury, but what he had experienced and what he had seen shocked him profoundly. He must have been an idealistic, highly emotional man with little actual knowledge of the world.

He did not tell me all this in its proper sequence, of course. It came out by fragments which I pieced together in my mind later on. As he talked I kept looking at his strange face and tried to find a word or a phrase which would describe it, but I could not. "Austerely sensual," was as close as I could come, but that, I realized, was pompous and high-flown; and it was not quite what I wanted, anyway. But Downey was talking again in his somewhat hoarse and somewhat hesitant voice.

"When I got back home, I felt that the end of the world had come, and that I was left alive by accident," he was saying. "I kept thinking that all the time. I had been sure, once, of what was evil and what was good, but I knew, now, that those things were only words, meaningless in themselves and taking significance from other words equally meaningless and equally subject to change. I was lost in a strange world that frightened me."

As Downey talked, I could imagine his efforts to readjust himself. He had hoped when he was discharged that a return to normal life would solve his problems, but he found very soon that that was impossible. He had nothing in common with his wife any more; the deep sense of understanding which had existed between them was gone. He began actually to hate her for what he considered her smug sense of right and wrong, her constant talk of religion. He got so he couldn't stand the sight of his children either. An overpowering feeling of restlessness came over him.

One night his wife got him to go to church with her. It was the first time he had been in a church since he had enlisted. He sat in his pew, slightly sickened, not believing any man could be as harsh and as stupid as the minister seemed. Then he got up, walked out of the church and went back home. When his wife arrived half an hour later she found him in their livingroom swinging an ax, smashing the furniture to bits. That same night Downey went to a friend of his, a lawyer, deeded everything he owned to his wife and children and left town.

As Downey told me his story, all jumbled up and not in its proper order, as I'm telling it to you, his voice was without emotion, and his body was quiet. Occasionally he moved his hand backward and forward on the arm of the chair, and occasionally he wet his full, sensual lips. Then suddenly he lowered his eyes. We sat there in silence, neither looking at the other. I offered him a cigarette, which he took. From the way he sucked it into his lungs I knew it was the first smoke he had had for a long time. I thought it better neither to offer comment on what he had told me, nor to ask him to continue. A few minutes later he got up and went back to his room.

After that, Downey came to see me often. He never talked so freely as he had the first time, but in the next week he did tell me a great deal about himself: After he had left his wife (he had never seen her since, and he had no wish to see either her or his children), he had gone to Chicago and had got a job as motorman on a streetcar. At night he went to the public libraries and took out books, books on philosophy and religion mostly, but he could find nothing in them that he wanted. Then —Downey thought this himself—he became slightly insane. He began writing obscene pamphlets in which he proved that there was no God; that there could be no God. Later on, he went to New York and worked in a restaurant as a dishwasher. At night he read or wrote his rambling, profane pamphlets. Occasionally he would talk to late-comers in the restaurant, trying to convince them, as he had convinced himself, that the skies were empty. But the taxi-drivers or the workmen to whom he talked laughed at him and tapped their foreheads.

From New York he drifted to Philadelphia, where he remained for a few weeks. But his restlessness came over him again. He had been in Omaha, New Orleans, Detroit, Denver, St. Louis, Kansas City and Seattle within a short time, but he remembered nothing of those places except the various furnished rooms he had lived in, and even they, because of their lack of individuality, had gradually merged in his mind into one composite room. Many times he could not find work, and more often than not he was hungry, but something inside him impelled him constantly forward. He did not know what he was seeking, or even that he was seeking anything. He simply knew when the impulse came over him that he must get away.

As he talked in my room, he could not remember the names of some of the cities where he had been. He would refer, often, to places as "where the man in the United Cigar store had a gold tooth in front," or, "where the landlady was in mourning for her daughter," identifying an entire community with one of its members.

As the years went by, he found it more and more difficult to get work. Then, too, he had started to drink pretty heavily. In Cleveland, Ohio, he met a waitress and they lived together for a time—not more than a month or so, I gathered—but he had left her, too. She had really loved him, he was sure, and he might have been happy with her, but when the urge to run away came over him he could not resist it.

Later, in Detroit, a man in a rooming-house started him using drugs, and after that his descent had been swift. He had quit reading. He had quit thinking. He worked when he could get work and stole or begged when he couldn't. There was nothing that he hadn't done, he told me, no degradation that he hadn't experienced. He told me these thnigs quietly, without self-consciousness and without shame, as if he were speaking clinically about another person whom we both understood.

The drugs-and-drinking period had lasted about three years, he thought, and then one morning in Frisco, in an agony of disgust with himself, he had signed as a seaman on a sailing vessel. His going to sea was not premeditated. He did it on impulse, without thought. He felt, dimly, that he might find in a foreign country what he had looked for and been unable to find in America. He did not find it, of course, but the trip improved his health, and when he returned to the United States, six months later, his desire for drugs had left him. After that he had gone to sea regularly for a few years, but he rarely made two voyages in the same steamer.

Then, finally, he had been unable to get a ship at all, but he managed to keep himself alive by doing odd jobs around the docks. Later he got a job as delivery boy for a grocery store. It was while he was so employed that he came to live in Mrs. Southworth's dingy rooming-house, about a month before I met him.

He told me all this over a period of days.

"What is it you want?" I asked. "What are you looking for?"

"I don't know," he said. "I wish to God I did know. If I knew that, I could lay down this heavy load and rest."

We sat smoking quietly. We had come to the point where we would sit quiet together for long periods. "Where did you learn wood-carving?" I asked casually. He looked at me, but he did not answer. "Mrs. Southworth told me that you were carving a block of wood," I continued, "and of course I saw you taking out those shavings that night."

His lips opened and he seemed on the point of telling me something, but he changed his mind. "I'll be going now," he said. When he reached the door he turned and came back to me: "You're not offended, are you?"

"Of course, I'm not," I answered; "why, of course, I'm not." Then he went out. "He'll tell me about the carving later, when he is ready to do it," I decided. I was correct, for sure enough he did tell me. My ship was out of drydock by that time and was going on loading-berth the next day. It was my last night in Mrs. Southworth's establishment, and my bag was almost packed when Downey rapped on my door. It was January, and the weather was cold. Outside a mist-like rain was falling. The wind flung the chill rain against my window in intermittent rushes, like the brushing of leaves.

I opened the door and Downey entered. I stood gaping, amazed at the change that had come over him. His step was brisk and his eyes were shining. He seemed to have dropped his sickness, his hunger and his despair like a shabby coat. There was a buoyancy, a joyousness about him that I could not understand, and which I was not prepared for. When he came into my room, his shoulders were straight and there was color in his lined, haggard face. He kept moving about and touching things with a surprised delight. His clothes were soaked, and I could see the raindrops clinging to his frail neck and chest, but he seemed unaware of the cold, as if there were something within that warmed him. He sat back in my chair and laughed deeply, the contented laugh of a happy man—it was the most restful sound I have ever heard—and began to talk slowly, trying to find words simple enough to describe his happiness. He raised his hands and brought the blunt tips of his fingers together.

"I have found what I have been seeking!" he said. "I have put down my load!"

For awhile he talked incoherently, but gradually I began to follow his sentences, and piece out his story. It was while working as a delivery boy for the grocery store, before I met him, that he had picked up a block of wood. He had been taking a walk along the bay front that Sunday afternoon, and he saw the block on the dirty beach, just out of reach of the tide. The wood was a golden brown color, and unlike any wood he had ever seen. Apparently it had grown in a far country and had been thrown overboard from some ship by a sailor. When Downey picked up the block and turned it over and over in his hands, he saw that the wood was strangely grained, and, as he examined it, he thought he could detect in its looped and whirled surface the outline of a head. When he discovered that, he sat down and began to trace with the blade of his pocketknife the figure in the wood.

He sat flat on the dirty sand, the block resting between his legs, and worked slowly. Before him was the bay and a small beach littered with driftwood, tin cans and grapefruit rinds, while behind him, somewhere in the distance, a switch engine was spotting cars of freight for a steamer working overtime. The rhythmical bumping of the cars, as the engine hit them and shoved them forward, came muffled and uncertain, and more and more indistinct, until, at last, the sound lost its meaning for Downey and became the booming of surf a long way off. And as he continued to work, the dirty beach disappeared also, and another and an older scene superimposed itself. This is the way Downey described the change to me:

"As I sat there carving on the block, I thought of myself not as a middle-aged delivery boy for a cheap grocery store, but as a naked brown man who had crawled out of the protection of his jungle for the first time to stare in amazement at the sea. Behind me stretched hot, misty swamps with purple and red flowers, larger than a man's head, swinging like bells from the trees. Birds, colored unbelievably, were screaming always on one persistent note, flapping back and forth between the ancient trees, or resting, balanced on the swinging lianas, their wings half flushed and ready for flight. Ferns grew as tall as cliffs, and there was a rich mist hanging over everything. And as I sat there looking into that jungle, a strange thing happened to me. I lost all sense of time and space and even of my own identity. I seemed so completely a part of the background I visioned. I could see my own body sitting there—a little, patient, brown man, making a god from a piece of curiously grained wood.

"Later, when it became dark, I returned to my room, carrying the block with me, stroking it with my hands. I had become obsessed with the block; so much so that on the following morning, when it was time to go to the grocery store, I found that I could not. I really made an effort to go out of the room and leave the figure which was taking shape under my hands, but it was impossible."

That had been three weeks ago and since then Downey had worked patiently. He knew nothing of wood-carving, he told me, and he had no tools to work with except his knife and a crude scraper which he had made out of a safety razor blade.

At first Downey had been somewhat ashamed of what he was doing, but as he continued to work the idea gradually took a firm hold on him. "Why shouldn't I make a god of my own?" he asked. "Why not? I could not accept the gods of other people." His eyes closed and his lips pressed forward with a faint quiver, as if recently touched, in love, by other and unseen lips. "What was there absurd about that?" he asked. He sat in his dark room hour after hour carving and whispering to himself. "I am creating a god of compassion and tenderness. I am not making him all-wise or all-just or all-powerful. I am creating an eager god who loves joy, laughter and dancing; not cruelty, not bloodshed. 'Sing!' he says. 'Sing and love and dance, for the world is a beautiful place and life is something strange which passes quickly!' "

Downey continued to talk, a slight, self-deprecatory smile on his lips. I did not interrupt him. There was nothing that I could say, after all. Suddenly he got up and raised his arms above his head in a gesture of complete adoration.

"Today I completed the figure and polished it with oil until it shone like a rich lamp in my room. I stood there looking at it. It was not a very good carving, but I had made it, I alone, and I loved it! Then I began to feel half ashamed because it had taken such a hold on my thoughts. I put the figure on the table in my room, and stood aside to examine it critically, with half-closed eyes; but before I understood what was happening, I found myself on my knees before it, my head thrown back, my hands pressed together, rocking from side to side. Words came tumbling out of me, words which I had not used for a long time: 'Lord! Lord!' I prayed. 'Heal me! Save me! Make me whole!'

"Then an essence flowed through my body. I could feel it moving about in my veins, washing me clean. I could feel tight things, buried in my body for a long time, being loosened and untied by the essence and smoothed flat again. My flesh tingled with a new life. Then, as the essence surged back and forth through me, like a river, all grief, disgust and shame were washed away, and a feeling of rest such as I had never before known came over me. I knelt before the figure for a long time, at peace, my heart swelling with joy and love as if it would burst through my side."

Downey got up and walked to my window and stared for a time at the river, seen indistinctly through the rain. It was still blowing, and gusts of wind swept the rain against my window with a faint sound, like thrown sand. He stood there, silent, watching the rain swirling over the river, watching the lines of black smoke from factories breaking under the force of the wind and coming together again. Then, after awhile, he began to talk in his joyous, new voice:

"A long time afterwards, I got up from my knees and went out and walked in the rain. I had forgotten how beautiful red brick could be, or the way wet asphalt reflected in a shallower world the things that surrounded it. I wanted to touch everything with my hands: the red bricks, the iron posts, the rough bark of trees. I wanted to feel everything, see everything, and hear everything again. And so I walked in the streets for hours, surprised that the world was so much lovelier than I had thought it; watching the way a tree bent against the wind, the shape of a cloud scurrying across the sky, or raindrops congealing and dripping slowly from the end of a green blind. Somewhere during my walk a woman came to a window and said to someone else within: 'Get the blue; blue wears longer.'

"As I walked the streets, I kept turning those words over and over in my mind. To me they possessed a beauty not of this world, a significance beyond the stretch of our dull senses." Downey laughed joyously and pressed his hands together. "Do you understand what I'm trying to tell you?" he asked.

"Yes," I said.

He was silent for a moment and then he continued: "Later on, I saw a man walking toward me. He was an old Negro, and he carried a sack filled with junk slung across his shoulders. I went over to him, to help him with his load, but he pulled away, as if I meant to rob him. I had wanted to tell him about my new happiness, and to share it with him, but when he pulled away, I saw how wrong I was. That was the mistake people had always made. I knew, then, that I must never show my god to anybody or even speak his name to another."

Again Downey walked in my small room. "I'm so happy," he said; "so perfectly happy. Nothing can ever touch me again. Nothing! Pain, hunger, old age, death—they're meaningless words, now! They're nothing to me at all!" Then he lifted his enraptured eyes and stared into the sky at a vision which I could not follow.

I got up and began to finish my packing, looking occasionally at Downey standing by the window, watching his exalted face. And I knew, then, for the first time that man is not yet a completed thing; that he is only part of other things which he cannot name and which he but dimly understands. He must have a master if he is to have peace, and if he loses one, he will not rest until he has found another. He talks eternally about freedom, but he can never be free, for he is a frail, lost creature, too weak as yet to walk unaided.

I closed my seabag and snapped the lock, saddened all at once because these things were true.

HEJDA
by Anaïs Nin

The unveiling of women is a delicate matter. It will not happen overnight. We are all afraid of what we shall find.

Hejda was, of course, born in the Orient. Before the unveiling she was living in an immense garden, a little city in itself, filled with many servants, many sisters and brothers, many relatives. From the roof of the house one could see all the people passing, vendors, beggars, Arabs going to the mosque.

Hejda was then a little primitive, whose greatest pleasure consisted in inserting her finger inside pregnant hens and breaking the eggs, or filling frogs with gasoline and setting a lighted match to them. She went about without underclothes in the house, without shoes, but once outside she was heavily veiled and there was no telling exactly the contours of her body, which were at an early age those of a full-blown woman, and there was no telling that her smile had that carnivorous air of smiles with large teeth.

In school she had a friend whose great sorrow was her dark color. The

---

From *Under a Glass Bell* by Anaïs Nin (Denver: Alan Swallow, 1961), pp. 86–95.

darkest skin in the many shaded nuances of the Arabian school. Hejda took her out into the farthest corner of the school garden one day and said to her: "I can make you white if you want me to. Do you trust me?"

"Of course I do."

Hejda brought out a piece of pumice stone. She very gently but very persistently began to pumice a piece of the girl's forehead. Only when the pain became unendurable did she stop. But for a week, every day, she continued enlarging the circle of scraped, scarred skin, and took secret pleasure in the strange scene of the girl's constant lamentations of pain and her own obstinate scraping. Until they were both found out and punished.

At seventeen she left the Orient and the veils, but she retained an air of being veiled. With the most chic and trim French clothes, which molded her figure, she still conveyed the impression of restraint and no one could feel sure of having seen her neck, arms or legs. Even her evening dresses seemed to sheathe her. This feeling of secrecy, which recalled constantly the women of Arabia as they walked in their many yards of white cotton, rolled like silk around a spool, was due in great part to her inarticulateness. Her speech revealed and opened no doors. It was labyrinthian. She merely threw off enough words to invite one into the passageway but no sooner had one started to walk towards the unfinished phrase than one met an impasse, a curve, a barrier. She retreated behind half admissions, half promises, insinuations.

This covering of the body, which was like the covering of the spirit, had created an unshatterable timidity. It had the effect of concentrating the light, the intensity in the eyes. So that one saw Hejda as a mixture of elegance, cosmetics, aesthetic plumage, with only the eyes sending signals and messages. They pierced the European clothes with the stabbing brilliancy of those eyes in the Orient which to reach the man had to pierce through the heavy aura of yards of white cotton.

The passageways that led one to Hejda were as tortuous and intricate as the passageways in the oriental cities in which the pursued women lost themselves, but all through the vanishing, turning streets the eyes continued to signal to strangers like prisoners waving out of windows.

The desire to speak was there, after centuries of confinement and repression, the desire to be invaded and rescued from the secretiveness. The eyes were full of invitations, in great contradiction to the closed folds of the clothes, the many defenses of the silk around the neck, the sleeves around the arms.

Her language was veiled. She had no way to say: look at Hejda who is full of ideas. So she laid out cards and told fortunes like the women of the harem, or she ate sweets like a stunted woman who had been kept a child by close binding with yards of white cotton, as the feet of the Chinese women had been kept small by bandaging. All she could say was: I had a dream last night (because at breakfast time in the Orient, around the first cup of dark coffee, everyone told their dreams). Or she opened a book accidentally when in trouble and placed her finger on a phrase and decided on her next course of action by the words of this phrase. Or she cooked a dish as colorful as an oriental market place.

Her desire to be noticed was always manifested, as in the Orient, by a bit of plumage, a startling jewel, a spangle pasted on her forehead between the eyes (the third eye of the Oriental was a jewel, as if the secret life so long preserved from openness had acquired the fire of precious stones).

No one understood the signals: look at Hejda, the woman of the Orient who wants to be a woman of tomorrow. The plumage and the aesthetic adornment diverted them like decoration on a wall. She was always being thrust back into the harem, on a pillow.

She had arrived in Paris, with all her invisible veils. When she laughed she concealed her mouth as much as possible, because in her small round face the teeth were extraordinarily large. She concealed her voraciousness and her appetites. Her voice was made small, again as the Chinese make their feet small, small and infantile. Her poses were reluctant and reserved. The veil was not in her timidities, her fears, in her manner of dressing, which covered her throat and compressed her overflowing breasts. The veil was in her liking for flowers (which was racial), especially small roses and innocent asexual flowers, in complicated rituals of politeness (also traditional), but above all in evasiveness of speech.

She wanted to be a painter. She joined the Academie Julien. She painted painstakingly on small canvases—the colors of the Orient, a puerile Orient of small flowers, serpentines, confetti and candy colors, the colors of small shops with metallic lace-paper roses and butterflies.

In the same class there was a dark, silent, timid young Roumanian. He had decadent, aristocratic hands, he never smiled, he never talked. Those who approached him felt such a shriveling timidity in him, such a retraction, that they remained at a distance.

The two timidities observed each other. The two silences, the two withdrawals. Both were oriental interiors, without windows on the external world, and all the greenery in the inner patio, all their windows open on the inside of the house.

A certain Gallic playfulness presides in the painting class. The atmosphere is physical, warm, gay. But the two of them remain in their inner patio, listening to birds singing and fountains playing. He thinks: how mysterious she is. And she thinks: how mysterious he is.

Finally one day, as she is leaving, he watches her repainting the black line on the edge of her eyes out of a silver peacock. She nimbly lifts up the head of the peacock and it is a little brush that makes black lines around her oriental eyes.

This image confounds him, ensorcells him. The painter is captivated, stirred. Some memory out of Persian legends now adorns his concept of her.

They marry and take a very small apartment where the only window gives on a garden.

At first they marry to hide together. In the dark caverns of their whisperings, confidences, timidities, what they now elaborate is a stalactitic world shut out from light and air. He initiates her into his aesthetic values. They make love in the dark and in the daytime make their place more beautiful and more refined.

In Molnar's hands she is being remolded, refashioned, stylized. He cannot remold her body. He is critical of her heaviness. He dislikes her breasts and will not let her ever show them. They overwhelm him. He confesses he would like her better without them. This shrinks her within herself and plants the seed of doubt of her feminine value. With these words he has properly subjugated her, given her a doubt which will keep her away from other men. He bound her femininity, and it is now oppressed, bound, even ashamed of its vulgarity, of its expansiveness. This is the reign of aesthetic value, stylization, refinement, art, artifice. He has established his domination in this. At every turn nature must be subjugated. Very soon, with his coldness, he represses her violence. Very soon he polishes her language, her manners, her impulses. He reduces and limits her hospitality, her friendliness, her desire for expansion.

It is her second veiling. It is the aesthetic veils of art and social graces. He designs her dresses. He molds her as far as he can into the stylized figures in his paintings. His women are transparent and lie in hammocks between heaven and earth. Hejda cannot reach this, but she can become an odalisque. She can acquire more silver peacocks, more poetic objects that will speak for her.

Her small canvases look childlike standing beside his. Slowly she becomes more absorbed in his painting than in her own. The flowers and gardens disappear.

He paints a world of stage settings, static ships, frozen trees, crystal fairs, the skeletons of pleasure and color, from which nature is entirely shut off. He proceeds to make Hejda one of the objects in this painting; her nature is more and more castrated by this abstraction of her, the obtrusive breasts more severely veiled. In his painting there is no motion, no nature, and certainly not the Hejda who liked to run about without underwear, to eat herbs and raw vegetables out of the garden.

Her breasts are the only intrusion in their exquisite life. Without them she could be the twin he wanted, and they could accomplish this strange marriage of his feminine qualities and her masculine ones. For it is already clear that he likes to be protected and she likes to protect, and that she has more power in facing the world of reality, more power to sell pictures, to interest the galleries in his work, more courage too. It is she who assumes the active role in contact with the world. Molnar can never earn a living, Hejda can. Molnar cannot give orders (except to her) and she can. Molnar cannot execute, realize, concretize as well as she can, for in execution and action she is not timid.

Finally it is Molnar who paints and draws and it is Hejda who goes out and sells his work.

Molnar grows more and more delicate, more vulnerable, and Hejda stronger. He is behind the scene, and she is in the foreground now.

He permits her love to flow all around him, sustain him, nourish him. In the dark he reconquers his leadership. And not by any sensual prodigality, but on the contrary, by a severe economy of pleasure. She is often left hungry. She never suspects for a moment that it is anything but economy and thinks a great abundance lies behind this aesthetic reserve. There is no delight or joy in their sensual contact. It is a creeping together into a womb.

Their life together is stilted, windowless, facing inward. But the plants and fountains of the patio are all artificial, ephemeral, immobile. A stage setting for a drama that never takes place. There are colonnades, friezes, backgrounds, plush drops but no drama takes place, no evolution, no sparks. His women's figures are always lying down, suspended in space.

But Hejda, Hejda feels compressed. She does not know why. She has never known anything but oppression. She has never been out of a small universe delimited by man. Yet something is expanding in her. A new Hejda is born out of the struggle with reality, to protect the weakness of Molnar. In the outer world she feels larger. When she returns home she feels she must shrink back into submission to Molnar's proportions. The outgoing rhythm must cease. Molnar's whole being is one total negation; negation and rejection of the world, of social life, of other human beings, of success, of movement, of motion, of curiosity, of adventure, of the unknown.

What is he defending, protecting? No consuming passion for one person, but perhaps a secret consuming. He admits no caresses, no invitations to love-making. It is always "no" to her hunger, "no" to her tenderness, "no" to the flow of life. They were close in fear and concealment, but they are not close in flow and development. Molnar is now frozen, fixed. There is no emotion to propel him. And when she seeks to propel him, substitute her élan for his static stagnation, all he can do is break this propeller.

"Your ambitions are vulgar."

(She does not know how to answer: my ambitions are merely the balance to your inertia.)

A part of her wants to expand. A part of her being wants to stay with Molnar. This conflict tears her asunder. The pulling and tearing bring on illness.

Hejda falls.

Hejda is ill.

She cannot move forward because Molnar is tied, and she cannot break with him.

Because he will not move, his being is stagnant and filled with poison. He injects her every day with this poison.

She has taken his paintings into the real world, to sell, and in so doing she has connected with that world and found it larger, freer.

Now he does not let her handle the painting. He even stops painting. Poverty sets in.

Perhaps Molnar will turn about now and protect her. It is the dream of every maternal love: I have filled him with my strength. I have nourished his painting. My painting has passed into his painting. I am broken and weak. Perhaps now he will be strong.

But not at all. Molnar watches her fall, lets her fall. He lets poverty install itself. He watches inertly the sale of their art possessions, the trips to the pawnbroker. He leaves Hejda without care. His passivity and inertia consume the whole house.

It is as if Hejda had been the glue that held the furniture together. Now it breaks. It is as if she had been the cleaning fluid and now the curtains turn gray. The logs in the fireplace now smoke and do not burn: was she the fire in the hearth too? Because she lies ill objects grow rusty. The food turns sour. Even the artificial flowers wilt. The paints dry on the palette. Was she the water, the soap too? Was she the fountain, the visibility of the windows, the gloss of the floors? The creditors buzz like locusts. Was she the fetish of the house who kept them away? Was she the oxygen in the house? Was she the salt now missing from the bread? Was she the delicate feather duster dispelling the webs of decay? Was she the silver polish?

Tired of waiting for her to get well—alone, he goes out.

Hejda and Molnar are now separated. She is free. Several people help her to unwind the binding wrapped around her personality first by the family life, then by the husband. Someone falls in love with her ample breasts, and removes the taboo that Molnar had placed upon them. Hejda buys herself a sheer blouse which will reveal her possessions.

When a button falls off she does not sew it on again.

Then she also began to talk.

She talked about her childhood. The same story of going about without underwear as a child which she had told before with a giggle of confusion and as if saying: "what a little primitive I was," was now told with the oblique glance of the strip-teaser, with a slight arrogance, the *agent provocateur* towards the men (for now exhibitionism placed the possibility in the present, not in the past).

She discards small canvases and buys very large ones. She paints larger roses, larger daisies, larger trellises, larger candied clouds, larger taffy seas. But just as the canvases grow larger without their content growing more important, Hejda is swelling up without growing. There is more of her. Her voice grows louder, her language, freed of Molnar's decadent refinement, grows coarser. Her dresses grow shorter. Her blouses looser. There is more flesh around her small body but Molnar is not there to corset it. There is more food on her table. She no longer conceals her teeth. She becomes proud of her appetite. Liberty has filled her to overflowing with a confidence that everything that was once secret and bound was of immense value. Every puerile detail of her childhood, every card dealer's intuition, every dream, becomes magnified.

And the stature of Hejda cannot bear the weight of her ambition. It is as if compression had swung her towards inflation. She is inflated physically and spiritually. And whoever dares to recall her to a sense of proportion, to a realization that there are perhaps other painters of value in the world, other women, becomes the traitor who must be banished instantly. On him she pours torrents of abuse like the abuse of the oriental gypsies to whom one has refused charity—curses and maledictions.

It is not desire or love she brings to the lovers: I have discovered that I am very gifted for love-making!

It is not creativity she brings to her painting: I will show Molnar that I was a better painter!

Her friendships with women are simply one long underground rivalry: to excel in startling dress or behavior. She enters a strained, intense competition. When everything fails she resorts to lifting her dress and arranging her garters.

Where are the veils and labyrinthian evasions?

She is back in the garden of her childhood, back to the native original Hejda, child of nature and succulence and sweets, of pillows and erotic literature.

The frogs leap away in fear of her again.

THE YOUNG MAN WHO LIVED ALONE

by Mohammed Mrabet

A man named Si Qaddour had been left a large tract of land by his father. There was a big house at one end of it where the family lived, and a half mile or so from the house there was a grove of trees. Here in the shade at the edge of a stream Si Qaddour's father had built a small house and arranged a garden around it. The old man had spent most of his time sitting in this garden, far from his family.

Si Qaddour was a busy man, and never went near the little house in the woods. His son, however, a youth of seventeen, like to smoke kif, and his grandfather's garden seemed to him the perfect place to do it. He began to spend more and more time there, until finally he moved out of his family's house altogether and went to live alone in the woods. Once a month he would go into the town and buy what he needed, such as matches, or a new pipe, or more kif. Each afternoon he walked to his father's house and got the food he would be eating that night and the next day.

His grandfather had made a pool in the garden, and it was beside the pool that the young man liked to sit. He would stay without moving for long periods of time, so that the birds would come and light near him. He had spent many months trying to become their friend. It took patience and intelligence, and a good deal of kif besides, to learn how to sit as he did, waiting for the birds to come. But usually they came, and sometimes they even perched on his shoulder. And it seemed to him that they were trying to talk to him, as if they believed he understood what they were saying with their chirping.

One day a group of relatives from another part of the country arrived to call on Si Qaddour and his family. Among them there was a young

---

From *M'Hashish* (San Francisco: City Lights Books, 1969), pp. 21–23, transcribed and translated by Paul Bowles.

mute girl. She sat with the rest of the family for a while, and then, growing restless, she got up and wandered outside. The orchards were beautiful, and so she took a walk. After a while she came to the grove of trees, and the path led her to the small house by the river.

As she went into the garden she saw the youth sitting by the pool with two birds on the ground in front of him. He seemed to be talking to them. The girl stood still, and her mouth opened in astonishment. The birds were chirping very loud. The young man listened, and appeared to be saying something to them. He raised his arms and the two birds flew away. Then he began to laugh. At that moment he looked up and saw the girl watching him from the other end of the garden. It seemed to him that he had never seen such a beautiful face.

He called to her: Who are you?

The girl put her hand in front of her mouth and shrugged her shoulders, to say that she could not speak. He went over to her and made gestures, and she showed that she understood.

What are you doing way out here in the woods? he wanted to know.

She made signs to say that her family were visiting at a big house beyond the orchards, and he told her it was his father's house.

He led the girl to the pool and told her to sit down. Then he made her some tea. As she drank he filled his pipe with kif and lighted it. He poured himself a glass of tea and sat smoking and looking at her.

The girl was making a great effort to say something to him, but he raised his hand and said: No. Don't try to talk. I want to dream a little.

They were both silent for a while, as the kif climbed into the young man's head and he listened to the sound of the river flowing by.

After a time he rose and said to the girl: Come with me. I'll show you the way back to my father's house.

They started to walk through the woods. He talked to her, and she answered by moving her hands. Suddenly a snake rose up in the middle of the path, as if it were going to strike at them. The girl saw it, and her fear was so great that she opened her mouth and screamed with all her force. The fear had loosened her voice.

The snake went to one side, and lay among the leaves by the edge of the path.

I speak now, said the girl. The youth looked at her, but he did not understand.

Soon he told her: Now we're out of the grove. And you can see the house up there. Just keep going.

Yes, she said, and she went on to the house, thinking: Now I can speak.

The young man turned around and went back to where the snake was waiting for him. He stopped and ran his hand along its back two or three times, and it slid away. Then he walked on to his garden and sat smoking kif by the pool.

Social

NEW LIFE AT KYEREFASO
by Efua Theodora Sutherland

Shall we say
Shall we put it this way

Shall we say that the maid of Kyerefaso, Foruwa, daughter of the Queen Mother, was as a young deer, graceful in limb? Such was she, with head held high, eyes soft and wide with wonder. And she was light of foot, light in all her moving.

Stepping springily along the water path like a deer that had strayed from the thicket, springily stepping along the water path, she was a picture to give the eye a feast. And nobody passed her by but turned to look at her again.

Those of her village said that her voice in speech was like the murmur of a river quietly flowing beneath shadows of bamboo leaves. They said her smile would sometimes blossom like a lily on her lips and sometimes rise like sunrise.

The butterflies do not fly away from the flowers, they draw near. Foruwa was the flower of her village.

So shall we say,

Shall we put it this way, that all the village butterflies, the men, tried to draw near her at every turn, crossed and crossed her path? Men said of her, "She shall be my wife, and mine, and mine and mine."

But suns rose and set, moons silvered and died and as the days passed Foruwa grew more lovesome, yet she became no one's wife. She smiled at the butterflies and waved her hand lightly to greet them as she went swiftly about her daily work:

"Morning, Kweku
Morning, Kwesi
Morning, Kodwo"

but that was all.

From *An African Treasury* (New York: Crown Publishers, Inc., 1960), edited by Langston Hughes, pp. 111–17.

And so they said, even while their hearts thumped for her:

"Proud!
Foruwa is proud . . . and very strange"

And so the men when they gathered would say:

"There goes a strange girl. She is not just stiff-in-the-neck proud, not just breasts-stuck-out-I-am-the-only-girl-in-the-village proud. What kind of pride is hers?"

The end of the year came round again, bringing the season of festivals. For the gathering in of corn, yams and cocoa there were harvest celebrations. There were bride-meetings too. And it came to the time when the Asafo companies should hold their festival. The village was full of manly sounds, loud musketry and swelling choruses.

The pathfinding, path-clearing ceremony came to an end. The Asafo marched on toward the Queen Mother's house, the women fussing round them, prancing round them, spreading their cloths in their way. "Osee!" rang the cry. "Osee!" to the manly men of old. They crouched like leopards upon the branches.

Before the drums beat
Before the danger drums beat, beware!
Before the horns moaned
Before the wailing horns moaned, beware!

They were upright, they sprang. They sprang. They sprang upon the enemy. But now, blood no more! No more thundershot on thundershot.

But still we are the leopards on the branches. We are those who roar and cannot be answered back. Beware, we are they who cannot be answered back.

There was excitement outside the Queen Mother's courtyard gate. "Gently, gently," warned the Asafo leader. "Here comes the Queen Mother.

Spread skins of the gentle sheep in her way.
Lightly, lightly walks our Mother Queen.
Shower her with silver,
Shower her with silver for she is peace."

And the Queen Mother stood there, tall, beautiful, before the men and there was silence.

"What news, what news do you bring?" she quietly asked.

"We come with dusty brows from our pathfinding, Mother. We come with tired, thorn-pricked feet. We come to bathe in the coolness of your peaceful stream. We come to offer our manliness to new life."

The Queen Mother stood there, tall and beautiful and quiet. Her fanbearers stood by her and all the women clustered near. One by one the men laid their guns at her feet and then she said:

"It is well. The gun is laid aside. The gun's rage is silenced in the stream. Let your weapons from now on be your minds and your hands' toil.

"Come maidens, women all, join the men in dance for they offer themselves to new life."

There was one girl who did not dance.

"What, Foruwa!" urged the Queen Mother, "Will you not dance? The men are tired of parading in the ashes of their grandfathers' glorious deeds. That should make you smile. They are tired of the empty croak: 'We are men, we are men.'

"They are tired of sitting like vultures upon the rubbish heaps they have piled upon the half-built walls of their grandfathers. Smile, then, Foruwa, smile.

"Their brows shall now indeed be dusty, their feet thorn-picked, and 'I love my land' shall cease to be the empty croaking of a vulture upon the rubbish heap. Dance, Foruwa, dance!"

Foruwa opened her lips and this was all she said: "Mother, I do not find him here."

"Who? Who do you not find here?"

"He with whom this new life shall be built. He is not here, Mother. These men's faces are empty; there is nothing in them, nothing at all."

"Alas, Foruwa, alas, alas! What will become of you, my daughter?"

"The day I find him, Mother, the day I find the man, I shall come running to you, and your worries will come to an end."

"But, Foruwa, Foruwa," argued the Queen Mother, although in her heart she understood her daughter, "five years ago your rites were fulfilled. Where is the child of your womb? Your friend Maanan married. Your friend Esi married. Both had their rites with you."

"Yes, Mother, they married and see how their steps once lively now drag in the dust. The sparkle has died out of their eyes. Their husbands drink palm wine the day long under the mango trees, drink palm wine and push counters across the draughtboards all the day, and are they not already looking for other wives? Mother, the man I say is not here."

This conversation had been overheard by one of the men and soon others heard what Foruwa had said. That evening there was heard a new song in the village.

"There was a woman long ago,
Tell that maid, tell that maid,
There was a woman long ago,
She would not marry Kwesi,
She would not marry Kwaw,
She would not, would not, would not.
One day she came home with hurrying feet,
I've found the man, the man, the man,
Tell that maid, tell that maid,
Her man looked like a chief,
Tell that maid, tell that maid,
Her man looked like a chief,
Most splendid to see,
But he turned into a python,
He turned into a python
And swallowed her up."

From that time onward there were some in the village who turned their backs on Foruwa when she passed.

Shall we say
Shall we put it this way

Shall we say that a day came when Foruwa with hurrying feet came running to her mother? She burst through the courtyard gate; and there she stood in the courtyard, joy all over. And a stranger walked in after her and stood in the courtyard beside her, stood tall and strong as a pillar. Foruwa said to the astonished Queen Mother:

"Here he is, Mother, here is the man."

The Queen Mother took a slow look at the stranger standing there strong as a forest tree, and she said:

"You carry the light of wisdom on your face, my son. Greetings, you are welcome. But who are you, my son?"

"Greetings, Mother," replied the stranger quietly, "I am a worker. My hands are all I have to offer your daughter, for they are all my riches. I have traveled to see how men work in other lands. I have that knowledge and my strength. That is all my story."

Shall we say,
Shall we put it this way,

strange as the story is, that Foruwa was given in marriage to the stranger.

There was a rage in the village and many openly mocked saying, "Now the proud ones eat the dust."

Yet shall we say,
Shall we put it this way

that soon, quite soon, the people of Kyerefaso began to take notice of the stranger in quite a different way.

"Who," some said, "is this who has come among us? He who mingles sweat and song, he for whom toil is joy and life is full and abundant?"

"See," said others, "what a harvest the land yields under his ceaseless care."

"He has taken the earth and molded it into bricks. See what a home he has built, how it graces the village where it stands."

"Look at the craft of his fingers, baskets or kente, stool or mat, the man makes them all."

"And our children swarm about him, gazing at him with wonder and delight."

Then it did not satisfy them any more to sit all day at their draughtboards under the mango trees.

"See what Foruwa's husband has done," they declared; "shall the sons of the land not do the same?"

And soon they began to seek out the stranger to talk with him. Soon they too were toiling, their fields began to yield as never before, and the women labored joyfully to bring in the harvest. A new spirit stirred the village. As the carelessly built houses disappeared one by one, and new homes built after the fashion of the stranger's grew up, it seemed as if the village of Kyerefaso had been born afresh.

The people themselves became more alive and a new pride possessed them. They were no longer just grabbing from the land what they desired for their stomachs' present hunger and for their present comfort. They were looking at the land with new eyes, feeling it in their blood, and thoughtfully building a permanent and beautiful place for themselves and their children.

"Osee!" It was festival-time again. "Osee!" Blood no more. Our fathers found for us the paths. We are the roadmakers. They bought for us the land with their blood. We shall build it with our strength. We shall create it with our minds.

Following the men were the women and children. On their heads they carried every kind of produce that the land had yielded and crafts that their fingers had created. Green plantains and yellow bananas were carried by the bunch in large white wooden trays. Garden eggs, tomatoes, red oil-palm nuts warmed by the sun were piled high in black earthen vessels. Oranges, yams, maize filled shining brass trays and golden calabashes. Here and there were children proudly carrying colorful mats, baskets and toys which they themselves had made.

The Queen Mother watched the procession gathering on the new village playground now richly green from recent rains. She watched the people palpitating in a massive dance toward her where she stood with her fanbearers outside the royal house. She caught sight of Foruwa. Her load of charcoal in a large brass tray which she had adorned with red hibiscus danced with her body. Happiness filled the Queen Mother when she saw her daughter thus.

Then she caught sight of Foruwa's husband. He was carrying a white lamb in his arms, and he was singing happily with the men. She looked on with pride. The procession had approached the royal house.

"See!" rang the cry of the Asafo leader. "See how the best in all the lands stands. See how she stands waiting, our Queen Mother. Waiting to wash the dust from our brow in the coolness of her peaceful stream. Spread skins of the gentle sheep in her way, gently, gently. Spread the yield of the land before her. Spread the craft of your hands before her, gently, gently.

"Lightly, lightly walks our Queen Mother, for she is peace."

Prophecy and Fulfillment

BELIEF in prophecy assumes the existence of a universe in which events occur in a way that is preordained and inflexible: it assumes that a plan or a design is at work in the affairs of men, that certain individuals have the power of foreseeing the form which the pattern will ultimately assume, and that man is powerless to prevent its fulfillment. The world of prophecy is thus a world of determinism, and it is eternally at war with what is rationalistic, skeptical, and mechanistic. The conflict is sharply and shrewdly dramatized in a story such as "The Death of Bed Number 12," where the narrator's wholly imaginary reconstruction of a fellow-patient's history finds striking corroboration in a single piece of physical evidence. Like the skeptical priest in "The Dragon," he has proved himself to be a better prophet than he would ever have imagined.

Because prophecy assumes a planned universe and the existence of supernatural forces, it has always played an important role in religion and mythology. In ancient Greece the gods were believed to speak prophecies through the mouths of mediums or priests, and certain places were thought to be particularly suitable for such revelations: thus, the Temple of Apollo at Delphi became the seat of the Delphic Oracle, which was listened to with great respect throughout the classical world. The story of Oedipus had its inception there in the prophecy—which he attempted in vain to circumvent—that he would murder his father and marry his mother.

An interesting feature of prophecy is that the individuals possessing the gift for such utterance are not held personally responsible for what they say. There is an obvious reason for this: if they were punished for telling the truth, they might be prevented by fear of punishment from telling it. On the other hand, the practice readily lends itself to abuse, for, given such immunity and a certain dramatic talent, an unscrupulous person can manipulate events to his personal advantage.

Actually, it is often believed of genuine prophets that they have no choice in determining the occasion and the circumstances of their revelations, any more than they have in deciding the nature of the prophecy. Since they serve merely as mouthpieces for destiny, these decisions are presumably made for them, and they are "possessed" for this purpose when necessary. Aeschylus dramatized seizures of this kind in the *Agamemnon,* in which Cassandra is made to prophesy almost against her will, and also in the *Eumenides.* On the other hand, in the *Antigone,* Tiresias, angered by Creon's insinuation that he has used his gift for private profit, chooses deliberately to reveal to the king the painful destiny that awaits him.

Prophecy was at least equally important in Hebrew religion, and two of the most famous prophets were Nathan, in the time of David and Solomon, and Elijah, in the reign of Ahab. From Scriptural accounts we infer that among the Hebrews the prophetic state was accompanied by particularly violent physical symptoms—convulsions and catalepsy, with temporary loss of personality. We are told that Saul, himself a prophet, was "turned into another man" when the spirit came upon him: "He too stripped off his clothes, and he too prophesied before Samuel, and lay naked all that day and all that night." (I Sam., 19:24).

Prophecy also figures importantly in medieval folklore and literature, particularly folk literature, both in Western and Oriental civilization. One of the most popular of all fairy tales, that of the Sleeping Beauty, involves the working out of a prophecy, while the legend of Saint Julian the Hospitaller, which appears in rather primitive form in the *Gesta Romanorum* (see "The Prophecy of the White Stag," reprinted in the Appendix) does likewise; this was apparently the source for Flaubert's remarkable story. The curious little tale by Li Fu-yen, "Predestined Marriage," comes from ninth-century medieval China.

Any theme so universal and so ancient is archetypal by definition, and, if antiquity alone were sufficient (which it is not—universality is also a necessary condition) to establish the archetypal quality of a literary theme, then there is almost none which has a clearer title, for one of the earliest extant specimens of conscious literary prose is a story from ancient Egypt entitled "The Doomed Prince"; unfortunately the condition of the papyrus manuscript, which dates from approximately 1200 B.C. and contains many lacunae, makes its inclusion in this collection impracticable.

In literary projection the theme of prophecy and fulfillment need not necessarily involve a specific prediction, though naturally the effect is more striking when this is the case—as with the three witches in *Macbeth* or the soothsayer in *Julius Caesar.* Any narrative or dramatic work that suggests a pattern of destiny is being fulfilled, or a design inevitably executed through the operation of some supernatural force or intelligence, reveals the presence of this archetype. The point may be illustrated by two works of Hawthorne, the first a novel, *The House of the Seven Gables,* and the second a short story, "Roger Malvin's Burial." The former involves a specific prediction in the form of a curse that works itself out through several generations, while the latter involves the scarcely less dreadful punishment of an individual who has failed to keep his oath to a deceased friend: no curse has been pronounced, but the unhappy man moves inevitably and quite unconsciously, as if propelled by a superior intelligence, to fulfill the destiny that has been decreed for him because of his betrayal. The one is no less archetypal than the other.

The archetypal theme of Prophecy and Fulfillment may occasionally overlap with that of Transformation, as in "The Legend of Saint Julian the Hospitaller," and the archetypal character of the Wise Old Man, encountered in the stories by Hesse and Hawthorne, may often combine with that of the Prophet, as happens in "Predestined Marriage."

THE LEGEND OF ST. JULIAN THE HOSPITALLER

by Gustave Flaubert

Julian's father and mother lived in a castle with a forest round it, on the slope of a hill.

The four towers at its corners had pointed roofs covered with scales of lead, and the walls were planted upon shafts of rock which fell steeply to the bottom of the moat. The pavement of the courtyard was as clean as the flagstones of a church. Long gutter-spouts in the form of leaning dragons spat the rain-water down into the cistern; and on the window-ledges of each storey, in pots of painted earthenware, a heliotrope or basil flowered.

A second enclosure made with stakes held a fruit-orchard to begin with, and then a flower garden patterned into figures; then a trellis with arbours where you took the air, and an alley for the pages to play mall. On the other side were the kennels, the stables, the bake-house, the presses, and the barns. A green and turfy pasture spread all round this, enclosed in turn by a stout thorn-hedge.

They had lived at peace so long that the portcullis was never lowered now. The moats were full of grass; swallows nested in the cracks of the battlements; and when the sun blazed too strongly the archer who paced all day long the rampart took refuge in his turret and slept like a monk.

Inside there was a sheen of ironwork everywhere; the rooms were hung with tapestries against the cold; the cupboards overflowed with linen; casks of wine were piled up in the cellars, and the oaken coffers creaked with the weight of bags of money. In the armoury, between standards and wild beasts' heads, could be seen weapons of every age and every nation, from the slings of the Amalekites and the javelins of the Garamantes to the short swords of the Saracens and Norman coats of mail. The chief spit in the kitchen could roast an ox; the chapel was as splendid as a king's oratory. There was even, in a secluded corner, a Roman vapour-bath; but the good lord abstained from using it, considering it a practice of the heathen.

Wrapped always in a mantle of fox skins, he walked about his castle, administering justice to his vassals and setting the disputes of his neighbours at rest. In winter he watched the snowflakes falling or had stories read to him. With the first fine days he rode out on his mule along the

---

From *Three Tales* by Gustave Flaubert, translated by Arthur McDowell (New York: Alfred A. Knopf, Inc., 1924), pp. 75–121. Reprinted by permission.

by-ways, beside the greening corn, and chatted with the peasants, to whom he gave advice. After many adventures he had taken a lady of high lineage as his wife.

Very white of skin she was, a little proud and serious. The horns of her coif brushed against the door lintel, and the train of her dress trailed three paces behind her. Her household was ordered like the inside of a monastery; every morning she gave out the tasks to the servants, inspected the preserves and unguents, span at her distaff or embroidered altar-cloths. By dint of prayer to God a son was born to her.

Then there were great rejoicings and a banquet which lasted three days and four nights, with the illumination of torches, the sound of harps, and strewing of green branches. They ate of the rarest spices, and fowls as large as sheep; a dwarf came out of a pasty, to amuse the guests; and as the throng was always increasing and the bowls would go round no longer, they were obliged to drink out of horns and helmets.

The lady who had just been made a mother was not present at this cheer. She stayed quietly in her bed. Waking one evening, she saw as it were a shadow moving under a ray of the moon which came through the window. It was an old man in a frieze gown, with a chaplet at his side, a wallet on his shoulder, and all the semblance of a hermit. He came towards her pillow and said to her, without opening his lips:

"Rejoice, O mother, thy son shall be a saint!"

She was just going to cry out, but he glided over the streak of moonlight, rose gently into the air and vanished. The songs of the banqueters broke out louder. She heard angels' voices; and her head fell back on the pillow, over which, framed with garnets, hung a martyr's bone.

Next morning all the servants were questioned and said they had seen no hermit. Whether it were a dream or reality, it must have been a communication from Heaven; but she was careful not to speak of it, fearing she might be taxed with pride.

The guests went off at morning twilight, and Julian's father was outside the postern gate, to which he had just escorted the last to go, when suddenly a beggar rose before him in the mist. He was a gipsy, with a plaited beard and silver rings on his arms, and fiery eyes. With an air of inspiration he stammered these disjointed words:

"Ah, ah! thy son! Blood in plenty! . . . Fame in plenty! . . . Blest always—the family of an emperor!"

And stooping to pick up his alms he was lost in the grass and disappeared.

The good castellan looked right and left, and called with all his might. No one! The wind blew shrill; the mists of morning flew away.

He put down this vision to a weary head, from having slept too little. "If I speak of it they will make a jest of me," he said to himself. Yet the glories destined to his son dazzled him, although the promise was not clear and he doubted even whether he had heard it.

The husband and wife each kept their secret. But they cherished their child, both of them, with an equal love; and, reverencing him as marked out by God, had an infinite care for his person. His cot was stuffed with the finest down; a lamp shaped like a dove burned continually above it, three nurses rocked him; and well swaddled in his clothes, with his rosy looks and blue eyes, a brocade cloak and a cap set with pearls, he looked a little Jesus. He teethed without crying at any time.

When he was seven his mother taught him to sing. To make him brave his father lifted him on to a big horse. The child smiled with pleasure and before long knew all about chargers.

A learned old monk taught him Holy Writ, the Arabic way of counting, the Latin letters, and how to make dainty pictures on vellum. They worked together high up in a turret away from all noise. The lesson over, they came down into the garden and studied the flowers, pausing at every step.

Sometimes a string of laden beasts was seen passing below in the valley, led by a man on foot dressed in the Eastern way. The castellan, recognizing him for a merchant, would send a servant out to him, and the stranger, taking heart, would turn out of his road. He would be brought into the parlour, where he drew out of his coffers strips of velvet and silk, jewels, perfumes, and curious things of unknown use; after which the worthy man went off, having taken a great profit and suffered no violence. At other times a band of pilgrims would come knocking at the gate. Their draggled garments steamed before the fire; and when they had been well fed they told the story of their travels: wanderings on shipboard over foamy seas, journeyings afoot in burning sands, the furious rage of paynims, the caves of Syria, the Manger and the Sepulchre. Then they would give the young lord scallop-shells from their cloaks.

Often the castellan feasted his old companions-at-arms. While they drank they called to mind their wars and the storming of fortresses, with the crash of warlike engines and the prodigious wounds. Julian listened to them and uttered cries; and his father had no doubt, then, that he would be a conqueror one day. Yet at evening, coming from the Angelus, as he passed between the bending rows of poor, he dipped in his purse with such modesty and so noble a mien that his mother thought surely to see him an archbishop in his time.

His place in chapel was by the side of his parents, and however long the offices might be he stayed kneeling at his stool, with his cap on the floor and his hands clasped in prayer.

One day, while mass was being said, he raised his head and saw a little white mouse coming out of a hole in the wall. It trotted along the first pace of the altar, and after making two or three turns to right and left fled by the way it had come. Next Sunday he was troubled by the thought that he might see it again. It did come back; and then every Sunday he watched for it, was troubled, seized with hatred for it, and determined to get rid of the mouse.

So, having shut the door and sprinkled some cake-crumbs along the altar steps, he took post in front of the hole with a little stick in his hand.

After a very long time a small pink nose appeared, and then the entire mouse. He struck a light blow, and stood lost in amazement at this tiny body which did not stir again. A drop of blood spotted the pavement. Julian wiped it off rapidly with his sleeve, threw the mouse away, and did not say a word to anyone.

There were all kinds of little birds which pecked at the seeds in the garden. Julian had the thought of putting peas into a hollow reed. When he heard the sound of chirruping in a tree he came up softly, lifted his pipe, and blew out his cheeks; and the little creatures rained down in such abundance on his shoulders that he could not help laughing in delight at his trick.

One morning, as he was going back along the curtain wall, he saw a fat pigeon on the top of the rampart, preening itself in the sun. Julian stopped to look at it, and as there was a breach in this part of the wall a fragment of stone lay ready to his hand. He swung his arm, and the stone brought down the bird, which fell like a lump into the moat.

He dashed down after it, tearing himself in the briars and scouring everywhere, nimbler than a young dog. The pigeon, its wings broken, hung quivering in the boughs of a privet. The obstinate life in it annoyed the child. He began to throttle it, and the bird's convulsions made his heart beat, filled him with a savage, passionate delight. When it stiffened for the last time he felt that he would swoon.

At supper in the evening his father declared that it was time for him to learn the art of venery, and he went to look for an old manuscript which contained, in questions and answers, the whole pastime of the chase. A master explained in it to his pupil the craft of breaking-in dogs, taming falcons, and setting snares; how to know the stag by his droppings, the fox by his footmarks, the wolf by his scratchings of the ground; the right way to discern their tracks, the manner of starting them, the usual places of their lairs, the most favourable winds, and a list of all the calls and the rules for the quarry.

When Julian could repeat all this by heart his father gathered a pack of hounds for him.

The first to catch the eye were twenty-four greyhounds from Barbary, swifter than gazelles, but prone to get out of hand; and then seventeen couples of Breton hounds, with red coats and white spots, unshakable in control, deep-chested, loud to bay. To face the wild boar and its dangerous redoublings there were forty boarhounds, as shaggy as bears. Mastiffs from Tartary nearly as tall as asses and flame-coloured, with broad backs and straight legs, were assigned to hunt the aurochs. The black coats of the spaniels shone like satin, and the yapping of the talbots matched the chanting of the beagles. In a yard by themselves, tossing their chains and rolling their eyes, growled eight Alain dogs, fearsome animals that fly at the belly of a horseman and have no dread of lions.

All of them ate wheaten bread, drank out of stone troughs, and bore sonorous names.

The falconry, maybe, was choicer even than the pack; for by dint of money the good lord had secured tiercelets of the Caucasus, sakers from Babylonia, gerfalcons of Germany, and peregrines taken on the cliffs at the edge of cold seas in far quarters of the world. They were housed in a big shed roofed with thatch, and fastened to the perching-bar in a row according to their size, with a strip of turf before them where they were placed from time to time to unstiffen their limbs.

Purse-nets, hooks, wolf-traps, and engines of every kind were artfully made.

Often they took out setters into the country, who quickly came to a point. Then huntsmen, advancing step by step, cautiously spread a huge net over their motionless bodies. At a word of command they barked; quails took wing; and the ladies of the neighbourhood who had been bidden with their husbands, the children, the handmaids, the whole company darted on the birds and easily caught them. At other times they would beat drums to start the hares; foxes fell into pits, or a trap would spring and take hold of a wolf's paw.

But Julian spurned these handy devices. He preferred to hunt far away from the rest with his horse and his falcon. It was almost always a great Scythian tartaret, white as snow. Its leathern hood was topped with a plume, bells of gold quivered on its blue feet; and it stood firmly in its master's arm while the horse galloped and the plains unrolled below. Julian, freeing the jesses, would suddenly let it go; the daring bird rose straight as an arrow into the sky; and you saw two specks, one larger and one smaller, circle, meet, and then vanish in the high blue spaces. The falcon soon came down, tearing a quarry, and returned to perch on the gauntlet with its wings a-quiver.

In that way Julian flew his falcons at the heron, the kite, the crow, and the vulture.

He loved to blow his horn and follow his hounds as they coursed along the sloping hills, jumped the streams, and climbed to the woods again; and when the stag began groaning under their bites he felled it cleverly, and was delighted by the fury of the mastiffs as they devoured it, hewn in pieces on its reeking hide.

On misty days he went down into a marsh to ambush the geese, otters, and wild duck.

Three squires waited for him from dawn at the foot of the steps, and though the old monk might lean out of his window and make signs to call him back Julian would not turn. He went out in the heat of the sun, under the rain, and amidst storms, drinking water from the springs out of his hand, munching wild apples as he trotted along, and resting under an oak if he were tired; and he came in at midnight covered in blood and mire, with thorns in his hair and the odour of the wild beasts hanging round him. He became as one of them. When his mother kissed him he took her embrace coldly, and seemed to be dreaming of deep things.

He slew bears with strokes of his knife, bulls with the axe, and wild boars with the pike; and once, even, defended himself with nothing but a stick against wolves that were gnawing corpses at the foot of a gibbet.

One winter morning he started in full trim before dawn, with a cross-bow on his shoulder and a quiver of arrows at his saddle-bow.

His Danish jennet, followed by two bassets, made the earth ring under its even tread. Drops of rime stuck to his cloak, and a fierce breeze blew. The sky lightened at one side, and in the pale twilight he saw rabbits hopping at the edge of their burrows. The two bassets dashed for them at once, jumping hither and thither as they broke their backs.

Soon after he entered a wood. At the end of a branch a grouse, numbed by the cold, slept with its head under its wing. With a back-stroke of his sword Julian cut off its two feet, and without stopping to pick it up went on his way.

Three hours later he found himself on the top of a mountain, which was so high that the sky seemed almost black. A rock like a long wall sloped away in front of him, cresting a precipice; and at the farther end of it two wild goats were looking down into the chasm. Not having his arrows at hand—he had left his horse behind—he thought he would go right down upon the goats; and stooping double, barefoot, he reached the first of them at last and plunged his dagger under its ribs. The other was seized with panic and jumped into the abyss. Julian leaped to strike it, and his right foot slipping, fell across the body of the first, with his face hanging over the gulf and arms flung wide.

He came down into the plain again and followed a line of willows bordering a river. Cranes, flying very low, passed overhead from time to time. Julian brought them down with his whip, not missing one.

Meanwhile the air had grown warmer and melted the rime; there were broad wreaths of vapour floating, and the sun appeared. Far off he saw a still lake glistening like a sheet of lead. In the middle of it was an animal which Julian did not know, a black-headed beaver. In spite of the distance he killed it with an arrow, and was vexed not to be able to carry off its skin.

Then he went on down an avenue of great trees, whose tops made a kind of triumphal arch at the entrance of a forest. A roebuck bounded out of a thicket, a fallow deer showed itself at a crossing, a badger came out of a hole, a peacock spread its tail on the grass; and when he had slain them all more roebuck, deer, badgers, peacocks and blackbirds, jays, polecats, foxes, hedgehogs, lynxes—an endless company of beasts—appeared and grew more numerous at every step. Tremblingly they circled round him, with gentle supplicating looks. But Julian did not tire of killing, by turns bending his cross-bow, unsheathing his long sword, and thrusting with his short, thinking of nothing, with no memory of anything at all. Only the fact of his existence told him that for an indefinite time he had been hunting in some vague country, where all happened with the ease of dreams. An extraordinary sight brought him to a halt. A valley shaped like an arena was filled with stags, who crowded close together warming each other with their breath, which could be seen steaming in the mist.

The prospect of a slaughter like this for a minute or two took Julian's breath away for pleasure. Then he dismounted, rolled up his sleeves, and began to shoot.

At the whistle of the first arrow all the stags turned their heads at once. Hollows opened in the mass, plaintive cries rose, and a great stir shook the herd.

The brim of the valley was too high to climb. They leaped about in this enclosure, trying to escape. Julian aimed and shot, and the arrows fell like rain shafts in a thunderstorm. The maddened stags fought, reared, and climbed on each other's backs; and the bodies and entangled antlers made a broad mound which crumbled and changed.

At last they died, stretched on the sand, their nostrils frothing, entrails bursting, and bellies slowly ceasing to heave. Then all was motionless. Night was close at hand; and behind the woods, in the interspaces of the boughs, the sky was red as a sheet of blood.

Julian leant back against a tree, and gazed with staring eyes at the enormous massacre; he could not think how it had been done.

Then across the valley, at the edge of the forest, he saw a stag with its hind and its fawn.

The stag was black and hugely tall; it carried sixteen points and a white beard. The hind, pale yellow like a dead leaf, was grazing; and the spotted fawn, without hindering her movements, pulled at her dugs. Once more the cross-bow sang. The fawn was killed on the spot. Then its mother, looking skywards, bellowed with a deep, heart-breaking, human cry. In exasperation Julian stretched her on the ground with a shot full in the breast.

The great stag had seen it, and made a bound. Julian shot his last arrow at him. It hit the stag in the forehead and stuck fast there.

The great stag did not seem to feel it; striding over the dead bodies, he came on and on, in act to charge and disembowel him; and Julian retreated in unspeakable terror. The monstrous creature stopped, and with flaming eyes, as solemn as a patriarch or judge, said three times, while a bell tinkled in the distance:

"Accurst! accurst! accurst! one day, ferocious heart, thou shalt murder thy father and thy mother!"

The stag's knees bent, his eyes closed gently, and he died.

Julian was thunderstuck, and then suddenly felt crushed with fatigue; disgust and boundless sadness came over him. He buried his face in his hands and wept for a long time.

His horse was lost, his dogs had left him; the solitude which folded round him seemed looming with vague dangers. Seized with alarm, he struck across country, and choosing a path at random found himself almost immediately at the castle-gate.

He could not sleep at night. By the flickering of the hanging lamps he always saw the great black stag. The creature's prophecy besieged him, and he fought against it. "No! no! no! it cannot be that I should kill them!" And then he mused: "Yet if I should wish to kill?" and he was afraid that the Devil might inspire him with the wish.

For three months his mother prayed in anguish by his pillow, and his father walked to and fro along the corridors with groans. He sent for the most famous master physicians, who prescribed quantities of drugs. Julian's malady, they said, was caused by a noxious wind, or by a love-desire. But the young man, in answer to all questions, shook his head.

His strength came back to him, and they took him out to walk in the courtyard, the old monk and the good lord each propping him with an arm.

When he had recovered altogether he obstinately refused to hunt. His father, hoping to cheer him, made him a present of a great Saracen sword. It was in a stand of arms, at the top of a pillar, and a ladder was needed to reach it. Julian went up. The sword was too heavy and slipped from his fingers, and in the fall grazed the worthy lord so close as to cut his mantle; Julian thought he had killed his father, and fainted away.

From that moment he dreaded weapons. The sight of a bare blade made him turn pale. This weakness was a sorrow to his family, and at last the old monk, in the name of God, of honour, and his ancestors, bade him take up the exercises of his gentle birth again.

The squires amused themselves daily at practising with the javelin. Julian very quickly excelled in this; he could throw his javelin into the neck of a bottle, break the teeth of a weather-vane, and hit the nails on a door a hundred paces off.

One summer evening, at the hour when things grow indistinct in the dusk, he was under the trellis in the garden and saw right at the end of it two white wings fluttering by the top of its supports. He made sure it was a stork, and threw his javelin. A piercing cry rang out.

It was his mother, whose bonnet with long flaps stayed pinned to the wall.

Julian fled from the castle and was seen there no more.

II

He took service with a passing troop of adventurers and knew hunger and thirst, fevers and vermin. He grew accustomed to the din of mellays and the sight of dying men. The wind tanned his skin. His limbs hardened under the clasp of armour; and as he was very strong, valiant, temperate, and wary he won the command of a company with ease. When a battle opened he swept on his soldiers with a great flourish of his sword. He scaled the walls of citadels with a knotted rope at night, swinging in the blasts, while sparks of Greek fire stuck to his cuirass and boiling resin and molten lead hissed from the battlements. Often a stone crashed and shivered his buckler. Bridges overladen with men gave way under him. Swinging his battle-axe to and fro, he got rid of fourteen horsemen. In the lists he overcame all challengers. More than a score of times he was left for dead.

Thanks to the favour of Heaven he always came out safely, for he protected clerks, orphans, widows, and, most of all, old men. When he saw one of them walking in front of him he called out to see his face, as though he were afraid of killing him by mistake.

Runaway slaves, peasants in revolt, fortuneless bastards, and venturous men of all sorts flocked under his banner, and he made an army of his own.

It grew, and he became famous. The world sought him out. He succoured in turn the Dauphin of France and the King of England, the Templars of Jerusalem, the Surena of the Parthians, the Negus of Abyssinia, and the Emperor of Calicut. He fought against Scandinavians covered with fish-scales, negroes with bucklers of hippopotamus hide, mounted on red asses, and gold-coloured Indians flourishing broadswords brighter than mirrors above their diadems. He subdued the Troglodytes and the Anthropophages. He went through such burning regions that the hair on the head caught fire of itself, like torches, in the sun's heat; through others so freezing that the arms snapped from the body and fell to the ground; and countries where there was so much mist that you walked surrounded by phantoms.

Republics in distress consulted him, and in colloquies with ambassadors he gained unhoped-for terms. If a monarch behaved too badly Julian was quickly on the spot and took him to task. He set free peoples and delivered queens immured in towers. He it was, no other, who slew the viper of Milan and the dragon of Oberbirbach.

Now the Emperor of Occitania, having triumphed over the Spanish Moslems, had taken the sister of the Caliph of Cordova as his concubine, and by her he had a daughter whom he brought up to be a Christian. But the Caliph, feigning a wish to be converted, came to return his visit with a numerous escort, put all his garrison to the sword, and threw him into an underground dungeon, where he used him cruelly to extort his treasure.

Julian hastened to his aid, destroyed the army of the infidels, besieged the town, killed the Caliph, cut off his head, and threw it over the ramparts like a ball. Then he drew the emperor out of prison and set him on his throne again, in the presence of all his court.

To require this great service the emperor presented him with basketfuls of money; Julian would have none of it. Thinking that he wanted more, he offered him three-quarters of his wealth, and was refused again; then the half of his kingdom; Julian thanked him and declined. The emperor was in tears of distress, seeing no way to show his gratitude, when he tapped his forehead and whispered in a courtier's ear; the curtains of a tapestry lifted and a maiden appeared.

Her large dark eyes gleamed like two gentle lamps; her lips were parted in a winning smile. The ringlets of her hair caught in the jewels of a half-opened robe, and under the transparent tunic the young lines of her body could be guessed. She was slim of figure, all daintiness and softness.

Julian was dazzled with love, the more because he had lived in great chastity till then.

So he took the emperor's daughter in marriage, with a castle that she held from her mother; and when the wedding was over he and his host parted, after a long exchange of courtesies.

It was a palace of white marble, in the Moorish fashion, built on a promontory in a grove of orange-trees. Terraces of flowers sloped to the edge of a bay, where there were pink shells that crackled underfoot. Behind the castle stretched a forest in the shape of a fan. The sky was blue unceasingly, and the trees waved by turns under the sea breeze and the wind from the mountains, which closed the horizon far away.

The rooms were full of shadow, but drew light from their incrusted walls. High columns, slender as reeds, supported their domed vaults, which were embossed in relief to imitate the stalactites in caves. There were fountains in the greater rooms, mosaics in the courts, festooned partitions, delicacies of architecture beyond number, and everywhere so deep a silence that one heard the rustle of a scarf or the echo of a sigh.

Julian made war no longer. He rested with a quiet people round him, and every day a crowd passed before him, making obeisances and kissing hands in the Eastern style.

In his purple dress he would stay leaning in the embrasure of a window, recalling his hunts of former days; and he would have liked to scour the desert after gazelles and ostriches, hide among the bamboos to wait for leopards, traverse forests full of rhinoceroses, climb the most inaccessible mountain-tops to take better aim at eagles, and fight with white bears on icebergs in the sea.

Sometimes, in dreams, he saw himself like our father Adam in the midst of Paradise, among all the beasts. He stretched out his arm against them, and they died; or else, again, they defiled before him, two by two according to their size, from the elephants and lions to the ermines and the ducks, as on the day when they entered Noah's ark. From the shadow of a cave he rained darts on them which never missed; other animals appeared; there was no end to them, and he woke with his eyes rolling wildly.

Among his friends there were princes who invited him to hunt. He always refused, thinking that by a penance of this kind he would turn aside his curse, for it seemed to him that the slaughter of animals would decide the fate of his father and mother. But it was a grief to him not to see his parents, and his other secret desire became impossible to bear.

His wife sent for jugglers and dancers to amuse him. She went out with him into the country in an open litter; and at other times they would lie in a boat and watch, over the side, the fish roaming in water as clear as the sky. Often she threw flowers in his face, or crouching at his feet drew music from a three-stringed mandolin; and then, laying her clasped hands on his shoulder, said timidly, "What ails thee then, dear lord?"

He did not answer, or broke into sobs. At last, one day, he confessed his horrible thought.

She fought against it, arguing very well. His father and mother, most likely, were already dead; but if he ever saw them again what chance or purpose could lead him to this abominable deed? His fear was causeless, then, and he should return to the hunt.

Julian smiled as he listened to her, but could not make up his mind to fulfil his desire.

One August evening they were in their chamber, she being just in bed and he kneeling down to pray, when he heard a fox barking, and then some light footfalls under the window. He caught a glimpse, in the dusk, of what seemed to be the shapes of animals. The temptation was too strong, and he took down his quiver.

She showed surprise.

"I do it to obey you," he said; "I shall be back at sunrise." Still, she was afraid of a disastrous venture.

He reassured her and went out, surprised at her inconsistent mood.

Soon afterwards a page came in to say that two strangers, as they could not see the absent lord, were asking instantly to see his lady.

And soon there entered the room an old man and an old woman, bowed and dusty, dressed in rough linen, each leaning on a staff.

Taking courage, they said that they were bringing Julian news of his parents. She leaned out of bed to listen.

But, having first exchanged a look, they asked her if he was still fond of them, and if he spoke of them at times.

"Ah, yes!" she said.

"Well, we are they!" they cried, and, being very weary and spent with fatigue, sat down.

The young wife felt no assurance that her husband was their son, but they proved it by describing some particular marks on his skin.

Then she leaped out of bed, called the page, and a repast was served to them.

They could scarcely eat, though they were very hungry; she observed, aside, how their bony hands trembled as they grasped the cups. They asked countless questions about Julian, and she answered all, but took care not to speak of the ghastly fancy in which they were concerned.

After waiting in vain for his return they had left their castle, and they had been travelling for several years after vague clues, without losing hope. So much money had been swallowed up by river-tolls and inns, the dues of princes and demands of thieves that their purse was emptied to the bottom, and now they begged their way. But what of that, when they would soon embrace their son? They extolled his happiness to have so fair a wife, and could not have enough of watching her and kissing her.

They were much astonished by the richness of the room, and the old man, after examining its walls, asked why the Emperor of Occitania's coat-of-arms was there.

"He is my father," she replied.

At that he started, remembering the gipsy's prophecy, while the old woman thought of the hermit's words. Doubtless their son's glory was but the dawn of an eternal splendour; and they both sat open-mouthed under the light of the great candlestick upon the table.

They must have been very handsome in their youth. The mother had kept all her hair, and its fine plaits hung to the bottom of her cheeks like drifts of snow. The father, with his height and his great beard, was like a statue in a church.

Julian's wife persuaded them not to wait for him. With her own hands she placed them in her bed, then shut the window, and they went to sleep. Daybreak was near, and little birds were beginning to sing outside.

Julian had crossed the park and walked through the forest with a springing step, enjoying the soft turf and mild night air. Shadows fell from the trees across the moss. From time to time the moonlight made white patches in the drives and he hesitated to go forward, thinking he saw a pool; or, again, the surface of the still ponds would itself be lost in the colour of the grass. There was a deep silence everywhere, and he found no trace of the animals which a few minutes earlier had been straying round his castle.

The wood thickened and grew profoundly dark. Puffs of warm air went by him, with relaxing scents. His feet sank among dead leaves, and he leaned against an oak to breathe a little.

Suddenly, from behind his back, a darker mass leaped out. It was a wild boar. Julian had no time to snatch his bow, and was as vexed as though it was a disaster.

Then, when he had left the wood, he saw a wolf stealing along a hedge. Julian sent an arrow after it. The wolf paused, turned round to look at him, and went on again. It trotted on, always at the same distance, stopping from time to time, and taking flight again as soon as Julian aimed.

In this way Julian went over an endless plain and a tract of sand-hills, and came out upon high ground which looked over a great breadth of country. Flat stones lay scattered on it from ruined vaults all round. His feet stumbled on dead bones, and in places there were worm-eaten crosses leaning mournfully askew. But forms stirred in the dim shadow of the tombs; and hyenas rose out of them, scared and panting. Their hoofs clattered on the pave-stones as they came up to Julian, sniffing at him and showing their gums with a yawn. When he drew his sword they went off at once in all directions, with a headlong, limping gallop which lasted till they vanished in the distance under a cloud of dust.

An hour later he met a savage bull in a ravine, lowering its horns and ploughing the sand up with its foot. Julian thrust with his lance at it under the dew-lap. The lance was shivered, as though the animal were made of bronze; he closed his eyes, expecting to be killed. When he re-opened them the bull had disappeared.

Then his heart sank for shame. A higher power was bringing his strength to nought, and he went back into the forest to regain his home.

The forest was tangled with creepers; and as he was cutting them with his sword a marten slipped sharply between his legs, a panther made a bound over his shoulder, and a snake wound its way up an ash tree. A huge jackdaw looked down at Julian out of its leaves, and on every side among the branches appeared a multitude of great sparks, as though the firmament had showered all its stars into the forest. They were eyes of animals—wild cats, squirrels, owls, parrots, monkeys.

Julian darted his arrows at them; the feathered shafts settled on the leaves like white butterflies. He threw stones at them, and the stones fell back without touching anything. He cursed, wanted to fight, shouted imprecations, and choked with rage.

And all the animals which he had been hunting appeared again and made a narrow circle round him. Some sat upon their haunches, others stood erect. He was rooted in the middle, frozen with terror, and impotent to move at all. With a supreme effort of will he took a step; the creatures on the branches spread their wings, those on the ground stretched their limbs, and all went on with him.

The hyenas walked in front, the wolf and the boar behind. The bull was on his right, swaying its head, while on his left the serpent wound through the grass and the panther arched its back and advanced with long, velvet-footed strides. He walked as slowly as he could to avoid irritating them; and as he went he saw porcupines, foxes, vipers, jackals, and bears come out of the dense undergrowth.

Julian began to run; they ran too. The serpent hissed, and the stinking creatures slavered. The wild boar's tusks prodded his heels, and the wolf rubbed the palms of his hands with his hairy muzzle. The monkeys pinched him and made faces, and the marten rolled over his feet. A bear swung its paw back and knocked his hat off, and the panther, which had been carrying an arrow in its mouth, let it fall in disdain.

Their sly movements gave peeps of irony. As they watched him out of the corner of their eyes they seemed to be meditating a plan of revenge; while he, deafened by the buzzing insects, lashed by the birds' tails, and smothered by the breath of the animals, walked with arms outstretched and eyes shut like a blind man, without even having strength to cry for mercy.

A cock-crow rang in the air, and others answered. It was day, and he recognized his palace roof beyond the orange-trees.

Then at the edge of a field he saw, three paces off him, some red partridges fluttering in the stubble. He unfastened his cloak and threw it over them as a net. When he uncovered them he found but one, long dead and rotten.

This deception infuriated him more than all the others. His thirst to kill swept over him again, and for want of beasts he would gladly have slain men.

He climbed the three terraces and burst open the door with a blow of his fist; but when he reached the staircase his heart unbent at the thought of his dear wife. She was alseep, doubtless, and he would take her by surprise.

He drew off his sandals, turned the lock gently, and went in.

The pale dawn came dimly through the leaded window-panes. Julian's feet caught in clothes lying on the floor; a little farther, and he knocked against a buffet still laden with plate. "Her supper, doubtless," he said to himself, and went on towards the bed, which he could not see in the darkness at the end of the room. He came close, and to kiss his wife bent down over the pillow where the two heads were lying side by side. Then he felt the touch of a beard against his mouth.

He drew back, thinking he was going mad, but came near the bed again, and as he felt about with his fingers they encountered long tresses of hair. To convince himself that he was wrong he passed his hand again slowly over the pillow. It was really a beard this time, and a man —a man lying with his wife!

In a fit of boundless fury he leaped on them, striking with his dagger; he stamped and foamed, roaring like a wild beast. Then he stopped. The dead folk, pierced to the heart, had not so much as stirred. He listened closely to their dying groans, which almost kept time together; and as they grew feebler another, in the far distance, took them up. Vague at first, this plaintive, long-drawn voice came nearer, swelled, rang cruelly; and he recognized in terror the belling of the great black stag.

And as he turned round he thought he saw his wife's ghost framed in the doorway, with a light in her hand.

The noise of the murder had drawn her there. In one wide glance she grasped it all, and fled in horror, dropping her torch. He picked it up.

His father and mother lay before him, stretched on their backs, with breasts pierced through; and their faces, in a gentle majesty, looked as though they were keeping a secret for ever. Splashes and pools of blood showed on their white skin, over the bed-clothes and the floor, and trickled down an ivory crucifix in the alcove. The scarlet reflection from the window, which the sun was striking, lit up these red patches and cast others, more numerous still, all round the room. Julian walked towards the two dead figures, saying to himself, and struggling to believe, that this thing could not be and that he was deceived by an error—by one of those resemblances which nothing can explain. Finally he bent down a little to look close at the old man, and saw between the unshut eyelids a glazed eye which scorched him like fire. Then he went to the other side of the couch where the other body lay, its white hair hiding part of the face. Julian passed his fingers under the plaits and lifted the head; and holding it at arm's length with one hand, while in the other he held up the torch, he looked at it. Drops of blood were oozing from the mattress and falling one by one upon the floor.

At the end of the day he came into his wife's presence; and in a voice not his own bade her first of all not to answer him, come near him, or even look at him. Under pain of damnation she must follow all his orders, which would not be gainsaid.

The funerals must be carried out according to injunctions which he had left in writing, on a prie-dieu in the chamber of the dead. He ceded to her his palace, his vassals, and all his possessions, not excepting even his clothes or his sandals, which would be found at the head of the stairs.

She had obeyed God's will in making the occasion of his crime, and she must pray for his soul, since from that day he ceased to exist.

The dead were sumptuously buried in an abbey church at three days' journey from the castle. A monk in shrouded hood followed the procession at a distance from the others, and no one dared to speak to him. He remained while the mass lasted, lying flat in the middle of the porch, with his arms making the form of a cross and his forehead in the dust.

After the burial he was seen to take the road leading to the mountains. He turned to look round several times, and finally disappeared.

III

He went onwards, begging his way throughout the world.

He held out his hand to the riders on the high-roads and bent his knee when he approached the reapers. Or he would stand motionless before the gates of courtyards, and his face was so sad that he was never refused alms.

In a spirit of humbleness he would tell his story; and then all fled from him, making the sign of the cross. In the villages which he had passed through before, the people, as soon as they recognized him, shut their doors, shouted abuse at him, threw stones at him. The most charitable of them placed a bowl on their window-sills and then closed the shutters so as not to see him.

Being repulsed everywhere, he shunned mankind, and fed on roots, plants, wayside fruit, and shell-fish which he gathered along the beaches.

Sometimes, at the turn of a hillside, he saw a jumble of crowded roofs under his eyes, with stone spires, bridges, towers, and a network of dark streets, from which a ceaseless hum rose up to him. A need to mingle with the life of others would draw him down into the town. But the brutal look in their faces, their noisy crafts and callous words, made his heart freeze. On festal days, when the great cathedral bells tuned the whole populace to joy from daybreak, he watched the folk issuing from their houses, and the dancing in public spaces, the beer fountains at the crossways, the damask hung before the lodgings of princes; and then at evening, through the lower windows, the long family tables where grandparents dandled little children on their knees. Sobs choked him, and he turned away towards the country.

He had thrills of love as he gazed at young horses in the meadows, birds in their nests, and insects on the flowers; all, at his approach, ran farther off, hid in terror, or flew swiftly away.

He sought deserted places. But the wind grated on his ear like the rattle of a death-agony; the dew-drops falling to the ground brought other, heavier drops to mind. Every evening the sun tinged the clouds blood-red, and each night the murder of his parents began again in dreams.

He made himself a hair shirt with iron spikes, and climbed on his knees up every hill which had a chapel at the top. But his pitiless thought dimmed the radiance of the shrines, and stung him even in his acts of mortification. He did not rebel against God for having brought the deed upon him, and yet the idea that he could have done it made him despair.

His own person filled him with such horror that in the hope of release he risked it among dangers. He saved the paralysed from fires and children from the bottom of chasms. The abyss cast him up; the flames spared him.

Time brought no relief to his suffering. It became intolerable, and he resolved to die.

And one day when he was by a spring, leaning over it to judge the water's depth, he saw opposite him on a sudden an emaciated old man, with a white beard and a look so dolorous that Julian could not keep back his tears. The other wept also. Without recognizing him exactly, Julian had a confused memory of a face like his. He uttered a cry; it was his father; and he thought no more of killing himself.

So with the burden of his recollections he travelled many lands, and came one day to a river, which, owing to its violence and a great stretch of slime along its banks, was dangerous to cross. No one for a long time had dared to make the passage.

An old boat, whose stern had been embedded, lifted its prow among the reeds. Julian examined it and found a pair of oars; and the thought came to him that he might use his life in the service of others.

He began by making a sort of roadway on the bank to lead down to the channel of the river; and he broke his nails in moving enormous stones, propped them against his waist to carry them, slipped in the mud and sank there, and nearly perished several times. Then he repaired the boat with pieces of wreckage, and made a hut for himself out of clay and tree-trunks.

The ferry came to be heard of and travellers appeared. They waved flags and hailed him from the other side, and Julian at once jumped into his boat. It was very heavy, and they overweighted it with baggage and loads of all kinds, without counting the beasts of burden, who made the crowding worse by kicking in alarm. He asked nothing for his labour; some of the passengers gave him remnants of food out of their wallets or worn-out clothes which they had no more use for. The brutal ones shouted blasphemies. Julian reproved them gently, and they retorted with abuse. He was content to bless them.

A little table, a stool, a bed of dry leaves, and three clay cups—that was the whole of his furniture. Two holes in the wall served for windows. On one side barren plains stretched away out of view, dotted with pale meres here and there; and in front of him the great river rolled its greenish waters. In spring the damp soil breathed an odour of decay. Then came a riotous wind that lifted the dust and whirled it. It found its way in everywhere, muddying the water and grating in the mouth. A little later there were clouds of mosquitoes, which pinged and pricked without ceasing day and night. And then came on appalling frosts which turned everything to the hardness of stone and roused a wild craving to eat meat.

Months glided by when Julian did not see a soul. Often he closed his eyes and tried to revive his youth in memory. The courtyard of a castle would rise before him, with greyhounds on a flight of steps, grooms in the armoury, and a fair-haired boy under a vine trellis between an old man dressed in furs and a lady wearing a great coif. Suddenly, the two corpses were there. He threw himself face downwards on his bed and kept murmuring with tears:

"Ah, poor father! Poor mother, poor mother!"—and fell into a drowsiness through which the mournful visions still went on.

When he was asleep one night he thought he heard someone calling him. He strained his ears and made out nothing except the roar of the water.

But the same voice cried again: "Julian!"

It came from the other bank, which amazed him, considering the breadth of the river.

A third time he was hailed: "Julian!"

And the loud voice had the tone of a church bell.

Julian lit his lantern and went out of the hovel. A wild hurricane was sweeping through the night. There was an intense darkness, pierced now and then by the whiteness of the leaping waves.

After a moment's hesitation Julian unfastened his moorings. The water instantly became calm, and the boat glided over it to the other bank, where a man stood waiting.

He was wrapped in a tattered cloth and his face was like a plaster mask, with eyes redder than coals. Holding the lantern to him, Julian saw that he was covered with a hideous leprosy; yet there was something of a royal majesty in his posture.

As soon as he entered the boat it sank prodigiously, overwhelmed by his weight. It rose again with a shake, and Julian began to row.

At every stroke the surf tossed the boat up by its bows. The water, blacker than ink, ran furiously against the planks on both sides. It hollowed into gulfs and rose into mountains, which the boat leaped over, only to fall back into the depths, where it spun round at the mercy of the wind.

Julian bent low, stretched his arms out, and propping himself against his feet swung back with a twist to get more power. The hail lashed his hands, the rain streamed down his back, he could not breathe in the fierce wind, and stopped. Then the boat drifted and was carried away. But feeling that there was a great matter at stake, an order which might not be disobeyed, he took up the oars again, and the clacking of the thole-pins cut through the stormy clamour.

The little lantern burned in front of him. Birds hid it from time to time as they fluttered by. But he always saw the eyes of the Leper, who stood, motionless as a pillar, at the stern.

It went on long, very long.

When at last they had entered the hovel Julian shut the door; and he saw the Leper sitting on the stool. The kind of shroud which covered him had fallen to his hips; and his shoulders, chest, and wizened arms were hardly to be seen for the scaly pustules which coated them. Immense wrinkles furrowed his brow. He had a hole in place of a nose, like a skeleton, and his bluish lips exhaled a breath as thick as fog, and nauseous.

"I am hungry!" he said.

Julian gave him what he had, an old piece of bacon and the crust of a black loaf. When he had devoured them, the table, the dish, and the handle of the knife bore the same spots that could be seen on his body.

Next he said, "I am thirsty!"

Julian went to get his pitcher, and it gave out an aroma, as he took it, which enlarged his heart and nostrils. It was wine—what happiness! But the Leper put out his arm and emptied the whole pitcher at a draught.

Then he said, "I am cold!"

And Julian, with his candle, set light to a pile of bracken in the middle of the hut.

The Leper came to warm himself, and as he crouched on his heels he trembled in every limb and weakened. His eyes ceased to gleam, his sores ran, and in an almost lifeless voice he murmured:

"Thy bed!"

Julian helped him gently to drag himself there, and even spread the canvas of his boat over him as a covering.

The Leper groaned. His teeth showed at the corners of his mouth, a faster rattle shook his chest, and as each breath was taken his body hollowed to the backbone.

Then he shut his eyes.

"It is like ice in my bones! Come close to me!"

And Julian, lifting the cloth, lay down on the dead leaves side by side with him.

The Leper turned his head.

"Take off thy clothes, that I may have thy body's warmth!"

Julian took off his clothes and lay down on the bed again, naked as when he was born; and he felt the Leper's skin against his thigh, colder than a serpent and rough as a file.

He tried to hearten him, and the other answered in gasps:

"Ah, I am dying! Come closer, warm me! Not with the hands; no, with thy whole body!"

Julian stretched himself completely over him, mouth to mouth and chest on chest.

Then the Leper clasped him, and his eyes suddenly became as bright as stars; his hair drew out like sunbeams; the breath of his nostrils was as sweet as roses; a cloud of incense rose from the hearth, and the waves began to sing. Meanwhile an abundance of delight, a superhuman joy flooded into Julian's soul as he lay swooning; and he who still clasped him in his arms grew taller, ever taller, until his head and feet touched the two walls of the hut. The roof flew off, the firmament unrolled—and Julian rose towards the blue spaces, face to face with Our Lord Jesus, who carried him to heaven.

And that is the story of St. Julian the Hospitaller, more or less as you will find it on a church window in the region where I live.

THE DRAGON

by Ryūnosuké Akutagawa

"Lord bless me!" said Uji Dainagon Takakuni.* "Awaking in a dream from my nap, I feel it's especially hot today. Not a breath of wind blows to shake even the wisteria flowers hanging from the pine branch. The murmuring of the spring, which at other times makes me feel cool, is nearly drowned out by the singing of the cicadas, and seems only to add to the sultry heat. Now I will have the servant boys fan me."

"Oh, you say people on the streets have gathered! Then I'll go too. Boys, follow me, and don't forget to bring the big fans."

"Greetings. I'm Takakuni. Pardon the rudeness of my scanty attire.

"Today I have a request to make of you, so I've had my coach stop at the tea-house of Uji. Lately, I've been thinking of coming here to write a story book as others do. But unfortunately I know no stories worth writing. Idle as I am, it bores me to have to rack my brains. So from today I plan to have you tell me the old stories so that I may put them into a book. Since I, Takakuni, am always around and about the Imperial Court, I shall be able to collect from all quarters many unusual anec-

---

From *Rashomon and Other Stories,* by Ryūnosuké Akutagawa, translated by Takashi Kojima (New York: Liveright Publishing Corp., 1952), pp. 102–19.

**Uji Dainagon Takakuni* (1087–1160). *'Dainagon'* was the government office of Chief Councilor of State in olden days. Uji Takakuni, the author of *'Konjaku Monogatari,'* has been traditionally, though not authentically, identified with the author of *'the Uji Shuishu'* (*'Gleanings from the Tales of Uji'*), from which Akutagawa took this story. (The notes throughout this story are the translator's. [Eds.])

dotes and curious stories. So you, good folks, troublesome though it may be, will you grant my request?

"You all grant my request? A thousand thanks! Then I will listen to your stories one by one."

"Here, boys. Start using your big fans so that the whole room may have a breeze. That will make us a little cooler. You, ironmaster, and you potter, don't be reserved. Both of you, step nearer to this desk. That woman who sells '*sushi,*' * if the sunlight is too hot for you, you'd better put your pail in a corner of the verandah. Priest, lay down your golden hand-drum. You, samurai, and you, mountain priest, there, have you spread your mats?

"Are you all ready? Then if you're ready, potter, since you are the oldest, you first tell us any story you prefer."

"We are greatly obliged for your courteous greeting," the old man replied. "Your Lordship graciously said that you would make a story book of what we humble folks are going to tell you. This is a far greater honor than I deserve. But if I should decline, Your Lordship wouldn't be pleased. So I'll take the liberty of telling you a foolish old story. It may be somewhat tiresome, but please listen to my tale for a while."

The old man began his story.

In old days when I was quite young, in Nara there lived a priest called Kurodo Tokugyo who had an extraordinarily large nose. The tip of his nose shone frightfully crimson all the year round, as if it'd been stung by a wasp. So the people of Nara nicknamed him Ohana-no Kurodo Tokugyo.† But because that name was too long, they came to call him Hanazo.‡ I myself saw him a couple of times in the Kofuku Temple in Nara. He had such a fine red nose that I, too, thought that he might well be scornfully called Hanazo.

On a certain night, Hanazo, that is, Ohana-no Kurodo Tokugyo, the priest, came alone to the pond of Sarusawa, without the company of his disciples, and set up, on the bank in front of the weeping willow, a notice-board which said in bold characters, "On March third a dragon shall ascend from this pond." But as a matter of fact, he didn't know whether or not a dragon really lived in the pond of Sarusawa, and needless to say, the dragon's ascension to heaven on March third was a black lie. It would have been more certain if he had said that no dragon would ascend to heaven. The reason why he made such needless mischief is that he was displeased with the priests of Nara who were habitually making fun of his nose, and he planned to play a trick on them this time and laugh at them to his heart's content. Your Lordship must think it quite ridiculous. But this is an old story, and in those days people who played such tricks were by no means uncommon.

The next day, the first to find this notice-board was an old woman who

---

* *sushi.* Boiled rice flavored with vinegar, often pressed into balls, and served with fish, fried eggs, etc.

† *Ohana-no Kurdo Tokugyo.* '*Ohana*' means a big nose. '*Kurodo*' means an official in the Imperial Archives. '*Tokugyo*' might mean a person accomplished in religious austerities.

‡ *Hanazo* might mean a big-nosed fellow.

came to worship Buddha at the Kofuku Temple every morning. When she neared the still misty pond, leaning on a bamboo cane with her rosary in her hand, she found the notice-board, which she had not seen under the weeping-willow the day before. She wondered why a board announcing a Buddhist mass should stand in such a strange place. But since she could not read any of the characters, she was about to pass it by, when she fortunately met a robed priest coming from the opposite direction, and she had him read it for her. The notice said, "On March third a dragon shall ascend from this pond." They were astonished at this.

The old woman was amazed. Stretching her bent body, she looked up into the priest's face and asked, "Is it possible that a dragon lives in this pond?" The priest assumed an air of still more composure and said to her, "In former times a certain Chinese scholar had a lump over his eyelid which itched terribly. One day the sky suddenly became overcast, and a thunder shower rained down in torrents. Then instantly his lump burst and a dragon is said to have ascended straight up to heaven trailing a cloud. Since a dragon could live even in a lump, tens of dragons could naturally live at the bottom of a big pond like this." With these words he expounded the matter to her. The old woman, who had always been convinced that a priest never lied, was astounded out of her wits, and said, "I see. Now that you mention it, the color of the water over there does look suspicious." Although it was not yet March third, she hurried away, scarcely bothering to use her cane, panting out her Buddhist prayers, and leaving the priest behind alone.

Had it not been for the people about him, the priest would have split his sides with laughter. This was only natural, for the priest was none other than the author of the notice-board, that is, Kurodo Tokugyo, nicknamed Hanazo. He had been walking about the pond with the preposterous idea that some gullible persons might be caught by the notice-board which he put up the night before. After the old woman left, he found an early traveler accompanied by a servant who carried her burden on his back. She had a skirt with a design of insects on it, and was reading the notice-board from beneath her sedgehat. Then the priest, cautiously stifling his laugh with great effort, stood in front of the sign, pretending to read it. After giving a sniff with his red nose, he slowly went back toward the Kofuku Temple. Then, in front of the big southern gate of the temple, by chance he met the priest called Emon, who lived in the same cell as he himself.

"You are up unusually early today," Emon said, furrowing his dark, thick, stubborn brow. "The weather may change."

"The weather may really change," Hanazo readily replied with a knowing look, dilating his nose. "I'm told that a dragon will ascend to heaven from the Sarusawa Pond on March third."

Hearing this, Emon glared dubiously at Hanazo. But soon purring in his throat, he said with a sardonic smile, "You had a good dream, I suppose. I was once told that to dream of a dragon ascending to heaven is an auspicious omen." So saying he tried to go past Hanazo, tossing his mortar-shaped head. But he must have heard Hanazo muttering to himself, "A lost soul is beyond redemption." Turning back with such hateful force that the supports of his hemp-thronged clogs bent for the moment, he demanded of Hanazo, in a tone as vehement as if he would challenge him to a Buddhist controversy, "Is there any positive proof that a dragon will ascend to heaven?"

Thereupon, Hanazo, affecting perfect composure, pointed towards the pond, on which the sun was already beginning to shed its light, and replied, looking down at him, "If you doubt my remark, you ought to see the notice-board in front of the weeping willow."

Obstinate as Emon was, his normal keen reasoning must have lost a little of its initial impetuosity. Blindly, as if his eyes were dazzled, he asked in a half-hearted voice, "Well, has such a notice-board been set up?" and went off in a thoughtful mood, with his mortar-shaped head to one side.

You may well imagine how this amused Hanazo, who saw him going away. He felt the whole of his red nose itch, and while he went up the stone-steps of the big southern gate with a sullen expression, he could not help bursting into laughter in spite of himself.

Even that first morning the notice-board saying "On March third a dragon shall ascend" had a great effect on the public. In the course of a day or two the dragon in the pond of Sarusawa became the talk of the whole town of Nara. Of course some said, "The notice-board may be somebody's hoax." Also at that time there spread in Kyoto a rumor that the dragon in the Shinsen-en had ascended to heaven. Even those who asserted that the prophecy on the notice-board was a hoax started to waver between belief and doubt as to the truth of the rumor, and began to think that such an event might possibly occur.

Just then an unexpected wonder took place. Less than ten days later the nine year old daughter of a certain Shinto priest who served the Shrine of Kasuga was drowsing, with her head in her mother's lap, when a black dragon fell like a cloud from heaven, and said in human speech, "At last I am to ascend to heaven on March third. But rest at ease, since I expect to cause no trouble to you townspeople." The moment she woke up, she told her mother about her dream. The talk that the little girl had dreamt of the dragon in the pond of Sarusawa caused a great sensation in the town. The story was exaggerated in one way and another: a child possessed of a dragon wrote a poem, a dragon appeared to such and such a shrine priest in a dream and gave him a divine revelation.

In the course of time, one man went so far as to say that he had actually seen a dragon, although no dragon could be expected even to have thrust his head above water. He was an old man who went to the market to sell fish every morning. At dawn one day he came to the pond of Sarusawa. Through the morning haze he saw the wide expanse of water gleam with a faint light under the bank where the weeping-willow stood and where the notice-board was set up. At any rate it was the time when the rumor of the dragon was on everyone's lips. So he thought that the dragon god had come out. Trembling all over with this half happy and half dreadful thought, he left his catch of river fish there, and stealing up, he held on to the weeping-willow and tried to look into the pond. Then he saw an unknown monster like a coiled black chain lurking ominously at the bottom of the faintly illuminated water. Probably frightened by human foot-steps, the dreadful monster uncoiled and disappeared somewhere in a twinkling. At this sight the man broke into a cold sweat, and returned to the place where he had left his fish, only to find that a score of fish, including some carp and eels which he was carrying to the market, had disappeared. Some laughed at this rumor, saying, "He was probably deceived by an old otter." But not a few said, "Since it's impossible for an otter to live in the pond which the dragon king rules and protects, the dragon king took pity on the life of the fish, and must have called them down into the pond where he lives."

In the meantime, the notice-board message "On March third a dragon shall ascend from this pond," came to be more and more talked about, and Hanazo, elated by this success, chuckled to himself, and dilated his nose. Time went on and the third of March drew near. Four or five days before the scheduled ascension of the dragon, to Hanazo's great astonishment, his aunt, a priestess in Sakurai in the province of Settsu, came up all the long way to Nara, saying that she wanted by all means to see the dragon's ascension. He was quite embarrassed, and resorted to frightening, coaxing and a thousand other means, to persuade her to go back to Sakurai. But she obstinately refused and stayed on without listening to his advice, saying, "I'm very old. If I can have a glimpse of the dragon king and worship him, I shall be happy to die." He could not now confess that out of mischief he himself had put up the notice-board. At last Hanazo yielded, and not only did he agree to take care of her until March third, but he had to promise her that he would accompany her to see the dragon god's ascension on the day.

Since even his aunt, the priestess, had heard of the dragon, the rumor must have spread to the provinces of Settsu, Izumi, and Kawachi, and possibly as far as to the provinces of Harima, Yamashiro, Omi and Tamba, to say nothing of the province of Yamato. The mischief he had done with the intention of playing a trick upon the people of Nara had brought about the unexpected result of deceiving tens of thousands of people in many provinces. When he thought of this, he felt more alarmed than pleased. While he was showing his aunt, the priestess, around the temples of Nara every day, he had the guilty conscience of a criminal hiding out of the sight of the police commissioner. But while on one hand he felt uneasy when he learned from hearsay on the streets that incense had been burnt and flowers offered before the notice-board, on the other, he felt as happy as if he had accomplished some great achievement.

Days passed by, and at last came the third of March, when the dragon was to ascend to heaven.

As his promise left him no alternative, he reluctantly accompanied his aunt to the top of the stone steps of the big southern gate of the Kofuku Temple, which commanded a bird's-eye view of the pond of Sarusawa. It was a clear and cloudless day, and there was not a breath of wind to ring even a wind-bell at a gate.

The spectators who had been looking forward to the day thronged in from the provinces of Kawachi, Izumi, Settsu, Harima, Yamashiro, Omi, Tamba and others, to say nothing of the city of Nara. Looking out from the top of the stone steps, he saw, as far as the eye could reach, a sea of people stretching in all directions to the end of the thoroughfare of Nijo in the hazy distance. All kinds of ceremonial headgear rustled in waves. Here and there ox-carts, elaborately decorated with blue or red tassels or in tasteful shades, towered over the mass of people, their roofs inlaid with gold and silver shining dazzlingly in the beautiful spring sunlight. Some people had put up sunshades, some pitched flat tents, others set up elaborate stands on the streets. The area in the vicinity of the pond, spread out under his eyes, presented a scene reminiscent of the Kamo festival, although out of season. Priest Hanazo who now saw this, had little dreamt that setting up a mere notice-board would cause such great excitement.

"What tremendous crowds of people!" Hanazo said in a feeble voice, looking back at his aunt as in great amazement. And he squatted down at the foot of the column of the large southern gate, apparently without even the spirit to sniff with his large nose.

But his aunt, the priestess, was far from able to read his innermost thoughts. Stretching out her neck so far that her hood almost slipped off, she looked around here and there, and chattered continually, "Indeed, the view of the pond where the dragon king lives is exquisite. Since such big crowds have turned out, the dragon god will be sure to appear, won't he?" and so on.

Hanazo could not keep on squatting at the foot of the column, so reluctantly he stood up, to find a large crowd of people in creased or triangular ceremonial head-gear on the stone steps. Then in the crowd, who did he recognize but Priest Emon looking intently toward the pond, with his mortar-shaped head towering conspicuously above the others. At this sight he suddenly forgot his wretched feeling. Amused and tickled by the idea that he had taken in even this fellow, he called out to him, "Priest," and asked him mockingly, "Are you here also to see the dragon's ascension?"

"Yes," Emon replied, looking backward arrogantly. Then, assuming an unusually serious look, his dark thick eyebrows growing rigid, he added, "He is slow in coming out."

Hanazo felt that the trick had overreached itself and his buoyant voice sank, and he looked vacantly down over a sea of people, as helpless as ever. But although a long time passed, there were no indications of the dragon ascending in the limpid surface of the water, which apparently had already become slightly warmer, mirroring distinctly the cherries and willows on the bank. Probably because masses of spectators were crowded for miles around, the pond today seemed smaller than usual, furthering impression that there could be no dragon.

But all the spectators waited patiently with breathless interest as if unconscious of the passage of hours. The sea of people under the gate spread wider and wider. As time went on, the ox-carts became so numerous that in some places their axles jostled one another. It may well be imagined from the preceding account how miserable Hanazo felt at this sight. But then a strange thing happened, for Hanazo began to feel in his heart that a dragon was really likely to ascend—at first, he began to feel that it might not be impossible for a dragon to ascend. Of course he was the author of the notice-board, and he ought not to have entertained any such absurd idea. But while he was looking at the surging of the ceremonial head-gear, he actually began to feel that some such alarming event might happen.

This may have been because the excitement of the multitude of people impressed Hanazo without his being aware of it. Or it may be that he felt guilty when he thought over the fact that his trick caused such great general excitement, and that without being aware of it, he began to desire in his heart, that a dragon should really ascend from the pond. Whatever the reason, his miserable feeling gradually faded away, though he knew quite well that it was he himself who had written the sentence on the notice-board, and he too began gazing at the surface of the pond as intently as his aunt. Indeed, had he not conceived such a fancy, he could not have remained standing under the large southern gate all day long, waiting for the impossible ascension of the dragon.

But the pond of Sarusawa, not a ripple rising, reflected back the spring sunlight. The sky was bright and clear with not a speck of cloud floating. Still the spectators, as closely packed as ever under sunshades and flat tents and behind the balustrades of stands, awaited the appearance of the dragon king in the throes of expectation, as if they had been unaware of the passage of time from morning to noon and from noon to evening.

Nearly half a day had gone by since Hanazo had arrived there. Then a streak of cloud like the smoke of a joss stick trailed in mid-air. Suddenly it grew larger and larger, and the sky which had been bright and clear became dusky. At that moment a gust of wind swept down over the pond and ruffled the glassy surface of the water into innumerable waves. Then in the twinkling of an eye, white rain came down in torrents before the spectators, prepared as they were, had time to scurry helter-skelter. Furthermore, terrific claps of thunder suddenly pealed, and flashes of lightning flew past one another like wefts of a fabric. Then hooked hands seemed to tear apart a cluster of clouds, and in the excess of their force they raised a spout of water over the pond. At that instant Hanazo's eyes caught a blurred vision of a black dragon more than one hundred feet long ascending straight into the sky, with its golden talons flashing. But this happened in a twinkling. After that, amidst a storm, cherry blossoms around the pond were seen flying up into the dusky sky. It hardly need be said that the disconcerted spectators, as they scurried away, formed waves of humanity which surged like the waves in the pond.

Eventually the torrential rain stopped and a blue sky began to peep through the clouds. Then Hanazo stared around him as if he had forgotten his large nose. Was the figure of the dragon which he had just seen an illusion? While he wondered, author of the notice-board as he was, he began to feel that the dragon's ascension was impossible. Nevertheless, he did actually see it. So, the more he thought over the event, the more mysterious it became. At that time, when he raised his aunt, who had been lying more dead than alive at the foot of the column near by, he was unable to conceal his bewilderment and fright. He asked her timidly, "Did you see the dragon?" His aunt, who had been stunned for a time, heaved a great sigh, and could do nothing but repeat her nod in fear. Presently in a trembling voice she answered, "Surely I did. Wasn't he a dragon, black all over, with only his golden talons flashing?"

So probably it was not only the eyes of Hanazo, or Kurodo Tokugyo, who saw the dragon. Yes, later it was said that most of the people of all ages and sexes who had been there on that day had seen the black dragon ascending to heaven in a dark cloud.

Later Hanazo confessed that the notice-board had been his own mischievous idea. But I am told none of his fellow-priests, not even Emon, believed his confession. Now did his notice-board hit the mark? Or did it miss? Ask Hanazo or Kurodo Tokugyo the Big Nosed, and probably he himself will be unable to reply to this question.

"What a mysterious story, indeed!" said Uji Dainagon Takakuni. "In the old days a dragon seems to have lived in that pond of Sarusawa. What! You cannot tell whether it did even in the old days? Yes, in the old days it must have lived there. In those times all people believed that dragons lived at the bottom of water. So, naturally, dragons ought to have flown between heaven and earth and at times ought to have appeared in mysterious forms like gods. But I would rather hear your stories than make my comments. The next story is the itinerant priest's turn, isn't it?"

"What?" Takakuni went on. "Is your story about a long-nosed priest called Ikeno-no-Zenchinaigu? That will be all the more interesting following the story of Hanazo. Now tell it to me at once . . ."

PREDESTINED MARRIAGE

by Li Fu-yen

Wei Ku of Tuling was an orphan from childhood. When he grew up he desired an early marriage but for a long time had difficulty in finding a suitable match. In the second year of Cheng Kuan (628) he had occasion to visit Chingho and on his way put up at an inn south of Sungeheng. One of the guests at the inn said that he knew of a retired official by the name of Pan Fang who had a daughter of marriage age; he said that

From *Traditional Chinese Tales*, translated by Chi-Chen Wang (New York: Columbia University Press, 1944), pp. 104–7.

if Ku was interested he should go to the Lung Hsing Temple west of the inn and there discuss the matter with Pan's middleman.

As Ku was eager for marriage, he went to the temple early the next morning when the slanting moon was still bright in the sky. There on the temple steps he found an old man sitting against a cloth bag and examining a book in the moonlight. Ku went up to him and looked at the book but could not read the writing.

"What kind of book are you reading, venerable sir?" Ku asked. "I have studied industriously from my youth and am familiar with all kinds of scripts, including the Sanskrit writing of the Western countries, but I have never seen anything like the writing in your book."

"Of course you have never seen anything like it," the old man said, smiling, "for it is not a book to be found in this world."

"What kind of a book is it then?" Ku asked, and the old man answered, "It is a book of the nether world."

"How does it happen that you, a man of the other world, have appeared in this one?"

"It is because you are abroad too early in the morning that you have encountered me, not that I have no business to be seen in these parts," the old man retorted. "For since it is the duty of officers of the nether world to govern the destinies of men, how can they avoid visiting their domain? As a matter of fact, the highways belong half to men and half to ghosts; only most men are not aware of it."

"What are your special duties?"

"The marriage bonds of the universe."

Ku was delighted on hearing this and said, "I was orphaned from childhood and it has been my desire to marry early so that I can rear a large family. But for more than ten years I have searched in vain for a suitable match. I am to meet some one here this morning to discuss a marital bond with the daughter of Pan Fang. Would you tell me, venerable sir, what are my chances of success?"

"You will have no success," the old man answered. "Your future wife is now only three years old and will not become your wife until she is seventeen."

Then Ku asked him what was in his bag, and he answered, "It contains red cords with which I tie together the feet of couples destined for each other. Once their feet are tied with these cords, they will eventually become husband and wife, even though their families are hereditary enemies or are separated by the gulf of varying fortunes or of remote distances. Your foot has been tied to that of the girl I allude to; there is no use in your looking elsewhere."

"Where is this future wife of mine and what does her family do?"

"She is the daughter of the vegetable woman who lives north of your inn."

"Can I see her?"

"Her mother always takes her to the market," the old man answered. "If you come with me I shall point her out to you."

When day came, Pan's emissary failed to appear. The old man closed his book, took his bag and walked away, with Ku following. When they came to the market, there was a woman with a three-year-old girl in her arms. She was repulsive in appearance, having only one eye; the child too, was quite unprepossessing. Pointing to the girl, the old man said, "There is your future wife!"

"I shall have her killed before I will marry her," Ku said angrily.

"It will be futile for you to try," the old man said. "She is destined to become a titled woman through the merit of her son." With this the old man vanished.

Ku sharpened up a knife and gave it to his servant, saying, "You are a very capable servant. If you will kill that girl for me, I shall give you ten thousand cash."

The servant took the knife and went to the vegetable woman's stall the next day. There without warning he struck the girl with his knife and then fled in the confusion.

"Did you kill her?" Ku asked his servant when he came back.

"I aimed at her heart," the latter answered, "but I struck her just above the eye."

For fourteen years more Ku tried in vain to find a suitable match. Then by virtue of his late father's meritorious service he was appointed an assistant to Wang Tai, the governor of Hsiangchou, and was charged with the administration of justice. He performed his duty so well that Wang Tai gave his daughter to him in marriage. She was about sixteen or seventeen and very beautiful. Ku was well pleased with the match, but was puzzled by a curious circumstance. His wife always wore a small piece of filigree over her eye which she never took off even when she bathed herself.

When after a year or so Ku asked her about it, she answered thus with an air of sadness: "I am the governor's niece, not his daughter. My father was the magistrate of Sungcheng at the time of his death. I was then only an infant. My mother and brother also died shortly afterwards. My nurse took compassion on me and took care of me. She was able to eke out an existence by growing vegetables on a piece of land that my father left and selling them in the market. When I was three years old I was struck by a murderous maniac and was left with a knife scar which I have to this day. That is why I wear this piece of filigree. Seven or eight years ago I was found by my uncle and so it happened that he married me to you as his daughter."

"Is your nurse blind in one eye?" Ku asked.

"Yes," she answered, "how did you know?"

Thereupon Ku told her the whole story. The couple thereafter treated each other with even greater respect and consideration. Later she gave birth to a son, whom they named Kun. He rose to be governor of Yenmen and by virtue of his position his mother was given the title Lady of Taiyuan.

One can see from this story that it is impossible to change one's destiny.

When the magistrate of Sungcheng heard this strange story, he conferred on the inn where Wei Ku had stayed the name "Inn of the Predestined Marriage" and inscribed those words on its sign board.

THE POOR THING

by Robert Louis Stevenson

There was a man in the islands who fished for his bare bellyful, and took his life in his hands to go forth upon the sea between four planks. But though he had much ado, he was merry of heart; and the gulls heard him laugh when the spray met him. And though he had little lore, he was sound of spirit; and when the fish came to his hook in the mid-waters, he blessed God without weighing. He was bitter poor in goods and bitter ugly of countenance, and he had no wife.

It fell in the time of the fishing that the man awoke in his house about the midst of the afternoon. The fire burned in the midst, and the smoke went up and the sun came down by the chimney. And the man was aware of the likeness of one that warmed his hands at the red peats.

"I greet you," said the man, "in the name of God."

"I greet you," said he that warmed his hands, "but not in the name of God, for I am none of His; nor in the name of Hell, for I am not of Hell. For I am but a bloodless thing, less than wind and lighter than a sound, and the wind goes through me like a net, and I am broken by a sound and shaken by the cold."

"Be plain with me," said the man, "and tell me your name and of your nature."

"My name," quoth the other, "is not yet named, and my nature not yet sure. For I am part of a man; and I was a part of your fathers, and went out to fish and fight with them in the ancient days. But now is my turn not yet come; and I wait until you have a wife, and then shall I be in your son, and a brave part of him, rejoicing manfully to launch the boat into the surf, skilful to direct the helm, and a man of might where the ring closes and the blows are going."

"This is a marvellous thing to hear," said the man; "and if you are indeed to be my son, I fear it will go ill with you; for I am bitter poor in goods and bitter ugly in face, and I shall never get me a wife if I live to the age of eagles."

"All this have I come to remedy, my Father," said the Poor Thing; "for we must go this night to the little isle of sheep, where our fathers lie in the dead-cairn, and tomorrow to the Earl's Hall, and there shall you find a wife by my providing."

So the man rose and put forth his boat at the time of the sunsetting; and the Poor Thing sat in the prow, and the spray blew through his bones

---

From *The Strange Case of Dr. Jekyll & Mr. Hyde. Fables: Other Stories & Fragments*, Tusitala Edition (London: W. Heinemann, 1924), pp. 109–14.

like snow, and the wind whistled in his teeth, and the boat dipped not with the weight of him.

"I am fearful to see you, my son," said the man. "For methinks you are no thing of God."

"It is only the wind that whistles in my teeth," said the Poor Thing, "and there is no life in me to keep it out."

So they came to the little isle of sheep, where the surf burst all about it in the midst of the sea, and it was all green with bracken, and all wet with dew, and the moon enlightened it. They ran the boat into a cove, and set foot to land; and the man came heavily behind among the rocks in the deepness of the bracken, but the Poor Thing went before him like a smoke in the light of the moon. So they came to the dead-cairn, and they laid their ears to the stones; and the dead complained withinsides like a swarm of bees: "Time was that marrow was in our bones, and strength in our sinews; and the thoughts of our head were clothed upon with acts and the words of men. But now are we broken in sunder, and the bonds of our bones are loosed, and our thoughts lie in the dust."

Then said the Poor Thing: "Charge them that they give you the virtue they withheld."

And the man said: "Bones of my fathers, greeting! for I am sprung of your loins. And now, behold, I break open the piled stones of your cairn, and I let in the noon between your ribs. Count it well done, for it was to be; and give me what I come seeking in the name of blood and in the name of God."

And the spirits of the dead stirred in the cairn like ants; and they spoke: "You have broken the roof of our cairn and let in the noon between our ribs; and you have the strength of the still-living. But what virtue have we? what power? or what jewel here in the dust with us, that any living man should covet or receive it? for we are less than nothing. But we tell you one thing, speaking with many voices like bees, that the way is plain before all like the grooves of launching: So forth into life and fear not, for so did we all in the ancient ages." And their voices passed away like an eddy in a river.

"Now," said the Poor Thing, "they have told you a lesson, but make them give you a gift. Stoop your hand among the bones without drawback, and you shall find their treasure."

So the man stooped his hand, and the dead laid hold upon it many and faint like ants; but he shook them off, and behold, what he brought up in his hand was the shoe of a horse, and it was rusty.

"It is a thing of no price," quoth the man, "for it is rusty."

"We shall see that," said the Poor Thing; "for in my thought it is a good thing to do what our fathers did, and to keep what they kept without question. And in my thought one thing is as good as another in this world; and a shoe of a horse will do."

Now they got into their boat with the horseshoe, and when the dawn was come they were aware of the smoke of the Earl's town and the bells of the Kirk that beat. So they set foot to shore; and the man went up to the market among the fishers over against the palace and the Kirk; and he was bitter poor and bitter ugly, and he had never a fish to sell, but only a shoe of a horse in his creel, and it rusty.

"Now," said the Poor Thing, "do so and so, and you shall find a wife and I a mother."

It befell that the Earl's daughter came forth to go into the Kirk upon her prayers; and when she saw the poor man stand in the market with only the shoe of a horse, and it rusty, it came in her mind it should be a thing of price.

"What is that?" quoth she.

"It is a shoe of a horse," said the man.

"And what is the use of it?" quoth the Earl's daughter.

"It is for no use," said the man.

"I may not believe that," said she; "else why should you carry it?"

"I do so," said he, "because it was so my fathers did in the ancient ages; and I have neither a better reason nor a worse."

Now the Earl's daughter could not find it in her mind to believe him. "Come," quoth she, "sell me this, for I am sure it is a thing of price."

"Nay," said the man, "the thing is not for sale."

"What!" cried the Earl's daughter. "Then what make you here in the town's market, with the thing in your creel and nought beside?"

"I sit here," says the man, "to get me a wife."

"There is no sense in any of these answers," thought the Earl's daughter; "and I could find it in my heart to weep."

By came the Earl upon that; and she called him and told him all. And when he had heard, he was of his daughter's mind that this should be a thing of virtue; and charged the man to set a price upon the thing, or else be hanged upon the gallows; and that was near at hand, so that the man could see it.

"The way of life is straight like the grooves of launching," quoth the man. "And if I am to be hanged let me be hanged."

"Why!" cried the Earl, "will you set your neck against a shoe of a horse, and it rusty?"

"In my thought," said the man, "one thing is as good as another in this world; and a shoe of a horse will do."

"This can never be," thought the Earl; and he stood and looked upon the man, and bit his beard.

And the man looked up at him and smiled. "It was so my fathers did in the ancient ages," quoth he to the Earl, "and I have neither a better reason nor a worse."

"There is no sense in any of this," thought the Earl, "and I must be growing old." So he had his daughter on one side, and says he: "Many suitors have you denied, my child. But here is a very strange matter that a man should cling so to a shoe of a horse, and it rusty; and that he should offer it like a thing on sale, and yet not sell it; and that he should sit there seeking a wife. If I come not to the bottom of this thing, I shall have no more pleasure in bread; and I can see no way, but either I should hang or you should marry him."

"By my troth, but he is bitter ugly," said the Earl's daughter. "How if the gallows be so near at hand?"

"It was not so," said the Earl, "that my fathers did in the ancient ages. I am like the man, and can give you neither a better reason nor a worse. But do you, prithee, speak with him again."

So the Earl's daughter spoke to the man. "If you were not so bitter ugly," quoth she, "my father the Earl would have us marry."

"Bitter ugly am I," said the man, "and you as fair as May. Bitter ugly I am, and what of that? It was so my fathers—"

"In the name of God," said the Earl's daughter, "let your fathers be!"

"If I had done that," said the man, "you had never been chaffering with me here in the market, nor your father the Earl watching with the end of his eye."

"But come," quoth the Earl's daughter, "this is a very strange thing, that you would have me wed for a shoe of a horse, and it rusty."

"In my thought," quoth the man, "one thing is as good—"

"Oh, spare me that," said the Earl's daughter, "and tell me why I should marry."

"Listen and look," said the man.

Now the wind blew through the Poor Thing like an infant crying, so that her heart was melted; and her eyes were unsealed, and she was aware of the thing as it were a babe unmothered, and she took it to her arms, and it melted in her arms like the air.

"Come," said the man, "behold a vision of our children, the busy hearth, and the white heads. And let that suffice, for it is all God offers."

"I have no delight in it," said she; but with that she sighed.

"The ways of life are straight like the grooves of launching," said the man; and he took her by the hand.

"And what shall we do with the horseshoe?" quoth she.

"I will give it to your father," said the man; "and he can make a kirk and a mill of it for me."

It came to pass in time that the Poor Thing was born; but memory of these matters slept within him, and he knew not that which he had done. But he was a part of the eldest son; rejoicing manfully to launch the boat into the surf, skilful to direct the helm, and a man of might where the ring closes and the blows are going.

THE DEATH OF BED NUMBER 12

by Ghassan Kanafani

Dear Ahmed,

I have chosen you in particular to be the recipient of this letter for a reason which may appear to you commonplace, yet since yesterday my every thought has been centred on it. I chose you in particular because when I saw him yesterday dying on the high white bed I remembered how you used to use the word 'die' to express anything extreme. Many is the time I've heard you use such expressions as 'I almost died laughing,' 'I was dead tired,' 'Death itself couldn't quench my love,' and so on. While it is true that we all use such words, you use them more than anybody. Thus it was that I remembered you as I saw him sinking down in the bed and clutching at the coverlet with his long, emaciated fingers, giving a convulsive shiver and then staring out at me with dead eyes.

But why have I not begun at the beginning? You know, no doubt, that I am now in my second month at the hospital. I have been suffering from a stomach ulcer, but no sooner had the surgeon plugged up the hole in my stomach than a new one appeared in my head, about which the surgeon could do nothing. Believe me, Ahmed, that an 'ulcer' on the brain is a lot more stubborn than one in the stomach. My room leads on to the main corridor of the Internal Diseases Wing, while the window overlooks the small hospital garden. Thus, propped up by a pillow, I can observe both the continuous flow of patients passing the door as well as the birds which fly past the window incessantly. Amidst this hubbub of people who come here to die in the serene shadow of the scalpel and whom I see, having arrived on their own two feet, leaving after days or hours on the death trolley, wrapped round in a covering of white; in this hubbub I find myself quite unable to make good those holes that have begun to open up in my head, quite incapable of stopping the flow of questions that mercilessly demand an answer of me.

I shall be leaving the hospital in a few days, for they have patched up my insides as best they can. I am now able to walk leaning on the arm of an old and ugly nurse and on my own powers of resistance. The hospital, however, has done little more than transfer the ulcer from my stomach to my head, for in this place, as the ugly old woman remarked, medicine may be able to plug up a hole in the stomach but it can never find the answers required to plug up holes in one's thinking. The day she said this the old woman gave a toothless laugh as she quietly led me off to the scales.

From *Modern Arabic Short Stories,* edited and translated by Denys Johnson-Davies (London: Oxford University Press, 1967), pp. 28–42. Reprinted by permission.

What, though, is such talk to do with us? What I want to talk to you about is death. Death that takes place in front of you, not about that death of which one merely hears. The difference between the two types of death is immeasurable and cannot be appreciated by someone who has not been a witness to a human being clutching at the coverlet of his bed with all the strength of his trembling fingers in order to resist that terrible slipping into extinction, as though the coverlet can pull him back from that colossus who, little by little, wrests from his eyes this life about which we know scarcely anything.

As the doctors waited around him, I examined the card that hung at the foot of his bed. I had slipped out of my room and was standing there, unseen by the doctors, who were engaged in a hopeless attempt to save the dying man. I read: 'Name: Mohamed Ali Akbar. Age: 25. Nationality: Omani.' I turned the card over and this time read: 'Leukaemia.' Again I stared into the thin brown face, the wide frightened eyes and the lips that trembled like a ripple of purple water. As his eyes turned and came to rest on my face it seemed that he was appealing to me for help. Why? Because I used to give to him a casual greeting every morning? Or was it that he saw in my face some understanding of the terror that he was undergoing? He went on staring at me and then—quite simply—he died.

It was only then that the doctor discovered me and dragged me off angrily to my room. But he would never be able to banish from my mind the scene that is ever-present there. As I got on to my bed I heard the voice of the male nurse in the corridor alongside my door saying in a matter-of-fact voice:

'Bed number 12 has died!'

I said to myself: 'Mohamed Ali Akbar has lost his name, he is Bed number 12.' What do I mean now when I talk of a human being whose name was Mohamed Ali Akbar? What does it matter to him whether he still retains his name or whether it has been replaced by a number? Then I remembered how he wouldn't allow anyone to omit any part of his name. Every morning the nurse would ask him, 'And how are you, Mohamed Ali?' and he would not reply, for he regarded his name as being Mohamed Ali Akbar—just like that, all in one—and that this Mohamed Ali to whom the nurse was speaking was some other person.

Though the nurses found a subject for mirth in this insistence on his whole name being used, Mohamed Ali Akbar continued to demand it; perhaps he regarded his right to possessing his name in full as being an insistence that he at least owned something, for he was poor, extremely poor, a great deal more so than you with your fertile imagination could conceive as you lounge around in the café; poverty was something engraved in his face, his forearms, his chest, the way he ate, into everything that surrounded him.

When I was able to walk for the first time after they had patched me up, I paid him a visit. The back of his bed was raised and he was sitting up, lost in thought. I sat on the side of the bed for a short while, and we exchanged a few brief, banal words. I noticed that alongside his pillow was an old wooden box with his name carved on it in semi-Persian style writing; it was securely tied with twine. Apart from this he owned nothing except his clothes, which were kept in the hospital cupboard. I remembered that on that day I had asked the nurse:

'What's in the old box?'

'No one knows,' she answered, laughing. 'He refuses to be parted from the box for a single instant.'

Then she bent over me and whispered:

'These people who look so poor are generally hiding some treasure or other—perhaps this is his!'

During my stay here no one visited him at the hospital. As he knew no one I used to send him some of the sweets with which my visitors inundated me. He accepted everything without enthusiasm. He was not good at expressing gratitude and his behaviour over this caused a certain fleeting resentment in me.

I did not concern myself with the mysterious box. Though Mohamed Ali Akbar's condition steadily worsened, his attitude towards the box did not change, which caused the nurse to remark to me that if there had been some treasure in it he would surely have given it away or willed it to someone, seeing that he was heading for death at such speed. Like some petty philosopher I had laughed that day saying to myself that the stupidity of this nurse scarcely knew any bounds, for how did she expect Mohamed Ali Akbar to persuade himself that he was inevitably dying, that there was not a hope of his pulling through? His insistence on keeping the box was tantamount to hanging on to his hope of pulling through and being reunited with his box.

When Mohamed Ali Akbar died I saw the box at his side, where it had always been, and it occurred to me that the box ought to be buried unopened with him. On going to my room that night I was quite unable to sleep. While Mohamed Ali Akbar had been deposited in the autopsy room, wrapped up in a white covering, he was, at the same time, sitting in my room and staring at me, passing through the hospital wards and searching about in his bed; I could almost hear the way he would gasp for breath before going to sleep. When day dawned across the trees of the hospital garden, I had created a complete story about him for myself.

Mohamed Ali Akbar was a poor man from the western quarter of the village of Abkha in Oman; a thin, dark-skinned young man, with aspirations burning in his eyes that could find no release. True he was poor, but what does poverty matter to a man if he has never known anything else? The whole of Abkha suffered from being poor, a poverty identical to Mohamed Ali Akbar's; it was, however, a contented poverty, a poverty that was deep-seated and devoid of anything that prompted one to feel that it was wrong and that there was something called 'riches.' And so it was that the two water-skins Mohamed Ali Akbar carried across his shoulders as he knocked on people's doors to sell them water, were the two scales which set the balance of his daily round. Mohamed Ali Akbar was aware of a certain dizziness when he laid down the water-skins, but when taking them up again the next morning he would feel that his existence was progressing tranquilly and that he had ensured for himself a balanced, undeviating journey through life.

Mohamed Ali Akbar's life could have continued in this quiet and ordered fashion, had fate emulated civilization—in not reaching faraway Oman. But fate was present even in far-off Oman and it was inevitable that Mohamed Ali Akbar should suffer a little from its capricious ways.

It happened on a scorchingly hot morning. Though the sun was not yet at the meridian, the surface of the road was hot and the desert blew gusts of dust-laden wind into his face. He knocked at a door which was answered by a young, brown-skinned girl with wide black eyes, and everything happened with the utmost speed. Like some clumsy oaf who has lost his way, he stood in front of the door, the water-skins swinging to and fro on his lean shoulders. Abstractedly he stared at her, hoping like someone overcome with a mild attack of sunstroke that his eyes would miraculously be capable of clasping her to him. She stared back at him in sheer astonishment, and, unable to utter a word, he turned his back on her and went off home with his water-skins.

Though Mohamed Ali Akbar was exceptionally shy even with his own family, he found himself forced to pour out his heart to his elder sister. As his mother had died of smallpox a long time ago and his father was helplessly bedridden, it was to his sister that he turned for help, for he had unswerving confidence that Sabika possessed the necessary intelligence and judgement for solving a problem of this sort. Seated before him on the rush mat, shrouded in her coarse black dress, she did not break her silence till Mohamed Ali Akbar had gasped out the last of his story.

'I shall seek her hand in marriage,' she then said. 'Isn't that what you want?'

'Yes, yes, is it possible?'

Removing a straw from the old rush mat, his sister replied:

'Why not? You are now a young man and we are all equal in Abkha.'

Mohamed Ali Akbar spent a most disturbed night. When morning came he found that his sister was even more eager than himself to set off on her mission. They agreed to meet up at noon when she would tell him of the results of her efforts, and from there they would both make the necessary arrangements for bringing the matter to completion.

Mohamed Ali Akbar did not know how to pass the time wandering through the lanes with the water-skins on his shoulders. He kept looking at his shadow and beseeching God to make it into a circle round his feet so that he might hurry back home. After what seemed an eternity, he made his way back and was met at the door by his sister.

'It seems that her mother is agreeable. But it must all be put to her father, who will give his answer in five days.'

Deep down within him Mohamed Ali Akbar felt that he was going to be successful in making the girl his wife. As far as he was able to imagine he began from henceforth to build up images of his future with this young and beautiful brown-skinned girl. His sister Sabika looked at the matter with a wise and experienced eye, but she too was sure they would be successful, for she was convinced that her brother's name was without blemish among the people of Abkha; she had, in addition, given a lot of attention to gaining the approval of the girl's mother, knowing as she did how a woman was able to put over an idea to her husband and make him believe that it was his own. Sabika, therefore, awaited the outcome of the matter with complete composure.

On the fifth day Sabika went to the girl's house in order to receive the answer. When she returned, however, her disconsolate face showed that she had failed. She stood in a corner of the room, unable to look Mohamed Ali Akbar in the eye, not knowing how to begin recounting what had happened.

'You must forget her, Mohamed Ali,' she said when she had managed to pluck up her courage.

Not knowing what to say, he waited for his sister to finish.

'Her father died two days ago,' continued Sabika, finding an opportunity in his silence to continue. 'His dying wish to his family was that they should not give her to you in marriage.'

Mohamed Ali Akbar heard these words as though they were addressed to someone else.

'But why, Sabika—why?' was all he could ask.

'He was told that you were a scoundrel, that you lived by stealing sheep on the mountain road, trading what you steal with the foreigners.'

'I?'

'They think you are Mohamed Ali,' said Sabika in a trembling voice she was unable to control. 'You know—the scoundrel Mohamed Ali? Her father thought that you were he . . .'

'But I am not Mohamed Ali,' he replied, palms outstretched like a child excusing himself for some misdeed he has not committed. 'I'm Mohamed Ali Akbar.'

'There's been a mistake—I told them at the beginning that your name was Mohamed Ali. I didn't say Mohamed Ali Akbar because I saw no necessity for doing so.'

Mohamed Ali Akbar felt his chest being crushed under the weight of the blow. However, he remained standing where he was, staring at his sister Sabika without fully seeing her. Blinded by anger, he let fly a final arrow:

'Did you tell her mother that I'm not Mohamed Ali but Mohamed Ali Akbar?'

'Yes, but the father's last wish was that they shouldn't marry her to you.'

'But I'm Mohamed Ali Akbar the water-seller, aren't I?'

What was the use, though, of being so stricken? Everything had, quite simply, come to an end, a single word had lodged itself in the gullet of his romance and it had died. Mohamed Ali Akbar, however, was unable to forget the girl so easily and spent his time roaming about near her house in the hope of seeing her once again. Why? He did not know. His failure brought in its wake a savage anger which turned to hate; soon he was no longer able to pass along that road for fear that his fury would overcome him and he would pelt the window of her house with stones.

From that day onwards he refused to be called by anything but his name in full: Mohamed Ali Akbar, all in one. He refused to answer to anyone who called him Mohamed or Mohamed Ali and this soon became a habit with him. Even his sister Sabika did not dare to use a contracted form of his name. No longer did he experience his former contentment, and Abkha gradually changed to a forbidding graveyard in his eyes. Refusing to give in to his sister's insistence that he should marry, a worm called 'wealth' began to eat its way into his brain. He wanted to take revenge on everything, to marry a woman with whom he could challenge the whole of Abkha, all those who did not believe that he was Mohamed Ali Akbar but Mohamed Ali the scoundrel. Where, though, to find wealth? Thus he decided to sail away to Kuwait.

The distance between Abkha and Ras al-Khaima is two hours by foot, and from Ras al-Khaima to Kuwait by sea is a journey of three days, the fare for which, on an antiquated boat, was seventy rupees. After a year or two he would be able to return to Oman and strut about proudly in the alleyways of Abkha wearing a snow-white *aba* trimmed with gold, like the one he had seen round the shoulders of a notable from Ras al-Khaima who had come to his village to take the hand of a girl the fame of whose beauty had reached all the way there.

The journey was a hard one. The boat which took that eager throng across the south and then made its way northwards to the corner of the Gulf was continually exposed to a variety of dangers. But ebullient souls accustomed to life's hardships paid no heed to such matters; all hands co-operated in the task of delivering safely that small wooden boat floating on the waves of the great sea. And when the sails of the ships lying in Kuwait's quiet harbour came into view, Mohamed Ali Akbar experienced a strange feeling: the dream had now fallen from the coloured world of fantasy into the realm of reality and he had to search around for a starting-point, for a beginning to his dream. It seemed to him that the fantasies nourished by his hate for Abkha and for which he now sought vengeance were not of sufficient moment. As the frail craft approached, threading its way among the anchored boats, he was slowly drained of his feeling and it appeared to him that his long dreams of wealth were merely a solace for his sudden failure and that they were quite irrational. The packed streets, the buildings with their massive walls, the grey sky, the scorching heat, the warm air of the north wind, the roads crammed with cars, the serious faces, all these things appeared to him as barriers standing between him and his dream. He hurried aimlessly through this ocean of people, conscious of a deep feeling of loss which resembled vertigo, almost convinced that these many faces which did not glance at him were his first enemy, that all these people were the walls obstructing the very beginning of the road to his dream. The story was not as simple as in Abkha. Here it was without beginning, without end, without landmarks. It seemed to him that all the roads along which he walked were endless, that they circuited a rampart that held everything—every single thing—within its embrace. When, at sunset, a road led him to the sea-shore and he once again saw the sea, he stood staring across at the far horizon that joined up with the water: out there was Abkha, enveloped in tranquillity. It existed, every quarter had its beginning and its end, every wall carried its own particular lineaments; despite everything it was close to his heart. He felt lost in a rush of scalding water and for the first time he had no sense of shame as he lifted his hand to wipe salty tears from his cheeks.

Mohamed Ali Akbar wept without embarrassment, perhaps for the first time since he grew up, involuntarily, he had been overcome by a ferocious yearning for the two water-skins he used to carry across his shoulders. He was still staring out at the horizon while night gradually settled down around him. It made him feel in a way that he was present in a certain place at a certain time and that this night was like night in Abkha: people were sleeping behind their walls, the streets bore the lineaments of fatigue and silence, the sea rumbled heavily under the light of the moon. He felt relief. Wanting to laugh and yet unable to, he wept once again.

Dawn brought him an upsurge of fresh hope. He rose and went running through the streets. He realized that he must find someone from Oman with whom he could talk and that he would, sooner or later, find such a person, and from there he would learn where he was destined to proceed, from where to make a start.

And so Mohamed Ali Akbar attained his position as errand boy at a shop and was provided with a bicycle on which to carry out his duties. It was from this bicycle that the features of the streets, the qualities of the walls, registered themselves in his head. He felt a certain intimacy with them, but it was an intimacy imposed upon a background of a forbidding impression that he was being dogged by the eyes of his sister Sabika, the chinks in the girl's window, and Mohamed Ali the scoundrel who, unwittingly, had caused such dire disaster.

Months passed with the speed of a bicycle's wheels passing over the surface of a road. The wealth he had dreamed of began to come in and Mohamed Ali Akbar clung to this tiny fortune with all his strength, lest some passing whim should sweep it away or some scoundrel lay his hands on it. Thus it was that it occurred to him to make a sturdy wooden box in which to keep his fortune.

But what did Mohamed Ali Akbar's fortune consist of? Something that could not be reckoned in terms of money. When he had collected a certain amount of money he had bought himself a diaphanous white *aba* with gold edging. Every evening, alone with his box, he would take out the carefully folded *aba,* pass his thin brown fingers tenderly over it and spread it before his eyes; on it he would spill out his modest dreams, tracing along its borders all the streets of his village, the low, latticed windows from behind which peeped the eyes of young girls. There, in a corner of the *aba,* reposed the past which he could not bring himself to return to but whose existence was necessary in order to give the *aba* its true value. The thin fingers would fold it gently once again, put it safely back in its wooden box, and tie strong cord round the box. Then, and only then, did sleep taste sweet.

The box also contained a pair of china ear-rings for his sister Sabika, which he would give her on his return to Abkha, a bottle of pungent perfume, and a white purse holding such money as God in His bounty had given him and which he hoped would increase day by day.

As for the end, it began one evening. He was returning his bicycle to the shop when he felt a burning sensation in his limbs. He was alarmed at the thought that he had grown so weak, and with such speed, but did not take a great deal of notice, having had spells of trembling whenever he felt exceptionally homesick for Sabika and Abkha; he had already experienced just such a sensation of weakness when savagely yearning for all those things he hated and loved and had left behind, those things that made up the whole of his past. And so Mohamed Ali Akbar hastened along the road to his home with these thoughts in mind. But his feeling of weakness and nostalgia stayed with him till the following midday. When he made the effort to get up from bed, he was amazed to find that he had slept right through to noon instead of waking up at his usual early hour. What alarmed him even more was that he was still conscious of the feeling of weakness boring into his bones. Slightly afraid, he thought for a while and imagined himself all at once standing on the sea-shore with the glaring sun reflected off the water almost blinding him, the two water-skins on his shoulders, conscious of a sensation of intense exhaustion. The reflection of the sun increased in violence, yet he was unable to shut his eyes—they were aflame. Abruptly he slid back into sleep.

Here time as usually understood came to an end for Mohamed Ali Akbar. From now on everything happened as though he were raised above the ground, as though his legs were dangling in mid-air: like a man on a gallows, he was moving in front of Time's screen, a screen as inert as a rock of basalt. His part as a practising human had been played out; his part as a mere spectator had come. He felt that there was no bond tying him to anything, that he was somewhere far away and that the things that moved before his eyes were no more than fish inside a large glass tumbler; his own eyes, too, were open and staring as though made of glass.

When he woke up again he realized that he was being carried by his arms and legs. Though he felt exhausted, he found the energy to recall that there was something which continued to be necessary to him and called out in a faint voice:

'The box . . . the box!'

No one, however, paid him any attention. With a frenzied movement he rose so as to get back to his box. His chest panting with the effort of getting to his feet, he called out:

'The box!'

But once again no one heard him. As he reached the door he clung to it and again gasped out in a lifeless voice:

'The box . . .'

Overcome by his exertions, he fell into a trance that was of the sea-shore itself. This time he felt that the tide was rising little by little over his feet and that the water was intensely cold. His hands were grasping a square-shaped rock with which he plunged downwards. When he awoke again he found himself clasping his old box tied round with cord. While spectres passed to and fro in front of him, a needle was plunged into his arm, and a face bent over him.

Long days passed. But for Mohamed Ali Akbar nothing really happened at all. The mercilessness of the pain continued on its way, and he was not conscious of its passing. He was conscious only of its constant presence. The sea became dissolved into windows behind wooden shutters low against the side of the street, a pair of china ear-rings, an *aba* wet with salt water, a ship suspended motionless above the waves, and an old wooden box.

Only once was he aware of any contact with the world. This was when he heard a voice beside him say:

'What's in the old box?'

He looked at the source of the voice and saw, as in a dream, the face of a young, clean-shaven man with fair hair who was pointing at the box and looking at something.

The moment of recollection was short. He returned to gazing silently at the sea, though the face of the clean-shaven, blond young man also remained in front of him. After this he felt a sudden upsurge of energy; for no particular reason things had become clear to him. He distinctly saw, for the first time since he had collapsed, the rising of the sun. It seemed to him that he was capable of getting up from his bed and returning to his bicycle. Everything had grown clear to him: the box was alongside him, bound round as it had always been. Feeling at peace, he moved so as to get up, when a crowd of men in white clothes suddenly descended upon him, standing round him and regarding him with curiosity. Mohamed Ali Akbar tried to say something but was unable to. Suddenly he felt that the tide had risen right up to his waist and that the water was unbearably cold. He could feel nothing. He stretched out his arms to seize hold of something lest he should drown, but everything slid away from under his fingers. Suddenly he saw the clean-shaven face of the blond young man again; he stared at him, somewhat frightened of him on account of his box, while the water continued to rise higher and higher until it had screened off that fair, clean-shaven face from his gaze.

'Bed number 12 has died.'

As the male nurse called out I was unable to free myself from Mohamed Ali Akbar's eyes staring out at me before he died. I imagined that Mohamed Ali Akbar, who refused to have his name mutilated, would now be satisfied at being merely 'Bed number 12' if only he could be assured about the fate of his box.

This, my dear Ahmed, is the story of Mohamed Ali Akbar, Bed number 12, who died yesterday evening and is now lying wrapped round in a white cloth in the autopsy room—the thin brown face that shifted an ulcer from my intestines to my brain and who caused me to write to you, so you don't again repeat your famous phrase 'I almost died laughing' in my presence.

Ever yours,

I haven't yet left the hospital. My health is gradually getting back to normal and the method by which I gauge this amuses me. Do you know how I measure my strength? I stand smoking on the balcony and throw the cigarette end with all my strength so that it falls along the strips of green grass in the garden. In past weeks the cigarette would fall just within the fourth strip, but today it was much nearer the sixth.

From your letter I understood you to say that you were in no need of being a witness to Mohamed Ali Akbar's death to know what death is. You wrote saying that the experience of death does not require the tragic prologues with which I described Mohamed Ali Akbar's life and that people die with far greater matter-of-factness: the man who fell down on the pavement and so let off the loaded pistol he had with him, whose bullet ripped open his neck (he was in the company of a strikingly beautiful girl), or the one who had a heart attack in the street one April evening, having become engaged to be married only a week before. Yes, that's all very true, my dear Ahmed, all very true, but the problem doesn't lie here at all, the problem of death is in no way that of the dead man, it is the problem of those who remain, those who bitterly await their turn so that they too may serve as a humble lesson to the eyes of the living. Of all the things I wrote in my last letter what I want to say now is that we must transfer our thinking from the starting-point to the end. All thinking must set forth from the point of death, whether it be, as you say, that of a man who dies contemplating the charms of the body of a wonderfully beautiful girl, or whether he dies staring into a newly-shaven face which frightens him because of an old wooden box tied round with string. The unsolved question remains that of the end; the question of non-existence, of eternal life—or what? Or what, my dear Ahmed?

Anyway, let's stop pouring water into a sack with a hole in it. Do you know what happened after I sent you my last letter? I went to the doctor's room and found them writing a report about Mohamed Ali Akbar. And they were on the point of opening the box. Oh, Ahmed, how imprisoned we are in our bodies and minds! We are always endowing others with our own attributes, always looking at them through a narrow fissure of our own views and way of thinking, wanting them, as far as we can, to become 'us.' We want to squeeze them into our skins, to give them our eyes to see with, to clothe them in our past and our own way of facing up to life. We place them within a framework outlined by our present understanding of time and place.

Mohamed Ali Akbar was none of the things I imagined. He was the father of three boys and two girls. We have forgotten that over there men marry early. Also, Mohamed Ali Akbar was not a water-seller, water being plentiful in Oman, but had been a sailor on one of the sailing ships that ply between the ports of the south and the Gulf, before settling down here quite a time ago.

It was in fact four years ago that Mohamed Ali Akbar arrived in Kuwait. After unimaginably hard effort he managed—only two months ago—to open what passed for a shop on one of the pavements of New Street. As to how he provided for his children in Oman, we simply don't know.

I read in the doctor's report that the patient had lost his sight six hours before death and so it would seem that Mohamed Ali Akbar had not in fact been staring into my face at the moment of his death as he was then blind. The doctor also wrote that as the address of the patient's family was not known, his burial would be attended solely by the hospital grave-diggers.

The doctor read out the report to his colleague. It was concise and extremely condensed, merely dealing in technical terms with the man's illness. The doctor's voice was lugubrious and colourless. When he had finshed reading he proceeded to untie the string round the box. At this point I thought of leaving the room, for it was none of my business: the Mohamed Ali Akbar I knew had died and this person they had written about was someone else; this box, too, was some other box. I knew for certain what Mohamed Ali Akbar's box contained. Why should I bother myself about some new problem?

And yet I was unable to go to the door, but stood in the corner, trembling slightly.

The box was soon opened and the doctor quickly ran his fingers through the contents. Then he pushed it to one side.

Fearfully I looked into the box: it was filled with recent invoices for sums owed by the shop to the stores which supplied it; in one corner was an old photo of a bearded face, an old watch strap, some string, a small candle and several rupees among the papers.

I must be truthful and say that I was sadly disappointed. Before leaving the room, though, I saw something that stunned me: the nurse had pushed aside Mohamed Ali Akbar's invoices and revealed a long china ear-ring that glittered. In a daze I went to the box and picked up the ear-ring. I don't know why it was that I looked at the nurse and said:

'He bought this ear-ring for his sister Sabika—I happen to know that.'

For a brief instant she stared at me in some surprise—then she laughed uproariously. The doctor, too, laughed at the joke.

You are no doubt aware that nurses are required to humour patients with stomach ulcers in case they should suffer a relapse.

Yours ever—

Initiation

IN anthropology, the term "initiation" refers to those rituals (sometimes called the "rites of passage") whereby an individual formally changes his status in some way; it involves the transition from one age or form of identity to another. In this sense birth, marriage, and death, together with the ceremonies that accompany them in most societies, are all types of initiaton, as is also the process, such as baptism or confirmation, by which an individual is received into a religious faith, a monastic order, or even a secret organization.

One of the commonest forms of initiation known to anthropology occurs when a youth formally becomes a man and is invested with the rights and obligations of an adult male. The rites employed on this occasion are astonishingly similar, even in places that are very widely separated: they include a period of seclusion from the non-initiated; an ordeal of some kind, frequently involving a mutilation such as circumcision, or the killing of a large and dangerous animal [1]; a feast or a dance; and a robing or anointment ceremony during which the individual is given a new name, as happens, for example, when a person joins a monastic order.

Underlying all of these rites is the idea of a second birth. Jane Harrison writes:

> With the savage to be twice-born is the rule. By his first birth he comes into the world; by his second he is born into his tribe. At his first birth he belongs to his mother and the women-folk; at his second he becomes a full-fledged man and passes into the society of the warriors of his tribe.[2]

The notion of rebirth is often suggested by some detail of the ceremony; thus, among the Kikuyus of East Africa, the youth's mother "stands up

---

[1] Such ordeals are often a feature of the Quest pattern (see headnote for The Search). In *The Hero With a Thousand Faces,* Joseph Campbell considers initiation as one of the stages in the progress of the hero archetype.

[2] Jane Harrison, cited by Edward Carpenter, *Pagan and Christian Creeds* (New York: Harcourt, Brace & World, 1920), p. 120.

with the boy crouching at her feet; she pretends to go through all the labor pains, and the boy on being reborn cries like a babe and is washed."[3] Some ceremonies also dramatize in various ways the death of the previous self, usually by symbolic actions whereby the individual is "killed" and later brought back to life.

Archetypes, of course, are not generated by anthropological custom; custom, on the contrary, expresses and confirms the archetype and fixes it in the racial memory. Similarly literature also confirms the archetype. When the initiation archetype is projected in literary form, no formal ritual need be involved. Mordecai Marcus writes:

> Only a very small proportion of works called initiation stories, or meeting the definitions for them, show adults testing or teaching the young. Ritual does occur in some initiation stories, but it is more often of individual than of social origin. Education is always important in an initiation story, but it is usually a direct result of experience rather than of indoctrination. One concludes that the initiation story has only a tangential relationship to the anthropologist's ideas of initiation.[4]

It is interesting to note, however, that in one of the stories which follows, "To the Mountains," the initiate kills a wolf, and, as has been said, the killing of a large, usually dangerous animal is a traditional feature of the initiation ceremony.

What is more important than the ritual elements of initiation in literature is that the candidate have at least a partial awareness that he has crossed a threshold and that this boundary will have the effect of forever separating him from the period of his boyhood. And even though the passage from innocence to knowledge is usually painful, especially nowadays (as William Coyle says, "Modern life and the modern imagination being what they are, the initiate's new knowledge is more likely to be unpleasant than otherwise."[5]), a story in which the candidate allows himself to be shattered by the experience is not truly a story of initiation. There must be awareness, but not defeat or annihilation, nor may the individual be inadequate constitutionally: Melville's Billy Budd, because of his excessive innocence, is, as Coyle correctly observes, not so much an initiate as a sacrificial victim.

The initiation archetype is very prominent in literature, sometimes appearing in the form of the discovery of evil, a theme with which it is obviously related—as in *Hamlet*. Other well-known examples from British literature are Wordsworth's "Prelude" (whose subtitle is "Growth of a Poet's Mind"), Dickens' *Great Expectations*, Joyce's "Araby" and *Portrait of the Artist as a Young Man*, and Conrad's *Heart of Darkness* and *The Shadow Line*. American literature yields even more

---

[3] Carpenter, *ibid.*

[4] Mordecai Marcus, "What Is an Initiation Story?," William Coyle (ed.), *The Young Man in American Literature: The Initiation Theme* (New York: Odyssey, 1969), p. 30.

[5] Coyle, "Introduction," *ibid.*, p. ii.

numerous and emphatic examples, and it is not entirely an accident that all but one of the stories we have selected for this category are by American writers. Coyle writes:

> Perhaps because Americans think of themselves as a youthful nation, their literature, especially fiction, has dealt preponderantly with youth. Exceptions can readily be found, but in general American writers have treated middle age in terms of frustration and old age in terms of pathos.[6]

Whatever the reason, American prose fiction is unusually rich in initiation archetypes, as is evidenced by such novels as *Huckleberry Finn, The Red Badge of Courage, The Catcher in the Rye,* and *The Member of the Wedding* (where the initiate, uncharacteristically, is a girl), and such short stories as Hawthorne's "Young Goodman Brown" and "My Kinsman, Major Molineux," Hemingway's "Indian Camp" and "My Old Man," Anderson's "I Want to Know Why," Faulkner's "The Bear," Steinbeck's "Flight," Fitzgerald's "The Freshest Boy," McCullers' "Wunderkind," and Porter's "The Circus" and "The Downward Path to Wisdom."

It should be mentioned that the initiation archetype combines occasionally with that of Transformation (spiritual) and with that of the Search, as in Hesse's "The Poet." The Wise Old Man, an archetypal character whom we have met in other sections, may also figure importantly in stories of the initiation type. Father Antonio in "To the Mountains" is such a figure.

---

[6] *Ibid.*, p. vii.

THE MAN WHO WAS ALMOST A MAN

by Richard Wright

Dave struck out across the fields, looking homeward through paling light. Whut's the use talkin wid em niggers in the field? Anyhow, his mother was putting supper on the table. Them niggers can't understan nothing. One of these days he was going to get a gun and practice shooting, then they couldn't talk to him as though he was a little boy. He slowed, looking at the ground. Shucks, Ah ain scareda them even ef they are biggern me! Aw, Ah know whut Ahma do. Ahm going by ol Joe's sto n git that Sears Roebuck catlog n look at them guns. Mebbe Ma will lemme buy one when she gits mah pay from old man Hawkins. Ahma beg her t gimme some money. Ahm ol ernough to hava gun. Ahm seventeen. Almost a man. He strode, feeling his long loose-jointed limbs. Shucks, a man oughta hava little gun aftah he done worked hard all day.

He came in sight of Joe's store. A yellow lantern glowed on the front porch. He mounted steps and went through the screen door, hearing it bang behind him. There was a strong smell of coal oil and mackerel fish. He felt very confident until he saw fat Joe walk in through the rear door, then his courage began to ooze.

"Howdy, Dave! Whutcha want?"

"How yuh, Mistah Joe? Aw, Ah don wanna buy nothing. Ah jus wanted t see ef yuhd lemme look at tha catlog erwhile."

"Sure! You wanna see it here?"

"Nawsuh. Ah wans t take it home wid me. Ah'll bring it back termorrow when Ah come in from the fiels."

"You plannin on buying something?"

"Yessuh."

"Your ma lettin you have your own money now?"

"Shucks. Mistah Joe, Ahm gittin t be a man like anybody else!"

Joe laughed and wiped his greasy white face with a red bandanna.

"Whut you plannin on buyin?"

Dave looked at the floor, scratched his head, scratched his thigh, and smiled. Then he looked up shyly.

"Ah'll tell yuh, Mistah Joe, ef yuh promise yuh won't tell."

"I promise."

"Waal, Ahma buy a gun."

"A gun? Whut you want with a gun?"

"Ah wanna keep it."

"You ain't nothing but a boy. You don't need a gun."

"Aw, lemme have the catlog, Mistah Joe. Ah'll bring it back."

Joe walked through the rear door. Dave was elated. He looked around at barrels of sugar and flour. He heard Joe coming back. He craned his neck to see if he were bringing the book. Yeah, he's got it. Gawddog, he's got it!

"Here, but be sure you bring it back. It's the only one I got."

"Sho, Mistah Joe."

"Say, if you wanna buy a gun, why don't you buy one from me? I gotta gun to sell."

"Will it shoot?"

"Sure it'll shoot."

"Whut kind is it?"

"Oh, it's kinda old . . . a left-hand Wheeler. A pistol. A big one."

"Is it got bullets in it?"

"It's loaded."

"Kin Ah see it?"

"Where's your money?"

"Whut yuh wan fer it?"

"I'll let you have it for two dollars."

"Just two dollahs? Shucks, Ah could buy tha when Ah git mah pay."

"I'll have it here when you want it."

"Awright, suh. Ah be in fer it."

He went through the door, hearing it slam again behind him. Ahma git some money from Ma n buy me a gun! Only two dollahs! He tucked the thick catalogue under his arm and hurried.

"Where yuh been, boy?" His mother held a steaming dish of black-eyed peas.

"Aw, Ma, Ah just stopped down the road t talk wid the boys."

"Yuh know bettah t keep suppah waitin."

He sat down, resting the catalogue on the edge of the table.

"Yuh git up from there and git to the well n wash yosef! Ah ain feedin no hogs in mah house!"

She grabbed his shoulder and pushed him. He stumbled out of the room, then came back to get the catalogue.

"Whut this?"

"Aw, Ma, it's jusa catlog."

"Who yuh git it from?"

"From Joe, down at the sto."

"Waal, thas good. We kin use it in the outhouse."

"Naw, Ma." He grabbed for it. "Gimme ma catlog, Ma."

She held onto it and glared at him.

"Quit hollerin at me! Whut's wrong wid yuh? Yuh crazy?"

"But Ma, please. It ain mine! It's Joe's! He tol me t bring it back t im termorrow."

She gave up the book. He stumbled down the back steps, hugging the thick book under his arm. When he had splashed water on his face and hands, he groped back to the kitchen and fumbled in a corner for the towel. He bumped into a chair; it clattered to the floor. The catalogue sprawled at his feet. When he had dried his eyes he snatched up the book and held it again under his arm. His mother stood watching him.

"Now, ef yuh gonna act a fool over that ol book, Ah'll take it n burn it up."

"Naw, Ma, please."

"Waal, set down n be still!"

He sat down and drew the oil lamp close. He thumbed page after page, unaware of the food his mother set on the table. His father came in. Then his small brother.

"Whutcha got there, Dave?" his father asked.

"Jusa catlog," he answered, not looking up.

"Yeah, here they is!" His eyes glowed at blue-and-black revolvers. He glanced up, feeling sudden guilt. His father was watching him. He eased the book under the table and rested it on his knees. After the blessing was asked, he ate. He scooped up peas and swallowed fat meat without chewing. Buttermilk helped to wash it down. He did not want to mention money before his father. He would do much better by cornering his mother when she was alone. He looked at his father uneasily out of the edge of his eye.

"Boy, how come yuh don quit foolin wid tha book n eat yo suppah?"

"Yessuh."

"How you n ol man Hawkins gitten erlong?"

"Suh?"

"Can't yuh hear? Why don yuh lissen? Ah ast yu how wuz yuh n ol man Hawkins gittin erlong?"

"Oh, swell, Pa. Ah plows mo lan than anybody over there."

"Waal, yuh oughta keep yo mind on whut yuh doin."

"Yessuh."

He poured his plate full of molasses and sopped it up slowly with a chunk of cornbread. When his father and brother had left the kitchen, he still sat and looked again at the guns in the catalogue, longing to muster courage enough to present his case to his mother. Lawd, ef Ah only had tha pretty one! He could almost feel the slickness of the weapon with his fingers. If he had a gun like that he would polish it and keep it shining so it would never rust. N Ah'd keep it loaded, by Gawd!

"Ma?" His voice was hesitant.

"Hunh?"

"Ol man Hawkins give yuh mah money yit?"

"Yeah, but ain no usa yuh thinking bout throwin nona it erway. Ahm keepin tha money sos yuh kin have cloes t go to school this winter."

He rose and went to her side with the open catalogue in his palms. She was washing dishes, her head bent low over a pan. Shyly he raised the book. When he spoke, his voice was husky, faint.

"Ma, Gawd knows Ah wans one of these."

"One of whut?" she asked, not raising her eyes.

"One of these," he said again, not daring even to point. She glanced up at the page, then at him with wide eyes.

"Nigger, is yuh gone plumb crazy?"

"Aw, Ma—"

"Git outta here! Don yuh talk t me bout no gun! Yuh a fool!"

"Ma, Ah kin buy one fer two dollahs."

"Not ef Ah knows it, yuh ain!"

"But yuh promised me one—"

"Ah don care whut Ah promised! Yuh ain nothing but a boy yit!"

"Ma, ef yuh lemme buy one Ah'll *never* ast yuh fer nothing no mo."

"Ah tol yuh t git outta here! Yuh ain gonna toucha penny of tha money fer no gun! Thas how come Ah has Mistah Hawkins t pay yo wages t me, cause Ah knows yuh ain got no sense."

"But, Ma, we needa gun. Pa ain got no gun. We needa gun in the house. Yuh kin never tell whut might happen."

"Now don yuh try to maka fool outta me, boy! Ef we did hava gun, yuh wouldn't have it!"

He laid the catalogue down and slipped his arm around her waist.

"Aw, Ma, Ah done worked hard alla summer n ain ast yuh fer nothing, is Ah, now?"

"Thas whut yuh spose t do!"

"But Ma, Ah wans a gun. Yuh kin lemme have two dollahs outta mah money. Please, Ma. I kin give it to Pa . . . Please, Ma! Ah loves yuh, Ma."

When she spoke her voice came soft and low.

"Whut yu wan wida gun, Dave? Yuh don need no gun. Yuh'll git in trouble. N ef yo pa jus thought Ah let yuh have money t buy a gun he'd hava fit."

"Ah'll hide it, Ma. It ain but two dollahs."

"Lawd, chil, whut's wrong wid yuh?"

"Ain nothin wrong, Ma. Ahm almos a man now. Ah wans a gun."

"Who gonna sell yuh a gun?"

"Ol Joe at the sto."

"N it don cos but two dollahs?"

"Thas all, Ma. Jus two dollahs. Please, Ma."

She was stacking the plates away; her hands moving slowly, reflectively. Dave kept an anxious silence. Finally, she turned to him.

"Ah'll let yuh git tha gun ef yuh promise me one thing."

"Whut's tha, Ma?"

"Yuh bring it straight back t me, yuh hear? It be fer Pa."

"Yessum! Lemme go now, Ma."

She stooped, turned slightly to one side, raised the hem of her dress, rolled down the top of her stocking, and came up with a slender wad of bills.

"Here," she said. "Lawd knows yuh don need no gun. But yer pa does. Yuh bring it right back t me, yuh hear? Ahma put it up. Now ef yuh don, Ahma have yuh pa lick yuh so hard yuh won fergit it."

"Yessum."

He took the money, ran down the steps, and across the yard.

"Dave! Yuuuuuh Daaaaave!"

He heard, but he was not going to stop now. "Naw, Lawd!"

The first movement he made the following morning was to reach under his pillow for the gun. In the gray light of dawn he held it loosely, feeling a sense of power. Could kill a man with a gun like this. Kill anybody, black or white. And if he were holding his gun in his hand, nobody could run over him; they would have to respect him. It was a big gun, with a long barrel and a heavy handle. He raised and lowered it in his hand, marveling at its weight.

He had not come straight home with it as his mother had asked; instead he had stayed out in the fields, holding the weapon in his hand, aiming it now and then at some imaginary foe. But he had not fired it; he had been afraid that his father might hear. Also he was not sure he knew how to fire it.

To avoid surrendering the pistol he had not come into the house until he knew that they were all asleep. When his mother had tiptoed to his bedside late that night and demanded the gun, he had first played possum; then he had told her that the gun was hidden outdoors, that he would bring it to her in the morning. Now he lay turning it slowly in his hands. He broke it, took out the cartridges, felt them, and then put them back.

He slid out of bed, got a long strip of old flannel from a trunk, wrapped the gun in it, and tied it to his naked thigh while it was still loaded. He did not go in to breakfast. Even though it was not yet daylight, he started for Jim Hawkins' plantation. Just as the sun was rising he reached the barns where the mules and plows were kept.

"Hey! That you, Dave?"

He turned. Jim Hawkins stood eying him suspiciously.

"What're yuh going here so early?"

"Ah didn't know Ah wuz gittin up so early, Mistah Hawkins. Ah wuz fixin t hitch up ol Jenny n take her t the fiels."

"Good. Since you're so early, how about plowing that stretch down by the woods?"

"Suits me, Mistah Hawkins."

"O.K. Go to it!"

He hitched Jenny to a plow and started across the fields. Hot dog! This was just what he wanted. If he could get down by the woods, he could shoot his gun and nobody would hear. He walked behind the plow, hearing the traces creaking, feeling the gun tied tight to his thigh.

When he reached the woods, he plowed two whole rows before he decided to take out the gun. Finally, he stopped, looked in all directions, then untied the gun and held it in his hand. He turned to the mule and smiled.

"Know whut this is, Jenny? Naw, yuh wouldn know! Yuhs jusa ol mule! Anyhow, this is a gun, n it kin shoot, by Gawd!"

He held the gun at arm's length. Whut t hell, Ahma shoot this thing! He looked at Jenny again.

"Lissen here, Jenny! When Ah pull this ol trigger, Ah don wan yuh t run n acka fool now!"

Jenny stood with head down, her short ears pricked straight. Dave walked off about twenty feet, held the gun far out from him at arm's length, and turned his head. Hell, he told himself, Ah ain afraid. The gun felt loose in his fingers; he waved it wildly for a moment. Then he shut his eyes and tightened his forefinger. Bloom! A report half deafened him and he thought his right hand was torn from his arm. He heard

Jenny whinnying and galloping over the field, and he found himself on his knees, squeezing his fingers hard between his legs. His hand was numb; he jammed it into his mouth, trying to warm it, trying to stop the pain. The gun lay at his feet. He did not quite know what had happened. He stood up and stared at the gun as though it were a living thing. He gritted his teeth and kicked the gun. Yuh almos broke mah arm! He turned to look for Jenny; she was far over the fields, tossing her head and kicking wildly.

"Hol on there, ol mule!"

When he caught up with her she stood trembling, walling her big white eyes at him. The plow was far away; the traces had broken. Then Dave stopped short, looking, not believing. Jenny was bleeding. Her left side was red and wet with blood. He went closer. Lawd, have mercy! Wondah did Ah shoot this mule? He grabbed for Jenny's mane. She flinched, snorted, whirled, tossing her head.

"Hol on now! Hol on."

Then he saw the hole in Jenny's side, right between the ribs. It was round, wet, red. A crimson stream streaked down the front leg, flowing fast. Good Gawd! Ah wuzn't shootin at tha mule. He felt panic. He knew he had to stop that blood, or Jenny would bleed to death. He had never seen so much blood in all his life. He chased the mule for half a mile, trying to catch her. Finally she stopped, breathing hard, stumpy tail half arched. He caught her mane and led her back to where the plow and gun lay. Then he stooped and grabbed handfulls of damp black earth and tried to plug the bullet hole. Jenny shuddered, whinnied, and broke from him.

"Hol on! Hol on now!"

He tried to plug it again, but blood came anyhow. His fingers were hot and sticky. He rubbed dirt into his palms, trying to dry them. Then again he attempted to plug the bullet hole, but Jenny shied away, kicking her heels high. He stood helpless. He had to do something. He ran at Jenny; she dodged him. He watched a red stream of blood flow down Jenny's leg and form a bright pool at her feet.

"Jenny . . . Jenny," he called weakly.

His lips trembled. She's bleeding t death! He looked in the direction of home, wanting to go back, wanting to get help. But he saw the pistol lying in the damp black clay. He had a queer feeling that if he only did something, this would not be; Jenny would not be there bleeding to death.

When he went to her this time, she did not move. She stood with sleepy, dreamy eyes; and when he touched her she gave a low-pitched whinny and knelt to the ground, her front knees slopping in blood.

"Jenny . . . Jenny . . ." he whispered.

For a long time she held her neck erect; then her head sank, slowly. Her ribs swelled with a mighty heave and she went over.

Dave's stomach felt empty, very empty. He picked up the gun and held it gingerly between his thumb and forefinger. He buried it at the foot of a tree. He took a stick and tried to cover the pool of blood with dirt—but what was the use? There was Jenny lying with her mouth open and her eyes walled and glassy. He could not tell Jim Hawkins he had shot his mule. But he had to tell something. Yeah, Ah'll tell em Jenny started gittin wil n fell on the joint of the plow. . . . But that would hardly happen to a mule. He walked across the field slowly, head down.

It was sunset. Two of Jim Hawkins' men were over near the edge of the woods digging a hole in which to bury Jenny. Dave was surrounded by a knot of people, all of whom were looking down at the dead mule.

"I don't see how in the world it happened," said Jim Hawkins for the tenth time.

The crowd parted and Dave's mother, father, and small brother pushed into the center.

"Where Dave?" his mother called.

"There he is," said Jim Hawkins.

His mother grabbed him.

"Whut happened, Dave? Whut yuh done?"

"Nothin."

"C mon, boy, talk," his father said.

Dave took a deep breath and told the story he knew nobody believed.

"Waal," he drawled. "Ah brung ol Jenny down here sos Ah could do mah plowin. Ah plowed bout two rows, just like yuh see." He stopped and pointed at the long rows of upturned earth. "Then somethin musta been wrong wid ol Jenny. She wouldn ack right a-tall. She started snortin n kickin her heels. Ah tried t hol her, but she pulled erway, rearin n goin in. Then when the point of the plow was stickin up in the air, she swung erroun n twisted herself back on it . . . She stuck herself n started t bleed. N fo Ah could do anything, she wuz dead."

"Did you ever hear of anything like that in all your life?" asked Jim Hawkins.

There were white and black standing in the crowd. They murmured. Dave's mother came close to him and looked hard into his face. "Tell the truth, Dave," she said.

"Looks like a bullet hole to me," said one man.

"Dave, whut yuh do wid the gun?" his mother asked.

The crowd surged in, looking at him. He jammed his hands into his pockets, shook his head slowly from left to right, and backed away. His eyes were wide and painful.

"Did he hava gun?" asked Jim Hawkins.

"By Gawd, Ah tol yuh tha wuz a gun wound," said a man, slapping his thigh.

His father caught his shoulders and shook him till his teeth rattled.

"Tell whut happened, yuh rascal! Tell whut . . ."

Dave looked at Jenny's stiff legs and began to cry.

"Whut yuh do wid tha gun?" his mother asked.

"Whut wuz he doin wida gun?" his father asked.

"Come on and tell the truth," said Hawkins. "Ain't nobody going to hurt you . . ."

His mother crowded close to him.

"Did yuh shoot tha mule, Dave?"

Dave cried, seeing blurred white and black faces.

"Ahh ddinn gggo tt sshooot hher . . . Ah ssswear ffo Gawd Ahh ddin. . . . Ah wuz a-tryin t sssee ef the old gggun would sshoot—"

"Where yuh git the gun from?" his father asked.

"Ah got it from Joe, at the sto."

"Where yuh git the money?"

"Ma give it t me."

"He kept worryin me, Bob. Ah had t. Ah tol im t bring the gun right back t me . . . It was fer yuh, the gun."

"But how yuh happen to shoot that mule?" asked Jim Hawkins.

"Ah wuzn shootin at the mule, Mistah Hawkins. The gun jumped when Ah pulled the trigger . . . N fo Ah knowed anythin Jenny was there a-bleedin."

Somebody in the crowd laughed. Jim Hawkins walked close to Dave and looked into his face.

"Well, looks like you have bought you a mule, Dave."

"Ah swear fo Gawd, Ah didn go t kill the mule, Mistah Hawkins!"

"But you killed her!"

All the crowd was laughing now. They stood on tiptoe and poked heads over one another's shoulders.

"Well, boy, looks like yuh done bought a dead mule! Hahaha!"

"Ain tha ershame."

"Hohohohoho."

Dave stood, head down, twisting his feet in the dirt.

"Well, you needn't worry about it, Bob," said Jim Hawkins to Dave's father. "Just let the boy keep on working and pay me two dollars a month."

"Whut yuh wan fer yo mule, Mistah Hawkins?"

Jim Hawkins screwed up his eyes.

"Fifty dollars."

"Whut yuh do wid tha gun?" Dave's father demanded.

Dave said nothing.

"Yuh wan me t take a tree n beat yuh till yuh talk!"

"Nawsuh!"

"Whut yuh do wid it?"

"Ah throwed it erway."

"Where?"

"Ah . . . Ah throwed it in the creek."

"Waal, c mon home. N firs thing in the mawnin git to tha creek n fin tha gun."

"Yessuh."

"Whut yuh pay fer it?"

"Two dollahs."

"Take tha gun n git yo money back n carry it t Mistah Hawkins, yuh hear? N don fergit Ahma lam you black bottom good fer this! Now march yosef on home, suh!"

Dave turned and walked slowly. He heard people laughing. Dave glared, his eyes welling with tears. Hot anger bubbled in him. Then he swallowed and stumbled on.

That night Dave did not sleep. He was glad that he had gotten out of killing the mule so easily, but he was hurt. Something hot seemed to turn over inside him each time he remembered how they had laughed. He tossed on his bed, feeling his hard pillow. N Pa says he's gonna beat me . . . He remembered other beatings, and his back quivered. Naw, naw, Ah sho don wan im t beat me tha way no mo. Dam em all! Nobody ever gave him anything. All he did was work. They treat me like a mule, n then they beat me. He gritted his teeth. N Ma had t tell on me.

Well, if he had to, he would take old man Hawkins that two dollars. But that meant selling the gun. And he wanted to keep that gun. Fifty dollars for a dead mule.

He turned over, thinking how he had fired the gun. He had an itch to fire it again. Ef other men kin shoota gun, by Gawd, Ah kin! He was still, listening. Mebbe they all sleepin now. The house was still. He heard the soft breathing of his brother. Yes, now! He would go down and get that gun and see if he could fire it! He eased out of bed and slipped into overalls.

The moon was bright. He ran almost all the way to the edge of the woods. He stumbled over the ground, looking for the spot where he had buried the gun. Yeah, here it is. Like a hungry dog scratching for a bone, he pawed it up. He puffed his black cheeks and blew dirt from the trigger and barrel. He broke it and found four cartridges unshot. He looked around, the fields were filled with silence and moonlight. He clutched the gun stiff and hard in his fingers. But, as soon as he wanted to pull the trigger, he shut his eyes and turned his head. Naw, Ah can't shoot wid mah eyes closed n mah head turned. With effort he held his eyes open; then he squeezed. *Blooooom!* He was stiff, not breathing. The gun was still in his hands. Dammit, he'd done it! He fired again. *Blooooom!* He smiled. *Bloooom! Bloooom! Click, click.* There! It was empty. If anybody could shoot a gun, he could. He put the gun into his hip pocket and started across the fields.

When he reached the top of a ridge he stood straight and proud in the moonlight, looking at Jim Hawkins' big white house, feeling the gun sagging in his pocket. Lawd, ef Ah had just one mo bullet Ah'd taka shot at tha house. Ah'd like t scare ol man Hawkins jusa little . . . Jusa enough t let im know Dave Saunders is a man.

To his left the road curved, running to the tracks of the Illinois Central. He jerked his head, listening. From far off came a faint *hoooof-hoooof; hoooof-hoooof; hoooof-hoooof*. . . . He stood rigid. Two dollahs a mont. Les see now . . . Tha means it'll take bout two years. Shucks! Ah'll be dam!

He started down the road, toward the tracks. Yeah, here she comes! He stood beside the track and held himself stiffly. Here she comes, erroun the ben . . . C mon, yuh slow poke! C mon! He had his hand on his gun; something quivered in his stomach. Then the train thundered past, the gray and brown box cars rumbling and clinking. He gripped the gun tightly; then he jerked his hand out of his pocket. Ah betcha Bill wouldn't do it! Ah betcha . . . The cars slid past, steel grinding upon steel. Ahm ridin yuh ternight, so hep me Gawd! He was hot all over. He hesitated just a moment; then he grabbed, pulled atop of a car, and lay flat. He felt his pocket; the gun was still there. Ahead the long rails were glinting in the moonlight, stretching away, away to somewhere, somewhere where he could be a man . . .

BLACKBERRY WINTER
by Robert Penn Warren

To Joseph Warren *and* Dagmar Beach

It was getting into June and past eight o'clock in the morning, but there was a fire—even if it wasn't a big fire, just a fire of chunks—on the hearth of the big stone fireplace in the living room. I was standing on the hearth, almost into the chimney, hunched over the fire, working my bare toes slowly on the warm stone. I relished the heat which made the skin of my bare legs warp and creep and tingle, even as I called to my mother, who was somewhere back in the dining room or kitchen, and said: "But it's June, I don't have to put them on!"

"You put them on if you are going out," she called.

I tried to assess the degree of authority and conviction in the tone, but at that distance it was hard to decide. I tried to analyze the tone, and then I thought what a fool I had been to start out the back door and let her see that I was barefoot. If I had gone out the front door or the side door she would never have known, not till dinner time anyway, and by then the day would have been half gone and I would have been all over the farm to see what the storm had done and down to the creek to see the flood. But it had never crossed my mind that they would try to stop you from going barefoot in June, no matter if there had been a gully-washer and a cold spell.

Nobody had ever tried to stop me in June as long as I could remember, and when you are nine years old, what you remember seems forever; for you remember everything and everything is important and stands big and full and fills up Time and is so solid that you can walk around and around it like a tree and look at it. You are aware that time passes, that there is a movement in time, but that is not what Time is. Time is not a movement, a flowing, a wind then, but is, rather, a kind of climate in which things are, and when a thing happens it begins to live and keeps on living and stands solid in Time like the tree that you can walk around. And if there is a movement, the movement is not Time itself, any more than a breeze is climate, and all the breeze does is to shake a little the leaves on the tree which is alive and solid. When you are nine, you know that there are things that you don't know, but you know that when you know something you know it. You know how a thing has been and you know that you can go barefoot in June. You do not understand that voice from

---

From *The Circus in the Attic and Other Stories* by Robert Penn Warren (New York: Harcourt, Brace & World, 1947).

back in the kitchen which says that you cannot go barefoot outdoors and run to see what has happened and rub your feet over the wet shivery grass and make the perfect mark of your foot in the smooth, creamy, red mud and then muse upon it as though you had suddenly come upon that single mark on the glistening auroral beach of the world. You have never seen a beach, but you have read the book and how the footprint was there.

The voice had said what it had said, and I looked savagely at the black stockings and the strong, scuffed brown shoes which I had brought from my closet as far as the hearth rug. I called once more, "But it's June," and waited.

"It's June," the voice replied from far away, "but it's blackberry winter."

I had lifted my head to reply to that, to make one more test of what was in that tone, when I happened to see the man.

The fireplace in the living room was at the end; for the stone chimney was built, as in so many of the farmhouses in Tennessee, at the end of a gable, and there was a window on each side of the chimney. Out of the window on the north side of the fireplace I could see the man. When I saw the man I did not call out what I had intended, but, engrossed by the strangeness of the sight, watched him, still far off, come along the path by the edge of the woods.

What was strange was that there should be a man there at all. That path went along the yard fence, between the fence and the woods which came right down to the yard, and then on back past the chicken runs and on by the woods until it was lost to sight where the woods bulged out and cut off the back field. There the path disappeared into the woods. It led on back, I knew, through the woods and to the swamp, skirted the swamp where the big trees gave way to sycamores and water oaks and willows and tangled cane, and then led on to the river. Nobody ever went back there except people who wanted to gig frogs in the swamp or to fish in the river or to hunt in the woods, and those people, if they didn't have a standing permission from my father, always stopped to ask permission to cross the farm. But the man whom I now saw wasn't, I could tell even at that distance, a sportsman. And what would a sportsman have been doing down there after a storm? Besides, he was coming from the river, and nobody had gone down there that morning. I knew that for a fact, because if anybody had passed, certainly if a stranger had passed, the dogs would have made a racket and would have been out on him. But this man was coming up from the river and had come up through the woods. I suddenly had a vision of him moving up the grassy path in the woods, in the green twilight under the big trees, not making any sound on the path, while now and then, like drops off the eaves, a big drop of water would fall from a leaf or bough and strike a stiff oak leaf lower down with a small, hollow sound like a drop of water hitting tin. That sound, in the silence of the woods, would be very significant.

When you are a boy and stand in the stillness of woods, which can be so still that your heart almost stops beating and makes you want to stand there in the green twilight until you feel your very feet sinking into and clutching the earth like roots and your body breathing slow through its pores like the leaves—when you stand there and wait for the next drop to drop with its small, flat sound to a lower leaf, that sound seems to measure out something, to put an end to something, to begin something, and you cannot wait for it to happen and are afraid it will not happen, and then when it has happened, you are waiting again, almost afraid.

But the man whom I saw coming through the woods in my mind's eye did not pause and wait, growing into the ground and breathing with the enormous, soundless breathing of the leaves. Instead, I saw him moving in the green twilight inside my head as he was moving at that very moment along the path by the edge of the woods, coming toward the house. He was moving steadily, but not fast, with his shoulders hunched a little and his head thrust forward, like a man who has come a long way and has a long way to go. I shut my eyes for a couple of seconds, thinking that when I opened them he would not be there at all. There was no place for him to have come from, and there was no reason for him to come where he was coming, toward our house. But I opened my eyes, and there he was, and he was coming steadily along the side of the woods. He was not yet even with the back chicken yard.

"Mama," I called.

"You put them on," the voice said.

"There's a man coming," I called, "out back."

She did not reply to that, and I guessed that she had gone to the kitchen window to look. She would be looking at the man and wondering who he was and what he wanted, the way you always do in the country, and if I went back there now she would not notice right off whether or not I was barefoot. So I went back to the kitchen.

She was standing by the window. "I don't recognize him," she said, not looking around at me.

"Where could he be coming from?" I asked.

"I don't know," she said.

"What would he be doing down at the river? At night? In the storm?"

She studied the figure out the window, then said, "Oh, I reckon maybe he cut across from the Dunbar place."

That was, I realized, a perfectly rational explanation. He had not been down at the river in the storm, at night. He had come over this morning. You could cut across from the Dunbar place if you didn't mind breaking through a lot of elder and sassafras and blackberry bushes which had about taken over the old cross path, which nobody ever used any more. That satisfied me for a moment, but only for a moment. "Mama," I asked, "what would he be doing over at the Dunbar place last night?"

Then she looked at me, and I knew I had made a mistake, for she was looking at my bare feet. "You haven't got your shoes on," she said.

But I was saved by the dogs. That instant there was a bark which I recognized as Sam, the collie, and then a heavier, churning kind of bark which was Bully, and I saw a streak of white as Bully tore round the corner of the back porch and headed out for the man. Bully was a big, bone-white bull dog, the kind of dog that they used to call a farm bull dog but that you don't see any more, heavy chested and heavy headed, but with pretty long legs. He could take a fence as light as a hound. He had just cleared the white paling fence toward the woods when my mother ran out to the back porch and began calling, "Here you, Bully! Here you!"

Bully stopped in the path, waiting for the man, but he gave a few more of those deep, gargling, savage barks that reminded you of something down a stone-lined well. The red clay mud, I saw, was splashed up over his white chest and looked exciting, like blood.

The man, however, had not stopped walking even when Bully took the fence and started at him. He had kept right on coming. All he had done was to switch a little paper parcel which he carried from the right hand to the left, and then reach into his pants pocket to get something. Then I saw the glitter and knew that he had a knife in his hand, probably the kind of mean knife just made for devilment and nothing else, with a blade as long as the blade of a frog-sticker, which will snap out ready when you press a button in the handle. That knife must have had a button in the handle, or else how could he have had the blade out glittering so quick and with just one hand?

Pulling his knife against the dogs was a funny thing to do, for Bully was a big, powerful brute and fast, and Sam was all right. If those dogs had meant business, they might have knocked him down and ripped him before he got a stroke in. He ought to have picked up a heavy stick, something to take a swipe at them with and something which they could see and respect when they came at him. But he apparently did not know much about dogs. He just held the knife blade close against the right leg, low down, and kept on moving down the path.

Then my mother had called, and Bully had stopped. So the man let the blade of the knife snap back into the handle, and dropped it into his pocket, and kept on coming. Many women would have been afraid with the strange man who they knew had that knife in his pocket. That is, if they were alone in the house with nobody but a nine-year-old boy. And my mother was alone, for my father had gone off, and Dellie, the cook, was down at her cabin because she wasn't feeling well. But my mother wasn't afraid. She wasn't a big woman, but she was clear and brisk about everything she did and looked everybody and everything right in the eye from her own blue eyes in her tanned face. She had been the first woman in the country to ride a horse astride (that was back when she was a girl and long before I was born), and I have seen her snatch up a pump gun and go out and knock a chicken hawk out of the air like a busted skeet when he came over her chicken yard. She was a steady and self-reliant woman, and when I think of her now after all the years she has been dead, I think of her brown hands, not big, but somewhat square for a woman's hands, with square-cut nails. They looked, as a matter of fact, more like a young boy's hands than a grown woman's. But back then it never crossed my mind that she would ever be dead.

She stood on the back porch and watched the man enter the back gate, where the dogs (Bully had leaped back into the yard) were dancing and muttering and giving sidelong glances back to my mother to see if she meant what she had said. The man walked right by the dogs, almost brushing them, and didn't pay them any attention. I could see now that he wore old khaki pants, and a dark wool coat with stripes in it, and a gray felt hat. He had on a gray shirt with blue stripes in it, and no tie. But I could see a tie, blue and reddish, sticking in his side coat-pocket. Everything was wrong about what he wore. He ought to have been wearing blue jeans or overalls, and a straw hat or an old black felt hat, and the coat, granting that he might have been wearing a wool coat and not a jumper, ought not to have had those stripes. Those clothes, despite the fact that they were old enough and dirty enough for any tramp, didn't belong there in our back yard, coming down the path, in Middle Tennessee, miles away from any big town, and even a mile off the pike.

When he got almost to the steps, without having said anything, my mother, very matter-of-factly, said, "Good morning."

"Good morning," he said, and stopped and looked her over. He did not take off his hat, and under the brim you could see the perfectly unmemorable face, which wasn't old and wasn't young, or thick or thin. It was grayish and covered with about three days of stubble. The eyes were a kind of nondescript, muddy hazel, or something like that, rather bloodshot. His teeth, when he opened his mouth, showed yellow and uneven. A couple of them had been knocked out. You knew that they had been knocked out, because there was a scar, not very old, there on the lower lip just beneath the gap.

"Are you hunting work?" my mother asked him.

"Yes," he said—not "yes, mam"—and still did not take off his hat.

"I don't know about my husband, for he isn't here," she said, and didn't mind a bit telling the tramp, or whoever he was, with the mean knife in his pocket, that no man was around, "but I can give you a few things to do. The storm has drowned a lot of my chicks. Three coops of them. You can gather them up and bury them. Bury them deep so the dogs won't get at them. In the woods. And fix the coops the wind blew over. And down yonder beyond that pen by the edge of the woods are some drowned poults. They got out and I couldn't get them in. Even after it started to rain hard. Poults haven't got any sense."

"What are them things—poults?" he demanded, and spat on the brick walk. He rubbed his foot over the spot, and I saw that he wore a black, pointed-toe shoe, all cracked and broken. It was a crazy kind of shoe to be wearing in the country.

"Oh, they're young turkeys," my mother was saying. "And they haven't got any sense. I oughtn't to try to raise them around here with so many chickens, anyway. They don't thrive near chickens, even in separate pens. And I won't give up my chickens." Then she stopped herself and resumed briskly on the note of business. "When you finish that, you can fix my flower beds. A lot of trash and mud and gravel has washed down. Maybe you can save some of my flowers if you are careful."

"Flowers," the man said, in a low, impersonal voice which seemed to have a wealth of meaning, but a meaning which I could not fathom. As I think back on it, it probably was not pure contempt. Rather, it was a kind of impersonal and distant marveling that he should be on the verge of grubbing in a flower bed. He said the word, and then looked off across the yard.

"Yes, flowers," my mother replied with some asperity, as though she would have nothing said or implied against flowers. "And they were very fine this year." Then she stopped and looked at the man. "Are you hungry?" she demanded.

"Yeah," he said.

"I'll fix you something," she said, "before you get started." She turned to me. "Show him where he can wash up," she commanded, and went into the house.

I took the man to the end of the porch where a pump was and where a couple of wash pans sat on a low shelf for people to use before they went into the house. I stood there while he laid down his little parcel wrapped in newspaper and took off his hat and looked around for a nail to hang it on. He poured the water and plunged his hands into it. They were big hands, and strong looking, but they did not have the creases and the earth-color of the hands of men who work outdoors. But they were dirty, with black dirt ground into the skin and under the nails. After he had washed his hands, he poured another basin of water and washed his face. He dried his face, and with the towel still dangling in his grasp, stepped over to the mirror on the house wall. He rubbed one hand over the stubble on his face. Then he carefully inspected his face, turning first to one side and then the other, and stepped back and settled his striped coat down on his shoulders. He had the movements of a man who has just dressed up to go to church or a party—the way he settled his coat and smoothed it and scanned himself in the mirror.

Then he caught my glance on him. He glared at me for an instant out of the bloodshot eyes, then demanded in a low, harsh voice, "What you looking at?"

"Nothing," I managed to say, and stepped back a step from him.

He flung the towel down, crumpled, on the shelf, and went toward the kitchen door and entered without knocking.

My mother said something to him which I could not catch. I started to go in again, then thought about my bare feet, and decided to go back of the chicken yard, where the man would have to come to pick up the dead chicks. I hung around behind the chicken house until he came out.

He moved across the chicken yard with a fastidious, not quite finicking motion, looking down at the curdled mud flecked with bits of chicken-droppings. The mud curled up over the soles of his black shoes. I stood back from him some six feet and watched him pick up the first of the drowned chicks. He held it up by one foot and inspected it.

There is nothing deader looking than a drowned chick. The feet curl in that feeble, empty way which back when I was a boy, even if I was a country boy who did not mind hog-killing or frog-gigging, made me feel hollow in the stomach. Instead of looking plump and fluffy, the body is stringy and limp with the fluff plastered to it, and the neck is long and loose like a little string of rag. And the eyes have that bluish membrane over them which makes you think of a very old man who is sick about to die.

The man stood there and inspected the chick. Then he looked all around as though he didn't know what to do with it.

"There's a great big old basket in the shed," I said, and pointed to the shed attached to the chicken house.

He inspected me as though he had just discovered my presence, and moved toward the shed.

"There's a spade there, too," I added.

He got the basket and began to pick up the other chicks, picking each one up slowly by a foot and then flinging it into the basket with a nasty, snapping motion. Now and then he would look at me out of the bloodshot eyes. Every time he seemed on the verge of saying something, but he did not. Perhaps he was building up to say something to me, but I did not wait that long. His way of looking at me made me so uncomfortable that I left the chicken yard.

Besides, I had just remembered that the creek was in flood, over the bridge, and that people were down there watching it. So I cut across the farm toward the creek. When I got to the big tobacco field I saw that it had not suffered much. The land lay right and not many tobacco plants had washed out of the ground. But I knew that a lot of tobacco round the country had been washed right out. My father had said so at breakfast.

My father was down at the bridge. When I came out of the gap in the osage hedge into the road, I saw him sitting on his mare over the heads of the other men who were standing around, admiring the flood. The creek was big here, even in low water; for only a couple of miles away it ran into the river, and when a real flood came, the red water got over the pike where it dipped down to the bridge, which was an iron bridge, and high over the floor and even the side railings of the bridge. Only the upper iron work would show, with the water boiling and frothing red and white around it. That creek rose so fast and so heavy because a few miles back it came down out of the hills, where the gorges filled up with water in no time when a rain came. The creek ran in a deep bed with limestone bluffs along both sides until it got within three quarters of a mile of the bridge, and when it came out from between those bluffs in flood it was boiling and hissing and steaming like water from a fire hose.

Whenever there was a flood, people from half the county would come down to see the sight. After a gully-washer there would not be any work to do anyway. If it didn't ruin your crop, you couldn't plow and you felt like taking a holiday to celebrate. If it did ruin your crop, there wasn't anything to do except to try to take your mind off the mortgage, if you were rich enough to have a mortgage, and if you couldn't afford a mortgage you needed something to take your mind off how hungry you would be by Christmas. So people would come down to the bridge and look at the flood. It made something different from the run of days.

There would not be much talking after the first few minutes of trying to guess how high the water was this time. The men and kids just stood around, or sat their horses or mules, as the case might be, or stood up in the wagon beds. They looked at the strangeness of the flood for an hour or two, and then somebody would say that he had better be getting on home to dinner and would start walking down the gray, puddled limestone pike, or would touch heel to his mount and start off. Everybody always knew what it would be like when he got down to the bridge, but people always came. It was like church or a funeral. They always came, that is, if it was summer and the flood unexpected. Nobody ever came down in winter to see high water.

When I came out of the gap in the bodock hedge, I saw the crowd, perhaps fifteen or twenty men and a lot of kids, and saw my father sitting his mare, Nellie Gray. He was a tall, limber man and carried himself well. I was always proud to see him sit a horse, he was so quiet and straight, and when I stepped through the gap of the hedge that morning, the first thing that happened was, I remember, the warm feeling I always had when I saw him up on a horse, just sitting. I did not go toward him, but skirted the crowd on the far side, to get a look at the creek. For one thing, I was not sure what he would say about the fact that I was barefoot. But the first thing I knew, I heard his voice calling, "Seth!"

I went toward him, moving apologetically past the men, who bent their large, red or thin, sallow faces above me. I knew some of the men, and knew their names, but because those I knew were there in a crowd, mixed with the strange faces, they seemed foreign to me, and not friendly. I did not look up at my father until I was almost within touching distance of his heel. Then I looked up and tried to read his face, to see if he was angry about my being barefoot. Before I could decide anything from that impassive, high-boned face, he had leaned over and reached a hand to me. "Grab on," he commanded.

I grabbed on and gave a little jump, and he said, "Up-see-daisy!" and whisked me, light as a feather, up to the pommel of his McClellan saddle.

"You can see better up here," he said, slid back on the cantle a little to make me more comfortable, and then, looking over my head at the swollen, tumbling water, seemed to forget all about me. But his right hand was laid on my side, just above my thigh, to steady me.

I was sitting there as quiet as I could, feeling the faint stir of my father's chest against my shoulders as it rose and fell with his breath, when I saw the cow. At first, looking up the creek, I thought it was just another big piece of driftwood steaming down the creek in the ruck of water, but all at once a pretty good-size boy who had climbed part way up a telephone pole by the pike so that he could see better yelled out, "Golly-damn, look at that-air cow!"

Everybody looked. It was a cow all right, but it might just as well have been driftwood; for it was dead as a chunk, rolling and roiling down the creek, appearing and disappearing, feet up or head up, it didn't matter which.

The cow started up the talk again. Somebody wondered whether it would hit one of the clear places under the top girder of the bridge and get through or whether it would get tangled in the drift and trash that had piled against the upright girders and braces. Somebody remembered how about ten years before so much driftwood had piled up on the bridge that it was knocked off its foundations. Then the cow hit. It hit the edge of the drift against one of the girders, and hung there. For a few seconds it seemed as though it might tear loose, but then we saw that it was really caught. It bobbed and heaved on its side there in a slow, grinding, uneasy fashion. It had a yoke around its neck, the kind made out of a forked limb to keep a jumper behind fence.

"She shore jumped one fence," one of the men said.

And another: "Well, she done jumped her last one, fer a fack."

Then they began to wonder about whose cow it might be. They decided it must belong to Milt Alley. They said that he had a cow that was a jumper, and kept her in a fenced-in piece of ground up the creek. I had never seen Milt Alley, but I knew who he was. He was a squatter and lived up the hills a way, on a shirt-tail patch of set-on-edge land, in a cabin. He was pore white trash. He had lots of children. I had seen the children at school, when they came. They were thin-faced, with straight, sticky-looking, dough-colored hair, and they smelled something like old sour buttermilk, not because they drank so much buttermilk but because that is the sort of smell which children out of those cabins tend to have. The big Alley boy drew dirty pictures and showed them to the little boys at school.

That was Milt Alley's cow. It looked like the kind of cow he would have, a scrawny, old, sway-backed cow, with a yoke around her neck. I wondered if Milt Alley had another cow.

"Poppa," I said, "do you think Milt Alley has got another cow?"

"You say 'Mr. Alley,' " my father said quietly.

"Do you think he has?"

"No telling," my father said.

Then a big gangly boy, about fifteen, who was sitting on a scraggly little old mule with a piece of croker sack thrown across the saw-tooth spine, and who had been staring at the cow, suddenly said to nobody in particular, "Reckin anybody ever et drownt cow?"

He was the kind of boy who might just as well as not have been the son of Milt Alley, with his faded and patched overalls ragged at the bottom of the pants and the mud-stiff brogans hanging off his skinny, bare ankles at the level of the mule's belly. He had said what he did, and then looked embarrassed and sullen when all the eyes swung at him. He hadn't meant to say it, I am pretty sure now. He would have been too proud to say it, just as Milt Alley would have been too proud. He had just been thinking out loud, and the words had popped out.

There was an old man standing there on the pike, an old man with a white beard. "Son," he said to the embarrassed and sullen boy on the mule, "you live long enough and you'll find a man will eat anything when the time comes."

"Time gonna come fer some folks this year," another man said.

"Son," the old man, "in my time I et things a man don't like to think on. I was a sojer and I rode with Gin'l Forrest, and them things we et when the time come. I tell you. I et meat what got up and run when you taken out yore knife to cut a slice to put on the fire. You had to knock it down with a carbeen butt, it was so active. That-air meat would jump like a bullfrog, it was so full of skippers."

But nobody was listening to the old man. The boy on the mule turned his sullen sharp face from him, dug a heel into the side of the mule and went off up the pike with a motion which made you think that any second you would hear mule bones clashing inside that lank and scrofulous hide.

"Cy Dundee's boy," a man said, and nodded toward the figure going up the pike on the mule.

"Reckin Cy Dundee's young-uns seen times they'd settle fer drownt cow," another man said.

The old man with the beard peered at them both from his weak, slow eyes, first at one and then the other. "Live long enough," he said, "and a man will settle fer what he kin git."

Then there was silence again, with the people looking at the red, foam-flecked water.

My father lifted the bridle rein in his left hand, and the mare turned and walked around the group and up the pike. We rode on up to our big gate, where my father dismounted to open it and let me myself ride Nellie Gray through. When he got to the lane that led off from the drive about two hundred yards from our house, my father said, "Grab on." I grabbed on, and he let me down to the ground. "I'm going to ride down and look at my corn," he said. "You go on." He took the lane, and I stood there on the drive and watched him ride off. He was wearing cowhide boots and an old hunting coat, and I thought that that made him look very military, like a picture. That and the way he rode.

I did not go to the house. Instead, I went by the vegetable garden and crossed behind the stables, and headed down for Dellie's cabin. I wanted to go down and play with Jebb, who was Dellie's little boy about two years older than I was. Besides, I was cold. I shivered as I walked, and I had goose-flesh. The mud which crawled up between my toes with every step I took was like ice. Dellie would have a fire, but she wouldn't make me put on shoes and stockings.

Dellie's cabin was of logs, with one side, because it was on a slope, set on limestone chunks, with a little porch attached to it, and had a little whitewashed fence around it and a gate with plow-points on a wire to clink when somebody came in, and had two big white oaks in the yard and some flowers and a nice privy in the back with some honeysuckle growing over it. Dellie and Old Jebb, who was Jebb's father who lived with Dellie and had lived with her for twenty-five years even if they never had got married, were careful to keep everything nice around their cabin. They had the name all over the community for being clean and clever Negroes. Dellie and Jebb were what they used to call "white-folks' niggers." There was a big difference between their cabin and the other two cabins farther down where the other tenants lived. My father kept the other cabins weatherproof, but he couldn't undertake to go down and pick up after the litter they strewed. They didn't take the trouble to have a vegetable patch like Dellie and Jebb or to make preserves from wild plum, and jelly from crab apple the way Dellie did. They were shiftless, and my father was always threatening to get shed of them. But he never did. When they finally left, they just up and left on their own, for no reason, to go and be shiftless somewhere else. Then some more came. But meanwhile they lived down there, Matt Rawson and his family, and Sid Turner and his, and I played with their children all over the farm when they weren't working. But when I wasn't around they were mean sometimes to Little Jebb. That was because the other tenants down there were jealous of Dellie and Jebb.

I was so cold that I ran the last fifty yards to Dellie's gate. As soon as I had entered the yard, I saw that the storm had been hard on Dellie's flowers. The yard was, as I have said, on a slight slope, and the water running across had gutted the flower beds and washed out all the good black woods-earth which Dellie had brought in. What little grass there was in the yard was plastered sparsley down on the ground, the way the drainage water had left it. It reminded me of the way the fluff was plastered down on the skin of the drowned chicks that the strange man had been picking up, up in my mother's chicken yard.

I took a few steps up the path to the cabin, and then I saw that the drainage water had washed a lot of trash and filth out from under Dellie's house. Up toward the porch, the ground was not clean any more. Old pieces of rag, two or three rusted cans, pieces of rotten rope, some hunks of old dog dung, broken glass, old paper, and all sorts of things like that had washed out from under Dellie's house to foul her clean yard. It looked just as bad as the yards of the other cabins, or worse. It was worse, as a matter of fact, because it was a surprise. I had never thought of all that filth being under Dellie's house. It was not anything against Dellie that the stuff had been under the cabin. Trash will get under any house. But I did not think of that when I saw the foulness which had washed out on the ground which Dellie sometimes used to sweep with a twig broom to make nice and clean.

I picked my way past the filth, being careful not to get my bare feet on it, and mounted to Dellie's door. When I knocked, I heard her voice telling me to come in.

It was dark inside the cabin, after the daylight, but I could make out Dellie piled up in bed under a quilt, and Little Jebb crouched by the hearth, where a low fire simmered. "Howdy," I said to Dellie, "how you feeling?"

Her big eyes, the whites surprising and glaring in the black face, fixed on me as I stood there, but she did not reply. It did not look like Dellie, or act like Dellie, who would grumble and bustle around our kitchen, talking to herself, scolding me or Little Jebb, clanking pans, making all sorts of unnecessary noises and mutterings like an old-fashioned black steam thrasher engine when it has got up an extra head of steam and keeps popping the governor and rumbling and shaking on its wheels. But now Dellie just lay up there on the bed, under the patch-work quilt, and turned the black face, which I scarcely recognized, and the glaring white eyes to me.

"How you feeling?" I repeated.

"I'se sick," the voice said croakingly out of the strange black face which was not attached to Dellie's big, squat body, but stuck out from under a pile of tangled bedclothes. Then the voice added: "Mighty sick."

"I'm sorry," I managed to say.

The eyes remained fixed on me for a moment, then they left me and the head rolled back on the pillow. "Sorry," the voice said, in a flat way which wasn't question or statement of anything. It was just the empty word put into the air with no meaning or expression, to float off like a feather or a puff of smoke, while the big eyes, with the whites like the peeled white of hard-boiled eggs, stared at the ceiling.

"Dellie," I said after a minute, "there's a tramp up at the house. He's got a knife."

She was not listening. She closed her eyes.

I tiptoed over to the hearth where Jebb was and crouched beside him. We began to talk in low voices. I was asking him to get out his train and play train. Old Jebb had put spool wheels on three cigar boxes and put wire links between the boxes to make a train for Jebb. The box that was the locomotive had the top closed and a length of broom stick for a smoke stack. Jebb didn't want to get the train out, but I told him I would go home if he didn't. So he got out the train, and the colored rocks, and fossils of crinoid stems, and other junk he used for the load, and we began to push it around, talking the way we thought trainmen talked, making a chuck-chucking sound under the breath for the noise of the locomotive and now and then uttering low, cautious toots for the whistle. We got so interested in playing train that the toots got louder. Then, before he thought, Jebb gave a good, loud *toot-toot*, blowing for a crossing.

"Come here," the voice said from the bed.

Jebb got up slow from his hands and knees, giving me a sudden, naked, inimical look.

"Come here!" the voice said.

Jebb went to the bed. Dellie propped herself weakly up on one arm, muttering, "Come closer."

Jebb stood closer.

"Last thing I do, I'm gonna do it," Dellie said. "Done tole you to be quiet."

Then she slapped him. It was an awful slap, more awful for the kind of weakness which it came from and brought to focus. I had seen her slap Jebb before, but the slapping had always been the kind of easy slap you would expect from a good-natured, grumbling Negro woman like Dellie. But this was different. It was awful. It was so awful that Jebb didn't make a sound. The tears just popped out and ran down his face, and his breath came sharp, like gasps.

Dellie fell back. "Cain't even be sick," she said to the ceiling. "Git sick and they won't even let you lay. They tromp all over you. Cain't even be sick." Then she closed her eyes.

I went out of the room. I almost ran getting to the door, and I did run across the porch and down the steps and across the yard, not caring whether or not I stepped on the filth which had washed out from under the cabin. I ran almost all the way home. Then I thought about my mother catching me with the bare feet. So I went down to the stables.

I heard a noise in the crib, and opened the door. There was Big Jebb, sitting on an old nail keg, shelling corn into a bushel basket. I went in, pulling the door shut behind me, and crouched on the floor near him. I crouched there for a couple of minutes before either of us spoke, and watched him shelling the corn.

He had very big hands, knotted and grayish at the joints, with calloused palms which seemed to be streaked with rust with the rust coming up between the fingers to show from the back. His hands were so strong and tough that he could take a big ear of corn and rip the grains right off the cob with the palm of his hand, all in one motion, like a machine. "Work long as me," he would say, "and the good Lawd'll give you a hand lak cass-ion won't nuthin' hurt." And his hands did look like cast iron, old cast iron streaked with rust.

He was an old man, up in his seventies, thirty years or more older than Dellie, but he was strong as a bull. He was a squat sort of man, heavy in the shoulders, with remarkably long arms, the kind of build they say the river natives have on the Congo from paddling so much in their boats. He had a round bullet-head, set on powerful shoulders. His skin was very black, and the thin hair on his head was now grizzled like tufts of old cotton batting. He had small eyes and a flat nose, not big, and the kindest and wisest old face in the world, the blunt, sad, wise face of an old animal peering tolerantly out on the goings-on of the merely human creatures before him. He was a good man, and I loved him next to my mother and father. I crouched there on the floor of the crib and watched him shell corn with the rust cast-iron hands, while he looked down at me out of the little eyes set in the blunt face.

"Dellie says she's might sick," I said.

"Yeah," he said.

"What's she sick from?"

"Woman-mizry," he said.

"What's woman-mizry?"

"Hit comes on 'em," he said. "Hit just comes on 'em when the time comes."

"What is it?"

"Hit is the change," he said. "Hit is the change of life and time."

"What changes?"

"You too young to know."

"Tell me."

"Time come and you find out everything."

I knew that there was no use in asking him any more. When I asked him things and he said that, I always knew that he would not tell me. So I continued to crouch there and watch him. Now that I had sat there a little while, I was cold again.

"What you shiver fer?" he asked me.

"I'm cold. I'm cold because it's blackberry winter," I said.

"Maybe 'tis and maybe 'tain't," he said.

"My mother says it is."

"Ain't sayen Miss Sallie doan know and ain't sayen she do. But folks doan know everthing."

"Why isn't it blackberry winter?"

"Too late fer blackberry winter. Blackberries done bloomed."

"She said it was."

"Blackberry winter just a leetle cold spell. Hit come and then hit go away, and hit is growed summer of a sudden lak a gunshot. Ain't no tellen hit will go way this time."

"It's June," I said.

"June," he replied with great contempt. "That what folks say. What June mean? Maybe hit is come cold to stay."

"Why?"

"Cause this-here old yearth is tahrd. Hit is tahrd and ain't gonna perduce. Lawd let hit come rain one time forty days and forty nights, 'cause He wus tahrd of sinful folks. Maybe this-here old yearth say to the Lawd, Lawd, I done plum tahrd, Lawd, lemme rest. And Lawd say, Yearth, you done yore best, you give 'em cawn and you give 'em taters, and all they think on is they gut, and, Yearth, you kin take a rest."

"What will happen?"

"Folks will eat up everthing. The yearth won't perduce no more. Folks cut down all the trees and burn 'em cause they cold, and the yearth won't grow no more. I been tellen 'em. I been tellen folks. Sayen, maybe this year, hit is the time. But they doan listen to me, how the yearth is tahrd. Maybe this year they find out."

"Will everything die?"

"Everthing and everbody, hit will be so."

"This year?"

"Ain't no tellen. Maybe this year."

"My mother said it is blackberry winter," I said confidently, and got up.

"Ain't sayen nuthin' agin Miss Sallie," he said.

I went to the door of the crib. I was really cold now. Running, I had got up a sweat and now I was worse.

I hung on the door, looking at Jebb, who was shelling corn again.

"There's a tramp came to the house," I said. I had almost forgotten the tramp.

"Yeah."

"He came by the back way. What was he doing down there in the storm?"

"They comes and they goes," he said, "and ain't no tellen."

"He had a mean knife."

"The good ones and the bad ones, they comes and they goes. Storm or sun, light or dark. They is folks and they comes and they goes lak folks."

I hung on the door, shivering.

He studied me a moment, then said, "You git on to the house. You ketch yore death. Then what yore mammy say?"

I hesitated.

"You git," he said.

When I came to the back yard, I saw that my father was standing by the back porch and the tramp was walking toward him. They began talking before I reached them, but I got there just as my father was saying, "I'm sorry, but I haven't got any work. I got all the hands on the place I need now. I won't need any extra until wheat thrashing."

The stranger made no reply, just looked at my father.

My father took out his leather coin purse, and got out a half-dollar. He held it toward the man. "This is for half a day," he said.

The man looked at the coin, and then at my father, making no motion to take the money. But that was the right amount. A dollar a day was what you paid them back in 1910. And the man hadn't even worked half a day.

Then the man reached out and took the coin. He dropped it into the right side pocket of his coat. Then he said, very slowly and without feeling: "I didn't want to work on your—farm."

He used the word which they would have frailed me to death for using.

I looked at my father's face and it was streaked white under the sunburn. Then he said, "Get off this place. Get off this place or I won't be responsible."

The man dropped his right hand into his pants pocket. It was the pocket where he kept the knife. I was just about to yell to my father about the knife when the hand came back out with nothing in it. The man gave a kind of twisted grin, showing where the teeth had been knocked out above the new scar. I thought that instant how maybe he had tried before to pull a knife on somebody else and had got his teeth knocked out.

So now he just gave that twisted, sickish grin out of the unmemorable, grayish face, and then spat on the brick path. The glob landed just about six inches from the toe of my father's right boot. My father looked down at it, and so did I. I thought that if the glob had hit my father's boot something would have happened. I looked down and saw the bright glob, and on one side of it my father's strong cowhide boots, with the brass eyelets and the leather thongs, heavy boots splashed with good red mud and set solid on the bricks, and on the other side the pointed-toe, broken, black shoes, on which the mud looked so sad and out of place. Then I saw one of the black shoes move a little, just a twitch first, then a real step backward.

The man moved in a quarter circle to the end of the porch, with my father's steady gaze upon him all the while. At the end of the porch, the man reached up to the shelf where the wash pans were to get his little newspaper-wrapped parcel. Then he disappeared around the corner of the house and my father mounted the porch and went into the kitchen without a word.

I followed around the house to see what the man would to. I wasn't afraid of him now, no matter if he did have the knife. When I got around in front, I saw him going out the yard gate and starting up the drive toward the pike. So I ran to catch up with him. He was sixty yards or so up the drive before I caught up.

I did not walk right up even with him at first, but trailed him, the way a kid will, about seven or eight feet behind, now and then running two or three steps in order to hold my place against his longer stride. When I first came up behind him, he turned to give me a look, just a meaningless look, and then fixed his eyes up the drive and kept on walking.

When we had got around the bend in the drive which cut the house from sight, and were going along by the edge of the woods, I decided to come up even with him. I ran a few steps, and was by his side, or almost, but some feet off to the right. I walked along in this position for a while, and he never noticed me. I walked along until we got within sight of the big gate that let on the pike.

Then I said: "Where did you come from?"

He looked at me then with a look which seemed almost surprised that I was there. Then he said, "It ain't none of yore business."

We went on another fifty feet.

Then I said, "Where are you going?"

He stopped, studied me dispassionately for a moment, then suddenly took a step toward me and leaned his face down at me. The lips jerked back, but not in any grin, to show where the teeth were knocked out and to make the scar on the lower lip come white with the tension.

He said: "Stop following me. You don't stop following me and I cut yore throat, you little son-of-a-bitch."

Then he went on to the gate, and up the pike.

That was thirty-five years ago. Since that time my father and mother have died. I was still a boy, but a big boy, when my father got cut on the blade of a mowing machine and died of lockjaw. My mother sold the place and went to town to live with her sister. But she never took hold after my father's death, and she died within three years, right in middle life. My aunt always said, "Sallie just died of a broken heart, she was so devoted." Dellie is dead, too, but she died, I heard, quite a long time after we sold the farm.

As for Little Jebb, he grew up to be a mean and ficey Negro. He killed another Negro in a fight and got sent to the penitentiary, where he is yet, the last I heard tell. He probably grew up to be mean and ficey from just being picked on so much by the children of the other tenants, who were jealous of Jebb and Dellie for being thrifty and clever and being white-folks' niggers.

Old Jebb lived forever. I saw him ten years ago and he was about a hundred then, and not looking much different. He was living in town then, on relief—that was back in the Depression—when I went to see him. He said to me: "Too strong to die. When I was a young feller just comen on and seen how things wuz, I prayed the Lawd. I said, Oh, Lawd, gimme strength and meke me strong fer to do and to in-dure. The Lawd hearkened to my prayer. He give me strength. I was in-duren proud fer being strong and me much man. The Lawd give me my prayer and my strength. But now He done gone off and fergot me and left me alone with my strength. A man doan know what to pray fer, and him mortal."

Jebb is probably living yet, as far as I know.

That is what has happened since the morning when the tramp leaned his face down at me and showed his teeth and said: "Stop following me. You don't stop following me and I cut yore throat, you little son-of-a-bitch." That was what he said, for me not to follow him. But I did follow him, all the years.

THE FOURTH DAY OUT FROM SANTA CRUZ

by Paul Bowles

Ramón signed on at Cádiz. The ship's first call was at Santa Cruz de Tenerife, a day and a half out. They put in at night, soon after dark. Floodlights around the harbour illuminated the steep bare mountains and made them grass green against the black sky. Ramón stood at the rail, watching. "It must have been raining here," he said to a member of the crew standing beside him. The man grunted, looking not at the green slopes unnaturally bright in the electric glare, but at the lights of the town ahead. "Very green," went on Ramón, a little less certainly; the man did not even grunt in reply.

As soon as the ship was anchored, scores of Hindu shopkeepers came aboard with laces and embroidered goods for the passengers who might not be going ashore. They stayed on the first-class deck, not bothering to go down below to third-class where Ramón was scullery boy in the passengers' *cocina.* The work so far did not upset him; he had held more exacting and tiring jobs in Cádiz. There was sufficient food, and although it was not very good, nevertheless it was better than what was taken out to the third-class passengers. It had never occurred to Ramón to want privacy in his living quarters, so that he was unmoved by the necessity of sharing a cabin with a dozen or so shipmates. Still, he had been acutely unhappy since leaving Cádiz. Except for the orders they gave him in the kitchen, the sailors behaved as if he did not exist. They covered his bunk with their dirty clothes, and lay on it smoking at night when he wanted to climb in and sleep. They failed to include him in any conversation, and so far no one had even made an allusion, however deprecatory, to his existence. One would have said that for them he simply was not present. To even the least egocentric man such a state of affairs can become intolerable. In his sixteen years Ramón had not been in a similar situation; he had been maltreated but not wholly disregarded.

Most of the crew stood at the prow smoking, pointing out bars to one another, as they scanned the waterfront. Partly out of perversity born of his grievance, and partly because he wanted to be by himself for a spell, Ramón walked to the stern and leaned heavily against the rail, looking down into the darkness below. He could hear an automobile

---

horn being blown continuously as it drove along the waterfront. The hills behind backed up the sound, magnified it as they threw it across the water. To the other side was the dim roar of the sea's waves against the breakwater. He was a little homesick, and as he stood there he became angry as well. It was inadmissible that this state of affairs should continue. A day and a half was too long; he was determined to force a change immediately, and to his undisciplined young mind kept recurring the confused image of a fight,—a large-scale struggle with the entire crew, in which he somehow finished as the sole victor.

It is pleasant to walk by the sea-wall of a foreign port at night, with the autumn wind gently pushing at your back. Ramón was in no hurry; he stopped before each café and listened to the guitars and shouting, without, however, allowing himself to be detained by the women who called to him from the darker doorways. Having had to clean up the galley after an extra meal had been served to sixty workmen who had just come aboard here at Santa Cruz, bound for South America, he had been the last to get off the ship, and so he was looking for his shipmates. At the Café del Teide he found several of them seated at a table sharing a bottle of rum. They saw him come in, but they gave no sign of recognition. There was no empty chair. He walked towards the table, slowed down a bit as he approached it, and then continued walking towards the back of the café. The man behind the bar called out to him: "You were looking for something?" Ramón turned around and sat down suddenly at a small table. The waiter came and served him, but he scarcely noticed what he was drinking. He was watching the table with the six men from his ship. Like one fascinated, he let his eyes follow each gesture: the filling of the little glasses, the tossing down of the liquor, the back of the hand wiping the mouth. And he listened to their words punctuated by loud laughter. Resentment began to swell in him; he felt that if he sat still any longer he would explode. Pushing back his chair, he jumped up and strode dramatically out into the street. No one noticed his exit.

He began to walk fast through the town, paying no attention to where he was going. His eyes fixed on an imaginary horizon, he went through the *plaza*, along the wide Paseo de Ronda, and into the tiny passages that lie behind the cathedral. The number of people in the streets increased as he walked away from the centre of town, until when he had come to what seemed an outlying district, where the shops were mere stalls, he was forced to saunter along with the crowd. As he slowed down his gait, he felt less nervous. Gradually he took notice of the merchandise for sale, and of the people around him. It suddenly occurred to him that he would like to buy a large handkerchief. Outside certain booths there were wires strung up; from these hung, clipped by their corners, a great many of the squares of cloth, their bright colours showing in the flare of the carbide lamps. As Ramón stopped to choose one at the nearest booth he became aware that in the next booth a girl with a laughing face was also buying a bandana. He waited until she had picked out the one she wanted, and then he stepped quickly over to the shopkeeper and pointing down at the package he was making, said: "Have you another handkerchief exactly like that?" The girl paid no attention to him and put her change into her purse. "Yes," said the shopkeeper, reaching out over the counter to examine the bandanas. The girl picked up her little packet wrapped in newspaper, turned away, and walked along the street. "No, you haven't!" cried Ramón, and he hurried after her so as not to lose sight of her in the crowd. For some distance he trailed her along the thoroughfare, until she turned into a side street that led uphill. It smelled here of drains and there was very little light. He quickened his pace for fear she would go into one of the buildings before he had had the opportunity to talk to her. Somewhere in the back of his mind he hoped to persuade her to go with him to the Café del Teide. As he overtook her, he spoke quietly without turning his head: "Señorita." To his surprise she stopped walking and stood still on the pavement. Although she was very near to him, he could not see her face clearly.

"What do you want?"

"I wanted to talk to you."

"Why?"

He could not answer.

"I thought—" he stammered.

"What?"

There was a silence, and then as she laughed Ramón remembered her face: open and merry, but not a child's face. In spite of the confidence its recalled image inspired in him, he asked: "Why do you laugh?"

"Because I think you're crazy."

He touched her arm and said boldly: "You'll see if I'm crazy."

"I'll see nothing. You're a sailor. I live here"; she pointed to the opposite side of the street. "If my father sees you, you'll have to run all the way to your ship." Again she laughed. To Ramón her laugh was music, faintly disturbing.

"I don't want to bother you. I only wanted to talk to you," he said, timid again.

"Good. Now you've talked. *Adiós.*" She began to walk on. So did Ramón, close beside her. She did not speak. A moment later, he remarked triumphantly: "You said you lived back there!"

"It was a lie," she said in a flat voice. "I always lie."

"Ah. You always lie," echoed Ramón with great seriousness.

They came to a street-light at the foot of a high staircase. The sidewalk became a series of stone steps leading steeply upward between the houses. As they slowly ascended, the air changed. It smelled of wine, food cooking, and burning eucalyptus leaves. Up above the city here, life was more casual. People leaned over the balconies, sat in dark doorways chatting, stood in the streets like islands among the moving dogs and children.

The girl stopped and leaned against the side of a house. She was a little out of breath from the climb.

"Tired?" he asked.

Instead of replying she turned swiftly and darted inside the doorway beside her. For a few seconds Ramón was undecided whether or not to follow her. By the time he had tiptoed into the dimly lit passageway she had disappeared. He walked through into the courtyard. Some ragged boys who were running about stopped short and stared at him. A radio was playing guitar music above. He looked up. The building was four storeys high; there were lights in almost all the windows.

On his way back to the waterfront a woman appeared from the shadows of the little park by the cathedral, and took his arm. He looked at her; she was being brazenly coy, with her head tilted at a crazy angle as she repeated: "I like sailors." He let her walk with him to the Café del Teide. Once inside, he was disappointed to see that his shipmates were gone. He bought the woman a manzanillo and walked out on her as she began to drink it. He had not said a word to her. Outside the night seemed suddenly very warm. He came to the Blanco y Negro; a band was playing inside. Two or three of the men from the ship were on the dark dance floor, trying to instil a bit of life into the tired girls that hung to them. He did not even have a drink here, but hurried back to the ship. His bunk was piled with newspapers and bundles, but the cabin was empty, and he had several hours in the dark in which to brood and doze, before the others arrived. The boat sailed at dawn.

They skirted the island next day,—not close enough to see the shore, but within sight of the great conical mountain, which was there all day beside them in the air, clear in distant outline. For two days the ship continued on a southwest course. The sea grew calm, a deep blue, and the sun blazed brighter in the sky. The crew had ceased gathering on the poopdeck save in the early evening and at night, when they lay sprawled all over it, singing in raucous voices while the stars swayed back and forth over their heads.

For Ramón life continued the same. He could see no difference in the crew's attitude towards him. It still seemed to him that they lived without him. The magazines that had been bought at Santa Cruz were never passed around the cabin. Afternoons when the men sat at the table in the third class *comedor*, the stories that were recounted could never be interpreted by any gesture in their telling as being directed at a group that included him. And he certainly knew better than to attempt to tell any himself. He still waited for a stroke of luck that might impose him forcibly upon their consciousness.

In the middle of the fourth morning out from Santa Cruz he poked his head from the galley and noticed several of the men from his cabin gathered along the railing at the stern. The sun was blinding and hot, and he knew something must be keeping them there. He saw one man pointing aft. Casually he wandered out across the deck to within a few feet of the group, searching the sea and the horizon for some object,—something besides the masses of red seaweed that constantly floated by on top of the dark water.

"It's getting nearer!"

"Qué fuerza!"

"It's worn out!"

"Claro!"

Ramón looked over their heads, and between them when they changed position from time to time. He saw nothing. He was almost ready to be convinced that the men were baiting him, in the hope of being able to amuse themselves when his curiosity should be aroused to the point of making him ask: "What is it?" And so he was determined to be quiet, to wait and see.

Suddenly he did see. It was a small yellow and brown bird flying crookedly after the boat, faltering as it repeatedly fell back towards the water between spurts of desperate energy.

"A thousand miles from land!"

"It's going to make it! Look! Here it comes!"

"No!"

"Next time."

At each wild attempt to reach the deck, the bird came closer to the men, and then, perhaps from fear of them, it fluttered down towards the boiling sea, missing the wake's maelstrom by an ever closer margin. And when it seemed that this time it surely would be churned under into the white chaos of air and water, it would surge feebly upward, its head turned resolutely towards the bright mass of the ship that moved always in front of it.

Ramón was fascinated. His first thought was to tell the men to step back a little from the rail so that the bird might have the courage to land. As he opened his mouth to suggest this, he thought better of it, and was immediately thankful for having remained quiet. He could imagine the ridicule that would have been directed at him later: in the cabin, at mealtime, evenings on the deck. Someone would have invented a shameful little ditty about Ramón and his bird. He stood watching, in a growing agony of suspense.

"Five pesetas it goes under!"

"Ten it makes it!"

Ramón wheeled about and ran lightly across to the galley. Almost immediately he came out again. In his arms he carried the ship's mascot, a heavy tomcat that blinked stupidly in the sudden glare of the sun. This time he walked directly back to the railing where the others stood. He set the animal down at their feet.

"What are you doing?" said one.

"Watch," said Ramón.

They were all quiet a moment. Ramón held the cat's flanks and head steady, waiting for it to catch sight of the fluttering bird. It was difficult to do. No matter how he directed its head it showed no sign of interest. Still they waited. As the bird came up to the level of the deck at a few feet from the boat, the cat's head suddenly twitched, and Ramón knew the contact had been made. He took his hands away. The cat stood perfectly still, the end of its tail moving slightly. It took a step closer to the edge, watching each movement of the bird's frantic efforts.

"Look at that!"

"He sees it."

"But the bird doesn't see him."

"If it touches the boat, the ten pesetas still go."

The bird rose in the air, flew faster for a moment until it was straight above their heads. They looked upward into the flaming sun, trying to shade their eyes. It flew still further forward, until, if it had dropped, it would have landed a few feet ahead of them on the deck. The cat, staring up into the air, ran quickly across the deck so that it was directly below the bird, which slowly let itself drop until it seemed that they could reach out and take it. Stretching its full length with the sudden force of a steel spring, the cat made a futile leap into the air. They all cried out, but the bird was too high. Suddenly it rose much higher; then it stopped flying. Swiftly they passed on beneath it as it remained poised an instant in the air. When they had turned their heads back it was a tiny yellow thing falling slowly downward, and almost as quickly they lost sight of it.

At the noonday meal they talked about it. After some argument the bets were paid. One of the oilers went to his cabin and brought out a bottle of cognac and a set of little glasses which he put in front of him and filled, one after the other.

"Have some?" he said to Ramón.

Ramón took a glass, and the oiler passed the rest around to the others.

TO THE MOUNTAINS

by Paul Horgan

Julio lay as quietly as he could, only his eyes kept moving, turning toward the open door that led into the other room, as if by looking there he could hear better what the women were saying. His brother Luis was asleep beside him. The same blanket of catskins covered them both. Luis could sleep no matter what. The firelight on the walls and the ceiling was enough to keep Julio awake, even if his mother were not weeping in the next room. It was a silent night outside, like all the other nights in this place of home.

"When the fire goes out I will go to sleep," thought Julio; his legs ached from holding them still. But he slept before the coals began to breathe their rosy lives to ash. And he dreamed of his world with much sorrow and love. The dream was a kind of memory that pursued him as if to be told again, a legend like one of the saints' lives, and thus worshiped.

Four nights ago his mother had given birth to a baby girl. Josefina

---

Martinez came nine miles from Bernalillo to assist. The father was in Mexico on a wagon train. The trade in the summer and autumn of 1800 was promising, and the weather very fortunate. Rosa's baby came with no one there but her two sons and Josefina, the midwife. They made a huge fire in the front room and left the door open so the heat would wave silently through. The boys stayed outdoors, shuddering like horses under the November moon. From within came the wafting firelight and the nimble sounds of repeated sufferings.

The great river lay beyond in the groves of cottonwoods. In the chill night the boys fancied they could hear river sounds . . . lappets of wave and shift of sand and suck of mud and the airy clamber of the huge heron as it heavied itself upward on bony wings. The chimney behind them blew fragrant sparks. Each boy felt like the deputy of his father. Luis was sixteen and Julio was thirteen. Luis was a stout boy, legs and arms like cottonwood branch, round and wieldy. He had pale eyes, and his glance never erred from guilt, the boy's guilt of accidental knowledge of the world. Julio was slender and something like a half-grown cat in his physical ways. He was wary and respectful of life's dangers. His eyes were black and so was his hair, and his face was dark. He had grown with caution, because fear slowly told him more as he grew up. Everything Luis did easily because he was older, Julio had to learn to do because he was younger, and thus everything was harder for him. The boys had no one but each other for companions, mostly; for they lived in the Rio Grande valley a ways out from the village of Bernalillo. They sometimes went there on horseback, when their father could spare the animals from work in the fields. Once, riding to town, Julio's horse had stamped and run wild, because a hunter in the tall saplings by the field near the river had shot his musket at a rising goose. Julio often dreamed of it, and the triumph of regaining the horse's head.

The brothers slept and the firelight faded down.

In the back room Rosa presently slept too, and Josefina sat watching her and the new baby.

Josefina was greatly girthed, with two circles of fat at her middle. She was heavy-faced and her eyes were kind, even when her tongue was sharp and filthy. Thus her character: good heart, from instinct; wicked mind, from dealings in the hard world.

The baby lay by its mother's side.

"The face of a piñon," thought Josefina, staring at the tiny brown head and the little open mouth that breathed so roundly.

The house was thick as a fortress, with adobe walls. It stood on a little green flat of land above the fields, beyond which lay the Rio Grande. Over it went two mighty cottonwoods planted a long time ago by the grandfather of this house, who himself had left the service of the Viceroy of New Spain to scratch his own land and yield it to his own sons. To the east the fields faded into mesa country, rising face of gravelly sand that held dusty bushes. The mesa rolled away and lifted hills where little pine trees grew. In morning, distant under the early sun, the pine trees seemed to exhale a blue air; and from the blue air rose the mountains, whose trees looked far away like scratches upon the face of blue rock. The mountains were miles away from the house of the family, and sometimes they were altogether hidden by weather: cloud, or rain, or wind alive with dust. At other times the mountains were momentously close, as if moved in golden light by the hand of God, and every canyon, every wind course and water hollow in the rock, stood clear to the eyes of the wondering brothers. Hardly a day of their lives failed to be somehow influenced by the mountains off there to the east. In the lush river valley, life seemed spontaneous, from black earth; and bedded woman. The boys would one day own the earth and know woman; and perhaps, as some men did, know something of the mystery of the mountains at the world's rim.

Josefina came into the front room to kick some more wood on the dying fire; for cold was quick to get through her petulant flesh.

She woke Julio; but he lay with his eyes shut, identifying the noises she made and the profane rumble of her musing. When she went back, he heard his mother speak sleepily; then the baby squeaked and began to cry, what sounded to him like a mortal utterance and farewell of that alien little life in his mother's bed.

"Yes, if you all four of you get through the winter, that will be one of God's little jokes," said Josefina, slapping her hands on her cold belly. "This house never gets warm; and nothing to cover with, those boys out there, freezing on the dirt floor with a dirty old catskin." . . .

"My husband will bring back plenty of money and furs and clothes from Mexico," said Rosa. But she began to cry again, and mumble little sad doubts against the baby's hot temple.

"So, I will stay as long as I can," said Josefina. "But you know that can't be forever. . . . Be quiet now. You will choke the baby. Here, I'll take her, though God knows she may freeze to death. Get back to sleep. I will warm her."

Josefina took the baby.

Julio leaned and crouched from his bed to see what they did. There was a coldly steady candle burning by the wooden saint in the corner of the bedroom. Josefina held the baby with one arm and with her other hand pulled her tight dress away in front, and her huge bosom lay open and cavernous with shadow. There at her warmest and most copious being, she laid the baby and folded her breasts to it, and drew her dress together and held her arms like a cradle. Her cheeks quivered at the striving touch of the baby, some pleasure deepened in her being; and for no reason that she could recognize, out of her assortment of past lives—midwife, servant, thief, and harlot—she began to blush.

Her eyes watered and she smiled and sighed.

Julio backed into his bed again. His brother Luis flinched and jerked like a dog that is tickled when it dozes. Julio held his breath for fear he wake Luis. Yet he wanted to talk to him. He wanted to stir his brother into a fury of doing: to save this family; to prove that it was not a world for women, that it was their own little tiny sister who so blindly threatened their mother's life and will and who opened the disgusting bosom of a fat witch to lie there for warmth!

So his thoughts were confused and furious.

His boyishness misjudged the stuff of the complaining fat woman, just as his heart was jealous for his mother.

The fire was alive again in little flames like autumn leaves. He could not sleep. He could not forget. He hated his fears. They were with him, vaguely enlivened by Josefina's talk.

It was not long before winter.

In the broken darkness of firelight, Julio lay awake and prayed until he was answered by the same thing that always answered prayers, the earliest voice he had been taught to recognize, which no one else had to hear, the voice of God Himself in his own heart. Father Antonio made him know when he was a very little boy that the stronger a man was the more he needed the guidance of God. So when he felt afraid and feeble alongside his mild strong brother, he had only to pray, and shut his eyes, and remember Jesus, Who would presently come to him and say, "I see you, Julio Garcia; it is all right. What is it?"

"The mountains, to the mountains," thought Julio in answer to his own prayer.

"Blessed is the fruit of thy womb, Jesus."

"What is in the mountains?"

". . . now and at the hour of our death."

"There is much that my brother and I can do in the mountains, and as soon as he awakens I will tell him; we will take my father's musket and go hunting; we will bring home skins to keep our little sister warm, and show our mother that this is a house of men, who do what is right, no matter how hard it is to do." . . .

"Amen."

Against the mica panes of the small deep window the early daylight showed like fog, silvery and chill. Luis jumped alive from sleep and went like a pale shadow to the dead fireplace, where he blew ashes off a few remote coals and, shivering in his bare skin, coaxed a fire alive. Then he found his clothes and got into them. He began to laugh at Julio, curled like a cat under the mountain catskins, waiting for warmth to get up to. Then he thought with pleasure of the work to be done outside; in the marching dawn; cold mist over the river; the horses stirring; animals to feed and release. He went out, already owner of the day.

Julio was awake all that time; and he squinted at the fire, judging nicely just when it would need more wood, lest it go out; and just when the room would be comfortable to arise into. He was soon up, listening for sounds in the other room. Presently Josefina came to make breakfast. She felt tragic in the cold morning, and her face drooped with pity for her heart which was abused.

"I am going home," said she.

"No, you can't do that," said the boy.

She looked at him with sad delight in his concern.

"Why can't I?—What do I get around here for my pains?—I was freezing all night."

"When my father comes home he will pay you plenty.—Luis and I can—We will bring you a glorious piece of fur."

"Oh, indeed: and where from."

"We are going to the mountains."

"—A pair of fool children like you?"

"Where is Luis? I must speak to him."

"He is out by the shed.—Yes, and another thing for your poor mama to worry about.—If she lives through the winter it will be very surprising."

"What do you mean!"

She had nothing to mean, and so she made it more impressive by quivering her great throat, a ridiculous gesture of melancholy.

Julio ran outside and found his brother. They did not greet each other but fell into tasks together.

The sky was coming pale blue over the river, and pale gold edges of light began to show around the far mountain rims. The house looked like a lovely toy in the defining light, its edges gilded, its shadows dancing.

"Luis."

"What."

"I have an idea."

"Well."

"—Did you feel cold at night?"

"No, but you would not lie still."

"I am sorry.—I heard Josefina talking to Mama."

"The poor old cow."

"Do you realize that we are so poor that we haven't got enough things to keep us warm, especially with the new baby here? And an extra woman in the house—she ought to stay with us until Mama is well again."

"What are you going to do about it?"

"You and I should take the musket and go to hunt cats in the mountains, and bring home enough furs to satisfy everybody."

"Yes," said Luis, without any surprise, "I have thought of that too."

"Then I can go?"

"I suppose so.—If you behave yourself. It's no child's errand, you know."

"Of course not.—Then you will tell Mama?"

"Why don't you?"

"—She wouldn't think I *knew*."

"All right."

Now the smoke was thick and sweet above the house.

The light spread grandly over the whole valley.

Luis went to his mother's bedside and leaned down. The baby was awake and obscurely busy against her mother's side.

"Mama."

"My little Luis."

"Julio and I are going to the mountains for a few days, to get some furs."

"No, no, you are both too young, that little Julio is just a baby, now, Luis, don't break my heart with any more troubles!"

"What troubles: we have no troubles!"

"Your father is gone, we have no money, my children shiver all night long, that Josefina is a fat crow. Father Antonio hasn't been near us since the baby was born." . . .

She wept easily and weakly. Luis was full of guilt, and ideas of flight. He leaned and kissed her cool forehead and laughed like a big man.

"—You'll see. My brother and I will come back like merchant princes."

"Then you are going?"

"Yes, Mummie, we'll go."

She stared at him in a religious indignation. This was her son! So even sons grew up and went away and did what they wanted to do, in spite of all the things women could think of to keep them back?

Later Julio came to say goodbye and she shamelessly wooed him to stay, with the name of God, and her love, and his pure dearness, and various coquetries; he felt a lump in his throat but he coughed over it, and kissed her, while she said:

"My poor little darling Julio, already running off from home!"

"But I tell you!" he said, and then he began to smart in the eyes, so he shrugged, like his father, and went to the other room, where he paused and said:

"Thank you, Josefina, for staying until my brother and I get back."

"—The devil takes many odd forms," she said with a pout.

The little house was full of shadows in the daytime, for the windows were deep and small, and this suggested how narrow, how cloudy the world was to those who lived there. There were facts within eyesight, and farther away than that there were rumors only, and in the heart there were convictions learned of life and ordered by heaven. But through earnings of their bodies and their spirits, they owned life, and loved it, as it used them.

They had two horses and the musket which their father had left at home before his last departure for Mexico, from Albuquerque, where the wagon trains set out. They had a rawhide pouch containing things to eat, loaves and chilis and dried meat. As soon as they were free of the little fields of home, Julio began to gallop; and Luis overtook him and, saying nothing, reached out for the halter and brought him down to a walk. Julio felt very much rebuked; he sat erect on his horse and squinted his eyes at the mountain rising so far ahead of them, and thought of himself as a relentless hunter, the snake of the sand hills, who is hungry only once or twice a year, and comes forth then with slow tremendous appetite to take whatever he desires from resistless owners.

The boys toiled over the land all morning.

They paused and looked back several times, touched by the change in the look of their farm, which lay now like a box or two on the floor of the valley; and they thought respectively, "When I have my farm, I shall want it to be on higher ground," and "What if something dreadful has happened since we left home, if the baby choked to death, or a robber came, I should never forgive myself."

But they turned again to the mountains, letting their dreams of personality fade.

The mountains looked strangely smaller as they advanced. The foothills raised the riders up, and from various slopes the mountain crowns seemed to lean back and diminish. The blue air in canyons and on the far faces of rock slides and broken mighty shoulders was like a breath of mystery over the familiar facts of memory.

"Let me carry the musket now for a while."

"No, we might as well decide that now. I am to have it all the time."

"Why, that isn't right!"

"No, I have had more experience with it. It is our only arm. Now be sensible."

"Just because I am the younger, you always do this way.—I tell you, I am an excellent shot."

"You may be. But I am nearly four years older, and—I just think it better this way."

"I wish I'd known before we started."

"Why don't you go back, then?"

"I will."

But they rode on together. Easily triumphant, Luis could afford to be indulgent; later on he rode close to Julio and knocked him on the back and winked.

"You think I am not as much of a man as you are," said Julio bitterly.

"Well, you're not."

"You'll see! I can show you!"

"A man always agrees to do the thing that is best for others."

"Well, whose idea was it, coming to the mountains to hunt skins for our family?"

"Sure. Yours."

The brothers' love for each other was equally warm, but derived from different wells of feeling.

Sometimes they felt only the love; at other times only the difference.

Now in afternoon, riding on the windy November plain, and knowing that before nightfall they would be in the very shadow of the nearest mountain reach, they felt their littleness on that world; and so they made their feelings and their thoughts big, and owned those wild rocks and that crown-cut skyline in their souls; and their spirits rose; and in the wilderness, with none but themselves to use and know, they had a certain giddiness. The air was lighter so high up above the river valley. They looked back. An empire of sand-colored earth; and there, in the far light, the river herself, furred with trees. They looked ahead; but, in doing that, had to look up, now.

It was a crazy giant land; a rock that looked like a pebble from here was higher than a tree when they got to it.

"We must find a place to leave the horses."

"What?"

"You idiot, we can't expect horses to climb straight up cliffs like that over there!"

"Sure, we'll find a place to leave them."

"—It must be nearly too late to go into the mountains tonight."

"We'll make a fire here."

"If it is clear enough tonight, they could see our fire from home."

"They could?"

The thought made Julio shiver. But then it was already getting chill. The sun was going down. Great colorful energies from its last heat began to shift and brood on the mountains, until a veil of rosy mist covered it all; and then slowly earth's own shadow climbed with vast measure up the mountain faces and left them the night.

They awoke the next morning under the cold mountains, and in their rested souls there was a mood of gods. They caught their horses and rode along the last little flat before the great rise; and before the sun was up over the rocky shoulder, they had found a little box canyon where there was a growth of straw-colored grass and through which there washed a small creek. Leading the horse, they walked far into the narrow shadowy canyon and at last Luis said:

"There."

"What."

"Here is the place to leave the animals. We can make a little fence down here, and then be safe when we go off to hunt."

"What will you build your fence with?"

"Some big rocks and then a lot of branches that will seem high to the horses."

"Where does that river come from, do you suppose?"

"If you'll stop talking long enough to get to work, we'll go and find out."

The light of builders came into their eyes, measuring, devising; after a few trials, they had a system for their work; they moved harmoniously. Given need, materials and imagination, nothing wanted. They grew warm and threw down their coats. The sun quivered in watery brilliance high beyond the rocky crown and then came into view, spilling such warmth and glory down the ragged slopes that the brothers hurried harder, enchanted by the job of life.

When they were done, they untethered the horses and took up their most valuable possessions—the food, the musket, the powder, balls, their knives, their tinder—and went up the canyon, following the creek. It led them into shadow; they had to wade; the rocks widened; sunlight ahead; then a miniature marsh with moss and creatures' tracks; then a little fall, which they heard, a whisper in diamond sunlight before they saw it, and under it a black pool plumbed by the sun to its still sandy floor.

The fall came down from a rocky ledge halfway up the face of a gray stone cliff.

The forest shadows beyond it, which they saw looking up, were hazy with sunlight and noon blue.

It was the shelf of still another world; the mountains seemed to be made of terraces leading up, and up, each into a new state of being; until to the brothers' souls, born of the obscure little farm in the river valley, far from cities and reliant upon God and priest for all further knowledge, it seemed that the last terrace of all must end at the very step to heaven.

"We'll swim!"

The fall drifted into the canyon and was wavered by the warm air reflected off the rocks about.

The boys took off their clothes and fell into the water; for a moment they hated the cold shock, and then they were happily claimed by the animal world. They were away from everything. They were let to their senses. They dived and splashed and bellowed, awakening the silences to echo, which only tempest and beast had awakened before them. This was a bath of a superman; not the idle, slow, muddy, warm current of the

Rio Grande, which suggested cows and babies paddling and hot mud drugging boys who swam in summer.

They came out into the warmer air and slapped until they were dry; then they dressed.

"Up there, we've got to get up there some way."

Luis pointed up to the higher world beyond the fall. There were gigantic pines standing in light-failing ranks; and behind them a great plane of rock shaggy with its own breakage.

So they retreated from the waterfall and went around it, climbing and clawing until they had gained the upper level. They stood to listen. Enormous and pressing, the quiet of the mountains surrounded them. Their eyes, so long limited to a tame river world, hunted ahead. They were explorers, so far as they knew. What no man has ever seen before! There was a mysterious sense of awe in the first eye that owned it.

As they passed in and out of shadow, they felt alternately cold and warm.

As they went, they were often forced by the huge silence to stop and let their own sounds die away.

They would laugh at each other at such moments, and then go on.

In midafternoon they thought they must plan to go back, since it took them so long to come. The horses would need company and perhaps protection against beasts.

The sun was yellower and cooler.

The way they had come no longer looked the same; coming, they had watched another face of it; now retreating, they had to look back often to recognize their course. They lost it, or thought they had, when they came to a bench of gray stone in a spill of light through branches. Then they looked aside, and saw the ledge curve and vanish in a stout hillside, and emerge a little farther on and there become the rocky shelf over which rustled their waterfall of the sunny noon.

"It is made by heaven for our purposes!" said Luis.

"Yes, it certainly is.—How do you mean?"

"Well, the cats probably come and drink and lie here, and other animals. We could be here on this shelf, you see."

"And fire down on them?"

"Sure."

"Jesus!"

"Come on."

They started along the ledge and then shagged back and nearly fell down to the canyon floor below when a boom of air and shock arose and smote them from a few feet ahead. It was the thunder of a great bald eagle who beat his way off the rocks and straight up over them, his claws hanging down, his hot red eyes sparkling for one tiny second in the light of the sky. Then he wheeled and raised his claws and extended his head and drifted off in a long slanting line like the descent of the mountain edge over which he vanished.

The boys were breathless.

It scared them.

It also hushed them; the grandeur of that heavy bird leaving earth for air.

"How I would love to get a bird like that!"

"To kill him?"

"Or at least get some of his feathers."

Julio moved forward and then crouched and called for his brother.

"Luis, look, hurry, here is what he had!"

They were looking at a partially picked mountain lion cub, off which the eagle had been feeding.

"Julio, you see now? Here is where the big cats will come. They will roam until they find it, and they will watch. The eagle carried off the baby cat. He'll come back, too!"

Julio did a thing like a very small boy. He kicked the carcass of the cub off the ledge into the shaly slide below.

"What did you do that for?"

"I don't know."

"It was wonderful bait! Now it's gone!"

"Well . . ."

"Oh, come on!"

The godlike temper and power of the day was gone for them both; Luis exasperated; Julio tired and guilty.

As they went down to the canyon where the waterfall seemed to stand, not fall, in a mist of blue shadow now that the sun was sinking, they looked up and saw the eagle so high that he seemed like a spiraling leaf. Luis shrugged and said:

"Oh, cheer up, I suppose he would have come back anyway and carried his supper off!"

But Luis, though he was again friendly, could not offset the chilling of the whole day; and the rocky clear cold cupping of night in those walled places closed over Julio and confirmed his hunger, his bitterness, his youthful rue at the turn of happiness into misery, like the turn of day into dusk.

All right, if everybody was older than he was, let them parade and give orders.

Time was his enemy, just as much as mountains, and needed conquering.

He could dream of pushing them all back, and making his mortal little grant to the world.

If Luis felt so superior, Julio would show him some day.

They scampered down the canyon as fast as they could, for where they had left the horses was like a station of home to them, and thus desirable; man's claim endowing the earth with his own virtue and responsibility.

To the boys, the mountains seemed to create the weather, to give it off like a part of mountainhood.

When it was dark enough, they looked for stars, and saw some; but clouds had come, and a damp, warmish wind, and the canyon talked in wind, trees keening, and now and then an almost silent thunder of a wind-blow when it met a high rock side of a hill.

By the last light of their fire, Luis examined his musket, to see that the day's toil over hard ground hadn't damaged it any.

"Let me see it," said Julio.

"What for?"

"Oh, can't I just *see* it?"

Luis handed it over.

Julio sighted along the barrel.

"She's a lovely one," he murmured. Then he gave it back, ready to go to sleep, chuckling with affection for Luis, who would be so surprised.

Straight above the canyon, but so high above, the wind went by all night long.

The campfire hardly felt the breath of it.

But the high places of the whole mountain system did, and there was a gather of some moist, soft, warmish air over the peaks; the stars blurred; the highest timber exhalant; the top naked rocks misted.

Dawn came with a ghostly diffusion of misty light; the slow march of shapes.

Julio was ready.

He rolled with almost infinite slowness to the ground, free of the blankets, and left Luis slumbering like a mummy who knew the cold of Mexican centuries.

He crouched and slowly went around the bed, and took up the musket and ammunition from his brother's side.

He sniffed the air and it was bittersweet with cold and some drifting new flavor.

He didn't know, in his excitement and caution, that it was the presage of snow.

He went up the canyon chewing on a hank of jerked meat from his pocket. He was abroad in his own wilderness, with his own gun; in effect, with his own destiny. He remembered yesterday's trail very well; and he toiled while the light grew; yet, there being no sun, everything had a new look, though he had seen it before. He came after a long time to the pool and the waterfall, There he stopped and looked back. Now he realized how far it was; how many hours divided him from Luis, who must have been awake and wondering hours ago.

What would Luis do?

Would he kick the hard ground in fury, and halloo for him?

Or would he set out in pursuit?

But which way would Luis decide to go?

Or perhaps he was weeping at the conviction that his beautiful young brother Julio had been carried off in the night by beasts of prey.

Then the image of a devouring lion shouldering a musket was too odd, and Julio laughed; then he smartly turned to see where another's laugh came from; then he laughed again, at his echo in the rocky room with the sky roof.

The waterfall was like a wraith made of heavier air than the gray essence that filled the intimate little canyon.

"The cats will come to the ledge," thought Julio, faithful to his brother's wisdom even though he outraged it.

He went around the long way, slowly going across the roll of the rocky hillside, and found himself then in the tall forest up there. There the air hung among the trees like heavy cloths among dark dripping pillars.

He knew that a hunter must wait; so he settled himself to do so on a tilted shelf of moss, between two big boulders, lacy with fern and dark with shadow.

His stomach was clutched by doubts and partly whetted hunger, and the enchantment of folly, and the burlesque of courage.

Hardest of all was to keep the silence of the mountains, lest he startle his game.

Many times he was ready to get up, relieve the ache of his set legs, and go back to Luis, and pretend that he had only wandered a few feet away from home but had oddly managed to get lost.

But he was afraid now.

He was afriad of the way the sky looked, dark, and soft, and wind very high up which pulled the clouds past the peaks as if tearing gray cloth on the sharp edges.

He was lost, really.

The musket was a heavy sin across his lap. It was loaded. Perhaps he should unload it and scamper back.

But then if a mountain cat came to the ledge, he would be helpless.

Then he remembered for the first time that he might be in danger from the animals.

It sent blood back through him, and he grew angry at such menace. "If they think they can hurt me, they are crazy, those wildcats!"

So he spent the early day and noon in thoughts of himself and his furies, while the peace of the forest was held, and the sky now came down in darkness and again blew upward in windy lets of silvery light.

And he stayed, watching.

He was so alone and silent that the first touch on his cheek out of the air startled him, and he faced his head quickly to look: but what had touched his cheek was the snow, shortly after noon.

It came down, dandled by the odd currents of airy wind in the irregular mountains, like white dust sifting through the ancient stand of trees up the mountainside.

Julio blinked at the spotty snow falling before his eyes, and he licked the delicious flakes that starred his lips.

The rocks were beginning to look white.

The distance was reduced. When he tried to peer as far as he would, his sight seemed to go so far and then turn back.

All suddenly, a most childish wave of lonesomeness broke over him, and he knew how far away he was, and how solitary; how subject to the mountains and to his own mortality, which was so dear to him now.

He got up.

Something else moved too, in the whitening world.

He saw it, obscurely dark against the white stone shelf below him in line of sight. It was a mountain lion coming down the ledge with beautiful stillness and almost the touch of snow in its own paws.

Its heart-shaped nose was along the ground, smelling the fresh snow and whatever it covered.

Julio lifted the gun, which was as light as he wanted it in this moment, and watched, and licked the snow off his upper lip. Then with his eyes wide open and his cheeks blown up, he fired.

He couldn't hear the lion cry, or the echo of the amazing blast through the canyons and the aisles. He was deaf from it. But he sat down behind his rock and watched while he reloaded, and saw the cat spilling its blood on the snow; and then gradually he could hear it moaning as his head cleared; and it cried and sounded like a huge kitten, which made his eyes water. Then it suddenly died. The snow continued on it passively, cooling the blood, and making it pale, and finally thickening over it entirely.

After a long time Julio came down from his rock and touched his game. He glanced around to see if any more cats happened to be there. There were none. He was exalted and indifferent. He rolled the heavy lion off the ledge down to the sloping hillside below it. There the snow was thinner. There he set to work to skin the cat, as he had watched his father skin animals at home, for fur, for rawhide.

His knife was so wet and cold that it tried to stick to his hands.

He was late in finishing.

He felt proud.

Maybe Luis would be annoyed, but not for long. To bring home the first fur? He had a loving warm tender heart for all animals, now that he had conquered one of the greatest. He felt that animals must love men in return, and serve them humbly.

Done, then, he returned to thoughts of others, and then he could have groaned aloud when he really imagined what Luis might feel.

Now with the heavying snow and the night beginning to fall in the middle of the afternoon, Julio stared and said:

"Do you suppose my brother is in danger because I took away his gun? What if he has been attacked? What if I had not had the gun when the lion came? It would be the same with him, without any protection!—Oh, my Jesus and my God, help me to get back in a hurry, and have him safe when I get there!"

Now the hunter could not scramble fast enough to undo what his day had done.

He shouldered his new skin which was freezing and heavy, and his gun and his supplies, and went down off the rocky hill. In the bottom of the chasm where the waterfall entered the stream, it was dark. The black water of the creek alone was clearly visible. The snow lay against him in the air when he went.

He stopped and called out, then turned to listen; but the spiraling flaky darkness was vastly quiet.

He hurried on and sobbed a few times but he said to himself that it was simply that he was cold; not that he was sorely afraid and sorry.

"Certainly I can see!"

But he paid for this lie when he struck a rock that cut his cheek and threw him down to the ground, where the soft copious snowfall went on secretly to change the mountains, to enrich stony hollows with soft concavities, to stand the bare ridges barer above snowy articulations.

He struggled to make a small fire, scratching twigs and needles and branches from the lee side of rocks, having to feel for his wants. At last he produced a flame, and his heart leaped up farther than it had fallen. The firelight on the snow was so lovely, so like a blessing, that he felt like a young child, yet not afraid any more. In the light he saw where he was and collected more branches, building craftily, to bring up his flames, until the canyon was roaring with light and heat at that spot.

He sat, then lay on his new fur, with the raw side down.

The snowflakes made a tiny, fascinating little hiss of death when they fell into the fire.

"Luis will be all right. I will get to him early in the morning, as soon as it is light, I shall start out."

He dozed and awoke; at last to see his fire gone. Then he knew he must stay awake.

What he knew next was so strange that he felt humble. In spite of trying not to, he had fallen asleep, and was then awakened afterward by wave after wave of sound, through the falling, falling snow which hushed everything but this clamor that had awakened him, the ringing of a bell. The bell clanged and stammered and changed with the wind; like the bell of the church at home, miles up the valley on a still hot summer Sunday morning, speaking to him, and everyone faithful within its sound.

"But this is not—there can be no church in these mountains!" he said in the blackest density of the snowfall that night.

And he listened again, but now heard nothing, nothing beyond the faint sense of hushing in the air made by the falling snow.

The bell was gone; it had served to awaken him; somewhere beyond this cold separating fall, it had rung out for him; true, even if it came to him as a dream of security and the dear refuges of the suffering.

He did not lie down again; but sat; marveling; sick for home and fervid with secret vows and wonder at the obstinacy of the world.

The snow continued with daybreak.

He set out again as soon as he could see a few feet in front of him. As the light grew, so did his sense of folly.

It was as if he had dreamed of the things that might happen to his brother Luis.

All this greatness of accomplishment disappeared. What good was this smelling and frozen catskin now? He threw it down by an icy rock and found that he could now run, trotting, without the awkward burden of the cat hide, which was stiff and slippery with its frozen leggings of fur which stuck out, ragged and indignant, the congealed ghost of the cat.

The snow died away as Julio hurried.

The wind became capricious and bitter. It scratched in long sweeps down the canyon and bore out over the open plains, which Julio could begin to see as the day grew and he toiled farther down the shadowy chasm.

He kept staring ahead for sight of the spare pines which stood by their camp.

He remembered seeing the pines against open sky the first night there, which meant that they were nearly out of the mountain's fold.

He thought he saw the sentinel trees once; broke into a hard run; and then stopped panting when he saw that the gray light on a wall of rock had looked for a moment like a misty sky out there over the plain.

His heart came into his mouth; and he trudged on, confused by the fashion in which a child's devices ended in nothing.

The musket was heavy and cold in his grasp. He had it still loaded. Perhaps he ought to shoot it off, a signal for his brother?

But he would call first.

He cried out, and stood to listen, his whole body turned sideways to hear an answer.

There was none.

The sound of his own voice seemed mournful.

Now he knew that the bell he had heard last night, waking him up during the snowstorm, was a miracle, sent to keep him from freezing to death in his sleep.

So he began to run again, and his heart nearly burst, he thought, with burdens of hope.

Perhaps there would be another miracle, to keep Luis safe and bring Julio back to him right away.

Julio crawled over the rocks that seemed cold enough to crack in the weather; he waded where he had to in the glazed creek; suddenly it was lighter, the sky lay before him as well as above him; and at last he looked down on the miniature meadow of the canyon mouth where the horses were fenced. There! Yes, there were the guardian pine trees.

"Luis, Luis, I am back!" he cried, but he choked and made only a sobbing sound. There was no fire burning at the camp; and Julio was thumped in the breast by fear again, as if Luis had gone back home with the two horses and left him as he deserved to be left, alone in the mountains where he had been such a fool.

He hurried and then saw the horses, far down the way.

Then he heard a voice, talking to him from a distance; no words; level, careful sounds; it sounded like Luis.

"Luis, where are you!"

Julio came down farther.

He squinted around, and then upward.

"I am glad to see you back. Stop where you are!"

"Luis!"

"Be careful."

At the same moment Julio heard how Luis spoke from the tree where he was hanging, and he saw, at the base of the tree, the wolf which sat staring upward perfectly quiet and ready.

The wolf was huge and looked like a dog, except that he was gray, the color of rock, which was why Julio didn't see him for the first little while.

The wolf must have heard him, for his ears were standing up and the fur on his spine was silvery and alive. Julio stood shocking-still and was perfectly sure that the wolf's eyes were straining toward him as far as they could without the turn of the head, and that the animal was ready to turn and attack him if necessary.

So there was a grotesque interval of calm and silence in the canyon.

Luis was hanging to the pine tree, which had a few tough fragments of branch about sixteen feet above the ground.

The sun tried to shine through the bitter and cloudy day.

Luis looked white and sick, half-frozen; his eyes were burning black in new hollow shadows.

"Julio," said Luis, as lightly as possible, never taking his eyes off the wolf; indeed, as if he were addressing the wolf.

"Yes, Luis," whispered Julio.

"You have the gun there with you, haven't you?" asked the older brother, in an ingratiating and mollifying tone, to keep the wolf below him still intent upon his first design.

"Yes, Luis."

"Well, Julio," said his brother with desperate charm, velvet-voiced and easy, "see if you can load it without making much disturbance, will you?"

"It is loaded, Luis."

"Oh, that is fine. Then, Julio, pray Jesus you can manage to shoot the wolf. Julio, be easy and steady now . . . don't.move.fast.or.make.any. noise. Julio, for.the.love.of.God . . ."

It was like coming back to the reward of his folly to Julio.

He held his breath, to be quiet.

He thought Luis was going to fall from the tree: his face was so white and starving; his hands so bony and desperate where they clutched.

"Why, of course I can shoot the terrible wolf," said Julio to himself, slowly, slowly bringing the musket around to the aim.

Luis from his tree against the gray pale sky went on talking in tones of enchantment and courtesy to the wolf, to keep alive the concentration, until Julio fancied the wolf might answer, as animals did in the tale of early childhood, "A Dialogue between Saint Philip and the Wicked Fox."

"We shall see, my friend Wolf, just sit there.one.more.minute.if you please until.my.brother gets the thing ready . . . it.is.better, Wolf, for you.to.want.to.eat.me.than.my.horses . . . Are.you.ready.Julio . . ."

The answer was the shot.

The wolf lashed his hindquarters around so that he faced Julio, whence the sound had come.

He roared and spat; but he could not move. His back was broken. He sat and barked and snapped his teeth.

Julio ran a little way forward, then was cautious. He stopped and began to reload.

Luis fell to the ground.

He had his knife ready.

But he could not move as quickly as he would. He was cold and stiff and cramped. He hacked his knife into the animal's breast, but the stab was shy and glancing. The wolf made a crying effort and scrabbled its shattered body forward and took Luis by the leg.

"Now Julio! Your knife!"

Julio dropped the musket and came down to them.

"Where? Luis!"

"Under his left forearm!"

"Wolf!" said Julio, and drove his knife.

It was all.

For a moment they all stayed where they were; panting, the brothers; the animal, dead, and slowly relaxing thus.

The flavor of danger was common to all three while it lasted undecided.

Now there was victory; and the brothers sweated and couldn't speak, but hung their heads and spat dry spit and coughed and panted.

"Well," said Luis, at last.

"Did he bite you bad?" asked Julio.

"No, he couldn't bite very hard, not even like a dog; he was too hurt."

"Let me see."

They peeled the cloth away from the leg just above the knee. The teeth had torn the cloth and the flesh. It did not hurt. It was numb. It bled very little. The skin was blue.

There was nothing to do to the leg except cover it again, they thought.

They took as long as possible at it, but they had presently to come to the story of the young brother's folly; and as soon as that was done, they felt elated: the one penitent and grave; the other pardoning and aware that the terrors of the experience were more useful to his young brother than any words of rebuke.

"—And I know right where I left the lion skin; we'll get it later!—We can get many more!"

Julio was ballooning with relief, now that it was all over and done with. He felt as he always felt after confession in church, airy and tall.

The physical misery in snow and wind and rocky mountain temper—this was their outer penalty. But the boys knew an inner joy at the further range of their doing. Simply being where they were, at odds with what menaced them—this was achievement; it was man's doing done, confirming the love for their family and bringing animal craft to protect it.

Late that day the sun did break through and a little while of golden light seemed to relieve the cold. It didn't snow again that night. They kept their fire high. Luis was oddly too lame to walk. But he was glad to lie and watch the flames; and to smile at Julio's serious bearing, full of thoughtful play in his face which meant plans and intentions.

The day after the snowstorm the valley itself came back in a kind of golden resurge of autumn. The house at the little farm was soaked with melting snow; running lines of dark muddy thaw streaked from the round-worn edges of the roof to the walls and the ground.

The temper of the river was warmer than the mountain weather. The willows and cottonwoods lost their snow by noon. The mountains were visible again, after the day of the blind white blowing curtain over the plain.

Not many travelers were abroad; but Father Antonio came down the road shortly after noon, and Josefina saw him, his fat white mare, his robe tucked above his waist, his wool-colored homespun trousers, and his Mexican boots. She went to tell Rosa that the priest was coming at last, and to stop crying, if that was all she was crying for.

The priest dismounted in the yard and let his horse move.

Josefina tidied herself in honor of the visit; and he came in, catching her at wetting her eyebrows. She immediately felt like a fool, from the way he looked at her; and she bowed for his blessing, furious at his kind of power over and against women.

"I didn't get your message about the baby until two days ago, and then I said nothing could keep me from coming as soon as I could. Isn't it fine! Where is he? Or is it a girl?—I hope you have a girl, already those bad boys of yours, where are they?"

Rosa felt as if authority had walked into her house and that she need have no further vague wonders and fears about surviving this life on behalf of her baby and her boys.

Father Antonio was a tall, very spare, bony man nearly fifty, with straw-colored hair, a pale wind-pinked face, and little blue eyes that shone speculatively as he gazed. He was awkward; he couldn't talk without slowly waving his great-knuckled hands in illustration of his mood; and he loved to talk, putting into words the great interest of his days. Everything suggested something else to him; he debated with himself as if he were two Jesuits, they said in Santa Fe, where he was not popular with the clergy because he preferred working in the open land among the scattered families of the river basin.

"Where are the boys?" he asked.

Rosa was at peace. Her cheeks dried and her heart seemed to grow strong. She felt a surge of calm strong breath in her breast. She was proud.

"They have gone hunting, they have been gone several days now. In the mountains."

Josefina lingered on the outside of a kind of sanctuary which the priest and the mother made, a spiritual confine which she could not enter, a profane and resentful woman. But she could toss her opinions into it.

"They are little fools, a pair of chicken-boned infants, crazy, going to the mountains. It snowed there for two days. They will never come back."

Rosa watched the priest's face, ready to be frightened or not, by his expression.

He glanced at Josefina, a mild blue fire.

"They are probably all right."

Josefina mumbled.

"How will a man ever know what goes on," asked Father Antonio, "unless he goes out and looks at it?"

"How long can you stay, Father?" asked Rosa.

"Till we christen the baby."

"But—"

"I'll wait till the brothers come back, so the baby will have a godfather."

"I—godmother," simpered Josefina on her outskirts, making a fat and radiant gesture of coquetry.

"Why not?" said the priest mildly, taking the sting out of her scandalous contempt.

It sobered her. She blushed.

"When your husband comes back in the spring with the wagon train," said Father Antonio, "you can send some money to my church."

"Gladly," said Rosa.

"Those must be big boys by now; I haven't seen them for months. Luis? Julio? That's right.—When I was a boy I had all the desires to go and look at what was over the mountains. Then when I was away, there, in Mexico, at the seminary, the world of this side of the mountains was just as inviting and mysterious. Eh? When I came back to go to work, everybody bowed to me and behaved properly as to a priest. But I always felt a little guilty for that, and went fishing or hunting. The animals had no respect for me, which was a relief, for they knew not of God, whose weight is something to carry, I can tell you!"

This was strange talk to the women.

"Next to catching a sinner and taking away his sin, I like best to fetch a trout, or play a long game of war with a beaver in the river pools.—So now I know why your two big brown babies went off to the mountains."

"Oh," thought the women. "That explains it."

Father Antonio stayed more than a week. The boys were missing. The priest would go and look at the mountains in all times of day, to see if he could see anything, even in his mind, which might be played with as news for the distracted mother.

But all he saw were the momentous faces of the mountains: light or the absence of light; at dawn, a chalky black atmosphere quivering with quiet air; at noon, silvered by the sun, the great rock wrinkles shining and constant; at evening, the glow of rose, as if there were furnaces within the tumbled stone which heated the surface, until it came to glow for a few moments and then, cooling to ashy black from the base upward, joined the darkening sky like a low heavy cloud.

"I have promised to stay for them, and I will," said the priest.

He spent the days making Rosa agree to get strong, until she finally arose from her bed and ordered her house again. He did the tasks of the outdoors. There was no need for Josefina to stay now; but stay she did, touched in her vanity by the godmotherhood which had been mentioned once.

She came in one day, still holding her arm over her eyes, as if staring into the distance, the golden chill of the open winter.

"I think I see them coming!" she cried.

They all went outdoors.

"You are crazy," said the priest.

They looked and looked.

The plain and the slow rise into the mountain lift was swimming with sunlight. They searched with long looks until they had to blink for vision.

"See! Like a couple of sheep, just barely moving," insisted Josefina, pointing vaguely at the mountains.

"Where!"

"Yes. I do see! She is right!—She must have Indian blood."

The mother was the last to see and agree.

There was an infinitesimal movement far on the plain, hardly perceptible as movement; some energy of presence, a dot of light and cast of shadow, just alive enough to be convincing. It was the hunters, coming on their horses on the second day's journey out of the mountains.

Late in the afternoon they arrived.

The marks of their toil were all over them.

To go and come back! This being the common mystery of all journeying, the mother could hardly wait for them to speak, to tell her everything.

She brought the baby, and the boys kissed her tiny furred head.

The priest gave them his blessing, and they bent their shaggy necks under it.

Josefina stared and then squinted at them, whispering something.

"Luis, you are hurt!"

"—Not any more."

"But you *were!*"

"I will tell you sometime."

"Now, now!"

"How long have we been away?"

"Ten days!"

The boys talked, confirming each other with looks.

Luis and the wolf; the bite; the fever; the body as the residence of the devil, and the raving nights. Julio and his amazing skill as a marksman; his reckless courage; the two of them together, after Luis's recovery, shagging up and down rocky barriers, mountain sprites, and their bag of skins.

"Look at that!"

They got and opened out their two packs of furs; and there were cats, the wolf, a little deer, and a middle-sized brown bear.

"Who got the bear!"

"*Luis,* it was wonderful; the bear was in a tree, watching us, and what made him, nobody knows, but Luis looked up, and whang! and boo! down fell the bear, and all it took was the one shot!"

"—But you should have seen Julio the time he saved my life, when the wolf was waiting for me to fall down; I was so cold and weak! Up in my tree!"

The silence was full of worried love: what had they not done!—But safe.—Yes, but what if!

The brothers looked at each other.

Nothing would ever be said about the other thing. Nobody ever managed to grow up without being foolish at some time or other.

"The nights were hardest, it was so cold!"

"We kept a fire going; we had to wake up every so often to fix it."

"The horses had a fight one day when we were gone hunting; they killed a small mountain cat that came down."

There were marvels to rehearse for many a time to come.

The priest thought,

"The boy Julio looks taller; I suppose it is only natural. Last time I was here he was . . ."

Luis took the baby sister to hold.

There was plenty of fur to keep her warm.

Julio sighed. It was a curiously contented and old man's comment.

Father Antonio felt like laughing; and he would have, but there was some nobility of bearing in Julio's little mighty shoulders that didn't deserve patronizing.

The priest glanced at Josefina.

He knew his materials like a craftsman.

He thought,

"Josefina sees—she even smells as a female—what has taken place in Julio. She stares at him and then squints and whispers to herself. It isn't *hers*, except in mind, and stir of flesh.—How little is secret! How much makes a life!"

The mother's arms were free of her infant. She went and hugged Julio, because, though she hardly thought it so clearly, she knew that he had gone and conquered the wilderness which was his brother's by birth. She knew that—and what lay behind it—as only a child's mother could know it; with defensive and pitying and pardoning love, so long as it might be needed.

"I wish I could write, now," said Luis.

"Why?"

"Then I would write to my father about it."

"But he could not read it."

"No, but he could get somebody to read it to him."

"Should I write and tell him about it for you?" asked Father Antonio.

"Oh, if you would, Father!"

"I'll be glad to. The minute I get back to my house where I have pens and paper. You have told me the whole adventure."

But when the priest did return home, and sit down, to keep his promise to the delighted brothers, what they had told him seemed to him man's story, and all he finally wrote was:

Dear Garcia,

Your wife has had a dear baby girl; and both are well and happy, with God's grace. Your two sons are proud of their family; and when you return, before hearing from their lips anything of their adventures during your absence, you will see that they are already proper men, for which God be praised in the perfection of His design for our mortal life.

THE BENCH

by Richard Rive

"We form an integral part of a complex society, a society in which a vast proportion of the population is denied the very basic right of ex-

---

From *An African Treasury*, edited by Langston Hughes (New York: Crown Publishers, Inc., 1960), pp. 128–33.

istence, a society that condemns a man to an inferior position because he has the misfortune to be born black, a society that can only retain its precarious social and economic position at the expense of an enormous oppressed mass!"

The speaker paused for a moment and sipped some water from a glass. Karlie's eyes shone as he listened. Those were great words, he thought, great words and true. Karlie sweated. The hot November sun beat down on the gathering. The trees on the Grand Parade in Johannesburg afforded very little shelter and his handkerchief was already soaked where he had placed it between his neck and his shirt collar. Karlie stared around him at the sea of faces. Every shade of color was represented, from shiny ebony to the one or two whites in the crowd. Karlie stared at the two detectives who were busily making shorthand notes of the speeches, then turned to stare back at the speaker.

"It is up to us to challenge the right of any group who willfully and deliberately condemn a fellow group to a servile position. We must challenge the right of any people who see fit to segregate human beings solely on grounds of pigmentation. Your children are denied the rights which are theirs by birth. They are segregated educationally, socially, economically. . . ."

Ah, thought Karlie, that man knows what he is speaking about. He says I am as good as any other man, even a white man. That needs much thinking. I wonder if he means I have the right to go to any bioscope, or eat in any restaurant, or that my children can go to a white school. These are dangerous ideas and need much thinking. I wonder what Ou Klaas would say to this. Ou Klaas said that God made the white man and the black man separately, and the one must always be "baas" and the other "jong." But this man says different things and somehow they ring true.

Karlie's brow was knitted as he thought. On the platform were many speakers, both white and black, and they were behaving as if there were no differences of color among them. There was a white woman in a blue dress offering Nxeli a cigarette. That never could have happened at Bietjiesvlei. Old Lategan at the store there would have fainted if his Annatjie had offered Witbooi a cigarette. And Annatjie wore no such pretty dress.

These were new things and he, Karlie, had to be careful before he accepted them. But why shouldn't he accept them? He was not a colored man any more, he was a human being. The last speaker had said so. He remembered seeing pictures in the newspapers of people who defied laws which relegated them to a particular class, and those people were smiling as they went to prison. This was a queer world.

The speaker continued and Karlie listened intently. He spoke slowly, and his speech was obviously carefully prepared. This is a great man, thought Karlie.

The last speaker was the white lady in the blue dress, who asked them to challenge any discriminatory laws or measures in their own way. Why should she speak like that? She could go to the best bioscopes and swim at the best beaches. Why she was even more beautiful than Annatjie Lategan. They had warned him in Bietjiesvlei about coming to the city. He had seen the skollies in District Six and he knew what to expect there.

Hanover Street held no terrors for him. But no one had told him about this. This was new, this set one's mind thinking, yet he felt it was true. She had said one should challenge. He, Karlie, would astound old Lategan and Van Wyk at the Dairy Farm. They could do what they liked to him after that. He would smile like those people in the newspapers.

The meeting was almost over when Karlie threaded his way through the crowd. The words of the speakers were still milling through his head. It could never happen in Bietjiesvlei. Or could it? The sudden screech of a car pulling to a stop whirled him back to his senses. A white head was thrust angrily through the window.

"Look where you're going, you black bastard!"

Karlie stared dazedly at him. Surely this white man never heard what the speakers had said. He could never have seen the white woman offering Nxeli a cigarette. He could never imagine the white lady shouting those words at him. It would be best to catch a train and think these things over.

He saw the station in a new light. Here was a mass of human beings, black, white and some brown like himself. Here they mixed with one another, yet each mistrusted the other with an unnatural fear, each treated the other with suspicion, moved in a narrow, haunted pattern of its own. One must challenge these things the speaker had said . . . in one's own way. Yet how in one's own way? How was one to challenge? Suddenly it dawned upon him. Here was his challenge! *The bench.* The railway bench with "Europeans Only" neatly painted on it in white. For one moment it symbolized all the misery of the plural South African society.

Here was his challenge to the rights of a man. Here it stood. A perfectly ordinary wooden railway bench, like hundreds of thousands of others in South Africa. His challenge. That bench now had concentrated in it all the evils of a system he could not understand and he felt a victim of. It was the obstacle between himself and humanity. If he sat on it, he was a man. If he was afraid he denied himself membership as a human being in a human society. He almost had visions of righting this pernicious system, if he only sat down on that bench. Here was his chance. He, Karlie, would challenge.

He seemed perfectly calm when he sat down on the bench, but inside his heart was thumping wildly. Two conflicting ideas now throbbed through him. The one said, "I have no right to sit on this bench." The other was the voice of a new religion and said, "Why have I no right to sit on this bench?" The one voice spoke of the past, of the servile position he had occupied on the farm, of his father, and his father's father who were born black, lived like blacks, and died like mules. The other voice spoke of new horizons and said: "Karlie, you are a man. You have dared what your father and your father's father would not have dared. You will die like a man."

Karlie took out a cigarette and smoked. Nobody seemed to notice his sitting there. This was an anticlimax. The world still pursued its monotonous way. No voice had shouted, "Karlie has conquered!" He was a normal human being sitting on a bench in a busy station, smoking a cigarette. Or was this his victory: the fact that he was a normal human being? A well-dressed white woman walked down the platform. Would she sit on the bench? Karlie wondered. And then that gnawing voice, "You should stand and let the white woman sit!" Karlie narrowed his eyes and gripped tighter at his cigarette. She swept past him without the slightest twitch of an eyelid and continued walking down the platform. Was she afraid to challenge—to challenge his right to be a human being? Karlie now felt tired. A third conflicting idea was now creeping in, a compensatory idea which said, "You sit on this bench because you are tired; you are tired therefore you sit." He would not move because he was tired, or was it because he wanted to sit where he liked?

People were now pouring out of a train that had pulled into the station. There were so many people pushing and jostling one another that nobody noticed him. This was his train. It would be easy to step into the train and ride off home, but that would be giving in, suffering defeat, refusing the challenge, in fact admitting that he was not a human being. He sat on. Lazily he blew the cigarette smoke into the air, thinking. . . . His mind was away from the meeting and the bench: he was thinking of Bietjiesvlei and Ou Klaas, how he had insisted that Karlie should come to Cape Town. Ou Klaas would suck on his pipe and look so quizzically at one. He was wise and knew much. He had said one must go to Cape Town and learn the ways of the world. He would spit and wink slyly when he spoke of District Six and the women he knew in Hanover Street. Ou Klaas knew everything. He said God made us white or black and we must therefore keep our places.

"Get off this seat!"

Karlie did not here the gruff voice. Ou Klaas would be on the land now waiting for his tot of cheap wine.

"I said get off the bench, you swine!!" Karlie suddenly whipped back to reality. For a moment he was going to jump up, then he remembered who he was and why he was sitting there. He suddenly felt very tired. He looked up slowly into a very red face that stared down at him.

"Get up!" it said. "There are benches down there for you."

Karlie looked up and said nothing. He stared into a pair of sharp, gray, cold eyes.

"Can't you hear me speaking to you? You black swine!"

Slowly and deliberately Karlie puffed at the cigarette. This was his test. They both stared at each other, challenged with the eyes, like two boxers, each knowing that they must eventually trade blows yet each afraid to strike first.

"Must I dirty my hands on scum like you?"

Karlie said nothing. To speak would be to break the spell, the supremacy he felt was slowly gaining.

An uneasy silence, then: "I will call a policeman rather than soil my hands on a Hotnot like you. You can't even open up your black jaw when a white man speaks to you."

Karlie saw the weakness. The white man was afraid to take action himself. He, Karlie, had won the first round of the bench dispute.

A crowd had now collected.

"Afrika!" shouted a joker.

Karlie ignored the remark. People were now milling around him, staring at the unusual sight of a black man sitting on a white man's bench. Karlie merely puffed on.

"Look at the black ape. That's the worst of giving these Kaffirs enough rope."

"I can't understand it. They have their own benches!"

"Don't get up! You have every right to sit there!"

"He'll get up when a policeman comes!"

"After all why shouldn't they sit there?"

"I've said before, I've had a native servant once, and a more impertinent . . ."

Karlie sat and heard nothing. Irresolution had *now* turned to determination. Under no condition was he going to get up. They could do what they liked.

"So, this is the fellow, eh! Get up there! Can't you read?"

The policeman was towering over him. Karlie could see the crest on his buttons and the wrinkles in his neck.

"What is your name and address! Come on!"

Karlie still maintained his obstinate silence. It took the policeman rather unawares. The crowd was growing every minute.

"You have no right to speak to this man in such a manner!" It was the white lady in the blue dress.

"Mind your own business! I'll ask your help when I need it. It's people like you who make these Kaffirs think they're as good as white men. Get up, you!" The latter remark was addressed to Karlie.

"I insist that you treat him with proper respect."

The policeman turned red.

"This . . . this . . ." He was lost for words.

"Kick up the Hotnot if he won't get up!" shouted a spectator. Rudely a white man laid hands on Karlie.

"Get up, you bloody bastard!" Karlie turned to resist, to cling to the bench, his bench. There was more than one man pulling at him. He hit out wildly and then felt a dull pain as somebody rammed a fist into his face. He was bleeding now and wild-eyed. He would fight for it. The constable clapped a pair of handcuffs on him and tried to clear a way through the crowd. Karlie still struggled. A blow or two landed on him. Suddenly he relaxed and slowly struggled to his feet. It was useless to fight any longer. Now it was his turn to smile. He had challenged and won. Who cared the rest?

"Come on, you swine!" said the policeman forcing Karlie through the crowd.

"Certainly!" said Karlie for the first time. And he stared at the policeman with all the arrogance of one who dared sit on a "European bench."

The Return to the Womb

LATE in his career, Freud theorized that two basic drives were involved in human behavior: the instinct toward life, which he called Eros, and the instinct toward death, which his followers have termed Thanatos. The former aims at creation through union; the latter at destruction through the reduction of organisms to an inanimate state. "If we suppose that living things appeared later than inanimate ones and arose out of them," he wrote, "then the death instinct agrees with the formula that we have stated, to the effect that instincts tend toward an earlier state of things." [1]

From this point of view, all human behavior may be regarded as a struggle between these two basic instincts, which express themselves as love and hate. The relationship between these two instincts is immensely complicated: an interaction rather than a simple struggle is involved, for they may either come into conflict, which is normal, or they may unexpectedly combine, so that we have behavior which is sadomasochistic. It is interesting to consider Tennessee Williams' powerful story, "Desire and the Black Masseur," in the light of the following observation by Freud:

> In biological functions the two basic instincts (love and death) work against each other or combine with each other. Thus, the act of eating is a destruction of the object with the final aim of incorporating it, and the sexual act is an act of aggression having as its purpose the most intimate union.[2]

---

[1] Sigmund Freud, "Libido and the Death Instinct," cited by Richard Ellmann and Charles Feidelson, Jr. (eds.), *The Modern Tradition: Backgrounds of Modern Literature* (New York: Oxford University Press, 1965), p. 565. Though this assumption accounts for the existence of Thanatos, it poses a problem where Eros is concerned, since the desire for union suggests that union was present originally. Freud (who was intrigued by Plato's idea that man was originally androgynous, and that the lover seeks union with his other half, from which Zeus, in anger, had separated him), finally became convinced that this was the case, though as a rationalist he was obliged to admit that it belonged to the realm of parapsychology.

[2] *Ibid.*, p. 564.

Freud saw an analogy between the interaction of these two basic drives in human life and the physical forces of attraction and repulsion in the inorganic world. Moreover, he theorized that the destructive instinct was capable of manifesting itself either outwardly, in the form of aggressive behavior, or inwardly, in the form of suicidal tendencies. In the latter case, the individual may or may not be aware of their existence: where such tendencies are partially neutralized by the life-instinct, the result may be what Menninger terms "chronic" or "slow" suicide, which reveals itself in such conditions as alcoholism, neurotic invalidism, and asceticism ("the very refinement of slow death" according to Menninger). An excessive proneness to accident or the so-called "will to fail," wherein the individual tends to make a career of failure, may also reveal the presence of a powerful death instinct. Perhaps the most fatal form is the progressive inability to take any interest or pleasure in life, often without any specific or obvious reason, indicating the complete victory of Thanatos over Eros. Mallea's protagonist, in "The Lost Cause of Jacob Uber," is unable to analyze his depression, but he feels, and feels rightly, that it is somehow connected with his inability to love.

It is this latter phenomenon, a kind of malaise or *tedium vitae* for which there may be no immediate or particular source, that the phrase "Return to the Womb" connotes and that appears with sufficient frequency in literature to justify our consideration of it as an archetype. The category thus excludes those kinds of suicide where a specific motive other than a strong death wish is apparent: for example, if a patient with terminal cancer decides to take what is left of his life, or a *kamikaze* pilot deliberately destroys himself and his plane to inflict massive injury upon the enemy, or an individual makes of himself a human torch to protest a political action, the archetype does not apply. It refers rather to the situation where an individual, feeling himself inadequate to the life-challenge, longs either consciously or unconsciously, and as it were atavistically, for a state of peace and security resembling that of the foetal condition, where he enjoyed the protection of the maternal womb and had no obligations or fears. The situation may or may not end fatally: the dramatic possibilities are naturally greater when it does, but this is by no means a requirement.

The womb metaphor is peculiarly appropriate to this regressive pattern of behavior. As Frederick J. Hoffmann comments:

> Within the limits of physical generation, the womb is the great and only area in which life is cherished and supported during its period of prenatal helplessness. It is perhaps natural to think of it as a source of renewal when the initial helplessness is duplicated in later social or psychic distress.[3]

To the victim of such distress darkness and liquid, two qualities of the womb, assume extraordinary value: it is no accident that Anthony

---

[3] Frederick J. Hoffman, *Freudianism and the Literary Mind,* 2nd ed. (Baton Rouge: Louisiana State University Press, 1957), p. 288.

Burns, in "Desire and the Black Masseur," instinctively seeks dimness and darkness (he particularly enjoys being "swallowed up" in the darkness of a movie-house), nor that the victims in both "The River" and "The Lost Cause of Jacob Uber" seek in water the remedy for their respective miseries. Water, which Jung has called the commonest symbol for the unconscious, is a traditional literary symbol for death and also, paradoxically, for life—indeed for the whole birth-death-resurrection cycle.

This archetype tends to occur less frequently in primitive cultures than in those more advanced and specialized, and its presence in the latter has tended historically to coincide with the development of secularism: the climate of Existentialism has been peculiarly favorable to it, as is evidenced by the kind of collective "nausea" of which Sartre wrote in his famous novel of the same name. But Renaissance examples are not lacking, and Hamlet's soliloquies sometimes involve a dialogue between Eros and Thanatos. When he cries, "O God, O God!/ How weary, flat, stale, and unprofitable/ Seem to me all the uses of this world!" he is expressing the very quintessence of the death instinct. Goethe explores the theme in *The Sorrows of Werther,* and Stendhal's Julien Sorel, in *The Red and the Black,* is yet another eighteenth-century example. The type is clearly portrayed by Dickens, Hawthorne, and Melville in the characters of Smike (*Nicholas Nickleby*), Ilbrahim ("The Gentle Boy"), and Bartleby ("Bartleby the Scrivener") respectively. Bartleby actually assumes the foetal position in his final sleep. Among the many twentieth-century European writers who have dramatized the death instinct we might mention Chekhov (*Three Sisters, The Sea-Gull,* and *Uncle Vanya*), Kafka ("The Burrow," and "Metamorphosis"), Mann ("Tristan," "Death in Venice," *Buddenbrooks,* and *The Magic Mountain*), and Joyce ("The Dead"). Kafka's "A Hunger Artist," appearing in the Search section, combines the Search for Perfection archetype with the Return to the Womb, to which it is obviously related. In poetry, the Return to the Womb was an obsessive theme with Dylan Thomas, who in his own career acted out his instinct for self-destruction until he achieved it. On this side of the Atlantic, Quentin, in Faulkner's *The Sound and the Fury;* Harry, in Hemingway's "The Snows of Kilimanjaro"; Captain Penderton, in McCullers' *Reflections in a Golden Eye;* Paul, in Cather's "Paul's Case"; and the other Paul in Conrad Aiken's "Silent Snow, Secret Snow"; and Brick in Tennessee Williams' "Three Players of a Summer Game" are all characters who have been dominated by the death wish. Williams has also explored this theme in some of his plays, perhaps most notably in *Cat on a Hot Tin Roof.*

VOLODYA
by Anton Chekhov

At five o'clock one Sunday afternoon in summer, Volodya, a plain, shy, sickly-looking lad of seventeen, was sitting in the arbor of the Shumihins' country villa, feeling dreary. His despondent thoughts flowed in three directions. In the first place, he had next day, Monday, an examination in mathematics; he knew that if he did not get through the written examination on the morrow, he would be expelled, for he had already been two years in the sixth form and had two and three-quarter marks for algebra in his annual report. In the second place, his presence at the villa of the Shumihins, a wealthy family with aristocratic pretensions, was a continual source of mortification to his *amour-propre*. It seemed to him that Madame Shumihin looked upon him and his *maman* as poor relations and dependents, that they laughed at his *maman* and did not respect her. He had on one occasion accidentally overheard Madame Shumihin, in the veranda, telling her cousin Anna Fyodorovna that his *maman* still tried to look young and got herself up, that she never paid her losses at cards, and had a partiality for other people's shoes and tobacco. Every day Volodya besought his *maman* not to go to the Shumihins', and drew a picture of the humiliating part she played with these gentlefolk. He tried to persuade her, said rude things, but she—a frivolous, pampered woman, who had run through two fortunes, her own and her husband's, in her time, and always gravitated towards acquaintances of high rank—did not understand him, and twice a week Volodya had to accompany her to the villa he hated.

In the third place, the youth could not for one instant get rid of a strange, unpleasant feeling which was absolutely new to him. . . . It seemed to him that he was in love with Anna Fyodorovna, the Shumihins' cousin, who was staying with them. She was a vivacious, loud-voiced, laughter-loving, healthy, and vigorous lady of thirty, with rosy cheeks, plump shoulders, a plump round chin and a continual smile on her thin lips. She was neither young nor beautiful—Volodya knew that perfectly well; but for some reason he could not help thinking of her, looking at her while she shrugged her plump shoulders and moved her flat back as she played croquet, or after prolonged laughter and running up and down stairs, sank into a low chair, and, half closing her eyes and gasping for

---

From *A Treasury of Great Russian Short Stories,* edited by Avrahm Yarmolinsky, translated by Constance Garnett (New York: Macmillan 1966), pp. 635–47. Also from *The Lady with the Dog* (London: Chatto & Windus).

breath, pretended that she was stifling and could not breathe. She was married. Her husband, a staid and dignified architect, came once a week to the villa, slept soundly, and returned to town. Volodya's strange feeling had begun with his conceiving an unaccountable hatred for the architect, and feeling relieved every time he went back to town.

Now, sitting in the arbor, thinking of his examination next day, and of his *maman,* at whom they laughed, he felt an intense desire to see Nyuta (that was what the Shumihins called Anna Fyodorovna), to hear her laughter and the rustle of her dress. . . . This desire was not like the pure, poetic love of which he read in novels and about which he dreamed every night when he went to bed; it was strange, incomprehensible; he was ashamed of it, and afraid of it as of something very wrong and impure, something which it was disagreeable to confess even to himself.

"It's not love," he said to himself. "One can't fall in love with women of thirty who are married. It is only a little intrigue. . . . Yes, an intrigue. . . ."

Pondering on the "intrigue," he thought of his uncontrollable shyness, his lack of mustache, his freckles, his narrow eyes, and put himself in his imagination side by side with Nyuta, and the juxtaposition seemed to him impossible; then he made haste to imagine himself bold, handsome, witty, dressed in the latest fashion.

When his dreams were at their height, as he sat huddled together and looking at the ground in a dark corner of the arbor, he heard the sound of light footsteps. Someone was coming slowly along the avenue. Soon the steps stopped and something white gleamed in the entrance.

"Is there anyone here?" asked a woman's voice.

Volodya recognized the voice, and raised his head in a fright.

"Who is here?" asked Nyuta, going into the arbor. "Ah, it is you, Volodya? What are you doing here? Thinking? And how can you go on thinking, thinking, thinking? . . . That's the way to go out of your mind!"

Volodya got up and looked in a dazed way at Nyuta. She had only just come back from bathing. Over her shoulder there was hanging a sheet and a rough towel, and from under the white silk kerchief on her head he could see the wet hair sticking to her forehead. There was the cool damp smell of the bathhouse and of almond soap still hanging about her. She was out of breath from running quickly. The top botton of her blouse was undone, so that the boy saw her throat and bosom.

"Why don't you say something?" said Nyuta, looking Volodya up and down. "It's not polite to be silent when a lady talks to you. What a clumsy seal you are though, Volodya! You always sit, saying nothing, thinking like some philosopher. There's not a spark of life or fire in you! You are really horrid! . . . At your age you ought to be living, skipping, and jumping, chattering, flirting, falling in love."

Volodya looked at the sheet that was held by a plump white hand, and thought. . . .

"He's mute," said Nyuta, with wonder; "it is strange, really. . . . Listen! Be a man! Come, you might smile at least! Phew, the horrid philosopher!" she laughed. "But do you know, Volodya, why you are such a clumsy seal? Because you don't devote yourself to the ladies. Why don't you? It's true there are no girls here, but there is nothing to prevent your flirting with the married ladies! Why don't you flirt with me, for instance?"

Volodya listened and scratched his forehead in acute and painful irresolution.

"It's only very proud people who are silent and love solitude," Nyuta went on, pulling his hand away from his forehead. "You are proud, Volodya. Why do you look at me like that from under your brows? Look me straight in the face, if you please! Yes, now then, clumsy seal!"

Volodya made up his mind to speak. Wanting to smile, he twitched his lower lip, blinked, and again put his hand to his forehead.

"I . . . I love you," he said.

Nyuta raised her eyebrows in surprise, and laughed.

"What do I hear?" she sang, as prima donnas sing at the opera when they hear something awful. "What? What did you say? Say it again, say it again. . . ."

"I . . . I love you!" repeated Volodya.

And without his will having any part in his action, without reflection or understanding, he took half a step towards Nyuta and clutched her by the arm. Everything was dark before his eyes, and tears came into them. The whole world was turned into one big, rough towel which smelt of the bathhouse.

"Bravo, bravo!" he heard a merry laugh. "Why don't you speak? I want you to speak! Well?"

Seeing that he was not prevented from holding her arm, Volodya glanced at Nyuta's laughing face, and clumsily, awkwardly, put both arms round her waist, his hands meeting behind her back. He held her round the waist with both arms, while, putting her hands up to her head, showing the dimples in her elbows, she set her hair straight under the kerchief and said in a calm voice:

"You must be tactful, polite, charming, and you can only become that under feminine influence. But what a wicked, angry face you have! You must talk, laugh. . . . Yes, Volodya, don't be surly; you are young and will have plenty of time for philosophizing. Come, let go of me; I am going. Let go."

Without effort she released her waist, and, humming something, walked out of the arbor. Volodya was left alone. He smoothed his hair, smiled, and walked three times to and fro across the arbor, then he sat down on the bench and smiled again. He felt insufferably ashamed, so much so that he wondered that human shame could reach such a pitch of acuteness and intensity. Shame made him smile, gesticulate, and whisper some disconnected words.

He was ashamed that he had been treated like a small boy, ashamed of his shyness, and, most of all, that he had had the audacity to put his arms round the waist of a respectable married woman, though, as it seemed to him, neither his age nor anything in his outward appearance, nor his social position gave him any right to do so.

He jumped up, went out of the arbor, and, without looking round, walked into the recesses of the garden furthest from the house.

"Ah! only to get away from here as soon as possible," he thought, clutching his head. "My God! as soon as possible."

The train by which Volodya was to go back with his *maman* was at eight-forty. There were three hours before the train started, but he would with pleasure have gone to the station at once without waiting for his *maman*.

At eight o'clock he went to the house. His whole figure was expressive of determination: what would be, would be! He made up his mind to go in boldly, to look them straight in the face, to speak in a loud voice, regardless of everything.

He crossed the terrace, the big hall and the drawing-room, and there stopped to take breath. He could hear them in the dining-room, drinking tea. Madame Shumihin, *maman*, and Nyuta were talking and laughing about something.

Volodya listened.

"I assure you!" said Nyuta. "I could not believe my eyes! When he began declaring his passion and—just imagine!—put his arms round my waist, I should not have recognized him. And you know he has a way with him! When he told me he was in love with me, there was something brutal in his face, like a Circassian."

"Really!" gasped *maman*, going off into a peal of laughter. "Really! How he does remind me of his father!"

Volodya ran back and dashed out into the open air.

"How could they talk of it aloud!" he wondered in agony, clasping his hands and looking up to the sky in horror. "They talk aloud in cold blood . . . and *maman* laughed! . . . *Maman!* My God, why didst Thou give me such a mother? Why?"

But he had to go to the house, come what might. He walked three times up and down the avenue, grew a little calmer, and went into the house.

"Why didn't you come in in time for tea?" Madame Shumihin asked sternly.

"I am sorry, it's . . . it's time for me to go," he muttered, not raising his eyes. "*Maman*, it's eight o'clock!"

"You go alone, my dear," said his *maman* languidly. "I am staying the night with Lili. Goodbye, my dear. . . . Let me make the sign of the cross over you."

She made the sign of the cross over her son, and said in French, turning to Nyuta:

"He's rather like Lermontov . . . isn't he?"

Saying goodbye after a fashion, without looking anyone in the face, Volodya went out of the dining-room. Ten minutes later he was walking along the road to the station, and was glad of it. Now he felt neither frightened nor ashamed; he breathed freely and easily.

About half a mile from the station, he sat down on a stone by the side of the road, and gazed at the sun, which was half hidden behind a barrow. There were lights already here and there at the station, and one green light glimmered dimly, but the train was not yet in sight. It was pleasant to Volodya to sit still without moving, and to watch the evening coming little by little. The darkness of the arbor, the footsteps, the smell of the bathhouse, the laughter, and the waist—all these rose with amazing vividness before his imagination, and all this was no longer so terrible and important as before.

"It's of no consequence. . . . She did not pull her hand away, and laughed when I held her by the waist," he thought. "So she must have liked it. If she had disliked it she would have been angry. . . ."

And now Volodya felt sorry that he had not had more boldness there in the arbor. He felt sorry that he was so stupidly going away, and he was by now persuaded that if the same thing happened again he would be bolder and look at it more simply.

And it would not be difficult for the opportunity to occur again. They used to stroll about for a long time after supper at the Shumihins'. If Volodya went for a walk with Nyuta in the dark garden, there would be an opportunity!

"I will go back," he thought, "and will go by the morning train tomorrow. . . . I will say I have missed the train."

And he turned back. . . . Madame Shumihin, *maman*, Nyuta, and one of the nieces were sitting on the veranda, playing vint. When Volodya told them the lie about missing the train, they were uneasy that he might be late for the examination next day, and advised him to get up early. All the while they were playing he sat on one side, greedily watching Nyuta and waiting. . . . He already had a plan prepared in his mind: he would go up to Nyuta in the dark, would take her by the hand, then would embrace her; there would be no need to say anything, as both of them would understand without words.

But after supper the ladies did not go for a walk in the garden, but went on playing cards. They played till one o'clock at night, and then broke up to go to bed.

"How stupid it all is!" Volodya thought with vexation as he got into bed. "But never mind; I'll wait till tomorrow . . . tomorrow in the arbor. It doesn't matter. . . ."

He did not attempt to go to sleep, but sat in bed, hugging his knees and thinking. All thought of the examination was hateful to him. He had already made up his mind that they would expel him, and that there was nothing terrible about his being expelled. On the contrary, it was a good thing—a very good thing, in fact. Next day he would be as free as a bird; he would put on ordinary clothes instead of his school uniform, would smoke openly, come out here, and make love to Nyuta when he liked; and he would not be a schoolboy but "a young man." And as for the rest of it, what is called a career, a future, that was clear; Volodya would go into the army or the telegraph service, or he would go into a chemist's shop and work his way up till he was a dispenser. . . . There were lots of callings. An hour or two passed, and he was still sitting and thinking. . . .

Towards three o'clock, when it was beginning to get light, the door creaked cautiously, and his *maman* came into the room.

"Aren't you asleep?" she asked, yawning. "Go to sleep; I have only come in for a minute. . . . I am only fetching the drops. . . ."

"What for?"

"Poor Lili has got spasms again. Go to sleep, my child, your examination's tomorrow. . . ."

She took a bottle of something out of the cupboard, went to the window, read the label, and went away.

"Marya Leontyevna, those are not the drops!" Volodya heard a woman's voice, a minute later. "That's lily of the valley, and Lili wants morphine. Is your son asleep? Ask him to look for it. . . ."

It was Nyuta's voice. Volodya turned cold. He hurriedly put on his trousers, flung his coat over his shoulders, and went to the door.

"Do you understand? Morphine," Nyuta explained in a whisper. "There must be a label in Latin. Wake Volodya; he will find it."

Maman opened the door and Volodya caught sight of Nyuta. She was wearing the same loose wrapper in which she had gone to bathe. Her hair hung loose and disordered on her shoulders, her face looked sleepy and dark in the half-light. . . .

"Why, Volodya is not asleep," she said. "Volodya, look in the cupboard for the morphine, there's a dear! What a nuisance Lili is! She always has something the matter."

Maman muttered something, yawned, and went away.

"Look for it," said Nyuta. "Why are you standing still?"

Volodya went to the cupboard, knelt down, and began looking through the bottles and boxes of medicine. His hands were trembling, and he had a feeling in his chest and stomach as though cold waves were running all over his inside. He felt suffocated and giddy from the smell of ether, carbolic acid, and various drugs, which he quite unnecessarily snatched up with his trembling fingers and spilled in so doing.

"I believe *maman* has gone," he thought. "That's a good thing . . . a good thing. . . ."

"Will you be quick?" said Nyuta, drawling.

"In a minute. . . . Here, I believe this is morphine," said Volodya, reading on one of the labels the word "morph . . ." "Here it is!"

Nyuta was standing in the doorway in such a way that one foot was in his room and one was in the passage. She was tidying her hair, which was difficult to put in order because it was so thick and long, and looked absent-mindedly at Volodya. In her loose wrap, with her sleepy face and her hair down, in the dim light that came into the white sky not yet lit by the sun, she seemed to Volodya captivating, magnificent. . . . Fascinated, trembling all over, and remembering with relish how he had held that exquisite body in his arms in the arbor, he handed her the bottle and said:

"How wonderful you are!"

"What?"

She came into the room.

"What?" she asked, smiling.

He was silent and looked at her, then, just as in the arbor, he took her hand, and she looked at him with a smile and waited for what would happen next.

"I love you," he whispered.

She left off smiling, thought a minute, and said:

"Wait a little; I think somebody is coming. Oh, these schoolboys!" she said in an undertone, going to the door and peeping out into the passage. "No, there is no one to be seen. . . ."

She came back.

Then it seemed to Volodya that the room, Nyuta, the sunrise and himself—all melted together in one sensation of acute, extraordinary, incredible bliss, for which one might give up one's whole life and face eternal torments. . . . But half a minute passed and all that vanished. Volodya saw only a fat, plain face, distorted by an expression of repulsion, and he himself suddenly felt a loathing for what had happened.

"I must go away, though," said Nyuta, looking at Volodya with disgust. "What a wretched, ugly . . . fie, ugly duckling!"

How unseemly her long hair, her loose wrap, her steps, her voice seemed to Volodya now! . . .

" 'Ugly duckling,' . . ." he thought after she had gone away. "I really am ugly . . . everything is ugly."

The sun was rising, the birds were singing loudly; he could hear the gardener walking in the garden and the creaking of his wheelbarrow . . . and soon afterwards he heard the lowing of the cows and the sounds of the shepherd's pipe. The sunlight and the sounds told him that somewhere in this world there is a pure, refined, poetical life. But where was it? Volodya had never heard a word of it from his *maman* or any of the people round about him.

When the footman came to wake him for the morning train, he pretended to be asleep. . . .

"Bother it! Damn it all!" he thought.

He got up between ten and eleven.

Combing his hair before the looking-glass, and looking at his ugly face, pale from his sleepless night, he thought:

"It's perfectly true . . . an ugly duckling!"

When *maman* saw him and was horrified that he was not at his examination, Volodya said:

"I overslept myself, *maman*. . . . But don't worry, I will get a medical certificate."

Madame Shumihin and Nyuta waked up at one o'clock. Volodya heard Madame Shumihin open her window with a bang, heard Nyuta go off into a peal of laughter in reply to her coarse voice. He saw the door open and a string of nieces and other toadies (among the latter was his *maman*) file into lunch, caught a glimpse of Nyuta's freshly washed laughing face, and, beside her, the black brows and beard of her husband the architect, who had just arrived.

Nyuta was wearing a Little Russian dress which did not suit her at all, and made her look clumsy; the architect was making dull and vulgar jokes. The rissoles served at lunch had too much onion in them—so it seemed to Volodya. It also seemed to him that Nyuta laughed loudly on purpose, and kept glancing in his direction to give him to understand that the memory of the night did not trouble her in the least, and that she was not aware of the presence at table of the "ugly duckling."

At four o'clock Volodya drove to the station with his *maman*. Foul memories, the sleepless night, the prospect of expulsion from school, the stings of conscience—all roused in him now an oppressive, gloomy anger.

He looked at *maman's* sharp profile, at her little nose, at the raincoat which was a present from Nyuta, and muttered:

"Why do you powder? It's not becoming at your age! You make yourself up, don't pay your debts at cards, smoke other people's tobacco. . . . It's hateful! I don't love you . . . I don't love you!"

He was insulting her, and she rolled her little eyes in alarm, clapped her little hands, and whispered in horror:

"What are you saying, my dear! Good gracious, the coachman will hear! Be quiet or the coachman will hear! He can overhear everything."

"I don't love you . . . I don't love you!" he went on breathlessly. "You've no soul and no morals. . . . Don't dare to wear that raincoat! Do you hear? Or else I will tear it into rags. . . ."

"Control yourself, my child," *maman* wept. "The coachman can hear!"

"And where is my father's fortune? Where is your money? You have wasted it all. I am not ashamed of being poor, but I am ashamed of having such a mother. . . . When my schoolfellows ask questions about you, I always blush."

In the rain they had to pass two stations before they reached the town. Volodya spent all the time on the little platform between two carriages and shivered all over. He did not want to go into the compartment because there the mother he hated was sitting. He hated himself, hated the ticket collectors, the smoke from the engine, the cold to which he attributed his shivering. And the heavier the weight on his heart, the more strongly he felt that somewhere in the world, among some people, there was a pure, honorable, warm, refined life, full of love, affection, gayety, and serenity. . . . He felt this and was so intensely miserable that a passenger, after looking in his face attentively, actually said: "You have the toothache, I suppose?"

In town *maman* and Volodya lived with Marya Petrovna, a lady of noble rank, who had a large flat and let rooms to boarders. *Maman* had two rooms, one with windows and two pictures in gold frames hanging on the walls, in which her bed stood and in which she lived, and a little dark room opening out of it in which Volodya lived. Here there was a sofa on which he slept, and, except that sofa, there was no other furniture; the rest of the room was entirely filled up with wicker baskets full of clothes, cardboard hatboxes, and all sorts of rubbish, which *maman* preserved for some reason or other. Volodya prepared his lessons either in his mother's room or in the "common room," as the large room in which the boarders assembled at dinnertime and in the evening was called.

On reaching home he lay down on his sofa and put the quilt over him to stop his shivering. The cardboard hatboxes, the wicker baskets, and the other rubbish, reminded him that he had not a room of his own, that he had no refuge in which he could get away from his mother, from her visitors, and from the voices that were floating up from the "common room." The satchel and the books lying about in the corners reminded him of the examination he had missed. . . . For some reason there came into his mind, quite inappropriately, Mentone, where he had lived with his father when he was seven years old; he thought of Biarritz and two little English girls with whom he ran about on the sand. . . . He tried to recall to his memory the color of the sky, the sea, the height of the waves, and his mood at the time, but he could not succeed. The English girls flitted before his imagination as though they were living; all the rest was a medley of images that floated away in confusion. . . .

"No; it's cold here," thought Volodya. He got up, put on his overcoat, and went into the "common room."

There they were drinking tea. There were three people at the samovar: *maman*, an old lady with tortoiseshell pince-nez, who gave music lessons; and Avgustin Mihailych, an elderly and very stout Frenchman, who was employed in a perfumery factory.

"I have had no dinner today," said *maman*. "I ought to send the maid to buy some bread."

"Dunyasha!" shouted the Frenchman.

It appeared that the maid had been sent out somewhere by the lady of the house.

"Oh, that's of no consequence," said the Frenchman, with a broad smile. "I will go for some bread myself at once. Oh, it's nothing."

He laid his strong, pungent cigar in a conspicuous place, put on his hat and went out. After he had gone away *maman* began telling the music teacher how she had been staying at the Shumihins', and how warmly they welcomed her.

"Lili Shumihin is a relation of mine, you know," she said. "Her late husband, General Shumihin, was a cousin of my husband. And she was a Baroness Kolb by birth—"

"*Maman*, that's false!" said Volodya irritably. "Why tell lies?"

He knew perfectly well that what his mother said was true; in what she was saying about General Shumihin and about Baroness Kolb there was not a word of lying, but nevertheless he felt that she was lying. There was a suggestion of falsehood in her manner of speaking, in the expression of her face, in her eyes, in everything.

"You are lying," repeated Volodya; and he brought his fist down on the table with such force that all the crockery shook and *maman's* tea was spilt. "Why do you talk about generals and baronesses? It's all lies!"

The music teacher was disconcerted, and coughed into her handkerchief, affecting to sneeze, and *maman* began to cry.

"Where can I go?" thought Volodya.

He had been in the street already; he was ashamed to go to his schoolfellows. Again, quite incongruously, he remembered the two little English girls. . . . He paced up and down the "common room," and went into Avgustin Mihailych's room. Here there was a strong smell of ethereal oils and glycerine soap. On the table, in the window, and even on the chairs, there were a number of bottles, glasses, and wineglasses containing fluids of various colors. Volodya took up from the table a newspaper, opened it and read the title *Figaro*. . . . There was a strong and pleasant scent about the paper. Then he took a revolver from the table. . . .

"There, there! Don't take any notice of it." The music teacher was comforting *maman* in the next room. "He is young! Young people of his age never restrain themselves. One must resign oneself to that."

"No, Yevgenya Andreyevna; he's too spoilt," said *maman* in a singsong voice. "He has no one in authority over him, and I am weak and can do nothing. Oh, I am unhappy!"

Volodya put the muzzle of the revolver to his mouth, felt something like a trigger or spring, and pressed it with his finger. . . . Then he felt something else projecting, and once more pressed it. Taking the muzzle out of his mouth, he wiped it with the lapel of his coat, looked at the lock. He had never in his life taken a weapon in his hand before. . . .

"I believe one ought to raise this . . ." he reflected. "Yes, it seems so."

Avgustin Mihailych went into the "common room," and with a laugh began telling them about something. Volodya put the muzzle in his mouth again, pressed it with his teeth, and pressed something with his fingers. There was the sound of a shot. . . . Something hit Volodya in the back of his head with terrible violence, and he fell on the table with his face downwards among the bottles and glasses. Then he saw his father, as in Mentone, in a top-hat with a wide black band on it, wearing mourning for some lady, suddenly seize him by both hands, and they fell headlong into a very deep, dark pit.

Then everything was blurred and vanished.

THE DREAMING CHILD

by Isak Dinesen

In the first half of the last century there lived in Sealand, in Denmark, a family of cottagers and fishermen, who were called Plejelt after their native place, and who did not seem able to do well for themselves in any way. Once they had owned a little land here and there, and fishing-boats, but what they had possessed they had lost, and within their new enterprises they failed. They just managed to keep out of the jails of Denmark, but they gave themselves up freely to all such sins and weaknesses—vagabondage, drink, gambling, illegitimate children and suicide—as human beings can indulge in without breaking the law. The old judge of the district said of them: "These Plejelts are not bad people; I have got many worse than they. They are pretty, healthy, likable, even talented in their way. Only they just have not got the knack of living.

And if they do not promptly pull themselves together I cannot tell what may become of them, except that the rats will eat them."

Now it was a queer thing that—just as if the Plejelts had been overhearing this sad prophecy and had been soundly frightened by it—in the following years they actually seemed to pull themselves together. One of them married into a respectable peasant family, another had a stroke of luck in the herring-fishery, another was converted by the new parson of the parish, and obtained the office of bell-ringer. Only one child of the clan, a girl, did not escape its fate, but on the contrary appeared to collect upon her young head the entire burden of guilt and misfortune of her tribe. In the course of her short, tragic life she was washed from the country into the town of Copenhagen, and here, before she was twenty, she died in dire misery, leaving a small son behind her. The father of the child, who is otherwise unknown to this tale, had given her a hundred rixdollars. These, together with the child, the dying mother handed over to an old washerwoman, blind in one eye, and named Madame Mahler, in whose house she had lodged. She begged Madame Mahler to provide for her baby as long as the money lasted, in the true spirit of the Plejelts, contenting herself with a brief respite.

At the sight of the money Madame Mahler got a rose in each cheek; she had never till now set eyes on a hundred rixdollars, all in a pile. As she looked at the child she sighed deeply; then she took the task upon her shoulders, with what other burdens life had already placed there.

The little boy, whose name was Jens, in this way first became conscious of the world, and of life, within the slums of old Copenhagen in a dark backyard like a well, a labyrinth of filth, decay and foul smell. Slowly he also became conscious of himself, and of something exceptional in his worldly position. There were other children in the backyard, a big crowd of them; they were pale and dirty as himself. But they all seemed to belong to somebody; they had a father and a mother; there was, for each of them, a group of other ragged and squalling children whom they called brothers and sisters, and who sided with them in the brawls of the yard; they obviously made part of a unity. He began to meditate upon the world's particular attitude to himself, and upon the reason for it. Something within it responded to an apprehension within his own heart: that he did not really belong here, but somewhere else. At night he had chaotic, many-coloured dreams; in the day-time his thoughts still lingered in them; sometimes they made him laugh, all to himself, like the tinkling of a little bell, so that Madame Mahler, shaking her own head, held him to be a bit weak in his.

A visitor came to Madame Mahler's house, a friend of her youth, an old wry seamstress with a flat, brown face and a black wig. They called her Mamzell Ane. She had in her young days sewn in many great houses. She wore a red bow at the throat, and had many coquettish, maidenly little ways and postures. But within her sunken bosom she had also a greatness of soul, which enabled her to scorn her present misery in the memory of that splendour which in the past her eyes had beheld. Madame Mahler was a woman of small imagination; she did but reluctantly lend an ear to her friend's grand, interminable soliloquies. After a while Mamzell Ane turned to little Jens for sympathy. Before the child's grave attentiveness her fancy took speed; she called forth, and declaimed upon, the glory of satin, velvet and brocade, of lofty halls and marble staircases. The lady of the house was adorned for a ball by the light of multitudinous candles; her husband came in to fetch her with a star on his breast, while the carriage and pair waited in the street. There were big weddings in the cathedral, and funerals as well, with all the ladies swathed in black like magnificent, tragic columns. The children called their parents Papa and Mamma; they had dolls and hobby-horses to play with, talking parrots in gilt cages, and dogs that were taught to walk on their hind legs. Their mother kissed them, gave them bonbons and pretty pet-names. Even in winter the warm rooms behind the silk curtains were filled with the perfumes of flowers named heliotrope and oleander, and the chandeliers that hung from the ceiling were themselves made of glass in the shape of bright flowers and leaves.

The idea of this majestic, radiant world, in the mind of little Jens merged with that of his own inexplicable isolation in life into a great dream, or fantasy. He was so lonely in Madame Mahler's house because one of the houses of Mamzell Ane's tales was his real home. In the long days, when Madame Mahler stood by her washtub, or brought her washing out into town, he fondled, and played with, the picture of this house and of the people who lived in it, and who loved him so dearly. Mamzell Ane, on her side, noted the effect of her *épopée* on the child, realized that she had at last found the ideal audience, and was further inspired by the discovery. The relation between the two developed into a kind of love-affair; for their happiness, for their very existence they had become dependent upon each other.

Now Mamzell Ane was a revolutionist, on her own accord, and out of some primitive, flaming visionary sight within her proud, virginal heart, for she had all her time lived amongst submissive and unreflective people. The meaning and object of existence to her was grandeur, beauty and elegance. For the life of her she would not see them disappear from the earth. But she felt it to be a cruel and scandalous state of things that so many men and women must live and die without these highest human values—yes, without the very knowledge of them—that they must be poor, wry and unelegant. She was every day looking forward to that day of justice when the tables were to be turned, and the wronged and oppressed enter into their heaven of refinement and gracefulness. All the same she now took pains not to impart into the soul of the child any of her own bitterness or rebelliousness. For as the intimacy between them grew, she did in her heart acclaim little Jens as legitimate heir to all the magnificence for which she had herself prayed in vain. He was not to fight for it; everything was his by right, and should come to him on its own. Possibly the inspired and experienced old maid also noted that the boy had in him no talent for envy or rancour whatever. In their long, happy communications, he accepted Mamzell Ane's world serenely and without misgiving, in the very manner—except for the fact that he had not any of it—of the happy children born within it.

There was a short period of his life in which Jens made the other children of the backyard party to his happiness. He was, he told them, far from being the half-wit barely tolerated by old Madame Mahler; he was on the contrary the favourite of fortune. He had a Papa and Mamma and a fine house of his own, with such and such things in it, a carriage, and horses in the stable. He was spoiled, and would get everything he asked for. It was a curious thing that the children did not laugh at him, nor afterwards pursue him with mockery. They almost appeared to believe him. Only they could not understand or follow his fancies; they took but little interest in them, and after a while they altogether disregarded them. So Jens again gave up sharing the secret of his felicity with the world.

Still some of the questions put to him by the children had set the boy's mind working, so that he asked Mamzell Ane—for the confidence between them by this time was complete—how it had come to pass that he had lost contact with his home and had been taken into Madame Mahler's establishment? Mamzell Ane found it difficult to answer him; she could not explain the fact to herself. It would be, she reflected, part of the confused and corrupt state of the world in general. When she had thought the matter over she solemnly, in the manner of a Sibyl, furnished him with an explanation. It was, she said, by no means unheard of, neither in life nor in books, that a child, particularly a child in the highest and happiest circumstances, and most dearly beloved by his parents, enigmatically vanished and was lost. She stopped short at this, for even to her dauntless and proven soul the theme seemed too tragic to be further dwelt on. Jens accepted the explanation in the spirit in which it was given, and from this moment saw himself as that melancholy, but not uncommon, phenomenon: a vanished and lost child.

But when Jens was six years old Mamzell Ane died, leaving to him her few earthly possessions: a thin-worn silver thimble, a fine pair of scissors and a little black chair with roses painted on it. Jens set a great value to these things, and every day gravely contemplated them. Just then Madame Mahler began to see the end of her hundred rixdollars. She had been piqued by her old friend's absorption in the child, and so decided to get her own back. From now on she would make the boy useful to her in the business of the laundry. His life therefore was no longer his own, and the thimble, the scissors and the chair stood in Madame Mahler's room, the sole tangible remnants, or proof, of the splendour which he and Mamzell Ane had known and shared.

At the same time as these events took place in Adelgade, there lived in a stately house in Bredgade a young married couple, whose names were Jakob and Emilie Vandamm. The two were cousins, she being the only child of one of the big shipowners of Copenhagen, and he the son of that magnate's sister—so that if it had not been for her sex, the young lady would with time have become head of the firm. The old shipowner, who was a widower, with his widowed sister, occupied the two loftier lower stories of the house. The family held closely together, and the young people had been engaged from childhood.

Jakob was a very big young man, with a quick head and an easy temper. He had many friends, but none of them could dispute the fact that he was growing fat at the early age of thirty. Emilie was not a regular beauty, but she had an extremely graceful and elegant figure, and the slimmest waist in Copenhagen; she was supple and soft in her walk and all her movements, with a low voice, and a reserved, gentle manner. As to her moral being she was the true daughter of a long row of competent and honest tradesmen: upright, wise, truthful and a bit of a pharisee. She gave much time to charity work, and therein minutely distinguished between the deserving and the undeserving poor. She entertained largely and prettily, but kept strictly to her own milieu. Her old uncle, who had travelled round the world, and was an admirer of the fair sex, teased her over the Sunday dinner-table. There was, he said, an exquisite piquancy in the contrast between the suppleness of her body and the rigidity of her mind.

There had been a time when, unknown to the world, the two had been in concord. When Emilie was eighteen, and Jakob was away in China on a ship, she fell in love with a young naval officer, whose name was Charlie Dreyer, and who, three years earlier, when he was only twenty-one, had distinguished himself, and been decorated, in the war of 1849. Emilie was not then officially engaged to her cousin. She did not believe, either, that she would exactly break Jakob's heart if she left him and married another man. All the same, she had strange, sudden misgivings; the strength of her own feelings alarmed her. When in solitude she pondered on the matter, she held it beneath her to be so entirely dependent on another human being. But she again forgot her fears when she met Charlie, and she wondered and wondered that life did indeed hold so much sweetness. Her best friend, Charlotte Tutein, as the two girls were undressing after a ball, said to her: "Charlie Dreyer makes love to all the pretty girls of Copenhagen, but he does not intend to marry any of them. I think he is a Don Juan." Emilie smiled into the looking-glass. Her heart melted at the thought that Charlie, misjudged by all the world, was known to her alone for what he was: loyal, constant and true.

Charlie's ship was leaving for the West Indies. On the night before his departure he came out to her father's villa near Copenhagen to say good-bye, and found Emilie alone. The two young people walked in the garden; it was moonlit. Emilie broke off a white rose, moist with dew, and gave it to him. As they were parting on the road just outside the gate, he seized both her hands, drew them to his breast, and in one great flaming whisper begged her, since nobody would see him walk back with her, to let him stay with her that night, until in the morning he must go so far away.

It is probably almost impossible to the children of later generations to understand or realize the horror and abomination which the idea and the very word of seduction would awake in the minds of young girls of that past age. She could not have been more deadly frightened and revolted had she found that he meant to cut her throat.

He must repeat himself before she understood him, and as she did so the ground sank beneath her. She felt as if the one man amongst all, whom she trusted and loved, was intending to bring upon her the supreme sin, disaster and shame, was asking her to betray her mother's memory and all the maidens in the world. Her own feelings for him made her an accomplice in the crime, and she realized that she was lost. Charlie felt her wavering on her feet, and put his arms around her. In a stifled, agonized cry she tore herself out of them, fled, and with all her might pushed the heavy iron gate to; she bolted it on him as if it had been the cage of an angry lion. On which side of the gate was the lion? Her strength gave way; she hung on to the bars, while on the other side the desperate, miserable lover pressed himself against them, fumbled between them for her hands, her clothes, and implored her to open. But she recoiled and flew to the house, to her room, only to find there despair within her own heart, and a bitter vacuity in all the world round it.

Six months later Jakob came home from China, and their engagement was celebrated amongst the rejoicings of the families. A month after she learned that Charlie had died from fever at St. Thomas. Before she was twenty she was married and mistress of her own fine house.

Many young girls of Copenhagen married in the same way—*par dépit*—and then, to save their self-respect, denied their first love and made the excellency of their husbands their one point of honour, so that they became incapable of distinguishing between truth and untruth, lost their moral weight and flickered in life without any foothold in reality. Emilie was saved from their fate by the intervention, so to say, of the old Vandamms, her forefathers, and by the instinct and principle of sound merchantship which they had passed on into the blood of their daughter. The staunch and resolute old traders had not winked when they made out their balance-sheet; in hard times they had sternly looked bankruptcy and ruin in the face; they were the loyal, unswerving servants of facts. So did Emilie now take stock of her profit and loss. She had loved Charlie; he had been unworthy of her love; and she was never again to love in that same way. She had stood upon the brink of an abyss, and but for the grace of God she was at this moment a fallen woman, an outcast from her father's house. The husband she had married was kind-hearted, and a good man of business; he was also fat, childish, unlike her. She had got, out of life, a house to her taste and a secure, harmonious position in her own family and in the world of Copenhagen; for these she was grateful, and for them she would take no risk. She did at this moment of her life with all the strength of her young soul embrace a creed of fanatical truthfulness and solidity. The ancient Vandamms might have applauded her, or they might have thought her code excessive; they had taken a risk themselves, when it was needed, and they were aware that in trade it is a dangerous thing to shy danger.

Jakob, on his side, was in love with his wife, and prized her beyond rubies. To him, as to the other young men out of the strictly moral Copenhagen bourgeoisie, his first experience of love had been extremely gross. He had preserved the freshness of his heart, and his claim to neatness and orderliness in life by holding on to an ideal of purer womanhood, in the first place represented by the young cousin whom he was to marry, the innocent fair-haired girl of his own mother's blood, and brought up as she had been. He carried her image with him to Hamburg and Amsterdam, and that trait in him which his wife called childishness made him deck it out like a doll or an icon; out in China it became highly ethereal and romantic, and he used to repeat to himself little sayings of hers, to recall her low, soft voice. Now he was happy to be back in Denmark, married and in his own home, and to find his young wife as perfect as his portrait of her. At times he felt a vague longing for a bit of weakness within her, or for an occasional appeal to his own strength, which, as things were, only made him out a clumsy figure beside her delicate form. He gave her all that she wanted, and out of his pride in her superiority left to her all decisions on their house and on their daily and social life. Only within their charity work it happened that the husband and wife did not see eye to eye, and that Emilie would give him a little lecture on his credulity. "What an absurd person you are, Jakob," she said. "You will believe everything that these people tell you—not because you cannot help it, but because you do really wish to believe them." "Do you not wish to believe them?" he asked her. "I cannot see," she replied, "how one can well wish to believe or not to believe. I wish to find out the truth. Once a thing is not true," she added, "it matters little to me whatever else it may be."

A short time after his wedding Jakob one day had a letter from a rejected supplicant, a former maid in his father-in-law's house, who informed him that while he was away in China his wife had a liaison with Charlie Dreyer. He knew it to be a lie, tore up the letter, and did not give it another thought.

They had no children. This to Emilie was a grave affliction; she felt that she was lacking in her duties. When they had been married for five years Jakob, vexed by his mother's constant concern, and with the future of the firm on his mind, suggested to his wife that they should adopt a child, to carry forward the house. Emilie at once, and with much energy and indignation, repudiated the idea; it had to her all the appearance of a comedy, and she would not see her father's firm encumbered with a sham heir. Jakob held forth to her upon the Antonines with but little effect.

But when six months later he again took up the subject, to her own surprise she found that it was no longer repellent. Unknowingly she must have given it a place in her thought, and let it take root there, for by now it seemed familiar to her. She listened to her husband, looked at him, and felt kindly towards him. "If this is what he has been longing for," she thought, "I must not oppose it." But in her own heart she knew clearly and coldly, and with awe of her own coldness the true reason for her indulgence: the deep apprehension, that when a child had been adopted there would be no more obligation to her of producing an heir to the firm, a grandson to her father, a child to her husband.

It was indeed their little divergences in regard to the deserving or undeserving poor which brought upon the young couple of Bredgade the events recounted in this tale. In summer-time they lived in Emilie's father's villa on the Strandvej, and Jakob would drive in to town, and out, in a small gig. One day he decided to profit by his wife's absence to visit an unquestionably unworthy mendicant, an old sea-captain from one of his ships. He took his way through the ancient town, where it was difficult to drive a carriage, and where it was such an exceptional sight that people came up from the cellars to stare at it. In the narrow lane of Adelgade a drunken man waved his arms in front of the horse; it shied, and knocked down a small boy with a heavy wheelbarrow piled high with washing. The wheelbarrow and the washing ended sadly in the gutter. A crowd immediately collected round the spot, but expressed neither indignation nor sympathy. Jakob made his groom lift the little boy onto the seat. The child was smeared with blood and dirt, but he was not badly hurt, nor in the least scared. He seemed to take this accident as an adventure in general, or as if it had happened to somebody else. "Why did you not get out of my way, you little idiot?" Jakob asked him. "I wanted to look at the horse," said the child, and added: "Now, I can see it well from here."

Jakob got the boy's whereabouts from an onlooker, paid him to take the wheelbarrow back, and himself drove the child home. The sordidness of Madame Mahler's house, and her own, one-eyed, blunt unfeelingness impressed him unpleasantly; still he had before now been inside the houses of the poor. But he was, here, struck by a strange incongruity between the backyard and the child who lived in it. It was as if, unknowingly, Madame Mahler was housing, and knocking about, a small, gentle, wild animal, or a sprite. On his way to the villa he reflected that the child had reminded him of his wife; he had a reserved, as it were selfless, way with him, behind which one guessed great, integrate strength and endurance.

He did not speak of the incident that evening, but he went back to Madame Mahler's house to inquire about the boy, and after a while, he recounted the adventure to his wife and, somewhat shyly and half in jest, proposed to her that they should take the pretty, forlorn child as their own.

Half in jest she entered on his idea. It would be better, she thought, than taking on a child whose parents she knew. After this day she herself at times dwelt upon the matter when she could find nothing else to talk to him about. They consulted the family lawyer, and sent their old doctor to look the child over. Jakob was surprised and grateful at his wife's compliance with his wish. She listened with gentle interest when he developed his plans, and would even sometimes vent her own ideas on education.

Lately Jakob had found his domestic atmosphere almost too perfect, and had had an adventure in town. Now he tired of it and finished it. He bought Emilie presents, and left her to make her own conditions as to the adoption of the child. He might, she said, bring the boy to the house on the first of October, when they had moved into town from the country, but she herself would reserve her final decision in the matter until April, when he should have been with them for six months. If by then she did not find the child fit for their plan she would hand him over to some honest, kindly family in the employ of the firm. Till April they themselves would likewise be only Uncle and Aunt Vandamm to the boy.

They did not talk to their family of the project, and this circumstance accentuated the new feeling of comradeship between them. How very different Emilie said to herself, would the case have proved had she been expecting a child in the orthodox way of women. There was indeed something neat and proper about settling the affairs of nature according to your own mind. "And," she whispered in her mind, as her glance ran down her looking-glass "in keeping your figure."

As to Madame Mahler, when time came to approach her, the matter was easily arranged. She had it not in her to oppose the wishes of her social superiors; she was also, vaguely, rating her own future connection with a house that must surely turn out an abundance of washing. Only the readiness with which Jakob refunded her her past outlays on the child left in her heart a lifelong regret that she had not asked for more.

At the last moment Emilie made a further stipulation. She would go alone to fetch the child. It was important that the relation between the boy and herself should be properly established from the beginning, and she did not trust to Jakob's sense of propriety on this occasion. In this way it came about that, when all was ready for the child's reception in the house of Bredgade, Emilie drove by herself to Adelgade to take possession of him, easy in her conscience towards the firm and her husband, but, beforehand, a little tired of the whole affair.

In the street by Madame Mahler's house a number of unkempt children were obviously waiting for the arrival of the carriage. They stared at her, but turned off their eyes, when she looked at them. Her heart sank as she lifted her ample silk shirt and passed through their crowd and across the backyard. Would her boy have the same look? Like Jakob, she had many times before visited the houses of the poor. It was a sad sight, but it could not be otherwise. "The poor you have with you always." But today, since a child from this place was to enter her own house, for the first time she felt personally related to the need and misery of the world. She was seized with a new deep disgust and horror, and at the next moment with a new, deeper pity. In these two minds she entered Madame Mahler's room.

Madame Mahler had washed little Jens and watercombed his hair. She had also, a couple of days before, hurriedly enlightened him as to the situation and his own promotion in life. But being an unimaginative woman and moreover of the opinion that the child was but half-witted, she had not taken much trouble about it. The child had received the information in silence; he only asked her how his father and mother had found him. "Oh, by the smell," said Madame Mahler.

Jens had communicated the news to the other children of the house. His Papa and Mamma, he told them, were coming on the morrow, in great state, to fetch him home. It gave him matter for reflection that the event should raise a great stir in that same world of the backyard that had received his visions of it with indifference. To him the two were the same thing.

He had got up on Mamzell Ane's small chair to look out of the window and witness the arrival of his mother. He was still standing on it when Emilie came in, and Madame Mahler in vain made a gesture to chase him down. The first thing that Emilie noticed about the child was that he did not turn his gaze from hers, but looked her straight in the eyes. At the sight of her a great, ecstatic light passed over his face. For a moment the two looked at each other.

The child seemed to wait for her to address him, but as she stood silent, irresolute, he spoke. "Mamma," he said, "I am glad that you have found me. I have waited for you so long, so long."

Emilie gave Madame Mahler a glance. Had this scene been staged to move her heart? But the flat lack of understanding in the old woman's face excluded the possibility, and she again turned to the child.

Madame Mahler was a big, broad woman. Emilie herself, in a crinoline and a sweeping mantilla, took up a good deal of room. The child was much the smallest figure in the room, yet at this moment he dominated it, as if he had taken command of it. He stood up straight, with that same radiance in his countenance. "Now I am coming home again, with you," he said.

Emilie vaguely and amazedly realized that to the child the importance of the moment did not lie with his own good luck, but with that tremendous happiness and fulfillment which he was bestowing on her. A strange idea, that she could not have explained to herself, at that, ran through her mind. She thought: "This child is as lonely in life as I." Gravely she moved nearer to him and said a few kind words. The little boy put out his hand and gently touched the long silky ringlets that fell forward over her neck. "I knew you at once," he said proudly. "You are my Mamma, who spoils me. I would know you amongst all the ladies, by your long pretty hair." He ran his fingers softly down her shoulder and arm, and fumbled over her gloved hand. "You have got three rings on today," he said. "Yes," said Emilie in her low voice. A short, triumphant smile broke upon his face. "And now you kiss me, Mamma," he said, and grew very pale. Emilie did not know that his excitement rose from the fact that he had never been kissed. Obediently, surprised at herself, she bent down and kissed him.

Jens' farewell to Madame Mahler at first was somewhat ceremonious in two people who had known each other for a long time. For she already saw him as a new person, the rich man's child, and took his hand tardily, her face stiff. But Emilie bade the boy, before he went away, to thank Madame Mahler because she had looked after him till now, and he did so with much freedom and grace. At that the old woman's tanned and furrowed cheeks once more blushed deeply, like a young girl's, as by the sight of the money at their first meeting. She had so rarely been thanked in her life. In the street he stood still. "Look at my big, fat horses!" he cried. Emilie sat in the carriage, bewildered. What was she bringing home with her from Madame Mahler's house?

In her own house, as she took the child up the stairs and from one room into another, her bewilderment grew. Rarely had she felt so uncertain of herself. It was, everywhere, in the child, the same rapture of recognition. At times he would also mention and look for things which she faintly remembered from her own childhood, or other things of which she had never heard. Her small pug, that she had brought with her from her old home, yapped at the boy. She lifted it up, afraid that it would bite him. "No, Mamma," he cried, "she will not bite me, she knows me well." A few hours ago—yes, she thought, up to the moment when in Madame Mahler's room she had kissed the child—she would have scolded him: "Fie, you are telling a fib." Now she said nothing, and the next moment the child looked round the room and asked her: "Is the parrot dead?" "No," she answered, wondering, "she is not dead; she is in the other room."

She realized that she was afraid both to be alone with the boy, and to let any third person join them. She sent the nurse out of the room. By the time Jakob was to arrive at the house she listened for his steps on the stairs with a kind of alarm. "Who are you waiting for?" Jens asked her. She was at a loss as how to designate Jakob to the child. "For my husband," she replied, embarrassed. Jakob on his entrance found the mother and the child gazing in the same picture-book. The little boy stared at him. "So it is you who are my Papa!" he exclaimed, "I thought so, too, all the time. But I could not be quite sure of it, could I? It was not by the smell that you found me, then. I think it was the horse that remembered me." Jakob looked at his wife; she looked into the book. He did not expect sense from a child, and was soon playing with the boy and tumbling him about. In the midst of a game Jens set his hands against Jakob's chest. "You have not got your star on," he said. After a moment Emilie went out of the room. She thought: "I have taken this upon me to meet my husband's wish, but it seems that I must bear the burden of it alone."

Jens took possession of the mansion in Bredgade, and brought it to submission, neither by might nor by power, but in the quality of that fascinating and irresistible personage, perhaps the most fascinating and irresistible in the whole world: the dreamer whose dreams come true. The old house fell a little in love with him. Such is ever the lot of dreamers, when dealing with people at all susceptible to the magic of dreams. The most renowned amongst them, Rachel's son, as all the world knows, suffered hardships and was even cast in prison on that account. Except for his size, Jens had no resemblance to the classic portraits of Cupid; all the same it was evident that, unknowingly, the shipowner and his wife had taken into them an amorino. He carried wings into the house, and was in league with the sweet and merciless powers of nature, and his relation to each individual member of the household became a kind of aerial love affair. It was upon the strength of this same magnetism that Jakob had picked out the boy as heir to the firm at their first meeting, and that Emilie was afraid to be alone with him. The old magnate and the servants of the house no more escaped their destiny—as was once the case with Potiphar, captain to the guard of Egypt. Before they knew where they were, they had committed all they had into his hands.

One effect of this particular spell was this: that people were made to see themselves with the eyes of the dreamer, and were impelled to live up to an ideal, and that for this their higher existence they became dependent upon him. During the time that Jens lived in the house, it was much changed, and dissimilar to the other houses of the town. It became a Mount Olympus, the abode of divinities.

The child took the same lordly, laughing pride in the old shipowner, who ruled the waters of the universe, as in Jakob's staunch, protective kindness and Emilie's silk-clad gracefulness. The old housekeeper, who had often before grumbled at her lot in life, for the while was transformed into an all-powerful, benevolent guardian of human welfare, a Ceres in cap and apron. And for the same length of time the coachman, a monumental figure, elevated sky-high above the crowd, and combining within his own person the vigour of the two bay horses, majestically trotted down Bredgade on eight shod and clattering hoofs. It was only after Jens' bed hour, when, immovable and silent, his cheek buried in the pillow, he was exploring new areas of dreams that the house resumed the aspect of a rational, solid Copenhagen mansion.

Jens was himself ignorant of his power. As his new family did not scold him or find fault with him, it never occurred to him that they were at all looking at him. He gave no preference to any particular member of the household; they were all within his scheme of things and must there fit into their place. The relation of the one to the other was the object of his keen, subtle observation. One phenomenon in his daily life never ceased to entertain and please him: that Jakob, so big, broad and fat, should be attentive and submissive to his slight wife. In the world that he had known till now bulk was of supreme moment. As later on Emilie looked back upon this time, it seemed to her that the child would often provoke an opportunity for this fact to manifest itself, and would then, so to say, clap his hands in triumph and delight, as if the happy state of things had been brought about by his personal skill. But in other cases his sense of proportion failed him. Emilie in her boudoir had a glass aquarium with goldfish, in front of which Jens would pass many hours, as silent as the fish themselves, and from his comments upon them she gathered that to him they were huge—a fine catch could one get hold of them, and even dangerous to the pug, should she happen to fall into the bowl. He asked Emilie to leave the curtains by this window undrawn at night, in order that, when people were asleep, the fish might look at the moon.

In Jakob's relation to the child there was a moment of unhappy love, or at least of the irony of fate, and it was not the first time either that he had gone through this same melancholy experience. For ever since he himself was a small boy he had yearned to protect those weaker than he, and to support and right all frail and delicate beings in his surroundings. The very qualities of fragility and helplessness inspired in him an affection and admiration which came near to idolatry. But there was in his nature an inconsistency, such as will often be found in children of old, wealthy families, who have got all they wanted too easily, till in the end they cry out for the impossible. He loved pluck, too; gallantry delighted him wherever he met it, and for the clinging and despondent type of human beings, and in particular of women, he felt a slight distaste and repugnance. He might dream of shielding and guiding his wife, but at the same time the little cool, forbearing smile with which she would receive any such attempt on his side to him was one of the most bewitching traits in her whole person. In this way he found himself somewhat in the sad and paradoxical position of the young lover who passionately adores virginity. Now he learned that it was equally out of the question to patronize Jens. The child did not reject or smile at his patronage, as Emilie did; he even seemed grateful for it, but he accepted it in the part of a game or a sport. So that, when they were out walking together, and Jakob, thinking that the child must be tired, lifted him on to his shoulders, Jens would take it that the big man wanted to play at being a horse or an elephant just as much as he himself wanted to play that he was a trooper or a mahout.

Emilie sadly reflected that she was the only person in the house who did not love the child. She felt unsafe with him, even when she was unconditionally accepted as the beautiful, perfect mother, and as she recalled how, only a short time ago, she had planned to bring up the boy in her own spirit, and had written down little memoranda upon education, she saw herself as a figure of fun. To make up for her lack of feeling she took Jens with her on her walks and drives, to the parks and the zoo, brushed his thick hair, and had him dressed up as neatly as a doll. They were always together. She was sometimes amused by his strange, graceful, dignified delight in all that she showed him, and at the next moment, as in Madame Mahler's room, she realized that however generous she would be to him, he would always be the giver. Her sisters-in-law, and her young married friends, fine ladies of Copenhagen with broods of their own, wondered at her absorption in the foundling—and then it happened, when they were off their guard, that they did themselves receive a dainty arrow in their satin bosoms, and between them began to discuss Emilie's pretty boy, with a tender raillery as that with which they would have discussed Cupid. They asked her to bring him to play with their own children. Emilie declined, and told herself that she must first be certain about his manners. At the New Year, she thought, she would give a children's party herself.

Jens had come to the Vandamms in October, when trees were yellow and red in the parks. Then the tinge of frost in the air drove people indoors, and they began to think of Christmas. Jens seemed to know everything about the Christmas-tree, the goose with roast apples, and the solemnly joyful church-going on Christmas morning. But it would happen that he mixed up these festivals with others of the season, and described how they were soon all to mask and mum, as children do at Shrovestide. It was as if, from the centre of his happy, playful world, its sundry components showed up less clearly than when seen from afar.

And as the days drew in and the snow fell in the streets of Copenhagen, a change came upon the child. He was not low in spirits, but singularly collected and compact, as if he were shifting the centre of gravitation of his being, and folding his wings. He would stand for long whiles by the window, so sunk in thought that he did not always hear it when they called him, filled with a knowledge which his surroundings could not share.

For within these first months of winter it became evident that he was not at all a person to be permanently set at ease by what the world calls fortune. The essence of his nature was longing. The warm rooms with silk curtains, the sweets, his toys and new clothes, the kindness and concern of his Papa and Mamma were all of the greatest moment because they went to prove the veracity of his visions; they were infinitely valuable as embodiments of his dreams. But within themselves they hardly meant anything to him, and they had no power to hold him. He was neither a worldling nor a struggler. He was a Poet.

Emilie tried to make him tell her what he had in his mind, but got nowhere with him. Then one day he confided in her on his own account.

"Do you know, Mamma," he said, "in my house the stairs were so dark and full of holes that you had to grope your way up it, and the best thing was really to walk on one's hands and knees? There was a window broken by the wind, and below it, on the landing, there lay a drift of snow as high as me." "But that is not your house, Jens," said Emilie. "This is your house." The child looked round the room. "Yes," he said, "this is my fine house. But I have another house that is quite dark and dirty. You know it, you have been there too. When the washing was hung up, one had to twine in and out across that big loft, else the huge, wet, cold sheets would catch one, just as if they were alive." "You are never going back to that house," said she. The child gave her a great, grave glance, and after a moment said: "No."

But he was going back. She could, by her horror and disgust of the house, keep him from talking of it, as the children there by their indifference had silenced him on his happy home. But when she found him mute and pensive by the window, or at his toys, she knew that his mind had returned to it. And now and again, when they had played together, and their intimacy seemed particularly secure, he opened on the theme. "In the same street as my house," he said, one evening as they were sitting together on the sofa before the fireplace, "there was an old lodging-house, where the people who had plenty of money could sleep in beds, and the others must stand up and sleep, with a rope under their arms. One night it caught fire, and burned all down. Then those who were in bed did hardly get their trousers on, but ho! those who stood up and slept were the lucky boys; they got out quick. There was a man who made a song about it, you know."

There are some young trees which, when they are planted, have thin, twisted roots and will never take hold in the soil. They may shoot out a profusion of leaves and flowers, but they must soon die. Such was the way with Jens. He had sent out his small branches upwards and to the sides, had fared excellently of the chameleon's dish and eaten air, promise-crammed, and the while he had forgotten to put out roots. Now the time came when by law of nature the bright, abundant bloom must needs wither, fade and waste away. It is possible, had his imagination been turned on to fresh pastures, that he might for a while have drawn nourishment through it, and have detained his exit. Once or twice, to amuse him, Jakob had talked to him of China. The queer outlandish world captivated the mind of the child. He dwelled with the highest excitement on pictures of pig-tailed Chinamen, dragons and fishermen with pelicans, and upon the fantastic names of Hongkong and Yangtze-kiang. But the grown-up people did not realize the significance of his novel imaginative venture, and so, for lack of sustenance, the frail, fresh branch soon drooped.

A short time after the children's party, early in the new year, the child grew pale and hung his head. The old doctor came and gave him medicine to no effect. It was a quiet, unbroken decline; the plant was going out.

As Jens was put to bed and was, so to say, legitimately releasing his hold upon the world of actuality, his fancy fetched headway and ran along with him, like the sails of a small boat, from which the ballast is thrown overboard. There were, now, people round him all the time who would listen to what he said, gravely, without interrupting or contradicting him. This happy state of things enraptured him. The dreamer's sick-bed became a throne.

Emilie sat at the bed all the time, distressed by a feeling of impotence which sometimes in the night made her wring her hands. All her life she had endeavoured to separate good from bad, right from wrong, happiness from unhappiness. Here she was, she reflected with dismay, in the hands of a being, much smaller and weaker than herself, to whom these were all one, who welcomed light and darkness, pleasure and pain, in the same spirit of gallant, debonair approval and fellowship. The fact, she told herself, did away with all need of her comfort and consolation here at her child's sick-bed; it often seemed to abolish her very existence.

Now within the brotherhood of poets Jens was a humorist, a comic fabulist. It was, in each individual phenomenon of life, the whimsical, the burlesque moment that attracted and inspired him. To the pale, grave young woman his fancies seemed sacrilegious within a death-room, yet after all it was his own death-room.

"Oh, there were so many rats, Mamma," he said, "so many rats. They were all over the house. One came to take a bit of lard on the shelf—pat! a rat jumped at one. They ran across my face at night. Put your face close to me, and I will show you how it felt." "There are no rats here, my darling," said Emilie. "No, none," said he. "When I am sick no more I shall go back and fetch you one. The rats like the people better than the people like them. For they think us good, lovely to eat. There was an old comedian, who lived in the garret. He had played comedy when he was young, and had travelled to foreign countries. Now he gave the little girls money to kiss him, but they would not kiss him, because they said that they did not like his nose. It was a curious nose, too—all fallen in. And when they would not he cried and wrung his hands. But he got ill, and died, and nobody knew about it. But when at last they went in, do you know, Mamma—the rats had eaten off his nose!—nothing else, his nose only! But people will not eat rats even when they are very hungry. There was a fat boy in the cellar, who caught rats in many curious ways, and cooked them. But old Madame Mahler said that she despised him for it, and the children called him Rat-Mad."

Then again he would talk of her own house. "My Grandpapa," he said, "has got corns, the worst corns in Copenhagen. When they get very bad he sighs and moans. He says: 'There will be storms in the China Sea. It is a damned business; my ships are going to the bottom.' So, you know, I think that the seamen will be saying: 'There is a storm in this sea; it is a damned business; our ship is going to the bottom.' Now it is time that old Grandpapa, in Bredgade, goes and has his corns cut."

Only within the last days of his life did he speak of Mamzell Ane. She had been, as it were, his Muse, the only person who had knowledge of the one and the other of his worlds. As he recalled her his tone of speech changed; he held forth in a grand, solemn manner, as upon an elemental power, of necessity known to everyone. If Emilie had given his fantasies her attention many things might have been made clear to her. But she said: "No, I do not know her, Jens." "Oh, Mamma, she knows you well!" He said: "She sewed your wedding-gown, all of white satin. It was slow work—so many fittings! And my Papa," the child went on and laughed, "he came in to you, and do you know what he said? He said: 'My white rose.' " He suddenly bethought himself of the scissors which Mamzell

Ane had left him, and wanted them, and this was the only occasion upon which Emilie ever saw him impatient or fretful.

She left her house for the first time within three weeks, and went herself to Madame Mahler's house to inquire about the scissors. On the way the powerful, enigmatical figure of Mamzell Ane took on to her the aspect of a Parca, of Atropos herself, scissors in hand, ready to cut off the thread of life. But Madame Mahler in the meantime had bartered away the scissors to a tailor of her acquaintance, and she flatly denied the existence both of them and of Mamzell Ane.

Upon the last morning of the boy's life Emilie lifted her small pug, that had been his faithful playmate, onto the bed. Then the little dark face and the crumpled body seemed to recall to him the countenance of his friend. "There she is!" he cried.

Emilie's mother-in-law and the old shipowner himself had been daily visitors to the sick-room. The whole Vandamm family stood weeping round the bed when, in the end, like a small brook which falls into the ocean, Jens gave himself up to, and was absorbed in, the boundless, final unity of dream.

He died by the end of March, a few days before the date that Emilie had fixed to decide on his fitness for admission into the house of Vandamm. Her father suddenly determined that he must be interred in the family vault—irregularly, since he was never legally adopted into the family. So he was laid down behind a heavy wrought-iron fence, within the finest grave that any Plejelt had ever obtained.

Within the following days the house in Bredgade, and its inhabitants with it, shrank and decreased. The people were a little confused, as after a fall, and seized by a sad sense of diffidence. For the first weeks after Jens' burial life looked to them strangely insipid, a sorry affair, void of purport. The Vandamms were not used to being unhappy, and were not prepared for the sense of loss with which now the death of the child left them. To Jakob it seemed as if he had let down a friend, who had, after all, laughingly trusted to his strength. Now nobody had any use for it, and he saw himself as a freak, the stuffed puppet of a colossus. But with all this, after a while there was also in the survivors, as ever at the passing away of an idealist, a vague feeling of relief.

Emilie alone of the house of Vandamms preserved, as it were, her size, and her sense of proportion. It may even be said that when the house tumbled from its site in the clouds, she upheld and steadied it. She had deemed it affected in her to go into mourning for a child who was not hers, and while she gave up the balls and parties of the Copenhagen season, she went about her domestic tasks quietly as before. Her father and her mother-in-law, sad and at a loss in their daily life, turned to her for balance, and because she was the youngest amongst them, and seemed to them in some ways like the child that was gone, they transferred to her the tenderness and concern which had formerly been the boy's, and of which they now wished that they had given him even more. She was pale from her long watches at the sick-bed; so they consulted between them, and with her husband, on means of cheering and distracting her.

But after some time Jakob was struck with, and scared by, her silence. It seemed at first as if, except for her household orders, she found it unnecessary to speak, and later on as if she had forgotten or lost the faculty of speech. His timid attempts to inspirit her so much appeared to surprise and puzzle her that he lacked the spirit to go on with them.

A couple of months after Jens' death Jakob took his wife for a drive by the road which runs from Copenhagen to Elsinore, along the Sound. It was a lovely, warm and fresh day in May. As they came to Charlottenlund he proposed to her that they should walk through the wood, and send the carriage round to meet them. So they got down by the forest-gate, and for a moment their eyes followed the carriage as it rolled away on the road.

They came into the wood, into a green world. The beech trees had been out for three weeks, the first mysterious translucence of early May was over. But the foliage was still so young that the green of the forest world was the brighter in the shade. Later on, after midsummer, the wood would be almost black in the shade, and brilliantly green in the sun. Now, where the rays of the sun fell through the tree-crowns, the ground was colourless, dim, as if powdered with sun-dust. But where the wood lay in shadow it glowed and luminesced like green glass and jewels. The anemones were faded and gone; the young fine grass was already tall. And within the heart of the forest the woodruff was in bloom; its layer of diminutive, starry, white flowers seemed to float, round the knotty roots of the old grey beeches, like the surface of a milky lake, a foot above the ground. It had rained in the night; upon the narrow road the deep tracks of the wood-cutters' cart were moist. Here and there, by the roadside, a grey, misty globe of a withered dandelion caught the sun; the flower of the field had come on a visit to the wood.

They walked on slowly. As they came a little way into the wood they suddenly heard the cuckoo, quite close. They stood still and listened, then walked on. Emilie let go her husband's arm to pick up from the road the shell of a small, pale-blue, bird's egg, broken in two; she tried to set it together, and kept it on the palm of her hand. Jakob began to talk to her of a journey to Germany that he had planned for them, and of the places that they were to see. She listened docilely, and was silent.

They had come to the end of the wood. From the gate they had a great view over the open landscape. After the green sombreness of the forest the outside world seemed unbelievably light, as if bleached by the luminous dimness of midday. But after a while the colours of fields, meadows and dispersed groups of trees defined themselves to the eye, one by one. There was a faint blue in the sky, and faint white cumulus clouds rose along the horizon. The young green rye on the fields was about to ear; where the finger of the breeze touched it it ran in long, gentle billows along the ground. The small thatched peasants' houses lay like lime-white, square isles within the undulating land; round them the lilac-hedges bore up their light foliage and, on the top, clusters of pale flowers. They heard the rolling of a carriage on the road in the distance, and above their heads the incessant singing of innumerable larks.

By the edge of the forest there lay a wind-felled tree. Emilie said: "Let us sit down here a little."

She loosened the ribbons of her bonnet and lay it in her lap. After a minute she said: "There is something I want to tell you," and made a long pause. All through this conversation in the wood she behaved in the same way, with a long silence before each phrase—not exactly as if she were collecting her thoughts, but as if she were finding speech in itself laborious or deficient.

She said: "The boy was my own child." "What are you talking about?" Jakob asked her. "Jens," she said, "he was my child. Do you remember telling me that when you saw him the first time you thought he was like me? He was indeed like me; he was my son." Now Jakob might have been frightened, and have believed her to be out of her mind. But lately things had, to him, come about in unexpected ways; he was prepared for the paradoxical. So he sat quietly on the trunk, and looked down on the young beech-shoots in the ground. "My dear," he said, "my dear, you do not know what you say."

She was silent for a while, as if distressed by his interruption of her course of thought. "It is difficult to other people to understand, I know," she said at last, patiently. "If Jens had been here still, he might perhaps have made you understand, better than I. But try," she went on, "to understand me. I have thought that you ought to know. And if I cannot speak to you I cannot speak to anyone." She said this with a kind of grave concern, as if really threatened by total incapacity of speech. He remembered how, during these last weeks, he had felt her silence heavy on him, and had tried to make her speak of something, of anything. "No, my dear," he said, "you speak, I shall not interrupt you." Gently, as if thankful for his promise, she began:

"He was my child, and Charlie Dreyer's. You have met Charlie once in Papa's house. But it was while you were in China that he became my lover." At these words Jakob remembered the anonymous letter he had once received. As he recalled his own indignant scouting of the slander and the care with which he had kept it from her, it seemed to him a curious thing that after five years he was to have it repeated by her own lips.

"When he asked me," said Emilie, "I stood for a moment in great danger. For I had never talked with a man of this matter. Only with Aunt Malvina and with my old governess. And women, for some reason, I do not know which, will have it that such a demand be a base and selfish thing in a man, and an insult to a woman. Why do you allow us to think that of you? You, who are a man, will know that he asked me out of his love and out of his great heart, from magnanimity. He had more life in him than he himself needed. He meant to give that to me. It was life itself; yes, it was eternity that he offered me. And I, who had been taught so wrong, I might easily have rejected him. Even now, when I think of it, I am afraid, as of death. Still I need not be so, for I know for certain that if I were back at that moment again, I should behave in the same way as I did then. And I was saved from the danger. I did not send him away. I let him walk back with me, through the garden—for we were down by the garden-gate—and stay with me the night till, in the morning, he was to go so far away."

She again made a long pause, and went on: "All the same, because of the doubt and the fear of other people that I had in my heart, I and the child had to go through much. If I had been a poor girl, with only a hundred rixdollars in all the world, it would have been better, for then we should have remained together. Yes, we went through much."

"When I found Jens again and he came home with me," she took up her narrative after a silence, "I did not love him. You all loved him, only I myself did not. It was Charlie that I loved. Still I was more with Jens than any of you. He told me many things, which none of you heard. I saw that we could not find another such as he, that there was none so wise." She did not know that she was quoting the Scripture, any more than the old shipowner had been aware of doing so when he ordained Jens to be buried in the field of his fathers and the cave that was therein —this was a small trick peculiar to the magic of the dead child. "I learned much from him. He was always truthful, like Charlie. He was so truthful that he made me ashamed of myself. Sometimes I thought it wrong in me to teach him to call you Papa."

"By the time when he was ill," she said, "what I thought of was this: that if he died I might, at last, go into mourning for Charlie." She lifted up her bonnet, gazed at it and again dropped it. "And then after all," she said, "I could not do it." She made a pause. "Still if I had told Jens about it, it would have pleased him; it would have made him laugh. He would have told me to buy grand black clothes, and long veils."

It was a lucky thing, Jakob reflected, that he had promised her not to interrupt her tale. For had she wanted him to speak he should not have found a word to say. As now she came to this point in her story she sat in silence for a long time, so that for a moment he believed that she had finished, and at that a choking sensation came upon him, as if all words must needs stick in his throat.

"I thought," she suddenly began again, "that I would have had to suffer, terribly even, for all this. But no, it has not been so. There is a grace in the world, such as none of us has known about. The world is not a hard or severe place, as people tell us. It is not even just. You are forgiven everything. The fine things of the world you cannot wrong or harm; they are much too strong for that. You could not wrong or harm Jens; no one could. And now, after he has died," she said, "I understand everything."

Again she sat immovable, gently poised upon the tree-stem. For the first time during their talk she looked round her; her gaze ran slowly, almost caressingly, along the forest scenery.

"It is difficult," she said, "to explain what it feels like to understand things. I have never been good at finding words, I am not like Jens. But it has seemed to me ever since March, since the Spring began, that I have known well why things happened, why, for instance, they all flowered. And why the birds came. The generosity of the world; Papa's and your kindness too! As we walked in the wood today I thought that now I have got back my sight, and my sense of smell, from when I was a little girl. All things here tell me, of their own, what they signify." She stopped, her gaze steadying. "They signify Charlie," she said. After a long pause she added: "And I, I am Emilie. Nothing can alter that either."

She made a gesture as if to pull on her gloves that lay in her bonnet, but she put them back again, and remained quiet, as before.

"Now I have told you all," she said. "Now you must decide what we are to do."

"Papa will never know," she said gently and thoughtfully. "None of them will ever know. Only you. I have thought, if you will let me do so, that you and I, when we talk of Jens—" She made a slight pause, and Jakob thought: "She has never talked of him till today"—"might talk of all these things, too."

"Only in one thing," she said slowly, "am I wiser than you. I know that it would be better, much better, and easier to both you and me if you would believe me."

Jakob was accustomed to take a quick summary of a situation and to make his dispositions accordingly. He waited a moment after she had ceased to talk, to do so now.

"Yes, my dear," he said, "that is true."

DESIRE AND THE BLACK MASSEUR

by Tennessee Williams

From his very beginning this person, Anthony Burns, had betrayed an instinct for being included in things that swallowed him up. In his family there had been fifteen children and he the one given least notice, and when he went to work, after graduating from high school in the largest class on the records of that institution, he secured his job in the largest wholesale company of the city. Everything absorbed him and swallowed him up, and still he did not feel secure. He felt more secure at the movies than anywhere else. He loved to sit in the back rows of the movies where the darkness absorbed him gently so that he was like a particle of food dissolving in a big hot mouth. The cinema licked at his mind with a tender, flickering tongue that all but lulled him to sleep. Yes, a big motherly Nannie of a dog could not have licked him better or given him sweeter repose than the cinema did when he went there after work. His mouth would fall open at the movies and saliva would accumulate in it and dribble out the sides of it and all his being would relax so utterly that all the prickles and tightenings of a whole day's anxiety

From *One Arm and Other Stories* by Tennessee Williams (New York: New Directions, 1954), pp. 83–94.

would be lifted away. He didn't follow the story on the screen but watched the figures. What they said or did was immaterial to him, he cared about only the figures who warmed him as if they were cuddled right next to him in the dark picture house and he loved every one of them but the ones with shrill voices.

The timidest kind of a person was Anthony Burns, always scuttling from one kind of protection to another but none of them ever being durable enough to suit him.

Now at the age of thirty, by virtue of so much protection, he still had in his face and body the unformed look of a child and he moved like a child in the presence of critical elders. In every move of his body and every inflection of speech and cast of expression there was a timid apology going out to the world for the little space that he had been somehow elected to occupy in it. His was not an inquiring type of mind. He only learned what he was required to learn and about himself he learned nothing. He had no idea of what his real desires were. Desire is something that is made to occupy a larger space than that which is afforded by the individual being, and this was especially true in the case of Anthony Burns. His desires, or rather his basic desire, was so much too big for him that it swallowed him up as a coat that should have been cut into ten smaller sizes, or rather there should have been that much more of Burns to make it fit him.

For the sins of the world are really only its partialities, its incompletions, and these are what sufferings must atone for. A wall that has been omitted from a house because the stones were exhausted, a room in a house left unfurnished because the householder's funds were not sufficient—these sorts of incompletions are usually covered up or glossed over by some kind of make-shift arrangement. The nature of man is full of such make-shift arrangements, devised by himself to cover his incompletion. He feels a part of himself to be like a missing wall or a room left unfurnished and he tries as well as he can to make up for it. The use of imagination, resorting to dreams or the loftier purpose of art, is a mask he devises to cover his incompletion. Or violence such as a war, between two men or among a number of nations, is also a blind and senseless compensation for that which is not yet formed in human nature. Then there is still another compensation. This one is found in the principle of atonement, the surrender of self to violent treatment by others with the idea of thereby clearing one's self of his guilt. This last way was the one that Anthony Burns unconsciously had elected.

Now at the age of thirty he was about to discover the instrument of his atonement. Like all other happenings in his life, it came about without intention or effort.

One afternoon, which was a Saturday afternoon in November, he went from his work in the huge wholesale corporation to a place with a red neon sign that said "Turkish Baths and Massage." He had been suffering lately from a vague sort of ache near the base of his spine and somebody else employed at the wholesale corporation had told him that he would be relieved by massage. You would suppose that the mere suggestion of such a thing would frighten him out of his wits, but when desire lives constantly with fear, and no partition between them, desire must become very tricky; it has to become as sly as the adversary, and this was one of those times when desire outwitted the enemy under the roof. At the very mention of the word "massage," the desire woke up and exuded a sort of anesthetizing vapor all through Burns' nerves, catching fear off guard and allowing Burns to slip by it. Almost without knowing that he was really going, he went to the baths that Saturday afternoon.

The baths were situated in the basement of a hotel, right at the center of the keyed-up mercantile nerves of the downtown section, and yet the baths were a tiny world of their own. Secrecy was the atmosphere of the place and seemed to be its purpose. The entrance door had an oval of milky glass through which you could only detect a glimmer of light. And even when a patron had been admitted, he found himself standing in labyrinths of partitions, of corridors and cubicles curtained off from each other, of chambers with opaque doors and milky globes over lights and sheathings of vapor. Everywhere were agencies of concealment. The bodies of patrons, divested of their clothing, were swathed in billowing tent-like sheets of white fabric. They trailed barefooted along the moist white tiles, as white and noiseless as ghosts except for their breathing, and their faces all wore a nearly vacant expression. They drifted as if they had no thought to conduct them.

But now and again, across the central hallway, would step a masseur. The masseurs were Negroes. They seemed very dark and positive against the loose white hangings of the baths. They wore no sheets, they had on loose cotton drawers, and they moved about with force and resolution. They alone seemed to have an authority here. Their voices rang out boldly, never whispering in the sort of apologetic way that the patrons had in asking directions of them. This was their own rightful province, and they swept the white hangings aside with great black palms that you felt might just as easily have seized bolts of lightning and thrown them back at the clouds.

Anthony Burns stood more uncertainly than most near the entrance of the bath-house. Once he had gotten through the milky-paned door his fate was decided and no more action or will on his part was called for. He paid two-fifty, which was the price of a bath and massage, and from that moment forward had only to follow directions and submit to care. Within a few moments a Negro masseur came to Burns and propelled him onward and then around a corner where he was led into one of the curtained-compartments.

Take off your clothes, said the Negro.

The Negro had already sensed an unusual something about his latest patron and so he did not go out of the canvas-draped cubicle but remained leaning against a wall while Burns obeyed and undressed. The white man turned his face to the wall away from the Negro and fumbled awkwardly with his dark winter clothes. It took him a long time to get the clothes off his body, not because he wilfully lingered about it but because of a dream-like state in which he was deeply falling. A faraway feeling engulfed him and his hands and fingers did not seem to be his own, they were numb and hot as if they were caught in the clasp of someone standing behind him, manipulating their motions. But at last he stood naked, and when he turned slowly about to face the Negro masseur, the black giant's eyes appeared not to see him at all and yet they had a glitter not present before, a liquid brightness suggesting bits of wet coal.

Put this on, he directed and held out to Burns a white sheet.

Gratefully the little man enveloped himself in the enormous coarse fabric and, holding it delicately up from his small-boned, womanish feet, he followed the Negro masseur through another corridor of rustling white curtains to the entrance of an opaque glass enclosure which was the steam-room. There his conductor left him. The blank walls heaved and sighed as steam issued from them. It swirled about Burns' naked figure, enveloping him in a heat and moisture such as the inside of a tremendous mouth, to be drugged and all but dissolved in this burning white vapor which hissed out of unseen walls.

After a time the black masseur returned. With a mumbled command, he led the trembling Burns back into the cubicle where he had left his clothes. A bare white table had been wheeled into the chamber during Burns' absence.

Lie on this, said the Negro.

Burns obeyed. The black masseur poured alcohol on Burns' body, first on his chest and then on his belly and thighs. It ran all over him, biting at him like insects. He gasped a little and crossed his legs over the wild complaint of his groin. Then without any warning the Negro raised up his black palm and brought it down with a terrific whack on the middle of Burns' soft belly. The little man's breath flew out of his mouth in a gasp and for two or three moments he couldn't inhale another.

Immediately after the passing of the first shock, a feeling of pleasure went through him. It swept as a liquid from either end of his body and into the tingling hollow of his groin. He dared not look, but he knew what the Negro must see. The black giant was grinning.

I hope I didn't hit you too hard, he murmured.

No, said Burns.

Turn over, said the Negro.

Burns tried vainly to move but the luxurious tiredness made him unable to. The Negro laughed and gripped the small of his waist and flopped him over as easily as he might have turned a pillow. Then he began to belabor his shoulders and buttocks with blows that increased in violence, and as the violence and the pain increased, the little man grew more and more fiercely hot with his first true satisfaction, until all at once a knot came loose in his loins and released a warm flow.

So by surprise is a man's desire discovered, and once discovered, the only need is surrender, to take what comes and ask no questions about it: and this was something that Burns was expressly made for.

Time and again the white-collar clerk went back to the Negro masseur. The knowledge grew quickly between them of what Burns wanted, that he was in search of atonement, and the black masseur was the natural instrument of it. He hated white-skinned bodies because they abused his pride. He loved to have their white skin prone beneath him, to bring his fist or the palm of his hand down hard on its passive surface. He had barely been able to hold this love in restraint, to control the wish that he felt to pound more fiercely and use the full of his power. But now at long last the suitable person had entered his orbit of passion. In the white-collar clerk he had located all that he longed for.

Those times when the black giant relaxed, when he sat at the rear of the baths and smoked cigarettes or devoured a bar of candy, the image of Burns would loom before his mind, a nude white body with angry red marks on it. The bar of chocolate would stop just short of his lips and the lips would slacken into a dreamy smile. The giant loved Burns, and Burns adored the giant.

Burns had become absent-minded about his work. Right in the middle of typing a factory order, he would lean back at his desk and the giant would swim in the atmosphere before him. Then he would smile and his work-stiffened fingers would loosen and flop on the desk. Sometimes the boss would stop near him and call his name crossly. Burns! Burns! What are you dreaming about?

Throughout the winter the violence of the massage increased by fairly reasonable degrees, but when March came it was suddenly stepped up.

Burns left the baths one day with two broken ribs.

Every morning he hobbled to work more slowly and painfully but the state of his body could still be explained by saying he had rheumatism.

One day his boss asked him what he was doing for it. He told his boss that he was taking massage.

It don't seem to do you any good, said the boss.

Oh, yes, said Burns, I am showing lots of improvement!

That evening came his last visit to the baths.

His right leg was fractured. The blow which had broken the limb was so terrific that Burns had been unable to stifle an outcry. The manager of the bath establishment heard it and came into the compartment.

Burns was vomiting over the edge of the table.

Christ, said the manager, what's been going on here?

The black giant shrugged.

He asked me to hit him harder.

The manager looked over Burns and discovered his many bruises.

What do you think this is? A jungle? he asked the masseur.

Again the black giant shrugged.

Get the hell out of my place! the manager shouted. Take this perverted little monster with you, and neither of you had better show up here again!

The black giant tenderly lifted his drowsy partner and bore him away to a room in the town's Negro section.

There for a week the passion between them continued.

This interval was toward the end of the Lenten season. Across from the room where Burns and the Negro were staying there was a church whose open windows spilled out the mounting exhortations of a preacher. Each afternoon the fiery poem of death on the cross was repeated. The preacher was not fully conscious of what he wanted nor were the listeners, groaning and writhing before him. All of them were involved in a massive atonement.

Now and again some manifestation occurred, a woman stood up to expose a wound in her breast. Another had slashed an artery at her wrist.

Suffer, suffer, suffer! the preacher shouted. Our Lord was nailed on a cross for the sins of the world! They led him above the town to the place of the skull, they moistened his lips with vinegar on a sponge, they drove five nails through his body, and He was The Rose of the World as He bled on the cross!

The congregation could not remain in the building but tumbled out on the street in a crazed procession with clothes torn open.

The sins of the world are all forgiven! they shouted.

All during this celebration of human atonement, the Negro masseur was completing his purpose with Burns.

All the windows were open in the death-chamber.

The curtains blew out like thirsty little white tongues to lick at the street which seemed to reek with an overpowering honey. A house had caught fire on the block in back of the church. The walls collapsed and the cinders floated about in the gold atmosphere. The scarlet engines, the ladders and powerful hoses were useless against the purity of the flame.

The Negro masseur leaned over his still breathing victim.

Burns was whispering something.

The black giant nodded.

You know what you have to do now? the victim asked him. The black giant nodded.

He picked up the body, which barely held together, and placed it gently on a clean-swept table.

The giant began to devour the body of Burns.

It took him twenty-four hours to eat the splintered bones clean.

When he had finished, the sky was serenely blue, the passionate services at the church were finished, the ashes had settled, the scarlet engines had gone and the reek of honey was blown from the atmosphere.

Quiet had returned and there was an air of completion.

Those bare white bones, left over from Burns' atonement, were placed in a sack and borne to the end of a car-line.

There the masseur walked out on a lonely pier and dropped his burden under the lake's quiet surface.

As the giant turned homeward, he mused on his satisfaction.

Yes, it is perfect, he thought, it is now completed!

Then in the sack, in which he had carried the bones, he dropped his belongings, a neat blue suit to conceal his dangerous body, some buttons of pearl and a picture of Anthony Burns as a child of seven.

He moved to another city, obtained employment once more as an expert masseur. And there in a white-curtained place, serenely conscious of fate bringing toward him another, to suffer atonement as it had been suffered by Burns, he stood impassively waiting inside a milky white door for the next to arrive.

And meantime, slowly, with barely a thought of so doing, the earth's whole population twisted and writhed beneath the manipulation of night's black fingers and the white ones of day with skeletons splintered and flesh reduced to pulp, as out of this unlikely problem, the answer, perfection, was slowly evolved through torture.

THE RIVER

by Flannery O'Connor

The child stood glum and limp in the middle of the dark living room while his father pulled him into a plaid coat. His right arm was hung in the sleeve but the father buttoned the coat anyway and pushed him forward toward a pale spotted hand that stuck through the half-open door.

"He ain't fixed right," a loud voice said from the hall.

"Well then for Christ's sake fix him," the father muttered. "It's six o'clock in the morning." He was in his bathrobe and barefooted. When he got the child to the door and tried to shut it, he found her looming in it, a speckled skeleton in a long pea-green coat and felt helmet.

"And his and my carfare," she said. "It'll be twict we have to ride the car."

He went in the bedroom again to get the money and when he came back, she and the boy were both standing in the middle of the room. She was taking stock. "I couldn't smell those dead cigarette butts long if I was ever to come sit with you," she said, shaking him down in his coat.

"Here's the change," the father said. He went to the door and opened it wide and waited.

After she had counted the money she slipped it somewhere inside her coat and walked over to a watercolor hanging near the phonograph. "I know what time it is," she said, peering closely at the black lines crossing into broken planes of violent color. "I ought to. My shift goes on at 10 P.M. and don't get off till 5 and it takes me one hour to ride the Vine Street car."

"Oh, I see," he said; "well, we'll expect him back tonight, about eight or nine?"

"Maybe later," she said. "We're going to the river to a healing. This particular preacher don't get around this way often. I wouldn't have paid for that," she said, nodding at the painting, "I would have drew it myself."

"All right, Mrs. Connin, we'll see you then," he said, drumming on the door.

A toneless voice called from the bedroom, "Bring me an icepack."

"Too bad his mamma's sick," Mrs. Connin said. "What's her trouble?"

"We don't know," he muttered.

"We'll ask the preacher to pray for her. He's healed a lot of folks. The

---

From *A Good Man is Hard to Find* by Flannery O'Connor (New York: Harcourt, Brace & World, Inc., 1955), pp. 30–52.

Reverend Bevel Summers. Maybe she ought to see him sometime."

"Maybe so," he said. "We'll see you tonight," and he disappeared into the bedroom and left them to go.

The little boy stared at her silently, his nose and eyes running. He was four or five. He had a long face and bulging chin and half-shut eyes set far apart. He seemed mute and patient, like an old sheep waiting to be let out.

"You'll like this preacher," she said. "The Reverend Bevel Summers. You ought to hear him sing."

The bedroom door opened suddenly and the father stuck his head out and said, "Good-by, old man. Have a good time."

"Good-by," the little boy said and jumped as if he had been shot.

Mrs. Connin gave the watercolor another look. Then they went out into the hall and rang for the elevator. "I wouldn't have drew it," she said.

Outside the gray morning was blocked off on either side by the unlit empty buildings. "It's going to fair up later," she said, "but this is the last time we'll be able to have any preaching at the river this year. Wipe your nose, Sugar Boy."

He began rubbing his sleeve across it but she stopped him. "That ain't nice," she said. "Where's your handkerchief?"

He put his hands in his pockets and pretended to look for it while she waited. "Some people don't care how they send one off," she murmured to her reflection in the coffee shop window. "You pervide." She took a red and blue flowered handkerchief out of her pocket and stooped down and began to work on his nose. "Now blow," she said and he blew. "You can borry it. Put it in your pocket."

He folded it up and put it in his pocket carefully and they walked on to the corner and leaned against the side of a closed drugstore to wait for the car. Mrs. Connin turned up her coat collar so that it met her hat in the back. Her eyelids began to droop and she looked as if she might go to sleep against the wall. The little boy put a slight pressure on her hand.

"What's your name?" she asked in a drowsy voice. "I don't know but only your last name. I should have found out your first name."

His name was Harry Ashfield and he had never thought at any time before of changing it. "Bevel," he said.

Mrs. Connin raised herself from the wall. "Why ain't that a coincident!" she said. "I told you that's the name of this preacher!"

"Bevel," he repeated.

She stood looking down at him as if he had become a marvel to her. "I'll have to see you meet him today," she said. "He's no ordinary preacher. He's a healer. He couldn't do nothing for Mr. Connin though. Mr. Connin didn't have the faith but he said he would try anything once. He had this griping in his gut."

The trolley appeared as a yellow spot at the end of the deserted street.

"He's gone to the government hospital now," she said, "and they taken one-third of his stomach. I tell him he better thank Jesus for what he's got left but he says he ain't thanking nobody. Well I declare," she murmured, "Bevel!"

They walked out to the tracks to wait. "Will he heal me?" Bevel asked.

"What you got?"

"I'm hungry," he decided finally.

"Didn't you have your breakfast?"

"I didn't have time to be hungry yet then," he said.

"Well when we get home we'll both have us something," she said. "I'm ready myself."

They got on the car and sat down a few seats behind the driver and Mrs. Connin took Bevel on her knees. "Now you be a good boy," she said, "and let me get some sleep. Just don't get off my lap." She lay her head back and as he watched, gradually her eyes closed and her mouth fell open to show a few long scattered teeth, some gold and some darker than her face; she began to whistle and blow like a musical skeleton. There was no one in the car but themselves and the driver and when he saw she was asleep, he took out the flowered handkerchief and unfolded it and examined it carefully. Then he folded it up again and unzipped a place in the innerlining of his coat and hid it in there and shortly he went to sleep himself.

Her house was a half-mile from the end of the car line, set back a little from the road. It was tan paper brick with a porch across the front of it and a tin top. On the porch there were three little boys of different sizes with identical speckled faces and one tall girl who had her hair up in so many aluminum curlers that it glared like the roof. The three boys followed them inside and closed in on Bevel. They looked at him silently, not smiling.

"That's Bevel," Mrs. Connin said, taking off her coat. "It's a coincident he's named the same as the preacher. These boys are J. C., Spivey, and Sinclair, and that's Sarah Mildred on the porch. Take off that coat and hang it on the bed post, Bevel."

The three boys watched him while he unbuttoned the coat and took it off. Then they watched him hang it on the bed post and then they stood, watching the coat. They turned abruptly and went out the door and had a conference on the porch.

Bevel stood looking around him at the room. It was part kitchen and part bedroom. The entire house was two rooms and two porches. Close to his foot the tail of a light-colored dog moved up and down between two floor boards as he scratched his back on the underside of the house. Bevel jumped on it but the hound was experienced and had already withdrawn when his feet hit the spot.

The walls were filled with pictures and calendars. There were two round photographs of an old man and woman with collapsed mouths and another picture of a man whose eyebrows dashed out of two bushes of hair and clashed in a heap on the bridge of his nose; the rest of his face stuck out like a bare cliff to fall from. "That's Mr. Connin," Mrs. Connin said, standing back from the stove for a second to admire the face with him, "but it don't favor him any more." Bevel turned from Mr. Connin to a colored picture over the bed of a man wearing a white sheet. He had long hair and a gold circle around his head and he was sawing on a board while some children stood watching him. He was going to ask who that was when the three boys came in again and motioned for him to follow them. He thought of crawling under the bed and hanging onto one of the legs but the three boys only stood there, speckled and silent, waiting, and after a second he followed them at a little distance out on the porch and around the corner of the house. They started off through a field of rough yellow weeds to the hog pen, a five-foot boarded square full of shoats, which they intended to ease him over into. When they reached it, they turned and waited silently, leaning against the side.

He was coming very slowly, deliberately bumping his feet together as if he had trouble walking. Once he had been beaten up in the park by some strange boys when his sitter forgot him, but he hadn't known anything was going to happen that time until it was over. He began to smell a strong odor of garbage and to hear the noises of a wild animal. He stopped a few feet from the pen and waited, pale but dogged.

The three boys didn't move. Something seemed to have happened to them. They stared over his head as if they saw something coming behind him but he was afraid to turn his own head and look. Their speckles were pale and their eyes were still and gray as glass. Only their ears twitched slightly. Nothing happened. Finally, the one in the middle said, "She'd kill us," and turned, dejected and hacked, and climbed up on the pen and hung over, staring in.

Bevel sat down on the ground, dazed with relief, and grinned up at them.

The one sitting on the pen glanced at him severely. "Hey you," he said after a second, "if you can't climb up and see these pigs you can lift that bottom board off and look in thataway." He appeared to offer this as a kindness.

Bevel had never seen a real pig but he had seen a pig in a book and knew they were small fat pink animals with curly tails and round grinning faces and bow ties. He leaned forward and pulled eagerly at the board.

"Pull harder," the littlest boy said. "It's nice and rotten. Just life out thet nail."

He eased a long reddish nail out of the soft wood.

"Now you can lift up the board and put your face to the . . ." a quiet voice began.

He had already done it and another face, gray, wet and sour, was pushing into his, knocking him down and back as it scraped out under the plank. Something snorted over him and charged back again, rolling him over and pushing him up from behind and then sending him forward, screaming through the yellow field, while it bounced behind.

The three Connins watched from where they were. The one sitting on the pen held the loose board back with his dangling foot. Their stern faces didn't brighten any but they seemed to become less taut, as if some great need had been partly satisfied. "Maw ain't goin to like him lettin out thet hawg," the smallest one said.

Mrs. Connin was on the back porch and caught Bevel up as he reached the steps. The hog ran under the house and subsided, panting, but the child screamed for five minutes. When she had finally calmed him down, she gave him his breakfast and let him sit on her lap while he ate it. The shoat climbed the two steps onto the back porch and stood outside the screen door, looking in with his head lowered sullenly. He was long-legged and hump-backed and part of one of his ears had been bitten off.

"Git away!" Mrs. Connin shouted. "That one yonder favors Mr. Paradise that has the gas station," she said. "You'll see him today at the healing. He's got the cancer over his ear. He always comes to show he ain't been healed."

The shoat stood squinting a few seconds longer and then moved off slowly. "I don't want to see him," Bevel said.

They walked to the river, Mrs. Connin in front with him and the three boys strung out behind and Sarah Mildred, the tall girl at the end to holler if one of them ran out on the road. They looked like the skeleton of an old boat with two pointed ends, sailing slowly on the edge of the highway. The white Sunday sun followed at a little distance, climbing fast through a scum of gray cloud as if it meant to overtake them. Bevel walked on the outside edge, holding Mrs. Connin's hand and looking down into the orange and purple gulley that dropped off from the concrete.

It occurred to him that he was lucky this time that they had found Mrs. Connin who would take you away for the day instead of an ordinary sitter who only sat where you lived or went to the park. You found out more when you left where you lived. He had found out already this morning that he had been made by a carpenter named Jesus Christ. Before he had thought it had been a doctor named Sladewall, a fat man with a yellow mustache who gave him shots and thought his name was Herbert, but this must have been a joke. They joked a lot where he lived. If he had thought about it before, he would have thought Jesus Christ was a word like "oh" or "damm" or "God," or maybe somebody who had cheated them out of something sometime. When he had asked Mrs. Connin who the man in the sheet in the picture over her bed was, she had looked at him a while with her mouth open. Then she had said, "That's Jesus," and she had kept on looking at him.

In a few minutes she had got up and got a book out of the other room. "See here," she said, turning over the cover, "this belonged to my great grandmamma. I wouldn't part with it for nothing on earth." She ran her finger under some brown writing on a spotted page. "Emma Stevens Oakley, 1832," she said. "Ain't that something to have? And every word of it the gospel truth." She turned the next page and read him the name: "The Life of Jesus Christ for Readers Under Twelve." Then she read him the book.

It was a small book, pale brown on the outside with gold edges and a smell like old putty. It was full of pictures, one of the carpenter driving a crowd of pigs out of a man. They were real pigs, gray and sour-looking, and Mrs. Connin said Jesus had driven them all out of this one man. When she finished reading, she let him sit on the floor and look at the pictures again.

Just before they left for the healing, he had managed to get the book inside his innerlining without her seeing him. Now it made his coat hang down a little farther on one side than the other. His mind was dreamy and serene as they walked along and when they turned off the highway onto a long red clay road winding between banks of honeysuckle, he began to make wild leaps and pull forward on her hand as if he wanted to dash off and snatch the sun which was rolling away ahead of them now.

They walked on the dirt road for a while and then they crossed a field stippled with purple weeds and entered the shadows of a wood where the ground was covered with thick pine needles. He had never been in woods before and he walked carefully, looking from side to side as if he were entering a strange country. They moved along a bridle path that twisted downhill through crackling red leaves, and once, catching at a branch to keep himself from slipping, he looked into two frozen green-gold eyes enclosed in the darkness of a tree hole. At the bottom of the hill, the woods opened suddenly onto a pasture dotted here and there with black and white cows and sloping down, tier after tier, to a broad orange stream where the reflection of the sun was set like a diamond.

There were people standing on the near bank in a group, singing. Long tables were set up behind them and a few cars and trucks were parked in a road that came up by the river. They crossed the pasture, hurrying, because Mrs. Connin, using her hand for a shed over her eyes, saw the preacher already standing out in the water. She dropped her basket on one of the tables and pushed the three boys in front of her into the knot of people so that they wouldn't linger by the food. She kept Bevel by the hand and eased her way up to the front.

The preacher was standing about ten feet out in the stream where the water came up to his knees. He was a tall youth in khaki trousers that he had rolled up higher than the water. He had on a blue shirt and a red scarf around his neck but no hat and his light-colored hair was cut in side-burns that curved into the hollows of his checks. His face was all bone and red light reflected from the river. He looked as if he might have been nineteen years old. He was singing in a high twangy voice, above the singing on the bank, and he kept his hands behind him and his head tilted back.

He ended the hymn on a high note and stood silent, looking down at the water and shifting his feet in it. Then he looked up at the people on the bank. They stood close together, waiting; their faces were solemn but expectant and every eye was on him. He shifted his feet again.

"Maybe I know why you come," he said in the twangy voice, "maybe I don't.

"If you ain't come for Jesus, you ain't come for me. If you just come to see can you leave your pain in the river, you ain't come for Jesus. You can't leave your pain in the river," he said. "I never told nobody that." He stopped and looked down at his knees.

"I seen you cure a woman oncet!" a sudden high voice shouted from the hump of people. "Seen that woman git up and walk out straight where she had limped in!"

The preacher lifted one foot and then the other. He seemed almost but not quite to smile. "You might as well go home if that's what you come for," he said.

Then he lifted his head and arms and shouted, "Listen to what I got to say, you people! There ain't but one river and that's the River of Life, made out of Jesus' Blood. That's the river you have to lay your pain in, in the River of Faith, in the River of Life, in the River of Love, in the rich red river of Jesus' Blood, you people!"

His voice grew soft and musical. "All the rivers come from that one River and go back to it like it was the ocean sea and if you believe, you can lay your pain in that River and get rid of it because that's the River that was made to carry sin. It's a River full of pain itself, pain itself, moving toward the Kingdom of Christ, to be washed away, slow, you people, slow as this here old red water river round my feet.

"Listen," he sang, "I read in Mark about an unclean man, I read in Luke about a blind man, I read in John about a dead man! Oh you people hear! The same blood that makes this River red, made that leper clean, made that blind man stare, made that dead man leap! You people with trouble," he cried, "lay it in that River of Blood, lay it in that River of Pain, and watch it move away toward the Kingdom of Christ."

While he preached, Bevel's eyes followed drowsily the slow circles of two silent birds revolving high in the air. Across the river there was a low red and gold grove of sassafras with hills of dark blue trees behind it and an occasional pine jutting over the skyline. Behind, in the distance, the city rose like a cluster of warts on the side of the mountain. The birds revolved downward and dropped lightly in the top of the highest pine and sat hunch-shouldered as if they were supporting the sky.

"If it's this River of Life you want to lay your pain in, then come up," the preacher said, "and lay your sorrow here. But don't be thinking this is the last of it because this old red river don't end here. This old red suffering stream goes on, you people, slow to the Kingdom of Christ. This old red river is good to Baptize in, good to lay your faith in, good to lay your pain in, but it ain't this muddy water here that saves you. I been all up and down this river this week," he said. "Tuesday I was in Fortune Lake, next day in Ideal, Friday me and my wife drove to Lulawillow to see a sick man there. Them people didn't see no healing," he said and his face burned redder for a second. "I never said they would."

While he was talking a fluttering figure had begun to move forward with a kind of butterfly movement—an old woman with flapping arms whose head wobbled as if it might fall off any second. She managed to lower herself at the edge of the bank and let her arms churn in the water. Then she bent farther and pushed her face down in it and raised herself up finally, streaming wet; and still flapping, she turned a time or two in a blind circle until someone reached out and pulled her back into the group.

"She's been that way for thirteen years," a rough voice shouted. "Pass the hat and give this kid his money. That's what he's here for." The shout, directed out to the boy in the river, came from a huge old man who sat like a humped stone on the bumper of a long ancient gray automobile. He had on a gray hat that was turned down over one ear and up over the other to expose a purple bulge on his left temple. He sat bent forward with his hands hanging between his knees and his small eyes half closed.

Bevel stared at him once and then moved into the folds of Mrs. Connin's coat and hid himself.

The boy in the river glanced at the old man quickly and raised his fist. "Believe Jesus or the devil!" he cried. "Testify to one or the other!"

"I know from my own self-experience," a woman's mysterious voice called from the knot of people, "I know from it that this preacher can heal. My eyes have been opened! I testify to Jesus!"

The preacher lifted his arms quickly and began to repeat all that he had said before about the River and the Kingdom of Christ and the old man sat on the bumper, fixing him with a narrow squint. From time to time Bevel stared at him again from around Mrs. Connin.

A man in overalls and a brown coat leaned forward and dipped his hand in the water quickly and shook it and leaned back, and a woman held a baby over the edge of the bank and splashed its feet with water. One man moved a little distance away and sat down on the bank and took off his shoes and waded out into the stream; he stood there for a few minutes with his face tilted as far back as it would go, then he waded back and put on his shoes. All this time, the preacher sang and did not appear to watch what went on.

As soon as he stopped singing, Mrs. Connin lifted Bevel up and said, "Listen here, preacher, I got a boy from town today that I'm keeping. His mamma's sick and he wants you to pray for her. And this is a coincident—his name is Bevel! Bevel," she said, turning to look at the people behind her, "same as his. Ain't that a coincident, though?"

There were some murmurs and Bevel turned and grinned over her shoulder at the faces looking at him. "Bevel," he said in a loud jaunty voice.

"Listen," Mrs. Connin said, "have you ever been Baptized, Bevel?"

He only grinned.

"I suspect he ain't ever been Baptized," Mrs. Connin said, raising her eyebrows at the preacher.

"Swang him over here," the preacher said and took a stride forward and caught him.

He held him in the crook of his arm and looked at the grinning face. Bevel rolled his eyes in a comical way and thrust his face forward, close to the preacher's. "My name is Bevvvuuuuul," he said in a loud deep voice and let the tip of his tongue slide across his mouth.

The preacher didn't smile. His bony face was rigid and his narrow gray eyes reflected the almost colorless sky. There was a loud laugh from the old man sitting on the car bumper and Bevel grasped the back of the preacher's collar and held it tightly. The grin had already disappeared from his face. He had the sudden feeling that this was not a joke. Where he lived everything was a joke. From the preacher's face, he knew immediately that nothing the preacher said or did was a joke. "My mother named me that," he said quickly.

"Have you ever been Baptized?" the preacher asked.

"What's that?" he murmured.

"If I Baptize you," the preacher said, "you'll be able to go to the Kingdom of Christ. You'll be washed in the river of suffering, son, and you'll go by the deep river of life. Do you want that?"

"Yes," the child said, and thought, I won't go back to the apartment then, I'll go under the river.

"You won't be the same again," the preacher said. "You'll count." Then he turned his face to the people and began to preach and Bevel looked over his shoulder at the pieces of the white sun scattered in the river. Suddenly the preacher said, "All right, I'm going to Baptize you now," and without more warning, he tightened his hold and swung him upside down and plunged his head into the water. He held him under while he said the words of Baptism and then he jerked him up again and looked sternly at the gasping child. Bevel's eyes were dark and dilated. "You count now," the preacher said. "You didn't even count before."

The little boy was too shocked to cry. He spit out the muddy water and rubbed his wet sleeve into his eyes and over his face.

"Don't forget his mamma," Mrs. Connin called. "He wants you to pray for his mamma. She's sick."

"Lord," the preacher said, "we pray for somebody in affliction who isn't here to testify. Is your mother sick in the hospital?" he asked. "Is she in pain?"

The child stared at him. "She hasn't got up yet," he said in a high dazed voice. "She has a hangover." The air was so quiet he could hear the broken pieces of the sun knocking in the water.

The preacher looked angry and startled. The red drained out of his face and the sky appeared to darken in his eyes. There was a loud guffaw from the bank and Mr. Paradise shouted, "Haw! Cure the afflicted woman with the hangover!" and began to beat his knee with his fist.

"He's had a long day," Mrs. Connin said, standing with him in the door of the apartment and looking sharply into the room where the party was going on. "I reckon it's past his regular bedtime." One of Bevel's eyes was closed and the other half closed; his nose was running and he kept his mouth open and breathed through it. The damp plaid coat dragged down on one side.

That would be her, Mrs. Connin decided, in the black britches—long black satin britches and barefoot sandals and red toenails. She was lying on half the sofa, with her knees crossed in the air and her head propped on the arm. She didn't get up.

"Hello Harry," she said. "Did you have a big day?" She had a long pale face, smooth and blank, and straight sweet-potato-colored hair, pulled back.

The father went off to get the money. There were two other couples. One of the men, blond with little violet-blue eyes, leaned out of his chair and said, "Well Harry, old man, have a big day?"

"His name ain't Harry. It's Bevel," Mrs. Connin said.

"His name is Harry," *she* said from the sofa. "Whoever heard of anybody named Bevel?"

The little boy had seemed to be going to sleep on his feet, his head drooping farther and farther forward; he pulled it back suddenly and opened one eye; the other was stuck.

"He told me this morning his name was Bevel," Mrs. Connin said in a shocked voice. "The same as our preacher. We been all day at a preaching and healing at the river. He said his name was Bevel, the same as the preacher's. That's what he told me."

"Bevel!" his mother said. "My God! what a name."

"This preacher is name Bevel and there's no better preacher around," Mrs. Connin said. "And furthermore," she added in a defiant tone, "he Baptized this child this morning!"

His mother sat straight up. "Well the nerve!" she muttered.

"Furthermore," Mrs. Connin said, "he's a healer and he prayed for you to be healed."

"Healed!" she almost shouted. "Healed of what for Christ's sake?"

"Of your affliction," Mrs. Connin said icily.

The father had returned with the money and was standing near Mrs. Connin waiting to give it to her. His eyes were lined with red threads. "Go on, go on," he said, "I want to hear more about her affliction. The exact nature of it has escaped . . ." He waved the bill and his voice trailed off. "Healing by prayer is mighty inexpensive," he murmured.

Mrs. Connin stood a second, staring into the room, with a skeleton's appearance of seeing everything. Then, without taking the money, she turned and shut the door behind her. The father swung around, smiling vaguely, and shrugged. The rest of them were looking at Harry. The little boy began to shamble toward the bedroom.

"Come here, Harry," his mother said. He automatically shifted his direction toward her without opening his eye any farther. "Tell me what happened today," she said when he reached her. She began to pull off his coat.

"I don't know," he muttered.

"Yes you do know," she said, feeling the coat heavier on one side. She unzipped the innerlining and caught the book and a dirty handkerchief as they fell out. "Where did you get these?"

"I don't know," he said and grabbed for them. "They're mine. She gave them to me."

She threw the handkerchief down and held the book too high for him to reach and began to read it, her face after a second assuming an exaggerated comical expression. The others moved around and looked at it over her shoulder. "My God," somebody said.

One of the men peered at it sharply from behind a thick pair of glasses. "That's valuable," he said. "That's a collector's item," and he took it away from the rest of them and retired to another chair.

"Don't let George go off with that," his girl said.

"I tell you it's valuable," George said. "1832."

Bevel shifted his direction again toward the room where he slept. He shut the door behind him and moved slowly in the darkness to the bed and sat down and took off his shoes and got under the cover. After a minute a shaft of light let in the tall silhouette of his mother. She tiptoed lightly across the room and sat down on the edge of his bed. "What did that dolt of a preacher say about me?" she whispered. "What lies have you been telling today, honey?"

He shut his eye and heard her voice from a long way away, as if he were under the river and she on top of it. She shook his shoulder. "Harry," she said, leaning down and putting her mouth to his ear, "tell me what he said." She pulled him into a sitting position and he felt as if he had been drawn up from under the river. "Tell me," she whispered and her bitter breath covered his face.

He saw the pale oval close to him in the dark. "He said I'm not the same now," he muttered. "I count."

After a second, she lowered him by his shirt front onto the pillow. She hung over him an instant and brushed her lips against his forehead. Then she got up and moved away, swaying her hips lightly through the shaft of light.

He didn't wake up early but the apartment was still dark and close when he did. For a while he lay there, picking his nose and eyes. Then he sat up in bed and looked out the window. The sun came in palely, stained gray by the glass. Across the street at the Empire Hotel, a colored cleaning woman was looking down from an upper window, resting her face on her folded arms. He got up and put on his shoes and went to the bathroom and then into the front room. He ate two crackers spread with anchovy paste, that he found on the coffee table, and drank some ginger ale left in a bottle and looked around for his book but it was not there.

The apartment was silent except for the faint humming of the refrigerator. He went into the kitchen and found some raisin bread heels and spread a half jar of peanut butter between them and climbed up on the tall kitchen stool and sat chewing the sandwich slowly, wiping his nose every now and then on his shoulder. When he finished he found some chocolate milk and drank that. He would rather have had the ginger ale he saw but they left the bottle openers where he couldn't reach them. He studied what was left in the refrigerator for a while—some shriveled vegetables that she had forgot were there and a lot of brown oranges that she bought and didn't squeeze; there were three or four kinds of cheese and something fishy in a paper bag; the rest was a pork bone. He left the refrigerator door open and wandered back into the dark living room and sat down on the sofa.

He decided they would be out cold until one o'clock and that they would all have to go to a restaurant for lunch. He wasn't high enough for the table yet and the waiter would bring a highchair and he was too big for a high chair. He sat in the middle of the sofa, kicking it with his heels. Then he got up and wandered around the room, looking into the ashtrays at the butts as if this might be a habit. In his own room he had picture books and blocks but they were for the most part torn up; he found the way to get new ones was to tear up the ones he had. There was very little to do at any time but eat; however, he was not a fat boy.

He decided he would empty a few of the ashtrays on the floor. If he only emptied a few, she would think they had fallen. He emptied two, rubbing the ashes carefully into the rug with his finger. Then he lay on the floor for a while, studying his feet which he held up in the air. His shoes were still damp and he began to think about the river.

Very slowly, his expression changed as if he were gradually seeing appear what he didn't know he'd been looking for. Then all of a sudden he knew what he wanted to do.

He got up and tiptoed into their bedroom and stood in the dim light there, looking for her pocketbook. His glance passed her long pale arm hanging off the edge of the bed down to the floor, and across the white mound his father made, and past the crowded bureau, until it rested on the pocketbook hung on the back of a chair. He took a car-token out of it and half a package of Life Savers. Then he left the apartment and caught the car at the corner. He hadn't taken a suitcase because there was nothing from there he wanted to keep.

He got off the car at the end of the line and started down the road he and Mrs. Connin had taken the day before. He knew there wouldn't be anybody at her house because the three boys and the girl went to school and Mrs. Connin had told him she went out to clean. He passed her yard and walked on the way they had gone to the river. The paper brick houses were far apart and after a while the dirt place to walk on ended and he had to walk on the edge of the highway. The sun was pale yellow and high and hot.

He passed a shack with an orange gas pump in front of it but he didn't see the old man looking out at nothing in particular from the doorway. Mr. Paradise was having an orange drink. He finished it slowly, squinting over the bottle at the small plaid-coated figure disappearing down the road. Then he set the empty bottle on a bench and, still squinting, wiped his sleeve over his mouth. He went in the shack and picked out a peppermint stick, a foot long and two inches thick, from the candy shelf, and stuck it in his hip pocket. Then he got in his car and drove slowly down the highway after the boy.

By the time Bevel came to the field speckled with purple weeds, he was dusty and sweating and he crossed it at a trot to get into the woods as fast as he could. Once inside, he wandered from tree to tree, trying to find the path they had taken yesterday. Finally he found a line worn in the pine needles and followed it until he saw the steep trail twisting down through the trees.

Mr. Paradise had left his automobile back some way on the road and had walked to the place where he was accustomed to sit almost every day, holding an unbaited fishline in the water while he stared at the river passing in front of him. Anyone looking at him from a distance would have seen an old boulder half hidden in the bushes.

Bevel didn't see him at all. He only saw the river, shimmering reddish yellow, and bounded into it with his shoes and his coat on and took a gulp. He swallowed some and spit the rest out and then he stood there in water up to his chest and looked around him. The sky was a clear pale blue, all in one piece—except for the hole the sun made—and fringed around the bottom with treetops. His coat floated to the surface and surrounded him like a strange gay lily pad and he stood grinning in the sun. He intended not to fool with preachers any more but to Baptize himself and to keep on going this time until he found the Kingdom of Christ in the river. He didn't mean to waste any more time. He put his head under the water at once and pushed forward.

In a second he began to gasp and sputter and his head reappeared on the surface; he started under again and the same thing happened. The river wouldn't have him. He tried again and came up, choking. This was the way it had been when the preacher held him under—he had had to fight with something that pushed him back in the face. He stopped and thought suddenly: it's another joke, it's just another joke! He thought how far he had come for nothing and he began to hit and splash and kick the filthy river. His feet were already treading on nothing. He gave one low cry of pain and indignation. Then he heard a shout and turned his head and saw something like a giant pig bounding after him, shaking a red and white club and shouting. He plunged under once and this time, the waiting current caught him like a long gentle hand and pulled him swiftly forward and down. For an instant he was overcome with surprise; then since he was moving quickly and knew that he was getting somewhere, all his fury and his fear left him.

Mr. Paradise's head appeared from time to time on the surface of the water. Finally, far downstream, the old man rose like some ancient water monster and stood empty-handed, staring with his dull eyes as far down the river line as he could see.

THE LOST CAUSE OF JACOB UBER

by Eduardo Mallea

I

One thing alone kept people from hating Jacob Uber: the undeniable fact that his entire life was overshadowed by suffering, a suffering so intense that in the end it destroyed him.

A small, thin man, Jacob Uber was very regular in his habits, and prone to worry about what he was going to say before he said it. Actually, he was afflicted like this only in the presence of casual acquaintances, whereas with his friends he was invariably quite at ease. Though burdened with a singular weariness of spirit, in the company of intimate acquaintances he struggled to escape from himself, and in rare moments of bliss he succeeded. Otherwise, this inner miasma had stifled him since childhood.

For years and years, all his yearnings had centered on ridding himself once and for all of this vitiated atmosphere which so weighed him down. But the wretched man could never sufficiently destroy the evil

From *The Kenyon Review*, Autumn 1944. Copyright by Kenyon College, 1944. Reprinted by permission of the author and publisher.

spirit within to achieve this reformation, and there were periods when he felt as though he were trailing his hateful self around much as a serpent drags his cast-off skin. It was painful, too, to observe how unalterable he considered the traits of character with which nature had endowed him, and with what charity he condemned them.

He was a solitary and a very melancholy man. Those who knew him as he went to and fro through the big city, apparently engaged in the same pursuits as everybody else, never suspected anything of the kind. On the contrary, they always thought of him as leading a very peaceful life, as pleasure-loving, easygoing, relatively satisfied, even though subject to the usual human afflictions. Beginning with his closest friend, a retired supervisor of tax collectors and a patron of artists, and ending, for example, with Señora Folan, who kept the office books up on the seventh floor, everybody thought that Jacob Uber's loneliness was due almost entirely to his bourgeois smugness, about which they joked in a good-natured way even when he was present.

Nothing could be more trivial than the life he led in Buenos Aires. One got the idea that he meekly conformed to any changes which might take place in his world, but in other respects went his own way, for he held a city job, lived in a small house in the southern ward, was very fond of the movies, and on Saturdays dined in a French restaurant where he ordered succulent dishes with such high-flown names as *aloyau rôti aux legumes panachées,* or *omelette à la Tour de Nisan,* together with a half bottle of Château-Margaux. For a time he looked forward all week long to this event; later, he continued to go to the restaurant through inertia, although he no longer found the cooking especially tasty.

He was quite young when he first started working for the city. His father had come from Europe—from Lyons—while still a boy and had been rapidly assimilated into the Argentine way of life. He had died of angina pectoris one afternoon, in a railroad station. Then Jacob Uber, taking advantage of the small patrimony that fell to his lot, went back to live in the very house where he had spent his infancy. In his last few years, his father had rented the house to a Belgian couple in order that he might spend the income from it on expensive liquors, and so young Uber had been forced to live in a *pension.* Yet when he came back to the tiny apartment, located directly above a carpenter's shop, and quite dilapidated, his heart sank and he had a premonition that bad luck and despair were to be his companions in these quarters.

He took delight in repainting the apartment every once in a while, doing the work himself and always using a new color scheme for each room. The chamber which his father had used, however, remained closed, unchanged, and full of his special belongings: a baroque chest, elaborate candelabra, and mirrors with heavily decorated frames. Once a month, Jacob opened the windows in this room and aired it, then once more sealed it up hermetically.

Up until then, Jacob Uber had been very retiring. He was little given to carousing and was always rather taciturn when he returned with groups of gay companions from the brothel district, where sinister madams had overwhelmed him with insincere compliments. Nor was he interested in dancing or sporting events; at the latter he was always depressed by the brutality of the public and the annoying atmosphere of irritation which hovered over the stadium when a contest came to an end. He did, however, get enjoyment out of his friendship with a number of women who worked in different parts of the city and whom he had come to know in a thousand casual and simple ways.

At the office, he worked obstinately, forcing his mind, by nature given to wandering and dreaming, to concentrate upon his work; deliberately bringing his eyes to rest on his typewriter keys and the banal label: "Shipper A—File C.Y.Z." He had never had any ambition to become an efficient employee but he did ardently aspire to submerge completely the thoughts to which he was prone and which so thoroughly exhausted him. Such thoughts always led him back to dwell on his isolation and soon resulted in vague but unbearable anxieties. His greatest agony was to picture the rest of humanity as dwelling in another world with which he had no tie at all except, perhaps, the superficial bonds of his purely physical life.

Once, just as dawn was breaking, he was forced to take refuge in a café, as if in flight from the streets and the city, and there he stayed, anxious, timid, his heart palpitating, sipping a glass of cognac and watching all the strange people seated around him, here and there at little tables, surrounded by blue smoke and the yellow halo of the lamps. Even among strangers like these a certain warmth circulated, while outside in the streets, at this hour of the night, he felt as though his soul were starving in the midst of a desert.

He always had the sensation of living in a stupor, with his eyes wide open, as stationary as a sea anemone. Mornings, as he was leaving for the office, he would drink in the air and sunshine with a certain sense of elation, but as soon as he entered the stream of people among whom he must spend his day, the very sight of their familiar faces produced a feeling of deep disgust, of total disillusionment, which showed through all his mechanical actions and superficial words. Superficial words! Had he, indeed, ever spoken any that were not superficial, any with real meaning? No. No, he realized that he had never had anybody to say them to, nor any opportunity for using them. He had never confided anything to anybody, never had become sufficiently initimate with any human being to feel like unburdening himself of what he considered the vapid story of his life.

When he was about thirty years old, this sensation of depression began to grow on him. He had usually been free from this type of egoistic preoccupation, but now he began to dwell at length on his responsibility as a man, and on his failure to make any sentimental attachments. For he felt that it was this failure which had shut him off in arid loneliness in a recondite world of his own. He thought of saving in order to travel, hoping that this would amuse him and help him to get away from himself; dreamed of giving up his position and beginning another life in which adventure might have a place. This idea gradually evaporated, however, as if even before he had made the slightest effort to put it into effect he were certain that it would fail. So he continued to bend over his files after his daily walk through the sunlit streets and his frugal breakfast at a cheap bar on Reconquista Street. Stooping over his desk, he would send out reports he had composed without the least thought as to what it all meant, while his eyes lingered on the typist's flying fingers and the anemic, skinny legs showing under her work table. He found himself wondering what this girl, Rebecca, would be like in an intimate situation and what motives lay behind her tense energy. Were there really human beings whose least gesture was not predicated on its dramatic effect, and did not have its origin in some seed of tragedy? Beyond doubt, he was living right among just such carefree people, so different from himself, and he envied them. He envied their ability to live outside themselves, since this made it possible for them to fling themselves headlong into a passionate interest in other people, sights, and things. And all the time he felt that he, on the contrary, was doomed to vegetate among familiar objects—a bed, a restaurant, an *aloyau rôti,* a roomful of lithographs and pictures he had cut out of magazines—objects for which he felt an affection never extended to any living thing. He took a melancholy view of himself as a human receptacle containing its own world, one with no outlets, a stagnant world where one mirage after another moves slowly by. Only his imagination showed any sign of activity. Instead of really living, he merely imagined, creating, in this inner world of his, objects and desires which began and ended solely with him.

On holidays, he would ride out into the country with his friend Lucas Mordach and they would stroll over the wide, monotonous prairies until dusk. Then they would come back to the bar in the station and sit down among groups of peaceful farmers, in winter ordering tea with anise, and in summer one of their delicious ices. Lucas Mordach was a very talkative, sensual person, an unusual fellow, always nibbling on calycanthus blossoms and filling his pockets with fragrant cedar buds. As they walked, his eyes would light up, he would open his mouth and take deep breaths, expressing unrestrained pleasure in the natural odors of the fields and shrubs and broad-crowned trees native to this region. As he walked along by Mordach's side, however, Jacob Uber never took any notice of the perfect form of an *ombú* or the "liturgic color" of the pines except when Mordach's nasal tones called them to his attention; instead he would stroll along flicking his trousers with a green switch, while a flock of images having nothing whatever to do with the landscape kept him company. They were sketchy bits of dramatization, mirages wherein events fitted together in a miraculous way, and vague dreams. He would imagine himself dressed up in farmer's boots, blue overalls with a bib, and a broad straw hat, coming over the horizon toward his own home, where he would be eagerly greeted by a wife and a small son in trousers too big for him, nibbling on some seeds. Over this home and these human beings, however, an omen of tragedy would always be hovering. He saw nothing else. The sun did not shine on this or that tree in the nearby meadows, but only his mirage. The same sort of thing happened whenever he went out to hunt partridges or to fish for trout in Lake Baldivén. On such occasions, his usual companion had a strong, hearty voice to which he would listen without really hearing a word. As they returned to the train he would exclaim, "What a fine day to go into the country!" and later, on the way back, his eyes would stare fixedly at the little houses along the track as they slid dizzily backward.

The powerful illumination of the city at night always amazed him and filled him with vague apprehension. What did he fear? When his surroundings began to lose their reality, he was inevitably overcome by fears of some dark catastrophe which he felt continually threatened him as a raging storm threatens an unprotected orchid. Then he would hunt for some refuge; go from bar to bar, and then from movie house to movie house, without ever paying any attention to what he was looking at except when the drama lent support to his own sophistries, or supplemented the fantasy which held sway over his mind at the moment.

II

His younger years were spent in this fashion and he always retained the feeling that all the world, with its varied phenomena and infinite mutations, had been but part of his own experience.

He finally came to believe that a life of introspection was the most noble and generous existence of all. For what more precious gift could one present to others than the qualities which fantasy and imagination built up within one? This reasoning, however, brought him face to face with that condition of solitude which he could not explain away and which became more pathetic with each passing moment.

Only once had he thought of marriage, of bringing into his mournful abode a cheerful and beloved companion, and he could never exactly understand what it was that happened, why he failed in his purpose. One Saturday night, at a party given by one of his childhood friends, Jacob Uber met Carlota Morel, a tall, blond woman with bright eyes, a kind of blithe gaiety in her manner, a proud carriage of her head, and small hands. She was fairly well educated, gave private lessons in languages, and read Hölderlin in the original. She was not concerned with what others thought about her, and was inclined to laugh off any criticism, in a jovial and authoritative manner. From the very first meeting, he felt that he had made an impression on her, for she talked to him intelligently and frankly about her early life, thus creating a rather sudden intimacy which flattered him. Soon he was inviting her to meet him two or three times a week at the Botanical Gardens or in Lexama Park or some of the other quiet, well-shaded sections of the city. One day she confessed to him, in an anxious mood: "I am not a happy person. I am always doing things I don't mean to. I spend my nights in frightful terror, in a state of apprehension, horrified by the emptiness of my life." Jacob Uber gazed at her earnestly, but answered nothing. He never told her about himself. He thought he loved her, and she saw in him a self-absorbed man, endowed with a quiet, courageous attitude toward life, strong and tender. Days, weeks, and months passed and he went on dreaming about her, glad when he saw her approaching but silent when they met. Finally, it got so they hardly spoke. One night, they entered a sordid hotel and took a room which boasted a large, forlorn bed, a washstand, and curtains of Orléans lace. Throughout the night, like old jaded lovers, they hardly said a word. Once, sadly caressing her hair, he cried: "I can no longer live without you, without this hair of yours which I shall love more and more as it grows white with age." He did not realize why he said just that, but as a matter of fact the idea of turning white with age was to him a symbol of the fading of their relationship, since when she was present she never conformed to the image of her which he set up when he was alone, with this image of her as he would like her to be. When he was with the real Carlota Morel, he yearned for the Carlota Morel his brain had created, the one that had taken shape in his dreams, his companion in solitude, the Carlota Morel who for months had been living in his apartment on Constitution Avenue, even though her voice and her flesh never entered there. Before this exotic companion he was exalted, but when he was with the actual Carlota Morel he felt only a desire to escape, to flee from her and go to the other, the Carlota whom he had created in her image. They returned several times to this sordid hotel, and one afternoon she asked him why they couldn't go to his apartment instead. Jacob Uber remained sunk in thought, avoiding any reply. He was wondering what an encounter between the two women would be like; an encounter in which, undoubtedly, the Carlota of his dreams would flee in horror. That would be a terrible thing to have happen. He shook his head at the very idea, mute, and she never knew why Jacob Uber would not take her to his home. It was easy to conjure up many reasons for his reluctance, and she soon forgot all about the incident.

One day, when they were strolling through a deserted street in the center of the city, they got into a dispute and began to argue fiercely. He could no longer control the irritation which overwhelmed him whenever he was with this woman, who seemed more and more a stranger each time they met. He was annoyed by his own silence in her presence, embarrassed because he never knew what to say to her during their strange meetings. And she was so chilled by his attitude that her mechanical actions betrayed her growing apathy. She walked on in her stately way, dwelling on her usual topics, going over once more the different stages of Hölderlin's progress toward insanity. It was that very night, as they were returning through the silent streets after a movie, that another discussion arose, and she, sensing that he was rebuking her, replied with a dominating gesture which expressed her unspoken defiance. Jacob Uber stopped abruptly, insisting obstinately, a spark of fury gleaming in his eyes, and then turned away and strode off in an abrupt and callous manner. He knew well enough that this was no way to demonstrate his manliness or fine sensibilities, or anything else, for that matter. But it was what he had longed to do, what he had been planning to do for a long time. That night, as he was getting into bed, the sheets felt fresher and he felt liberated from a burden, at peace with the ideal which he had been cherishing. That night as he slept, an odor of apples came to him from the hotel next door, and the aroma struck him as something new, hitherto unknown.

The next day, he felt like a different man. From then on he worked happily, singing and whistling. His sudden alacrity became the butt of sly jokes which his office companions aimed at him, especially Nancel, who stuttered, and so made them all the funnier. He really did feel like another man, happy, freed from the weight which each meeting with the language teacher had imposed on him. Now, almost unconsciously, he gave his full attention to the mysterious companion whom he secretely carried everywhere with him—a beautiful, wealthy woman whom he could evoke at any time, summoning her to his side, drinking in her presence with delight. He adored this woman, who had the physical features of Carlota Morel but who responded rapidly to his will, who glided sensuously along beside him, reserved, dressed in garments of his choice, at any given moment making the precious gesture he felt in need of, and demanded. For a fortnight he felt completely happy, with no sense of remorse or regret. He took pleasure in walking through the city alone or with some of his male friends. As they climbed up the streets to the north of an evening, or traversed the market district in the mornings, he scarcely heard what was going on, for he was far away, creating new worlds for his adventures with that other Carlota Morel. After his five hours of work were over each day he would sit on some café terrace near the Congressional Building, and there he would remain motionless for hours before a glass of beer. Although, as night drew near, the traffic would get very heavy, he was rarely distracted in the least by the passersby. Once in a while his gaze would follow the feet of some man who was walking past, and then he would suddenly look away, his eyes fixed upon the distance.

But all this soon changed. The transformation was so sudden that it threw his mind into confusion. He could never explain it to himself, or define the change, much less interpret the reasons for this new state of mind. Nor could he say exactly when it was that he began to hate the image of Carlota which he had carried about in his imagination, and to revert to the real woman, the language teacher whom he had treated with such despotic brutality. In fact, he felt a profound resentment against himself and a powerful longing for the woman whom he had thrust out of his life but who now became his constant obsession. He kept thinking that he must have been mistaken, that each time they were together in that sordid hotel or in their rambles through the city, he had actually felt real pleasure, genuine satisfaction. This thought robbed him of sleep, overwhelmed him with an inner disquietude; he began to work reluctantly. One day, when the head tax collector—a bald, apoplectic, watery-eyed old man named Señor Olda—called him into his office, Jacob Uber just stood there, sunk in a strange apathy, unable even to listen or reply coherently because he was thinking about the woman he had driven out of his life. Señor Olda looked at him over his spectacles, and undoubtedly noticing that his thoughts were far away, shouted in his hoarse, vulgar voice: "Look here, repeat what I was just saying. These instructions are mighty important and they must be carefully obeyed!" Jacob Uber would have liked to vanish from the scene, just suddenly disappear. He leaned a hand on the edge of the broad desk and smiled vaguely in a manner which certainly made him look very stupid. "Go on, repeat them," the inspector demanded. "I don't quite understand you," Jacob Uber admitted. Then Señor Olda became furious and, raising his eyes to heaven in protest, told Jacob Uber to get out, and began to rave at the number of idiots that cluttered his department.

Jacob was forever getting into situations like these. He came to be known as a strange, absentminded man, for he could never cease blaming himself for his conduct with Carlota Morel, the woman he had treated with such inhuman indifference. He would walk sadly through the streets, reliving their hours together, and feeling that he would give anything in the world to caress once more that smooth head which he had forsaken, that head on which gray hairs were beginning to appear. "How cruel I was," he would mutter, thinking of the moment when she used to appear, a little late for her appointment to meet him at a certain corner, how they used to walk through the streets in the moonlight, protected from the serious difficulties of life by the simple fact of being together; how alert and intelligent she appeared, talking to him about Hölderlin's marvelous life and his pathetic decline into insanity. But he had banished all that from his life, and now all he had was this barren loneliness, an endless, aimless future haunted by these phantom memories. Moreover, he took care never to mention it to anybody, lest he fail to impart to his tale the exaltation, the force, the ardor with which his imagination embellished it. He was so upset by all this that his pallor began to excite pity for him among others. Every night he would walk along the street on which that sordid hotel stood and walk up and down, enjoying in his imagination what had never given him any satisfaction at the time. He would stop and look up at the hotel's front, with its narrow balconies beyond which one could look into rooms strewn with odd pieces of clothing. He could picture himself entering the hotel with Carlota Morel; but now it was always the real Carlota Morel, the tall, blond woman with shining eyes who set his senses afire. Once, he even got up courage to enter and asked the clerk for a room he remembered on the fourth floor, with draped curtains of worn velvet and an advertising calendar on one wall, next to a pretentious copy of an oil painting, and there he remained alone until nightfall, seated in a cretonne-covered armchair, the blinds drawn to shut out the daylight.

This mood lasted for some time. But he never tried to look her up; he was so engulfed in lethargy that he made not a single step to catch up with her. Finally this obsession with old memories began to disappear, and Jacob Uber once more felt free. Strange things kept happening to him in other phases of his life. He was constantly assailed by terrible attacks of exhaustion and restlessness and suffered in silence from causes he could not clearly define. More than once he visited a chapel on the green slopes of the Retiro in the northern part of the city, drawn there by some obscure force, although his mind constantly wandered from the liturgy. Always in a terrible state of indecision, he was incapable of adopting any special faith or of making up his mind as to what he did believe so that he could take a definite stand.

Thus days passed by and he could never find an opportunity to express the general human kindliness that he felt, by some concrete act of courtesy toward another person. A deep-seated, secret yearning made him want to make friends, to create something artistic, but it was all based on purely vague feelings, too broad, never brought to a focus. As a result, his desire for friendship was dissipated before he ever found a friend, and he never experienced any well-rooted, lasting attachment. This continual harboring of desires which bore no fruit, of barren aspirations, tortured him. His affair with the language teacher had taken place when he was twenty-eight and she about thirty-four, but by the time he had caught up with her age, Jacob Uber was living in his house on Constitution Avenue like mere vegetation endowed with a soul, to all appearances unnaturally inert, but, within, continually on the watch. Women were inevitably attracted by his eyes, which were beautiful in a virile way, large, eloquent, and with such depth that they hinted at an earnest and lofty purpose in life. Their gaze, however, was so distant and absent-minded that after a while they became merely tiresome and monotonous.

This state of concentration on abstract subjects had become so much a part of his nature that he was always dwelling in his inner thoughts. By the time he was thirty-nine years of age he no longer ate in order to live, but in order to sustain this constant distortion of everything created by his imagination, in which he took a languid delight. At times he would suddenly become aware that he was speaking of these imaginary happenings as though they were real. Once, in a Spanish restaurant, a bank clerk who was eating lunch at a table near his invited Jacob Uber to join him on a walking tour of the northern provinces, stopping at cheap inns and observing the curious folkways of both peasants and townspeople of the region. He agreed to the notion and immediately suggested that they plan to include the old houses along the river and the little baroque churches peculiar to northern Argentina. "We will have to leave before the end of this month if we want to avoid cold weather," the clerk reminded him. "All right, that's fine," replied Jacob Uber with an affable and animated smile. But as soon as he had started off alone along the streets lined with big commercial houses, he began to find fault with himself. Why had he agreed in such a hurry? Why had he raved on in such a puerile way, talking so effusively about a trip he had no intention of taking? He was angry with himself for having indulged so deplorably in the lies which his imagination conjured up. And yet the very certainty that he would never take such a trip made him look away from the world around him—from this avenue with its incessant, violent activity, where every face was stamped with strong determination—and plunge headlong into the thought of those little northern towns, so delightfully cradled under the shelter of broad-topped trees below the peaceful Andean foothills. That afternoon as he worked, his secret thoughts dwelled constantly on such an imaginary landscape.

On Saturday nights he would arrange with some of his companions to dine at a *café chantant* on Florida Street where they would be joined by two or three women of easy virtue but not too promiscuous. One, called Elsa, had sensual lips and untidy blond hair; another was a slender Hungarian with drooping eyelids, who translated stories for an evening paper. Sometimes the group was augmented by two sisters, both divorced, and the sweetheart of a certain politician, a lady with cold, cautious eyes that inspired fear in them all. They would pass the evening talking and laughing. Jacob Uber never gave up hope that he might discover some hidden beauty in one of these women, some spark of the spirit, something capable of elevating her for the moment above the common clay, and capable of inspiring her with faith in her unusual qualities. Days went by, however, and these meetings, enlivened by noisy orchestras, resulted in nothing more than tiresome gorging and indigestion. One by one, the women came to his house and became his mistresses, but it was inevitably a crude, boresome, abrupt and brutal affair in the eyes of Jacob Uber—a *Mene, mene, tekel upharsin.* Just bodies and more bodies, all inhabited by a gray specter, bodies imbued with impalpable death; bodies lying exhausted upon the bed while his own imagination went on its way, creating, withdrawing, separating his being from this other being, dividing the waters from the waters as on the second day of creation, dividing his withdrawn self from the body near at hand, motionless, tangible. He was amazed to find how fleeting was his contact with his flesh, although surrounded by perfect solitude. His distress consisted in taking possession of these women in the flesh without being himself present in the spirit; without being *aware* of the event. His eyes would wander and find no place to rest, like the eyes of a condemned man. Perhaps, if in place of the body which at that moment cast a vague glow in the dark of the room, it had another body—those other lips, laughter, tremors, and voice—the lips, laughter, and tremors of someone other than the woman at hand. . . Then the women would dress over near the door of his father's bedroom, so full of memories and dust, either protesting that he keep away, or not noticing him at all.

He had a vision of himself, a rather terrified one, in headlong flight which had no beginning and no end, divorced from the land, the sky, the air, the water—from passion, faith, and friendship—projecting his entity denuded of all roots into a universe where his spirit sailed along its course, vagrant and passive. Once he stood in absorption, smitten, before an engraving representing the dead Ophelia floating on a lake of white lotus blossoms, as if he realized that this image might refer directly to the inert submersion of his own spirit. Desperately at times he longed to find something to which he could anchor, which would make him take root somewhere, irrevocably—some passionate love, or belief, or order of society—something so far-reaching and profound that it would carry him with it and he would find himself in contact with the rest of the world. But every time, he would recant, escape, refuse to listen to the temptation of a broader, more distant vision, and revert to a kind of stupor filled with hallucinations.

III

It was not until after he had become head tax collector that he showed symptoms of a physical breakdown. He began to suffer nightly from spells of suffocation which would wake him from sleep with a terrible feeling of oppression. Soon this developed into an obstinate heart condition. When Jacob Uber left his office at six he would be overcome by his fear of the suffocating sensation, which he knew was bound to visit him that night, and this continual dread had its effect on him. He began to lose interest in conversation and his meals. The friend who had occupied an adjoining table in the Spanish restaurant, now that he had become aware of Uber's sullen and preoccupied taciturnity, no longer even bothered to speak to him. Yet, once dinner was over, Jacob found it hard to endure his solitude. He would travel any distance to visit his favorite office companions who happened to be alone in the world as he was.

While he was at the office, he avoided suggesting that they go out together, in the vain hope of getting along without such companionship at least part of the time. When he happened to run into one of them on the street, however, he preferred to walk along without saying a word. This naturally bored his companion. Again, midnight would come and he would find nobody inclined to wander through the streets with him in this strange fashion. Then he would turn to the districts where traffic was still heavy, where there were crowds and plenty of life—the dock areas, the well-illuminated but evil sections of the city. As long as he did not go to bed, he did not feel so bad; he suffered no crisis, and his symptoms were less acute, confined to a dazed sort of melancholy.

He used to wind up in a café where a strangely fascinating comedienne with a harsh voice sang her numbers over and over again until daybreak. This woman, advertised on the big yellow posters as Lola Cifuentes, wore a black, spangled dress carelessly fastened over her soft shoulders and possessed a certain savage elegance. She sang with eyes fixed, pupils concentrated, standing like a priestess close to the piano on which an athletic, blond Dutchman tried to exhibit his training as a gymnast. Jacob Uber would struggle to fix his attention on the people assembled there, scattered around in booths and at tables, submerged in the heavy atmosphere. But his mind persisted in imbuing the various personalities—men who smoked while they conversed or argued with each other, and showy women with tired faces—with a reflection of his own illness, the complex forms of his own case, the destiny which he had to face. At one moment he would decide that he was getting better, then he would feel sure that there was no way out of his condition, that he was getting worse, that he was done for, that he would wind up, once and for all, in a state of complete loneliness. Meantime, the woman's hoarse voice seemed to blend with the piano, to take on its high metallic tones, its sound of worn-out strings. When the first light of day began to filter into the bar, Jacob Uber would drain the last portion of his small glass of cognac which he had been sipping for hours, and return to his house, where he would fall into a sudden, thoroughly exhausted sleep.

His physician, a Dr. Fogueral, frightened him by insisting that what he needed was a more hygienic way of life and immediate, rigorous treatment. He advised him to enter a quiet *pension* at Palermo, run by a friend of his. Disheartened, Jacob Uber gave up his rooms, put a few possessions in a small white leather valise, and wrote the tax collectors' department that he was forced to ask for a leave of absence because of his health. He was so full of dark thoughts that when he got into a taxi he had hired to take him to this guesthouse in Palermo, instead of giving the address, he absent-mindedly asked the chauffeur: "Is your mistress at home?" as if he were talking to the maid. Then he awoke from his woolgathering and smiled feebly as if to beg the chauffeur's pardon.

As he drove along, he looked back over the city with the sky so high above, at its trees shading the big avenues, and the far-reaching sidewalks. Blobs of light seemed to expand and float through the dusk, breaking forth into great sheaves of red glow which were reflected in the long, straight city gutters by a vague brick-red coppery hue. Jacob Uber saw the afternoon slinking off in all its desperate misery. Above the buildings, over the vast horizontal expanse, he heard a tremendous clamor rising from the multivoiced and cosmic throat of Buenos Aires.

The house at Palermo proved to be white, gleaming, and totally bare of extraneous ornaments. The hostess came out to greet him, sporting a dress rich with black lace but entirely out of style, with too tight a belt, and wide, billowing flounces. Her eyes gleamed in lively fashion above excessively painted cheeks. Jacob Uber followed her through bare, whitewashed corridors. His room had a window from which he could look far down over a great slope leading to the river. Lights were springing up here and there. The hostess inquired as to what he wished to drink with his meals, and then went on to express her amazement at Jacob Uber's likeness to Lincoln in his youth. She would have liked to linger on for further comments, but her guest's face betrayed his weariness and boredom. She noiselessly closed the door. Jacob Uber opened one of the built-in wardrobes and, taking his extra suit from the valise, hung it up. Then he approached the mirror and stood there for some time, looking at himself. His untidy hair falling in wisps over his forehead accentuated the pallor of his face, already showing the ravages wrought by his bad nights. After this period of self-contemplation, he took out his books and placed them here and there on the tables. Several times he went to the window to survey his surroundings—to watch the dark birds winging their way toward the river, or to examine a nearby weathercock. He was especially interested in the assortment of windows in the houses below—windows with venetian blinds, French, baroque, and Byzantine windows.

The tiled roof of a factory and the cupola of a small church peered through the evening dusk. Far off, a flock of sea gulls wheeled in wide concentric flight. Night was creeping up from the river, advancing to engulf him and all that lay about him.

He looked over the furnishings of his rooms a number of times, and then sat down in an armchair upholstered in faded leather and discolored where the hands of former guests had rested. He felt sad and desolate. He raised his head, resting it on the low back, and closed his eyes, remaining in this position until nocturnal gloom had completely filled the room, admitting only the glow from the mirror in which the moonlight found reflection. He had a painful premonition that something agonizing was about to happen to him; yet he wished to get well, to live, at least a while longer, amidst all that he so painfully cherished.

He had turned on the light and was holding one of his few books when, after a discreet knock on the door, an imbecilic-looking maid entered the room. Her red hair was disheveled, and she had an air of being in a sort of trance. Her name was Ercilla, she said. Then she began to set a small, round table which she moved out of a corner into the center of the room. She left to fetch his dinner and came back with a portion of boiled fish and a bottle of milk. She remained watching him, in a dreamlike state, while he ate, picking at his food as if he suspected it, his large white body slightly stooped over his plate. Uber asked her some questions about the house, and she replied with monosyllables, her hands hanging listlessly against her gray skirt.

Time and again this same scene took place. The long days spent in that house were gloomy, far too gloomy for Jacob Uber. He lay about languidly, not caring when a strip of his flabby back showed through a rent in his shirt. Every third day, very early in the morning, he received a visit from Dr. Fogueral. He was a man of few words who said that he was dedicated to philosophy, but who in reality saw the final reason for things only in the viscera, which seemed to him a labyrinth in the face of which he never stopped being frightened, never stopped wrinkling his brow. Every morning after breakfast, Jacob Uber went out to get a little sunshine, walking through the deserted streets beyond the arid Plaza Italia. He had come to hate the tax collectors' office and never went near it even to pay a call, but these short strolls depressed him just as much. Each tree, each human being, each house showed him how far away he was from them all, and how little communication there was between them and the island on which he lived. What a bitter and difficult period he was going through! He constantly had a feeling that though everything in the world originates and exists through an act of love, he had tried to confine this love to his own little island, thus walling himself in more and more, instead of seeking his salvation through a spontaneous abandonment, a surrender of body and soul. Now he sensed that it was too late, and each time he thought of this a great sob would tear him asunder.

Yet he wanted to live. He took good care of the body which he had always loved so much, so solitary and imprisoned in its own fortress. He followed directions carefully, and while the doctor was listening to his heart through a stethoscope he would scan the doctor's face to see what could be read there. In vain he tried to distract himself. He could not read. Each day, he became more intent on the idea of his own sterility, and would hardly say a word to the hostess during her frequent visits to his room. He spent hours gazing at the lights of the city, at the long rows of windows at the top of the big buildings which differed from each other only in their varying degrees of insolent importance, and at the river. He watched the people hurrying past, bent on their own affairs, while he had nothing to look forward to.

In some streets a great solitude lingered, like some poor creature abandoned by time. The portals of the business houses remained hermetically sealed, watched over by the pallid splendor of the moon. This solitude, created by local atmospheric conditions, took on various forms and stalked mournfully through the streets at night.

At times he was harassed by the idea that the thing he had missed most in life was just the fact that his creative powers had never been fertilized by reality. He would observe the sunlight striking on the stones, or bringing out the green in the leaves, and reflect how apparent was its fertilizing effect on them, while he had never borne any fruit.

This led him to believe that he was no longer of any use, except for death, and a slow death at that, and the instinct for self-preservation which formerly had such a hold on him began to change into something approaching complete resignation. What a terrible transmutation was death! At first he was afraid of it. He would leave his room in search of fresh air, light, human faces, whenever he thought of this death which was beginning to haunt him. But later it seemed to him that he had been passing through an arid land whose only inhabitants were grief and discouragement.

The streets appeared barren and destitute of all color, nor did the faces which he studied in passing show any warmth; even the noisy bars were hostile and cold. Winter was already gnawing at the pallid trunks of the plantain trees, and the city dwellers sought refuge early. He would return slowly through the interminable parallel streets, fixing his attention on the blackened ornaments above the eaves and the regular, hermetic buildings. Finally the man's internal disintegration brought to his face an expression of mingled sorrow and acerbity.

His heart no longer functioned properly. He felt weaker each day and had to force himself to eat. The doctor had nothing good to report and merely recommended that he rest and keep as quiet as possible. But each day he was becoming more painfully aware that he was withdrawing further from his fellow beings, that he was receding, gradually disappearing from the scene. He now felt as if he were no longer of this world, as if his spirit had left its channel and was wandering without anchor, floating on the surface of his memories.

If he could only get a grip on something stable. But what? One afternoon, wandering back and forth in his room, he thought of his old love, the teacher, Carlota Morel. He dwelt with some pleasure on the idea of holding this hope before him, of still opening up this pleasant horizon onto a new life; thinking that when he got a little better he would look her up, that he would hunt everywhere until he found her—even though she were married and had a family. The essential thing was to get to her and tell her with passionate urgency all his unspoken thoughts which otherwise would necessarily remain secret and inhibited. They could still walk together through the city for a while. Perhaps she would again relate her tales of Hölderlin. Perhaps he would be able to see her proudly held head and her lively, sparkling eyes against a background of invading twilight.

This hope gave Jacob Uber new courage on which to feed. His face lost its harsh expression, was perceptibly softened. He felt peaceful, reconciled with himself. For three days he breathed the air of the city with greater happiness. Every face that his eyes fell upon—a poor man's, a policeman's, this or that woman's—seemed to come to life again, to suddenly burst into flower. Everything in the city took on new vitality, and in some corner of that city was Carlota Morel, if only he could run across her.

For several weeks he seemed to have entered a new life. He felt much better, and the doctor authorized him to return home. His wasted features, angular now and almost ascetic, though still somewhat wistful, were again visited by occasional smiles. He was happy to leave, and tipped the maid well. On the evening before his departure he had a long talk with his hostess. She appeared in his room, resplendent in lace and ribbons, a whalebone-supported collar holding her head rigidly erect, every gesture replete with vital energy, and exhaling a strong odor of brilliantine and cold cream with each movement she made. She and Jacob Uber exchanged some theories as to the probable outcome of the war which was then hovering over the world and which the lady considered as a divine punishment.

Hostess and maid said farewell to him one sunny morning at the street door, while another boarder, draped in a dark-red bathrobe, watched them from the vestibule. After thanking her effusively for all her kindness to him, Jacob Uber left, quite willing to quit that house forever.

IV

He lived for a fortnight in veritable happiness. Everything seemed to him bright and marvelous. Life talked to him in an unknown tongue. He was even glad to handle once more the dust-covered papers which had been accumulating on his desk in the tax collector's office. His imagination abandoned its prey for the time being, and Uber looked on the universe with fresh eyes. Now he appeared attentive and loquacious with his comrades and invited them to dinner at his house on Constitution Avenue. They drank considerably, and after dinner, in his stammering way, Nancel proposed a toast "to the return of the prodigal." After the feast, Uber accompanied them to the Caucaso, a Russian night club, where all of them cheerfully drank a lot more and let some of the women sit on their laps, pointing out Uber as their host and suggesting that they take turns kissing him. This the women did most generously. Jacob Uber smiled, seated at the head of the table with Nancel at his left and an Irishman, McCormack, completely drunk, at his right. The night club was a square room with tables running parallel to the wall and one long bench inside. In the corner opposite the entrance was the small platform for the orchestra. The leader of the band was a Tartar type who laughed and sang as he rattled a tambourine, dressed in a Cossack costume with two rows of decorations across his chest. The tables were so placed as to leave a space in the center for dancing, and the first of this merry group to enter it was McCormack, who gave the spectators a disorderly, nightmarish exhibition. His legs kept folding under him, and the young blonde whom he had taken for a partner had to use superhuman strength to keep him on his feet. Finally, McCormack fell flat on his face; Jacob Uber's companions applauded him wildly, while Jacob smiled without moving. The Tartar leader advanced a few steps and helped the blonde lift up the Irishman, who was as helpless as a stuffed doll. "What a fine party!" exclaimed Nancel. The women, wineglasses in their hands, threw themselves backward in convulsions of laughter.

Somehow or other, when he had left the party, Jacob Uber felt sadder than ever. He brooded over the fact that he had not joined in more heartily, that he had remained shut up within himself, after all; and he felt again that his sky, his earth, his ties with all the outside world were merely a dark projection of his spirit and had nothing to do with his own concrete and elemental being. Therefore, he reasoned, it was useless to hope to sublimate himself in outside interests. It was useless to seek modes of escape from this sense of self-suffocation which was bound to destroy him. His recent hopes had been mere illusions, as transitory and insubstantial as his earlier one had always been—a mere reaction from his physical improvement.

Then he fell into a state of continual affliction. Like a starved body which consumes itself from within, he began to lose all desires. He felt abandoned by all, left alone with his own imaginings. At times he could hardly hold back his sobs, and since this happened at the most unexpected times, he was forced to withdraw from all contact with other people. He could never confide all this to anybody, anybody at all. What good would it do, besides, to give way to such self-pity?

One December afternoon the crisis arrived. He had passed two nights without sleep, full of anxiety, absorbed in the deleterious effect of his uselessness. He had lost the very last of his desires—his appetite had left him; at dinnertime he merely tasted a little red wine and some slices of black bread with ham. The waiters in the restaurant made no attempt to question him, and he nibbled away in silence. That afternoon he did not return to his office, but took a walk along the shore road, walking for almost three hours, until he felt an immense fatigue invade both body and mind. Finally, he reached the estuary. Walking on along its edge he could see up above him, the green slopes of a ravine, rich in luxurious vegetation—here dark shadows, and there green lozenges of fresher, brighter tints. Within, he bore an awful sense of weeping. And a fear, a fear! But he could not turn back now; never more could he return to the world he had known. He could no longer go back to that realm where he was an outsider and where he felt as if he were smothering in the dark.

As he passed beneath one of the highest ravines, he saw two girls up there, dressed in white frocks, walking arm in arm, their beautiful bare heads exposed to the gentle breezes. He sat down and listened to the distant croaking of the frogs beyond the fields of sugar cane which had been planted between the green ravines along the estuary. Suddenly, as if he heard a voice calling or perhaps because he was overcome by a horrible wave of fear, he got up and began to run, his eyes fixed on the distant horizon, as if entranced. Reaching the edge of the water, he flung himself on into the river, producing a noise like applause in the water, which rose up in agitation around him. Then he swam out on that vast, becalmed sea over which such silence had reigned up to now. . . . He swam, and as he swam he wept with frightful anguish, abandoned to his infinite, forlorn despair. How many times, a mere child, he had swum in that river! Death was one place where at last he could enter and find rest, find something real, inexorably real. Suddenly he stopped swimming and began to shout. His cry echoed far. The water opened for a second, then once more presented to the supreme calm of falling dusk its normally motionless and colorless surface.

APPENDIX

ROBERT OF CYSILLE
from the *Gesta Romanorum*

Robert, king of Sicily,* brother to Pope Urban and to Valemond emperor of Germany, was among the most powerful and valorous princes of Europe; but his arrogance was still more conspicuous than his power or his valour. Constantly occupied by the survey of his present greatness, or by projects for its future extension, he considered the performance of his religious duties as insufferably tedious; and never paid his adorations to the Supreme Being without evident reluctance and disgust. His guilt was great; and his punishment was speedy and exemplary.

Once upon a time, being present during vespers on the eve of St. John, his attention was excited by the following passage in the Magnificat; "*deposuit potentes de sede, et exaltavit humiles.*" † He inquired of a *clerk* the meaning of these words; and, having heard the explanation, replied that such expressions were very foolish, since he, being the very flower of chivalry, was too mighty to be thrown down from his seat, and had no apprehension of seeing others exalted at his expense. The clerk did not presume to attempt any remonstrance; the service continued; Robert thought it longer and more tedious than ever; and at last fell fast asleep.

His slumber was not interrupted, nor indeed noticed by any of the congregation, because an angel having in the mean time assumed his features, together with the royal robes, had been attended by the usual officers to the palace, where supper was immediately served. Robert, however, awaked at the close of day; was much astonished by the darkness of the church, and not less so by the solitude which surrounded him. He began to call loudly for his attendants, and at length attracted the notice of the sexton, who, conceiving him to be a thief secreted in the church for the purpose of stealing the sacred ornaments, approached the door with some precaution, and transmitted his suspicions through the keyhole. Robert indignantly repelled this accusation, affirming that he was the king; upon which the sexton, persuaded that he had lost his senses, and not at all desirous of having a madman under his care, opened the door, and was glad to see the supposed maniac run with all speed to the palace. But the palace gates were shut; and Robert, whose temper was never very enduring, and was now exasperated by rage and hunger, vainly attempted by threats of imprisonment, and even of death, to subdue the contumacy of the porter. While the metamorphosed monarch was venting his rage at the gate, this officer hastened to the hall, and falling

---

*** This version of the medieval romance of Robert of Sicily represents an adaptation of the story "How the Proud Emperor Was Humbled."**

† "He has deposed the powerful from their high places and has exalted the humble."

on his knees, requested his sovereign's orders concerning a madman, who loudly asserted his right to the throne. The angel directed that he should be immediately admitted; and Robert at length appeared, covered with mud, in consequence of an affray in which he had flattened the porter's nose, and had been himself rolled in a puddle by the porter's assistants.

Without paying the least attention to the accidental circumstances, or the clamours of the wounded man, who loudly demanded justice, he rushed up to the throne; and though a good deal startled at finding not only that, and all the attributes of royalty, but even his complete set of features, in the possession of another, he boldly proceeded to treat the angel as an impostor, threatening him with the vengeance of the pope and of the emperor, who, he thought, could not fail of distinguishing the true from the fictitious sovereign of Sicily.

"Thou art my fool!" said the angel;
"Thou shalt be shorn, every deal
Like a fool, a fool to be;
For thou hast now no dignity.
Thine counsellor shall be an ape;
and o * clothing you shall be shape.—
He shall ben thine own fere:

Some wit of him thou might lere,
Hounds, how so it befalle,
Shall eat with thee in the hall.
Thou shalt eaten on the ground;
Thy 'sayer shall ben an hound,
To assay thy meat before thee;
For thou hast lore thy dignity."

He cleped a barber him before,
That, as a fool, he should be shore,
All around like a frere,
An *handle-brede* ** above the ear;
And on his crown maken a cross.†
He gan cry and make noise;
And said they should all abye,
That did him swich villainy, etc.

Thus was Robert reduced to the lowest state of human degradation; an object of contempt and derision to those whom he had been accustomed to despise; often suffering from hunger and thirst; and seeing his sufferings inspire no more compassion than those of the animals with whom he shared his precarious and disgusting repast. Yet his pride and petulance were not subdued. To the frequent inquiries of the angel, whether he still thought himself a king, he continued to answer by haughty denunciations of vengeance, and was incensed almost to madness, when this reply excited, as it constantly did, a general burst of laughter.

---

* One; i.e., in one.

** A hand's breadth.

† The custom of shaving fools, so as to give them in some measure the appearance of friars, is frequently noticed in our oldest romances.

In the mean time, Robert's dominions were admirably governed by his angelic substitute. The country, always fruitful, became a paragon of fertility; abuses were checked by a severe administration of equal justice; and, for a time, all evil propensities seemed to be eradicated from the hearts of the happy Sicilians—

Every man loved well other;
Better love was never with brother.
In his time was never no strife
Between man and his wife:
Then was this a joyful thing
In land to have swich a king.

At the end of about three years arrived a solemn embassy from Sir Valemond the emperor, requesting that Robert would join him on holy Thursday, at Rome, whither he proposed to go on a visit to his brother Urban. The angel welcomed the ambassadors; bestowed on them garments lined with ermine and embroidered with jewels, so exquisitely wrought as to excite universal astonishment; and departed in their company to Rome.

The fool Robert also went,
Clothed in loathly garment,
With fox-tails riven all about:
Men might him knowen in the rout.
An ape rode of his clothing;
So foul rode never king.

These strange figures, contrasted with the unparalleled magnificence of the angel and his attendants, produced infinite merriment among the spectators, whose shouts of admiration were enlivened by frequent peals of laughter.

Robert witnessed, in sullen silence, the demonstrations of affectionate regard with which the pope and the emperor welcomed their supposed brother; but at length, rushing forward, bitterly reproached them for thus joining in an unnatural conspiracy with the usurper of his throne. This violent sally, however, was received by his brothers, and by the whole papal court, as an undoubted proof of his madness; and he now learnt for the first time the real extent of his misfortune. His stubbornness and pride gave way, and were succeeded by sentiments of remorse and penitence.

We have already seen, that he was not very profoundly versed in Scripture history, but he now fortunately recollected two examples which he considered as nearly similar to his own; those of Nebuchadnezzar and Holofernes. Recalling to his mind their greatness and degradation, he observed that God alone had bestowed on them that power which he afterwards annihilated.

"So hath he mine, for my gult;
Now am I full lowe pult;
And that is right that I so be:
Lord, on thy fool have thou pitè

"That error hath made me to smart
That I had in my heart;
Lord, I 'leved not on thee:
Lord, on thy fool have thou pitè.

"Holy writ I had in despite;
Therefore reaved is my right;
Therefore is right a fool that I be:
Lord, on thy fool have thou pitè," etc.

The sincerity of his contrition is evinced, in the original, by a long series of such stanzas, with little variation of thought or expression; but the foregoing specimen will, perhaps, suffice for the satisfaction of the reader.

After five weeks spent in Rome, the emperor, and the supposed king of Sicily, returned to their respective dominions, Robert being still accoutred in his fox-tails, and accompanied by his ape, whom he now ceased to consider as his inferior. When returned to the palace, the angel, before the whole court, repeated his usual question; but the penitent, far from persevering in his former insolence, humbly replied, "that he was indeed a fool, or worse than a fool; but that he had at least acquired a perfect indifference for all worldly dignities." The attendants were now ordered to retire: and the angel, being left alone with Robert, informed him that his sins were forgiven; gave him a few salutary admonitions, and added—

"I am an angel of renown
Sent to keep thy regioun.
More joy me shall fall
In heaven, among mine feren all,
In an hour of a day,
Than here, I thee say,
In an hundred thousand year;
Though all the world, far and near,
Were mine at my liking:
I am an angel; thou art king!"

With these words he disappeared; and Robert, returning to the hall, received, not without some surprise and confusion, the usual salutations of the courtiers.

From this period he continued, during three years, to reign with so much justice and wisdom that his subjects had no cause to regret the change of their sovereign; after which, being warned by the angel of his approaching dissolution, he dictated to his secretaries a full account of his former perverseness, and of its strange punishment; and, having sealed it with the royal signet, ordered it to be sent, for the edification of his brothers, to Rome and Vienna. Both received, with due respect, the important lesson: the emperor often recollected with tenderness and compassion the degraded situation of the valiant Robert; and the pope, besides availing himself of the story in a number of sermons addressed to the faithful, caused it to be carefully preserved in the archives of the Vatican, as a constant warning against pride, and an incitement to the performance of our religious duties.

KING ROBERT OF SICILY

A Legend Retold by F. J. Harvey Darton

In Sicily there was a noble King, named Robert.* Men called him 'Great' and 'the Conqueror'; he was fair and strong and powerful, and the prince of all knighthood in his day. But he was also filled with pride, and thought no man his equal. His brothers were Pope Urban in Rome and Valemond, Emperor of Germany.

It chanced one day, on the eve of St John's Day, King Robert went to church to evensong; but, as was his wont in that holy place, he thought more of his worldly honour than of humbleness before God. As he sat there he heard the words of the service:

'He hath put down the mighty from their seat, and hath exalted the humble and meek.'

'What mean these words?' he asked of a learned clerk.

'Sire, they mean that God can with ease make men in high places fall low, and bring the lowly into high places. He can bring this to pass in the twinkling of an eye.'

'That is a false tale,' said the King. 'Who hath power to harm me? I am the flower of chivalry; I may destroy my enemies as I will. There is no man that lives who may withstand me.'

Thus he spoke, and thus he thought in his heart; and while he thought, a deep sleep came on him as he sat in his kingly seat. Evensong drew to an end, and still King Robert of Sicily slept. All men went out of the church, and left him sleeping: and they knew not that the King was not with them, for in his place there appeared an angel, in the King's likeness, clad in the King's robes, wearing the King's crown; and the angel was taken for the King and returned to the King's palace, and feasted there, all the court having great gladness in his presence.

Night fell upon King Robert as he lay in church, and at length he woke, alone. He cried for his serving men, but no man came. He cried again, but there was no answer, until at last the sexton heard and came to the church door. When he perceived a man in the church, he cried angrily: 'What do you here, false knave? You are here with intent to rob!'

'I am no thief! I am the King!' answered King Robert. 'Open the church door that I may go to my palace.'

The sexton, at these strange words, believed that he had to deal with a madman, and opened the church door in haste. King Robert ran out as if indeed he were mad, and rushed to his palace. But he was now in

---

* This is a modern retelling of the legend of the Proud Emperor.

ragged clothes and none knew him as he pushed his way angrily into the great hall of the palace. And there on the throne sat the angel in the likeness of the King.

'Who are you who comes before us so rudely?' asked the angel King.

'You know well who I am,' answered King Robert. 'I am King, and King will I be, whatever you do. You sit in my place wrongfully. The Pope is my brother, and the Emperor of Germany is my brother. They will uphold me.'

'You are a fool, you are without the dignity of a King,' said the angel. 'You shall be shorn like a fool, and you shall become my fool. For councillor you shall have an ape, who shall be clad as a fool, like you; he shall be your brother. Perchance you may learn wisdom of him. You shall eat from the ground, like the dogs, and they shall share your plate.'

The angel summoned a barber, who cut King Robert's hair like a fool's, bare to within a hand's breadth of his ears. He stormed and shouted, and cried that he would be avenged upon them all, but to no avail. Everyone scorned him, and laughed at him.

So the mighty King Robert of Sicily, for his pride, was put down from his seat, and could fall to no lower estate. He was below the meanest serving man. He knew hunger and thirst, for the dogs fed from his plate, and he was brought nigh to starvation before he would eat after them. And every day the angel called him, and asked scornfully, 'My fool, are you King?'

Yet King Robert would not abate his pride. 'I am King,' he would answer. 'Though I am cast down, yet am I the King.'

'You are my fool,' said the angel.

Meanwhile King Robert's dominions prospered. The angel ruled justly and wisely. There was great plenty in the land, and men dwelt in peace with one another.

Thus for three years the angel reigned. Then there came an embassy from the Emperor, proposing to the King that they should go together to visit their brother the Pope. The angel welcomed the ambassadors, and feasted them; and at length he set out with them for Rome. In his train rode Robert of Sicily, clad in fool's motley; and on his shoulder sat a grinning ape. The angel was clad all in white, and sat upon a white steed richly caparisoned, so that he looked truly a King; but the fool was a sight for jeering laughter.

They came to Rome, and the Pope and the Emperor welcomed the angel as their brother, with great splendour and rejoicings. At their meeting King Robert could not contain himself, but rushed among them, crying eagerly on his brothers to recognize him.

'This is no King,' he said, pointing to the angel. 'He has taken my crown and my throne and my kingdom by some trickery. I am Robert of Sicily, your brother.'

But the Pope and the Emperor would have none of him. His words seemed but another proof of his madness.

And now, when all men cast him off, even his own brothers, King Robert began to feel true repentance in his heart. 'Alas,' he cried, 'how low have I fallen: I am more forlorn than any man alive.' Then he thought how he had come to this pass; how in his pride he had said,

'No man hath power to bring me low;' and, behold, he was lower now than his humblest servant.

'For my evil pride I am set in this sorry case, and it is right that I should be thus. Lord, on Thy fool have pity. I repent of my sin. I alone did wrong, for I was filled with pride and despised Thy word. Have pity on Thy fool, O Lord.'

Thus King Robert repented of his pride; and peace came into his heart.

In five weeks' time the angel once more returned to Sicily, with the fool still in his train. When they came to the royal palace, the angel called King Robert before him, and asked him, as of old, 'Fool, are you King?'

'No, sire,' answered King Robert.

'What are you then?' asked the angel.

'Sire, I am your fool,' answered King Robert.

Then the angel went into his private chamber, and summoned King Robert thither to him; and they were alone together.

'You have won God's mercy,' said the angel. 'God has forgiven your pride. Henceforth serve and love Him: think of the lowly estate to which you were cast down, and how lowly is even a King by comparison with the King of Heaven. Know now that I am an angel, sent to keep your kingdom from harm while you learnt humility. I return to joy in Heaven; you are the King.'

The angel vanished. Then King Robert, now again in his kingly robes, returned to the hall of the palace, and was received once more without question as King.

For three years he reigned wisely and well until he received warning, in a dream, that the hour of his death was near. Then he wrote down all the story of his fall from high estate, and sent it to his brothers, that they and all men might know that God alone has true power; and this is the tale that has been handed down concerning him.

THE PREDICTION OF THE STAG
from *Tales of the Monks*

A certain soldier, called Julian,* unwittingly killed his parents. For being of noble birth, and addicted, as youth frequently is, to the sports of the field, a stag which he hotly pursued suddenly turned round and addressed him: "Thou who pursuest me so fiercely shalt be the destruction of thy parents."

These words greatly alarmed Julian, who feared their accomplishment even while he disavowed the probability. Leaving, therefore, his amusement, he went privately into a distant country, and enrolled himself in the bands of a certain chieftain. His conduct, as well in war as in peace, merited so highly from the prince he served, that he created him a knight, and gave him the widow of a castellan in marriage, with her castle as a dowry.

All this while, the parents of Julian bewailed the departure of their son, and diligently sought for him in all places. At length they arrived at the castle, and in Julian's absence were introduced to his wife, who asked them what they were. They communicated without reserve the occasion of their search, and their sorrow for an only child. Convinced by this explanation that they were her husband's parents—for he had often conversed with her about them, and detailed the strange occurrence which induced him to flee his country—she received them very kindly; and in consideration of the love she bore her husband, put them into her own bed, and commanded another to be prepared elsewhere for herself.

Now, early in the morning, the lady castellan went to her devotions. In the mean time Julian returning home, hastened, according to custom, to the chamber of his wife, imagining that she had not yet risen. Fearful of awaking her, he softly entered the apartment, and perceiving two persons in bed, instantly concluded that his wife was disloyal. Without a moment's pause, he unsheathed his sabre, and slew both.

Then he hurried from the chamber, and accidentally took the direction in which the church lay, and by which his wife had proceeded not long before. On the threshold of the sacred building he recognized her, and struck with the utmost amazement, inquired who they were that had taken possession of his bed. She replied that they were his parents; who, after long and wearisome search in pursuit of him, arrived at his castle the last evening.

From *Tales of the Monks*, from the *Gesta Romanorum*, edited by Manuel Komroff, The Library of Living Classics (New York: Tudor Publishing Co., 1939), copyright 1928, pp. 34–36. Reprinted by permission.

* This tale is the original source of Flaubert's "St. Julian the Hospitaller." [Eds.]

The news was as a thunderbolt to Julian; and unable to contain himself he burst into an agony of tears. "Oh!" he exclaimed. "Lives there in the world so forlorn a wretch as I am? This accursed hand has murdered my parents, and fulfilled the horrible prediction which I have struggled to avoid. Dearest wife, pardon my fatal suspicions, and receive my last farewell; for never will I know rest, until I am satisfied that God has forgiven me."

His wife answered, "Wilt thou abandon me then, my beloved, and leave me alone and widowed? No—I have been the participator in thy happiness, and now will participate in thy grief."

Julian opposed not, and they departed together towards a large river, that flowed at no great distance, and where many had perished. In this place they built and endowed a hospital, where they abode in the truest contrition of heart. They always ferried over those who wished to cross the river, and received great numbers of poor people within the place.

Many years glided by, and, at last, on a very cold night, about the mid-hour, as Julian slept, overpowered with fatigue, a lamentable voice seemed to call his name, and beg him in dolorous accents to take the speaker across the river. He instantly got up, and found a man covered with the leprosy, perishing for very cold. He brought him into the house, and lighted a fire to warm him; but he could not be made warm. That he might omit no possible means of cherishing the leper, he carried him into his own bed, and endeavoured by the heat of his body to restore him.

After a while, he who seemed sick, and cold, and leprous, appeared enveloped in an immortal splendour: and waving his light wings, seemed ready to mount up into heaven.

Turning a look of the utmost benignity upon his wondering host, he said, "Julian, the Lord hath sent me to thee, to announce the acceptance of thy contrition. Before long both thou and thy partner will sleep in the Lord."

So saying, the angelic messenger disappeared. Julian and his wife, after a short time fully occupied in good works, died in peace.

UNEXPECTED REUNION

Johann Peter Hebel

A good fifty years ago or more, in Falun,* which is in Sweden, a young miner kissed his pretty young fiancée and said to her: "On St. Lucy's Day our love will be blessed by the hand of the pastor, and then we shall be man and wife and we'll build a little nest of our own."

"And peace and love shall live there," said his pretty fiancée with an endearing smile, "for you are my one and all, and without you I'd rather be in the grave than anywhere else."

But before St. Lucy's Day had arrived, when the pastor called out for the second time in the church: "Does anyone know any reason why these two should not be joined together in marriage? . . ." Death spoke up. For though the youth had passed by her house the next morning in his black miner's outfit (miners always wear their death garb), and knocked at her window as always and bade her good-morning, he was never again to wish her good-night. He did not come back from the pit.

The same morning she happened to sew for him a black kerchief with a red border for the wedding day. But as he never came, she laid the kerchief aside and cried for him, and never forgot him.

Meanwhile the city of Lisbon, in Portugal, was destroyed in an earthquake, and the Seven Years' War ended, and the Emperor Francis I died, and Poland was divided up, and the Empress Maria Theresa passed away, and Struensee was decapitated, America became free, and the united French and Spanish might proved unable to subdue Gibraltar. The Turks locked General Stein up in the Veteran's Cave in Hungary, and the Emperor Joseph died, too. King Gustav of Sweden conquered Russian Finland, and the French Revolution and the Long War began, and Leopold II went also to his grave. The British bombarded Copenhagen, and the peasants sowed and reaped. The miller was grinding his meal, the smithies were hammering, and the people of the mines kept digging for metal ores in their underground workshop.

And when the miners of Falun, in the year 1809—in June, somewhere around St. John's Day—were about to make an opening between two shafts a good six hundred feet below the earth, they found in the diggings and vitriol-water the body of a young man, completely permeated with iron sulphate, but otherwise unimpaired and unaltered so that one could fully recognize his features and tell his age as if he had just died an hour before or dozed off a little at his job.

---

* This is a story that Hoffman undoubtedly read before he wrote "The Mines of Falun." [Eds.]

He was brought to the surface, and as his father, mother, friends, and acquaintances were all long dead, nobody recognized the sleeping youth or knew anything of his tragedy until the arrival at the place of the former fiancée of the miner who one day had gone on his shift and had never returned.

Gray and shriveled, she came on a crutch, and recognized her betrothed, and more with rapture than with sorrow she sank down upon the body of her beloved. And only after she had recovered from a long upheaval of emotions did she say: "It is my fiancé, for whom I've mourned these fifty years, and whom God has let me see once again before I die. A week before our wedding he went into the earth, and he never came back."

The hearts of all the bystanders were seized with grief, and they wept when they saw the fiancée of long ago, now a withered figure of spent old age, and her betrothed still in his youthful beauty, and how after fifty years the flame of young love once more awoke in her breast—but no longer did the beloved open his lips for a smile, nor his eyes for a glance of recognition—and how she had him carried at last to her little room, as the only one who belonged to him and had a right to him, while his grave was being prepared in the churchyard.

The next day, when the grave had been readied and the miners came to get him, she unlocked a little box, tied the black silk kerchief with the red border around his neck, and then accompanied him in her Sunday best, as if this were her wedding day and not the day of his interment.

Then as he was laid into his grave in the churchyard, she said: "Sleep well now for yet a day or ten in the cool wedding bed, and may time not be long for you. I have still only a few things to attend to, and shall come soon, and soon again it will be day. What the earth has relinquished once, it will not refuse to yield a second time," she said as she walked away, and, for the last time, looked back.

INDEX

About the Authors

A native of New Orleans, Oliver Evans has spent much of his life traveling abroad. He received his B.A. degree from Louisiana State University and his M.A. from the University of Tennessee. The first teaching position of his distinguished career was at Athens College (Greece), and he has also lectured at Ohio State University, Vanderbilt University, the University of Nebraska, the City College of New York, and the University of Illinois. A Fulbright lecturer at Chulalongkorn University in Bangkok, Mr. Evans has received several grants from the Authors League of America, an exchange fellowship at the University of Milan, Italy, and in 1961 was a co-recipient of the Poetry Society of America's Reynolds Lyric Award. Included in his varied collection of published works are *Young Man with a Screwdriver* (poetry, with an introduction by Tennessee Williams), *New Orleans* (history), a translation of Machiavelli's *La Clizia, Carson McCullers: Her Life and Work, The Ballad of Carson McCullers, Forster's 'A Passage to India': A Critical Analysis,* and *Anaïs Nin.* Mr. Evans is currently Professor of English at San Fernando Valley State College.

Born in Atlanta, Georgia, Harry Finestone received his B.A. from Emory University and his M.A. and Ph.D. from the University of Chicago. After teaching at Washington State University, Roosevelt University, the University of Virginia, and the University of North Carolina at Greensboro, Mr. Finestone joined the faculty of San Fernando Valley State College in California where he was professor and chairman of the Department of English and is currently the Dean of Academic Planning. Mr. Finestone has also served as a Fulbright lecturer at the University of Oslo, President of the English Council of California State Colleges, and was a member of the board of the National Council of Teachers of English. In the summer of 1970 he was the director of the National Seminar of English Department Chairmen and has been appointed director again for the summer of 1971. Mr. Finestone specializes in the study of American literature and literary criticism and has been a regular contributor to *American Literary Scholarship,* the editor of *Bacon's Rebellion: The Contemporary Newsheets,* and has written an instructor's manual for Lionel Trilling's *Literary Criticism: An Introductory Reader.* He is currently completing an edition of essays on Henry James' *The Wings of the Dove.* He lives, with his wife and three children, in Northridge, California.

A Note on the Type

The text of this book was set on the Linotype in a new face called Primer, designed by Rudolph Ruzicka, earlier responsible for the design of Fairfield and Fairfield Medium, Linotype faces whose virtues have for some time now been accorded wide recognition. The complete range of sizes of Primer was first made available in 1954, although the pilot size of 12 point was ready as early as 1951. The design of the face makes general reference to Linotype Century (long a serviceable type, totally lacking in manner or frills of any kind) but brilliantly corrects the characterless quality of that face. The book was designed by Pedro Noa and was composed, printed, and bound by Kingsport Press Inc., Kingsport, Tennessee.